The Fifth Sorceress

VOLUME I

of

THE CHRONICLES OF BLOOD AND STONE

Robert Newcomb

BANTAM PRESS

LONDON · NEW YORK · TORONTO · SYDNEY · AUCKLAND

TRANSWORLD PUBLISHERS
61–63 Uxbridge Road, London W5 5SA
a division of The Random House Group Ltd

RANDOM HOUSE AUSTRALIA (PTY) LTD
20 Alfred Street, Milsons Point, Sydney,
New South Wales 2061, Australia

RANDOM HOUSE NEW ZEALAND LTD
18 Poland Road, Glenfield, Auckland 10, New Zealand

RANDOM HOUSE SOUTH AFRICA (PTY) LTD
Endulini, 5a Jubilee Road, Parktown 2193, South Africa

Published 2002 by Bantam Press,
a division of Transworld Publishers.
First published in the United States by The Ballantine Publishing Group,
a division of The Random House Group Inc.

A catalogue record for this book is available from the British Library.
ISBN 0593 049616

Printed in Great Britain by
Clays Ltd, Bungay, Suffolk

1 3 5 7 9 10 8 6 4 2

For Joyce, mon raison d'être.
Because she understands.

True peace of mind comes only when my heart and actions are aligned with true principles and values. I shall forsake not, to the loss of all material things, my honor and integrity. I shall protect the Paragon above all else, but take no life except in urgent defense of self and others, or without fair warning. I swear to rule always with wisdom and compassion.

—THE SUCCESSION OATH OF THE FIRST REIGNING
MONARCH OF THE KINGDOM OF EUTRACIA, MADE TO
THE DIRECTORATE OF WIZARDS UPON THE PEACE
FOLLOWING THE SORCERESSES' WAR

To ignore the past is to solicit disrespect.
To ignore the present is to invite laziness.
To ignore the future is to beg disaster.

—EUTRACIAN PROVERB

Contents

The Fifth Sorceress

Prologue:
The Sea of Whispers

. . . and a great war shall come to pass, in which many shall die before the easing of its flames. The dark side of the conflict, those of the Pentangle, shall come to defeat before finding their Fifth, and only after the discovery of the Stone and the Tome by their enemies. The banishment of those of the Pentangle shall occur upon the sea from which few have returned . . .

—PAGE 2,037, CHAPTER ONE OF THE PROPHECIES OF THE TOME

The once-proud war galleon was named the *Resolve*, and she listed drunkenly in the nighttime sea, her seams slowly failing while she tried to hold back the brackish ocean that pressed relentlessly against her sides. Her ship's wheel tied off on each side and her sails belayed, she rolled awkwardly at the mercy of the elements. The crew had tried to keep the ship's lanterns lit, but the squalls of rain kept extinguishing them, finally forcing a surrender to larger torches both fore and aft. The firelight cast oddly shifting shadows upon her gently rolling hulk, revealing areas of scorched and destroyed deck and railing.

The old wizard in the rain-soaked gray robe was named Wigg, and he looked with tired eyes down the length of the galleon from his stand in the stern as lightning occasionally scratched across the cloudy, starless sky. Three of the galleon's masts lay broken at impossible angles upon the rain-soaked deck, intertwined with frayed, seared rigging that snaked randomly about in the wind as if it had a life of its own. He watched with sadness as even the saltwater spray coming over the gunwales had no effect upon the blood that had dried there.

The war has been hard on this ship, he reflected. *At least the bodies were taken ashore before we were ordered to sail.* The urgency of their orders had left no time to make repairs. Strangely, once at sea, those same repairs hadn't seemed so important.

He turned, the wet, braided wizard's tail of gray hair falling forward over his shoulder, and glanced toward the restless ocean and to the lines from the galleon, which held in tow a much smaller vessel. The second boat followed behind in jerky, hesitant intervals, like a petulantly dallying child not really wanting to catch up to a scolding parent. Gray, froth-tipped waves occasionally licked up and over the sides of the fragile craft. For the hundredth time he wondered if it would be seaworthy. And for the hundredth time he reminded himself that it probably didn't matter.

There were thirty-one of them on board, not counting the prisoners in the hold below, and none of them had spoken since the tattered sails had been dropped from the lone remaining mast and the ship's wheel tied off, leaving them adrift in the stormy sea. The remainder of the ship's company was evenly divided between seamen and military officers. They now stood before him in two neat lines awaiting their orders, anxious to relieve themselves of their burden.

He beckoned to the captain of the guard, painfully remembering once again that the man had no right arm, another casualty of the war. The old one knew this man to be a loyal officer, but tonight the look in the captain's eyes told the wizard that this officer, no matter how true, was hesitant to discharge his duties. The same disconcerting look was on the face of each man that stood with him. The old wizard watched as the captain approached slowly, his black cape wet and sticking to the collar of his breastplate.

"Bring them up," Wigg said simply.

The captain blinked his eyes in the rain. Despite the loss of an arm there was neither man nor blade that he feared, but this was different. All night he had been trying to summon the courage to ask the question. And all night he had been reminding himself that second-guessing the orders of any of those in the gray robes was never wise. Cautiously, he began to put words to his fears. "Forgive me, Lord, but are you sure they have been sufficiently weakened?" he asked. They had been sailing due east for fifteen days, and during that time they had severely limited the prisoners' rations as per the wizard's orders. He searched the old man's eyes with his own, even himself unsure of what he wanted to hear.

"We have no choice," Wigg said gently. He understood only too well the other man's apprehension, for it was in his own mind, also. The wizard glanced anxiously upward as another crooked tree branch of lightning tore across the sky, followed by the inevitable rumbling of thunder.

"I have my orders from the Directorate. Besides, you know as well as I that fifteen days into the Sea of Whispers is the farthest we can go. Even if we were to pause here and wait, we could easily drift past the point of safety. This far out, the sea is bottomless. No anchor ever made could hold us here."

He looked past the captain's armless shoulder and into the frightened eyes of the seamen and officers. He was not pleased to see that fear was now turning into restlessness. "If we were to go farther into these waters the crew would mutiny," he added, raising an eyebrow for emphasis as he turned his gaze back to the officer standing nervously before him. "And perhaps rightly so. No, we must finish this now, whatever the outcome."

The captain bowed shortly and commanded a small company of officers to follow him below. The wizard looked back out to sea, not anxious to face the ones they were to bring up on deck. There had already been so much death and suffering.

May the task I am about to perform produce no more, he thought.

He closed his eyes and ran one hand down his creased, rain-soaked face, deeply inhaling the heavy, salt-laden air, remembering the past that he would much rather forget. The four prisoners belowdecks had been the leaders and the most difficult to capture, their followers protecting them to the very end at the cost of their lives. They had ruthlessly conducted a scorched-earth policy from which it would take generations to recover. Thankfully, as far as he and the recently formed Directorate knew, all the rest of their confederates had perished in the insurrection.

The flat, iron-braced door to the hold suddenly lurched up and over, falling backward noisily onto the shattered, rain-slick deck. One by one, four women emerged, their bare feet shackled in irons, their hands manacled in front of them. Even as powerful as he knew himself to be, he felt a chill go up his spine as the soldiers prodded the prisoners into line before him. Each in turn raised her face. He could feel the hate in their eyes bore its way into his brain, reminding him once again of who and what they were.

Sorceresses of the Coven.

The blond, the redhead, and the two brunettes stood unsteadily but defiantly before him on the slippery, rolling deck. Their once-luxurious gowns were torn and scorched, and their hair was disheveled, matted against shoulders and breasts. He tried not to notice the Pentangle that appeared upon each dress in faded gold embroidery.

The rationing of food and water over the last fifteen days had produced the desired effect. He had hated having to give the order to restrict their nourishment, but it was the only remotely humane way to maintain control over them. They looked thinner and weakened. Weakened, he hoped, to the point that they were now powerless. At the very least, enough so that he could overcome their combined efforts if need be. For unlike his Brothers, the females of endowed blood had found a way to join their power, making them far more dangerous when together. He had petitioned the Directorate for hours to have at least one more wizard accompany him in this madness, but they had declined. Too many from their ranks had already died, they said. Therefore, as he was the most powerful of them, the task had fallen to him alone. He took a deep breath, looking into their malevolent eyes, taking stock of what he saw in them.

Weakened, yes. Humbled, never.

He chose then to glance at the thirty men lined up behind the women, wondering if he would see lust in their eyes, hoping he would not have to waste any of his power trying to control them, too. But the only emotion he saw on their faces was fear. Fear bordering on terror.

He turned his attention to the woman at the end of the line to the right. Tall and still shapely, despite the effects of near starvation, she was exquisitely beautiful. The streaks of premature gray in her black hair only gave her a more dominating demeanor. It had been a decade since he had last seen her, but it seemed she hadn't aged a single day. Rather nervously, he now noticed that it appeared as if none of the others had, either. This one was the most powerful of the Coven, he knew. The leader of the leaders. He stepped before her, carefully searching her face. When she brought her hazel eyes up to his, they seemed to glow in the dim light of the torches. He had always been drawn to those eyes, no matter how many times he looked at this woman. Hers was a countenance born to give orders, a fact the wizard was all too familiar with.

She bluntly spat into his face.

"Wizard bastard," she hissed. "I shall live to see you dead."

Without emotion, he wiped the spittle from his face. It was mixed with blood.

Exhausted, she bent over unsteadily upon the rain-slickened deck, coughing up more blood with the simple exertion of having spoken even so few words. Despite her crimes, part of the old wizard's heart wanted to go out to her, but he pulled back his emotions. He had his orders, and he knew that it was imperative that he complete his task now, while he still could.

The woman to the leader's right was also dazzling, despite her current physical condition. The jet-black hair that fell, knotted and filthy, to her waist could have been made of strands of silk, and the almond-shaped eyes dominated the exotic, delicate face. She smirked at him as she seductively raised her manacled hands upward, coyly brushing her breasts, only to throw her hair over one shoulder. He tried not to watch as the wind swayed it enticingly back and forth behind her.

He increasingly wondered how many of the supposedly unbelievable legends about them were actually true. *How far had their version of the craft progressed?* he asked himself. Sadly, such thoughts only increased his concern for the now-vulnerable men standing behind them.

The exotic one turned toward her leader to help her to stand upright. But the leader roughly pushed her Sister's help away, preferring to rise on her own. The wizard knew she would refuse to show weakness in any way. Once again holding herself upright, albeit with obvious difficulty, she raised her hazel eyes to his.

The rusty manacles came up between them as she held a broken and dirty fingernail before his face.

"Your Brothers all think you have won," she breathed hoarsely. She tilted her head ominously as a crooked smile spread across her parched, cracked lips. She narrowed her eyes. "Tell me, Wizard, are you yourself so sure?"

Wigg struggled to remain emotionless. He slowly took two paces back and a step to the left to once again face the center of the row of women. He remained outwardly calm but was left with the hollow, stabbing feeling that she had somehow knowingly tapped into his greatest fear. Had he not known her for almost his entire life, her words would not have affected him so. She never made idle threats; she wouldn't waste the time.

The lightning was more frequent now and the rain came harder, occasionally flying sideways and stinging his face, the salt of the sea air invading his nostrils and lungs. He must complete his orders now, before the weather worsened and made the galleon's return impossible. Raising his voice against the wind, he addressed the four manacled women who stood before him, the mangled ship rocking heavily back and forth beneath them.

"You have been collectively tried and found guilty of crimes against humanity," he began, looking sternly into all four pairs of eyes in turn. "The charges include inciting civil war, revolution, murder, the rape and torture of both sexes, and systematic pogroms of military and civilian citizens alike." He paused, tears running down his face, the water from his eyes tumbling to join the water from the sky already there. "The physical and psychological damage you have done will take generations to repair. We can see no end to the calamities you have caused." Each pair of eyes remained defiant and unrepentant.

He paused. *So be it.*

"Despite the overwhelming demands from the populace that we

separate each of you from your heads, the Directorate has chosen to be compassionate." He steeled his resolve, still not believing what he was about to say. "Therefore, it is the order of the Directorate that you be exiled for the remainder of your lives. Be forewarned that should you ever return, the Directorate claims the right to kill you on sight. Nonetheless, may the Afterlife have mercy on your souls." The words made him teeter on the edge of being physically ill. Not because the punishment was so severe, but because it was so forgiving.

A cry of protest immediately arose from the ranks of crewmen and officers, and after a gesture from the wizard, the captain had to stand fast to silence them. As the shouting subsided, they stood together in shocked disbelief, their lines now ragged and disorganized. The restlessness in their eyes was beginning to turn to blatant anger.

He glanced toward the Coven's leader for her reaction. A brief look of shock had passed across her face like a summer storm, only to be replaced a split second later by narrowed eyes, a slight nodding of her head, and a faint smile of understanding.

"Of course," she said, taking triumphantly dead aim at him with her words. "Your oath. We're weakened. You must obey your ridiculous vows." The menacing smile widened. "That oath will one day be your undoing." Her gaze darted overboard to the tossing waves. "So it is to be done here, in the Sea of Whispers." She again lowered her head as she shook it back and forth knowingly. "A clever solution, wizard. Hypocritical, but clever. I commend you."

Ignoring the insults, the wizard commanded that the skiff in tow be hauled alongside and secured to the galleon. A rope ladder was lowered down the length of her rain-soaked hull and into the smaller craft as the storm fought violently to separate the two. Crewmen anxiously scrambled like a small army of busy ants as they readied the skiff, anxious to be done with it. Casks of hardtack, salted meat, potable water, and two lanterns were lowered in. Oars and the components of a rudimentary mast, sail, and rudder were also carefully lowered down, but left unassembled.

At the direction of the wizard, the captain of the guard unlocked the shackles and manacles, freeing the women. The captain dropped the manacles noisily to the deck as the women began to flex and rub their wrists, blinking their eyes in the rain. He then beckoned three of his officers forward, ordering them to draw their swords, as he also did. A sword point to each of their backs, the women began to shuffle stiffly toward the now-open gunwale gate.

The wizard watched as each of the first three turned to look him in the eye before clambering down the crude rope ladder and into the skiff. Their leader was the last. As she turned to face the wizard for the last time she pulled a wet shock of mixed gray-and-black hair away from her face, curling it behind one ear. Being free of her irons seemed to have somehow emboldened and partially energized her, and he found it unsettling to see her confidence beginning to return. Partway down the ladder she paused, continuing to hold his eyes in hers. Once again the damaged fingernail waggled threateningly.

"Your new, so-called Directorate has miscalculated, Wizard," she gloated. "The food and drink will give us strength. My first order shall be to set sail back to our homeland and plan your death." She spat again, and a combination of blood and spittle ran slowly down the side of the galleon and into the sea.

Then, to the captain's puzzlement, the wizard extended the first two fingers of his left hand, pointing them at either side of the rope ladder. Immediately, the ropes on each side began to uncoil and separate, causing her to fall the remaining distance into the skiff. He then pointed to the heavier lines securing the skiff to the galleon. The captain watched in amazement as the heavier lines immediately separated in two and the skiff and the galleon began to drift apart.

The wizard turned quickly to the captain of the guard. "Set sail," he said. "Due west. Home. Free the ship's wheel, and be quick about it. We have no desire to travel any farther into the Sea of Whispers than we already are."

Visibly shaken, Wigg walked once again to his favorite spot at the stern of the ship and leaned against the rail. He looked up at the stern torch. Narrowing his eyes, he caused it to extinguish. The rain was abating, and with the torch out he could see that the clouds were gradually parting and the usual three red moons were rising into view, bathing the calming sea in their customary, rose-colored translucence. Looking at the familiar moons, he took comfort in the fact that despite what he and his countrymen had endured, some things never changed.

He could now easily make out the dark shape of the receding skiff. As he continued to look, a yellow light suddenly winked on from the craft. One corner of the wizard's mouth turned upward in recognition, his suspicions confirmed. He had purposefully given them no physical means to bring flame to the lanterns. He also knew that light would be their most immediate need in order to prepare their small craft to make way against the storm. Therefore, they must have summoned the remainder of their collective power to conjure forth flame to light the lanterns. That would leave them completely weakened; also, the light would give him a way to identify their position for the last task he was to fulfill. He remained silent and motionless as the captain of the guard came to lean against the rail beside him.

"So you were right," the soldier said slowly to the old one. "They did have a small reserve of power." He paused. "But my conscience forces me, Lead Wizard, to tell you that this is a mistake." The captain's eyes were neither angry nor resentful, but sadly skeptical. "We had all assumed that they were due for execution. The only thing we couldn't fathom was why we were risking our own lives to take them out to sea in this barely adequate craft." He again paused, watching the small yellow light as it slowly grew smaller still. "Now we know."

He turned his face to the wizard. Young eyes that had already seen too many of the horrors of life hungrily searched the wizard's profile for answers. None came. He decided to express his opinion anyway.

"Many of my officers who have lost loved ones in the hostilities feel they have been cheated by not letting their swords take their vengeance. I must admit that I also do not understand. Those women were the last of their kind. Each of those bitches should have been killed, and the pieces thrown to the sharks."

The old one in the soaked gray robe didn't answer, but continued to watch the receding light, as if he were temporarily lost in the past. He had no need to verbalize to the captain the unspoken sentiments that each knew he shared with the other, and the wizard's legendary silence could be deafening. After what seemed an eternity to the young soldier, the wizard named Wigg finally took a deep breath and broke out of his reverie as if he were speaking only to himself.

"We gave them a chance once, long ago," he mused. He smiled at the look of surprise on the young captain's face. Sometimes the wizard forgot that he was so old, and the war had lasted so long. The death and the dying had seemed such an interminable part of his life that it was easy to forget he had ever enjoyed a peaceful existence before the outbreak of war. The offer he spoke of had been made before this man was even born. He sighed. "But you wouldn't know about that. As their numbers and power grew, we offered to share power equally, and in peace. But they refused and chose war. With them it was all or nothing. Wizard against sorceress. Male against female. Light against dark." He slowly shook his head. "We are very fortunate to have prevailed." He paused, his index finger rubbing back and forth across his lip as if making a decision.

"With the sorceresses gone I am now at liberty to tell you certain things," Wigg began. "Once the final four had been captured, we were forced to restrict their sustenance so as to be able to control their joined power and make them stand trial," he said slowly, the truth of it obviously causing him both pain and frustration. "However, after the trial and the women being so weakened, the Directorate collectively ruled that execution would be tantamount to murder." He turned his aquamarine eyes once again toward the captain. "And our vows forbid murder. Because of his power, it is forbidden for a wizard to take a life other than in urgent self-defense or without prior warning. Life imprisonment was considered, but posed too many ethical problems. The indefinite imprisonment of the sorceresses would have dictated continuance of their weakened state, resulting in certain death from disease, and therefore would also have constituted murder. A true wizard's conundrum. Exile was the only choice. And the Sea of Whispers was the only answer. Here there was an outside chance, as far as we knew, for their survival." He shook his head sadly. "She was right about one thing, you know. It was a clever choice. Hypocritical, but clever."

"But what stops them from doing as their leader said?" the captain pressed. "You have given them virtual freedom with their own craft, oars and sail, and food and drink. Their power will return, and they'll set sail for home." He shook his head in his disbelief of the Directorate's foolishness, while at the same time trying to control his anger. He couldn't believe so many had died only to see these women set free upon the ocean. "Fifteen days is not a long time."

"To them, it will be an eternity," the old one said. He smiled. In his frequent conversations with the young captain, he was reminded of one of his father's favorite sayings, which had often been repeated to him in the early days of his training in the craft. *If youth only knew how, and if old age only could.* And even though it seemed so long ago now, the phrase always proved just as trustworthy as ever.

"The provisions are not as they seem," Wigg said simply. "I altered them. The number of casks that were lowered into the skiff appeared to be enough food and drink for weeks. But if you were to ask any of your men who did the work, you would be told that each of the containers was suspiciously light. Indeed, even if rationed there is only enough for five days at best. The false appearance of that much sustenance was designed to make them climb into the skiff willingly, and anxious to be off." He returned his gaze to the yellow light as the *Resolve* began to gain way slowly, the tattered and scorched rigging now raising her best sails up the lone remaining mast. He again remembered that many of the sails themselves were also badly damaged. It would be a slow trip home. He looked carefully into the face of the captain. "Do you now understand?"

The captain smiled, nodding slowly. "Of course. The first thing they will try to do will be to eat and drink their fill. They will want their power back. But when they discover the shortages, they will have to ration themselves." He smiled broadly at the image. "Their power will not increase." Proud of himself, the captain laughed aloud to the ocean, thinking the riddle solved.

His smile faded again as he saw the wizard silently staring at him with those infernally blue eyes of his. There must be more to it. He had often been told that the mental processes and physical actions of wizards were piled upon each other in seamless intricacy, carefully constructed layers of thought and deed. Trying to understand the ones in the gray robes was like trying to peel an onion: A layer was removed, only to reveal another beneath it. It was never easy to fully understand them. Few outside of the craft ever tried.

"And can you imagine what else, Captain?" the wizard asked. The younger man could tell that Wigg expected more from him, but he was unable to give it. The old one again raised an eyebrow. "No? Consider their plight. Their hold belowdecks had barred windows. They knew when it was day or night. Therefore, they also knew that we were fifteen days out." He laced his fingers and rested his forearms on the rail. "It is common knowledge that no ship has ever survived a journey of greater than that distance into the Sea of Whispers, even when wizards were aboard. And no one knows why. The ships just never returned. The women only have enough food, even if rationed, for five days. In their already-weakened state, an attempt to travel the extra ten days west toward home would result in death from starvation. Or rather, suicide. Their only answer will be to travel east, into the unknown despite the danger, in the hope that they strike landfall in no more than five days."

Layers of thought and deed, the captain thought to himself. But he still saw anxious concern in the old face as though there was more yet to do. The answer was quick in coming.

"Captain, please go to my quarters and fetch the teak box you will find in my locker. Take care not to drop it."

Upon returning with the box the young officer watched the wizard remove what appeared at first to be an ordinary velvet bag. From the velvet bag came forth a bowl of blue glass, slightly larger around than the outstretched fingers of the old man's hand. It looked to be as fragile and ancient as the wizard himself.

Closing his eyes and balancing the bowl upside-down upon his thumb and fingertips, the old one stretched his arm to the sky. For a long silent moment the wizard waited, and something in the captain told him not to move or speak. In the rose-colored light from the trio of moons, the small skiff, with its faint yellow light, was now visible.

The wizard suddenly raised the bowl higher. As he did so the ocean beneath the skiff took the exact shape of the bowl, surrounding the sorceresses' little boat perfectly in its center, lifting the small craft high over the surface of the ocean at the top of a tall column of seawater. No sooner had the captain's mouth fallen open than the wizard dropped the leading edge of the bowl forward. The huge, distant bowl of ocean water responded immediately, spilling the skiff down the forward falling rush of water and carrying it east, away from the galleon at least one entire league.

The skiff's lantern vanished from sight in the distance.

The wizard raised, tipped, and lowered the bowl nineteen more times in a row. Then he unexpectedly cast the bowl to the deck, showering it into pieces. As it flew apart, the captain, his mouth still agape, saw a faint blue light start to glow from the pieces, and an unusual aroma came to his nostrils that reminded him of lily petals and ginger. The broken shards then suddenly combined into a quickly rising, brilliant azure vortex that careened upward, whistling hauntingly through the rigging and sails, eventually fading into nothingness.

The wizard finally opened his eyes, exhausted, leaning against the rail for support.

The captain closed his mouth. His knees were trembling.

"Soon they will be an additional twenty leagues farther to the east," the old one said, finally satisfied. "The destruction of the bowl ensures that the process cannot be reversed, even by them. Any thought of their return to our shores should now be extinguished." He silently prayed for all of the future generations of his homeland that what he had just said would come to pass. But secretly, he wondered if it had been enough.

He turned around, looking west once more and down the length of the *Resolve*'s decks, the braid of wet gray hair turning with him, and he lowered his head in fatigue.

As the galleon limped west, the captain's mind once again embraced the realization about those with endowed blood that he would not soon forget.

Layers of thought and deed, he said to himself, shaking his head.

Layers of thought and deed.

Dawn broke harshly over the small craft as it bounced freely in the waves, revealing a clear, sun-filled sky. Various casks of food and water lay opened and partially consumed upon the deck of the skiff, gently bumping back and forth.

The first to wake was the leader, her black-and-gray hair spread crazily over her face and breasts. Pushing her hair back, she tried to stand, angrily remembering she was still tied down. They had quickly secured one another to the deck as the wizard had begun to push them to the east. She loosened her bonds and sat up. She had understood his plan when the first of the casks had been opened, even before the giant waves had begun. She fruitlessly searched the barren horizon with her eyes, thinking.

Wizard bastard.

I will live to see you dead. Someday you will pay. You all will pay, including any of the inferior male offspring you may spawn.

She splashed saltwater on the faces of her Sisters, awakening them. Coughing and blinking, they loosened one another's bonds and sat up. Sullenly, the three other women raised their eyes toward hers in silent concern.

Squinting toward the morning sky, their leader noted the position of the rising sun. Slowly raising her arm, she pointed out over the empty ocean. "Make sail," she said hoarsely. "We head east."

Looking nervously among themselves they reluctantly did as she ordered, and the small craft began to make way, each woman aboard knowing instinctively that heading east was the only choice. The only chance.

The exotic one with the long black hair raised her dark, almond eyes to her mistress, silent questions implicit on her sensual face. The leader looked down at her, the food and drink having already begun to restore the gleam in her manic, hazel eyes. She tenderly placed a palm to one of the woman's cheeks.

"Even if we perish, my Sister," she said with her crooked smile, "never forget the one of us who sacrificed everything to a lifetime of seclusion in order to stay behind in our homeland." For the last time she turned her eyes west toward her lost home, searching the endless, invisible line where the turquoise sky met the darker blue of the sea.

"At least one of us still thrives there."

She bent to pick up an oar.

PART I

The Kingdom of Eutracia,
327 Years Later

CHAPTER

One

The Tome shall be read first by a seed of the victors who, years later, shall become the sworn enemy of those same victorious ones. The sire of this seed shall, having abandoned the victor's cause, live as an outcast. The six of the craft who remain shall select one from their midst to lead them in peace for sixteen score and seven years, choosing, in turn, many who shall wear the stone. From the seed of one of those who wear the stone shall come the Chosen One, first preceded by another.

The azure light that accompanies the births of the Chosen Ones shall be the proof of the quality of their blood . . .

—PAGE 478, CHAPTER ONE OF THE VIGORS OF THE TOME

True peace of mind comes only when my heart and actions are aligned with true principles and values. I shall forsake not, to the loss of all material things, my honor and integrity. I shall protect the Paragon above all else, but take no life except in urgent defense of self and others, or without fair warning. I swear to rule always with wisdom and compassion.

The succession oath played over and over again in his head like a bad nursery rhyme. He couldn't get it out of his mind no matter what else he thought about. No matter how hard he tried. That was why he had come this morning to his favorite place.

To be alone in the Hartwick Woods.

He reached behind his right shoulder for another throwing knife, gripping its handle automatically and smoothly bringing his right arm up and over in a swift circle, releasing the blade in yet another trajectory. It twirled unerringly toward the target he had carved in the huge old oak tree. And as he now stood looking at the blade that lay buried next to the others he had thrown, he knew that the fact it would accurately find its mark had been a foregone conclusion.

He had been doing this all morning. His right arm was sore, his body and face were covered in a light sheen of sweat, and he was dirty from head to toe.

He didn't care.

He pushed the comma of longish black hair back from his forehead and ran his hand through it to where it grew long down the back of his neck. Looking down at his clothes, he suddenly realized just how filthy he really was. He was wearing what he always wore when he came up here: the black leather knee boots and trousers, with the simple black vest that laced in the front across his bare chest. The vest that always allowed plenty of free arm movement for his practice with the knives.

True peace of mind comes only when your heart and actions are aligned with true principles and values. I shall forsake not, to the loss of all material things . . .

He watched the next knife wheel toward the target, swiftly burying itself alongside the ones already there.

Prince Tristan the First of the House of Galland, heir apparent to his father, King Nicholas the First of the kingdom of Eutracia, stood alone in the woods, practicing with his knives and thinking over what his future was about to bring. In thirty days he was to become king of Eutracia, succeeding his father to the throne at the occasion of his father's abdication ceremony. It always occurred on the thirtieth birthday of the king's firstborn son, and had been a joyous custom of Eutracia for over the last three hundred years, ever since the end of the Sorceresses' War. But there were no more sorceresses in Eutracia to fight, and peace and prosperity had reigned ever since—in no small part due to the continual guidance given to the reigning king by the Directorate of Wizards. But there was just one problem.

He wasn't looking forward to his thirtieth birthday.

And he didn't want to be king.

He also did not wish to be counseled by wizards for the remainder of his life. No matter how he tried, he just couldn't get the truth of his feelings out of his head. Nor could he forget the oath that the old ones would make him take at the ceremony when he succeeded to the throne. He would then be forced to follow in the footsteps of his father until *his* firstborn son turned thirty years old. He sighed. He didn't have any sons yet.

He didn't even have a wife.

Another throwing knife whistled through the air, clanking into place alongside its brothers in the battered and gnarled old tree.

Panting lightly, he reached over his shoulder for one more from the specially designed quiver that lay across his right shoulder blade, but found it empty. His face sullen, he walked slowly to the oak to recover his knives. He had chosen this tree because it was the one closest to the sheer rock face of the cliff, its branches reaching out into space over the valley. That meant that whenever he missed, his knives would fly over the steep precipice and be lost forever. Proper punishment for a bad throw, he thought. And he had been throwing for over three hours now.

None of them had gone over the side.

Now standing at the very edge of the cliff, he took the time to wipe the sweat from around his eyes and slowly leaned one arm against the nearest branch of the tree. He looked down toward Tammerland, the city of his birth, and to the Sippora River, which snaked through the city on its way to the Cavalon Delta at the east coast, where the great river lazily released itself into the Sea of Whispers. Tammerland, the capital city of Eutracia, lay peacefully along either side of the Sippora's banks. He could see the royal palace easily from here because of its strategic placement upon higher ground and because of the brightly colored flags that flew from its towers and ramparts. And he could also pick out the markets and squares of the city that surrounded it. They would be teeming with life this time of day. He smiled, imagining the mothers and daughters at market, haggling with the vendors for the ingredients of their families' evening meals. But his smile faded. *His* evening meal would be taken as usual with his parents, twin sister, and brother-in-law in the great dining hall of the palace. He loved them all very much, but they would be angry with him tonight—and their criticisms were something he would rather avoid. Perhaps he would take a simple evening's meal tonight in the kitchen with the staff, as he was so fond of doing these days. Somehow those people always seemed so much more real to him.

He had defiantly ignored his requisite daily classes with the wizards to come here today, and to be alone. They were all probably out looking for him right now, but they would be wasting their time. This place was almost impossible to find. He sighed in resignation as he pulled the knives from the tree. Unstrapping the quiver from around his chest, he draped it over his left shoulder, replacing the dirks one by one until they were arranged to his liking.

This art of the knives, at least, was his and his alone. He had designed the quiver himself, along with the throwing knives. The palace leathersmith and blacksmith had only been too happy to help the prince with their construction. The black leather baldric went comfortably around and under each of his armpits, and the quiver joined to his vest in the back with a silver buckle, securely holding up to a dozen of the special throwing knives just behind his right shoulder.

Then had come the hours and hours of practice, which at first had been very defeating. He had foolishly begun in the military training yards, in full view of the Royal Guard. He had realized immediately that this was a mistake, as he had watched so many of his early throws bounce harmlessly off their target. So, to avoid embarrassment, he had taken his practice to the woods. That had been seven years ago, and he had come to the forest virtually every afternoon since, after his daily classes with the wizards were over. No one had seen him throw a dirk since that day he left the courtyard, and know one knew the expert that he had become.

Sometimes instead of just practicing, he walked through the woods quietly in search of game. Bringing down larger animals was difficult, and meant a well-thrown head shot was usually needed. It was something that required even greater skill if the animal was moving, but now even moving targets had become little challenge for him. The largest game he had ever killed had been a hugely antlered stag. After killing it with a single throw to the head, he had neatly quartered the animal in the woods and given the meat to the townspeople living at the edge of the forest—the forest that had become his second home.

But his most dangerous quarry had been a large, charging wild boar. They were prevalent in the Hartwick Woods, and it was not uncommon to hear of the occasional hunting party that had lost a member to the awful cloven hooves and sharp, curved tusks before it could be killed. He had come upon the creature unknowingly, and the kill had become necessary rather than voluntary. Tristan's boar had stood across an open field from him, snorting and glaring with enraged eyes. The prince had remained motionless until the awful thing had begun its charge. His right arm had then become a curved blur of speed as the whirling dirk cleaved the boar's skull directly between the eyes, stopping it dead in its tracks only ten feet from where Tristan held his ground. He had left the carcass to rot in the field, thankful that he had made a good throw. He probably wouldn't have gotten another.

Still gazing down at Tammerland, once again leaning against the outstretched tree branch and lost in his memories, he didn't hear the thing that came up behind him before it was too late. Without warning, he was violently pushed forward from behind.

Out into the air and over the cliff.

Instinctively, his right arm wrapped around the tree limb while his left arm held the quiver to his shoulder. He frantically hung by one arm, swinging crazily in the air, at least a thousand feet above the valley floor. He closed his eyes for a moment, trying to shut down the fear, trying not to look down.

Someone had just tried to kill him, and looking down would be the completion of a death sentence.

Using his left hand, he placed the quiver strap around his neck. He was then able to bring both hands to the limb. His strength was beginning to ebb, but the old limb, at least for the time being, was holding his weight.

I thank the Afterlife, his terrified mind shouted.

Carefully, one hand after the other, he began to reverse direction on the limb to face his attacker. As he came around, he wondered if he would be able to hold on with only his left hand and secure and throw a dirk with his right at the same time. He would without question kill the person who was standing there before he swung himself back to the cliff.

If he could swing himself to the cliff.

As his body came around, he managed to hang on with his left hand and take a dirk with his right, praying he would be able to throw it without losing his grip. The limb bending and straining under his weight, he quickly finished the turn, bringing both his weapon and his eyes up to kill whoever it was that had tried to murder him.

It was his horse.

Pilgrim, his dappled gray stallion with the white mane and tail, stood at the edge of the cliff, looking at him with spirited, huge black eyes. The horse pawed the ground twice with his left front hoof and snorted softly at him, as if he had already put up with quite enough of Tristan's foolishness and was more than ready to go back to the stables. Nudging Tristan from the back had been one of his favorite habits ever since he was a colt. But this spot had definitely not been the place for it.

Tristan hung in stark terror a thousand feet above the surface of the valley from a lone tree branch, slowly losing his strength. Carefully managing to replace the dirk in his quiver and his right hand upon the branch, he looked tentatively to the left where the limb joined the trunk, trying to see if it was dried or decayed. He groaned inwardly when he saw the dry crack, and there was no way to tell if it was strong enough for what he had planned. He couldn't simply stretch his legs to the cliff. It was too far away. He would have to swing his body back and forth to gain the momentum to reach the ledge. It was the only way. Slowly, his eye on the crack, he began to swing from his arms the same way he had seen the court acrobats do so many times before, the bark starting to painfully twist off in his hands. Each time he swung his outstretched legs a little harder. Each time a little more bark came off in his now-raw palms. Each time a little more sweat began to flow into his eyes. And each time he had a little less strength.

The crack split open another inch.

Just two more swings should do it, he prayed. *I beg the Afterlife, just two more.*

His release from the branch on the second swing came at the precise moment the crack split all the way open, the shards of the joint becoming a twisted, tortured rope of exposed wood. He flew through the air toward the cliff, his face finally striking the end of Pilgrim's muzzle as the horse bolted backward in surprise. Tristan went down hard on one knee, the momentum carrying him over on his back, finally hitting the back of his head hard upon the ground.

Moments later, dazed, his eyes out of focus and his face strangely wet, he raised his hand to check his face for blood. There was none. The twisted and torn tree limb lay innocently upon his lap, and he tossed it to one side.

He wanted to kiss the ground.

Pilgrim's lips once more nuzzled his master's face. The stallion had definitely had enough of this and wanted to go home. Tristan sat up, looking at the impatient Pilgrim, and began to laugh softly, then harder, finally bursting with the sheer joy of being alive. He laughed at himself harder still, imagining the looks on the faces of all six wizards of the Directorate when they realized they had no king to fill the throne at the abdication ceremony. He still didn't want to be king, but there had to be an easier way out of it all than this. And in truth he loved to tease them, but he didn't want to die doing it. At least he had temporarily forgotten their ridiculous oath.

He slowly stood, wondering if anything was broken, and collected the scattered dirks. He was all right, but he would be sore for a week. When he placed his hands to either side of Pilgrim's muzzle, the horse flinched his head to one side in pain. The stallion's nose would be sore for a while, also. Served him right. Putting his arms around the horse's neck and his mouth against the animal's ear, he smiled.

"Next time we come up here, if you don't behave yourself I shall have to tie you to a tree," he said gently.

Pilgrim whinnied softly and brushed the longish center of his dappled head against the prince's shoulder.

Tristan glanced to the left across the open glade to where he had hung the saddle and bridle over a convenient tree limb. Upon arriving he always took the saddle and bridle off, allowing the horse to roam freely. Pilgrim never went far, and had been trained from a colt to always return at Tristan's first whistle. The prince hobbled stiffly across the clearing, removing the saddle and saddlebag from the tree, placing them on the soft grass in the shade. Looking up at the sun, he saw it was now early afternoon.

He removed his quiver and lay down in the grass with his saddle as a pillow. Reaching into one of the saddlebags, he pulled out a pair of carrots.

Upon hearing Tristan's whistle, the stallion trotted over immediately. He carefully took the outstretched carrot from his master's hand with his long, uniform teeth and munched contentedly, watching the prince eat his. This was another of one of their little rituals, and sometimes there was some carrot left over. Deciding he wasn't really hungry anyway, Tristan offered the last half to the stallion. Pilgrim bent his head down and nuzzled Tristan's face again, this time unceremoniously leaving little bits of wet carrot all over it. Tristan laughed a little, wiping off his face. He would have laughed harder, but his ribs were beginning to hurt.

"Go away," he said. "I know I need a bath, but I don't want it coming from you."

Retrieving yet another carrot from the bag, Tristan slowly drew it before Pilgrim's nostrils and then promptly threw it to the other side of the clearing. He smiled as the stallion ran off after it anxiously, his head and tail held high. Tristan's previous mount, a mare, had died giving birth to Pilgrim after having been bred by one of the finest studs in the kingdom. From that moment on, the young prince and colt had been inseparable. Sometimes the horse seemed to be the best friend he'd ever had. Next, of course, to his twin sister Shailiha, and Wigg, Lead Wizard of the Directorate. He lay back down on the grass and watched the clouds go by. An odd one came into view, rather crookedly reminiscent of the old wizard's profile, and he smiled.

Wigg, his mentor and friend. Lead Wizard, and therefore assumed by many to be the most learned and powerful of the Directorate. And the one he most enjoyed poking fun at. Wigg would be angry with him beyond all reason. But the thought of the six wizards of the Directorate seeing him hanging over a cliff so close to the abdication ceremony started him laughing all over again. *King Tristan the First, Lord of the Swinging Tree Branches,* he thought to himself. He laughed aloud until the recurring fire in his ribs forced him to stop.

Still looking at the sky, his mind drifted to the Directorate as a whole. The Directorate of Wizards, endowed advisors to the reigning king of Eutracia. He envisioned each of their faces in turn. Wigg, Egloff, Tretiak, Slike, Killius, and Maaddar. The ancient heroes who had been responsible for bringing victory in the Sorceresses' War of so long ago. They were all over three hundred years old, two of them now over four hundred, each protected from the ravages of old age by the esoteric

enchantments they themselves had conjured near the end of the insurrection. The enchantments were effective only upon those with endowed blood, and had been instrumental in the final victory. Their use
was reserved exclusively for the Directorate of Wizards and the reigning king if he so chose; not even the lesser rural wizards could avail
themselves of the health-sustaining incantations known as time enchantments. That was as much as Tristan knew.

But what he did know as a certainty was that on his thirtieth birthday, Tristan's father would abdicate and join the Directorate, making
seven. Then Nicholas' life, also, would be protected by the time enchantments, as well as by the powerful jewel called the Paragon that so
augmented the exceptional power of the wizards of the Directorate.
Tristan's mother Morganna would therefore sadly but gracefully die before her husband, leaving him to a life of perpetuity with the Directorate.

And Tristan would rule.

He sighed. He had to admit that he loved them all, despite how
much fun he made of it. But it did little to increase his desire to
be king.

The Directorate's first order of business after Tristan became king
would be to try to influence him to take a queen, hoping for the birth
of a son to succeed him in thirty years, whereupon Tristan would join
the Directorate with his father. At the end of the Sorceresses' War, the
Directorate had selected a well-respected citizen of endowed blood to
become the first Eutracian king, a new government had been formed,
and the process had led on from there. By tradition, if the reigning king
had no sons, another endowed citizen was selected, and the process
began anew. And so it had gone for over three hundred years of peace
and prosperity. It had always been the choice of the abdicating monarch
to decide whether or not to join the Directorate, and thereby receive
training in the craft and be protected by the time enchantments. Until
Tristan's father, none had chosen to do so, preferring to die of old age
with their queens.

In addition to this precedent-setting decision, Nicholas had been
the first and only king to preannounce the fact that his son would also
join the Directorate when his time came. And although the young prince
had questioned and protested the decision many times, he was told by
the Directorate and his father only that this was the way it must be. He
had heard a rumor once that the decision had been made at the exact
moment of his birth, but anytime he had asked his parents or the wizards about it, they had given him no reply. Finally, he had stopped argu-
ing and glumly accepted his fate.

As Tristan continued to watch the sky, his mind turned from affairs of state to affairs of the heart. Even though he didn't have a wife—he should soon say "queen," he reminded himself—there had nonetheless been many women in his life. He sighed. Far too many, according to his parents. Even his twin sister Shailiha, his most staunch defender of what some would call his recent disregard for his royal duties and responsibilities, had begun to criticize him about his romantic dalliances.

But the prince had always been kind to those women who hoped to capture his heart. Because of his good looks and royal position, the realm was positively overflowing with women who were more than willing to try. Sometimes, during his public appearances at court, he couldn't decide which flapped faster, their batting eyelashes or the unfolded fans that each of them always seemed obligated to flutter while trying to cool the quick blush of their cheeks. Many, to the increasingly obvious chagrin of both his family and the Directorate, had ended up in his bed.

But he had never fallen in love.

None of the women he had encountered so far had moved him to the point of wanting more than a brief dalliance. It wasn't that he was cold or uncaring toward them. He treated them kindly, and always ended his affairs like a gentleman. That was simply his nature. He laced his fingers behind his sore head, cushioning it from the saddle, and watched as a particularly interesting cumulus floated over. Reminding himself that at least there had been no scandalous pregnancies, he sighed.

Sadly, it was just that no woman had ever really made him ache in her absence to the point of distraction, or hunger in her presence to the point of pain. Deeper, in his heart of hearts, he truly hoped that one day it would be different. Secretly, he wished that he could be as happy as his sister. Shailiha was his elder, something that she was overly fond of teasing him about. He was equally fond of teasing her back, claiming that even though she had preceded him into this world by only eight minutes, one day he would be king and have dominion over her. But truthfully he wished his life were more like hers. She was very happily married to Frederick, commander of the Royal Guard, one of Tristan's best friends. And she was now five and a half months pregnant, the entire royal family and court excitedly awaiting the blessed event. But most of all he envied the fact that she would never have to rule. He smirked upward at the afternoon sky. At least his parents, King Nicholas and Queen Morganna, had raised *one* heir that pleased them.

Then, sadly, there was also the matter of his studies and royal duties as prince.

He had been educated in all matter of things his entire life by the wizards in preparation for his succession of his father as king. And although the realm had been at peace for over three centuries and had acquired no foes since, he had also been scrupulously trained in the art of war by the Royal Guard. After the Sorceresses' War, the Directorate had wisely vowed never to allow the nation's guard down again. Operating under the assumption that those who do not learn from history are condemned to repeat it, they had decreed that the history of the war be taught to each and every Eutracian schoolchild, and a term of service in the Royal Guard be mandatory for each able-bodied man in the kingdom, with the option of choosing it as a life's career. Plaques and monuments, almost always of the finest marble, dotted the countryside at the sites of many of the most important battles of the war. They were at the same time both sad and greatly respected places, as most of them marked the scenes of the massacres of long-since dead wizards and their slaughtered troops. Therefore, by tradition, the Royal Guard stood vigilantly at the ready to defend the realm against any potential threat, training relentlessly toward that end. But Tristan was sure that during his reign, as had been true for so long now, he would never have to call upon them for any reason.

Especially the defense of the realm.

He yawned, running his fingers again back through the longish black hair and over the painful bump that had resulted from his leap back to the cliff. Once he was king, the wizards would probably make him cut his hair in a more appropriate style. And then, when he eventually joined the Directorate, they would have him grow the customary wizard's tail of braided hair down the back of his neck. Depressed, he realized that all he had ever wanted was to have a normal life, but it had never been allowed him. Nor would it ever be.

The classroom training that had come to him from the wizards had been presented in many forms. Eutracian history and civics, basic laws of the realm, reading and writing the language, and so on. Following that had come studies in the kingdom's culture: her music, literature, and the arts. Then had come the requisite training in the negotiation and arbitration of the endless requests and bickering between the dukes who represented the seven different duchies that made up the kingdom and contributed to her welfare with their taxes. Politics was not his strong suit, and he still had much to learn, with very little time remaining in which to learn it. He reflected glumly upon the wisdom of taking an entire day away from his studies to come up here, only to lie in the luxurious grass of a high mountain glade. The back of his head was now throbbing badly. Perhaps overall he had done himself more harm than good today.

But his smile returned when he thought about the other side of his training—the physical side. His education with the Royal Guard had been his one true love, and he had, at the great pride of his drill officers, excelled at almost everything. Swordsmanship, archery, dagger use, horsemanship, hand-to-hand combat, and survival skills, among many other things. These had made up the basic war education in which he had found the most joy.

He could still remember his father's thunderous voice castigating him when, at eighteen years of age, he had asked to be relieved of his duties as prince and be given a commission in the Royal Guard, instead. And despite his father's rebuke, Tristan had foolishly continued to press him to honor his request. It was only when his father had finally taken him aside into the ornate anteroom of the royal quarters and spoken to him in private that he had finally understood. That was the day he had learned that his mother, Queen Morganna, had almost died while giving life first to his twin sister, and then to him. As a result, she could bear no more children. Therefore, because of Nicholas' unprecedented desire to join the Directorate and to be followed by his only son Tristan, the young man's fate was sealed first as prince, then king, and finally as a wizard of the Directorate itself.

It was the only time in his life that he had seen his father cry.

Crying, trying to make his son understand.

And so he had cooperated, abjectly resigning himself to the fate that was to be his, taking as much joy as possible in the physical side of his training and unhappily but stoically enduring his academic studies and position at court as best he could. But over the last few years, something had changed. Sometimes he could now feel the power of the endowed blood coursing through his veins. He shook his head in consternation. *Endowed blood,* he thought to himself. *That which allows the learning of the craft.*

At times it seemed that his blood had a life of its own, streaming anxiously through his body and brain as if begging him to hurry through his reign so as to finally begin his wizard's training with the Directorate and bring the power forth. And when this feeling came upon him, as it seemed to do so often of late, nothing else in the world made him feel so alive. But no matter how much he begged them, the wizards of the Directorate had adamantly refused his requests to train him in his power at this stage in his life. *You must become king first,* they had always said. They had openly admitted that none of them could remember any other royal heirs with endowed blood who had behaved quite like this at such an early age. And yet they had never explained either his unusually premature requests or their adamant refusals.

Tristan glanced back down from the sky, across the clearing and at the beauty that surrounded him. The Season of New Life was in full bloom, and was his favorite. It seemed to have come early to Eutracia this year, thankfully freeing the cities and countryside from the grip of the snow and the cold. Then followed the Season of the Sun, when all of the plants and crops started to mature, followed by the Season of Harvest, when the crops were picked before the cold winds and snow set in again. And finally came the Season of Crystal that blew snow and cold down upon the land from the high surrounding mountain ranges, finally giving way to allow the cycle to repeat.

He looked at the violet and blue leaves of the bugaylea trees that framed the clearing at the edge of the woods, as did the pink trillium blossoms that grew so thickly here, virtually covering the first few paces into the forest floor. A covey of rare, three-winged triad larks suddenly took flight from their nests high in the trees, each one's trio of blue-and-white wings beating gracefully up and away against the sky as they called out to one another. It all reminded him of how much he wished his life at the royal residence could have this type of symmetry and simplicity. Each living being here in the Hartwick Woods seemed to know and, more importantly, accept its place in the Afterlife's great plan.

And then his eyes went wide, and the breath caught in his lungs.

He couldn't believe what was suddenly before him.

It was a very rare occurrence to see them; most Eutracians went their entire lives enviously only hearing others describe their great beauty. Some claimed that they were only a myth. Still others declared that they had been created by the wizards and, as such, only those trained in the craft were able to see them. He held his breath and lay as still as death, so as not to frighten them away. For the first time in his life, he had the privilege of watching them dart to and fro in the warm afternoon sunshine.

The Fliers of the Fields.

Dozens of the giant butterflies soared and careened effortlessly on the afternoon breeze, each of their diaphanous wings as far across as a man's forearm, the body and head delicately posed between them. They darted and swayed with such speed he couldn't understand what kept them from colliding, but they never did. Red, green, blue, black, white, yellow, and violet, some a single hue and others multicolored, they flashed by unerringly over the fresh, green grasses of the clearing. To catch a quick glimpse of them once in a lifetime was miracle enough. But to see them now, for this long a time, was unheard of.

It was then that he saw Pilgrim at the other edge of the clearing, shaking his head and mane as he whinnied and pawed the ground. Without notice, Pilgrim abruptly charged into the center of the glade, clearly intrigued. The giant butterflies, instead of flying away in fear as had always been reported to be their nature, were now unmistakably teasing the horse. And Pilgrim was responding in kind, jumping, running, and bucking all over the field as the game progressed. The butterflies' beauty was so great and the game so fascinating, Tristan didn't know whether to laugh or cry, but laughter won as Pilgrim fruitlessly tried to catch them.

And then the giant butterflies were gone.

They careened away, leaving the clearing in a great, curving turn, flying single file into the woods with astonishing speed. It happened so quickly that it was almost as if they were of one mind. Then, to Tristan's initial amusement, Pilgrim turned frantically after them, knocking down tree branches and making a noisy entrance into the woods. Tristan smiled, knowing the stallion would chase them for only a short distance into the forest and then finally turn back to his master.

But he didn't.

He kept on going, finally out of sight.

Tristan stood up, ignoring his pain, the smile on his lips beginning to fade. He gave the customary whistle, but Pilgrim still did not appear. Concerned, he put two fingers into his mouth and whistled harder, but the horse was gone.

His mood now turning to genuine concern, Tristan pulled the bridle and reins from the tree branch and slung them across his shoulder. Then, clutching his quiver full of dirks, he began running across the field, toward the same spot where the Fliers of the Fields and the stallion had entered the forest.

He had to find the horse. Tristan's trot broke into a full run as his worry increased. At least it was easy to follow the trail. The heavyset horse left shoe prints in the soft earth, not to mention the wide trail of crushed trillium blossoms.

A sudden, terrible thought seized him. Suppose he came upon Pilgrim and the stallion was injured? There were many burrowing creatures in these woods, and their entrance holes into the forest floor were numerous. If the unknowing stallion stepped into one, he would go over and down, breaking his leg like a dry twig. Worse yet, Tristan would have to put the horse to death, with no humane means to do it. Back in Tammerland if a horse went down, a wizard would be called upon to dissipate the animal's mind into a painless, sudden death. But here, in these strange woods, he would somehow have to kill the horse himself, and all he had with him was his dirks—too small to do the job properly. It also frightened him to know that the edge of the cliff ran parallel to the horse's headlong run. In these dense woods, if the Fliers of the Fields changed course and suddenly flew out into the air over the cliff, the horse would not see the edge in time and run straight off. His mind sheered away from the images. They were too awful to contemplate.

Keep running, his frightened mind shouted to him. *The trail exists and has not changed course. Pilgrim is all right.*

He ran on, harder. At least another half league, he thought.

Tristan, his body now completely bathed in sweat, began to lose his bearings. Despite the shade from the dense trees, the forest seemed unusually hot. Fetid, heavily scented air made it difficult to breathe, and the undergrowth had become much thicker, branches and vines pulling at his hair and clothing like outstretched fingers, threatening to take him down. He realized suddenly that he had never entered this area of the forest before. Perhaps it was just his imagination, but the whole forest seemed unfamiliar and full of strange sensations. The bridle and reins were bouncing irritatingly across the back of his shoulder as he ran, and the pain in his legs was increasing, throbbing in unison with the quick beating of his heart.

He also had the chilling sensation that the harder he ran, the less progress he was making. He stopped and bent over, panting, trying to ease the fire in his lungs.

Standing still, he stole a precious moment to examine the forest more closely. Discouragingly, Pilgrim's trail still led away, up a small rise a short distance away. As his breathing slowed, he looked about slowly.

He thought he must be hallucinating.

Everything in this part of the forest was giant in size. Unfamiliar-looking trees reached endlessly toward the sky, with branches so thick that the ground below was occasionally lost in virtual darkness. Shimmering slivers of prismed sunlight randomly found their way to earth as the breeze shifted the great branches overhead. It would have taken at least five men holding hands to surround even the smallest of these enormous, ancient trees, and each of their partially exposed and snaking roots were at least three times the width of his thigh. The pink trillium blossoms, normally about the size of his palm, were now the size of dinner plates, and vines as thick around as ale kegs hung from the great heights all the way to the ground.

The forest floor was like the deepest, most luxurious carpet of the royal palace, and everywhere the colors were indescribable. The reds, greens, and violets of the foliage somehow seemed to become even more luminous as random silver pillars of sunlight occasionally stabbed down at them. He took a deep breath through his nostrils; even the texture of the air had suddenly changed and now seemed perfumed, a wonderfully aromatic combination of scents.

It was like walking into a dream.

Exhausted and dripping with sweat, he was amazed to see a nearby mushroom that was the size of a dinner table. He walked over and gently started to sit down. Unbelievably, it held his weight. He dropped the bridle on the soft forest floor and, still holding his quiver, tried to regain his breath.

Tristan once again looked up toward the path of widely spread foliage that marked the horse's trail. It went about fifty paces forward in a basically straight line, leading up to a small rise and disappearing upon what appeared to be a plateaued clearing. He sighed, strapped the quiver in its usual place around and across his back, picked up the reins and bridle, and resignedly started up the trail. Too tired to run, he walked quickly to the top of the rise.

When he finally stood at the top, what he saw made his jaw drop.

He was standing at the edge of a small circular clearing, bordered on all sides by tall trees with colorful foliage. Directly across from him on the other side of the glade was Pilgrim, standing dead still, intensely watching something. The horse looked calm and apparently unhurt, aside from some scrapes and scratches obtained during his frantic chase through the woods. His chest was heaving and dripping with sweat, and his muzzle was lathered with foam from the exertion of his run. And although Tristan was relieved to see him, it wasn't the stallion that now so fascinated the prince.

It was the butterflies.

Immediately next to where Pilgrim was standing at the edge of the clearing was a huge embankment. It stood strangely all upon its own, its right and left sides gently sloping down over some distance back to the level of the ground. Its edges were matted with the same pink trillium blossoms and soft, deep grasses that had covered the forest floor. Embedded in its center was a strange, square, gray shape that Tristan could not identify because it had long since been encroached upon and almost completely covered by odd, variegated vines. Had the butterflies not drawn the prince's attention to it, he would surely never have noticed it at all.

Perched upon the vines, resting entirely at peace, were the Fliers of the Fields, their only movement the occasional gentle opening and closing of their wings.

Tristan approached Pilgrim slowly, placing the bridle over his head and the bit into the horse's mouth. He led the stallion to the other side of the clearing and tied the reins securely around the branch of a tree. Pilgrim whinnied softly and once again pushed his head against his master as if apologizing for all the trouble that he had caused. The prince smiled and rubbed the horse's ears.

Walking back to the embankment, Tristan gently approached the butterflies. He had never heard of anyone having the opportunity to see them motionless at such a close distance. As he came even closer, they remained quiet and clinging to the vines, their closeness to each other composing a riotous pattern of color. Strangely, they almost seemed to welcome his presence.

And then he watched one disappear.

Not fly away, but truly disappear, as if it had just melted into and become one with the embankment. He watched, fascinated, as the next one crept carefully upward to the exact same spot and disappeared as well. Stepping closer still, he realized that they were, in turn, folding their wings together and slowly slipping through a vertical gap in the gray expanse beneath the vines. He now also saw that the grayness was a man-made wall of fieldstone. It looked to be hundreds of years old. He watched in awe, as one by one the Fliers of the Fields disappeared through the gap in the stone wall.

And then they were gone.

Tristan pushed aside some of the vines. The stone wall seemed to have been built without mortar. One narrow but rather tall stone had apparently loosened and fallen inward, allowing enough space for the Fliers of the Fields to enter.

Curious, he put one eye to the space but could see nothing beyond it. Inside, it was as dark as night. He selected a dirk from his quiver and tried to pry loose the stone to the right of the hole to get a better look. Even without mortar, it remained solidly in place. He removed the dirk and replaced it in the joint just below the same stone, and this time he thought he noticed it move a little bit. Bracing his legs and leaning forward at the waist, he put all his weight against the knife.

The result was completely without warning.

An entire section of the wall collapsed inward, and Tristan fell forward into the dark emptiness with it. Except this time, there was no tree branch on the other side to save him.

Nor was there any floor.

Down he fell, end over end, some of the loose stones following behind him into the pitch-black nothingness.

CHAPTER
Two

"I told you not to come." The old wizard's tone was not particularly polite. He did not mean it to be. "A woman in your condition should not be away from the palace midwives, much less sitting on top of a horse."

He watched ruefully as she turned awkwardly in her sidesaddle, trying to become more comfortable as their horses, side by side, took them deeper into the woods. He had been present at her birth, and had watched her grow into the beautiful, strong-willed woman he now saw before him. The long blond hair framed an intelligent face, strong but still feminine; her hazel eyes always seemed to dance with curiosity and love of life. And as uncomfortable as he knew she may be, he also knew she would never admit it.

He characteristically raised an eyebrow. "I needn't remind you that you are in the fifth moon of your pregnancy."

Shailiha, Tristan's twin sister, knew that the old one was right but couldn't bring herself to admit it. She needed to be here, and there was very little in this world that would have succeeded in stopping her.

When Tristan had not reported to the Wizards' Conservatory this morning as usual, the Directorate had immediately sent a runner to the stables. When they learned that Tristan's favorite mount was missing, as well as his saddle, they had decided to begin a search. For the headstrong prince to go off alone after his daily classes was not usually a cause for alarm, but his behavior of late had put everyone on edge, and his attendance was required that night at an important function at the palace. Shailiha would not have known of his disappearance but for the fact that she was already in the stables, tending to her favorite brood-mare's newborn foal.

After overhearing the wizards' runner question the stable boy, she had followed the fellow back to the Directorate's chambers and demanded answers from the old ones. When she had learned her brother was missing she had announced to them all in no uncertain terms that she would go find him, alone if need be, and an argument had ensued. But after the wizards had gone so far as to threaten to throw a containment warp around her if necessary to prevent her from leaving on her own, she finally agreed to a compromise. She could go, but Wigg would accompany her. At least he had given her time to fetch a basket of food and drink.

Leather creaked as she turned once again in her saddle. She loved her brother more than anything on earth, except perhaps for the unborn child she was carrying. Despite all that, if he was unhurt when they found him, she would be tempted to ask the old wizard to punish him rigidly. *Today of all days,* her troubled mind thought. She shook her head. If they didn't find him soon, this time he'd be in real trouble, future king or not.

She frowned. As the date of her father's abdication ceremony drew near, Tristan somehow seemed to get into more and more trouble, and she was determined to keep today's incident from their parents. Fortunately, her husband was on maneuvers all day with the Royal Guard and wouldn't miss her. The only other inhabitants of the palace who knew of her brother's disappearance were his teachers, the Directorate of Wizards, and she had sworn them to secrecy with a look that could have frozen water. Now Wigg, the most powerful of them, rode beside her, and she had to admit, if only to herself, that his company was a relief. She always felt safer around Wigg.

She looked to her right, at the old wizard's craggy profile. Over three hundred years old, he was still one of the most powerful men in the kingdom. The tan, creased face held a thin mouth, and under arched brows were bright aquamarine eyes that never missed a thing. His gray hair, pulled back from a widow's peak, ended in the traditional Directorate wizard's tail of braided hair that fell down his back. Simple gray robes draped loosely over his still-muscular body, and the hands that held his horse's reins were large and strong. It suddenly occurred to her that when he was young—before the application of the time enchantments—he probably would have been one of the most handsome men she had ever seen, almost as handsome as Tristan. She smiled to herself, knowing that the old wizard's gruff exterior belied how much he cared for her welfare. She loved him dearly and had all of her life.

Shailiha grinned to herself, remembering how Wigg, when they had gone to fetch their horses, had sworn the terrified stable boy to secrecy. Flicking his finger, the Lead Wizard had turned the poor fellow upside down in midair, ankles together, suspending him headfirst above that morning's freshly steaming pile of horse manure. Before setting him right, Wigg had promised to lower him in slowly, headfirst, should they return to learn the poor boy's lips had slipped. Once again, she smiled. By this time, his fellow stable hands probably thought the poor fellow had somehow gone mute. No one, she was sure, wanted to have to explain to the king and queen yet another of Tristan's indiscretions. She shifted gently in her sidesaddle as her mare stepped around a fallen log.

Beside her, Wigg reached into the small leather pouch that he wore around his waist. She had seen him put it on just before they left the palace. After crossing the plain that surrounded the city and entering the mountainous woods beyond, he had begun to reach into this pouch now and then and remove a couple of fingers full of an oddly colored powder she'd never seen before. He had then casually sprinkled the powder on the ground alongside his horse. Although very curious, she knew better than to ask the wizard about his craft. And so, without comment, she had simply watched the little ritual occasionally unfold as he rode along with her.

"Tell me, Wigg, why does he do it?" she asked now. Her brother's rebellious behavior of late truly disturbed her, and although she thought she understood him, for some reason she had a feeling Wigg understood him better. She watched her mare gently shake a fly from her head as they rode on.

Wigg changed the reins from his left hand to his right and spoke without turning to her. "Do you mean, why does he ignore his duties, prefer the war college over his academics, choose to associate with commoners instead of the court, unnecessarily harass the Directorate, and disappear into the woods with those odd knives of his all the time?" His voice was deep and resonant. "And why does he continue to bed women from all over the realm and yet take no wife?"

He paused and shook his head, letting his criticisms settle into her mind. "And why," he said finally, "and most importantly, does he purposely continue to defy his parents, the king and queen, and the very Directorate itself every time he disregards his duties?" He rose up slightly in his saddle, stretching and arching his back like a cat and taking his time about it, as if to tease her by withholding the answer. But when he turned toward her, she saw that the infamous aquamarine eyes were sad rather than mischievous. "The answer is more simple than you may think, my dear," he said, carefully measuring his words. "He doesn't want to be king." He once again faced forward.

Shailiha's breath caught momentarily in her throat, but upon considering it, she had to admit that the wizard might be right. Although
Tristan had never told her, all the signs had long been there. She wondered if, despite the strength of the prince's feelings, her brother had
kept them to himself to spare everyone else. That would be like him.
She began to feel her sisterly anger at him melt into sympathy. She tried
to imagine spending almost a lifetime as king and then a potential eternity as a wizard of the Directorate, never wanting to be either. He must
regard his future as life imprisonment, she thought, and in thirty days
his sentence was to begin.

Once again, she decided to dare question the wizard. "How can
you be so sure he doesn't want to be king?" she asked. In truth, she
knew the old one was right. She had known him too long and knew
better. In reality, she just wanted to know how it was he had found out
the truth before she had.

"Often the most complex of puzzles can be unlocked with the key
of simplicity," he mused, running his free hand down the length of his
face. He dropped some powder along the path. "It's simple. He told me."

She briefly felt her cheeks flush. At first she felt hurt that Tristan
could confide such a thing to Wigg but not to her, but her concern for
Tristan quickly outweighed the pain of her exclusion. As was her habit
when perplexed, she tentatively bit her lower lip.

Wigg could see the coming questions in her eyes. He could also see
that the woods were thickening and changing—and he became more
and more concerned the farther in they went. He could sense they were
coming closer to Tristan, but not yet close enough.

"He simply confided in me," the old one said. "It was upon the occasion of his twenty-ninth birthday, and he came to my chambers in
anger. We talked for a long time, and I learned that, for him, it was as if
some year-long hourglass had suddenly been turned over in his head. In
just one year he would be king, and nothing could stop it. The reality of
it all had finally sunk in. With so little time left before his coronation, I
suppose his recent actions have been a form of denial for him. A last
stab at freedom, if you will." He paused, considering his next words.
"Sometimes it seems that Tristan's problems lie more in what he won't
do rather than what he will, and like it or not, he *will* become the king
of Eutracia." He reached up to rub the neck of his black gelding. "But
the real problem is that if he truly does not want to become king, when
he does finally take the throne he will rule poorly, despite the Directorate, and Eutracia cannot afford that."

Shailiha considered the old one's words as she looked toward the
sun, putting the time at midafternoon. With the woods gradually grow-

ing denser, brightness was becoming more difficult to find, and the air was thicker and sweeter. She decided to change the subject.

"Wigg, how do you know where to go?" she asked hesitantly.

As far as she could tell, since they had entered the woods he had taken them in a basically straight line. But at one point, he had brought his horse to a stop and closed his eyes for a time, and then made a distinct turn to the left. He had not turned since then.

The wizard pulled back on his reins, halting his gelding. He looked as if he had had quite enough of her intrusive questions. Shailiha, stopping beside him, wondered if she had angered him. The wizard looked into her eyes. He had the deepest eyes she had ever seen. He was Lead Wizard of the Directorate; she couldn't begin to understand how much knowledge and power he had accumulated after more than three hundred years of practice at the craft.

"With training, endowed blood can sense other endowed blood," he replied simply. "I can tell we're getting closer to him. For some time now he has remained still. I only hope that he does not move again. The reason I fought the idea of you accompanying me was twofold. First, the close presence of your endowed blood makes it more difficult for me to sense him." He raised his eyebrow. "Your being his twin makes it doubly hard, because your blood is so similar."

For the first time the princess felt a twinge of guilt about forcing her presence upon the old wizard today. *Twins.* There had always been so much about her hereditary connection to Tristan that she didn't understand, that had never been explained to her, that had solicited no answers no matter how many questions she had asked over the years. She had been wondering lately whether the abdication ceremony would bring forth any solutions, but where the Directorate was concerned, one never knew. And it was this curiosity mixed with her love of life that usually managed to overcome her less-tenacious sense of royal decorum. She was famous for it, as was Tristan.

"Do you mean that you can smell him?" she asked, unconsciously wrinkling her nose.

He smiled benevolently at her incomprehension.

"No, not in the way that you mean. Rather, my mind can respond to his presence. The closer I come to him, the stronger the response. Actually, it is only a small thing." He made a throwaway gesture with his hand, as if the whole idea were unimportant and therefore unworthy of discussion, and set his horse moving with a light kick.

"And the second reason?" she prompted, trotting briefly to catch up.

"What second reason?" he asked testily. But she had known him long enough to ascertain when his hearing was becoming selective.

"The second reason you did not want to bring me. What was it?"

Wigg scowled. "If you must know, there are things in these woods. Unpleasant things. Or at least there used to be. I haven't come to this forest for at least a hundred years, so don't expect any detailed descriptions from my memory." He turned his face back to the ever-thickening forest.

Shailiha dismissed his gruffness, turning her mind once again to her brother. She felt perfectly safe with Wigg. She realized that perhaps she was being naive, but she couldn't imagine anything the old one couldn't do, including protecting her with his life. She looked down to her riding habit, placing an affectionate hand on her protruding abdomen. That also meant protecting her unborn child. Soon Tristan would take the throne, and she would be a mother. Her husband, Frederick, was already bursting with pride.

Looking around at the passing woodlands, she suddenly realized that while she had been so lost in conversation with the wizard, the forest had changed strikingly in appearance. The woods were much thicker, and she began to see foliage here and there that was unfamiliar to her, and more brilliantly colored. The terrain was sloping ever upward, and long, thin, variegated vines now hung from the tops of the trees almost to the forest floor. The ground was soft and lush. Oddly, the air was much warmer here, despite the fact that the thickening trees permitted less and less sunlight, and the pleasantly sweet aroma she had noticed earlier continued to permeate the air. Still, Wigg kept them on a basically straight line.

Shailiha's mind turned back to the palace they had left only a few hours ago, to her mother and father, the king and queen, and to all of the other people who lived there. She never ceased to be amazed at how many it took to oversee everything and to help the king to rule. From the royal family, the Directorate, and the Royal Guard, all the way down to the lowliest stable boy now sworn to secrecy by Wigg and including the hundreds of people in-between, each had their place and their responsibility in the scheme of things. And all of them were diligently working now toward one common goal; the abdication ceremony of her father, King Nicholas, and Tristan's concurrent coronation as the new king. It was a grand and joyous event that was always anxiously awaited by the populace. The preparations had been going on for months.

This evening there was to be a royal inspection of the ceremony preparations in the Great Hall. Literally hundreds of people would be milling about waiting for them, each hoping to please the royal entourage with his or her work. There would be decorators, advisors, entertainers, chefs and pastry makers, maidservants and cleaners, not to mention the entertainers, musicians, and curious dukes, duchesses, and diplomats from the various provinces of Eutracia. She sighed slowly, letting her breath out in a long stream. There would also be the usual covey of available women who hoped to catch the prince's eye.

Was it possible that Tristan had run away permanently instead of just for the day? Did he hate the prospect of being king to such an extent that he would go into hiding? *Would he do such a thing to all of us?*

Totally nonplussed, her head began to reel with the unsettling, new set of complications and repercussions. Who would break the news to her parents, if Tristan was truly gone? And who would succeed her father, King Nicholas, without Tristan to fill the void? The terrifying prospect of becoming the queen of Eutracia suddenly loomed before her. The realm had never had a queen. But if Tristan had indeed disappeared, she remained the only heir of endowed blood from the union of her parents, and her mother had long since been unable to give birth. Would the Directorate simply choose another of the Eutracian citizens to become king, as they had done in the past? Or would they force her to take the throne in light of the fact that she was pregnant and might give birth to a son of their family's endowed blood? Then, in another thirty years, Eutracia would once again have a king. Upon his succession, would she be forced to join the Directorate by her father's decision regarding Tristan's fate? And as what? A sorceress? Wasn't that what they used to call women who were trained in the craft? But there had been no sorceresses in Eutracia since the training of women of endowed blood had been banned at the end of the Sorceresses' War, over three hundred years earlier. What, then, would become of her?

A tear began to trace a shiny path down one cheek. *Tristan, where are you?*

As if reading her mind, Wigg gently extended one of his hands to her face, wiping away the tear, his previously harsh demeanor temporarily faded.

"Don't worry, little one," he said comfortingly. "We shall find him. He doesn't know I can sense his location, and it is only a matter of time, especially if he is not on the move. Most probably he has simply forgotten tonight's festivities."

A small clearing had appeared in the midst of the ever-thickening forest. It looked like a good place to stop. He hated the idea of taking time to rest, but feared the princess may need it. Neither did he mention to her that Tristan could probably survive alone in these woods indefinitely if he chose to, perhaps avoiding even the old wizard himself. No one knew these woods like Tristan.

Wigg lowered his eyes slightly before speaking his next carefully measured words. "If he refuses to return of his own free will to fulfill his duties, the situation will become difficult, and even though I love him as I would my own child, I may have to take action to ensure his return. I have a great responsibility to your father."

Just as Shailiha began to wonder what type of action Wigg was referring to, her bay mare abruptly stopped walking, then began to paw the ground nervously, snorting and shaking her head back and forth, rattling her bridle. Wigg's black gelding reared up and whinnied loudly. Despite any prodding from their riders, the two horses refused to advance into the clearing.

With a quick gesture from Wigg, Shailiha stopped trying to spur her horse onward. He put an index finger vertically across his lips to indicate silence, and she nodded. Wigg quickly dismounted, holding his reins firmly in one hand as he walked forward and turned to face the gelding. Closing his eyes, he placed his right hand flat upon the horse's forehead for a moment. Immediately, the gelding began to calm down, while Shailiha's mare still continued to dance about. Fearing for her unborn child, she started to dismount. But, as if seeing her through his closed eyes, Wigg immediately stretched his other arm forward, gesturing to her to stay in her saddle.

She watched Wigg as he abruptly turned away to look into the clearing. Then, completely amazed, she watched the color immediately drain from his face. Automatically, the princess lifted her eyes to follow his gaze . . . and began to shake uncontrollably, bile rising in her throat and making her feel as if she might vomit.

It was something out of a nightmare, and its eyes were focused directly on Wigg.

It was too large and misshapen to be a man. Yet it stood on two legs and had arms like a man. The huge, elongated head held insane, bloodshot eyes, but there was no nose, only slits in the skin where a man's nostrils would be. On each side of the bald head were flat, elongated ears, the earlobes ending in long, ragged points of skin. Hanging from each corner of the mouthful of dark and decaying teeth was a perfect white incisor fang as long as her index finger. Lathered drool ran from the mouth to the chin, and down to its hairy chest in long white strings. Its only clothing was a leather-fringed warrior's skirt, which did little to hide the grotesque, misshapen male genitals beneath it. Its own dried excrement clung darkly to its legs, and each of the highly elongated fingers and toes ended in long, tearing talons. Around its neck hung an odd chain of small round orbs. Gasping, Shailiha realized they were a collection of desiccated eyeballs. It held in its hands a terrible battle ax such as she had never seen. The long, black helve was randomly patterned with dried blood, and its top was crowned with a cracked human skull. From each of the skull's temples a shiny silver ax blade extended outward at right angles. The sun streaming through the treeless clearing glinted menacingly off their highly polished edges.

She looked again at the nightmare's eyes. They weren't just insane. They held something else—something she could only describe as an insatiable, uncontrollable need.

From the center of the clearing it stared unflinchingly at Wigg for what seemed an eternity, its chest heaving. Another string of white drool snaked wetly from its chin to the ground.

Then, without warning, the thing raised the battle ax high above its head and charged headlong at the old wizard. Its speed was amazing. Crossing the clearing in an instant, it let forth a deranged battle scream. Terrified, Shailiha watched as Wigg stood frozen before his horse, almost as if he were willingly embracing his own death. Finally, at the last possible instant, the wizard seemed to regain his senses and rolled nimbly to the right across the field, the silver, wheeling blur of the battle ax barely missing his head. The ax blades continued their deadly swath downward, cleaving point-blank into the black gelding, slicing horsehide, bone, and muscle. The horse screamed. Blood erupted everywhere as the head and neck finally tore away from the shoulders. Its legs helplessly kicking, the gelding lost his brief struggle with death in midair and crashed sideways upon the ground.

For a moment the thing stood looking at the carnage of the horse, the blood running from the helve down its forearms and finally dripping from its elbows into a puddle upon the ground. A sickening grin began to walk the length of its grotesque mouth as yet more drool, pink with splattered blood, fell to its chest.

It turned once more toward Wigg and raised the ax over its head for another charge.

But this time, as the battle ax reached the zenith of its swing, the wizard raised his arms and the ax was pulled out of the creature's hands and flew sideways across the clearing like a pinwheel, landing squarely at Wigg's feet. Shailiha watched, panic-stricken, as the old one calmly made no attempt to pick it up when the thing charged at him again, this time extending its bare hands and sharp talons.

The princess shook with the realization that the wizard was about to die before her eyes.

Instead, though, Wigg pointed to the ax and it rose hauntingly into the air. He quickly extended his fingers, and the ax flew across the clearing, end over end, in a black-and-silver blur.

With a sickening crack, one of the ax's blades buried itself into the thing's forehead. The creature fell over onto its back, dead. Yellowish brain matter began to ooze from the shattered skull.

Then immediately came the thunder and lightning. She thought at first she must be hallucinating, to see lightning on such a calm day. It streaked its way across the expanse of the otherwise clear sky in convoluted patterns she had never imagined possible, followed by thunder that pounded through the air, shaking everything in the forest. Then she heard a strange noise, and once again looked out at the thing that lay in the middle of the clearing—the thing that Wigg had killed.

From around its great, shattered skull came a hissing sound as the yellow fluid from its head bled out into the grass. An inexplicable shroud of fog began to rise up from the turf around the head, bringing up into the air a stench so malodorous that she was forced to lower her face, covering her nose and mouth.

Shailiha found herself dumbly looking down to find wet, sticky blood and pink pieces of horseflesh all over her clothes. Blankly rubbing her protruding abdomen, she lifted her hand to see her palm and fingers covered with the horrible mixture. She began to vomit.

The last thing she remembered was Wigg's hands reaching up to catch her as she fell from her saddle.

*T*he sounds of his weeping awakened her. It came from somewhere off in the distance, yet it was very distinct. *How odd.* Opening her eyes, she saw fluffy clouds upon the bright blue canvas of an afternoon sky, floating behind the orange and green leaves of a hypernia tree. *How beautiful.* But she was going to be sick again. She rolled onto her side and just let it happen. As her mind began to clear, she realized she was lying on the soft grass under a tree on one side of the clearing.

Suddenly she remembered. The clearing. The . . . thing. She sat bolt upright and looked around. The creature that had tried to kill Wigg still lay dead where it had fallen, the handle of the battle ax rising into the air from the thing's smashed, grotesque forehead. The odd shroud of fog that had inexplicably gathered around it was still there. To her left, the remains of Wigg's beheaded horse lay at pitifully impossible angles in a huge pool of its own dark-red blood. She looked down over her riding habit and gently rubbed her abdomen, praying to the Afterlife that her unborn child had not been injured. Somehow her clothes and hands had been wiped clean, or as close to clean as someone could have done under the circumstances.

She heard the sound of sobbing. Slowly rising to her feet, she was amazed to see Wigg sitting back upon his heels in the grass next to the dead creature, crying over it almost uncontrollably. With his hands covering his face and his head bent over, tears dripped from between his fingers and onto his robes, creating dark-gray blotches. His shoulders were shaking.

Shailiha walked up to the old one, trying not to look at the mangled corpse that lay between them both. Without speaking, she laid one hand upon his shoulder and bent down to look at him. Uncovering his face, the wizard finally took her hands in his, stood, and led her out of the clearing.

He took her to where he had placed the saddle and tack after removing it from the murdered horse. The saddle blanket was spread upon the ground, and Shailiha rather awkwardly sat down upon it, relieved to be off her feet, for she thought she might soon fall down, anyway. It occurred to her that she had never in her life seen a wizard cry, nor had she ever heard of one doing so.

Wigg slowly sat down next to her. Reaching out, he gently spread open the upper and lower lids of her right eye, and examined it. Satisfied, he reached into the sleeve of his robe and produced a clean, recently picked plant root.

"Suck on this from time to time, little one," he said compassionately.

As she obediently took the root from him and placed it in her mouth, a pleasantly sweet flavor emerged.

At her questioning look he said, "It will help with the vomiting."

His tears apparently suspended for the moment, he placed the palm of his left hand on her abdomen and closed his eyes. After several seconds, he opened them again. "Your child is well," he said. He rubbed his hands together as he looked back out to the clearing. "We have been fortunate."

She reached out to wipe a tear from his cheek. He had saved her life, but she understood none of what had happened.

"Wigg, what *was* that thing?" she asked urgently. "Why did it try to kill you?" She lowered her eyes. "And why do you cry so?" She looked out into the clearing. "It's dead. You should be happy."

Without speaking, Wigg rose to his feet and walked the short distance to where he had tied the princess' mare to a tree. Reaching into the food basket tied to the saddle, he brought forth a dark green bottle of ale and returned to the blanket to sit cross-legged before Shailiha.

He removed the cork and took a long draft of the ale. His eyes went back to the corpse in the field, and he suddenly seemed to be far away. He was still looking out at the body when he finally said, "He was my friend."

A look of shock spread over Shailiha's face. If she had not been with child, she would have taken a drink of the ale herself. She quickly removed the root from her mouth.

"Your *friend*?" she exclaimed. "That hideous thing just tried to kill us!"

Wigg turned back to her, his face beginning to regain its usual strength and composure. She was relieved to see that Wigg was becoming Wigg again.

"Phillius," he said softly. "That hideous *thing*, as you call it, that lies dead in the clearing at my own hand was my friend, and his name was Phillius."

He took another draft of ale. She was glad to see him finally smiling gently into her eyes. Perhaps the ale was helping. He sighed. "It requires some explanation." His voice had become barely audible.

Shailiha arranged her legs into a more comfortable posture, raised her eyes to the old one, and tilted her head slightly. She was willing to invest the time to hear his explanation, whatever it was, and it was clear by her demeanor that she was not to be denied.

The wizard pressed his lips together in a tight half smile and let out a deep breath as if he had been holding it in for years.

"The creature that lies dead in the field is called a blood stalker," he began. "It is a mutant product of the Sorceresses' War, protected from then until now by what are called time enchantments. We had thought him and all of his kind long since dead. There hasn't been a confirmed sighting of a blood stalker in over three centuries." He rubbed his lower lip back and forth slowly. *How could one of their time enchantments have lasted this long?* his racing mind asked. *This should not be possible.*

"I thought you said his name was Phillius?"

"It was. In truth, Princess, he was my friend and my mentor." He looked down at his hands as he laced his fingers before speaking again. "He was a wizard."

"A wizard?" she exclaimed. "That ghastly thing? No wizard ever looked like that. It's impossible." She was quite surprised that he was being so forthcoming with his answers. She knew he would not even have considered speaking to her of this if she had not been of endowed blood. The wizards of the Directorate, those six who had the greatest responsibility for victory in the Sorceresses' War, preferred never to speak of their wartime experiences. Coming to the conclusion that she was about to hear a rare wizard's story of the war, she schooled herself to look more respectful.

He took another draft of the ale, cognizant of the subtle change in her demeanor.

"During the war, many wizards died," he began. "At that time we actually were fearful that male endowed blood would become extinct. We never knew how many of us there were because then, unlike now, no birth records were ever kept. A child was simply known as either 'endowed' or 'common.' He or she could either be trained in the craft, or not. There was as yet no Directorate, and as far as we knew, the jewel called the Paragon did not exist. Wizards helped to train each other in the craft, but we were widely dispersed across the countryside, with no real sense of organization except for those of us living in the palace at Tammerland. Training was haphazard at best, and the craft itself was in only a rudimentary form of development. This is one of the reasons why the sorceresses almost won. They were better organized and had succeeded in pushing the boundaries of magic farther than we had, and were thus more powerful than we were. But because of the discovery of the Paragon, their advantage was not to last." He paused once again to take another swallow of ale.

He frowned at his next thoughts. "It is not widely known today, but the sorceresses tried, whenever possible, not to kill wizards—they preferred to take them alive."

Before he continued he once again looked at his hands, the same hands that had just killed his one-time friend. "Captives of unendowed, or 'common' blood, often were pressed into service in the sorceresses' armies. But the various fates that the endowed ones suffered were far beyond description. Some were killed outright, some tortured for the sorceresses' pleasure, and some turned into blood stalkers like poor Phillius. Others were left alive for yet different purposes." He turned his attention toward the crushed skull of the corpse in the field, and to the strange fog that had surrounded it. It had been over three hundred years since he had seen such a haze, and it brought him no pleasure to have seen one again today.

"What other purposes?" she asked gently.

He looked back at her with tired aquamarine eyes.

"Breeding. Because the union of two endowed people is the most likely to produce an endowed child, they raped the wizards repeatedly, hoping for a pregnancy that would yield a special girl child to raise as a sorceress. The male babies were simply killed outright. We never understood the importance of such a child to them. Had they not spent so much of their power and their time trying to achieve this birth, we may never have prevailed. Inadvertently, they gave us the one thing we needed most: time." Again he paused, as though not wishing to relive the painful memories.

The princess looked at the corpse lying in the hot afternoon sun. The fog around the body had dissipated, and hungry flies had begun to gather around the exposed brain to settle in dark clumps upon the yellow fluid. Feeling sick again, she returned her gaze to the old one, still feeling full of questions. This time it was she who wished to change the subject.

"Surely Phillius, if he was a wizard, did not always look like that?" she asked. She put the root back into her mouth.

Wigg shook his head. "No. At one time he was a strong, handsome man. The change in his appearance was part of the mutation process forced upon him by the sorceresses. During the war, it was said that the process was so painful and happened so quickly that many of the wizards simply went insane. In that case, they had no use and they were killed. Only the strongest of them could withstand the transformation. Phillius was one of those, and his capture was a sad day for all of us."

Wigg closed his eyes. He knew that had Phillius survived he would have been an invaluable member of the Directorate, and his wisdom was sorely missed.

"Then how did you know it was him?" she queried. She was becoming more interested with every word.

Wigg took another swallow of the ale, replacing the cork. He stood without speaking and walked to the dead blood stalker. Carefully avoiding the yellow fluid in the grass, he lifted up the inside of the thing's left forearm so Shailiha could see it from where she was. He pointed with his other hand to an odd, bright red birthmark, then gently laid the forearm back upon the ground before returning to the princess.

"I had known Phillius since I was a child," he explained as he sat down again. "That birthmark had always been a part of him. I saw it when he first raised his ax."

She carefully considered her next words.

"Is that why you hesitated?" She regretted the question the moment it left her lips, but she had to know.

He drew himself up and looked into her questioning face. "Do you doubt me because you yourself might have been killed? I am fully aware of my responsibilities, Princess, and I have successfully protected many others who came into this world long before you."

She looked down at the blanket. He smiled and put a finger beneath her chin, raising her eyes up to his. As long as he had known this one, he had admired her spirit. Clearly, she and her brother were twins in more ways than one.

"The truth is, you were never in any danger. To answer your question, yes, that is why I hesitated. But he was only after me. Once I was dead, he would have totally ignored you. Blood stalkers pursued only males of endowed blood, and of them only those who had already been trained in the craft. Their entire existence was to serve solely as the sorceresses' assassins, with only wizards as their prey. Clever, when you think about it."

"If I was not in danger, then what would it have done after it had killed you?"

Wigg looked briefly over Shailiha's shoulder as he pursed his lips. "Eaten the dead horse. Raw."

She thought she was going to be sick again. She sucked once more at the root.

"Is that why you named them blood stalkers?" she asked.

"We did not name them—their creators did. The sorceresses stripped them of all their powers except sensing us, and then gave them inordinate strength, supplying each one with the rather creative battle ax that you saw him carry. It is said that the skull atop each of the battle axes is the skull of the blood stalker's first victim. That is why it had such a discernible crack in its top."

"There was a smell." She wrinkled up her nose. "When you killed him, there was an awful smell, and steam came up from around him. I saw it. It was terrible."

Wigg looked out again at the remains of what had once been his friend, noticing that the grass all around the smashed skull's perimeter had turned black. He looked away. The only way to remember this, he knew, was to hold tight to the knowledge that had Phillius been able to choose, he would have chosen death. Ultimately, Wigg had been able to give him at least that much. He knew it was this realization that would help both him and the Directorate deal with some of the pain.

"During the transformation, the brain matter always turned yellow and became acidic," he said. "When his skull parted, the odor was released. Early on, we tried to retrieve them from their transformations to return them back to human form. But we always failed. Before the discovery of the Paragon, the sorceresses were just too strong for us. Many wizards, some more capable than myself, died in the attempts to reverse the process. It took us time, but sadly all we really learned was that the fastest way to kill one was to crush the skull. But the sorceresses knew that, too, and were able to use even that technique against us." He picked a blade of grass and idly began to shred it between his fingers.

"What do you mean?"

"As I said, the yellow brain matter is acidic. That's why you saw the foggy steam. It was burning into the grass as he lay there. If it touches human skin, even the smallest amount, it is instantaneously fatal." He paused. "Another gift from the sorceresses."

She had more questions, and she could have asked them all day. If nothing else, Princess Shailiha was known for being inquisitive.

"What about the thunder and lightning? The sky remained clear. What I saw was impossible."

Wigg smiled and placed the tip of a long, ancient index finger squarely on the end of the princess' nose.

"Too many questions, Shailiha," he lectured. His left eyebrow came up again. "Have you forgotten why we came out here in the first place?"

Her cheeks flushed. Of course she had not forgotten about her brother! She tossed her long blond hair over one shoulder. "Please, just tell me about the thunder and lightning," she begged. She was too curious to stop now. "And, oh, why did you put your hands on your poor horse's face? Last questions, I promise."

For several moments he simply looked at her without speaking. She had been through a great deal already today, and Tristan was still missing. There was much yet to do. He noticed there were still bits of blood in her hair, and reminded himself that they must do something about that before they returned to the palace.

"It's a bargain," he said finally. He looked slowly up at the sky as he thought about his reply.

"Every time a blood stalker is killed, there is the same strange atmospheric event. Massive thunder and lightning of a highly unusual type, without dark clouds or rain. During the war, we could only surmise that it served to inform the sorceresses of the death of one of their own. Sadly, I have seen it myself too many times." *But there is another, darker reason,* he thought. *One I cannot yet share with you.*

He couldn't blame the princess for her curiosity. Those of endowed blood always had an insatiable desire to learn the craft, and she was no different. But since the Sorceresses' War, the teaching of the craft to females had been strictly forbidden.

"As for the horse, I was trying to sense from the poor animal the reason, the danger, that was preventing them both from going any farther." He frowned. "I got my answer."

He promptly stood up. Without explanation he walked to the center of the field and stood near the corpse. He examined the handle of the battle ax and finally found a spot clear of the awful acid, by which he could hold it. He methodically wiped the weapon in the grass and laid it to one side of the clearing. Then he pulled the hood of his simple gray robe down over his head, partially hiding his face. Walking back to stand before the remains of his one-time friend, he clasped his hands before him and bowed his head. Immediately, the corpse burst into bright azure flames that rose high into the air, and the stench became much worse. He then went to the remains of the murdered gelding and repeated the process. On his way back to Shailiha, he beckoned her to stand, then picked up the blanket, basket, and tack, and began to saddle the mare. Leaving her horse tied to the tree, he helped the young woman into her sidesaddle. Then, to her surprise, he turned and walked away without saying a word, passing the burning, stinking corpse and disappearing into the smoke.

If I am not upwind of the dead, I shall never sense the blood of the living, he thought to himself.

Stepping out of the smoke on the other side, Wigg stopped, holding his hands out before him, his eyes closed. He could sense Tristan's presence. But it was much weaker than before, as if being blocked by something. Worry began to crowd into the corners of his mind.

Returning to Shailiha, he untied the mare and began to lead it across the field in the direction of Tristan's presence. There was much more that he could have told her, but he chose to remain silent. He would have to swear both her and her brother to secrecy about the blood stalker before they returned to Tammerland. But the presence of the gruesome thing had unnerved him. Despite the Directorate's hopes that all of the blood stalkers had perished, Phillius had somehow prevailed for over three centuries.

He suddenly stopped short, wondering. It could be even worse. He had recently heard of the unexplained disappearances of several of the lesser rural wizards. Phillius might not have simply survived in hiding all of those years. A cold shudder shot through him, as the unwanted thoughts surprised his mind.

Phillius might actually have been dead, and suddenly recalled, he thought.

Turning back for one last glimpse of the burning corpse, he raised his free hand, palm open. Shailiha watched, her mouth agape, as the bloody battle ax rose into the air, flying in a straight line this time, its long black handle slapping directly into Wigg's palm. They turned and walked on through the smoke.

$\mathcal{W}$hen Tristan awoke, the first sensations that came to him were those of pain and noise. Pain throughout his entire body—and a noise he could not identify. Both crashed in upon his still-groggy mind like dual awakening explosions. He opened his eyes to find only blackness. The combination was at once both intolerable and terrifying.

I pray to the Afterlife, please do not let me be blind, Tristan prayed.

His face felt wet, and some kind of liquid was running down into his eyes. Realizing he was on his back, he began to raise himself up. It took three tries before his swimming head finally allowed him to sit upright. There was pain in every part of his body, and still he could not see. Dazed and disoriented, he had no memory of how he got here. *Wherever here is,* he wondered.

Running his hand across his forehead, he felt the fluid between his fingertips. It was thick enough to be blood, and it was warm to the touch like blood—but he could feel no wound. He hurt everywhere. Blindly, he used his hands to wipe his face off as best he could.

The ever-present noise was overwhelming. A great and terrible rushing noise, he finally decided. But in the pitch-black void, he could not quite place the sound. It was at this point that his eyes began to adjust to the small amount of light. Joyously, he began to pick out odd shapes in the gloom.

I can see. Thank the Afterlife, I can see.

Turning his head, he was now able to begin to make out the weak shaft of light as it cast dimly downward from the hole in the wall above. It gave off only enough light for him to determine that there was a set of broken stone steps beneath it, leading down toward the blackness near where he sat. They looked to be about forty feet high. And then it came back to him. The chase for Pilgrim. The butterflies on the wall. And falling through into the black nothingness.

Standing slowly, he was able to determine that nothing was broken. But the pain in his joints and muscles was almost debilitating. Looking up at the dimly lit hole high in the wall he could see that he had fallen a long way, probably hitting the steps several times on the way down.

He seemed to be in an underground cavern. A deep one. At the bottom. For safety's sake, he got down on his hands and knees and began crawling toward the spot where he estimated the stone steps would touch the ground. Upon reaching them there was enough light to see that the steps were indeed at least a hundred feet tall, and stopped at the top where he had fallen in. He didn't know whether he trusted them to hold his weight, but any fool could see he had little choice.

Cautiously, he began crawling up the steps like a toddler. Slowly and painfully he made it to the top, all the while his eyes adjusting to the strengthening light, the strange indescribable loudness of the rushing noise fading away behind him. Eventually he stood on the last step, facing the jagged hole he had broken in the wall when he had fallen through. Lifting his foot over the crumbling stones, he stepped back into the clearing, glad for the second time that day to be alive. He had no idea how long he had been unconscious, but squinting at the sun, he estimated at least two hours to have gone by. He breathed a sigh of relief when he saw Pilgrim, still tied to the tree where he had left him.

When the prince reached his horse, Pilgrim immediately rubbed the length of his face against his master's shoulder and whinnied softly, as if impatient to be untied.

Tristan smiled. But even smiling hurt.

"No, I won't let you run free again," he said softly into the stallion's ear. "Not keeping you tied up is the cause of all my troubles today. You're staying here."

Ignoring his aching body, he returned to the hole in the wall and began to loosen more stones, allowing additional light to enter the depths below. After a good half hour, he very gingerly stepped back through the hole and onto the first of the stone steps. He couldn't see much, but thought he could make out a shape near the bottom.

He loosened a few more stones and peered down again, trying to make out the shape. It looked as if it was mounted on the wall near the bottom of the steps.

A torch!

Carefully, slowly, he made his way back down, not knowing whether he was doing the right thing. His mind and body had certainly had enough punishment for one day, but his curiosity was overpowering him. The great rushing noise filled his ears again, hammering his senses with all its fury. It seemed always to go onward, unabated and unrelenting. And yet the sound was frustratingly familiar.

When he reached the bottom step, he could see that his discovery was indeed a wall torch. Tristan never traveled into the woods without flint, which he now produced from his pants pocket. Reaching up, he was barely able to take down the torch from the wall. He could tell it had not been lit in a long time, but it still smelled of oil. Leaning it up against the stone steps by its wooden handle, he struck his flint, and the torch erupted into flame. He turned the torchlight toward the darkness.

What he saw made the breath leave his lungs in disbelief.

He was standing on the floor of a huge, oddly shaped underground cavern, at least several hundred feet long in each direction, as well as high. Stalactites of every color and description hung from the ceiling, some so long they almost reached the floor. Some of their older brothers had in fact already found the floor some time long ago, creating here and there the impression of marvelously beautiful stone columns connecting the floor and ceiling. But it was still too dark to see very far. And the noise went on and on, roaring in his ears.

Looking to the wall at his left he saw another torch, and then another and yet another, their shadows extending like fingers along the murky lengths of the cavern walls. He lit many of them in a row, the noise growing louder all the time as he walked farther into the depths of the cave, until finally he extinguished and dropped the torch in his hand, and turned from the now-illuminated wall to face the interior of the chamber.

It was the most arresting example of nature he had ever seen.

The waterfall was about the same height as the steps he had fallen down—about forty feet. It was at least an equal distance wide. Springing from a tunnel in the opposite wall of the cavern, the water traveled about twenty feet across a smooth horizontal stone precipice before finally falling gracefully into a large stone pool at the bottom. Tristan immediately realized that the waterfall was the source of the noise, and that he had been prevented from identifying the sound because of the way it bounced randomly from wall to wall across the cavern. He shook his head. Had the falls been outdoors, he would have recognized the sound instantly.

At the opposite end of the pool, the water ran out through a low tunnel in the rock. It occurred to him that the water's exit tunnel would ensure that the pool would never overflow, leading him to wonder whether the waterfall was man-made. *But who could have made this?* he wondered. He stood transfixed.

Looking around at the walls, he noticed a great variety of plants and flowers that he had never seen before; the floor itself was covered with thick, green foliage. Every plant was huge, and the colors were incredibly vibrant. He began to walk closer to the falls, but suddenly stopped himself in midstride.

How have these things grown here without sunlight? he asked himself. *So much of this is impossible. Yet here they are.*

Looking further, he saw that high upon the walls near the ceiling there were words carved into the rock in a language that was completely foreign to him. The strangely oblique writing completely encircled the rim of cavern.

Making his way back to the stone steps, he saw that they ended not far from the edge of the pool. His foot struck against something hard. Hard and sharp. He jumped back instinctively, only to realize that he had found his dirks and quiver, which he'd lost when he fell. Relieved, he began to collect the dirks, eventually finding all of them and returning them to the quiver, which he buckled on in its usual place across his right shoulder.

Suddenly, he felt dizzy. Slowly, he sat down upon the bottom step to try to clear his mind. Mesmerized, he watched as the water seemed to dance and play in the flickering light of the torches, turning and undulating strangely as if it were alive. A sudden, intense curiosity about the water came to him. He looked to the top of the falls where the water fairly jumped off the precipice, falling downward, ever downward, separating itself on the way to the pool into drops that looked more like sparkling crystals than liquid. And, oddly, each drop seemed to have a pink cast. He reasoned it must be because of the torchlight and the many reflected colors of the plants. The longer he sat looking, the more intrigued he became, almost as if the pool of water was calling to him, beckoning him to join it as it cascaded into the pool. And the longer he watched, the more inviting the water became.

Its allure was becoming irresistible.

Without thinking, he rose and began to remove his clothes. His leather knee boots, trousers, black vest, quiver, and undergarments soon all lay in a dirty pile at his feet. Serenely detached, he watched himself walk forward. It was as if in a dream that he saw his feet go to the edge of the dark, rolling water. He was at the far end, near the steps, where the water seemed the calmest, and he stood there naked for a moment, calmly looking down at his reflection as if he were looking at someone else. He saw his longish black hair, the high cheekbones, what some would describe as the cruel mouth, and the slim, muscular body all dancing in the reflected light of the torches. Then he tilted his face toward the ceiling, closed his eyes, and calmly jumped feetfirst into the pool.

This part of the pool was deep. When he surfaced, he swam a little distance over to shallower water. He laid his head back against the cool, slick side of the stone pool and closed his eyes.

The effect was unexpected, but far from unpleasant.

Despite the fact that the stone wall surrounding the pool was quite cool, the water itself was warm, much warmer in fact than he would have guessed water from an underground spring to be. It seemed to surround and caress his naked body of its own will. As inexplicably as it had arrived, his dizziness began to fade, along with all of the other aches and pains he had garnered this day. The longer he lay in the warm pool, the better he felt. In time not only did his pains completely vanish, but he also began to feel a resurgence of energy and strength, and with it a lightening of his mood and an increase in his confidence. Mixed with the wonderful sensations of warmth and strength was the ever-present sound of the falls tumbling into the pool. He was becoming used to the sound—in fact, he was starting to find it reassuring and actually quite beautiful.

He smiled. It was really quite extraordinary. And suddenly, he became aware of a new, unmet need: a sudden powerful thirst, such as he had never known. Thinking back, he realized that it had been hours since he had drunk anything. He joined his hands together to gather up a cup of pool water, and slowly opened his eyes as he brought the liquid to his lips.

It was then that he saw the Fliers of the Field.

He barely noticed the water trickling out of his hands as he gazed at them gathered on the far side of the pool. There had to be at least a dozen of them perched in a quiet line at the water's edge, their wings a riot of colors that reflected into the pool from the torches. They had either not noticed his presence or, for some reason, were not fearful of him in these surroundings. Occasionally each would slowly lower and raise its huge, expressive wings while the others remained quiet at the edge of the pool. Then he realized the reason for their presence.

They're drinking from the pool!

As if in response to his thoughts, all the giant butterflies rose into the air at once, heading straight for him. They circled his head, swerving and dipping to and fro as if teasing him to join them, just as they had done to Pilgrim. And then, as fast as they had come, they swirled single file up the stone steps to the light, taking turns squeezing through the broken wall, and were gone. He smiled to himself. Unlike his impetuous horse he would not chase after them.

The prince of Eutracia remained alone in the warm pool. He felt wonderful, except for his raging thirst. He had never felt anything like it. It was almost as if the water were begging to be consumed by him. No other need—no hunger, no pain, no pleasure—had in his entire life ever been this compelling. His breath became ragged and uneven as his body and mind joined in the almost sexual need for the fluid that swirled around him. He looked longingly again at the water.

The butterflies. Was their amazing size due to drinking the water? He dared not drink.

With more willpower than he had ever before summoned forth, he turned and pulled himself out of the water to stand naked and dripping at the pool's edge. His chest was heaving with exhaustion. Once out of the water his body and mind began to calm, and the awful thirst abated. But his earlier ache and pains remained gone, and he continued to feel unusually strong. More than a little confused, he began to dress.

Clothed once again, he thought to at least wash the mud from his knee boots before going back to the palace. He slowly bent over and cupped some of the water in his hands, then turned toward the wall of flickering torches.

What he saw made him jump back in fright, the liquid tumbling from his hands to splash on the ground at his feet.

The water was a deep red. He had not been able to see his own cupped hands through it. *It was like holding a handful of blood,* he realized. He quickly wiped his hands down the length of his dirty pants. Suddenly he realized that this must have been the fluid that he had wiped from his face when he had fallen down the stairs. Apparently he had landed close enough to the pool to be splashed by some of the spray from the falls.

He had seen all he wanted to of this place for one day.

Nervously, he walked past the wall torches, planning to extinguish the first one deepest in the cave, then each of the others in turn on his way back to the stone steps. But when he reached the farthest torch, his eyes fell upon something that he had not noticed there the first time.

He was standing before a large, squarely cut entrance to a tunnel. It was obviously man-made, at least ten feet high and fifteen feet across. A rectangular panel had been carved into the stone above it and contained the same type of writing that he had seen on the other walls of the caves. He took the torch from the wall and moved closer. Standing directly in front of the tunnel's entrance, he raised the torch higher to try to look down the passage, but he could not see anything except an endless black void. The inside of the tunnel was silent and unyielding, and seemed to go forever. He stood there for a moment, unmoving, wondering what he should do. Glancing back to the hole at the top of the stone steps, he saw that the afternoon sunlight was still coming through, meaning that he had some daylight left before he had to return. Extending the torch, he walked forward into the tunnel, his mind full of questions.

Abruptly, he found his answer.

As soon as he crossed the plane of the passageway there was a sharp noise, a flash of light, and his body was hurled backward through the air at least a dozen feet. At the same time an indescribable pain shot through his entire body. He was turned over in midair and landed hard, facedown on the floor of the cavern. The flaming torch was still in his hand, close to his face. Too close. Moving the torch away, he rolled over onto his back and slowly sat up. There was a dirty, copperlike taste in his mouth, and as he spat, he saw that his saliva was mixed with blood. He wiped his mouth as clean as he could and spat again as he stood up. Strangely, neither the fall nor the cut had hurt at all.

His mouth twisted ironically as he once again pushed the comma of dark hair off his forehead. Staring back toward the tunnel, he saw that everything was as it had been. Everything except him. Then an idea struck him.

Looking around, he found a hand-sized rock and picked it up. Moving near the wall of torches, he stood at an angle to the tunnel entranceway, instead of directly before it. With an underhand toss, he sent the rock flying toward the portal.

The reaction was immediate. As soon as the rock crossed the plane of the portal there was another loud crack, a split-second flash of white light, and the rock was repelled backward almost the entire length of the cavern to fall on the cavern floor in pieces.

Why, then, am I not in pieces, too? he asked himself.

He shook his head in resigned disbelief. He had no idea what he had just seen or what had just happened, and he found himself laughing aloud at the realization that the same was true about a great many things this strange day. But one thing he knew without question.

He had more than enough desire to leave this place.

Extinguishing the torches one by one, he made his way back to the stone steps. In the dim light of the retreating sunshine that came feebly in through the broken wall at the top, he climbed the stairs and finally exited into the warm and welcoming afternoon air. The natural light felt good on his face.

He was to find that replacing each of the stones in the wall was more laborious than taking them down, and it took more time than he had expected. At last, lightly covered in perspiration and his clothes dirtier than ever, he had retreated a few steps to admire his handiwork when something tugged at him from the back of his memory. Something was missing, but he couldn't remember what. As had been his habit since he was a child, he closed his eyes and relaxed completely, emptying his mind so the thought would come to him, rather than him chasing it. Finally, it surfaced.

Pulling out one of his dirks, he set to work on the wall until the slit for the giant butterflies was open again. Then he walked back across the field. Untying the stallion from the tree, he rubbed the horse's ears affectionately as Pilgrim pawed the ground with one of his front hooves.

"Yes, I know I've been gone a long time," Tristan said affectionately. "And yes, I know you are very thirsty." He pursed his lips and ran one hand back through his thick, dark hair as he looked back one last time at the stone wall. "So am I. But we're not going to drink anything here."

He easily jumped up on the horse's bare back and they crossed the clearing, entering the woods at the same spot from which they had come out. He would have to go back down to the lower glade to gather his saddle and gear. Looking down at himself, he realized that his trousers were stained red where he had wiped the strange water from his hands. He wondered if the stains would ever come out. Glumly, he reminded himself that everyone would be furious with him back at the palace. He had not planned to be gone this long. But he decided to tell no one what he had found, not even Wigg.

He would come back here before his coronation. Something in his heart and mind told him that he must—and soon. There was so much he wished to know about this place. And until he learned more, he would tell no one what he had seen.

A bastard quotation from somewhere in his past suddenly came to mind: *Leave only footprints. Take only memories.*

Pilgrim began to carry him back down the mountain.

*W*igg sat thinking, cross-legged on the soft grass of the upper forest glade, his eyes closed and the basket of food next to him. He was not pleased with the conclusions that flowed through his mind. Far too much had already happened, including the appearance of the blood stalker. Certain circumstances already seemed out of his control, and therefore out of the control of King Nicholas and even of the entire Directorate.

When he searched his mind for Tristan's presence—and the prince was clearly closer now—the texture of what he was sensing had been altered. Irrevocably. Which meant that something major had happened to Tristan that had changed him in a profound way.

Given the wizard's knowledge of the Hartwick Woods, there was one particularly unsettling answer. But the old one's mind sheered away from that possibility. Partly because it was so complicated and would produce so many problems. And partly because, for Tristan's sake, he simply did not want to believe it.

We're so close now, Wigg reflected. *Only thirty days to the coronation. I beg the Afterlife, please let me find him unchanged.*

When Wigg and the princess had entered the glade in search of Tristan, they had immediately seen the prince's saddle and blanket on the ground. Sensing Tristan's presence coming steadily closer, Wigg had decided to wait here for him. Shailiha, still shaken and exhausted, had immediately gone to sleep under a tree with Tristan's saddle as her pillow. Wigg had gone to the opposite edge of the cliff to think, and to wait.

His very old but sharp eyes had missed nothing. He had discovered the damaged oak that had served as Tristan's throwing target, the twisted branch that had obviously been torn from the same tree, and the matted and disturbed grass just a few feet from the precipice of the cliff. They all gave him pause. It was the cliff's edge upon which he had chosen to sit and think.

He turned to check on Shailiha as she lay sleeping. Her impending pregnancy did little to disturb her great beauty. Her long, golden blond hair and her tall, exquisite form had come directly from her mother, Queen Morganna. But her hazel eyes, sensuous mouth, and happy, compassionate nature were all her own. He shook his head sadly, thinking of how little Shailiha and her twin brother Tristan knew of their ultimate potential. How much had been kept from them both, and how it had broken his heart every day to have to keep such secrets from them. He cast his eyes to the valley far below, and farther out to the capital city of Tammerland, which had been his home for over three hundred years. The view was spectacular. If this was where Tristan always came to be alone, the old one could understand why.

An odd analogy came to his mind and he smiled, shaking his head slowly. He and the country that he loved so much were in many ways so alike. Both so old. Both so full of secrets. And both so isolated. Eutracia was bordered on the east by the Sea of Whispers—the sea that had never been crossed. Hundreds had tried to traverse it, but no one had ever sailed farther than fifteen days and returned, not one. All were assumed lost. The same fate had befallen all of the sea voyages that had attempted to head too far north and south. And although the Sea of Whispers was bountiful in her goodness to Eutracian fisherman living in the ports that dotted the coastline, no one ever tried anymore to sail completely across it. No one even knew why it was called the Sea of Whispers. It just was. Wigg, haunted by memories of his own fateful time upon that mysterious sea, turned his thoughts inland.

The northern, western, and the southern borders provided equally frustrating obstacles. The ominous Tolenka Mountains formed a continuous, semicircular boundary from the north coast to the west down to the south coast and once again back to the sea that had never been crossed. Iron gray and snowcapped, their jagged outline scratched the sky in every direction save east to the sea. They were so high, in fact, that every expedition had been forced to turn back when the air became too thin to breathe, even for wizards. And no pass had ever been found. The Tolenkas, like the Sea of Whispers, had also proven to be uncrossable. And so Eutracia had always existed on her own.

Sadly, he reminded himself, there was no written history before their victory in the Sorceresses' War. So little was known about those times. It was only upon the wizards' triumph in that awful conflict that scribes had been ordered to begin to record public events. The Eutracian citizens believed that the members of the Directorate, protected by time enchantments, were the only remaining link to the prewar past. This was untrue. And there were still more secrets that must be kept, adding to his burden. Slowly, as was his habit, he picked a blade of grass and began to shred it between his long fingers.

Hundreds of thousands of people had lived peacefully in Eutracia for over three centuries. The kingdom contained seven duchies, each overseen by its own duly elected duke, and each with its own capital city. The king in Tammerland reigned over all of them, and over the years, each king, with the aid of the Directorate, had ruled with compassion and grace. In only a matter of weeks, Tristan would take the throne. And in only a matter of seconds now, the old wizard sensed, Tristan would enter the glade, and his questions would be answered.

As if the prince's arrival had been prearranged, Wigg turned around calmly to watch Tristan ride bareback into the clearing, and the old one's heart felt as if someone had suddenly shattered it to pieces, his worst possible fears realized.

He has discovered the Caves of the Paragon, the old wizard thought, horrified.

There could be no question. The azure aura that could be seen only by a wizard as highly trained as Wigg was radiating outward from all around the prince's body. Wigg shuddered and went cold inside. The prince's trousers showed long, red stains down each side. A very distinctive red. And the stains could have only come from one place: the water of the Caves.

I have not seen this aura surround anyone or anything since the twin births of Tristan and his sister, Wigg ruminated. And then an ancient quote from the past slipped gently into his mind. *"The azure light that accompanies the births of the Chosen Ones shall be the proof of the quality of their blood . . ."*

Upon seeing Wigg, Tristan stopped short. Looking around, he saw Shailiha sleeping peacefully. He walked Pilgrim to edge of the clearing and tied him, and then sat down next to the wizard. They sat for what seemed to be a long time, each of them staring out over Tammerland while the sun slowly set, neither one knowing what to say. It was Tristan who finally broke the silence. He pointed to the basket.

"Have you eaten?" he asked simply. Wigg shook his head. Tristan produced a large wedge of cheese from the basket and began to eat. He was starving. Tentatively he added, "I'm sure everyone is angry with me." He turned and studied the wizard's profile for a moment. "I truly had expected to be back at the palace by now."

"But?" Wigg turned and raised the infamous eyebrow, staring at the prince through the glow that the young man was obviously unaware of. *Good,* the wizard thought. *At least for now he cannot see it.*

Tristan gave Wigg his best look of nonchalance. "I was detained."

"I see. Would you care to talk about it?"

"No, Lead Wizard, I would not."

Tristan desperately wanted to change the subject but didn't know how. The old wizard decided not to press the issue. It would be difficult enough to explain both the blood stalker and Tristan's discovery of the Caves to the king and to the Directorate tonight, as he knew he must do.

Wigg reached into his robes and produced part of the twisted oak branch that had been torn from the tree. "Your clothes are filthy," he said with distaste. He held the limb before Tristan's face. "Perhaps this had something to do with it?" He turned the branch over in his hand a few times, still looking at the prince.

As foolish as he felt about it, Tristan breathed an inward sigh of relief, sensing that this topic was much safer than a conversation about the falls. He explained the incident of being pushed out over the cliff in graphic detail, the words tumbling from his mouth between bites of cheese. He reached for the bottle of ale. It had been a long day.

When Tristan finished, Wigg remained silent, shredding yet another piece of grass between his ancient fingers.

"Next time I'll tie up my horse," the prince offered.

Wigg shook his head and cast his eyes to the horizon past Tammerland.

"There shall be no need," he said. "The king of Eutracia does not have to come here."

Before Tristan could respond, they both heard Shailiha begin to stir. Wigg quickly pointed his left hand toward her, and she peacefully drifted back into a deep sleep. He had no desire for her to overhear their conversation. They both turned back toward the view of the valley.

"Why is she here?" Tristan finally asked. "She shouldn't be out of the palace in her condition, and everybody knows that. I can't believe my parents would let her come out here with you."

"For better or worse, your parents do not know," Wigg said simply. "Only she, myself, and the Directorate know. And the stable boy who saddled your horse." His eyebrow launched upward into its familiar display of sarcasm. "But I don't think he will be saying anything."

Tristan bit his lip. He was beginning to feel pangs of guilt about coming up here today. But despite that, he knew he had made a wonderful discovery, and he had never felt so strong and vibrant in his life. That part of it all he refused to feel guilty about.

The old wizard sighed. "And as for why she came with me . . . well, it is because she loves you so much. They all do. Your entire family and Directorate of Wizards itself would go to the ends of the world for you." He paused. "Although sometimes I don't know why. Not with the way you've been behaving lately." He looked directly into the prince's dark-blue eyes. "We were almost killed this afternoon while trying to find you." Wigg turned his gaze back out to the valley.

Tristan drew a sharp breath, but before he could speak, Wigg had begun to tell him about the encounter with the blood stalker, being careful to reveal only what he had told Shailiha. Any more was for the ears of his Directorate only, and his king. Wigg pointed to a tree at the side of the clearing, up against which he laid the stalker's battle ax.

"I kept his calling card."

Seeing the ax, Tristan felt truly ashamed. But working against that emotion were other emotions of equal, if not greater, energy. Ever since he had left the stone pool of the falls, two desires had struck his heart as surely as he knew the sun would rise the next morning. First was the need to return there as soon as possible. Second was the overpowering hunger to learn, a thirst to drink in all the knowledge of the craft he could find. And the feeling had been steadily increasing ever since he had left the cavern.

He needed the knowledge of magic.

He turned toward Wigg, waiting for the old one to face him.

Unafraid, he wanted to look directly into the wizard's eyes when he asked him.

As if he knew what Tristan's sudden desires were, yet also chose not to fulfill them, the old one continued to gaze out at the distance. But in his heart the wizard knew what was coming.

Tristan drew a breath. Somehow, inside of him, he knew that once he asked, there would be no retreat. No going back.

"Wigg, tell me, please. I need to know about your craft."

The old wizard's mind was racing. *And so it begins. It wasn't supposed to happen this way.*

Wigg turned to look at the prince. The azure aura that emanated from Tristan's head and body had, impossibly, become even more luminescent. Silently, Wigg gave thanks to the fact that he would be the only one in the kingdom to see it. Only those of endowed blood—and then only one who was as highly trained as himself—could recognize the aura. Even the other wizards of the Directorate would not see it. Wigg looked at Tristan with suddenly sad and tired eyes. The young prince had no idea what he had done, and the old one knew he must choose his words with care. He looked imperiously down his nose at the young man, determined to remain in control of the conversation.

"Until this moment, my prince, you've never expressed anything but disdain for the throne, and rather rude requests for the teaching of the magic that may follow the king's reign. Even your previous questions about the craft have, upon occasion, seemed ingenuine to us." He knew the second part was not true, but he kept his eyes on Tristan and schooled his face to show no emotion. "What is the reason for this apparent change of heart?"

Tristan drew both knees up under his chin and joined his hands in front of him, not knowing how to answer the question without revealing his discovery of the falls. Finally, in a less commanding voice he said, "I suppose it is the story of the blood stalker that has aroused my interest. I have never heard of one before."

Wigg sniffed. "I see."

The wizard was sure now that Tristan would not reveal his secret visit to the falls unless it was literally dragged out of him. And deep down the old one knew why. But he considered Tristan's request and decided to give the prince some rudimentary explanations—no more.

He changed his position so that he was sitting facing Tristan, and beckoned the prince to do the same. As they sat face-to-face, Wigg felt almost blinded by the azure aura around Tristan, and also by the need, the hunger, that was in the younger man's eyes. From this day on, the wizard knew, the man before him would never be the same.

"Magic begins with blood, Tristan," he began slowly. "It has always been this way, even before the Sorceresses' War, and before the commencement of written history and the organized recording of births." He gathered his robes closer around him to ward off the chill of the coming night.

"Children are born either 'endowed,' or 'common,' " the wizard continued. "As you know, both you and your sister are of endowed blood, as are both of your parents. The union of two parents of endowed blood always produces progeny of endowed blood. Only one in a thousand births from a mixed union—common and endowed—results in an endowed offspring." He raised both eyebrows. "Endowed blood is necessary to the mastery of magic. Trying to teach it to one of common blood is like trying to teach your stallion to play the harp."

Tristan smiled at the image, but he was becoming impatient. This talk of Wigg's was something that he already knew, that everyone in Eutracia knew.

Sensing the prince's impatience, Wigg continued. "The craft is divided into two parts, or schools of thought, if you will. The first is called the Vigors. This is the beneficent side of the craft, and requires great selflessness and sacrifice. It is the school of magic to which each of the wizards of the Directorate have taken their vows. Simply put, the Vigors teach those facets of the craft that produce charity, kindness, and deeds for others. It is the only type of magic practiced by wizards." He paused, gathering his thoughts, watching the setting sun slowly drop into the horizon before he finally spoke again.

"The other side of the craft is called the Vagaries. It is practiced only for power and greed, and the depravities of its execution know no bounds. It is said that complete mastery of the Vagaries always results in madness. During the war, the sorceresses practiced only the Vagaries, the wizards only the Vigors." He picked at the hem of his robe. "The Vagaries are the most dangerous of all aspects of the craft—not more powerful than the Vigors, but far more destructive. And destruction was the tool needed most by the sorceresses to accomplish their goals." A brief look of sorrow passed across the wizard's face, and he sighed. "For you see, Tristan, it is always far more harmful to achieve one's ends by taking, rather than by giving." His voice sounded sad and far away.

"Did you ever know such a person, Wigg?" Tristan asked. "A true master of the Vagaries?"

The old one raised himself up a little and looked straight into the prince's eyes. "Unfortunately, Tristan, I have," he answered. "And it was clear that the beginnings of the Vagaries' madness had begun to manifest themselves in its lead practitioner. She was the most purely evil person I have ever known—but she was also the most brilliant."

Tristan found himself stymied for a moment. For as long as he could remember, he had been under the impression that endowed males were more naturally powerful than their female counterparts. Finally, he asked, "Can women therefore become as powerful as men in their use of the craft?"

"Oh, yes," Wigg answered. "An endowed female who studied with equal intent could be just as dangerously powerful as any male, provided her blood was the quality of his. Before the war, both men and women of endowed blood were allowed to learn and practice the craft. The women called themselves sorceresses, and a collection of such sorceresses was called a coven. Males of endowed blood who practiced the craft called themselves wizards. The two names imply exactly the same thing, the only difference being gender. Most people do not realize that, because the training of women in the craft was outlawed, for better or for worse, at the end of the Sorceresses' War."

The wizard looked out at Tammerland. It was that wonderful time of twilight when the orange of the sun's rays could still be seen, melting upward into the ever-darkening black of the night. The three red moons would soon be up, and the night creatures of the Hartwick Woods would begin to stir.

"What makes one wizard or sorceress more powerful than another?" Tristan asked.

"In that, it is much like anything else. First, of course, ability is determined by the quality of one's blood. Added to this is the pupil's intelligence, and the quality and duration of training. But the overriding variable is blood purity. The stronger the blood, the better the pupil. The better the pupil, the more powerful the resulting wizard or sorceress."

Tristan continued to press. "And how is it, Wigg, that you and the other members of the Directorate have never died? I know of people in Tammerland who say you and the other members have not aged one bit in their entire lifetime."

"We are protected by what are called time enchantments. But the public perception of this is misleading, Tristan. It is true that the enchantments keep us impervious to disease and old age, but time enchantments do not necessarily equate to immortality. If you and I both jumped off this cliff, at the bottom of it I would be just as dead as you. The time enchantments were developed to protect our land from those who practiced the Vagaries, who were also close to perfecting the same enchantments. Not for selfish reasons. The war seemed to be interminable, and we were losing so many wizards. If by chance we could win the war, we wanted to ensure that this sort of thing could never happen again. True, we granted ourselves seeming immortality, but in return we pledged the remainder of our lives to the Vigors only, and to ensuring Eutracian peace."

Tristan was beginning to see the wizard in a new light, despite the fact that he had known him for almost thirty years. The old one had lived over ten times that long, and almost all of it in the service of his country.

"The various aspects of the craft are infinite, Tristan. For both the Vigors and the Vagaries. Spells, enchantments, incantations, transformations, potions, divinations, symbols—the list goes on and on. And each thing in nature has its own place in the craft. Thus, the study of the craft is infinite and, for those of us with endowed blood, irresistibly compelling."

"Are the Vagaries still practiced?" Tristan asked, looking genuinely concerned.

"No. Its practitioners were all either killed or banished, and the volumes and scrolls containing their teachings were burned." The need to lie to the prince sent a stabbing pain through Wigg's heart, but in this, too, the old one had no choice. There was so much he would have liked to tell him. The prince's situation was so unique—the first ever such case in the recorded history of Eutracia, and, as such, to be handled with the greatest of care, lest they risk the destruction of the entire kingdom. Tristan had been carefully, very carefully, watched from the moment of his birth, as had his sister. In truth Wigg knew that Tristan had good reason to feel like a specimen in some bottle, despite the fact that he was a fully grown man.

Tristan dropped his knees to the ground to sit cross-legged. For a moment he hesitated, unsure. Finally, he asked, "Wigg, may I ask you a personal question?"

The wizard's eyes narrowed. "Nothing precludes you from asking, just as nothing precludes me from remaining silent."

"Are you the most powerful of all the wizards?" The words seemed to hang in the air between them like a sudden, cold breeze.

Wigg sighed. "To answer your question, I don't really know. I am considered to be the most powerful and learned of the Directorate, but there are other wizards, including rural wizards, within the population of Eutracia. We do not follow the progress of such wizards—the task would be too great. Besides, it is not our job. There was, however, during the war, a wizard who was as powerful as me . . ." His voice trailed off, and his eyes seemed far away again. He lowered his voice farther still. "As I said before, it was also believed that the mastery of the Vagaries would eventually lead the practitioner to madness. And although the Vagaries are no longer being practiced, they still exist, nonetheless."

"I'm still not sure that I understand," Tristan said, mulling over the wizard's words.

Indeed, Wigg thought, looking compassionately into the prince's dark eyes. *How could you be expected even to begin to understand that which has taken the finest wizards of the realm over three centuries to unravel? Perhaps a demonstration would be the best way in which to instruct you now.*

"Magic is everywhere, Tristan," the wizard continued. "Even though it cannot be seen. In this aspect it is much like the air we breathe, constantly surrounding us yet invisible, making us blissfully unaware of its presence and usually quite unable to see it. Magic indeed has substance and shape, as does the air. But do not be misled. I'm not talking about the effects of the craft, or the result of its use. I'm speaking of the craft itself, of what it *really is*. There is a true, interwoven consistency to its energy and its existence, and it can be literally seen, each of the two sides, both the Vigors and the Vagaries." He pursed his lips for a moment, finally making up his mind. "Allow me to demonstrate."

Wigg once again turned toward the valley. The three red moons had finally risen, and the lights from the city and the palace could be seen. Darkness was falling quickly. To the prince's great curiosity, the wizard suddenly stood and apparently began collecting his thoughts, the hem of the gray robe of his office slowly waving back and forth gently in the evening breeze. He closed his eyes and raised his arms to the sky as if in supplication, bowing his head.

The effect was mesmerizing.

To Tristan's disbelief the sky began to lighten. A gigantic glow began to coalesce. As he watched, it gently started to spin and to turn on its axis. It was becoming a brilliant golden orb, with offshoots here and there of the palest white radiating outward from its center, bathing everything in radiance. From time to time golden droplets of energy would trickle from the slowly spinning orb and fall into the valley, dissipating into nothingness. *The Vigors,* Tristan's mind exclaimed. *It is too beautiful to be anything but the beneficent side of the craft.*

Wigg turned back to face the prince and, as if reading his mind, said, "Yes, Tristan, the Vigors, gathering and materializing in their physical form. Magnificent, isn't it?"

"But how is such a thing possible?" the prince whispered reverently.

Without answering, the wizard once more raised his arms, and a darker, more menacing form began to take form in the night sky. As the effect grew in size to match the Vigors, it too began to coalesce and spin, but the effect this time was far different—frightening, horrifying, in fact.

Now the same size and shape as the Vigors, the dark shape seemed to push the other orb aside, as if attempting to make room for itself in the night sky. Black and foreboding, it was as grotesque as the Vigors were beautiful. Droplets of dark, menacing energy dripped casually from its pitch-black, shining sides, and bright scratches of lightning shot through the ebony orb's center, occasionally lighting up the interior of the sphere, showing the complexity of its macabre form. Instinctively the prince knew what it was, and also knew that it was to be feared.

The Vagaries, he thought, mesmerized, as it turned there ominously before him. *The dark side of the craft. It has to be.*

Completely entranced, Tristan watched as the two great orbs began to move about the night sky. They would slowly, repeatedly begin to attract one another, as if somehow needful of each other. But then, suddenly, just as they were about to touch, they would unexpectedly, violently, repel one another, and the process would continue. In some ways it was almost a pitiful thing to watch, the never-ending attempts to join and the always-failing struggles to stay together, only to be thrust apart, over and over again.

He stood there speechless, his blood calling out to him as never before.

He was finally able to find his voice and ask the question. "How is it that they seem to attract, only to eventually repel one another?"

"Each thing in nature has its opposite," the wizard said calmly as he stood before the orbs. "Male and female, light and dark. And so it goes throughout the entire scheme of the world as we know it. The two sides of the craft are no different. But, unlike the other examples I just mentioned, the Vigors and the Vagaries cannot join. Indeed, if any aspect of either one is used in combination with the other, the result would be calamitous—a rent, or tear, if you will, in the fabric of each. For as long as we have known of their existence they have been in this perpetual state of similar, yet separate, permanence." He paused, the weight of his words seemingly heavy upon his heart. "If each, at the same time, had a tear large enough, it is said that it could release the powers of one to join with those of the other, and that such an uncontrolled occurrence would be the end of all we know. This is yet another reason why we wizards took the vows. To prevent any one of us from trying to combine the two schools."

He turned to look at Tristan, and the prince could feel that the wizard was about to tell him something of great importance. "It is also said that there are invisible corridors that connect the two sides of the craft, that virtually join the orbs," Wigg continued. "And that until those corridors are traveled through by one of the endowed, neither side of the craft, no matter how powerful it seems to be individually, has even a smattering of the dynamism it would display if the two were joined. This, then, is the ultimate goal of the craft of magic, Tristan. That is, the harmonious joining of the Vigors and the Vagaries, and their control and proper use thereafter." *And the Chosen One shall come, and through the use of his sanguine, perfect blood he shall one day traverse the corridors of the craft, and bring the two sides together without the breaching of their fabrics,* he thought.

"And therefore, when you think of the craft, it is proper to imagine it as these two opposites. Turning forever in time, waiting to be properly joined," Wigg said softly. "And, in addition, when you think of the Vigors, know that this is the craft of the wizards; and when you think of the Vagaries, know that this was the craft of the sorceresses, when they lived."

"But surely there were women who chose to practice the craft of the sake of good?" Tristan asked.

"Oh, indeed," Wigg answered. "Especially before the war. And just as there were women practicing the craft for the sake of the good, there were endowed men using it for evil. But once the battle had been won, it was forbidden by the Directorate for women to be trained in the craft. I now believe this policy is wrong, as do others of the Directorate, and we have decided that this issue should be formally addressed after your coronation. We feel it is a decision that the king should help us make. You are to be that king." He raised the infamous eyebrow at the prince. "As is the case with many such issues, you will have some tall thinking to do."

Tristan thought to himself quietly for a moment. "Perhaps if women were to be trained, and I think they should, then as a prerequisite we could ask them also to submit to the death enchantments. That would be fair, would it not?"

"Yes, Tristan." Wigg smiled, pleased that the prince had come to the same conclusion the Directorate had already arrived at. "It would."

Wigg raised his hands, and the gigantic, glowing orbs began to dissipate, finally fading away until only the ordinary night sky remained. The prince continued to sit in the grass in awe of what had just transpired.

"But once again do not be misled, Tristan," the wizard added, still gazing across the valley. "Magic is not without its limits, and neither am I. Just like you, I need food to eat, water to drink, and air to breathe. And, just like you, I can be killed. The power of the magic employed is limited by the power of the practitioner and the strength of the practitioner's ethics, or, in the case of the Vagaries, the practitioner's *lack* of ethics. Wizards of the Directorate have taken vows of poverty, service to king and country only, and are sworn to limit their studies solely to the practice of the Vigors. So you see, we do have limits, even though they are self-imposed. I cannot always do a thing simply because I would like to."

Still stunned from what he had just witnessed, Tristan nonetheless found himself overtaken by a different concern. "Has a prospective wizard of the Directorate ever not taken the vows?" he asked softly.

Wigg thought for a moment before answering.

"Yes, there was one who did not take the vows. After the rest of us had submitted to the vows he disappeared, and we always assumed he had found the call of the Vagaries too strong to resist, and had abandoned our cause to satisfy his own greed, voluntarily falling into league with the sorceresses. Because of his actions, we unanimously decided then and there to make the vows irreversible. You see, each of the two branches of the craft are also subdivided into two other subdoctrines, namely Achievement and Reversal. This makes a total of four very separate and distinct disciplines. As I said, the study of magic is infinite. One could spend an entire lifetime learning just one of the subdoctrines of just one of the two schools. Those were very dark days, and the stakes were very high. The fate of the known world hung upon we few remaining wizards making the right decision, and then doing the right thing." He paused. "That is why, in addition to the time enchantments, we also invoked, as a group, voluntary enchantments of death." With that, he sat back down on the grass next to the prince.

Tristan was stunned, his mind full of questions. *Death enchantments?*

"But surely, after all these years, there have been more than that one male who refused to take the vows!" he exclaimed.

"Some did. Some even practiced the dark side of the craft," the wizard said. "Thus the death enchantments."

"Does this mean you know when you are to die?" he asked. Like his twin sister, he couldn't imagine a world without Wigg in it.

The wizard bothered a loose thread at the hem of his robe. He replied softly. "In a manner of speaking, yes. But not in the way you think. An enchantment is an Achievement for which there is no known school of Reversal. In other words, it lasts indefinitely. The death enchantments were fashioned in such a way that if any wizard who has accepted them breaks any part of his vows or practices any form of the Vagaries, either known or unknown to the others, he immediately dies. We of the Directorate never showed other wizards anything of the Vagaries, of course. But against the chance of one learning of them from the sorceresses, the vows and the death enchantments were placed upon them before any serious training in the craft could commence."

Wigg sighed. "We instituted the death enchantments among ourselves because we would brook no more betrayals," he added sadly. "We could not—not and see Eutracia survive." He paused for a moment, considering his next words. "True, we perhaps could have delayed the taking of the vows long enough to use some of the Vagaries ourselves to help influence the outcome of the war. But we decided we would actually prefer to lose the war by following what we believed to be right, rather than see the Vagaries flourish. In addition, we had no idea what the aftereffects of such a decision would be. And we certainly did not need a group of wizards addicted, as it were, to the use of the Vagaries, even if that meant victory. A true case of the ends not justifying the means."

"Then how is it that you are able to show me the Vagaries without perishing from the death enchantments?" Tristan asked.

His mind is so quick, Wigg thought to himself. *But we always knew that it would be.*

The wizard smiled. "Because calling forth the Vagaries to show themselves is not the same thing as attempting to use them," he said simply. "Had I called upon their powers to produce an act of the craft, now or at any other time, I would be as dead as the blood stalker I killed this afternoon."

Wigg's various references to death suddenly prompted a different source of curiosity within the prince as he sat there in the grass. For his entire life, virtually everyone he had known, himself included, had made mention from time to time of the Afterlife, the nebulous place to which people's souls were supposedly carried after death. But he had never heard anyone actually explain its meaning, and he seriously doubted whether anyone could—anyone but one of the wizards, perhaps. He had long felt that the Directorate knew more of it than they chose to reveal, just as he had always been so sure of their same recalcitrance regarding the craft. But something also told him that just now, sitting here in the grass next to the Lead Wizard, was not the time to ask about this particular subject.

Tristan sat back on his heels in the grass, which was now wet with the evening dew, examining his emotions. Coupled with his thoughts of the Afterlife ran a feeling of sadness mixed with one of great debt to the wizard seated next to him, and to all of the Eutracians who had come and gone before him. As he returned his gaze to the valley, he saw that some of the torch lights had begun to twinkle more brightly within the city limits of Tammerland. There was so much more he wished to know. Somehow, in his heart of hearts, he knew now there always would be.

So it was Tristan who broke the silence. "And what of the Paragon itself, Wigg?" he asked. "I do not understand the importance of it in all this." He could picture it in his mind as he spoke, the mysterious, square-cut blood-red stone that had hung from around his father's neck on a gold chain for as long as the prince had been able to remember. And as unyielding as the wizards of the Directorate were in giving up information about the craft, it was commonly known that the subject of the Paragon was the topic about which they had always been the most taciturn. Even Tristan knew only what was common knowledge about the stone—which was very little, to say the least. He knew that it had been discovered near the end of the Sorceresses' War and had not only been essential in the victory, but somehow was also tied to the ongoing powers of the wizards of the Directorate themselves. Even as father to son the king had never spoken to him of it, despite the young man's many questions. Now his newfound need to know told him that these small scraps of information were not enough.

Wigg kept his gaze focused steadily upon the lights of the city. *It is in this that I must be the most careful of all,* he heard his mind say. Finally, he spoke.

"It is not appropriate for me to say a great deal more about the Paragon at this time, Tristan," he said slowly. "I will not add greatly to the knowledge that I know you already have about the stone, except to explain why it always hangs about the neck of the king for safekeeping, rather than being worn by one of the wizards. It was decided early on that none of the wizards of the Directorate should be personally entrusted with it, because at that time we had no idea what effect it could have upon an individual wizard's powers. Because the recent trauma of the war was still fresh in our minds, we agreed that no one already trained in the craft should be allowed to wear the stone, lest it consolidate too much power into the hands of one person. Therefore, an untrained person of endowed blood was always chosen. Remember, we were still very unsure what might develop within an endowed who was very proficient in the craft *and* who also wore the Paragon." *And we still are, my prince,* he thought to himself. *For you shall be the first to do so.* Wigg paused, considering his next words. Then, taking a long breath of the cool night air, he continued with his discourse.

"It has therefore long been Eutracian custom that this person, the wearer of the Paragon, shall be the king and thereby always kept close to the wizards. And due to the necessity of keeping the stone alive, the king must always be one of endowed blood. It is for reasons of safety that the king's training in the craft begins only *after* he leaves office, has removed the Paragon from his person, and has taken the vows of the Directorate, including the acceptance of the death enchantments. The only person who can remove the stone from around the king's neck is the king himself, and that happens only when the monarch's son turns thirty and succeeds him." He turned to look at the prince and pursed his lips. "If there is no son to succeed him, then, as you already know, the Directorate chooses a worthy candidate of endowed blood from the populace to become the new king. This, as I am also sure you know, was the case with your father."

Once again the words seemed to hang in the air between them for a long time as they looked out into the encroaching darkness of the valley. Wigg could easily remember the look on the face of the startled young Nicholas when the entire Directorate of Wizards had arrived at his door, offering him the crown.

"But there is something else you should know," the wizard said, almost reluctantly. "There is a mate to the stone. Not another stone, but a great book, called the Tome of the Paragon." Wigg's brow furrowed. *Perhaps I am telling him too much in one day. And this has been a very unusual day already. But soon the Paragon will be around his neck instead of his father's, and these things will be revealed to him anyway.*

"The Tome and the Paragon were discovered at the same time, Tristan," he continued, "and either one is useless without the other." *Time to test him again,* the Lead Wizard thought. He tilted his head slightly as he looked into the prince's eyes. "Can you imagine where they were discovered?"

Tristan looked down at the toes of his dirty knee boots, considering his options. He couldn't remember a single time that he had ever lied to Wigg, and he still felt that he had not technically lied to the old one so far today—but he had come close. Lying was not in his nature and never had been. Heretofore, his mind had made no connection between the Paragon and the caves he had discovered. After all, what could the Paragon have to do with an underground waterfall? Just the same, when he searched his heart, he felt that he could not reveal what he had discovered today, whether it had anything to do with the Paragon or not.

"No," he said quietly.

Wigg again pursed his lips, nodding his head. "I understand," he said. *More than you could ever know,* he thought. Sitting again in silence, the wizard realized that the daytime sounds of the Hartwick Woods had at some point given themselves over to the nighttime singing of tree frogs.

Wigg spoke at last. "No more questions. It is late. We must leave now in order to be back in time for the inspection ceremony." He moved closer to the prince, his aquamarine eyes steadily boring into Tristan's darker blue ones. "You will speak to no one of the things that have been discussed here this night." Slowly, he pointed a finger at the sleeping princess. "She will awaken now. Go to her while I saddle the horses."

He watched Tristan walk to her, the azure aura still about the prince's body. It looked even brighter now in the quickly gathering darkness.

Shailiha began to sit up, blinking. Immediately she jumped to her feet, her eyes full of tears, and hugged Tristan fiercely.

Wigg turned back to take a last look out over the now-dark valley and the distant, twinkling lights of Tammerland. *We have long feared this day, and now it has come. May the Afterlife grant us the wisdom to prevail.*

He stood to collect the battle ax and to saddle the two horses. Tristan helped Shailiha up onto Pilgrim as the old one mounted the princess' bay mare. They walked, three abreast, with Tristan on foot, to the place at the woods' edge from which they had emerged. Tristan again decided to ask the wizard a question and have some fun with him at the same time.

"Tell me, all-knowing, all-seeing Lead Wizard, how do we know where to go? As many times as I have been to this spot, I have never done so in the dark. It could take us all night to get back, even if we can see the path back down at all. Wizard or no wizard."

Despite the prince's jab, Wigg smiled and reached into the leather pouch that hung from around his waist. In the dark, Tristan thought he could see the wizard remove a small handful of a powdery substance. Holding the powder in the flat of his hand, Wigg took a deep breath and blew upon it, sending it toward the woods in front of them.

Upon touching the forest floor, the powder became luminescent in the night. A sparkling, twinkling iridescent blue streak was igniting itself and snaking all the way down the mountain, marking a clear path through the woods.

Tristan was stunned. Looking into the old one's eyes, he whispered, "Wigg, how is such a thing possible?"

Wigg gazed calmly at Tristan and Shailiha.

"I thought by now you both knew," he said, raising the familiar eyebrow. "It's magic."

Three

She had been traveling over winding and dusty Eutracian roads for more than six days now. She always hated traveling this way, without her chef or her maidservants. It was so common.

As the ornate carriage pulled by the six matching black stallions bumped and tossed along the dusty road to Tammerland in the gathering twilight, the lone occupant once again swore a silent oath to herself.

Soon I will never again travel to kneel before anyone. They will travel to kneel before me.

Natasha of the House of Minaar, duchess of the province of Ephyra, looked down at the blue silk gown she was wearing and carefully smoothed out two of the unruly white ruffles she found at the hem. There was no Pentangle upon her dress, nor had any of her clothes carried that beloved sign for the last three hundred years, but that would soon change. It was imperative that she look the part tonight. She was on her way to an audience with Queen Morganna, and to attend the inspection of the preparations for the upcoming royal abdication ceremony.

Ilendium, her home and the capital city of the province of Ephyra, was located at the foot of the Tolenka Mountains to the north. Ilendium was also known for its amazing deposits of marble, the finest in the kingdom. It was altogether true that, in terms of size, Ephyra was one of the lesser of the Eutracian duchies. But because of its marble quarries it was nonetheless one of the richest, and the abundance of its subsequent tax contributions to the realm always insured the small province an unusually lofty place in the hierarchy of Eutracian court politics.

That part of it all had been instrumental to Natasha's plan from the beginning.

Her seduction of and subsequent marriage to the doddering and ancient Duke Baldric of the House of Minaar had been almost embarrassingly easy to devise, giving her the one thing that she needed most to fulfill her destiny, and the destiny of her Sisters.

The married title of duchess of Ephyra, and the acceptance and access to the royal court at Tammerland.

From her traveling vanity case she produced a folding mirror with which to check her appearance, but the occasionally bumping carriage made it too difficult to hold the mirror still. Lowering and tying off the carriage window shades, she casually laid the mirror upon the red velvet seat next to her.

She tilted her head slightly, and the mirror rose steadily into the air to hang before her face. There, that was better.

She smiled at the thought that soon she would be able to give up this particular face, just as she had given up so many others over the last three hundred years. Just the same, she had been particularly happy with this appearance. The floating mirror showed a countenance framed by shiny brown ringlets that reached down past her shoulders, finally curving inward at their ends upon the swell of her ample breasts. Raising a finger, she vainly touched the beauty mark that she had so carefully placed near the left corner of her mouth. She was particularly fond of this birthmark, it having been the final touch to this particular creation of self. The lips were sensuous and full, and the dark, hooded eyes staring back at her from the mirror were of a deep and lustrous brown, with almost overly long and seductive lashes. She smiled.

As planned, poor old Duke Baldric had been immediately smitten, and they had married within a year of their introduction. Owner of the largest and most profitable of all the marble quarries in the province, he had been elected duke of Ephyra over thirty years ago, winning every reelection for the position since. He was greatly loved by the citizens of Ephyra, a fact that had no importance for Natasha at all except that she was able to keep her title of duchess, and the freedom and power that went with it. Their wedding day had been six years ago, and she longed for the day when she would soon be free of him, and free of so much else here that she had hated since her childhood. For the last six years she had simply smiled back at him innocently each time he had told her that she hadn't aged a single day since their wedding. And although the poor fool had unsuspectingly done his best to give them children, she only tolerated his inadequate and unexciting lovemaking because it served to strengthen the disguise of her marriage.

Keeping herself barren had also been a simple thing. Producing progeny with one of unendowed blood was not part of her plans, nor would it ever be. No matter, she thought. There had been many younger and more vital men in her bed to amuse her since her wedding day. It always made her laugh to imagine the looks that would have come upon their faces had she told any of them how old she truly was. But that was unimportant. There would always be more, especially since her husband's existence would soon be coming to an end.

Satisfied with her appearance, she narrowed her eyes, and the hovering mirror obediently folded in midair and slipped itself back into the vanity case. Pointing to the window shades, she watched them roll themselves back up into place.

She laid her head back against the velvet upholstery, closed her eyes, and silently blessed the beloved endowed blood streaming through her veins, at the same time cursing the wizard bastard who had been her father. She then smiled to herself, proud of the part she was about to play, and proud of who she had become.

A sorceress.

The fact that she was the only living sorceress in Eutracia was itself unparalleled. But it was her special talent of changing her appearance upon which she prided herself the most. This chameleonlike ability, as well as the time enchantments that protected her, had been essential in helping her to keep both herself and her secrets alive, time after time, for more than three centuries.

For Natasha of the House of Minaar was a Visage Caster, able to change her appearance to suit any need, or for that matter, any mood.

As the duchess of Ephyra, it was commonplace for her to visit Tammerland as an emissary of her husband. During her frequent visits to the palace she had always taken special care to be as charming as possible, cultivating the friendship of the queen and arranging useful political alliances at court. She was in constant need of any and all information regarding the royals and the Directorate that she could gather, and there were many in and around the court at Tammerland who were only too happy to provide it, assuming that the price was right. And Natasha always paid, and paid handsomely, with either the coin of the realm or with her body, whichever was most useful at the given moment. She had even managed to arrange the occasional audience with the unwitting wizards of the Directorate. It had taken her a long time to master the sorceress' warp that she had so carefully constructed about herself, the warp that allowed her to hide the quality of her blood from detection by the wizards. That warp had always been an essential part of the masquerade, just as her Sisters had taught her it would be. Despite how much she hated all wizards, she knew it was paramount that they feel comfortable in her presence, and that her secret remain intact.

She thought first of the royal family, and of what would happen to them. It brought a smile to her lips to think that she might save the prince for some pleasure of her own before it all ended. It had been so long since she had lain with a man whose blood quality was the equal of hers. And then her mind turned to each of the six wizards in turn, and to what the future would soon to bring them, as well. To the wizards who had defeated her teachers, who had banished her Sisters from their birthrights. To the infestation that now controlled Eutracia. And especially to Wigg, Lead Wizard, the greatest of the parasites.

It had been especially important to arrange this particular trip to Tammerland correctly, and to make sure that her otherwise useless husband remained at home on their estate in Ephyra. The intestinal bout that poor Duke Baldric had suddenly acquired had been childishly easy for her to conjure, and she had actually enjoyed inflicting it upon him. Not only would the doddering old fool be physically incapacitated, but he would be unable to bear the long carriage ride to the royal inspection ceremony. Indeed, he himself had insisted that traveling to Tammerland in a bumpy carriage to view a simple inspection of the abdication preparations was now completely out of the question. Which, of course, had suited her purposes perfectly. Natasha needed to be quite alone this evening if she was to accomplish all that was expected of her by her Sisters. Failing was not an option. She needed to be able to move amongst the other guests at the ceremony unescorted and of her own free will, so that she could be in the most advantageous position to observe the members of the royal family and the Directorate of Wizards. Indeed, at some point in the evening it was critically important that she become physically close to each of them. The timing must be perfect. There would be no second chance to try again before the die was finally cast.

As she laid her head lazily against the luxurious upholstery, her mind began to drift back in time to the sequence of events that had led her to this day, and to the even more important days that lay soon enough ahead. The fact that her name was not really Natasha was of no importance. After all, she had acquired and lost so many names over the last three hundred years that she wouldn't be able to remember half of them if she tried. Besides, she wanted nothing from the man who had been her father, including his name. No, names were not important. But what *was* important was that at the very young age of only five years she alone had been the first one to be able to read the Tome.

The Tome. The great book of all books that had accompanied the discovery of the Paragon. She had simply picked it up and begun reading it even after all of the greatest wizard minds of the realm had tried so hard to do the same thing. Tried and failed.

She would never forget the look upon the face of her bastard wizard father as he had come into that secret room, only to see his little girl perched in a huge chair with the very Paragon itself around her neck, reading calmly from the great Tome as though she had been speaking and writing its strange language all her life. Nor would she ever forget the rejected feeling of being pushed aside by all of the other wizards in their great haste to try again to read the book—to read the book and therefore help themselves to victory in their struggle against the ones they had called the sorceresses. She had read the book first. The book that before that day had always been gibberish, even to the most brilliant of wizards, including Wigg.

She had also been only five years old when the pretty ladies had first come to her. The pretty ladies who never aged. They had taken her with them to live, and she was happy about it because she had already been angry with her father and the other wizards. She sneaked away with them gladly, and had never returned.

And then had come her training.

She was special because of her blood, the four of them had said. Special and very pretty. And one day, if she worked very hard, she could grow up to be just like them. *Just like them.* How those words had so wonderfully swollen her heart, and how hard she had worked at everything the pretty ladies had taught her to do. And she *had* learned, beyond even the expectations of the four women whom she had taken to her heart as her Sisters. As her family.

But then, twenty years later, the dark days of the war had come. Because of the wizards' discovery of Paragon, her Sisters were losing their struggle. And it was decided that, instead of joining them in the conflict and revealing her identity, she would be left behind, in case all was lost. The cruel wizards had forgotten about her existence, her Sisters had said, and it was best that it remain that way. Even her father, they had told her, had forgotten about her. And thus her additional training as a Visage Caster had begun: so that she could be safely left behind, alone if need be, to keep their version of the craft alive and to serve her teachers should the need ever arise. Behind the veil of a thousand faces.

From the safety of her newly altered first change of appearance, she had watched in horror as her Sisters were first tried and then banished from their birthrights, convicted as common criminals to be set adrift upon the Sea of Whispers. For many weeks afterward she had remained hidden from the population of Eutracia, beside herself with grief, mourning her Sisters' deaths. After that, she constantly moved from place to place as they had instructed her, changing her appearance as necessary to keep the secret of her identity, unsure of what to do. And then, at last, the first message had come to her mind, the first of many such mental joinings that would follow. She could still remember the joy she felt the first time the voice of her eldest Sister had suddenly rung in her ears from somewhere far away. *We live,* the voice said. *Wait and become stronger. There shall be need of you, and you must watch for the Chosen Ones to come. Watch so that we may know, also.*

And the Chosen Ones *had* come, almost thirty years ago, just as the Tome had predicted.

And now her sisters knew also.

Smiling, Natasha of the House of Minaar slipped on her white silk elbow gloves and listened casually as her driver presented her papers of transit to the Royal Guard manning the gate just outside the moat of the royal palace at Tammerland. Her smile widened as she heard the driver finally urge the stallions ahead, over the bridge to the palace.

A sorceress of the Coven had just passed through the palace gates.

*T*he castle was coming alive with visitors and workers, he thought. There must have been two hundred people in this room alone. *And here I sit in my dirty clothes, for all of them to see.*

Tristan sat glumly in one of the ornate chairs that stood in several rows just outside the anteroom to the royal chambers. Physically, he still felt marvelous after his visit to the falls, but he was very worried about the discussions that he guessed were now taking place on the other side of the huge double mahogany doors. Without being told, he knew that the Directorate of Wizards were in closed chambers with his father, no doubt discussing his behavior of today. Upon reaching the palace Wigg had immediately stomped away, gray robes flying as he went down the palace halls, the look on his face granting him a wide berth in all of the hubbub. And Shailiha, after giving Tristan a stern but thoughtful look, had also left, presumably to retire to her own chambers to prepare for the ceremony and report the events of her equally amazing day to her husband, Frederick.

Tristan had great admiration for Frederick, not only as his brother-in-law, but also as the commander of the Royal Guard. In truth, they owed each other much. It had been Tristan who had first introduced him to his sister. And it had been Frederick who had personally given the young prince much of his training at the war college. Sadly, Tristan supposed that even Frederick would be angry with him this time, since Shailiha had been involved. Frederick loved her more than life.

Bored, the prince slowly looked around at the plush decorations that adorned this area of the royal residence. It was customary for a new king, upon taking the throne, to redecorate the palace to suit his taste. King Nicholas had given this responsibility to Morganna, and it was the unanimous opinion of Tammerland's citizens that the queen had done an exquisite job. The palace contained over six hundred rooms, some of which Tristan had never even visited. Amazingly, the queen had personally overseen the decoration of each of them. Marble of every possible color from the quarries at Ilendium could be seen everywhere, and ornate and colorful stained-glass windows and skylights had been used extensively to give the previously foreboding structure a lighter and more welcoming air. Oversized tapestries and paintings hung in virtually every room, and it had also been Morganna's idea to add a great library to one wing of the palace and to make its use available to everyone in the city. Even though he had lived here his entire life, Tristan never ceased to be amazed at the castle's sheer size. In addition to the spacious living quarters of the royal family, there were also various rooms of government administration and the headquarters and war rooms of the Royal Guard. Looking again at the double doors, he reminded himself that the living quarters, libraries, and other private rooms of the wizards of the Directorate were also contained within these walls, off-limits to everyone except the king.

The great room in which Tristan now sat anxiously waiting was called the Chamber of Supplication, usually reserved for the dozens of assorted citizens who arrived almost daily at the palace, asking for this favor or that from the king or, occasionally, even from the Directorate of Wizards. Sometimes the supplicants received audiences, and sometimes they did not. Either way, this room was a place of waiting and therefore, to Tristan, a place of boredom, despite its magnificent decor. The prince knew he was in trouble, but he couldn't imagine what the wizards and his father had been discussing for so long. Wigg had told him curtly to sit here until he was called, and despite the fact that the inspection ceremony was to begin shortly, he had as yet seen no sign that might indicate he would be summoned before the king and Directorate anytime soon.

His return to the city with Wigg and Shailiha had been uneventful, despite the embarrassment at being seen in this dirty and disheveled state when they should have been inside the palace preparing for the ceremony. When they had reached the palace, the Royal Guard had immediately come to attention and ushered them across the moat, motioning aside the many carriages and pedestrians that were trying to cross. Tristan enviously took notice, as he always did, of the soldiers' numerous weapons and various uniforms. Regardless of his rank, each wore a shiny silver breastplate etched with the image of a Eutracian broadsword, its blade running from the upper left corner of the chest armor down to the lower opposite right corner and ending there at the sword's highly decorated gold hilt. Above the beautiful broadsword lay the image of a roaring lion, painted in black. These two images comprised the heraldry that was of the House of Galland. A long, pleated black cape was attached to either shoulder of the breastplate and hung down each soldier's back. Each time Tristan saw the armor he wished he could spend more time in it instead of tending to his royal duties. Duties that would only increase soon, when he was king.

The palace was already teeming with the guests who were to join in the inspection ceremony and the countless palace workers who were responsible for making sure the ceremony came off smoothly. Everyone hustled by as if in a desperate hurry, off to this task or that, with some if not all of them taking notice that the prince was sitting there alone, in very dirty and, to say the least, unusual clothes. He reflected glumly that he was still even wearing his quiver, with its dirks plain for all to see. To make matters worse, each of the people passing by in the noisy hall apparently felt a civil responsibility to stop and chat. So far he had made polite conversation with visiting dukes and duchesses, noblemen and their ladies, officers of the Royal Guard, and maidservants and cooks, to name a few. He shook his head. There would be hundreds of people at the ceremony tonight, many of whom he would not know and would have to be introduced to. And despite the fact that he did not want to be king, he regretted meeting them for the first time dressed like this. For if the Directorate and the king did not summon him soon, he would have no time to change his clothes for the inspection ceremony.

He looked down in resignation at the strange red stains on his black breeches, and then at the swirling patterns in the rose-colored marble floor. Lost in his memories of the underground falls and his worries about his predicament, he didn't see or hear the woman approach until the almost obscenely high-heeled and equally polished sapphire shoes were only inches away from his own filthy leather boots.

"Good evening, Your Highness." The soft, velvety voice came from above.

Tristan stood, as he had so often done already this evening, to address yet another of his subjects, and found himself looking into the deep brown eyes of Natasha of the House of Minaar, duchess of Ephyra. She curtsied perfectly and extended her left hand for the customary kiss.

"How wonderful it is to see you again," she said demurely. "Tell me, how are your mother and father?" she asked, her eyes never wavering from his. She seemed to take absolutely no notice of Tristan's embarrassing appearance. Either she was being polite to one of the royal family, or she actually liked the way he looked tonight. Tristan thought it was the latter.

He had never liked this woman, despite the fact that since her marriage to Duke Baldric she had somehow become a good friend of his mother's. He reminded himself of the fact that she was obviously much closer to his own age than to that of her husband, and also of the reputation she had slowly garnered since her marriage. It had been whispered in political circles for years that she had taken many lovers, but she was nonetheless received courteously at court due to the importance of the province of Ephyra to the nation as a whole. His mother apparently either did not know of the woman's indiscretions, or chose to be gracious enough to ignore them. He groaned inwardly. *Time to be prince again.*

Bowing slightly, Tristan took her left hand in his right but held it there for a time, purposely forcing her to remain uncomfortably bent at the knees just a little longer than was customary. Finally, after taking his time in gently brushing his lips against the smooth white silk of her gloved hand, he smiled into her eyes.

"Please rise, Duchess," he said without pretense. As she rose slowly to her full height, he was reminded of how tall and striking she was. Ignoring the inquiry about his parents, he asked, "You are here for the inspection ceremony, no doubt? Tell me, is your husband the duke attending the ceremony with you this evening?" At the mention of her husband, the prince thought he saw a brief look of tension pass across her eyes, but if it had, it was gone in an instant.

"No, Your Highness," she answered, a somehow unconvincing expression of concern temporarily taking over her countenance and then vanishing as fast as it came. An opened fan had appeared in her right hand, and it began to move the air gracefully across the cleavage that rose above the low neckline of her magnificent blue gown. "And if it pleases Your Highness, please call me Natasha. Unfortunately, the duke was suddenly taken ill with some sort of nasty intestinal bout, just before we were to leave Ilendium for the trip to Tammerland." She smiled with her eyes over the fan as it continued its seductive path back and forth. Had this woman been anyone else the prince might have been intrigued and only too glad to join her in the beginnings of a flirtation, despite the fact that she was married. But not with her. And not tonight.

"Perhaps I could have one of the court physicians sent to your estate to tend to him," Tristan offered casually, deciding to keep the subject of her husband foremost in the conversation. He folded his arms across the laces of the dirty vest that he suddenly realized did little to conceal the fact that he had nothing on underneath it. "It would seem the least we could do for such a close friend of my mother's."

Her smile showed perfect teeth in the flickering candlelight of the chandeliers. "Thank you, Your Highness, but I have a feeling that as soon as I return home, the malady will leave him as quickly as it came." She tilted her head slightly to one side. A hidden meaning, perhaps? If it was, he didn't understand it. She once again curtsied.

"And now if you will excuse me, Your Highness, I am late for a visit with the queen. It has been months since I have visited the palace, and she has granted me the rare honor of a private audience. But I do so look forward to continuing our conversation later, after the ceremony. Could you be so kind as to point the way to the royal chambers?" The ever-present fan sent some of her perfume his way.

"Of course, Duchess," he said. "The royal quarters are in the west wing of the palace, where you will no doubt find her." Looking around, he summoned a lieutenant of the Royal Guard forward, resplendent in his dress uniform for the evening. Tristan felt shabby by comparison, but still the duchess' intent eyes never left his.

The lieutenant approached the prince and saluted crisply. "Your Highness," he said simply.

"Please escort the duchess to my mother's quarters," Tristan ordered him. Turning back to Natasha, he noticed her outstretched hand. Sighing inwardly, he again brushed his lips against the back of the gloved hand and bowed.

The look in Natasha's dark eyes now seemed even more bold, possibly due to the fact that she was about to take her leave of him. Her head still tilted slightly, she slowly looked him up and down. When her eyes at last returned to his, her tongue darted out playfully to touch the beauty mark at the left corner of her mouth. Then, turning away with the lieutenant, she was suddenly gone.

Tristan was standing there alone, smiling and quietly shaking his head, when a different voice—a deep, rich male voice—came up from behind him.

"A wink from a pretty girl at a party doesn't always result in climax," he heard it say, "but only a fool won't take the opportunity to find out."

He turned around to the familiar voice and smiled to find Frederick of the House of Steinarr, his brother-in-law and one of his best friends, smiling broadly at him. He stood before a small contingent of the Royal Guard, each of them already in dress uniform. "I've heard about that one," Frederick said slyly, watching her walk away. From the first day they had met, Frederick had inexplicably refused to address the prince formally, instead treating Tristan as an equal. And it was precisely that endearing measure of disrespect that had made him one of the prince's closest friends. A great, hulking bear of a man, Frederick always seemed too large for his uniform. But underneath that uniform was pure warrior, perhaps the best fighter of the realm, and now the commander of the Royal Guard. Tristan had never had a brother, but if he could have, he would have chosen this man. He smiled again into the face that was framed by the short brown hair and the great forest of brown beard.

"So how long have you been standing there?" the prince asked. He felt even more out of place in his dirty clothes as he stood next to the company of colorful soldiers.

"Long enough to know that you're obviously slipping," Frederick retorted. He stepped closer to Tristan, out of earshot of his troops. "I had heard you had a bad day, but I never thought I would live to see you *this* tired. When I finally saw her open her mouth that last time, I thought she was going to undress you with her teeth."

"No, thanks," Tristan said, wryly shaking his head. "I already have enough trouble."

"So I have heard." Frederick's smile evaporated, and he seemed genuinely concerned. "And by now most of the palace has heard, as well. Not the details, mind you, but enough to know that the seven rather powerful men behind those portals are not particularly happy with you just now." He tilted his head in the direction of the double mahogany doors. "I have spoken to your sister, and I know how worried she is about you. Apparently the two of you, each in your own way, have had quite a day."

Frederick's appearance suddenly had Tristan feeling rebellious again. "Walk with me," he said to Frederick, despite Wigg's imperious command to stay put until he was called for. "I want to stretch my legs."

Tristan's brother-in-law narrowed his eyes in disapproval. "Won't Wigg be angry?" he asked. "From what I've heard, that old wizard is already upset with you enough."

"He's the supreme, all-knowing Lead Wizard of the Directorate isn't he?" Tristan asked sarcastically. "If he can find me in all of the Hartwick Woods, then he can certainly find me in this drafty old palace." He turned on his heel and purloined two crystal wineglasses from a serving tray that one of the waiters held as he bustled by, offering one to Frederick. Next, Tristan stopped another of them and promptly commandeered an entire bottle. "Reinforcements," he said proudly. "Let's go."

As the prince sauntered along the ornate marble halls with Frederick, it felt good to be away from the hubbub and out on his own again. He quickly drank a full glass of wine, and then another, Frederick doing the same. Eventually they stopped before a large staircase, walked down it, and found themselves standing in the midst of one of the queen's many magnificent gardens. The stars were out, as were the three red moons, and the night sound of the tree frogs could be heard all around them. The prince found the peacefulness reassuring.

Tristan poured himself some more wine and turned to Frederick. "They're all pretty concerned, aren't they?" he asked.

"Not just them," Frederick said, "but your sister and I, as well. And we have a right to be. Sometimes it seems you care more about your horse than you do your family. Do you want to go into more detail about what really happened up there today?"

Normally, Tristan would gladly have told Frederick about his bizarre experiences. But today something stopped him. He wasn't even sure himself what exactly had transpired in those caves.

"I probably couldn't explain what happened to me today if I tried," he replied. "All I really want right now is to relax a little and forget it before Wigg, the grand inquisitor, comes looking for me again. You know, he can be a huge annoyance. I know he means well, as do the others of the Directorate, but sometimes I just want to be Tristan the citizen, not Tristan the prince." He smiled conspiratorially. "All too often I quite enjoy doing exactly what they tell me not to," he added, the wine beginning to swim in his head. "And if Wigg can't find me tonight, then they can all go to thunder, the whole lot of them."

Tristan and Frederick had met during the prince's training in the Royal Guard, and the two had become so close that Frederick eventually took over personal responsibility for all of Tristan's training. As a result they were without doubt the finest two swordsmen in the realm, with Frederick holding only a slight edge due to his size and strength. It had been a logical step for the prince to introduce Frederick to his sister Shailiha, and the romance had blossomed from there. Everyone in the royal family had approved, and the two had been married the following year in one of the largest ceremonies ever seen in Eutracia. A year later Shailiha was pregnant with her first child, and the entire kingdom was in joyous expectation of a new royal family member.

Smiling, Tristan put the wine bottle aside and punched Frederick on the arm, hard, as was his custom.

Perhaps it was the wine, or perhaps the fact that the two of them had such a healthy rivalry in all things physical. In any event, the challenge had been made, and Frederick smiled knowingly as he uncoupled the silver breastplate from his chest. He immediately struck the prince in the chest so hard that Tristan dropped his wine glass and fell to the ground.

And so it began. In a second, they were on top of each other like a pair of schoolboys at play. Tristan jumped up and grabbed Frederick from behind, only to find himself back down on the ground again.

Frederick promptly tried to jump on top of him, only to discover that the prince was gone and standing above him, grinning wickedly. Too late, Frederick saw that the bottle had reappeared in Tristan's hand, and before he could escape the inevitable, his head had been drenched in wine.

"There!" the prince shouted happily. "That serves you right for making my sister pregnant, you scoundrel!" Soon the two of them were laughing so hard that Frederick needed help up, but Tristan was barely able to give it, as they found themselves slipping and sliding in the mud created by the spilled wine and the crushed flowers that lay in ruins around them. Eventually the prince fell down next to Frederick, and the two of them sat there in the mud, laughing. Tristan grabbed a small handful of mud and pushed it into the side of Frederick's cheek. They were now both completely filthy, Tristan even worse than before, and they each felt as if their laughter would never stop.

Frederick finally found his footing and stood up, still laughing. "You're in a particularly rebellious mood today." He snickered. "May the Afterlife help you once the Directorate gets their hands on you tonight! But in case you have forgotten, I have other places to go, and other things to attend to. There is still much to do this evening, and that doesn't include spending any more time with the likes of a ne'er-do-well such as you!" He looked down at Tristan's dirty vest and red-stained trousers with a look of mock superiority, quite understanding that he was equally dirty. He started to strap on his breastplate. "You might also consider a change of clothes." He chuckled. "In case you have forgotten, this evening is all about you." He waved a great tree trunk of an arm at the edifice of the brightly lit palace. "And despite how grand I'm sure tonight will be, I'm told that it's nothing compared to the actual coronation itself." He shook his head slightly as he looked down at the recalcitrant member of the royal house who sat in the mud at his feet, and one corner of his mouth came up. "Take care of yourself," he said ruefully, thinking of the Directorate. "I believe there may be much more to come for you this night that you may not be pleased with. And now a good evening to you, Prince Filthy." Frederick then smiled, bowed mockingly to the prince, and slowly walked back into the palace.

Tristan stood and watched as Frederick made his way back into the palace. *A good man,* the prince thought. *And the father of Shailiha's unborn child.*

But Tristan's good mood slowly began to dissipate as he resignedly made his way back through the crowds, his head slowly clearing from the wine. He tried to ignore the even more bizarre looks he received as he negotiated his way down the halls and back to the Chamber of Supplication. The ornate, congested room seemed even busier than before, but blessedly there was as yet no sign of Wigg.

Once more alone and lonely in a crowd of hundreds, Tristan resignedly sat down in one of the plush supplicant's chairs and cast his eyes apprehensively to the double mahogany doors at the other side of the room.

Four

Tristan had indeed been correct in guessing that Wigg was in a foul mood. In truth the wizard realized he had no right to be angry with Tristan, or Shailiha either, for that matter. Instinctively he knew that the prince must have found the Caves by accident, except *how* he had found them the old one could not imagine. No one had visited the Caves for centuries. Until today. Of all of the people to have gone there, Tristan was the worst possible choice for so many reasons. And now, this close to the coronation, was the worst possible time. In addition, the appearance of the blood stalker had badly unnerved the old wizard, partly because a stalker had not been seen in over two centuries, and partly because it had been his old friend Phillius. He knew it was not anger at the prince and his sister that drove his emotions. It was worry for the future.

Now he stood before the Directorate of Wizards and King Nicholas in the rather dark but luxurious meeting room deep below the palace. This was one of the secluded places where the seven of them came to discuss matters of importance, and Wigg had specified this room because he knew he could allow no one to overhear, just as he could tolerate no interruptions.

He looked at the six of them seated at the highly polished circular conference table, the other wizards on either side of him and King Nicholas on the throne at the center of the far side. The king's usually regal bearing was tense with concern for his son as he pulled with worry upon his iron-gray beard. He was already dressed in the ermine-trimmed dark-blue velvet robes of his office in preparation for the inspection ceremony. Wigg was comforted to see the ever-present Paragon hanging around Nicholas' neck on the usual gold chain. The square-cut bloodred stone sent out shimmering highlights of deep scarlet even in the dim light of the subterranean room.

Wigg looked to the other five wizards, his friends of so long. Tretiak, Egloff, Killius, Maaddar, and Slike. Their traditional plain gray wizard's robes stood out in stark contrast to the king's richer clothing.

How do I begin this? the old wizard thought. *What I tell them here today will forever change all of our lives.* He took a breath to speak, but the king, no longer able to contain his worry, spoke first.

"Wigg," he began quietly, "I can only assume that this meeting is of great importance, given the fact that the inspection ceremony is less than two hours away." He looked around the table at the others. "And, since the prince has been missing all day, we can only assume that our presence here concerns him." He leaned forward intently, the Paragon gently swinging back and forth on the chain around his neck, then looked Wigg dead in the eye. "I have asked the other wizards of the Directorate seated here about my son's whereabouts today, but all I get in return are concerned, polite stares." He slowly laced his fingers before continuing. "Tell me, Lead Wizard, is my son safe?"

"Indeed, Sire, he is well, as is your daughter, who was also with me today." Wigg paused, wondering how to continue. "Yes, both your children are well, and back here at the palace awaiting your orders." He looked down at his long, gnarled fingers, then raised his eyes back up to those of his king. "But as to whether any of us are to *remain* safe is a question that I truly cannot answer at this time."

Before any of the others could ask him what he meant, Wigg turned and left the room. In a moment he returned holding the blood stalker's battle ax and tossed it unceremoniously upon the conference table. It screeched and scratched its way along the varnished wood for a few feet before stopping in the center, some of its various brain-matter stains still visible. The head of the ax slowly tipped to one side and finally came to rest upon the sharp edge of one of its shiny blades.

Before any of the other six men could speak he dryly added, "For any of you who do not remember, I don't recommend touching any of the places stained in yellow." He sat down heavily in his high-backed wizard's chair and let out a long sigh.

The room had become as silent as a tomb.

Nicholas' eyes went wide. He seemed to be about to speak, but then apparently found his last remaining measure of patience and drew back, obviously deciding to wait for the explanation to come to him. The five other wizards of the Directorate initially showed surprisingly little outright emotion at the sudden appearance of the ax, but Wigg could see the color draining from their faces.

Tretiak was the most powerful of the Directorate next to Wigg. He was also Wigg's best friend among the wizards and the man the Lead Wizard had known the longest. He was the first to speak.

"Where?" he asked simply, in his low, commanding voice.

"The Hartwick Woods," Wigg replied. He had been sure that this would be the first question asked, just as he had been equally sure that Tretiak would be the one to ask it. Tretiak gave Wigg a hard look. There was a meaning to the location, and they both knew it.

"And we can presume that you killed him?" Tretiak calmly continued, turning his gaze from the ax back to Wigg.

"Yes," Wigg said sadly. "But there is more that you must know. The stalker carried a red birthmark upon the inside of his left forearm." He paused. "It was Phillius."

At the mention of the dead stalker's human name, mouths dropped open and several of the wizards turned to each other in disbelief. Wigg let only a moment slip by before commanding their attention by speaking again.

"As for the identity of the skull atop the ax, although it undoubtedly belonged to a wizard, there is, of course, no telling who he was. I suggest that, out of respect for Phillius' first victim of endowed blood, the ax be taken apart and the skull be placed to rest in the Graves of the Unknown in the wizards' crypt. As a precaution, I destroyed the body of Phillius by fire, as has always been the custom." He looked down. "In addition, I know that all of you, including our king, are aware of the recent disappearances of a number of the lesser rural wizards over the course of the last several months. I do not profess to know whether Phillius acted alone, but I believe it fair to say that we at least have our answer regarding their recent vanishings."

From the left side of the table next to the king, Slike looked up at Wigg, his green eyes full of questions. "Blood stalkers were maintained by time enchantments," he said incredulously. A look very close to horror began to creep into his eyes. "Do you suppose it possible that—"

"I don't know," Wigg purposely interrupted, sure that he could guess the remainder of Slike's question, but not ready to enter into the inevitability of that discussion. "Whether he somehow survived in hiding for over three centuries, which I doubt, or whether he was recently recalled no one can say at this time, and further speculation in this regard is pointless." He folded his hands before him and looked solemnly at the others. As Lead Wizard he meant to have control of this meeting. "Besides," he continued, "it is my unpleasant duty to inform you of an even more threatening occurrence this day."

The old wizard began to steel his mind for what he knew must come next. *These wizards have been my friends for centuries,* he thought sadly. *How do I tell them this? I beg the Afterlife, how will the king react to such news of his own son?*

Controlling his composure as best he could, he decided there was no other way to say it. Looking at each of them in turn, he simply said, "I am certain beyond a doubt that Prince Tristan has discovered and entered the Caves of the Paragon."

First came a deathly silence. But soon after it was replaced by the highly uncustomary sound of disorganization as the five wizards urgently began to talk to each other in a loud confusion of various conversations. Wigg was about to raise his voice and silence them when suddenly the flat of Nicholas' hand pounded so hard and loud upon the table next to the ax that the gruesome weapon bounced several inches into the air, then landed back on the table, silencing them all.

The king was trembling in a combination of rage and fear. His last reserve of patience regarding his son was obviously gone, at least for today. The room was once again awash in a tense silence that seemed to permeate everyone and everything in it.

"Wigg, please tell me, how is it that you know this?" Nicholas asked. His normally strong voice was a barely audible whisper.

"Regrettably, Sire, there can again be no mistake. Even before I encountered the prince this afternoon, I could sense that something in his blood had changed, and the feeling became even stronger as the princess and I came closer to him. Then when he came out of the woods into full view I knew for certain. The azure glow is all about him, make no mistake, and it is a particular glow my eyes have not seen since the day of his birth. And until today I had not seen an azure aura that bright since the night I shattered the bowl to seal the fates of the sorceresses of the Coven." *This is the first time the sorceresses have been openly spoken of among ourselves in over three centuries,* he thought. *How strange it all seems to have them suddenly thrust into our thoughts once again.*

He looked at the other wizards and saw that tears filled the eyes of some. The two who remained the most composed, Maaddar and Tretiak, sat looking down at their hands, presumably to spare their king any further embarrassment. Wigg could always count on Tretiak.

Nicholas sat back heavily into his chair, and it was apparent to all that the weight of the world had just landed upon his shoulders. Inwardly Wigg winced at the thought of the additionally unsettling information that he must now put before them all. *Salt into the wounds,* he thought. He got up from his chair and stood behind it, placing his hand on top of the chair back where his name had been so intricately carved into the wood.

"I am sorry to have to inform everyone here that there is still more to tell you." Anyone looking hard enough would have been able to see the muscles in his jaw clenching. "The prince's clothes are stained in red. *The* red. Again, I am sad to say that there can be no mistake. I believe he has either bathed in or at the very least washed some parts of himself in the water of the stone pool. I need tell no one in this room that these actions are without precedent. We are truly walking into the unknown, and we have been innocently led there by one of endowed blood whom we all love very much." He paused and gazed directly at the king, so that Nicholas could not escape his meaning. "We must all try to remember that sentiment in the difficult days ahead." As he had hoped, he saw the king's countenance begin to soften.

"Unfortunately, we must also assume that Tristan has seen, if indeed did not also try to enter, the Tunnels of the Ones Who Came Before," he continued. His brow furrowed. "Have any of the members of the Directorate felt a disturbance in the wizard's warp that guards the tunnels' entrance?" None of the wizards spoke. "Good. However, it must be said that this afternoon I myself felt a definite shudder against the warp at the gateway to the tunnel. Perhaps I felt it only due to my closer proximity to the Caves. But I can also tell you with certainty that the tunnel portal has not been breached. The Tome is intact."

"Wigg," Nicholas began again, "will the azure glow be about him always?" There was both concern and a bit of uncharacteristic timidity in the usually commanding voice.

"No, Your Highness," Wigg said with compassion. "I am pleased to say that the aura will be gone from him in a few days. I do not believe that it can remain without repeated visits to the Caves. And I'm sure everyone agrees that under no circumstances can the prince return there."

Wigg laced his long, ancient fingers together upon the back of the chair. "It is also a good thing that no one other than myself will be able to discern the glow. Even the prince himself cannot see it. We should, therefore, be able to contain the secret among the men in this room. The unenlightened populace and even the rural wizards would never understand its meaning. And any explanation might cause only misunderstanding, perhaps even alarm and riot."

Egloff had a question. "Does Tristan now illustrate an even greater interest in the craft?" he asked. "For as long as I can remember, we in this room have been of the opinion that touching the water in an uncontrolled manner may unleash a desire to learn such as we have never seen. If I am not mistaken, I believe the Tome itself makes mention of it." A smallish man who was always concerned with details, Egloff placed the ends of his thumb and middle finger of one hand against either side of his long nose and closed his eyes, his mind already deep into his unparalleled memory of the Tome. After observing his knowledge and eccentricities for over three hundred years, the other wizards knew it best to allow him to think without interruption. Egloff was known among them as the Master of the Tome, and if any one of them knew the answer to a question about the great book, it would be him.

"Yes," he said, finally breaking the silence and opening his eyes. "I remember now. The Tome does indeed mention it in one of the later chapters of the Vigors. Tell us Wigg, does the hunger burn as bright in his eyes as the Tome foretells?"

"This, my friends, was the last thing that it was my unfortunate duty to tell you," Wigg said slowly. "Yes, his eyes are alive with it. Just as his mind is alive with forming questions and his tongue is equally alive with asking them. And given the nature of his birth, I fear that this, unlike the aura, will not go away anytime soon. He may become completely unmanageable. Perhaps he has even done irreparable harm to himself. Only time will tell."

The Lead Wizard took a long, deep breath. Once again he searched the king's face for a clue as to how Nicholas would deal with all of this. There was only one thing to do, of course, and each wizard in the room knew it.

"Sire," Wigg said gently, "I feel it is time that we addressed Tristan directly. He is, of course, your son and your blood, but I believe I speak for the Directorate and for the nation as a whole when I say that Tristan must be forbidden to go near the Caves. We must also take the responsibility of watching him very carefully until the coronation."

The path was obvious, but ultimately the decision had to be Nicholas'. Wigg remained silent, as did the other wizards, waiting for the hopefully inevitable order.

Nicholas drew himself up in his throne once again, his regal posture reinstated, and looked Wigg in the eye.

"Lead Wizard," he said quietly, "go and bring the prince to us."

Without speaking Wigg stood, turned on his heel, and began walking to the door.

Still seated in the supplicant's chair, Tristan wasn't aware of anyone behind him until he felt the tap on his right shoulder. He turned around to see Wigg standing over him. He had neither heard nor seen Wigg's approach. Most times, people never did.

"Your father has summoned you to appear before himself and the Directorate," the wizard said. Tristan looked glumly up into Wigg's unforgiving gaze, knowing there was no way out.

Tristan's heart sank. "What about the inspection ceremony?" he countered. "Don't we all have to appear very soon in the Great Hall?" It wasn't much of an excuse to get out of the meeting, but it was all he could think of.

"The ceremony can come later," the old one said. "And will, make no mistake. But this comes first. Besides, how do you think it could be held without you, your father, and the Directorate?"

Tristan glumly accepted his fate and rose to his feet. He had taken only one step toward the double mahogany doors when he heard the old wizard call out to him again.

"We're not going that way," Wigg said. He blatantly looked the prince up and down, noticing how much dirtier Tristan had become. Tristan's appearance would do nothing to improve the king's mood. "Follow me and be quiet. Try not to live up to any of our expectations." The wizard turned away from the direction of the double doors and began to walk out of the Chamber of Supplication in the opposite direction, with the glum-looking prince of all Eutracia in tow.

After crossing the rose-colored marble floor of the chamber, they entered the hall outside. People were still scurrying about in preparation for the ceremony, and upon seeing Wigg many of them lowered their heads and gave him a wide berth. But the Lead Wizard seemed to take no notice of anyone at all as he led Tristan farther and farther down the long marble hall, finally turning into an area that was relatively unknown to the prince.

Wigg finally stopped before a heavy wooden door decorated with brass trim. The old wizard narrowed his eyes, and Tristan could hear the insides of the door lock turn over once, then twice more. Wigg opened the door and walked through, beckoning Tristan to follow him into what appeared to be a large oak-paneled library, complete with many book-lined shelves and writing desks. Each of the desks held an oil lamp and was surrounded by comfortable-looking chairs. It occurred to the prince that he had never seen this room before, but then again there were many in the huge palace he had not seen. He shrugged. To him, it was just one more that he could cross off his list of unknowns. The old wizard shut the door and once again narrowed his eyes as the prince heard the lock secure itself. Somehow the knowledge came to Tristan that probably only a wizard could ever open that door.

Wigg crossed the stone floor to one of the many decorative oak panels that lined the right-hand wall. He reached up and placed the first two fingers of each hand upon four knots that Tristan had taken to be part of the decorative woodwork. The old one closed his eyes, then almost immediately opened them again and stepped back from the wall. To Tristan's amazement the entire paneled section began to revolve slowly and silently on a pivot that apparently ran vertically through its left side, revealing a dimly lit entranceway.

"Don't just stand there with your mouth open, or you'll catch dragonflies," the wizard said in a castigating tone. "Follow me." Wigg walked into the entranceway to the right of the pivot and was gone.

Tristan crossed the library and looked into the entranceway. There he saw Wigg impatiently waiting for him in yet another oak-paneled room. Lit by a single wall sconce containing an oil lamp, the room was only about the size of a scullery maid's broom closet. After testily beckoning Tristan forward, Wigg reached to his right and pulled a tasseled velvet cord that hung through a hole in the corner of the ceiling. The revolving door dutifully swung shut.

Almost immediately the prince felt his knees buckle slightly. He had the distinct feeling that he was falling, although looking down he could see that he was still standing firmly upon the floor of the little room. But despite the fact that neither he nor anything else in the room seemed to be moving, he was still sure he somehow detected the presence of motion. He smirked at Wigg. "More magic, Lead Wizard?" he asked.

Wigg could not help but let a small smile escape past his prickly demeanor. "Actually, no," he said. "Rather, this is a new invention, courtesy of the Directorate. It works on hydraulics. Water power, not magic. One of Wizard Maaddar's hobbies. He likes to call it the gravitating chamber." His smile faded as he gave Tristan a more controlled look. "As I might have thought you would have learned today, magic isn't the answer to everything. True, we are moving. Downward. Several stories *below* the level of the palace." He paused. "You are sworn to secrecy about anything and everything you may see or hear from this point forward, including the presence of this moving room." He turned his attention once again forward to the paneled door before them.

"But there is nothing below the first floor in this section of the palace," Tristan said. "All of the subterranean floors such as the kitchen, the sculleries, and the servants' quarters are elsewhere, far from here." He was sure of it. He had, after all, lived here all of his life.

Just after he finished speaking, the strange sensation of moving without going anywhere suddenly stopped, and the oak-paneled door began to pivot open again.

As it opened wider, the old wizard gestured toward the opening and blandly said, "Nothing below this section of the palace, eh? Really? Why don't you try telling *them* that?"

Tristan found himself staring through the open door into a world he had never known existed. He was dumbfounded. He looked back at the wizard in disbelief, but the old one simply walked out through the door ahead of him, motioning for the prince to follow.

They were standing in some sort of circular underground court-yard. It was constructed of the most beautiful light-blue Ilendium mar-ble he had ever seen. It appeared to be some sort of central crossroads for at least a dozen or more seemingly endless hallways that led off it at regular intervals like spokes from the hub of a wagon wheel. It was amazing. And the place was full of wizards. There were young ones, old ones, thin ones, and fat ones, but he noticed that although they were all dressed in the customary plain gray wizard's robes, none of them had the wizard's tail of braided hair that usually fell down the back of the neck.

He of course was familiar with all of the wizards of the Directorate, just as everyone in the kingdom was, even if only by name. But other than Wigg he saw none of them in this room. He could only reason that since he had never seen any of these other men before and because they had no wizard's tails, they therefore must be the lesser rural wizards from around the realm that Wigg had mentioned. But he had no idea that there had ever been so many of them, and had no clue what they were all doing here. Each seemed to be quietly going about his own business, some in hushed conversation, and some simply passing through on the way down to another hall. None took any particular notice of the visitors except for the occasional bow of respect to Wigg.

"Wigg, where *are* we?" Tristan asked, his voice barely audible. He stood transfixed. Never in his life had he experienced such an amazing day as this. He wasn't sure that he ever wanted to again.

"We are now standing in the crossroads of the Redoubt of the Di-rectorate. It is a secret place of learning and respect for the craft, and for the past. I suggest you behave accordingly." Wigg motioned for Tristan to walk with him down one of the great hallways, and continued to speak as they went.

"This place was constructed at the end of the Sorceresses' War, and its purpose is the furtherance of the craft via the teachings of the Vig-ors." He turned his hawklike gaze upon Tristan. "You *do* remember the Vigors?" he asked unnecessarily.

"At the end of the war, the nation was in shreds," he went on. "Famine, pestilence, and crime were rampant. The legions of the Royal Guard had been virtually decimated, as had the population of wizards. At that time there was much more that needed to be done than the newly formed Directorate could accomplish on its own. The Redoubt was established by the Directorate in order to train and dispatch wizards to help bring peace and order once again to the countryside and the cities in a compassionate, rather than martial, manner. And this practice of sending forth wizards has continued ever since." He pushed the er-rant braided tail of gray hair back over a shoulder as he walked.

"The wizards you see here have all been trained in the craft and taken the vows of the Vigors in this center of learning. When a male of endowed blood wishes to learn the craft he must always do so here, under our tutelage, so that we may make sure he is taught the Vigors only, and with the proper amount of self-control and respect for the past." The infamous eyebrow rose again. "Two things that you seem to have a distinct lack of lately." His gaze shifted back to the long hallway as they walked along.

"Once they have accepted the vows and the death enchantments, they are trained in the craft. Anyone refusing to take the vows is summarily rejected. Those who do go through training are sent back into the countryside dressed as peasants. They are empowered to perform as many good deeds as they deem appropriate for the benefit of the populace at large—all within reason, of course. They must go about the rest of their lives without alerting the citizens to the fact that they are wizards. A benevolent secret society, if you will. They have nowhere near the power of a wizard of the Directorate, and it is purposely planned to be this way."

"But can't the Vigors be used for selfish reasons, too?" Tristan asked innocently. "Haven't any of them ever tried?"

"Oh, yes," Wigg sighed. "No system is perfect. But the number of Consuls is very large now. When they are out in the field, they see each other often in the scheme of things. The abuse of the Vigors by one would would probably come to the attention of the others. And those, in turn, would inform us—or so we would hope. Such things were known to happen in the early history of the Brotherhood, but are now very rare."

Wigg clasped his hands behind him and looked down at the rich marble floor as they continued on along the seemingly endless hallway. "They are not protected by time enchantments, Tristan. They live and die just as any normal citizen of the realm would. Such wandering rural wizards are called the Consuls of the Redoubt. By sending them forth in this way everyone, endowed or common, has something to gain from the craft."

Wigg sighed, for the question was one the Directorate had long struggled with during the formation of the brotherhood of Consuls. "To understand why we did not give them time enchantments, one must have lived through the period of war that we had," he answered. "A harsh decision—perhaps too harsh. But we were very afraid of the craft being used against us once again. Right or wrong, we of the Directorate felt that, for the safety of Eutracia, both the higher applications of the craft and the gift of the time enchantments should be kept strictly among ourselves—among only those we knew we could trust. As to whether the Consuls desire time enchantments, or resent not having them, well, the only thing I can say is that if that is their motivation for joining, they join for the wrong reasons. Those who do join us, knowing the limitations about to be placed upon them, do so with a purity of heart. In short, they know the rules going in. And the Directorate may expel any who seem unfit."

He gave Tristan a meaningful look. "This process is the closest thing to an organized religion that Eutracia has, and as such must be monitored carefully."

Tales of such lesser wizards were not uncommon, but they were always assumed to be mere myth, since in each and every case following their supposed accomplishments they were reported to have vanished without a trace. Now Tristan knew why.

"Do they all know each other upon sight?" he asked.

"There are so many of them now that it is probably impossible for any one of them to know all of the others," Wigg said. "Therefore, before they are sent out into the world they are each given a tattoo. It is a likeness of the Paragon, and it is placed high up on their right arms. This way it can be hidden by their clothes, but if one consul wishes to prove his identity to another of his brothers he may do so, and without the more obvious use of magic."

As he walked along next to Wigg, Tristan noticed that many of the hallway doors were open, revealing the interiors of some of the rooms. When he was able to catch a quick glimpse into them as he walked by, he was stunned at what he saw. Several of the rooms appeared to be immense libraries and places of quiet study, lined floor to ceiling with huge and dusty books, many of which were titled in the same obscure language he had discovered circling the ceiling of the cave. Other rooms seemed to be storerooms: he saw containers of herbs and fluids, charts, scrolls, and symbols drawn upon parchment that hung randomly upon the walls. Still other rooms seemed to be fairly luxurious living quarters, presumably where the consuls resided during their training and subsequent visits back to the Redoubt.

But when he looked through an open pair of great double doors that had appeared at his right, he stopped dead in his tracks.

It was a schoolroom.

The large, bright chamber was filled with young boys of varying ages, from toddler up to what looked to be as old as ten. There had to be at least forty of them in the attractively painted room. They were not being tended to by nurses or maidservants as one might have expected, but rather by yet more wizards, who watched and cared for the children as attentively as if they were their own. *Perhaps they indeed are their own,*

Tristan thought. But the most amazing thing of all was the fact that the children weren't simply playing. The longer he stood there watching them, the more certain he became that, despite the playful aspect to their behavior, they were learning.

And some of them were executing aspects of the craft.

He stood there, mesmerized. He saw a pair of boys happily playing catch with a brightly colored ball, except they weren't using their hands to throw and catch it as it flew back and forth between them. Instead, it simply stopped in midair when it reached one of the boys, then flew back again to the other. They couldn't have been more than six years old, effortlessly laughing and playing at magic as if it were second nature to both of them.

At the back of the room, he saw a boy of about ten standing alone with his eyes shut. He appeared to be doing absolutely nothing. Nothing, that is, until Tristan looked down at the boy's feet and realized that the child had levitated himself at least a foot off the floor. Still more boys were seated on the marble floor in a semicircle, listening intently to an older wizard who was showing them a parchment full of symbols.

Tristan heard Wigg clear his throat. He turned quickly and looked directly into the ageless aquamarine eyes.

"A *nursery*?" he asked incredulously. "Whose children are these?" He turned once more back to the room, as if to reassure himself that he was not seeing things.

"Nursery, nursery, let me think," the old wizard said, enjoying the chance to tease the prince. "Yes, I do believe that's what they call a roomful of tutored children, isn't it?" He smirked at Tristan. "And to answer your question, yes, you are right in your assumption that these are the children of wizards. Or, to be more precise, the endowed sons of the consuls of the Directorate. Of course not all of the consuls' children are endowed. Consul wizards are, in many respects, just like everyone else, Tristan. Remember, they are not protected by time enchantments. After leaving the Redoubt, they take on occupations that suit them, blending back into society. Sometimes they fall in love, marry, and have children. Eventually they die, just like ordinary people. As the membership of the consuls grew over the centuries since the war, more and more of them began to bring their sons of endowed blood with them when they came here to visit." He ran an ancient hand down the length of his hawklike face as he recalled the distant, cherished memories.

"The bond between a wizard and his child is a particularly strong one, and it is not uncommon for the son of a wizard to wish to travel with his father, rather than be left behind at home with his mother. It seemed only the right thing to do when we decided to construct a nursery. With our supervision and permission, the fathers began to use this room to show their sons the ways of the craft. To our knowledge, such a thing had never been done before. It wasn't until we observed so many male children of endowed blood interacting in one place that we began to understand the true value of the Consuls' Nursery, as it is now called. Even these young boys before you, happily at play, have taken the Vows of the Consuls and are taught only the Vigors." He turned a compassionate gaze toward the roomful of peaceful boys.

Tristan's mouth turned up into a smile when he tried to imagine what Shailiha's reaction would be if she could ever see this amazing place. A thought came to him. "If Shailiha's child is a boy, will he come to this place to learn?" He genuinely hoped so.

And just how does one answer such a question as that? the old wizard thought. *How does one explain to this young man that the quality of both his and his twin sister's blood makes these children seem as mere dullards?* He shook his head imperceptibly.

"We need to be going now," he said, rather rudely ignoring the prince's question. "Are you forgetting that there are others who are waiting for us?"

If only I could, Tristan wished to himself as the wizard's words snapped him back to reality.

Wigg reached out to shut the huge double doors, and began once again to walk down the interminable hall in silence with Tristan alongside him.

The door that Wigg and Tristan finally stopped before did not look like any of the others they had passed. This door was the largest yet, and the front of it was intricately inscribed with the same odd writing that he had seen in the cave and on the bindings of some of the books here in the Redoubt. Had Tristan not been so apprehensive about his meeting with his father and the Directorate, he would have taken the opportunity to ask the old wizard what the writing meant. As it was, he now found himself much more concerned with who was behind the great door rather than what was engraved upon it.

Wigg gave Tristan a quick but compassionate look before he knocked twice, softly. When the door opened, he walked through, then motioned for Tristan to follow. With a sense of finality, the door shut heavily behind them.

The conference room was not particularly large, but what it lacked in size it more than made up for in elegance. From the center of the high ceiling hung a single gold chandelier of oil lamps that gave a subdued beauty to the room. Paintings and tapestries covered much of the four mahogany-paneled walls. It struck him that since no women were allowed here, the decor could not have been suggested by his mother and therefore, presumably, reflected his father's taste. In the center of the room, his father and the other wizards of the Directorate were seated around a large, circular conference table. He recognized the battle ax of the blood stalker upon it, and noted the scratches in the table's varnish where it had come to rest. A warm fire danced softly in a light-blue marble fireplace that ran along the length of the right-hand wall, its burning wood occasionally popping and snapping, the only sound in the otherwise palpable silence. The fire gave warmth and familiarity to a room that otherwise, he was sure, would show no friendliness to him.

Wigg walked over to his chair and sat down. There were no more seats in the room, suggesting to Tristan that visitors were few and far between. He walked to the fire and blatantly turned his back to the seven men in the room as he held his hands before the flames. Until now, he had not realized how cool it was this far below the palace.

Nicholas sat in his throne looking at his son's dirty back and the odd knives arrayed across it, wondering how things could ever have come to this. Never before had he been so disappointed in Tristan. It wasn't just the prince's actions of today. Indeed, his son's discovery of the Caves had probably been an accident. But added to Tristan's general disregard for the things that mattered so much to the future of the nation, today's revelations had somehow all become too much for the king to bear. Despite the fact that Tristan had long since grown into manhood, Nicholas was near the breaking point with his son. He loved Tristan more than his own life, and he knew the feeling would never leave his heart. But instinctively he also knew that his relationship with Tristan was about to change, and there was nothing either of them could do about it. *Long-since dusty hopes are about to float away upon the invisible ink of time,* he thought.

"Turn around and face us, Tristan," the prince heard his father say. It wasn't the request of a father to a son. It was a command from a king to one of his subjects.

Tristan turned back toward the men. He was acutely angry. He'd had quite enough of being ordered about today. To hide his emotion, he looked down at his trousers and tried to brush away some of the red stains, but they remained persistently in place. Finally giving up on his appearance, he faced his father, ready to accept whatever it was that was about to come his way.

"Don't bother with the stains," the king began, his eyes boring into those of his son. "They will never come out."

Tristan was stunned. *How could he possibly know that?* his mind asked.

"Thanks to the wizards in this room, you are a very well-educated young man," his father said. "Therefore, let us pay you the compliment of being blunt. You've made a lot of mistakes lately."

"I know," the prince said without hesitation. "I'm beginning to enjoy them."

"We don't have time for your insolence, Tristan." The king was shocked. Never before had his son spoken to him this way. Wigg gave Nicholas a hard look.

"We need to ask you some questions, my son," the king continued in a somewhat softer vein. "And we expect to receive truthful answers."

"Not until I get some of my own," Tristan said firmly. He glanced at the Lead Wizard. "Wigg has been kind enough to tell me of some things today, and I thank him for that." Wigg could tell that the prince's eyes were burning brightly with a need to learn, the azure glow about him as strong as ever.

"But it isn't enough," Tristan went on, achingly. He could literally sense his endowed blood coursing through his veins, and he still felt incredibly strong from his time in the water beneath the falls.

"What is it you would choose to know?" Wigg asked gently, raising an eyebrow.

"What I've *always* wanted to know!" Tristan burst out. He shook his head in frustration. "The things that I have begged you all to tell me since I was old enough to speak! Are you all deaf? Or are you all simply mad?" He felt in the grip of something he didn't understand. The hunger to learn that had been with him since this afternoon was suddenly exploding in his head. The deep, visceral need to know more about magic, and about himself.

"Why—no, *how* is it that I am different from everyone else?" the prince shouted. His eyes narrowed, and his hands balled up into tight fists. "Why is my father the first king in all of Eutracian history to decide to join the Directorate and watch his wife die of old age? Why am I the first son of a king to be told that he, too, must join the Directorate at the end of his reign, when every single king before me has had the power to choose for himself?" He frantically searched each pair of eyes in turn, but no one spoke. Surprised to find his cheeks wet with tears, he turned back toward the fireplace.

Wigg noticed that Nicholas was about to speak, but the old wizard quickly placed his index finger across his lips, indicating silence. Nicholas closed his mouth and reluctantly nodded back.

Wigg's heart was breaking for Tristan, but he realized that they must leave the prince alone just now. They all needed to see whether Tristan could come out of his rage by himself and begin to control the effects of the blood that was racing through him. It was imperative that the prince answer of his own free will. *Despite the combined powers of the Directorate, had this one already been trained in the craft he could have killed us all at once with a single thought,* the old one ruminated. *The Chosen One will come, but he shall be preceded by another—the prophecy is not only true, it is now upon us.*

Wigg gratefully saw the prince's breathing begin to slow, and his sharp eyes noticed one of Tristan's tears as it sadly fell to scatter like broken crystal upon the marble floor. The old one looked at Nicholas and nodded.

"Tristan," Nicholas began gently, "I am truly sorry for all that you have been through, and all that you may yet have to endure. But believe me when I say that every man in this room loves you, none more than myself, and that everything that has occurred in your life, indeed even the things that have *not* occurred, have all been for a reason." He looked questioningly at Wigg. The Lead Wizard closed his eyes briefly in affirmation.

"Please turn around, my son," Nicholas said quietly.

Tristan slowly did as he was told, his chest heaving from his tirade and the strength of his emotions. His cheeks were still shiny from his tears, and the anger still seeped through. But Wigg could see that the prince was once again more himself.

"Tristan," the king asked, gazing into his son's eyes, "how is it that your trousers are stained in red?"

Tristan groaned inwardly. *All I wanted of today was to keep my secret and hope to someday go back to the falls. Now they are about to take that away from me, too.*

Beaten and exhausted, the prince of Eutracia stood before them and finally, reluctantly, told them everything. The butterflies, the chase for Pilgrim, and falling into the cave. He went on, telling them of his exploration of the cavern, his swim in the strange water, and of being repelled backward at the portal of the tunnel. He left nothing out. When he was done, he didn't know whether he felt better or worse. For a long time the room remained bathed in silence, the only sounds once again the occasional snap of the wood as it burned in the fireplace.

Wigg turned his attention back to the men seated before him. "The first imperative is to reestablish the wizard's warp that once protected the wall that the prince inadvertently fell through. Tretiak, as the second most powerful among us, you are best suited for that job." How the warp guarding the wall had been breached was a source of great concern to Wigg, but he did not wish to speak of it now. He could only imagine that it had been the quality and strength of the prince's blood that had enabled him to unknowingly break through the barrier.

He turned his gaze once more to the prince. "I am sorry to have to say this Tristan, but we must forbid you to ever go near the Caves again. The stakes for all of us are much too high."

Somehow Tristan had expected to hear this, and he thought that his heart would break at the very idea of it. But suddenly a different concern seized him.

"Wigg, if the warp is reconstructed in front of the wall, how will the Fliers of the Fields receive their sustenance? Will they die?"

Wigg let out a sigh and clasped his hands in his lap. "I don't really know, Tristan," he said, shaking his head. He stood, walked over to the prince, and put an affectionate hand upon the young man's shoulder. "They were never supposed to go in there in the first place. Either way, we must recreate the warp."

Nicholas stood slowly and walked over to the two of them. He looked at Wigg. "It is obviously past the time when the ceremony should have begun. All of our guests and the palace servants have probably long since wondered what has happened to us. Please notify them that the ceremony has been postponed one hour. In addition I should like the queen, Shailiha, and Frederick to join Tristan and myself here, in this room, as soon as possible." The king turned his dark eyes back to his son. "I'm sorry, Tristan, but it appears that not only will you have to face the immediate concerns of the Directorate, but those of your family, as well." He looked with disdain at Tristan's dirty red-stained black breeches and leather vest. "And," he added sadly, "it also appears that you will have to attend the ceremony dressed as you are."

As Tristan wearily ran a hand through his thick, dark hair, Nicholas continued to gaze deeply into the deep blue eyes of his son, the man whom he loved more than anyone else in the world. Instinctively, he reached out to pull the prince to him in a long embrace, and was glad to find it being returned.

"I want complete privacy during this meeting with my family," he told Wigg. "We will all be along shortly."

Wigg bowed slightly at the waist. "As you wish, Sire."

The king and the prince watched as the elderly, powerful wizards dutifully exited the room. Then Nicholas turned to face the great fireplace, his back to his son, as the flames slowly started to burn themselves out.

I pray to the Afterlife, please let us survive the events of today, he thought sadly.

Tristan and Nicholas did not have to wait very long. In what seemed to the prince to be a very short amount of time there came a knock on the heavy door, and Wigg appeared with Morganna,

Frederick, and Shailiha. The Lead Wizard silently ushered the visitors into the room. Then, after giving the prince a rather pinched, concerned look, he left, quietly closing the door behind him.

The looks upon the faces of the rest of his family quickly told the prince that not only had the three of them never visited this part of the palace, but that Wigg had told Morganna and Frederick all that had transpired today. At the behest of Nicholas each of them took a seat at the table, Tristan included. The silence in the room was palpable, and Tristan felt even more alone now than when he had first come into this chamber and confronted the wizards of the Directorate. *The wizards are powerful,* he heard his heart whisper to him, *but it is my family that I hold most dear.* Only Shailiha and the recently bathed Frederick managed slightly encouraging smiles in his direction, while everyone waited for the king to speak.

They didn't have to wait long.

"Tristan," the king began as if reading his son's mind, "do you love us?"

The question hit the prince like a thunderbolt. How could his father ask him such a thing? Before he started to speak he knew his voice was about to crack, and it did. "Yes, Father," he began softly. "My family is the most important thing to me in the world."

Nicholas then unexpectedly leaned forward in his chair, gripped the chain of the Paragon just above the stone itself, and held the bloodred jewel out toward the prince. It twinkled in the light of the fireplace.

"And this stone?" the king asked, no small measure of regal command in his voice. "How is it that you feel about this?"

"It is the stone that I will soon wear around my neck, just as you have done ever since you turned thirty," the prince answered, entirely unsure of the meaning behind his father's question. "Other than that, there is really very little that I know about it."

Suddenly more frustrated with his son than ever, Nicholas looked down at the jewel that he had worn for so long—the same stone he longed to see around the neck of his only son, where for so many years the wizards had said it rightfully belonged. *How do I tell him these things?* the king asked himself. *How do I this day tell him how concerned his parents are for him, when all that he hungers to know cannot, will not, be told to him until the day of his coronation?*

Nicholas let go of the Paragon and leaned back in his chair, sighing slightly. "It is no secret to the people here in this room, or to the directorate of Wizards, that you do not wish to be king. But you *shall* be the king, and in a very short time. And what I must tell you now is that if you do not change and show your willingness to take on the responsibility that is about to be thrust upon you, you will rule poorly, and neither the nation nor your family can survive that. Trust me when I say that, for reasons I cannot this day explain, your reign will be unique to all of Eutracian history." Nicholas' face seemed to soften a bit as he considered his next words. "Too many good people have died trying to protect the Paragon to let it be worn by one who will not fulfill his duties.

"I ordered Shailiha and Frederick here with us today so that they may also hear these things," he continued. "So that they may know that your mother and I hold their interests in our hearts, as well. It is their futures and the future of their unborn child that you must also bear in mind, that you will one day be responsible for. I know it is not the way you wish things to be. I also know that you believe the world has been unfair to you, and in many ways, perhaps it has. But in time you will understand why."

Tristan looked over to his sister and her husband, and could see the two sympathetic but concerned faces that stared back at him. *Their worry is not only for me,* he realized, *but now for their child, as well.* It was becoming abundantly clear to him that the king meant to have his way in this. The prince looked hesitantly back to the face of his father.

Nicholas once again took the Paragon in his hand, and Tristan could see the deep, red color of the stone between the king's strong fingers. Nicholas looked to Morganna, his queen, and into her blue eyes that lay just below the tumbling, shoulder-length blond hair. *My queen. Tristan and Shailiha's mother,* he thought to himself. *The love of my life. You are half of all that he is, and all that he can become. Help me make him understand, in that way in which only you can.*

Morganna gazed knowingly into the eyes of her husband. Then her face purposely hardened, and she looked at the prince.

"The simple truth is, my son, that the stone is not meant to be worn by one who is unwilling to shoulder his responsibilities." She knew that she must go on, no matter how much her words pricked them both. "The stone is meant to be worn by a *man.* One who is, indeed, man enough to honor it with his courage, and his resolve."

The strained look on her son's face told her that she was finally getting through, and she chose her next words with care, knowing that the speaking of them would cause her an equal, if not greater, amount of pain. "I will repeat your father's question. 'Do you love us?' Do you love the people in this room enough to give of yourself and become the king of Eutracia, the king that this nation deserves?" She paused, deciding to risk the gamble. "Or need we ask the wizards to find another man of endowed blood to wear the stone?"

Or need we ask the wizards to find another man of endowed blood to wear the stone . . . His mother's seemingly impossible words echoed in his mind for what felt like an eternity, their sheer, startling simplicity rattling him to his core. Finally overcome by the strength of his emotions, the prince suddenly realized how he must have always appeared not only to his family but to his subjects, as well.

Tristan slowly stood and walked over to Morganna. Going down on bended knee, a tear reappearing in the corner of one eye, he lowered his head and kissed the hem of his mother's gown.

"I still do not know what measure of a monarch I can become, Mother," he said softly. "But never, never doubt my love for my family or my kingdom, or the willingness to do what I must to protect them. I shall wear the stone." His head still bowed, the next words came out in a whisper. "But please, Mother, also understand that I know I have much to learn."

Morganna smiled into the face of her husband and saw that his eyes were once again shiny with tears. She placed an affectionate hand upon her son's lowered head.

For now, she thought to herself, *that is all we can ask.*

PART II

The Nation of Parthalon

Five

The delicacy of revenge is a feast that must be served at the proper moment; neither too soon, nor too late, for its preparation must be perfect. In this matter, timing is everything.

—THE FIRST MISTRESS OF THE COVEN, FROM HER PRIVATE DIARIES

She smiled as the bullwhip snapped through the morning air. As second mistress of the Coven, she could have used her powers to punish him, but doing the physical work herself was always so much more pleasurable. She was an expert at this by now, and could easily lay the tight leather of the black woven whip anywhere she wished upon his naked back. Indeed, the design she was creating in his flesh was already beginning to take shape. As the whip whistled through the air, several drops of his blood splattered randomly across the room, some of it landing upon the hand that held the whip.

She touched the point of her outstretched tongue to the blood on her wrist and, smiling, closed her mouth.

The slave had not satisfied her needs, and for this they always paid. This particular young man had done her the indignity of not even becoming erect, and to her mind had therefore humiliated her. But then he had made the ultimate mistake: He had laughed at *her*.

Succiu, second mistress of the Coven, stood naked in the luxurious quarters of her bedroom in the Recluse, her breasts rising and falling with the exertion of her labors. When the slave had mocked her, her anger had immediately crossed over into the realm of hysteria. But despite the strength of her emotions, her aim with the whip had so far been perfect. So anxious was she to punish the slave that she had neither dressed nor taken the man to the Recluse dungeon as was usually her custom. Now, in examining the lines of blood across his back, she could see that her labors were only partially complete. Five more lashes would do it.

Suddenly the naked slave groaned and his body went slack in the iron manacles that circled his wrists and led to the elaborate ceiling via the chains. He hung there, his head lying to one side as if he were dead.

She threw an errant handful of jet-black waist-long hair over one shoulder and cast her exotic, almond-shaped eyes down at the dwarfed hunchback that was squatting on the floor at her feet. He looked up at her like an obedient dog on a leash.

"Check him, Geldon," she said simply as she slowly drew the length of the whip back to her and began coiling it into a circle. "This one is too strong to be dead yet." Her voice, controlled and smooth as silk, had a sensual, smoky quality to it.

For the thousandth time the dwarf extended his pudgy fingers to touch the shiny iron collar that ran around his neck, and to feel the jeweled chain that ran from it to the iron ring embedded in the marble floor. No one had to remind him of how many of these rings his mistress had ordered installed in the various floors of the Recluse so that she could take her personal slave wherever she pleased and imprison him in plain view of the others. She tilted her head and silently commanded the iron ring embedded in the marble floor to open itself, allowing the dwarf to free the chain. Geldon dutifully picked up the ornate chain and walked across the room to face the slave.

"He lives, Mistress," he said respectfully. "His chest rises and falls." He was careful not to say too much and further anger his Mistress.

"Good," she said casually, her eyes on both the slave and the dwarf at the same time. "Awaken him. I am not finished with my artwork, and we wouldn't want him to miss the experience."

The dwarfed hunchback shuffled to his mistress's bath and retrieved a bucket of cold water. Standing on a stool, he poured the water over the head of the slave, saving a small portion of it. Then, as the slave began to regain consciousness, he held the man's head back by the hair and without warning poured the rest of the water into the slave's throat and lungs, choking him. His mistress liked it better that way. Coughing and gagging, the blond man in the chains twisted and convulsed in his shackles as he tried to expel the water and fill his lungs with air, a pink mixture of blood and water spraying violently across the room from his mouth. Finally, the focus began to reappear in his eyes and he once again hung more upright, his bloody toes only inches off the marble floor.

The second mistress of the Coven walked around to face him. She had chosen him from the Stables this morning not just because he was a particularly handsome Parthalonian, but because of the insolent look in his eyes. She had thought that the kind of fire she had seen there might finally provide her with a specimen who could ultimately satisfy her rather exotic tastes. But in the end, this one had proven an even greater disappointment than the others. She ordered Geldon back to his place near the ring in the floor and narrowed her eyes, causing the iron circle to close through the last loop in the dwarf's chain, once again securing him there.

Grasping the handle of her whip, she placed the end of it beneath the slave's chin and raised his face up to hers. She was pleased to see the hatred and fire burning there as hot as ever.

"Sorceress bitch!" he shrieked as loud as he could. But his voice came out only as a whimper of ragged breath. "I shall never service you." He spat blood from his mouth onto her face and chest.

Completely unperturbed, she looked down at his groin. "With performance such as this, I daresay you are right." She laughed. Suddenly her expression hardened as she put less than an inch between their faces, this time speaking between clenched teeth. "You have no doubt seen the scars upon the backs of the others in the Stables who have displeased me in this way?" She touched a finger to one of his blood spots that had splattered upon her left breast, and again touched the finger to the tip of her waiting tongue. "Soon you will look just the same as they do, Stefan," she said coyly, crisscrossing the handle of the whip on his right cheek in a miniature version of the design that she had begun to imprint forever on his back. "I do my best work upon your back instead of your face so that I will not have to look at your ugly scars the next time you lay atop of me." The handle of the whip continued its maddening course across his cheek. "Consider yourself lucky."

From somewhere deep within him, the slave managed a smile. "I already do, you repulsive whore. Better to be scarred for life for not having serviced you than to have lain with one of the bitches who have enslaved us." Somehow he actually found the strength and courage to laugh at her again. "Someday we shall kill you all," he sneered. His breath had become even more ragged as he turned and twisted helplessly in the manacles.

"If you are talking about your comrades beyond the confines of these walls, you would do better to turn your mind to other things," she said, apparently quite sure of herself. "Like pleasing me." The handle of the whip began to undulate back and forth suggestively around his genitals.

Stefan collected as much blood and saliva in his mouth as he possibly could and sprayed it into the sorceress's face.

"Very well, then," Succiu said happily.

The second mistress of the Coven once again walked around to the back of the slave, and for a moment admired her handiwork. Then she viciously executed the last five strokes of the whip as hard as she could, finally on the last stroke using her powers to treble the strength in her arm. As she placed the whip so unerringly upon his back she could feel the distant, overpowering ecstasy of the Vagaries begin to rise in her veins, just as the First Mistress had told her it would over three centuries ago when her training in the darker arts had begun. And now she was a true sorceress, almost as powerful as her mistress, and the rapture she felt in her blood and her loins as she punished the slave drove her on even harder. Once again the slave groaned and slipped into unconsciousness.

The man's blood was now running freely down to his buttocks from the five perfect triangles that she had cut into his back with the whip. The triangles that together made up the beloved five-pointed star, the Pentangle.

The symbol of the Coven.

"I am done with this one," she said casually to the seated dwarf. Without looking, she pointed a lazy finger to the ring in the floor, and once again it opened. "Take him back to the Stables with the others. But first, draw my bath. This one has made rather a mess of me." She walked over to the great canopied four-poster bed and slipped a silk robe over her tall form, apparently not caring that the various spots of blood on her naked body were blotting through here and there.

"Yes, Mistress," the dwarf gurgled, as he trudged into the huge bathroom. She returned to stand before the hanging body of the unconscious slave and carefully scrutinized him the way a butterfly collector might examine a new specimen. *This one was strong,* she thought. *As strong as one of common blood could be. Because of being trapped here in this miserable land it has been more than three hundred years since I have lain with a man of endowed blood. But that is about to change.*

"Your bath is ready, Mistress," Geldon pronounced as he reentered the room.

"Good," Succiu said quietly, as she continued to examine the slave. "Time to wake him up."

Geldon winced, knowing what was expected of him. Walking back into his mistress's bath, he collected a handful of sea salt, then returned to stand once again upon the stool, this time directly behind the slave. This was the part he hated the most. Looking up to Succiu, he waited for her curt nod. Then he dutifully opened his hands and quickly rubbed the white grains into the many gaping slashes that had been carved into the man's back by Succiu's whip.

The effect was almost instantaneous.

The slave named Stefan was immediately brought back to consciousness, and he twisted and turned in his manacles, his eyes bulging from his head as he screamed insanely at the top of his lungs. When the screaming finally stopped, the whimpering began. And then the whimpering finally stopped, and the crying began. Succiu shook her head disparagingly and once again stepped before the slave, placing a sickeningly affectionate hand to one of his cheeks as she looked into his eyes. The slave named Stefan recoiled spasmodically at her touch.

"There now, isn't that better?" she cooed, smiling crookedly into his eyes. "We want those scars to heal just right so that you will remember your little lesson here today, don't we?" She turned her attention to the dwarf. "We wouldn't want him to develop a nasty infection, now would we, Geldon? If that were to happen, he might never be able to come back."

"No, we wouldn't want an infection, Mistress," the dwarf repeated obediently.

She looked hard into the slave's eyes. "I think you should thank Geldon for the kindness he has just shown you, don't you agree?"

With a final effort, he raised his face to hers. "No, bitch," he breathed. The final, almost quiet statement of defiance had taken everything the man had. He fainted again, going limp in the manacles.

Succiu's eyes once again hardened as she began to walk toward her bath. "Take him away from here. Back to the Stables with the other weaklings of his kind who also have no endowed blood. And then come back here quickly and clean all of this up. My bedroom is a disgrace." Stopping at her bed, she narrowed her eyes and caused a pink silk sheet to float into the air and land on the floor beneath the dangling, bloody toes of the inert slave.

"Wrap him up in that," she said sarcastically. "It wouldn't do to have a mess down the hallways, now would it?" She tilted her head slightly, and the manacles sprang open, sending the slave crashing to the marble floor. "And after you have cleaned this room, wait outside the door for me. You are to accompany me to a meeting this afternoon." She turned her back on him. "Just don't be loitering about in here when I come out of my bath."

"Yes, Mistress, I mean no, Mistress," the short one murmured. "I shan't be here when you come out."

She rather disinterestedly watched him drag the bloody body out of the room and close the huge doors behind him. Smiling to herself, she then luxuriously turned and, stretching her lithe body like an alley cat, walked to her bath.

After inserting one toe into the water, she knew that the dwarf had gotten the temperature just right. Very hot. She slowly lowered herself the rest of the way in before realizing she was still wearing the bloody silk robe. Smiling, she closed her eyes and made it vanish. No matter. She could conjure a hundred more just like it if she chose to.

Looking to her left, she gestured with a long fingernail to open the stained-glass windows to her bathroom. She had to admit that the Parthalonian countryside was every bit as beautiful as Eutracia had been 327 years ago, before their forced exile. But Parthalon was different. The people the sorceresses had found here had been little more than ignorant peasants, and the Coven had taken great pains to ensure that it stayed that way. There had been neither a tradition of royalty nor a standing army here, such as had been inflicted upon Eutracia by the so-called Directorate of Wizards. Her eyes narrowed. The mere thought of those wizards made her heart beat faster with hate.

Enslaving Parthalon had actually been very easy, she remembered, especially in light of the fact that there had been no presence of endowed blood here. Their defenses had been feeble at best. Thousands had died all manner of hideous and imaginative deaths, but before too long the people had bowed to the four mistresses as their rulers. It had actually been rather amusing. Most of the people had been terrified of the thing called magic, having never seen it before, and they had stayed that way to this day, cloaked in a blind fear that the Coven had no intention of removing.

But the absence of endowed blood had proven to be a sword that could cut both ways. Although the entire country had easily come under the Coven's control, there were no men of endowed blood here with whom to procreate. None of mistresses would ever dream of conceiving a child with one of these churlish cretins. And so the quest for the birth of a special female child of endowed blood from someone among the four of them had been lain aside as impossible, and the Coven had tried a different approach. It would take centuries, they knew, but it was the only way. And now, over three hundred years later, they were so close to completing their goal—as long as everything happened exactly as planned, and at the appropriate time.

Suddenly an interesting thought came to her. *Time. Such an invincible enemy, such an indispensable ally. Even time itself we can now manipulate, just as it also manipulates us.* She laid her head back against the cool marble of the huge tub and closed her eyes, lost in her thoughts.

Their slaves had been taken at random from the population as needed—for forced labor, or for other . . . uses. Indeed, the name "the

Stables" had been her idea for the area of the Recluse where they kept those particular male and female slaves. And only beautiful ones. They did not serve in the traditional roles that one would expect of a palace. No, the ones like Stefan all served the Coven as sexual entertainment. *Except for the First Mistress,* she thought. Again the corners of her mouth turned up into a smile. This had been her idea, and there must be hundreds of them of both sexes in the Stables by now, with three of the four mistresses making great use of the privilege. As a precaution they were tended to by deaf mutes only, and thus there could be no knowledge among the populace of the Stable slaves' existence or purpose.

But what the populace knew or didn't know really was of no importance. All of the more traditional servants and workers in the Recluse were slaves who had been taken from the countryside. The huge Recluse itself, the fortress home of the Coven, had been built with slave labor from Parthalon. When it was completed, all the workers had been put to death so that the inner layout of the castle remained a secret. With the exception of her personal slave, Geldon, once a native of Parthalon was taken into the Recluse there was only one way for him or her to leave.

Dead.

As she carefully washed the blood from beneath her nails, her thoughts turned to those days and nights over three centuries ago that she and her sisters had endured trying to cross the Sea of Whispers. She smiled at the brilliant bargain the first sorceress of the Coven had made to ensure their safe passage when the four of them had at last discovered the hideous reason the sea had never been crossed. At the same time she blessed the First Mistress' mastery of the Vagaries, without the knowledge of which that same bargain could never have been struck. And soon, very soon, they were to cross the Sea of Whispers again for the first time in over three hundred years. They had to return to Eutracia at last because the one they had left behind, although useful, did not possess the blood quality necessary to become the fifth mistress—the one that they had needed so badly and for so long in order to complete their plans.

And then the wizards who had banished them would pay. She reveled in the thought.

After leaving her bath and brushing her long, dark hair, she walked naked through her quarters to the huge closets that held her wardrobe. Opening the doors, she quickly decided upon red for today. This afternoon's upcoming meeting was of the greatest importance, and this magnificent gown had long been her favorite. As she dressed, she turned her attention toward the room. Geldon had returned and cleaned it as she had ordered, and was no doubt waiting at the other side of the doors for her to appear. He was the perfect servant, and not for the first time she smiled at her luck in finding him.

It had been during one of her earliest visits to the Ghetto of the Shunned.

From the first the Coven had needed a place to confine certain unwanted members of the population, even after the country had been successfully overwhelmed. The problem had been solved very simply by selecting a rather large city just south of the Recluse, conjuring a very high and inescapable wall around it, and then killing all of the citizens inside, whether they had been useful or not. There simply had been no need to sort them all out, and so the Coven exterminated them by means of a plague. This conveniently left the mistresses with vacant living quarters large enough to hold approximately two hundred thousand souls.

Then the crippled, the sick, the retarded, the criminal, and everyone else that the Coven deemed simply undesirable were forced into the Ghetto and left to fend for themselves. The results were inevitable: crime, filth, disease, and inbreeding. From the very beginning, relegation to the Ghetto had been an irreversible death sentence. And it had indeed proven itself to be a powerful tool for controlling the actions of the population, especially until provisions for a standing army had been conceived. The simple threat of life in the Ghetto usually made grown men tremble in their boots.

Although the other Sisters strictly avoided the Ghetto as not worth their time, Succiu visited there often, actually enjoying the change from her wonderful gowns into rags and walking the Ghetto at night in the light of the three same red moons that had illuminated her homeland. She enjoyed seeing the poverty and the desperation, enjoyed anonymously witnessing the occasional rape or murder. Guarded by her powers, she walked among the Ghetto's inhabitants without fear, occasionally killing at random simply to sharpen her skills.

She probably would have missed Geldon altogether had it not been for the sound of shattering glass. All of the storefronts in the Ghetto had long since been looted, and Succiu couldn't imagine that there was any glass left to break.

Curious, she turned a corner into yet another dark street. Looking up and down it, she finally noticed a bit of movement. The feet of a child in rather odd boots were all that could be seen sticking out of a smashed storefront window, toes down and wriggling, as though the child were scrambling after something. Curious, she reached out and grabbed the child's collar, launching him backward into the mud and glass that covered the street. What she had mistaken for a child she now saw was a dwarf, wincing in pain at having fallen on the hump between his shoulders. She casually placed one of her boots at the base of his throat.

"What were you doing?" she demanded.

He spat upon her leg, defiant. She increased the pressure of the boot on his throat, not really caring whether he lived or died. She could have used her powers to kill him a hundred different ways, but for the moment she was enjoying herself.

"Just one more chance," she said calmly.

"Cat," was the only word he could muster.

She lightened the pressure on his throat. "What do you mean, 'cat'?"

"You know what I mean." He panted. "There's no food here anymore. I'm hungry. We all are. Cats be good eatin'. One of 'em ran into the store here. Make three meals out of a cat, I can, especially if it's a big tomcat. Now, thanks to a street whore of the Ghetto, I'm still hungry!"

"Eating cats are you, little man?" she gloated, maintaining the pressure on his throat. "My last meal was highland pheasant with raptor's eggs."

"Not just a whore, but a lying whore," he snarled. "That be only outside food, and only for the rich, at that!"

She released her foot. "Get up."

He was perhaps all of three and a half feet tall, with dark hair, filthy clothes, and pudgy, greasy fingers. But she sensed a hidden intelligence in him. A perfect nocturnal creature of the Ghetto, he would be able to come and go virtually unnoticed. Such a person could be useful.

"What was your crime?" she asked.

"Robbery. I stole some bread for my family. We were starving. But they're all dead now."

The twisted mental image of a dwarfed hunchback trying to hide a loaf of bread that was the size of his arm brought a smile to her face. Growing even more curious, Succiu circled the dwarf as she examined him. The first finger of her left hand toyed with her bottom lip as the seed of an idea came to her.

"How would you like to leave this place? For services rendered, of course?"

"No street whore of the Ghetto has the power of freedom," he said sarcastically.

Succiu was beginning to feel that some instruction was in order.

"That's no way to speak to a mistress of the Coven," she said quietly, pointing a finger at the dwarf.

"Mistress of the Coven, my arse!" He laughed. One of his fingers came up in an obscene gesture.

She had noticed the lantern hook earlier, long since looted of its oil lamp. It was fastened to the shop wall just to the left of the broken door. It looked sturdy enough, and if it was not, she would make it so.

Deliberately, almost gently, she levitated the dwarf up and back through the air toward the shop, and neatly hung him upon the hook through the back of his muddy coat. She turned her exotic head this way and that, examining him as if he were some kind of prize she had just won at a Eutracian province fair. Still defiant and not understanding the gravity of his situation, he wiggled all four limbs at once as if trying to obtain some form of purchase in the humid night air. Finally, he became still. But she could see that it was a stillness born of defiance.

"Bitch!" he spat venomously.

"Still don't believe me, little man?" she asked. "I would have thought this small demonstration might have convinced you."

"No cheap magic trick will convince me you've a true sorceress' power." He glared. "Besides, the mistresses of the Coven all live in a grand castle. Everybody knows that. No, you're a street whore. Better looking than the others here, I grant you, and a whore with more tricks up her skirt than most, but a cheap street whore just the same."

A smile came to her lips, exposing her perfect, white teeth to the moonlight. "What is your name, little man?" she asked, arms akimbo.

"Geldon."

"Well, Geldon, it seems I have taken an interest in you. And, as I have said, I *am* a mistress of the Coven. But no matter. If you do not accept my offer, you will perish. Simple. And the secret that I sometimes walk the Ghetto by night will die with you." She laughed at the irony. "Such a little man with such a big secret!"

He tried to spit at her again, but was unable to reach her. "For the last time, bitch, leave me be, leave me!" he screamed fruitlessly. "Go find some other poor fool to rent your crotch to!"

At last, she decided.

With her arms spread to the stars, her back arched, and her eyes closed, she began the incantation:

> " 'Tis your blood that is sought;
> 'Tis heat to be wrought;
> No god or man can end my toil;
> No savior may cause this enchantment to spoil.
> I command your blood essence to writhe and churn;
> You shall feel your very soul to burn."

Two shafts of bright blue light shot from her hands, joined, and impaled the dangling dwarf to the wall. Immediately he began to tremble.

The second mistress of the Coven was executing a Blood Pox.

For the first time, true terror began to escape from the dwarf's beady eyes as his little body shuddered, then began to shake more violently. Sweat streamed from his face and hands, and his clothing actually began to wrinkle from the heat as the temperature of his blood rose.

"Agree to my request soon, or I will take you past the point of no return," Succiu hissed, watching her handiwork. "It is not a pretty sight." She laughed. "But by then, of course, you will already be blind."

Still, the dwarf refused to speak. As he shook more violently against the clapboards of the building, Succiu continued to raise the temperature of his blood, the shaft of blue light becoming more intense in the dark night. She could swear she was beginning to see the toes of his boots starting to curl.

A stream of urine began to run down the inside of his left leg, then to his boot, and finally to the ground, forming a stinking, steaming, pinkish puddle beneath him. Then he started to scream. His body convulsed against the wall.

"I agree," he said faintly.

"You'll have to do better than that." She laughed. "Address me correctly!"

"I agree, Mistress!" he screamed, his eyes rolling back in his head. She noticed a trickle of blood from one ear running down the side of his squat neck.

Immediately the shaft of blue light vanished, and Geldon crashed to the wooden sidewalk. Succiu stepped neatly around the pools of perspiration, urine, and blood, and stood over the scarcely breathing dwarf. With a smile, she bent down gracefully, touched a finger to the blood on the left side of his face just below the ear, and placed a drop of it on her tongue.

From that moment on, he was hers.

Taking him back to the Recluse, she had protected him with time enchantments and healed him to make him more useful. With two exceptions. She left his hunched back. And she left him impotent and sterile—results of the extreme blood temperature. Once he was well enough, she began using him to do her hunting for her. Hunting the Parthalonian countryside for the slaves that now made up the population of the Stables. And she had purposely left him broken. Teasing him with the possibility of a cure ensured that he would remain faithful.

She had instructed the Recluse maidservants to clean him, clothe him, and give him quarters. The First Mistress, upon seeing Geldon, had ordered him from the castle and rebuked Succiu for having brought him into their midst without permission. She found the hunchbacked dwarf disgusting to look at, not to mention an inferior life form, being a male of unendowed blood. But when Succiu had outlined her plans for using the dwarf to help her populate the Stables, Failee had relented, provided that Geldon was to be controlled and not left to wander the magnificent hallways of the Recluse at his own discretion. Succiu had gladly agreed and initiated the idea of the rings, thereby both humiliating the dwarf and condemning him to a life of servitude wearing the hated collar.

Smiling into the mirror as she admired herself in the stunning red gown, she knew that she would soon be gone from this place. Then she would have no need for the dwarf, and she could kill him.

After a final look of approval at her reflection, she walked to the door. Opening it, she reached down and picked up the end of the jeweled leash that the dutiful dwarf was holding up to her in both palms. Then she led the way down the hall, the dwarf waddling as best he could in order to keep up.

A's Failee ascended the circular stone staircase, her mind raced. Moisture dripped from the dark stone walls, occasionally hissing as it fell into the wall torches. If the entire Coven was not present at the appointed hour, she would see to it that they were punished with some mild form of the Vagaries.

It would be her pleasure.

Eventually she reached the top of the staircase and stood before the great double mahogany doors. The Pentangle had been inlaid into each of the doors in brass, and magic was required to enter. These were the doors to the Coven's Chamber, the highest and most private area of the Recluse.

As First Mistress of the Coven she had purposely decided to be late, to keep the other mistresses waiting. She uncurled one of her long fingers toward the doors and commanded them to open. To further illustrate the point of her leadership, she levitated herself and slowly glided into the room, finally coming to a stop in front of her throne and gently hovering there in dominance of the others already seated.

She was relieved to see that the other mistresses of the Coven were dutifully in attendance, each one in her prescribed throne. One throne was placed at each point of the oddly shaped five-cornered table. Two thrones remained blatantly empty. One was Failee's, into which she gracefully lowered herself. The other throne had been empty for centuries. No one had sat in it since the first day it had been brought to this room, over three hundred years ago.

Ironically, the darkness of the meeting's agenda was completely off-set by the light and airy beauty of the room. The walls and floor were of the finest blanched white marble. Paintings and sculptures in a variety of styles and colors were strategically placed about. One entire wall of the great room had been given over to leaded stained-glass windows that were now shut, and highly patterned rugs lay here and there upon the marble floor. Several gold oil lamp chandeliers hung from the ceiling, giving the room a soft, golden touch as twilight slowly advanced with the coming of night.

Without speaking, she looked in turn into each of the faces of her Sisters, the other mistresses who had been with her so long and had gone through so much. To her immediate right in a stunning red gown sat Succiu, second mistress of the Coven. On Succiu's right was Vona. Her straight, red hair did little to detract from the intensity of her blue eyes. An emerald representation of the Pentangle hung around her neck on a gold chain. The last was Zabarra, the youngest of them but one of the most powerful. She was also one of the most sarcastic. Her green eyes smiled at Failee as she played with the end of one of her blond ringlets.

Failee continued to gaze at the three other women. They appeared to be younger than she, since the time enchantments had come to her later in life. She smiled herself knowingly. The wizards, too, had been older at the time they had discovered the time enchantments. *Like me, they appear mature,* she thought. *And always will.*

But the three before her she had chosen as her most trusted follow-ers not only because of their power but also because of their relative youth and vitality—vitality that would be forever preserved by the time enchantments. The fact that they were younger and less experienced did not concern her, since she knew she would have all of eternity to train them. And she did not envy their eternal youth and beauty. *After all,* she thought, *they shall never possess the power that I do.*

"You're late," Vona said almost casually, her face a curious mix-ture of courtesy and impertinence. "Has it now to become the custom to keep other Sisters waiting for the beginning of such an important meeting?"

"Your tone tells me that perhaps you need a visit to the Stables, Vona," Failee said easily, but her hazel eyes stared commandingly into Vona's deep-blue ones. She tossed back heavy, dark hair that was shot through with streaks of premature gray. "After all, they are there for your unlimited enjoyment, are they not?"

Failee could see the anger begin to rise in Vona's face, but before the redhead could answer she was interrupted by a different voice. A male voice.

"Good evening, Mistress," Geldon gurgled as he trudged out from behind Succiu's throne.

Succiu slapped the dwarf across the face with the back of her hand. He went down hard upon the marble floor, his cheek bleeding from the cut put there by the ornate gemstone ring that Succiu always wore on the third finger of her left hand. Failee saw Geldon's eyes blaze red for a moment before slowly returning to their usual look of controlled servitude.

"How dare you speak to the First Mistress without being spoken to first!" Succiu hissed, her eyes narrowed into slits. "Perhaps I should simply take you back to that awful place where I found you." She threw one side of her long black hair over her shoulder as if in contempt of his very presence. Geldon slowly rose back up to his feet.

"Even though you insist upon being around that gruesome creature, at least you are keeping it on a leash," Zabarra said, shaking her head, her eyes to the ceiling. The tip of her right index finger remained lost inside the end of one of her ringlets as she spoke. "We are fully aware that he does all of the scouting for us, but must you always bring him here, as well?"

"Take care, Sister," Vona cautioned. "One day he will turn on you."

Succiu laughed impulsively. "Really, Vona?" she retorted. "And just how would he accomplish that? After all, he's only a man. And a little, mortal, emasculated one at that."

"Enough of this," Failee snapped, once more in command of the meeting. "Our guest should by now be waiting outside the door. Zabarra, please bring in Commander Kluge."

Zabarra went to the double doors and opened them, letting a tall man into the room. He walked slowly to the front of the table and stood quietly. His name was Kluge, and he was the commander of the Minions of Day and Night, the personal army of the Coven.

Unkempt but clean black hair streaked with gray fell past his shoulders. The dark, neatly trimmed mustache and goatee surrounded a firm mouth, and intelligent eyes, piercingly dark to the point of almost being black, seemed never to miss a thing. He was a tall, muscular man, almost handsome, except for the whitish scar that ran from the outside corner of his left eye, down his cheek, and into the small forest of his goatee. The energy and strength apparent in him were always kept under tight control, yet it always seemed as if simply looking at him could somehow cause one harm.

Upon his promotion to commander, Failee had given him permission to wear black. The sleeveless, black leather tunic revealed strong, scarred chest and arm muscles. Silver-trimmed forearm gauntlets, also black, ended at the first knuckle of each hand. Just above the first knuckle of each finger were spiked, silver finger rings, designed for stabbing and slashing at close quarters. Black leather boots trimmed in silver and a shiny winged helmet with horizontal eye slits held under the left arm completed the picture.

The curved, sheathed sword at his side was the mainstay of the Minion warrior. The sword, called a dreggan, looked like an ordinary sword, but at the touch of a lever built into the hilt, the blade would extend with great force up to another foot. During running swordplay, in which proper distancing was crucial, a Minion could surprise his opponent with the sudden appearance of an extra foot of swinging, flashing steel that had not been there before; or he could place the dreggan against the opponent's body and suddenly impale him with no apparent effort. A blood groove always ran down the blade's shiny, silver edge. It was fabled to be so sharp that when a silk scarf had once been thrown into the air in jest, it had been neatly halved by a well-turned dreggan before it hit the ground.

But the last of Kluge's weapons was the one that Failee found the most intriguing.

The returning wheel.

Hanging from Kluge's right hip was a silver hub, from which protruded flat, curved blades, equally distanced apart. When properly thrown, the returning wheel could slice through a victim cleanly and then return in a large circle to its owner. To be in the midst of a battle amid a flurry of returning wheels brought obvious danger not only to the enemy, but also to the Minions themselves. The proper use of a returning wheel took years to perfect, and Kluge was an expert. Failee glanced at the glove that Kluge wore over his right hand. The palm of the black leather glove was padded with lead, which allowed the returning wheel to be safely plucked back out of the air upon its return. The pad of Kluge's glove had long since been permanently stained with blood.

The other mistresses were also watching Kluge as he stood quietly at attention, waiting to be addressed. Succiu's eyes in particular roamed his face and body. She licked her lips, slowly.

Yet the most amazing of Kluge's attributes were barely visible, rising only slightly above each of his shoulders from the rear. Failee herself had been responsible for this anomaly. As a master of the Vagaries, she had worked for over a decade to produce just the right combination of blood mix from other creatures with incantations of her own to create this particular attribute, making sure it was both inheritable and completely functional. Since then, each member of the Minions of Day and Night had been born with the same amazing feature.

Wings.

Not the feathered wings of birds. Not light, fluffy, and hollow of bone. Instead, these dark, leathery wings were strong enough to break an enemy's back. Open, each wing stretched half again as far as an outstretched arm. After a few quick paces, a Minion warrior could leap into the air and fly, covering great distances. Given enough portable food and water, Minion warriors could remain aloft uninterrupted for up to two days and two nights.

Early on it had become obvious to the Coven that trying to conscript and train an army of the male weaklings of this strange land would be impossible. And so they had decided to use a different method to ensure themselves of warriors who would someday be worthy of their plans.

They would breed them.

It had begun with the abduction of several handpicked men and women of the populace. They had been forced to mate continuously under the supervision of Failee and an occasionally voyeuristic Succiu, to begin the growth of what would become a population of well-trained male warriors. Failee eliminated the problem of inbreeding through incantations of her own design. Any child with a deformity or ailment was immediately put to the sword. Females were used for breeding only, relegated to the brothels inside the various Minion fortifications that had begun to dot the countryside. Women who were infertile or past their childbearing years were assigned other duties, such as cooking, learning to make weapons, or serving as midwives in the birthing houses.

To better control the female population within the fortifications, the women's wings were clipped and their feet bound. To produce the largest number of warriors in the shortest amount of time the Coven had cast time enchantments of acceleration and deceleration upon them, forcing the boys and girls to reach puberty faster than normal, and the adults to age more slowly than normal, thus widening the window of opportunity for breeding. The results had surpassed even Failee's expectations.

The man who now stood before the Coven was their selection to command it all. The only authority he recognized was the Coven itself.

"Commander Kluge, you may approach," Failee said gently.

Kluge immediately bent to one knee, his head bowed. "I live to serve," came the short, deep-voiced reply. He stood and stepped nearer the table, where he once more waited to be spoken to.

"Please inform us of the status of your command, Commander," Failee said. "Leave out nothing. The time of your proving will shortly be upon us."

Kluge placed the highly polished helmet on the floor and folded his hands in front of himself, gathering his thoughts.

"Yes, Mistress. The current number of men under arms stands at one hundred fifty thousand, seven hundred and ten. Additionally, as you know, this now increases daily at a rate of approximately two hundred, due to the great effectiveness of the time enchantments. Births are upward of about double that amount, less of course the execution of the newborn undesirables and death from natural causes." Always the political animal, he paused, carefully glancing at each of the mistresses in turn, making sure he was addressing them as a group. As usual, however, his eyes seemed to linger a bit longer upon Succiu than the others.

"Foot soldiers, approximately sixty thousand. Elite assassins, twenty thousand. Captains of ocean-going warships, one thousand. Warship warriors, fifty thousand. Officers, eight thousand. Archers, two thousand. The remaining number of troops are divided into the usual support staff—cooks, blacksmiths, armorers, healers, and so on.

"As for the status of the Minion population including females for breeding, the current situation is good. There is very little disease and virtually no crime. The brothels have many new additions, and the visitation rate by the troops is as high as I have ever seen it. As a result, the birthrate is high. The construction of additional birthing houses with the usual complements of midwives and nursery guardians may be in order if this continues, but I must also add that if here are any problems at all, these are good ones to have.

"Training of the warriors continues relentlessly. Those injured in training and no longer capable of battle are housed in separate quarters, and used for siring purposes only. This serves two purposes. First, it is a reward for their service. And second, it prevents the number of males available for breeding from continuing to dwindle. We have lost far more warriors than usual in recent months—warriors who would have normally sired children. These losses are due to the vastly increased training to the death that I have seen fit to order in preparation for our mission. But I feel that the results have been worth the losses. The current male/female ratio is approximately even, making for a total Minion population of just over three hundred thousand. Officers of importance have, at your request, been secretly briefed that they are about to engage in a campaign, although they are unaware, as am I, of the specific nature of the confrontation." He turned and addressed Failee specifically. "All is ready."

Failee rose from her throne and glided to the largest of the stained-glass windows. As she pointed a finger, the double windows gently opened outward. She took a breath of the sweet Parthalonian early-evening air, gazing west into the sunset toward her homeland of Eutracia, out toward the Sea of Whispers that separated the two lands. The northern coastline of Parthalon was just visible from here, one reason the Coven had selected this area for the Recluse: so that they could never forget the centuries-ago war, the loss of so many of their Sisters at the hands of the wizards, and the desperate search to find a way across the supposedly uncrossable sea. They had washed ashore like peasants in a land no Eutracian knew existed, much less had ever set eyes on. The burning desire to return and reclaim their power set fire to her soul each time she viewed this ocean. Only four mistresses remained from the hundreds she had loved, lost, and left behind. *Soon, my dead Sisters,* she thought. *So many shall pay. Pay for the sins of their ancestors.*

It was the Season of New Life in Parthalon, and the beautiful countryside was blooming. The three red moons rose in the sky here each evening, just as they had in Eutracia. The bugaylea trees were just coming to full color, their leaves turning gracefully in the wind. A gorgeous squadron of black-and-yellow honeybees, growing in this land to the size of a man's hand, flew by noisily just below the open window. But her sorceress' heart yearned for Eutracia.

Her mind turned briefly to the man standing behind her. How could such a blunt instrument as Kluge ever understand the full motives behind this undertaking? She gently smiled to herself, knowing that it didn't matter, that his loyalty and the performance of the warriors and the warships were all the mistresses required of him. Indeed, she thought, the subtleties of the ultimate prize would be totally lost on Kluge. He lived only for war. Had she herself not bred him to be so?

She had seen Succiu's eyes roam over Kluge's body, and she knew why. Smiling, the memories of so long ago began to fill the corners of her mind.

As she continued to stare out at the Parthalonian countryside, one memory in particular came back to her, one that she had taken the luxury of revisiting often during these last, important days. Her mind began to drift happily back to over three hundred years ago, during the war in Eutracia when she had first taken the knowledge of the Vagaries from the wizards.

It had been in Florian's Glade, a city recently taken by the Coven. The captured wizard had been brought to her as a delightful surprise, and she had ordered him to be bound to a chair in the center of the town square in preparation of her interrogation of him.

But this one was strong, she knew, and she therefore decided first to try another way to convince him to give up his secrets rather than simply trying to force the knowledge from him. She smiled to herself, luxuriating in the irony of the moment and the solution that had so conveniently offered itself up.

For the Coven already had his daughter.

As Vona dragged the young girl forward to face her father in his simple but unforgiving prison in the sun, Failee gave him one brief, awful chance to save his only child. She stared down into his amazingly potent eyes and issued her stark, excruciating demand.

"Give all of your knowledge to me," she said quite simply, "or you shall witness your only child, your beautiful daughter of endowed blood, perish before your eyes."

At first the wizard was dumbstruck to see before him the daughter he had thought dead for so long, and the tears that began to form in the corners of his eyes ran down his cheeks and into the thirsty dirt of the courtyard. But strangely, he did not speak. He lowered his head in defeat.

But then his countenance hardened, as he became certain of the path he must take regardless of his personal feelings. He looked the First Mistress in the eyes, trying at the same time to avoid the eyes of his only child.

"No," he said simply. He spat as hard as he could into Failee's face, his heart tearing in two, knowing that he had just condemned his daughter to death.

Upon a short nod from Failee, Vona immediately grabbed the now-screaming girl by the hair and dragged her into a nearby house. The begging and shrieking were horrifying, and seemed to go on and on forever as if the sorceress was taking her time with her grisly task, enjoying her work. The wizard, powerless against the combined talents of the Coven, struggled pitifully in his chair, trying to escape while the unthinkable happened. And then all went quiet as Vona walked back out into the center of the square with a bloody dagger in one hand and a lock of his daughter's blond hair in the other.

She threw it into his face, laughing.

At that point the torture had started. And the Vigors and Vagaries that were so painfully ripped from the wizard's mind became an essential part of the powers of the Coven. As Failee's torture of the wizard progressed, her powers and understanding of the craft grew, and she willingly passed on the basic tenets of the darker side of the craft to her Sisters, the three females of endowed blood whom she had chosen to be her closest allies and to help her rule Eutracia after they had taken the kingdom.

She could still remember the moment when she finally broke through his mind and found what it was she had been searching for.

You have done it, her heart cried out. *You have broken the most powerful of them all!* And then she had smiled at him yet again, and had spoken the words intended to pierce his heart like daggers.

"You are now completely mine," she said softly, almost reverently, to the wizard as he sat there in his chair of torture, unable to move.

And for the next several months she had walked unfettered through his mind, his power, his very soul, learning and taking, committing psychic rape and delving into what she was sure was every part of his subliminal being, and his talents.

In addition she had also found the incantation that she had now so long held to her breast. The one that would, very soon, prove to be so invaluable to their mission.

And then, surprisingly, the acute, unfulfilled desires had come. One day, while struggling to understand one of the more arcane passages of the Vagaries, she and the others had all felt the unexpected stirring of their loins. The hugely sexual, needful longings had been intensified by an insanely irresistible desire to inflict those same sexual needs upon others.

Of both genders.

And with the resultant acts of depravity had come to Failee the shocking, absolute certainty that it was, indeed, these blissful feelings of ecstasy that truly helped augment their power. That the quality of their blood and, therefore, their ability to employ the Vagaries became stronger each time they indulged themselves in yet greater forms of sexual wickedness. And that to fulfill completely her potential as a true mistress of the Vagaries she must gladly obey that dark side of the craft, and willingly surrender to the depravities it was calling upon her and her sisters to perform. Failee had therefore encouraged such predilections, this sickness of the soul and of the body. Encouraged them, in fact, to such an extent that the construction of the Stables had been a necessity, rather than an indulgence.

Strangely, perhaps because the First Mistress was the most powerful of the Coven, the greater her understanding of the Vagaries became, the more her own sexual longings had begun to lessen and finally to dissipate, leaving her with only a pure, unadulterated need for the perfection of the craft. Her sexual needs had been replaced by a calmness, an inner peace, that she now knew only a true adept of the Vagaries could attain. But she continued to encourage the carnal activities of the others, hoping that one day they, too, would ascend to her level of superiority.

But in the end the sorceresses had lost. Lost the war that they had tried so hard to fight and win. And only because it had been the bastard wizards who had first found the stone and the Tome.

Reluctantly she turned from the window, glided back to her throne, and sat down. No one else in the room had spoken or moved. Failee's personal reveries were legendary, and her silence could be deafening. Kluge, the commander of the Minions, stood patiently waiting for her to speak, as did the others. Her mind finally came out of the past and began to concentrate upon the present.

"Of most importance, Commander, is the condition and state of the warships. Tell us, what is their battle status?"

"The vessels of which you speak have come under the highest scrutiny of all, Mistress," he assured her. His eyes flicked briefly to the others at the table. "They have been checked, sailed, and checked again. One thousand strong. Each captain has been handpicked and rigorously trained. As per your orders, the captains have been given the best of Minion quarters, food, wine, and females for recreation. The holds of each vessel are filled to capacity with the appropriate weapons, and each of the captains has spent time familiarizing himself with the capricious nature of the maritime winds. Water and provisions for the journey have been set aside, and will be loaded when I am given a sailing date. We have also taken the liberty of fashioning a death's head to the prow of each ship, which has heightened morale even further. Each man is anxious for the campaign to begin."

"What are your casualty estimates?" she asked. She knew that it was an unfair question, given the fact that Kluge had not been fully informed of the nature of the mission. Nonetheless she wanted him to answer first, to see if his numbers came close to those of her own.

"The officers corps and I estimate losses of at least twenty thousand, given the as-yet-unknown nature of the resistance. However, as you are aware, those losses will not be of equal proportion throughout the ranks. The highest proportion of deaths will occur among the Elite Assassins, since they are always the first to attack. Those wounded beyond help shall be put to the sword. Any remaining wounded still suitable for breeding shall be brought home, as per your orders. The balance of the casualties we expect to be rather evenly divided among the other types of warriors. Even though we have the element of surprise and the prizes that we seek shall be, as you have informed me, all in one place, due to the nature of the timing the entire Eutracian Guard shall be present. And although the Guard has not fought an actual battle in over three hundred years, they, too, as you have informed me, train relentlessly." He paused briefly, as if unsure of his next sentence. Finally, it came. "Mistress, may I ask a question of you?"

"Speak."

"If I may, I have two questions. First, how is it that my ladies know so much of the kingdom of Eutracia after such a great amount of time has passed? In fact, how can we be sure that the kingdom even continues to exist?" He waited to let the question sink in.

"And the second?"

He once again uncharacteristically paused. The asking of the second question, if phrased improperly, would seem to question both the wisdom and the authority of the Coven, a position in which he had no desire to find himself. Although he knew of his great value to the women in this room, he also knew with equal certainty that any one of them could kill him as easily as she could draw her next breath, and some of them would not hesitate to do so.

He lowered his gaze to an intersection of blocks in the white marble floor, searching his mind for the correct words. He must be careful in this, he knew. He raised his head, doing his best to divide his two dark eyes among the eight others that were so keenly regarding him.

"Please understand, Mistress," he began, "my question is as much from my officers corps as from myself," he said. "It is just that they press me constantly for an answer, and I—"

"Enough!" Failee interrupted. She lowered her eyes and slowly shook her head back and forth. Although usually controlled, she was running out of patience and had little time for a commander who could not come to the point. Time, above all, was now the Coven's most precious commodity.

"Ask your question or lose your tongue," she said almost gently. Succiu's mouth turned upward into a smirk.

Recognizing her tone, Kluge dropped again to one knee and bowed his head. "Forgive me, Mistress, but what is the prize we seek?" It was only now that he raised his head and looked into Failee's eyes. Gratefully, he saw her face relax slightly, the beginnings of a small smile coming to her lips. He stood.

Without answering, Failee's right hand emerged from her robe and reached across the table to draw closer to herself several arcane objects. A square, jeweled box with the sign of the Pentangle upon its lid was first. This was followed by a tall crystal goblet. Lastly, she picked up and placed before herself a large amphora, also made of crystal. The amphora was filled with water. Oddly, he realized he had not remembered seeing any of these objects until Failee had reached for them.

The First Mistress slowly filled the goblet from the amphora, watching the water pour out and down. Once the goblet was filled, the amphora once again vanished from the table. The other mistresses sat quietly watching, as if in reverence.

Failee raised her right arm, pointing her index finger straight down toward the center of the thick, dark table. Immediately the table began to separate, splitting down the center. The two sections of the table turned hauntingly toward the wall, until they joined again in the shape of a long rectangle. Each of the thrones, including the empty one, also moved, carrying each sorceress around the newly formed table until they were all on one side, facing the same direction. The empty throne was in the center. Geldon, Succiu's slave, was located at the far end of the table, still sitting on the floor, chained to the same spot.

For a moment Kluge imagined that he must be losing his wits, for the seated mistresses were facing a wall of the chamber that he did not remember being there before. It was in stark contrast to the rest of the room. Unlike the other walls, which were of blanched marble, this one was made of the most highly polished black marble he had ever seen. When he looked upon it, the black depths seemed endless. In addition he noticed that the room was beginning to further darken as the oil lamp chandeliers dimmed, no doubt yet another act of Failee's.

Failee turned in her throne to address Kluge, who was still standing in the same place, behind the table. She waved her hand, beckoning him forward. "Commander, come to the end of the table," she ordered. Kluge obeyed, walking in the half-light to stand next to Zabarra's throne. Zabarra, her finger still toying with a blond ringlet, bowed her head slightly, acknowledging his presence.

Failee smiled, spreading her hands upon the table before her. "As to your questions, Commander, the proof of our *supposed* knowledge of Eutracia will soon come to you in the form of a demonstration. You see, there is one in Eutracia who is still loyal to us. What that person sees, I can also see. What that person hears, I can also hear."

Kluge couldn't help but notice that her mood had changed. She almost seemed lost in her own thoughts.

"As to your second question—that is, what prize we seek—well, I do believe that you are in for somewhat of a surprise. The prize, or should I say prizes, shall also be illustrated to you shortly by way of a demonstration. But, to be polite, the true answer is that we seek only three things. First, a woman. Second, a gemstone. And third, a chalice of water."

Kluge was stunned. Twenty thousand estimated casualties and a campaign of this magnitude to accomplish a mere kidnapping and the theft of a gemstone? Were they insane? Any woman they desired, for any reason whatsoever, could easily be taken from the Parthalonian citizenry. And gemstones? Although he had not seen it done, he had to believe that any one of the Sisters could conjure up gemstones of any quantity and quality imaginable. He could feel his face turning red, but couldn't decide whether it came from rage or embarrassment.

To his mind now came the worst question of all. What to tell his troops? During the preparations for this campaign he had overheard the excited talk in the barracks of plunder, gold, the conquest of foreign lands, and the taking by force of women without wings. Some fool had even begun a rumor that the surviving warriors of the supposed occupation force would be allowed to divide the conquered lands and claim them as their own. Had Kluge known who it was, he would have killed him himself. How could he ever explain to his troops the concept of returning with nothing more than these few meager demands of the Coven? And he couldn't even begin to understand the need for a simple chalice. He took a deep breath and held himself steady, barely able to control himself while he waited, knowing that all eyes were upon him.

Succiu, in particular, had been watching Kluge, understanding and enjoying his frustration. She had seen the muscles of his left hand contract around the hilt of his sword and watched his lips press together as the muscles in his jaw clenched. As her eyes roamed over him, the tip of her tongue gently searched out one corner of her mouth, and she languidly crossed her long legs beneath her gown. Vona would not be the only one to have a visitor from the Stables this evening.

Failee lifted the lid of the box on the table. Removing a pinch of finely ground violet powder, she dropped it into the crystal goblet. Although the fluid in the goblet did not change color, it began to roll and undulate, as though a storm were tossing a small, self-contained ocean. A dense gray fog rose from the goblet, cascading over the rim and then farther downward, to collect upon the table.

Vona, Succiu, and Zabarra stood and approached Failee as she laid her arms along the length of the armrests of her throne and let her hands dangle over the intricately carved raven's claws at each end. As Kluge watched, Vona and Succiu each produced two small leather belts, while Zabarra picked up the fogging goblet and watched attentively. Kluge couldn't believe his eyes as he watched Succiu and Vona use the belts to secure Failee's ankles to the throne legs and her wrists to the raven's claws. They finished their work and waited dutifully.

"I am ready," Failee said firmly, gazing at the black marble wall before them. Obediently, Zabarra raised the goblet to Failee's lips. She drank timidly at first, taking only a small sip, as if apprehensive. Kluge had never known Failee to be afraid of anything, but this situation was apparently different. She then took another, larger swallow from the offered cup, this time seeming to much more enjoy both the flavor and the experience. Zabarra then placed the goblet on the table next to the box and went back to her throne, as did the other two.

The room became very cold. It had become more difficult to breathe, as though the air had become thinner, and all about the room came shimmering cascades of light moving to and fro, seemingly at their own will.

Failee's head was bowed slightly forward, her eyelids covering the upper half of each of the hazel irises. Still she was focused intently upon the black marble wall. Strands of her dark, gray-streaked hair were now matted to her forehead with perspiration, despite the coldness of the room. Even in the dim light, Kluge could plainly see the vein in her left temple begin to throb. She was straining both hands and feet against the belts that held her to the throne, and it was apparent that she was fighting something. But what? As her sworn protector, he felt compelled to reach out and free her from her bonds, but he restrained himself, fearing that any interference at this point might only invite his own death. A drop of the crimson liquid that had somehow lingered in the corner of Failee's mouth broke free and began to snake crazily downward toward her chin. Except for the ragged breathing of the First Mistress, the room was bathed in total silence.

Just then there came another sound. Kluge heard a strange scraping noise, like stone against stone, and looked to the domed ceiling of the chamber to see one of the ceiling stones moving by itself, down and over, creating a hole to the sky directly over Failee's head.

Failee raised her head back up, still concentrating on the black wall, once again calm and in control. She delicately licked the crimson fluid from her chin. She began to smile.

Without warning a rectangular shaft of blue light shot down out of the sky, making a loud grating sound, as if it were scratching the very air through which it passed. It shot directly downward to the top of Failee's head. The effect was immediate.

Her eyes were changing.

Kluge watched in a combination of fascination and horror as the irises and pupils of Failee's eyes began to become translucent and then disappear altogether, leaving only the whites of her eyes. Then, slowly, the white began to change to black, the same endless black as the wall. Kluge began to break into perspiration, and his breathing quickened.

But more was to come.

Small pinpricks of light began to emanate from her eyes, like stars in a dark night sky, but they were too close together and far too numerous to count. The pinpricks of light began to join into one, and then the single band of white light began to move toward the black marble wall.

Failee finally spoke, apparently once again in full control of her faculties. She let out a throaty laugh. "And now, Commander, the answer to your first question. I believe you asked me how we could have such absolute knowledge of Eutracia after the passing of over three hundred years. An understandable request. But first, Sisters, please remove my bonds."

The three other mistresses rose from their thrones and began removing the belts that held Failee. She remained stone-still, the light from her eyes continuously moving with almost agonizing slowness to the black marble wall, the ever-present shaft of blue light still shining down on the top of her head. When the light from her eyes had traversed approximately half of the distance to the wall it stopped, hovering in midair. Vona, Zabarra, and Succiu returned to their thrones.

Kluge noticed that both the goblet and the small square box had vanished from the table.

Failee raised her arms, palms up, as if in supplication, her eyes unmoving. "Commander," she said in a low but commanding voice, "I present to you the palace at Tammerland, capital city of the kingdom of Eutracia."

Immediately the shaft of brilliant light from Failee's eyes screamed through the air, covering the remaining distance to the black wall in a bare second. When it reached the black marble, it became an impossible mixture of liquid and light, rolling and surging out in every direction, covering the wall in a golden glow. There came a great crashing noise, similar to but not exactly like thunder. The light from Failee's eyes disappeared, and the wall was bathed in the most excruciatingly bright white light he had ever experienced. Instinctively he raised his hands to cover his eyes. When he finally sensed the light was gone, he slowly lowered his hands and found himself standing before the most amazing image he had ever seen.

It was like looking through a different pair of eyes and into a different life. Or, to be more precise, other lives. He was watching and hearing, in life-sized dimensions, scenes being played out as they were happening—hundreds of leagues away, across the Sea of Whispers in the kingdom of Eutracia. He stood transfixed.

The room he was looking at was larger than he had ever seen, so huge that although it was filled with hundreds of people it seemed almost empty. Even his visits to the Recluse had not prepared him for such splendor. The great square hall was covered by a domed ceiling of stained glass through which light cascaded in a dizzying array of colors; the floor was a vast sea of black-and-white checkerboard marble squares. Giant variegated marble columns, so thick around that it would take ten men holding hands to surround just one, flanked the entire length of two of the opposing walls from ceiling to floor. Scores of golden chandeliers and standing candelabras waited to be lit. Several large indoor fountains playfully shot streams of water into the air to tumble back into surrounding pools of fish of every color and description. A grand dais at one end of the hall identified this not only as a large gathering and meeting room, but as a throne room, as well. And a musicians' pit on the left of the dais held about twenty well-dressed men and women tuning and practicing their various instruments, many of which he had never seen before, creating a riotous cacophony of sounds.

In the center of the raised dais sat two ornate thrones, one larger than the other—presumably meant for the rulers. To their right was a neat row of six smaller, less ornate thrones, each with a name handsomely engraved upon the top of the back. The names were so clear that he could read them easily: Wigg, Tretiak, Egloff, Slike, Killius, and Maaddar. Advisors to the king and queen, he assumed.

A ruby-red velvet runner ran from the steps of the dais and down the center of the entire length of the great hall. Sofas, tables, and chairs of every description and color were placed strategically about the room for the comfort of the occupants, and scores of floor-to-ceiling windows opened inward to welcome the warm Eutracian sunlight and breezes.

Occasionally the entire scene would go completely black for a split second and then instantly return. The effect was unnerving until Kluge realized that he was looking through another person's eyes, and that the person must be blinking. Indeed, the viewer was now turning his head, as if in search of something in particular. Occasionally the entire scene would move dizzyingly up and down as the viewer nodded to other people in the room. Whoever the mistresses' confederate was, he was certainly well received at the Eutracian court. However, whatever conversations were passing between them were drowned out by the practicing musicians.

The experience of looking into another world in this way was going to take some getting used to. But no matter how disorienting the effect might be, Kluge's eyes remained glued to the wall. He was privy to a preview of his upcoming battleground, a secret look at his soon-to-be enemies. The experience was invaluable. The knuckles of his left hand were white with anticipation as he gripped the hilt of his dreggan.

The people moving about the room were fascinating. Dozens of women seemed to be decorating the great hall as if in preparation for some upcoming event. There were flowers, tapestries, potpourri, and garlands. Kitchen staff of every conceivable duty were milling about a great, long dining table, so long in fact that he could not see the end of it, with too many chairs to count. They were fussing over the crystal, china, centerpieces, and seating arrangements. Occasionally they would dart in and out of the hall through large double doors in a nearby wall, presumably leading to the kitchens. A great banquet must be in preparation, he thought. The image was so clear and close he could almost smell the food. In addition, crowds of well-dressed citizens and noblemen with their ladies had begun to pour into the room. The entire scene was happy, festive, and anticipatory. *But in anticipation of what?* his restless mind wondered.

As the viewer turned to pan the scene for them, Kluge began to pick out entertainers of every description practicing their particular disciplines in small, scattered clusters around the room. Harlequins pranced, jumped, and told what appeared to be jokes and riddles. Jugglers were tossing all manner of objects between themselves. Magicians were randomly making things appear and disappear, and acrobats bounded across the floor. He noticed with particular interest a troop of scantily clad female dancers practicing for each other, exuding stark sexuality at every turn. His eyes narrowed. It had long been forbidden for the Minions to take a woman without wings: It was considered a waste of their valuable seed when they could be producing more male infants for the Minions. The prospect of a woman without dark, leathery wings excited him, as he knew it would also excite his troops. He silently hoped that when the battle was over, the Coven would allow the Minions to indulge in a different kind of conquest.

But it was the soldiers who interested him the most. There were at least one hundred of them in the hall, and from their bearing and uniforms he assumed them to be some contingent of the royal bodyguard, assuming that there was one, and therefore the best the realm had to offer. They milled about the great room with controlled detachment, their eyes missing nothing. He looked them over when he had the chance and decided that these were men who would be chivalrous in battle. *Good,* he thought. *That means more of them will die.*

He saw black-pleated capes and silver breastplates with designs upon them. Each of their highly decorated baldrics held scabbards, each of the scabbards holding gleaming sword hilts, most of the swords accompanied by silver battle axes and daggers hanging from the waist. Each man looked fit and ready. *Very pretty,* Kluge thought to himself. He smiled, feeling ready for battle, anxious to give his dreggan another taste of blood. Eutracian blood. He wondered idly when the last time was that a Eutracian soldier had seen battle. And with so many of the Guard in the room, where, then, was their commander?

The sounds coming from the hall were becoming increasingly distracting. As if she had read his mind, Failee pushed her right palm toward the image; the sound stopped, while the scene continued.

"It is almost time for our friends to enter," she said carefully. A strange smile began to twist along the length of her mouth in anticipation. "I have made it quiet so as to inform you of your battle orders, Commander. Listen well." As if addressing no one in particular, she added, "Time to move toward the door."

The viewer in the hall began to move toward a grand entranceway just to the right of the dais. Within moments, two liveried attendants, one on each side of the large doors, simultaneously began mouthing announcements, striking golden pikes against the floor to command the attention of the crowd. Momentarily, the double doors opened and the crowd hushed.

"Pay close attention, Commander," Failee whispered. It was the most quiet yet at the same time the most commanding order she had ever given him. "All of the people you are about to see, save one, are to die by your hand personally."

A group of about ten men and women entered the room, causing the liveried servants to bow and the crowd in the great hall to draw forward. At first the view was partially obscured by the throng, but as they parted to allow the small company access to the hall he could begin to take his time examining each of them, as an attacking animal might take stock of its prey. He could quickly see that they were an interesting group.

A man and woman, each of about sixty years, walked by the viewer and down the length of the velvet runner. The man turned and lowered his head in acknowledgment of the viewer, smiling in recognition. His bearing was unmistakably regal, and Kluge could tell that this man was used to being in command. Iron-gray hair and eyes complemented a beard of the same color, helping to make up an intelligent face. His rather heavyset body was clothed in robes and trimmed with the beautiful fur of an animal with which Kluge was not familiar.

But of greater interest to the commander was the jewel the man wore around his neck on a gold chain, hanging down to his breastbone. It was unlike any other stone that Kluge had ever seen. He was familiar with prisms and enjoyed their power of refracting sunlight, but this one was different. The square-cut gemstone not only refracted the light but actually shredded it into a kaleidoscope of color, ever shimmering. It was about the size of a robin's egg, and moved back and forth with the motion of the heavyset man's body. The effect was mesmerizing.

The woman next to him, despite her advancing age, was very beautiful. She was dressed in a full-length gown of deep blue; her pearl necklace and earrings perfectly matched the off-white lace at the cuffs and bodice of her gown. Blond hair with hints of gray curled down to frame each side of the compassionate, attractive face. She had come so close to the viewer that Kluge had been easily able to pick out the gentle crow's feet at the outer corners of her expressive blue eyes. She carried her rather full but still attractive figure gracefully, balancing her extended fingertips upon the back of the fur-robed man's outstretched hand as they moved through the crowd. They turned a corner into a forest of people and were gone.

Failee finally broke the silence. "Those two pretenders who just went by are Nicholas the First, king of Eutracia, and Morganna, his queen, both of the House of Galland. They are to die." Her voice had lowered as the words seemed to drip like acid from her tongue. She looked into Kluge's eyes and added, "Kill them any way you desire. They are yours to do with as you please." Kluge lowered his head slightly in acknowledgment.

Looking back at the Eutracian scene, Kluge noticed some pushing and shoving among the persons in the rows nearest the edges of the pathway. For some distance down its length, young women of every description, most of them holding fans, were trying to get as close as possible to the entourage. In some cases they were unsuccessful, but in most instances were allowed by the Guard to come to the front of the crowd as though it was the usual custom. As he turned his attention to the next person to walk down the runner, he understood why.

The handsome man following the king and queen was tall and moved smoothly, with a naturally athletic gait. Thick black hair formed a comma down over the left eye, the rest rather haphazardly pushed back and worn long. Below the finely drawn dark eyebrows, smiling dark-blue eyes moved naturally among the crowd, pausing occasionally to make note of this person or that. High cheekbones lay above slightly hollow cheeks, and a straight nose lay just above a sensuous mouth. Taken as a whole, the effect was piratical. He was slim and muscular, with a rather wide chest descending into narrow hips, which in turn blended smoothly into long, powerful legs. In his face could be seen some resemblance to the king and queen. Kluge guessed his age to be at least thirty years.

But despite the man's good looks, it was his clothes that stood out.

The knee-high black boots were muddy, as were the tight red-stained trousers. Blood, perhaps, Kluge mused. The black leather vest was much like the one Kluge wore, except the well-aged leather was dry and cracked in some places, and spotted with mud. At first glance the man looked more like an assassin of the royal court than a member of it. But if he was an assassin, then why was he without a weapon? Then, as the man turned the corner, Kluge saw the ingenious weapons that lay across the man's back. A black leather sling, much like an arrow quiver but shorter and wider, lay along the man's right shoulder blade, holding almost a dozen silver, flat-bladed throwing knives in a row. The handles of the blades did not quite reach each up to the top of the shoulder, and thus had not been visible from the front. Indeed, if the man had chosen to wear a cape they would not have been visible at all. He looked incredibly out of place in the hall, as though he had arrived late and had no time to change his dress, or simply didn't care how he looked. Kluge thought that it was a little bit of both. As he continued to move into the room, women curtsied and smiled, trying to attract his attention as their multicolored fans twitched back and forth hurriedly, like a flock of hummingbirds' wings.

"Prince Tristan the First of the House of Galland," Failee said indifferently. "Son of Nicholas and Morganna. It is said that he is highly intelligent, yet takes seriously neither his station nor his duties in life. He has made no secret of the fact that he has no desire to be king. To us he is relatively unimportant. Yet, for reasons which I shall not concern you with, it is extremely important that he die." The corners of Kluge's mouth turned up slightly, pleased that the prince would presumably present a greater threat to his skills than would his parents. He always enjoyed a challenge.

He cast a pair of jealous eyes toward Succiu, for the express purpose of determining her reaction to the prince. Her eyes were locked upon Tristan, and as she toyed with the ends of her long, black hair, her tongue was intently circling her lips. *She is intrigued by this royal whelp,* Kluge thought angrily. *It's the quality of his endowed blood that attracts her. Blood that I do not, and never will, possess.* He turned his attention back to the prince. *One more reason to take great pleasure in killing him.*

Following Prince Tristan came another man and woman together, her arm linked happily through his. The man was unusually large and about the same age as Tristan, with brown hair cut very short and slightly thinning at the temples. As though it had been grown in compensation, a very thick brown beard covered his face. Like King Nicholas, he was also dressed in robes of fur. The overall effect was somewhat reminiscent of the wild bears that Kluge was fond of hunting in the outer reaches of Parthalon. With a warrior's eye Kluge knew that this man would be able to move his large bulk easily, perhaps even gracefully. He had a military bearing about him.

The woman next to him, presumably his wife, was a perfect mixture of Queen Morganna and Prince Tristan—tall and blond, like the queen, but with Tristan's high cheekbones and sensuous mouth. Kluge suddenly grasped the fact that she was the prince's twin. She had lustrous, hazel eyes, and a strong jawline. This one had courage, he thought, and would not be afraid to speak her mind simply because she was a woman. She seemed to smile almost perpetually in a genuine way, showing perfect, white teeth. But of greater interest to Kluge was the cut of her ornate red gown.

She was pregnant.

As an ambitious young officer rising through the ranks of the Minions, Kluge had spent a great deal of time overseeing the birthing houses of the various Minion fortifications. That experience had taught him to estimate the chronology of a pregnancy. He guessed this woman's unborn child to be somewhat less than six moons.

As the man and woman were slowly engulfed in the adoring crowd and slipped from view, Failee spoke again. "Princess Shailiha, also of the House of Galland, daughter of Nicholas and Morganna, twin sister to Tristan. Accompanied by her husband Frederick, of the House of Steinarr. He is commander of all of the Royal Guard, and now a member of the royal family by marriage. It is said that he personally trained Tristan in the combative arts. He, also, is to die." She paused, as if enjoying herself. "The princess, however, requires greater explanation."

An even more icy demeanor came over each of the mistresses, an expression that smacked of extreme anticipation, as if something or someone for which they had been waiting all of their lives were about to arrive.

Kluge looked back at the unfolding scene to see a small company of elderly, gray-haired men enter the hall and solemnly walk down the red runner. They neither smiled nor acknowledged the crowd in any way. Each wore the same simple, gray hooded robe, and walked with hands folded before him. Some had beards and some did not, but they all sported identical braided tails of gray hair that fell from the back of their heads to the center of their backs.

Upon the appearance of these six, the mistresses had become visibly angry. Failee's hands were balled up into fists, her knuckles white. In a barely audible whisper, she recited the names of the men as they passed with a hatred that to Kluge spoke volumes.

"Wigg, Tretiak, Egloff, Slike, Maaddar, and Killius. The Directorate of Wizards, advisors to King Nicholas. Together with the king they rule the infestation that Eutracia has become." She paused. "Kill all of them. But be warned, their deaths will not come easily." She raised a long, painted fingernail before Kluge's face. "They must be dealt with first, and swiftly. We shall explain how. Given enough time to react, these six grandfatherly looking old men will give both you and your Minions more trouble than the entire Eutracian Guard. If your timing is imprecise, you will, before they are finished with you, wish that you had never been born."

Wizards. Bane to the Coven. The male counterparts to sorceresses. The diseased balance of power that had kept the more gifted female gender, and therefore the more powerful side of magic, from ruling completely, as was its proper destiny. This much Kluge knew from private conversations with Succiu. He also knew, painfully, that a sorceress not only would not, but indeed could not ever fall in love with a male of unendowed blood. *The type of blood I and all the Minions of Day and Night possess,* he ruefully reminded himself. *And if the Minions cannot be so blessed, than we shall spill the so-called endowed blood of the wizards from one end of the palace to the other.*

He stared at the wizards, seated on their thrones, and burned each one into his memory. Since it appeared that the mistresses had known these wizards personally, the wizards must also have discovered the use of time enchantments in order to have survived this long. There was obviously a history between these two groups of mystics. A very bad one indeed to have fueled such hatred for over three hundred years. The so-called "brilliant" wizards of Eutracia. He wondered how clever they would consider themselves to be if they knew that they were being watched at this very moment. *This campaign is not about the conquest of new lands as much as it is about the settling of old debts,* he realized. *And now, for me, it is also about the destruction of male endowed blood.* Once again he looked to Succiu. *Especially the blood of the prince,* he thought bitterly.

As the entire scene moved back and forth before his eyes, Failee spoke. "Commander," she said carefully, "now that you have been introduced to the people of importance, we shall explain your task to you in detail." She stopped, as though trying to make a decision. "Due to the importance of the hour, I grant you the right to speak fully, and at any time." She slowly turned, looking for a reaction from her Sisters. But Kluge knew Failee well enough to know that it wouldn't matter—her mind was made up.

"The scene you are now watching illustrates the final preparations for the abdication ceremony of Nicholas the First. This great hall also serves as the throne room. Curious situation, isn't it? In Eutracia, abdication is a celebration, not a crisis of the regime." She looked at Kluge. "When you are finished, not only will there be a *genuine* crisis of the regime, but we shall have turned the abdication ceremony into an abduction ceremony." Zabarra and Vona smiled, delighted with their mistress' play on words.

"The abdication ceremony always takes place upon the thirtieth birthday of the male heir to the throne. It is concluded with a great banquet and ball. The tradition has been the same since the time of our exile. Nicholas' father, however, was not king before him. The king who preceded Nicholas had no sons, his wife the queen being barren. Therefore, as tradition demands, a commoner of endowed blood was selected to become king. In this case, the Directorate chose Nicholas. Although of very highly endowed blood, as is his wife, they are still, to us, just filthy peasants." She paused, letting her words sink in.

"As I was saying, the abdication ceremony occurs upon the prince's thirtieth birthday, simultaneously removing the king from power and installing his son as the new sovereign, whereupon the retiring king may choose to join the Directorate and begin training as a wizard. At that time he would also become protected by time enchantments. Nicholas is the first king of endowed blood ever in the history of Eutracia to decide to do so. He has also preordained Tristan's fate by declaring that

Tristan, upon the thirtieth birthday of *his* son, shall also join the Directorate under the same circumstances. We are aware of the unique reasons for this, but it is of no concern to you. Present at the abdication ceremony shall be the entire royal family, the Directorate of Wizards, the entire Eutracian Royal Guard both inside and outside of the palace for protection, and various important citizens, including each of the dukes of the various provinces and their wives." She sneered contemptuously. "They also enjoy the disgusting habit of inviting, by lottery, two thousand common citizens of the population to join in the celebration. How egalitarian of them." She paused. "Take your enjoyment upon the citizens any way you choose. Just be sure the wizards are all disposed of first, then the royal family. Except Shailiha, of course.

"We leave the logistics of the attack to you," she continued. "It should be simple, actually. Not only will you have overwhelming numbers but the element of complete surprise, as well. We leave it to you to find the most efficient way into the palace. With the exception of Shailiha, kill everyone of the royal house. Leave no stragglers."

Kluge smiled to himself. From the first viewing of the throne room his military mind had already grasped the best way in. As far as he was concerned, taking prisoners of war, military or civilian, had never been an option.

"I already know how to enter, Mistress," he replied. "It will be extremely effective."

"Good," Failee said. She looked at Vona. "Have you brought the documents?"

Vona stood and handed Kluge a leather satchel with the Pentangle embroidered on the top. She smiled knowingly. "Inside you will find complete plans of the palace, and maps of the Eutracian countryside. We trust that they are completely accurate."

Kluge could only imagine two sources for such information. First, the Sisters' collective memories, the strength of which he trusted absolutely. And second, their confederate at the Eutracian court.

Vona returned to her throne. Failee unexpectedly stood, stretched her muscles, and went to stand before the Eutracian scene, folding her arms over her breasts. Kluge realized that once the mental link to her confederate at court had been accomplished, Failee was able to move about the room at will, the blue light from above following her, something that frankly surprised him. And why not? Today had been full of nothing if not surprises. He was once again able to catch occasional glimpses of the royal family moving through the crowd, inspecting the arrangements for the upcoming ceremony. A flash of the princess' red gown reminded him of his orders.

"I assume, Mistress, that since part of my quest is for a woman, that the woman in question is the princess . . ." He let the statement hang in the air.

Failee looked at him. "Yes, Commander, you are correct. The orders regarding her are explicit. The princess is to be abducted and brought to Parthalon. But hear me well. Of the utmost importance is the order that not a drop of her blood is to be spilled, nor is she is to be harmed in any way. Also, make sure that your warriors have had their fill of Eutracian women in any manner they desire. I insist their needs be satisfied before Shailiha boards the officers' warship to return to Parthalon. They are to have nothing to do with her."

Curious, Kluge continued with his questions. "Obviously, Mistress, you know of her pregnancy. Is there any particular significance in this of which I should be informed?"

"A delightful surprise to us all," Failee said, her head turning as she tried to keep her eyes on Shailiha. "The princess' pregnancy only makes her presence even more rewarding. In a few moons' time she is to have a daughter. That baby girl is special, and is also to become ours."

She plucked a grape from a bowl of fruit that had suddenly appeared on the table out of nowhere. Tilting her head, she began to skin the grape with a long, painted fingernail. Behind her, the scene on the wall began to shift. They were once more looking at the dais. As the viewer in the hall walked closer to the thrones, Kluge saw the rectangular marble altar that sat before them. The white marble was intricately carved, and the top was covered with a violet runner, made of velvet, reaching to the floor at either end. In the center of the runner sat a golden chalice.

"And now to the second prize which we seek," Failee said simply. "I distinctly remember you admiring the gemstone that hung around the neck of King Nicholas. Did you notice its unusual effect on the light? How it seemed to shimmer as if it has a life of its own. Well, in fact, Commander, it does. It has been known for centuries as the Paragon of Eutracia, and if you fail to do your job correctly, it will kill you and everyone else in the great hall in the twinkle of an eye. You are to recover the stone. You are also to recover and return the chalice that you see before you, taking care not to spill so much as one drop of its water any more than you would spill a drop of the blood of Shailiha. Shailiha, the Paragon, the chalice, and the water in it are all of equal importance. If you cannot return here with each of them intact, do not come home at all. Trust me when I say that it would be far more preferable to fall on your own dreggan in disgrace in an alien land than to return to us a failure in any way." She walked back to Kluge and stood next to him. Turning to face his profile, she delicately plopped the peeled grape into her mouth. "Under no circumstances shall you or anyone under your command touch or drink any of the water from the chalice, no matter how appetizing it may seem. And appetizing it shall be." Kluge turned his eyes to the crooked smile upon her face. "For one of unendowed blood to touch or drink the water of the Caves of the Paragon is a sure invitation to an agonizing death."

Kluge stood there silently, trying to fathom the reasons behind his bizarre battle orders. The Princess Shailiha, her unborn child, this so-called Paragon of Eutracia, and a simple gold chalice filled with inde-scribable red water. How was he supposed to recover all of the fluid without spilling so much as a drop? Would the mistresses even know if he tried to replace it? And he ached for the loss of the plunder of Eutra-cia. From the splendor of the scene before him, this surely was a king-dom of riches to be had. But despite his avarice, he would perform as he was told. He was, after all, the commander of the Minions. And his loyalty, like that of his warriors, had been unfailingly bred into him.

Zabarra rose from her throne and stood before the viewing wall, ever toying with one of her blond ringlets. "If I may interrupt, Sisters," she said, more to Failee than the group as a whole. "It is now time the commander learned how to retrieve the Paragon from King Nicholas." She smiled, drawing a line across her throat with a long fingernail. "Af-ter all, separating the Paragon from Nicholas is not as simple as separat-ing Nicholas from his head. And although his head is expendable, the Paragon is not." She glanced at Failee, and her expression grew more se-rious. "May I continue?"

For the first time today, Kluge noticed that Failee had begun to look tired. In fact, it was the first time in his life he ever remembered seeing her so. He assumed that the maintenance of the mental link to her confederate at the Eutracian court was heavily taxing her powers. Now she walked to her throne and sat down. "You may continue," she said simply.

"First there is an issue of which my other two Sisters and I feel it is imperative to speak," Zabarra said. She looked quickly to both Succiu and Vona before continuing. Then she looked directly into Failee's eyes.

"We must once again voice our protest over your instructions to our confederate in Eutracia to recall and set free certain of the blood stalkers and screaming harpies," she said firmly. "Although we realize that we probably will not change your opinion in this matter, we none-theless feel that your decision was unwise. There seems, at least to the three of us, no reason for these actions that can further our cause. To provoke the Directorate in this way only raises the possibility of show-ing our hand and far outweighs any damage, no matter how well de-served, that can be caused to the wizards. We respectfully request that you withdraw your decision and use them to ravage the land *after* the attack."

Kluge was stunned. *Blood stalkers and screaming harpies?* He had no idea what she was talking about. But even more surprising was the fact that the other three sorceresses were challenging a decision of Failee's.

The First Mistress turned her hazel eyes upon Zabarra and was obviously trying hard to control her temper. She looked at the other two women and then back at Zabarra. "They are to pay," she said, trembling with anger, her voice a mere whisper. "And I have decided that it does no harm to toy with them a bit, and kill a few of them beforehand. That is my final decision, and there will be nothing more said of it." She leaned forward, putting her hands flat upon the table, her normally beautiful face contorted into a contemptuous sneer. "Now, are you going to continue briefing the commander, or shall I be forced to demonstrate to the three of you a rather unpleasant use of the Vagaries?"

As though the conversation had never taken place at all, Zabarra positioned herself between the table and the viewing wall. She bent over slightly, exposing the ample cleavage above the bodice of her ornate, rust-colored gown. Kluge refused to let his eyes drift down. Zabarra had always been dangerous, he reminded himself, because she loved to play games, and he knew from previous experience that her mood could change drastically in the blink of an eye. He gazed into her green eyes without smiling, tacitly telling her that he was not amused.

She straightened with a pout. "You wish to be all business today," she said to him in mock disappointment. "Very well. Since that is how you prefer it, then listen carefully, for I shall only instruct you in this once." She turned and pointed to the gold chalice that rested upon the marble altar.

"This is known as the Chalice of the Abdication Ceremony," she began, "and has no great significance other than that during the ceremony it is always the traditional resting place of the water from the Caves of the Paragon. The Paragon of Eutracia, as Sister Failee has explained to you, indeed has a life of its own. But, as is true of any life, it must be nurtured and sustained. While it is worn around the neck of a person with endowed blood, it harvests strength from that person, and returns that strength back to the wearer many times over. That is why the wizards of the Directorate do not allow one of their own to wear it, because it would engender an unheard-of amount of power in one of endowed blood who had also been trained in the craft. But a person of endowed blood who has not been trained in the craft cannot amplify his power with the stone, because there is no knowledge of magic to strengthen.

"It is impossible, even for a sorceress, to kill anyone while they are wearing the stone. In addition it is quite impossible to remove it from his person. Only the bearer of the Paragon has the power to lift the gold chain and the stone over his head."

She placed her hands flat upon the table, bending over and placing her face very close to his. He could smell the jasmine in her hair. "So you see, my dear commander, things are not as simple as they may have first appeared." She reached out and squeezed his right biceps. Hard. Despite Kluge's own unusual strength, her grip hurt, serving to remind him of the amazing amount of purely physical strength that any one of these women could produce. "I'm afraid that when it comes to the Paragon, these big, strong muscles of yours are not the answer. In this case, the brute force you pride yourself on simply is of no use." She released her iron grip on his arm and backed away, apparently pleased with her sarcasm.

Kluge decided it was time to speak. He had questions that he must have the answers to if he was to be completely successful in this madness. "Then, pray tell, Mistress, how indeed do we remove the stone from the king?" he asked courteously.

She slowly shook her head, again in a manner that could easily be taken as insulting. "I knew your mind couldn't possibly come to this conclusion on its own," she said nastily. "If no one can remove the stone from Nicholas, then the good and cooperative King Nicholas shall have to give it to us himself." As she emphasized the last words of her sentence, she bounced the end of her index finger off the point of Kluge's nose several times, as if she were reprimanding a misbehaving child.

Then her tone became more grave. "During the ceremony Nicholas will remove the Paragon himself and hand it to Wigg, Lead Wizard of the Directorate." She fairly spat out the last words of the sentence. "As I said, the Paragon has a life of its own, and therefore requires sustenance from its host. As a result, when it is removed from its wearer, it immediately begins to die." She waved a dismissive hand in front of his face. "Once again, however, I shall not waste my time trying to educate you with things that are so far beyond your ken."

"Cannot Nicholas simply place the Paragon around Tristan's neck, and therefore let it take its sustenance from its new wearer?" Kluge asked.

Zabarra turned upon him angrily, having temporarily forgotten that Failee had given him permission to speak at will. She stopped herself, reining in her emotions. One corner of Kluge's mouth turned upward into an almost imperceptible smile.

Zabarra simply sighed. "If you knew anything at all, you would also know that what you suggest is quite impossible. Simply put, because the

Paragon has been with Nicholas for so long, it requires a brief amount of time to ready itself before joining with a new host. Time to return to a 'virgin' state, if you will."

Kluge scratched the back of his neck, lost in thought. He was now genuinely interested in the puzzle that lay before him. "Then how is it, Mistress, that the Paragon does not die in the interim without a host?" he asked.

Zabarra pointed to the chalice. "The Paragon is placed in the chalice and covered with the water of the Caves. The water and the Paragon have a special bond. It was very long ago when the life-giving properties of the Caves were first discovered, and since that time they have been coveted by many." Her gaze seemed to drift away temporarily to another place, another time. Quietly, sadly, she added, "Wars have been fought over it." Regaining her composure, she said, "The water in the chalice sustains the Paragon, and the same water can go on doing so for only a certain amount of time without being replenished. When the water has changed from red to clear, the Paragon is once again ready and can be placed around the neck of the new king."

Her green eyes leveled an even harsher gaze upon Kluge. "This shall be the time of your attack—precisely when the Paragon is placed in the chalice, and the royal family and the Directorate of Wizards are at their most vulnerable. When the stone is immersed in the water the wizards are completely without their powers, as are we. This is why you and your troops have been chosen to take initial control of the situation in our stead. However, if you act either too soon, before the Paragon is immersed, or too late, after the Paragon is retrieved, you won't have to worry about the Royal Guard." She raised an eyebrow to make her point. "The Directorate will once again be in full possession of their abilities, and you and your grotesque Minions will die. Horribly."

Kluge ignored the implied insult and turned his head imperceptibly toward Succiu. Oddly, he noticed what appeared to be a look of concern. Such a look upon her usually mischievous face was rare. He had at first felt that his battle orders were complete, but after seeing her expression he wondered if there was even more yet to come.

As if on cue, Zabarra returned to her throne and Failee once again stood. She walked to the front of the marble viewing wall, and for a time watched the images of happy people busily preparing for a celebration. Then she faced the entire group.

"Commander," she began earnestly, "Mistress Succiu is to accompany you on your mission."

Kluge's head snapped involuntarily toward Succiu in disbelief, trying to read her face for clues. He once again found that of concern, but for whom? As a sorceress, she couldn't possibly be concerned for her own welfare. Succiu, he knew all too well, was far too powerful and vicious for that. But it did explain something that had been troubling him.

Several months ago the Coven had ordered the construction of a very special warship. Instead of being built for battle it had been built for luxury and speed, and included two amazingly beautiful staterooms. One of these staterooms had no windows, and its outer door could be bolted only from the outside. He now knew that this particular stateroom was meant for Shailiha. Apparently, the other was to become the private quarters of Succiu. The two rooms had a connecting door, lockable only from Succiu's side.

Failee folded her arms over her breasts. "After your initial mission is complete, you are to stay in Eutracia for two more suns. During this time, the Minions are to lay waste to as much of the population as possible. Your warriors may take whatever pleasure they desire from the females. Just make sure they are not negligent regarding their overall orders. You are also to kill all livestock and burn any and all available structures and crops to the ground, save the palace itself. We may eventually have a use for it. In short, you are to destroy as much of Eutracia as possible. But understand this well. It is imperative that you spend no more than two suns' time in doing so. Upon the morning of the third sun, you are to return home." Failee's face looked as hard as stone.

She turned back to the scene on the wall before speaking. "Basically, your orders are simple, and can be summed up in two sentences: Remove the Paragon, the princess, the chalice, and the water as instructed. And, excepting Princess Shailiha and our ally at court, if it moves, kill it."

Questions were still scratching at the back of Kluge's mind, and since they had not been addressed, he felt it necessary to ask.

"Mistress," he began quietly, "if I may, I have several more questions."

Vona's red hair rippled across her shoulder as she turned to face Kluge. "You have too many questions for my taste," she said harshly. "Just take your flying gargoyles and go do your job."

Failee seemed to be more forgiving. "What are they, Commander?" she asked.

"First, if I may know the reason that Mistress Succiu is to accompany us?" He thought he might choke just getting the words out. "And second, without knowing the identity of your confederate at the Eutracian court, how am I to ensure his safety from my warriors? And, forgive me, Mistress, but we have often heard it said throughout Parthalon that the Sea of Whispers is uncrossable, that no voyage of any duration has ever returned home. How then are we to ensure our safe passage over and back?" He once again cast his eyes down the entire length of the table to make sure he had not slighted any of them.

"You have answered your second and third questions with your first, Commander," Failee said easily. "Mistress Succiu will be able to point out our friend at court, because she is familiar with our confederate's most recent countenance."

Kluge's head was spinning. *Most recent countenance? What does that mean?* He decided it was better not to ask. Failee used her long fingernails to surgically remove another red grape from the bowl of fruit and delicately placed it into her mouth, unpeeled this time.

"And as far as crossing the Sea of Whispers is concerned, the Coven has done it once before. And done it in a way that will ensure our continued success at our leisure. Mistress Succiu is familiar with the means to cross. You have simply to follow her orders. But there is yet one more reason for the second mistress to accompany you."

A glance at Succiu's face showed him that her usually malevolent smile had returned. Whatever her duties in Eutracia were to be, he could tell she was looking forward to them.

For the first time Kluge realized that the mistresses had never referred to their ally at court by any gender. He was left wondering whether it was a man or a woman. He shrugged his shoulders slightly. It was apparently unimportant to his orders.

Finally, Failee seemed to be satisfied. With an unexpected wave of her arms, the scene at the Eutracian court vanished, and the limitless depths of the black marble wall returned. The blue shaft of light through the ceiling also vanished, and the ceiling stone that had been suspended in the air for so long now began to scratch its way back into place.

Kluge watched as the rectangular table morphed back into its original five-pointed shape, the thrones moving back to their original positions. He looked at Failee. She seemed somehow refreshed. Except for the mild fatigue on her face, it was as if none of it had ever happened. Picking up the packet of maps, he walked over to the spot where he had lain his helmet and picked it up, once again holding it beneath his left arm and standing at attention.

The sorceresses were looking at him as if they expected him to speak. But there was no reason for him to. His most important questions had been answered. His mission was abundantly clear, and he would carry it out as effectively and as ruthlessly as possible. And after seeing Succiu's reaction when the prince of Eutracia had walked by, he recognized that the mission had now taken on an unmistakably personal flavor, as well.

Failee stood and walked up to him, holding his eyes steady in the hazel irises of her own.

"Commander," she said quietly, "give me your sword."

Kluge grasped the hilt of his dreggan and drew it from its scabbard, the curved blade making its unusual signature sound in the air. The blade's song hung for a long time in the stillness of the chamber and then finally faded away, as if it had a life of its own that was not anxious to be extinguished. The chamber then became as silent as death.

Upon taking possession of his sword, Failee took a step closer. She studied his face for a moment.

"Kneel," she said softly, menacingly.

He immediately went down on one knee, lowering his head.

Without hesitation, Failee snatched a handful of the long, gray-streaked hair at the back of his head and snapped his face back as if his neck had been a dry tree branch, placing the tip of the dreggan hard at the base of his throat. A drop of his blood formed at the point of the blade and ran into the shallow trough of the blood groove, beginning a slow but inexorable journey toward the hilt. Succiu licked her lips.

"I bred you for this myself, Kluge," Failee hissed, her eyes narrowed. It was the first time in his life she had ever called him by his name instead of his rank. "You are mine to do with as I wish." She frowned darkly. "Do you understand your orders?"

"Yes, Mistress." Had she been a mortal he could easily have killed her with a single blow, despite the blade at his throat. But not a sorceress, and certainly not Failee. There was something even more frightening about her than the sword she held to his throat. Looking up into her manic, hazel eyes, he wondered once again if she was mad.

She used her power to treble the strength in her arm, stretching Kluge's neck backward almost to the breaking point. Her eyes went wide.

"In just over a week you sail for Eutracia," she whispered.

"Yes, Mistress," he whispered hoarsely. "The Minions of Day and Night shall prevail."

The pain in his neck was excruciating, but he knew he must not flinch. If this was a test of his nerve, so be it. He had come too far to be proven unworthy of his mission. He watched her thumb slowly cover the blade release lever in the hilt of the dreggan. If she pressed the lever now, the point of the dreggan's blade would enter beneath his jaw and violently exit through the top of his skull. He held fast, holding her deep, mystical eyes on his.

Failee twisted his hair even tighter and moved the dreggan imperceptibly forward. "The Minions shall prevail?" she asked. Her eyes were crazed and seemed to look right through him. "See that they do, Commander," she whispered. "See that they do."

PART III

Tammerland

CHAPTER

Six

The Chosen One shall come, preceded by another. And the knowledge that he seeks he shall one day demand of the one who recovers the stone. And those of the Pentangle, the ones who practice the Vagaries, shall require the female of the Chosen Ones, and shall bend her to their purpose.

—PAGE 1237, CHAPTER ONE OF THE VAGARIES OF THE TOME

Tristan awoke to find her still lying beside him, her back to him and the warm curve of her buttocks pressed into his groin. When he opened his eyes, he found that his face was only inches from her long blond hair. It had the delicate texture of corn tassels, and as he moved his face even closer he could smell the lingering jasmine in her hair, just one of the many things about her that had attracted him last night. Slowly taking back possession of his right arm, he gently slid it from beneath her. As expected, she only stirred slightly and murmured something in her sleep, once again lost to her dreams. Sweet ones, he hoped.

He reached behind him to gather up more of the silk-covered pillow beneath his head and sat up a little, only to remember that he had consumed too much wine at last night's inspection ceremony. Thankfully the room was not spinning nor was he ill, but there was something more than a faint pounding in his head from the fine red wine that had flowed like water last night. The wine had come from the vineyards of Florian's Glade, the finest grape-producing area of the realm, southwest of Tammerland. *Only the best for the heir apparent,* he thought. But if not having to become king would mean drinking only cheap wine for the rest of his life, it would have been a price he would gladly have paid.

He turned his face back to the beautiful young woman next to him, remembering the events of last evening. Her name was Evelyn of the House of Norcross, and he faintly remembered something about her father being a wealthy landowner in the area of Farplain, in the center of the kingdom. She had come to the inspection ceremony with her parents out of a sense of curiosity, as so many of the guests had. They were staying at one of the many inns in the city, and her parents had left her behind at the ceremony last night, apparently pleased that she was so lost in conversation with the prince. He rubbed his hand over his face, wondering what their mood was like this morning after discovering that their daughter's bed had not been slept in. He found himself sincerely hoping that her father was not more than a casual acquaintance to the king.

She had come to his quarters very willingly, as women always did, and they had laughingly fallen into each other's arms almost immediately. Twice more in the night she had reached out for him, and he had obeyed. But as usual, for him it had not been love.

She stirred and turned his way. He put his fingers through her hair and lifted it from her forehead, kissing her lips gently. Her blue eyes opened, slowly at first, and then quickly the rest of the way as the realization of her surroundings came to her and the memories of last night began to transform themselves into something more than a small measure of embarrassment. She immediately pulled the dark-blue silk sheet up over her breasts, as though he had never seen them before. He smiled, running a hand back through his hair.

"It isn't as though I'm not familiar with them, you know," he said gently, a smile upon his lips. "Besides, I don't remember anything about them for which you should be ashamed." He kissed the end of her nose and watched the apprehension in her face begin to melt away.

"Good morning, Your Highness," she said tentatively. She looked around in amazement at the sumptuous decorations of his private bedroom, still holding the sheet up to her chin like a shield in battle. "Apparently we fell asleep last night," she said, a hint of mischief crowding into the corners of her mouth.

"Yes," Tristan said smiling, his hand once again in her hair. "And we did a good deal more, as well."

He got out of bed and stood slowly, stretching his muscles as he walked naked to the balcony of his bedroom. Despite his unusual experiences of the previous day and the events surrounding the celebration last night, he had awakened early, just as the sun was starting to find its way over the horizon in the east. Stretching and waking the rest of his body, he remembered that the great sense of physical strength and mental well-being that he had garnered from his time in the Caves had gradually diminished and had been replaced by wine as the evening went on, and this morning he was sore and lame from all of the bumps and jolts he had taken during his adventures. He made a mental note to himself to check on Pilgrim, as well.

Now standing upon his balcony and looking down at the golden glow of the morning as it slowly blossomed into a new day, all his experiences in the Hartwick Woods seemed to be a dream. But one thing remained as strong and as real as ever: His intense hunger to learn the craft was still with him, coursing through his veins of endowed blood more strongly than he had ever known.

He turned around and walked back to stand beside the bed, looking down into her face. "Is there anything you would like before you leave?" he asked with the best of intentions.

She smiled up to him lazily and reached for his groin. "All I have the right to ask for is that you once again serve one of your humble subjects," she said softly.

He bent over, reached under the silk sheet for her, and put his lips on hers.

*T*he sound made by two swords in combat is like no other in the world, Tristan thought as he parried yet another and even stronger of Frederick's thrusts. *An ironic thing, a sword, being both the taker and the protector of life.* But there was no more time to occupy his mind with such luxuries, for Frederick had set upon him yet again, and the swords they were practicing with were real.

They had been at it for almost an hour now in the training yard of the Royal Guard, and given the relative importance of their positions in the realm, a crowd of spectators, mostly other members of the Guard, had formed around the outer edges of their area of contest and had begun to cheer on their respective favorites. It occurred to Tristan between ragged breaths that the two of them had managed to turn a simple training exercise into a blatant contest, complete with spectators. Where Frederick was stronger, Tristan was quicker. Where Frederick was tougher, Tristan was smarter. Each of them was determined to make the other yield without bloodshed, but so far neither had been able to gain a clear advantage. This particular training area was one of both Tristan's and Frederick's favorites because it was also full of training obstacles that an opponent could hide behind, jump over, and use or throw to his advantage, just as might occur in real combat.

Frederick's broadsword whistled through the air at him again, this time from overhead. Tristan stepped quickly, not back but directly forward, and turned on his heel 180 degrees to end up standing virtually neck-to-neck with Frederick, and facing the same way. He quickly extended his arms and cut his sword around his body in a plane level with the ground as if to cut Frederick in two, but again the larger, older man was not to be denied. Frederick stepped back with almost unheard-of speed for a man his size, missing Tristan's sweep altogether, and stabbed his sword directly at the prince's midsection. Another sharp parry from Tristan, and they once again found themselves on equal footing, swords raised, their dirty faces smiling at each other as they slowly circled.

After doing his gentlemanly duty by watching Evelyn depart this morning in one of the palace carriages, Tristan had decided to shake off the cobwebs of the previous evening by joining the Guard in some training, and Frederick had been the willing recipient of the prince's need for exercise. Tristan had hoped that it would help take his mind off the upcoming abdication ceremony. Evelyn, although lovely, had not proven to be an important enough occurrence in his life to change his outlook about the future, and he doubted he would see her again.

And so he had taken to the Royal Guard training grounds to sweat his depression out of himself.

The two friends circled each other slowly, each trying to decide the right time to strike again. "You're getting too old for this," Tristan taunted. "But I suppose it's good that I give you the benefit of my great expertise while I still can, since you will soon be spending all of your time attending the changing of the diapers instead of the changing of the Guard." He smiled nastily and waggled the point of his sword in front of Frederick's face. "But don't worry, Brother-in-law," he continued. "I'm sure in my position as king I can persuade my sister to let you out of the palace once in a while—say, once every other month or so."

With unexpected speed, Frederick launched himself at Tristan. But the prince gave no ground, and they found themselves locked against each other, their swords crossed between their bodies, their grimacing faces only inches apart.

"At least I showed up dressed for the occasion last night." Frederick grunted, straining against Tristan's surprising strength. "I couldn't tell whether you were part of the royal family or just a particularly grubby servant. I almost ordered you to fetch me a glass of wine, but then again, I heard you had plenty of that yourself."

Then, suddenly, Frederick did something odd. Instead of carrying on the fight he looked directly over Tristan's shoulder. The prince saw his friend's face fall, as if Frederick had just seen something horrible. Tristan started to turn his own eyes to the right, but that was exactly what Frederick had been hoping for. In the split second that Tristan's attention was diverted, Frederick stopped straining against the prince and reached down to Tristan's right ankle, quickly pulling it up and over, launching the prince to the hard ground on his back in the dust of the training yard. Frederick's blade was at Tristan's throat in an instant.

"Do you yield?" It wasn't as much a question as a command.

It was over, the prince knew. There could be no escape from this position, and truth be known, had Frederick really wanted him dead Tristan would have been so several moments ago, a bloody hole where his larynx used to be. "I yield," he said begrudgingly. Then Tristan looked up in momentary horror as the point of Frederick's broadsword came hurtling straight down at his face, only to bury itself finally in the ground about three inches away from his right temple.

Despite the fact that it was the prince who had lost, the crowd erupted in hoots, applause, and catcalls. Tristan smiled. These men were his friends, and he wouldn't have had it any other way.

Frederick's great bear's paw of a hand came to pull Tristan back up to his feet. The two of them began to brush the dust off themselves. Frederick smiled broadly and put an affectionate arm around the prince's shoulders, and the two walked side by side to the well on one edge of the courtyard.

"That was quite a trick," Tristan said, first pouring a carafe of water over his head and then shaking some of the water out of his hair. He raised the carafe high and took several long swallows from it before looking again at Frederick. "When did you learn that?"

"That wasn't a trick, it was a *technique*," Frederick said rather impatiently. "And when I learned it isn't as important as how I learned it." He took the offered carafe from Tristan. "You're missing the point again. Although you did very well today, probably better than anyone else in the Guard could have, you still spend too much time looking at my face during battle. As I have told you repeatedly, keep your eyes on my abdomen, so that you can more quickly tell where both of my arms and legs are, and when they are about to move against you." He paused, looking into the dark-blue eyes of the brother-in-law he had come to love so much. "After all, it isn't my face that can harm you, it's my sword."

"I'm not so sure about that," Tristan said with an expression of mock seriousness. "Have you looked in the mirror lately?"

Frederick flat-handed the prince so hard on his left shoulder that Tristan almost fell off the bench. After the two of them had stopped laughing, Frederick's face became more serious. "Truthfully, Tristan, are you all right? A lot of people are worried about you, and not just those of us in the family. I have heard from several places this morning that the wizards of the Directorate are virtually beside themselves with you. And I have it on good authority that they're in yet another of their famous closed-door sessions with your father right now. What in the name of the Afterlife did you *do* yesterday up in those woods to get everyone into such an uproar? I haven't seen them all this upset since that time you were found in your bedchambers pursuing your 'studies' with one of your nannies." After a brief and knowing smile between men, Frederick's face grew grave again. "Seriously, is there anything you would like to talk about? You know I am always here to help." He looked down in obvious distaste at the prince's clothes. "And are you ever going to get out of those?"

Although he had of course bathed, Tristan was wearing pretty much the same clothes he'd had on the day before, complete with quiver and dirks. He had replaced the red-stained trousers with another clean pair just like them this morning and tucked them into his knee boots, as was his habit. But now, of course, he was covered from his boots to his shoulders in dirt again.

Tristan moved a pebble back and forth across the ground with the toe of one of his boots, groaning inwardly. He had come here to forget his responsibilities for a while, not to be reminded of them. And he knew that Frederick was only trying to help, no doubt partly at the urging of Shailiha. But he was in no mood to discuss his experiences, let alone at liberty to. His heart was aching at the thought of not being able to return to the Caves. And how could he ever make anyone else understand what he had been through yesterday, when he didn't even understand it himself? It depressed him to know that few answers would be quick in coming from the wizards, given the tone and substance of his meeting with them yesterday. He turned his gaze upon the one hundred or so men of the Royal Guard who were training in various weapons in the large expanse of the courtyard, and once again his heart yearned for the simple life of a soldier. He looked back up at Frederick.

"I can't tell you about yesterday," he said bluntly, shaking his head in frustration. "I don't even understand what happened myself. I just have to try to accept the fact that I am to become king whether I like it or not. But I have decided to spend the last few days of my so-called freedom here with you, on the training fields. I've had enough of wizards and schooling to last me for the rest of my life, and if they don't like it, I don't particularly care." He knew full well that what he meant was only his formal schooling, rather than any training in the craft that they might give him. The desire for that burned fiercely in his being, but it was not something he could explain to Frederick, a person of unendowed blood. And once again it depressed him to know that, given the

wizards' tone of yesterday, no doubt his training in the craft was probably even farther away than ever.

He looked down at himself. There wasn't much right now about
his life that he felt he could truly control, except perhaps for the way he
looked. These clothes not only reminded him of the falls, but more accurately reflected his real personality than any of the pompous robes
they could bestow upon him. He turned back to Frederick.

"As far as my clothing is concerned, I may just stay in these for a
while, maybe even after I'm king." He paused as a small smile finally
started to come back to his lips. Leaning in conspiratorially to Frederick, he said, "After I'm king, I expect they would have a very hard time
getting me out of them, anyway."

The rumble of thunder interrupted him. But it wasn't thunder—
rather, something like it but not quite exactly the same. As Tristan and
Frederick began to look around, the noise became louder, and the closer
it came the more it seemed to turn into a kind of great rushing roar of
moving air. They could feel the wind against their faces now as they
turned to look. But before either one of them could discern the source
of the noise, something else happened.

The sun disappeared, and the courtyard was bathed in darkness.

Stunned, they both turned to try to find the cause of the great
shadow. Tristan automatically put a hand over his eyes in anticipation of
looking into the sun, but the sun wasn't there.

Something was blocking it.

It was then that the awful creature flew out of the direct line of
the sun and came to rest noisily upon the wall of the courtyard, directly
before them and approximately thirty feet above the ground. A deafening, semihuman scream came from it, as if it wished to announce its
presence.

Tristan grabbed Frederick by the shoulders and dragged him back
to the center of the training grounds, away from the hideous beast. "Get
Wigg!" he screamed into Frederick's ear. "Now! Run!"

Frederick looked into Tristan's eyes in seeming incomprehension
and then suddenly was gone, running as fast as he could toward the
archway in the wall on the opposite side of the yard.

Tristan turned back to the thing that had perched on the wall and
stared dumbly at it in disbelief. *Wigg, you must hurry,* he heard his brain
scream back at him.

It was like a giant bird of prey, but there ended any similarity to
anything Tristan had ever seen. Perched upon the wall, it had to be at
least thirty feet high from its claws to the top of its head. Its claws were
the talons of eagles, but each individual talon was at least a meter long,

and each foot had four instead of the three a Eutracian eagle would have. The black feathers were huge, each of them at least two to three meters long, and were ruffled and unpreened, seeming to lie upon the great bird in disarray. The thing screamed again, the sound so deafening that for a moment afterward he could hear nothing else, not even the hurried shouting of orders by the officers of the Guard who were standing behind him. It was the unnerving call of a hawk in flight coupled with the insane screams of a terrified woman, and it reverberated throughout the entire courtyard. Several of the Guard came to stand between him and the awful thing, ready to protect him with their lives, if necessary.

It screamed yet again as it extended its horrible wings and jumped to the left a little, trying to find a more advantageous position upon the wall. The wings stretched to each side at least twice as far as its body was tall; dark and grotesque, they were covered with black scales instead of feathers. The sickening stench that came to Tristan's nostrils every time it spread its wings was overpowering. But the most terrifying part of the beast was the head itself: It had the face of a woman.

And it appeared to be insane.

The face was ancient, gray, and wrinkled in a thousand places. Dark, sunken eyes not unlike those of a bird peered out from deep pockets, and the gray hair was brittle, long, and coarse, flying this way and that with the wind.

Again it stretched its wings and let forth a scream. Tristan could now clearly make out what he thought he had seen at first, but had not wanted to believe. Two rows of yellow pointed teeth lined the inside of the creature's mouth, each tooth at least six inches long. They showed ominously each time the thing screamed. And below the chin was an equally disturbing feature: a gullet. Dark, wrinkled skin loosely hung down, swaying sloppily with each movement of the creature's head. Occasionally the beast would duck down and sideways just like a bird, its movements jerky and hesitant, but incredibly fast. The thing moved its head again, and Tristan saw the leathery sides of its throat come together and then once again separate.

Its gullet was empty.

Then, without warning, it jumped down into the courtyard with lightning speed and grabbed one of the Guard in the four sharp talons of its right foot. It brought the screaming and bloody soldier up before its beady eyes and looked at the man curiously, turning its horrible head this way and that before half jumping, half flying back to the top of the wall.

Tristan had already begun to run to the rack of longbows and arrows, but by the time he turned back, it was too late.

Holding the screaming soldier in its talons, the monster pushed him into the giant maw of its mouth and hungrily bit him in two. It screamed again as if in pain, then tore off the breastplate that covered the man's chest and threw it angrily into the courtyard. Greedily it began to devour the lower half of the body.

Several feet of the still-screaming soldier's intestines fell to the courtyard floor, awash in blood.

Trying to fight back a wave of nausea, Tristan notched an arrow on the string of the longbow and aimed it at the thing's breast. Others of the Guard followed suit. Immediately he let the arrow fly, and it coursed in a true line, striking the monster exactly where the prince had estimated its heart to be. But the arrow did not penetrate very deeply, and the creature simply looked down at the shaft in its breast as if it were a mere nuisance. It extended its wings and screamed, dropping the lower torso of the soldier upon the wall next to it. Bending down its awful woman's face, it gripped the arrow with its teeth, pulled it out, and spat it away. More arrows lodged in the seemingly impenetrable feathers, but none seemed to be having any effect.

It began to eat the soldier's head now, drooling bits of bone and brain out of its awful mouth and down its chin.

A lieutenant of the Guard suddenly appeared before Tristan. The prince recognized him as Lucius, one of Frederick's best. "Your Highness, what are your orders?" he pleaded. "Nothing we do seems to harm it."

But Tristan was given no time to answer. The creature jumped into the midst of the soldiers to capture another one, but this time it missed, tearing the man's arm off at the shoulder. It quickly reached down, took the bloody stump in its claws, and then, screaming in defiance, launched itself back to its gory perch on the stone wall.

As if in a dream, Tristan watched Lucius and some of the other officers pull the poor mangled soldier back to the relative safety of the crowd. And then, purposely, he began to walk across the bloody ground, moving closer to the wall.

Several of the soldiers shouted to him to return, but he held up one of his hands, indicating silence. Oddly, even the creature grew rather still as it watched Tristan walk so deliberately toward it. The monster stretched its wings in defiance, screaming even louder, its awful woman's face contorting and its stench now becoming even more unbearable.

Just three more paces should do it, Tristan thought. *There are only two vulnerable targets. I beg the Afterlife, let my aim be true.*

His right foot touched the ground twice more, and the moment he stopped, his right arm became a curved blur of speed, reaching up and over for the first of his dirks. It came into his hand like second nature, and then almost before he knew he had thrown it, he saw the knife twirling toward the creature. For a bare second he held his breath. Then, as he watched, the blade sickeningly buried itself to the hilt in the left eye of the horrible woman-face.

It was said for decades afterward that the scream the men heard in the courtyard that day was unlike any sound that had ever been experienced in all of Eutracia. In a shrieking combination of insane pain and anger, the thing reached up and used its dark talons to pull the dirk from where its left eye used to be, blood and vitreous matter snaking crazily down its face.

Then it jumped from the wall to the courtyard, almost unfazed, and faced the prince.

Just as Tristan was about to throw another dirk he felt strong hands on both of his arms, pulling him back to the crowd. He tried to turn and face whoever it was, but he had never felt such strength before, not even from Frederick, and he was being literally hauled back to safety on the backs of his heels. When he was released at last, he found himself looking into the stern face of Wigg.

Wasting neither time nor words, Wigg bullied past the prince and began to walk toward the wounded beast with slow, measured steps. A deadly silence began to overtake the courtyard—even the monster made no sound. *It's almost as if the two of them recognize each other,* Tristan thought.

Suddenly Wigg stopped and raised his arms.

"Once again we meet," he said to it in a quiet voice. "You and your kind have avoided death far too many times. But not today. Today you are mine."

As the creature began again to scream, bolts of azure light shot from Wigg's hands. The light coalesced upon reaching the monster and began to surround it, trapping it within a brilliant blue cube. Wigg then lowered his hands and the cube began to change, bands of empty space alternating with the bands of glowing blue light, creating a cage of iridescent azure bars.

Tristan realized that for the first time in his life he was witnessing the creation of a wizard's warp.

The desperate creature began to smash its body violently against the sides of the warp in panic, apparently realizing what was happening. But no matter how furiously it fought, the warp never moved.

Wigg slowly began to join his hands together, and Tristan's mouth dropped open as he saw the warp, with the awful thing still inside it, begin to collapse. The creature screamed out in agony as the walls of the warp began to crush it. Its head was forced over to one side as the left-hand wall closed in on it and first broke its neck, then crushed its skull. The screaming stopped. When the walls of the warp were a little more than a yard apart, Wigg stopped joining his hands. Tristan saw the life finally go out of the thing's remaining eye, its blood and crushed organs pushed out between the slender bars of glowing light in a sickening mixture of red and pink.

And then came another horrible sound. An incredible din far more overwhelming than the awful screaming of the bird.

The sky darkened momentarily and then lightning shot across the sky in that Tristan had never dreamed possible. The thunder boomed until he thought his eardrums might burst, forcing him to place his hands over his ears. And then, as quickly as it had come, the sky lightened, and all was quiet.

Stunned, Tristan slowly walked up to where Wigg was standing and stood next to him, looking at the mangled remains inside the amazing, glowing azure box.

"A screaming harpy," Wigg said simply, without looking at the prince. "That *was* going to be your first question, wasn't it?"

In fact, that was not what Tristan had intended to ask first. He was much more interested in the glowing azure box than the monster. He turned to Wigg.

"The magic that you used to kill it—that was a wizard's warp, wasn't it?" he asked the old one.

"Yes," Wigg replied as he began to walk closer to the carnage. Reaching between the glowing azure rods, he carefully pulled Tristan's dirk out of the harpy's eye. The old wizard turned the throwing knife this way and that as he examined it in the afternoon sun. When he finally looked back at the prince there was a modicum of respect in his eyes. The old one also noticed that the glow that had surrounded the prince since his visit to the caves had blessedly disappeared.

"Warps are very useful, Tristan," he said, turning his attention back to the knife. "They are, simply put, powerful fields of protection and containment that can be modified at will." He looked at the dead thing inside the glowing box before turning his infamous eyes once again upon the prince. "After your reign, I will teach them to you."

After your reign, Tristan groaned to himself. That day seemed hundreds of years away to him. He decided to ask the second and perhaps more obvious question. "Why is it I have never heard of a screaming harpy before?"

Wigg let out a long sigh. *First a blood stalker, and now a screaming harpy,* he thought, his face unable to hide his concern. *And both of them appearing so close to the day of the abdication.*

"Harpies are indigenous to Eutracia," he told the prince as the men behind Tristan began to crowd closer to get a look at the awful thing that they had been unable to kill. "They have been in this land since long before the Sorceresses' War, and originally made their nesting places in the southern reaches of the Hartwick Woods, where the forest borders the plains of Heart Square."

Tristan knew the Hartwick Woods well enough but had spent little time in the larger, grass plain that was shaped in a square, thus earning its name.

"But harpies did not always have the faces of women," the old one continued, "nor were they always this vicious. During the war they were caught and trained by the sorceresses to plague and frighten the population into submission before the Coven tried to occupy a particular region. If they could kill or frighten away some of the people beforehand, then the sorceresses' task was just that much easier. Frankly, I am not particularly surprised that one or two of them still exist, despite the fact that one has not been sighted for over a century and a half." He winced inwardly at the lie, but with so many standing before him and hanging on his every word, he had no choice. He decided to change the subject.

Wigg walked back to Tristan and handed him his dirk, which the prince placed back into the quiver. "I have never seen you use one of those before," the wizard said with a short nod of approval. "You seem to be quite proficient with them. But let me give you a word of advice about taking a life, even a life as disgusting as the thing that is now trapped in my warp. Every time you use your dirks, or sword, or bow to take a life, try to think not of whom or what you are killing, but rather whom or what you are allowing to live. It will help with the eventual guilt that all those of our blood must deal with afterward. Endowed blood isn't just a gift; it's a responsibility. And sometimes it weighs heavily, indeed."

Instinctively, Tristan knew the old one was right. He always was. But more than that, the prince also had begun to feel that taking any life, even in self-defense and when apparently absolutely necessary, was not always the correct way to resolve conflict. Perhaps that was one of the reasons for his hunger to learn the craft. A short part of the wizard's vows now came back to him: *take no life except in urgent defense of self and others, or without fair warning.* He thought that he was perhaps beginning to understand.

Tristan watched as the wizard raised his hands before the warp. Immediately it began to dissolve, fading away into nothingness as the mangled creature inside dropped to the dust of the courtyard floor. Wigg motioned for Frederick to step forward.

"The orders I am about to give you are very specific, and must be followed to the letter," he said sternly. "Order your men to cut the carcass into at least a dozen pieces, and then bury each piece in its own hole, each at least thirty feet apart from the others and no less than fifteen feet deep. Cart the pieces of the carcass at least one full league away from the city before digging the holes. And the entire process must be completed before nightfall. Do you understand?" His eyes were unflinching.

"Yes, Lead Wizard," Frederick said dutifully. Inching closer to the wizard and lowering his voice, he asked, "But why must we take such precautions? Isn't it already dead?"

"Screaming harpies have been known to regain life, even if dismembered, and especially if the various body parts were few and were laid to rest near each other." The infamous eyebrow came up like a weapon. "You don't want to have to relive this little episode, do you, Commander?"

"No, of course not, Lead Wizard," Frederick blurted, more than a little surprised. "All shall be done as you order." He turned on his heel and began to give a few of his troops the orders, as others of them began to lay sheets over the bodies of the dead soldiers.

"A good man," Wigg said to himself after the prince's brother-in-law had walked away. "But he limits his imagination to only what he sees before him on a daily basis, instead of allowing for the possibility of whatever his mind can conceive."

As Tristan turned to start back to the palace, he was surprised to see his father and the five remaining wizards of the Directorate standing before him.

"I have never seen you throw one of those before, Tristan," Nicholas said with no small amount of pride in his voice. "You are very good at it." He turned his attention to the Lead Wizard. "Perhaps if we returned to the palace, you and the other wizards could explain to me just what it is that has happened here," he said rather sternly. "I think we need to talk."

He once again addressed the prince. "And as for you, Tristan," he said, "as soon as you've had a chance to clean up and change your clothes, your attendance is required before the queen." He leaned closer, smiling. "Don't worry; you're not in trouble, for once. She simply has not had an opportunity to see you much in the last few days, and would like to take tea with you and your sister this afternoon."

Tristan hated taking tea, and his father knew it. When he started to open his mouth in protest, the king immediately cut him off with a wave of his hand. "You're going," he said, smiling with mock ferociousness.

Tristan, his father, and the Directorate all turned away from the grisly job that the soldiers were now performing upon the screaming harpy and began to walk back to the palace.

*S*he reached up and moved an errant gray thread of wool a bit more to the right. It had been placed in the wrong spot, she could now see, and needed to be farther away from the shadowed area she was trying to create. *This one would do well in the king's private bedchamber,* she thought as one of her five handmaidens handed her more of the thick yarn. *The equestrian theme suits him, and since he has never seen this particular tapestry it will come as a surprise.*

Queen Morganna of the House of Galland stood up from her velvet upholstered sitting chair and walked away from the large, rectangular loom that was before her. She needed to gain the perspective that sitting before the loom and doing the actual act of creating the tapestry always denied her.

She turned to the plump, elderly woman on her right who had faithfully served as her senior handmaiden for the last thirty years. "What do you think, Marlene?" she asked. "Is it too dark?"

Standing beside her queen, Marlene could see the faults in the work. "Perhaps a bit too much so around the area of the horse's head, Your Highness," she replied earnestly. "Other than that I think it is a fine piece, as usual."

"And you, Shailiha, do you also agree?" the queen asked. Shailiha stood next to her, observing the tapestry and gently gliding her hand across her swollen abdomen in what had become an automatic gesture of maternal love. *I shall soon be a grandmother,* Morganna thought with pride. *And perhaps someday Tristan will put aside his capricious ways and add to our family some children of his own.* But then a darker thought began to invade her mind, and she tried her best not to let it show through. *Provided the fears of the wizards do not come to pass, as they have warned my husband,* she thought.

"Yes." Shailiha smiled back. "Too dark. But I think you already knew that, didn't you, Mother?" she answered playfully.

"Yes," the queen answered softly. "I suppose so."

Queen Morganna had spent the greater part of this afternoon doing two of the things that gave her the most joy: creating tapestries and spending time with her daughter.

Morganna had learned the secrets of the great weaving looms long ago from her now-departed mother and aunts, before she had met Nicholas and was still a peasant. Some at court thought it a waste of such an important person's time, but no one could deny that she had talent. The various tapestries she had created over the years hung in many of the rooms of the palace and were also sometimes auctioned off at great balls, the money used to support the several orphanages in Eutracia. But this one was special. It was to be a gift to her husband.

And then the screaming harpy had come.

After hearing about the death of the harpy and the part Tristan had played in it she had felt a sudden, compelling urge to see him, and to know he was well. She had therefore requested that the king summon him to her earlier than she had first planned, to take tea with her and Shailiha. She smiled. It was just the kind of thing that Tristan so hated.

As if preordained for this very moment, the soft knock at the door came once, then twice.

"Enter," she said simply, her eyes still grazing across the field of the cloth mural.

A uniformed member of the Guard, one of two who were always stationed just outside her door wherever she might be, entered the room and bowed. "Begging your pardon, Your Highness, but the prince is outside the door, and says that you called for him."

"Thank you, Jeffrey. Show him in," she said. Turning to her five handmaidens, she said, "You are all dismissed for the afternoon." Smiling at Marlene in particular, she added, "I shan't put you through any more of my artistic ramblings today."

"As you wish, Your Highness," Marlene said as she began to shoo the reluctant ladies from the room. Joining the queen in her quiet time was always one of the best ways to catch up on the palace gossip, and the very subject of that gossip was about to enter the room. None of them, including Marlene, really wanted to leave.

The senior handmaiden leaned in toward the queen, a knowing smile on her face. "You realize, of course, the position you now put me in," she said teasingly. "For the next two days they will all hound me mercilessly for any news of the prince that might come my way."

Morganna smiled back at her friend and confidante of so many years. "He has been so busy getting into trouble lately, I wouldn't know where to begin even if I chose to tell you."

Marlene winked knowingly and curtsied, then turned to hustle the remaining handmaidens out of the room like a mother hen trying to retain control of her wandering brood of chicks. They all curtsied as they passed the prince, and the queen watched her son bow to them and smile courteously. The younger of the handmaidens twittered and blushed. Morganna shook her head and raised a knowing eyebrow at Shailiha. It was always the same.

Despite his choice in clothing and the fact that he was again dirty from head to toe, the queen smiled with pride. Regardless of his recent misbehavior, she loved this one more than her life. Shailiha had always been the stable one, the obedient one, the respectful one, but Tristan had always been her favorite, right or wrong. Over the last two days he seemed to have developed a more mature and commanding demeanor, and after hearing about his adventures, she knew why.

She walked up and embraced him, kissing him upon his right cheek.

"Sit down, Tristan," she said, "and I will have some tea sent in." She motioned him to a small but elegant sitting area that faced two very large, open, stained-glass windows, from which could be seen the Eutracian countryside.

Before sitting down, Tristan reached up to her cheek and used the underside of his thumb to wipe away a small smudge that he had left there. He had rushed to change and wash—he must have missed some dirt on his cheek. "The queen mustn't be seen like this," he said, smiling into the eyes he loved so much. "The palace wags will talk. And given the fact that I have already supplied them with so much lately to talk about, let's not give them any more."

He turned to Shailiha with a look that he hoped would garner him some sympathy, but his sister simply smiled back cattily, enjoying his discomfort. He playfully narrowed his eyes. "I suppose you're here because you want to be," he whispered. "As for me, I'd rather face one of Wigg's interminable lectures in the Wizards' Conservatory than take tea, even if it is with the two of you."

Morganna, her attention once again upon the tapestry, said, "Why don't the two of you go out on the balcony? I shall join you when the tea arrives. Besides, I want to get this dark area repaired, before I lose the light."

Tristan, with his sister in tow, begrudgingly walked to the stained-glass balcony doors and opened them wide. After watching his sister gently lower herself into one of the high-backed upholstered chairs, he sat in one next to her, crossed his long legs, and looked out to the tranquil scene below.

Still looking out over the balcony, he whispered, "Are you going to tell me, or shall I have to command one of the wizards to torture it out of you?"

Shailiha looked over to his sharp profile to find a look of playful nastiness on his face.

"Tell you what?" she asked. She bit her upper lip to keep from smiling, obviously having trouble controlling either the urge to reveal a secret or her enjoyment of his discomfort, or both. The prince thought it was both.

Behind him, he heard his mother call for Jeffrey.

"Yes, Your Highness?" the guard asked.

"Please send for tea and scones for three," she said simply.

"Yes, Your Highness," the short reply came.

"I really don't want any tea, Mother," the prince said over his shoulder in his most apologetic manner. Tristan hated the idea of taking tea, of sitting around holding dainty china in the air while eating with the points of his teeth and pretending to be polite to the kinds of people who generally attended such things—even if those people were, in this case, only his sister and mother.

"Then don't drink any," the queen called with a laugh. "Besides, the reason I asked for the two of you to meet me in private wasn't really about having tea."

Tristan felt something inside of him slip a little. *I'm probably due for another of their talks regarding the last couple of days,* he reflected glumly. *What could my mother say to me that all of the others already have not?* He sat patiently next to his teasing sister for as long as he could without saying anything more, but eventually he simply had to ask.

"You know why we're here, don't you?" He looked conspiratorially into Shailiha's eyes, begging for a clue.

Shailiha's expression changed slightly, from one of mischief to one of affection. "Yes," she whispered back. "I never could keep a secret from you, and you know it. I do indeed know why we are here, but that is for Mother to say, not me." She cast her eyes down and rubbed her hand across her unborn. Suddenly, her hazel eyes flew open.

"What's wrong?" Tristan asked quickly.

"Nothing, really." Shailiha smiled. "She just kicked. She has been doing rather a lot of that lately."

"She?" Tristan asked.

"Oh, yes," Shailiha said softly. "My baby is a girl. I just know it. Don't ask me how, but for some time I have sensed that it will be a girl, with blond hair like mother and me. And green eyes like Frederick's, of course."

"Tristan," she then softly asked, looking a bit more seriously into his face. "Will you do me a favor?"

"Of course," he replied. "Anything—you know that. I always have, and I always will."

She reached out to take his hand, and before he could comment or pull it back she placed it lightly upon her abdomen, where hers had been only a moment before. As if Shailiha could command it, the baby kicked, and Tristan jumped back a little in surprise. *I have never before felt life within another,* he realized. *Somehow it makes the fact that she is pregnant just that much more real.*

"I placed your hand there for a reason, Brother," she said softly.

"And that is?"

"To show you that the consequences of one's action have very real effects upon the lives of others, as Father tried in his own way to tell you in the room below the palace. I do not say these things simply to drive home the painful points that Father made before, but to tell you that I believe I am the only person in the world who truly understands you. I hope and pray with all of my heart that you will heed that which your family has told you." She smiled softly into his eyes as she searched her mind for the proper analogy. "This kingdom is about to become yours, and you must grasp it firmly, yet tenderly, the way a man would hold the woman he loves most, never letting her go."

She has a special way about her, especially when it comes to loving and understanding me, he thought. *She always has.* He slowly removed his hand from her and smiled into the lovely face before him. *My sister. My twin, and my best friend.*

"I will do my best, Shailiha," he said, fearing that his voice was about to crack. "For you, anything. Wherever you may go, whatever may happen. For you, anything."

A knock came on the door, and after a greeting from the queen two liveried servants entered with a silver tray holding two pots of tea and a plate filled with scones. The queen thanked them, and they bowed and left the room. Morganna beckoned for her children to leave the balcony and rejoin her in her private quarters.

The queen poured herself a cup and tentatively tasted it, making sure it wasn't too hot. "I understand you have been very busy lately," she said to Tristan as they each took a seat around the small table now loaded with tea and scones.

Tristan turned rather uncomfortably in his chair as he watched Shailiha bite her lip, trying to control an impending smile. He turned back to the queen. "If you are referring to the Caves, Mother, that wasn't really my fault."

"The Caves?" Morganna asked innocently. "No, your father has already told me all about that, and I leave the handling of such things to him and the Directorate." She smiled knowingly into his dark-blue eyes. "I was referring to Evelyn of the House of Norcross."

Tristan swallowed. Hard. He was certain that he must be blushing, but surely this couldn't be the only reason she asked him here. Evelyn wasn't the first of those his mother had known about. And he would rather face a thousand screaming harpies than have to discuss his private matters of the heart with either of his parents or his sister.

"Don't worry, Tristan. Your secret is safe with us," his mother said lightly, pressing one of her hands against his crimson cheek. She and

Shailiha had always been more forgiving of the prince's dalliances than had been Nicholas or the Directorate—after all, they were women and could better understand the effects he had on so many of the young ladies of the realm. And she could tell that his heart was breaking at the thought of becoming king, and then a wizard of the Directorate. There was so little about any of it she could do.

"I also heard about the harpy. Are you sure you are all right?" She glanced over at his shoulder, thinking of the knives he so often carried there. "Your father says you are very good with those knives of yours," she said encouragingly. "I think he now better understands why you carry them."

Tristan shrugged. "It was really Wigg who killed it," he said, almost apologetically. "I just did what I could." He watched while she took another sip of tea. "Mother, is there a special reason you asked me here today?" he asked.

Morganna smiled to herself, once again reminded that the man sitting before her was not only her son, but also a very special person, indeed. She rose and walked a short way over to a mahogany writing desk that sat against the opposite wall. Opening the top drawer, she took out a velvet-covered box. She returned to her chair and held the small box in her lap with both hands.

"This was to be a gift to you from your father, your sister, and me after your coronation as king," she began quietly, "but we have decided to give it to you now, instead. Your father wanted to be here, but many important affairs have commanded so much of his attention of late that Shailiha and I decided we would present it to you ourselves." She handed him the box and, smiling, sat back in her chair.

Tristan took the box from his mother and slowly opened the lid.

What he saw took his breath away, and he could feel his eyes begin to tear.

Inside the box was a piece of gold jewelry on a gold rope chain. But not just any jewelry. Hanging from the chain was a small medallion, and engraved upon it was a broadsword with a fancy hilt, superimposed with a roaring lion. The heraldry of the House of Galland, the same as appeared upon breastplates of the Royal Guard. He took it from the box and held it before him as he watched it turn in the light. He had never seen anything so beautiful in his life.

Morganna could tell instantly that he was pleased. "We had it made for you last month, as we knew the time of your father's abdication was coming near. Please wear this with the Paragon, which will be placed around your neck that day, as a token of the love of your family." She blinked back the tears that threatened when she thought about what she could *not* tell him. *How do I tell my son that I must give this to him now, because of what the wizards have told us? That if we do not show our love for our children now, we may soon never be able to again?*

Tristan placed the chain and medallion around his neck, and he looked down at the jewelry as it twinkled against the black leather of his vest.

"Thank you, Mother," he said, his voice cracking slightly. "I shall wear it always, no matter where my life leads me." Turning to his sister, he could see tears in her eyes. "And thank you, Shailiha," he said softly. "For everything."

Shailiha cast him a knowing smile through her tears.

Even though he does not realize the full impact of what he just said, I could never have asked for more, Morganna thought. *Wear it well, my son, with or without us.*

She stood and beckoned him toward her. Tristan immediately rose and embraced his mother, but as he did so she made sure that neither of her children could see the lone tear that had begun to wend its way down her cheek.

The many oil sconces and chandeliers burned brightly in the ornate meeting room, and the hour was late. The heavy, self-imposed burden of complete silence reigned over everything as the many men sat there in their dark-blue robes, waiting for their revered teachers. It was rare for the Directorate to call such an impromptu meeting, especially at this hour of the night, and every one of the men in the rather stuffy, ornate room knew it. Something was afoot.

Before being allowed entry to the room each of them had been made to stand before the Lead Wizard himself and raise the sleeve of his robe, showing Wigg the tattoo of the Paragon upon his upper right arm. They had also been asked to perform some small use of the craft, in order to prove that they were in fact endowed and truly belonged here. Therefore the process of admittance to the meeting had taken hours to perform. Such precautions were a rarity, indeed.

There were several hundred of them in attendance, and although they were only a fraction of their total numbers they nonetheless represented the best of their kind. These hand-chosen men were the finest, the most highly trained of their brotherhood, other than the wizards of the Directorate.

The meeting room they had been summoned to was sumptuous, and the delicate, light-blue Ephyran marble of the walls, ceiling, and floor belied the serious, questioning attitude of those who had been ordered to attend. This room was in the farthest reaches of the Redoubt and was used only very rarely, when absolute security was required. The scent of anticipation swirled heavily upon the air.

Finally and without fanfare, the Directorate of Wizards entered the room from a door at the end of the hall and, all except for Wigg, walked to a row of high-backed chairs upon the raised dais at one end of the room. Wigg, Tretiak, Killius, Maaddar, Egloff, and Slike—the ancient heroes of the Sorceresses' War. Each of them wearing his gray robe of office and his braided wizard's tail falling down the center of his back, they stared politely out at the crowd. One by one they took their chairs, except for Wigg. The Lead Wizard remained standing and turned to address the group. The room somehow became even more still as Wigg looked out upon their numbers, rather unsure of how to begin. *We have never asked such a thing of them before,* the Lead Wizard thought. *We have never asked them to kill. And I am not sure myself how to ask them to perform the tasks that only they are now capable of accomplishing.*

"Consuls of the Redoubt," Wigg began, raising his voice so that all could hear. "Time is short; therefore I shall be brief. It is my unfortunate task to inform you all that our nation is being plagued by creatures the likes of which we have not seen for hundreds of years. They have already killed several of the Royal Guard, and are no doubt responsible for the mysterious disappearances of several of your brothers over the course of the last few months. Since those of you here are without the aid of time enchantments, you have probably never seen the beings of which I now speak. But rest assured they do once again exist, apparently roaming the countryside at will, and the Directorate is asking your help to protect the citizenry from them."

The consuls turned to one another with puzzled looks upon their faces, but none of them spoke as they waited respectfully for the Lead Wizard to resume his address.

"The creatures of which I speak are the blood stalker, which seeks out and destroys males of endowed blood, and the screaming harpy, the giant bird of prey with the head of a woman. We believe that an unknown disturbance in the natural flow of the craft has reactivated some of these beings, and we now ask your help in destroying them." It pained the old wizard to lie to these brothers of endowed blood who sat so respectfully before him. But he had no choice.

"As you know, the coronation of the prince is almost upon us. It is for this reason that we are unable to use the Royal Guard in this endeavor, since their attendance at the palace shall be needed for matters of security, including controlling the crowd. Due to the unsurpassed popularity of both the prince and the king, the attendance is expected to exceed all known records. Under normal circumstances the Directorate itself would have helped guide you in this charge, but we, too, must remain at the palace, for the same reasons as the Guard."

"Those of you who were selected to be here this night were chosen because of your long years of service and your relatively higher abilities in the craft," he continued. "I charge each of you to select eleven others, taken from members not present, and to form small companies of a dozen each. Each of these squads is to go out across the nation in search of these monsters, to destroy them wherever they are found."

Wigg turned around slightly and gestured to the other wizards seated behind him. "The Directorate will give you detailed training in how best to kill these nightmares, but let me say this first: The blood stalker can only be killed by crushing its skull. And the yellow brain matter that flows from it is fatal. Under no circumstances are you to allow it to touch your skin. The harpy, on the other hand, has no such danger in its bodily fluids but is infinitely stronger, larger, and therefore more difficult to kill. The best methods for its destruction are fire or the use of a wizard's warp, crushing it to death." He paused, thinking of the warp he had used to kill the harpy.

"And lastly," he said more slowly, "know that many of you in this room may not be coming back, that you may quite possibly perish in these attempts. We have no idea how many of these beings are loose in the nation, but we are reasonably sure that there are far more than the two we have already dispatched." He paused, lowering his head slightly. "May the Afterlife grant you the wisdom to prevail."

And may all of us, each and every one, survive the events of the next few days.

CHAPTER

Seven

K luge shuddered, partly out of sexual need and partly out of emotional longing as she slowly licked the unusually tender area high up on one of his wings, the small spot at the top that she knew from experience was a Minion area of sexual pleasure. They had been at sea for fourteen days now, and she had said little about their mission, other than occasionally making sure they were on course for the proper area of the Eutracian coast and verifying that all the other warships were dutifully following. Even today, when she had casually ordered him to her stateroom, and she had alluded to no more than a discussion of their mission.

Naked, Succiu slid up closer behind him as he sat on the edge of the large bed. She rather painfully bit the side of his neck as she hungrily watched his sexual excitement come to fruition.

"I assume, Mistress, that my presence here involves more than simply receiving my orders for tomorrow," he said, trying to contain both his sarcasm and his intense longing for the second mistress. He had heard stories of those who had not pleased her, and despite how much he enjoyed these times with her, he had no desire to join the ranks of lesser men who had not risen to the challenge. He would do as he was told.

She threw a shock of her long, silken hair back over one shoulder and reached languidly around him, her long, painted nails teasing his groin.

"You assume correctly, Commander," she said coyly. "It has been too long since we have joined, and despite our closeness during the last fourteen days, until now I had never been able to find the right moment. As you are aware, the First Mistress does not know of the times that we share together in this way, and would indeed not be pleased to learn of it. But, then again, she does not need to know, does she?"

Kluge shook his head slightly. Both he and the second mistress were well aware of the fact that when Failee had first perfected the Minions, the First Mistress had forbidden any such contact between her creations and the Coven, or the Minions and the native women of Parthalon, for that matter. All mating must be strictly for the purposes of siring more warriors, she had said. *And it is exactly like Succiu to rebel against her,* Kluge thought to himself. *Especially when it come to her needs of the flesh.* The first few times she had ordered him to lie with her he had feared for his life and had been barely able to perform. But, with the passage of time, not only was he at least partially able to satisfy her amazing hungers but he had come to want her heart, as well.

"You continue to dare to defy Failee in this way, even now, at this most important of times?" Kluge asked. He knew that Succiu was deadly, and that he must obey her orders to the letter, whatever they may be. But he also had no desire to have the First Mistress learn of their trysts and punish him with death, simply for submitting to the beauty before him.

"Failee is my problem, not yours," she said dismissively.

Slowly uncoiling her long legs from beneath her, she moved away from him and sat up on the bed, holding her knees in front of her. For a brief moment something in her countenance had changed—become even more conspiratorial. It was almost as if Succiu regarded Failee as something of a challenge, and a welcome one at that.

"The First Mistress long ago abandoned her earthly pleasures and turned her talents solely toward the mastery of a certain aspect of the craft," she continued coyly. She began to circle the inside of his ear maddeningly with her tongue. "But I, the second mistress, refuse to be bound by her constraints in this regard," Succiu continued. "Besides, aren't you pleased?"

"Of course, Mistress," he answered automatically.

"But business before pleasure. Turn around and face me," she ordered.

He turned around on the black silk sheets and found himself gazing directly into the dark, almond eyes. She was looking at him with dead seriousness, the playfulness now completely gone.

"Tomorrow is a very special day," she said. "We shall have been at sea for fifteen days with favorable winds at our backs, and so we must prepare. Listen carefully, for my orders are very explicit, and must be followed to the letter. If tomorrow does not proceed exactly as planned, you will have no need to worry about your attack, for we will all be dead and no trace of us, not even of our armada, will be found."

Kluge immediately understood the reference: the Sea of Whispers. The ocean that could never be crossed. His knowledge of it was limited only to what he had heard from the Parthalonian nationals, and the brief mention of it by Failee during his meeting with the Coven.

"What I am about to tell you is for your ears only, and even then it will not be complete," Succiu began seriously. "Much of what will happen tomorrow to ensure our crossing will become apparent to you then. In addition, should any of your officers learn the nature of tomorrow's events beforehand it might prove unsettling to them, and there is no need of that." She paused, looking into his eyes, obviously expecting him to agree.

"I understand, Mistress," he said purposefully.

"Good," she said without emotion. "Besides, a full explanation of tomorrow could take hours, and I have other plans for the use of our evening together." Her tongue licked her upper lip while her eyes grazed over his body. It was not love for him that she was displaying, he knew, but simply a need that she would order him to fulfill. *As a master would command a slave,* he thought. *And despite the fact she knows how much I love her, she will let me occasionally possess her body but never her heart, for the blood that runs through my veins is not endowed.*

She returned to her more businesslike demeanor. "Tomorrow at dawn, forty dead Parthalonian slaves will be brought to our vessel. One each from forty of our warships. They will be brought to us in skiffs by the captains of these vessels, and are to be laid naked in four rows upon the deck of this command ship." She spoke as casually as if she were discussing what the weather might be like tomorrow.

Kluge stared at her, speechless. *Forty dead slaves to be brought here?* His mind reeled. He couldn't possibly imagine the purpose of such a thing.

"Just before dawn, each one of the dead slaves will have been murdered in their sleep personally by the captain of each of the forty vessels, then stripped naked. The slaves were handpicked and put on board each of the ships by Failee herself before we sailed, and each of the warship captains were informed of their individual orders long ago. One of your tasks tomorrow will be to retain order among your troops and officers when the bodies are brought aboard. Our survival depends upon it."

The killing of captive slaves that were purposely brought upon a Minion mission? His brain fairly screamed the bizarre nature of it at him. Why bring them at all, if only to kill them now, halfway across this mysterious sea? And Minion warriors had certainly seen their share of dead slaves. Succiu knew that. So why would there be difficulty in maintaining order? Too stupefied to respond, he just sat there in abject disbelief of what he was hearing.

Regardless of the fact that she could sense the incomprehension and confusion in his eyes, her gaze became no more compassionate as she went on with her instructions.

"After the events of tomorrow, the reasons for these actions shall be clear," she said. "Actually, I am more than certain that you will agree with me when I say that there was absolutely no other choice. At dawn I want you standing next to me on deck, and I will do my best to explain as events unfold. The only thing I shall tell you now is that tomorrow you will become one of the very few who understand why it is called the Sea of Whispers."

For the first time in his life, he thought he could sense fear in her voice.

She got out of bed, walked naked to the ornate sideboard beneath the stained-glass windows of her cabin, and poured herself a glass of wine. She turned to him and raised the bottle questioningly, but he shook his head. Shrugging her shoulders, she came back up behind him in the great bed and took a sip.

"Assuming we survive tomorrow and we have crossed this horrible sea, I shall order that we drop our sails and congregate approximately one and a half day's sail from the Eutracian coast," she continued, apparently now lost in her thoughts. "That will be the day of the abdication ceremony. The closest Eutracian soil will then be a peninsula called Far Point. It is an area that is surrounded by dangerous reefs and therefore typically not used by Eutracian fishermen. Thus, it is highly unlikely that our fleet will be seen, especially under the coming cover of darkness. There are to be absolutely no lanterns lit. During the course of that day, you are to arm your warriors and give each of your officers their attack orders. Leave nothing out, especially the importance of taking Shailiha alive, and the capture of the Paragon. It will then be their individual responsibilities to return to their ships and inform their respective troops of their orders. That same afternoon, the Minions will fly for the coast, which should take no more than five or six hours. Six of your strongest are to carry a specially designed litter in which you and I will be transported."

"We shall fly under my direction directly to the woodlands surrounding the palace at Tammerland, just out of sight of the Royal Guard that shall be stationed in and around the palace for security during the abdication ceremony," she continued. "By the time we reach the palace, night will already have fallen, but the abdication ceremony will not yet have begun. At my order, you will then begin your attack. As you know, the precise timing of the attack is crucial—that is, the moment the Paragon has been immersed in the water of the chalice. Our ally at the Eutracian court shall already be inside attending the ceremony, and will inform me mentally of the precise moment."

Kluge thought of the mind-link he had witnessed between Failee and their ally at the Eutracian court. Apparently more than one of the Coven was trained in this particular talent.

"After the battle," she continued, "we will light a series of signal fires in a nearby coastal area called the Cavalon Delta, and our captains will approach the coast and moor there." She took another sip of the wine, and then set the glass upon her bed stand. She raised her dark eyes up to him again. "But first, we must survive tomorrow."

Her eyes seemed to glaze over briefly, and Kluge could see raw hunger once again begin to build there. But it was not sexual desire. It was the intense need to return to her homeland, bringing as much death as possible with her. He very much doubted the wisdom of asking her any questions just now, despite the fact that he had so many.

Kluge then watched as her expression began to evolve into a different, more erotic, and even more commanding hunger. She picked up the wineglass and walked around the edge of the huge bed, kneeling down before him.

"Poor Kluge," she whispered teasingly, as she smiled up at his dark face. "I know how you feel about me, and how you would like to possess me in a way other than simply the physical, but it's quite hopeless, don't you see?" She took another sip of the wine, clearly enjoying the opportunity not only to use his body, but also to insult his mind. "Your blood simply does not entice me the way endowed blood does. But that is not to say you are without your uses."

Endowed blood, Kluge thought. *That which I do not have.* His mind went back in time to the unique, hungry look in Succiu's eyes when she had so carefully observed the prince of Eutracia during the Coven's meeting in the palace. *He and his endowed blood shall die slowly,* Kluge promised himself. *Much more slowly than the others.*

He closed his eyes as Succiu poured the warm, red wine onto his abdomen and hungrily began to lick it from his groin.

*K*luge looked out across the calm sea as he stood alone in the bow of the command warship. The sky was clear, the wind at their backs strong and steady, and the sea itself the very picture of good sailing. He rubbed one gloved hand down the length of his tired face, drinking in the refreshing sea air. She had used him for hours last night, and he had willingly obeyed. Afterward he had found it impossible to sleep; instead he had wandered the decks for the rest of the night, wondering what possible threat she could have been referring to.

He turned to look down the length of the warship. Forty dead bodies lay on the main deck in four neat rows of ten each. Just as she had said, the forty captains of the preselected ships had all arrived at dawn with their respective cargoes of death, each in a small skiff that the captain had piloted himself. The dead men had been hearty and strong; the women had been tall, young, and beautiful; the children were perfect miniatures of the adults. There seemed to be an approximately even number of men, women, and children. *Handpicked, indeed,* he thought.

The captains had sailed their individual skiffs back to their ships, and the entire armada had now taken the shape of a V, like a flock of geese, with the command warship in the lead. Whatever Succiu planned on encountering, it was plain that she wanted her ship to arrive first.

Kluge had already instructed each of his officers according to Succiu's orders, telling them not to be surprised at whatever they witnessed this day, that all would happen as the Coven expected. He had felt more than a little foolish before his troops when he had not been able to tell them what *was* expected, however. Now, as he watched his men go about their morning tasks, Traax, his second in command, appeared before him. An unusually large and efficient officer, Traax had been appointed to the position immediately after Kluge's promotion to commander by the Coven.

"Permission to speak, my lord," he said simply, looking with clear, green eyes into the much darker eyes of his leader.

Kluge nodded.

"A status report, my lord," Traax began, standing stiffly at attention. "We make way unimpeded at approximately ten knots, the wind stays steady, and we are on the proper course. We make good progress. The warriors are interested in but not afraid of your warning of this morning. Minion warriors fear nothing, even the unknown."

Kluge began to respond, but before he could speak the first word, he was interrupted by a voice from behind him.

"Thank you, Traax. That will be all," Succiu said without emotion. She walked to the bow to stand with Kluge facing the west, the rising sun upon their backs.

"Yes, Mistress," Traax said obediently. He bowed briefly and returned to his duties on the main deck.

This was the first time Kluge had seen her this morning, and as expected, there was no hint in her face whatsoever of what had passed between them last night. *Such beauty,* he thought. *Beauty I am occasionally allowed to take, but never to possess.*

She stood there next to him for some time without speaking, simply watching the waves as they splashed and divided against the prow of the ship. He could feel the sun beginning to warm the back of his neck . . . and then things began to change.

The balmy morning air turned chilly; it seemed to grow distinctly colder with each second that passed. Kluge turned around to look toward the stern of the boat, wondering if they were being engulfed by a sudden storm front, but the weather behind them remained as perfect as that which lay before them.

And then the wind stopped.

It didn't just slow down, or start to give out in little gusts as would often be the case—it simply stopped. There was absolutely no breeze; the sea became as smooth as glass. The great warship slowly came to a stop. A deadly silence reigned over everything as Kluge looked down to see his warriors looking about in amazement, their breath streaming out in long, vaporous clouds because of the intense cold.

The second mistress of the Coven stepped before Kluge and looked into his dark eyes with a determination that he had never before seen there, despite his many dealings with her. "We have arrived," she said to him, her voice almost a murmur. "Belay the sails, tie off the ship's wheel, and be quick about it." She inched her face even closer to his. "And remind those flying monkeys of yours that they are to take absolutely no action unless it is specifically ordered by me." She turned away from him and began to cast her eyes slowly across the smooth, unmoving waters that surrounded the warship.

Kluge motioned to Traax, who was at his side in an instant. After giving his second in command the orders, Kluge watched as the sails came down and the wheel was tied off, making the ship entirely subject to the mercy of the waves. Except there were no waves, and the great ship now sat virtually motionless in the dark-blue water.

And then came the fog.

Unlike any he had ever seen, it rolled over them with great speed, seemingly from nowhere, engulfing them in its presence. Thick and gray, it seemed to have a life of its own and clung, cold and wet, to their clothes and skin. Reaching out into the air, he extended his fingers and rubbed them together. The fog seemed to have body to it, a silky texture that he could actually feel between his fingers. Turning toward Succiu, he could barely see her, even though they were less than three feet apart. *How is fog able to have substance?* his soldier's mind shouted at him. *Such a thing is not possible.* And then the fog began to take shape.

Gradually, he began once again to be able to pick out Succiu in the gloom as the fog started to coalesce and take form around certain areas of the warship. From bow to stern, it gathered on either side of the ship in two distinct columns that seemed to rise up out of the ocean. Occasional glimpses through the fog showed him that the weather beyond was as clear as it had been, and that the fog was isolated only around the ship.

Then, as he turned his attention back to the two growing pillars of fog, his mouth dropped open.

The great columns of fog had taken the shape of human arms rising out of the depths of the ocean. At the end of each arm was a gigantic gray hand, with ancient, gnarled fingers that ended in long, cracked, and broken fingernails. The great gray arms began moving in different directions. One of them went forward to the bow, and the other went astern. Paralyzed by amazement, Kluge could barely move his head to watch them, and his ragged breath came faster, streaming out of his mouth in cloudy bursts as it struck the increasingly frigid air. He could not remember ever being so cold in his life.

It was then that the great gray hands grasped the ship.

The forward hand and arm wrapped around the bow, and the arm and hand in the rear covered the stern of the warship in its grasp.

The ship sat in the ocean totally immobilized. The huge, gnarled hands, their grips firm, stopped moving, and all traces of fog except for that which made up the terrible arms and hands now vanished. The surrounding ocean was once again in clear view.

Succiu turned again to Kluge, the expression on her face nervous but not panic-stricken, as he had thought it might be. It was almost as if she had been expecting this.

"Follow me to the gunwale, Commander," she said, apparently in complete control of her voice. She walked across the bow deck of the ship, Kluge following, and gestured for him to look down into the dark blue water of the ocean.

The water all around the ship had suddenly begun to bubble and roil, as if someone or something were either breathing beneath it or trying to come to the surface, or both. Kluge watched, transfixed, as the beginnings of oval shapes started to become visible just beneath the surface of the ocean. And then the bubbling and churning stopped, and what was left in the momentarily calm waters was the most hideous scene he had ever witnessed

They were faces, dozens of huge faces that were each at least ten feet across, lying flat in the ocean just a couple of feet below the surface, staring blankly up at the sky. Each of the faces was different, yet they were all somehow the same. They floated and bobbed without moving away from the ship, and simply lay there in ghostly silence. They were bodiless.

The flesh of the faces was a horrible mixture of sea green and dark red, streaked with ancient wrinkles and boils. Where eyes and mouths would be were only dark, empty holes that seemed to go on forever as the faces shimmered in the light without actually changing position in the water.

Turning away from his mistress, Kluge thought he might be ill.

Looking down at his warriors, he saw that many of them were gazing over the sides of the ship in amazement, dreggans drawn. Others had gone both fore and aft to examine the great arms and hands that still held the ship prisoner. Succiu came to stand with him.

"Order them to stand fast and put their weapons away immediately," she commanded. "No dreggan in the world, no matter how sharp, can defeat either fog or myth."

Kluge gave the order to Traax, then turned his attention back to the ocean. The horrible faces were still there, floating just below the surface.

Succiu read the bewilderment in his face. "They are the Necrophagians," she said in a low voice. "The Eaters of the Dead. And soon they will make their demands upon us."

Kluge stood transfixed, beginning to understand. He glanced at the forty corpses in the neat piles upon the main deck of the ship. It was then that he began to hear the whispers.

"Pay us our bounty, or we shall take your bodies and your ships," the faces said, in the strangest of voices that had ever reached his ears. There were many voices speaking at once, in complete conformity, yet so softly that they could barely be heard. *The Sea of Whispers,* he realized.

Succiu looked with apparent calm down into several of the faces as she began to speak.

"You do not remember me?" she asked softly. "I am one of the four who were allowed to cross without payment, some three hundred twenty-seven years ago." She paused as the faces remained silent, moving back and forth beneath the waves. "I demand you honor the bargain made then, the bargain of the tenfold times four."

A seemingly interminable silence followed, the only sounds the light lapping of the sea against the sides of the ship.

"The bargain of the tenfold times four shall be honored," the collective voices said at last, the many mouths moving at the same time. "But first we require proof of your personage, that you are indeed who you say you are. If acceptable proof is not forthcoming, we shall take your ships, and then your bodies."

A look of concern passed over Succiu's face, but she quickly regained her composure.

"A test of identity was never part of the bargain," she said boldly. "And if I refuse?"

"Then watch and learn, Sorceress," the many whispers came at once.

Immediately Kluge heard a snapping noise, and as he turned around he saw that the great hand that was gripping the stern of the ship had begun to tighten its grasp, sending smashed and splintered wood that had once been the upper railing and deck of the stern flying off into the ocean and down upon the lower decks of the ship. He turned in horror to his mistress.

"Very well," she said finally. Kluge watched the awful hand release its grip slightly as yet more pieces of the ship fell crackingly downward. Succiu walked back to the gunwale and looked down at the repulsive, floating faces. She raised her hands to the sky.

"Then watch and learn, Eaters of the Dead!" she screamed.

Two bolts of blue light shot from her hands, joined, and plunged into the dark blue of the ocean a short distance beyond where the farthest of the grotesque faces lay just beneath the waves. Every man on the warship, and he assumed those behind them in the other ships as well, stood in awe as the second mistress of the Coven commanded the ocean to rise. A great body of the water leapt into the sky, separating itself from the sea to form a tall column of blue liquid that hovered there as she began to move her hands back and forth as if she were creating a work of art. She continued to twist and turn the moving, living, column of water this way and that until she was satisfied, and the gaze of every man aboard locked upon the image that now hung in space before them.

It was the Pentangle, the sign of the Coven, formed of seemingly living, breathing turquoise water, suspended at least one hundred feet above the surface of the ocean. Kluge watched in awe as it dripped, twinkled, and revolved in the bright sunlight of the afternoon.

It was magnificent.

Kluge turned to his troops to see that they were, to a man, suddenly down on bended knee before the image. He, too, went to one knee.

"This is the symbol of my Sisterhood, and you would do well to remember it, for I do not wish to be inconvenienced this way each time I or one of my Sisters chooses to cross this sea," she said brazenly to the faces in the water. "Not only could no other women produce it, but also none others would dare. It should serve as proof enough of my personage."

"We accept your proof," the many soft whispers said at once through the hideous black maws of their mouths. "Pay us your tribute and you may continue to cross."

Succiu closed her fingers into fists and dropped her hands to her side. Instantly the shimmering blue Pentangle dropped into the ocean. She turned quickly to Kluge.

"Lower the dead bodies over the side of the ship," she ordered harshly. "Twenty to each side. Then make ready to hoist the sails and untie the ship's wheel. We have no desire to remain here any longer than we must."

Kluge quickly ran down to the main deck next to the rows of bodies and gave the orders. The Minion warriors began heaving the corpses over the side of the ship while others started to work on the sails and wheel. He also gave an order that the ships behind them be signaled to do the same. He ran back up to take his place next to his mistress at the edge of the gunwale.

"This, Commander," she said excitedly, "is what would have happened to us had the Coven not struck that bargain of over three centuries ago. First, the Necrophagians would have pulled our ships under, and then, once we were dead, feasted upon both us and the Parthalonians."

Kluge looked down into the ocean, fascinated. The many faces beneath the water were moving like a pack of sharks at a feeding frenzy. The bodies were sucked downward when each of the awful mouths opened, and sometimes were cut in half despite the absence of any visible teeth. The ocean water around the ship swirled and churned red with blood, and occasionally a human organ that contained air would rise to the surface, only to be taken again by one of the sickening mouths. At last the red-stained sea calmed, and the faces began to disappear from view. Kluge turned automatically to look at each end of the ship and thankfully saw that the huge gray arms and hands were dissolving.

"Set sail," she commanded him. "The same heading as before. You will find that the weather and winds will once again become favorable." No sooner had she spoken than the temperature rose back to normal and the wind was against their backs again, filling the sails, snapping them open against the bright blue cloudless sky. The armada began to move.

"Now you and every man aboard this ship know not only why it is called the Sea of Whispers, but why it has been uncrossable. You are to swear all of your warriors to silence against penalty of death regarding their knowledge of this since we do not want any information regarding how to cross to be given to Eutracia, especially to the wizards," she told him. She leaned against the gunwale, lost in thought as she spoke as much to herself as to Kluge.

"The Necrophagians made themselves first known to the Coven as we tried to cross the Sea of Whispers some three hundred twenty-seven years ago, after we had been banished from Eutracia by the bastard wizard named Wigg," she said venomously. "They tried to take our small craft, and us with it, to be devoured. The Eaters of the Dead usually demand that their victims first choose among themselves who is to be killed, adding to the game, before the dead body or bodies are thrown overboard. But Failee, although unable to defeat them, was able to beguile them into a bargain."

"The bargain of tenfold times four," Kluge responded knowingly.

"Yes," she said, the sea wind blowing her long, dark hair. "The bargain of tenfold times four. Failee promised them that in return for our safe passage that day, she would promise to pay a bounty of ten times each one of us, or forty, each time the Coven or one of its members desired to cross. Thus, the need for the forty dead slaves. But there were risks. Because of the ongoing fear of this ocean by Parthalonian fishermen, we had always assumed that the Eaters of the Dead were still here, but we could not know for sure whether they would either remember or even honor our bargain. Luckily, they did."

"Who are they?" he asked.

"Failee believes that they were at one time wizards. They had to be, to have that much power. It occurred to us that they may have been condemned by some higher power to this permanent fate of living beneath the sea and feasting upon the dead, but none of us knows for sure. The important thing is that we got across." She glanced up to the destroyed deck and railing at the stern of the ship, and her eyes glazed over as her mind took her back in time to a similar galleon of so long ago. *The ship that the then newly formed Directorate of Wizards used to imprison us, and from which they set us adrift in this awful place,* she thought.

A concern occurred to Kluge that he felt should be addressed, especially after the events of this afternoon.

"I assume, Mistress, that since we are eventually returning to Parthalon by sail, we will encounter this same obstacle again," he said carefully, trying not to overstep his bounds.

"Of course," she replied, looking almost cheerfully into his dark eyes. "But this time our bounty will be different, and will cost nothing of value to us."

"How so?"

"Because we will be bringing with us forty dead Eutracians, of course," she said, laughing. A distinctly predatory look came into her eyes. "Perhaps we will include the bodies of the Directorate of Wizards for good measure," she added, obviously quite pleased with the idea.

"Keep us on this heading all night," she told him as she looked to the west. The sun was starting to hiss its way slowly into the ocean and pour forth a beautiful orange-and-red inferno into the darkening sky. Soon the stars would be out.

"In addition, assign a work detail of your warriors to begin repairing the stern of the ship. I want it set right as soon as possible." Then, in an uncustomary display of feelings, she added, "The damage brings me unpleasant memories that I have no desire to revisit."

"Yes, Mistress," he replied, bowing slightly.

"We have another fifteen days' sail to the coast of Eutracia, and after today nothing can stop us between here and there." She turned on her heel and was gone.

Kluge was left standing alone in the bow of the ship, watching the finishing sunset as he tried to comprehend all that had happened this day.

He was left with the distinct feeling that there would be much more to come.

*K*ing Nicholas took another deep breath of air from the warm Eutracian afternoon as he galloped his stallion down the little rise and toward the bubbling stream. The horses would need some water by now, and this would be a good place to stop and talk to the lead wizard, whom he had invited to join him on his ride. As the king's horse bent down to drink from the stream, Wigg finally caught up to him, also walking his mount into the cool water. For a silent moment they watched their horses drink long and deep, as each man wondered how to begin the conversation that they both knew must come.

Nicholas had purposely chosen to be outside and away from the palace so he could be absolutely sure there were no other ears to hear what would be said. As of late he had come to distrust even his personal conference room in the Redoubt of the Directorate, although if someone had asked him, he probably wouldn't have been able to say exactly why. It was just a feeling, and ever since the appearances of the blood stalker and the screaming harpy, his sixth sense had been growing stronger by the day. It had been almost than four weeks since Wigg had dealt with the harpy, and the abdication ceremony was now only two days away.

Nicholas looked down at the Paragon that had been around his neck for so many years. *Only two more days in my safekeeping,* he thought, *and then it will be passed to Tristan.*

He tied the reins to the saddle and jumped down into the river. Walking a few feet from the horses, he bent down and, with cupped hands, scooped up water to rub across his face and neck. Then, leaving his horse to drink, he walked out of the stream and sat down on the bank beneath a tree. The Lead Wizard followed him.

Wigg gathered his robes around himself as he sat down next to his king. He selected and picked a long blade of green grass that he began to shred carefully between his ancient fingers, as was his custom.

"I assume, Sire, that since neither of us really need the exercise and since there is still so much to do before the ceremony, there is a good reason why we are sitting on the banks of a stream today?" he asked without looking up.

Nicholas pulled absentmindedly on his gray beard as he looked into his friend's eyes. "I want to know, once and for all, whether there is anything of importance that you have not told me," he said simply, still worrying his beard. "The appearances of the stalker and harpy have, as you know, disturbed me greatly. And the abdication ceremony is only two days hence. What aren't you telling me?"

"Did I not deal with each of them in an effective manner?" Wigg asked, knowing full well that the deaths of the creatures was not what the king was referring to.

"Don't fence with me, Lead Wizard," the king said gruffly. "I am trying to ensure the safety of my family, and I am having misgivings about the ceremony."

"We have discussed all of this before, Your Highness," Wigg countered gently. "And the report that the Directorate gave you following the death of the harpy was the best of the conclusions that could be drawn. Are we marching down a path of destruction? Only time will tell. But you know as well as I that under no circumstances can we either postpone or cancel the ceremony. Due to the nature of his birth, Tristan is the very *future* of endowed blood in Eutracia, and nothing can stop that. We have known of his coming since the first translations of the Tome, over three hundred years ago. We just didn't know when." His heart went out to Nicholas. He could only imagine how powerless the king must feel right now, especially in light of the appearances of the stalker and the harpy, two of the Coven's most effective tools during the war of so long ago. *The Chosen One shall come, but he shall be preceded by another,* he thought. *Two days left.*

"I know all of that," Nicholas said almost angrily. "And I have read the Directorate's report a dozen times, telling me that the Coven probably didn't survive the Sea of Whispers those hundreds of years ago and even if they had that there is no conceivable way back, even if those bitches *are* still alive." He ran a hand through his dark gray hair. "But this is my family we're talking about. Can't we at least move the location of the ceremony to somewhere more remote and isolated, where it would be more difficult to find us?"

"The entire Directorate is in complete agreement on this point as well, Sire," Wigg said gently, trying to make him understand. "Moving the ceremony would mean moving the entire Royal Guard for protection, something which does not happen overnight. And besides, there is no safer place in the kingdom than the palace, with its walls, moat, and drawbridge."

Nicholas looked up to see a flock of Eutracian geese flying north, calling to each other noisily as they went. *How I wish it could be that simple,* he thought. *Just to collect up my family and fly them away to safety.*

"Then if it must be in the palace and the date cannot be changed, why not hold the ceremony in the depths of the Redoubt? Wouldn't we all be safer there?" Nicholas asked. "Since we sent forth the consuls to try to help protect the citizenry from the stalkers and harpies, the Redoubt is now deserted. Would it not be perfect for our use?"

Wigg closed his eyes, remembering that the thought processes of those who had not been trained in the craft could be so scattered. He looked compassionately up at his king. "That idea, too, was considered briefly by the Directorate after the consuls left, and then was also quickly rejected," he said simply. He reminded himself that this king had never had to fight a battle, much less a war, and he needed to be patient with him.

"Why?"

"For one thing, the Redoubt was constructed to be a place of learning, not a fort from which to defend one's realm. The Guard would be virtually useless while trying to navigate the many corridors. In addition, none of the populace could be invited, as usual, to the ceremony due to the secret nature of the Redoubt. What would you tell your nation?" He paused, hoping that the king understood. "The Directorate fully understands and appreciates your concern, for while the Paragon is in the chalice we, too, are vulnerable. But despite all that, we can see no way to proceed other than by following tradition."

Nicholas shook his head in frustration.

"Is Tristan still adamant about wearing those same dark clothes of his, instead of the traditional ceremonial robes of his upcoming office?" he asked.

"Yes." Wigg sighed. "And I see little that we can do at this point to change his mind. Considering all of the decisions about his life that have already been made against his will, I suggest we honor his demand.

I daresay he will wear those things even to the ceremony and well beyond, into his reign." He paused and picked another blade of grass. "Besides, in the scheme of things, what does it matter?"

I can't really blame him, the king thought. *My own beginnings were humble. Perhaps it is only fitting that my son serve as king in the clothes of the people.*

Nicholas' mind went back to the early days of his youth, when he had been a smith. A simple smith, at the outskirts of Tammerland, living with his parents. He still had the muscular arms and broad chest of his craft. A smith, just like his father before him, and his father before him. And then had come the day when he had looked up from his anvil and hammer to see the Wizards of the Directorate standing before him, impossibly telling him that he had been selected as king. That the king before him had a barren wife, and that there was no prince to succeed him.

And that on the previous night their king had died in his sleep.

And then he had met and married Morganna, the most beautiful woman he had ever seen, and Tristan and Shailiha had followed. His own parents were gone now, but they had lived to see their son become king, just as he would see his son do the same. *Today he is my son,* he thought, *and two days from now he will be my king.*

Seeming to have made up his mind, Nicholas stood, and Wigg stood with him. The king looked into the wizard's ancient aquamarine eyes in a way that Wigg had never seen before.

"Lead Wizard," he began, "if the worst befalls us, can you at least save my children? They are the ones of the greatest importance." The question was painfully simple, and the wizard thought his heart might break merely at hearing it asked. A blatant tear was tracing its way down Nicholas' cheek, the first of the king's that Wigg had ever seen.

"In truth, Your Majesty, I can only do my best," the old wizard said. "But I love them both like the children I was never blessed to have, and will protect them at the cost of my own life, if necessary."

Nicholas reached out and put his hand on the old one's shoulder for a moment. Then he turned and headed back to his horse, the Lead Wizard of the Directorate following slowly behind him.

Eight

✝

Tristan stood rather uncomfortably on the raised dais, facing what he guessed to be at least four thousand finely dressed people standing expectantly on the black-and-white-checkered floor of the Great Hall. And he knew that there were thousands more waiting outside of the palace, with members of the Royal Guard gently but firmly holding them back. The great room smelled pleasantly of potpourri, fresh-cut flowers, and anticipation.

It was late evening. The many lighted chandeliers and candelabras gave the room a golden, surreal presence, and seemed somehow to accentuate the colorful, ornate clothing of the visitors. Tristan, however, was still in his usual outfit, complete with his quiver of dirks, and he smiled slightly to himself at having made good upon his promise of wearing these garments to the abdication ceremony. When he, his family, and the Directorate of Wizards had first entered the room, he had seen the expected surprise at his appearance. But by now the finger-pointing and hushed tones had virtually all subsided.

He had never known any room of the palace to have ever been so beautiful. Frederick had been right when he said that the rehearsal preparations would be nothing compared to the actual ceremony itself. The thousands of visitors commanded almost every square inch of the floor, along with one hundred or so of the Royal Guard. The musicians and entertainers were huddled together near the orchestra pit. All eyes were glued upon the people on the dais as everyone waited for the ceremony to begin.

The time of my coronation is finally here, he thought solemnly. He glanced down at his clothes. *If it is a king I must be, then it is a king of the common people that I shall strive to remain.*

He looked into the crowd, scanning for faces that he knew, and saw that there were many. There was Natasha, the duchess of Ephyra, and her husband, Duke Baldric. Rather embarrassingly, he came upon the face of Evelyn of the House of Norcross, standing uncomfortably near the dais with her mother and father. She smiled up at him knowingly, and he managed a little smile back. Her father, the prince saw, didn't quite seem to share her great admiration for Tristan just now, despite the fact that the young man was about to become king. Tristan looked away. There were also a great many of his personal friends from the Royal Guard present in the room, as well as the seemingly countless people from throughout the realm whom his father and the Directorate had made sure he met during the course of his youth.

Inwardly, he sighed. It was going to be a long night.

Before him stood the marble altar with the red velvet runner and the gold Chalice of the Abdication Ceremony. Behind him, his mother and father were seated next to each other on their respective thrones. His father was wearing his official robes, the dark-blue velvet with the white ermine collar. As always, the Paragon could be seen hanging from around his neck. His mother looked as beautiful as ever in a white gown with matching elbow gloves. To Tristan's right sat the wizards of the Directorate in their row of thrones, and to his left stood Frederick and Shailiha, arms linked, both beaming with pride.

And just in front of him, between himself and the altar, stood Wigg, Lead Wizard of the Directorate and, therefore, the conductor of the ceremony.

Wigg turned to address the throng, and his voice cut through the air of the Great Hall.

"Ladies and their gentlemen, citizens of Eutracia, members of the Royal Guard, friends," he began earnestly. "It is my great privilege to welcome you to the most prestigious and solemn of all the ceremonies in our realm, the abdication of the reigning monarch and the subsequent coronation of the heir apparent in his place. Tonight history shall be made, just as it has been made in much the same way in each generation since our victory in the Sorceresses' War centuries ago. Part of what we do here tonight is in remembrance of those dark days, and of the many beloved ancestors who were lost in that great struggle. May what we do here this night not only immortalize their contributions, but also contribute to another period of peace and prosperity for our nation."

At this the crowd broke out into a long period of applause, punctuated by encouraging shouts and friendly waves of admiration. Tristan caught Evelyn's admiring gaze, and turned his attention back to the Lead Wizard.

"This marks the end of the reign of King Nicholas the First, and the beginning of the reign of his son, the heir apparent, King Tristan the First of Eutracia."

The crowd erupted into wild cheering, waving and calling out the prince's name, as Tristan moved up to stand beside Wigg. He could also hear shouts of "Long live the king!" The noise was deafening.

They're talking about me, he thought. *I have never heard anyone call me "king" before. I can't believe this is happening, even though I know it is. It's like a dream.*

Wigg lifted one of two beautiful golden amphorae that were sitting on the altar next to the Chalice of the Abdication Ceremony. He raised the amphora high.

"In this vessel I hold the sacred water," he said simply, and the crowd hushed. The fascination in their eyes reminded Tristan that no one outside of the Directorate and the royal family had any knowledge whatsoever of the water, or of the Caves from which it had come. As Wigg slowly poured it into the chalice, the strange and wonderful fluid tumbled and undulated with a life of its own, just the way it had surrounded Tristan's body in the Caves that day thirty days ago. At the sight of the water, his blood surged with desire for the craft, and he stood beside Wigg even more transfixed than the spectators.

Wigg solemnly turned to King Nicholas.

"Your Highness," he said gently, in an almost fatherly tone, "it is time for the Paragon."

Nicholas looked down at the shimmering, bloodred stone that had been around his neck continuously for more than thirty years. He then looked to his wife Morganna, the love of his life. With a long sigh that was part sadness and part determination, he lifted the stone and the gold chain from around his neck. Tristan noticed that just as soon as the stone had left his father's person it began to lose some of its luster; it no longer caught and refracted the light as he was so used to seeing it do. Wigg took the stone gently in his hands and held it before the crowd.

The Lead Wizard lifted the chain and the stone high into the air, and immediately the room went completely silent.

"The Paragon, ladies and gentlemen," he began. "That which gave us the courage and the hope to prevail in the Sorceresses' War, and which to this day grants the Directorate its power to help our sovereign rule with wisdom and compassion for all of our people."

Tristan watched, mesmerized, as the wizard poured approximately half the water from the first amphora into the second one. Wigg placed the stone into the vessel he was still holding aloft, then set the amphora back on the table beside its mate. Almost immediately the prince thought he could see the water around the stone begin to lose its color as the stone took on an even deeper red and began once again to collect the light of the room. As the seconds passed, a shaft of light slowly rose from the stone, moving higher and higher into the room until it touched and perfectly encircled the stained-glass domed ceiling and bathed it in a beautiful bloodred glow.

It was astounding.

Tristan knew what was coming next. Wigg would turn to him and begin reciting, line by line, the succession oath. Then would follow a period of approximately two hours while the Paragon remained in the water and readied itself for its new host. It was during this time that the royal family and the Directorate usually mingled with the crowd and made their personal greetings. And then, when the Lead Wizard had ascertained that the stone was ready, the royal entourage would reclaim the dais, and Wigg would place the Paragon around Tristan's neck and proclaim him king, the process complete. Afterward, the dancing and feasting would begin, and run on unfettered until dawn.

Tristan looked down briefly at the gold medallion that already hung around his neck—the medallion that his mother had given him, the one with the broadsword and lion engraved upon it. Soon the Paragon would be lying next to it, both of them close to his heart.

Wigg turned directly to face him, and Tristan decided to look out once again at the crowd of people for the last time as their prince. He again saw Evelyn, beaming proudly, and also several of his friends from the Guard who were looking up at him in a way that he had never seen before. They were no longer seeing him as the prince with whom they had enjoyed training in the yards, he realized. They were looking at him as their king.

Wigg, his back still to the crowd, suddenly but deliberately cleared his throat. Tristan dutifully turned to the old wizard, and he thought he could see the beginnings of tears forming in the famous aquamarine eyes. But then the hint of moisture was gone, and the wizard began Tristan's vows.

"True peace of mind comes only when my heart and actions are aligned with true principles and values," Wigg said, waiting for Tristan's identical reply. In the space between lines, the Great Hall was as silent as a tomb.

"True peace of mind comes only when my heart and actions are aligned with true principles and values," Tristan repeated.

"I shall forsake not, to the loss of all material things, my honor and integrity," Wigg said.

"I shall forsake not, to the loss of all material things, my honor and integrity."

"I shall protect the Paragon above all else . . . I shall protect the Paragon above all else . . . I shall protect the Paragon above all else . . ."

Just as the executioner's ax falls, just as the horse trips and the rider knows he is going down, just as the archer's fingers loose the arrow— whenever the portent of disaster arrives and the entire world begins to spin in a terrifying kind of slow motion, the words that one hears at that precise moment can go on almost forever in one's head, a sickening, un- forgettable prelude to disaster.

Tristan did not know it, but his world was about to be changed forever.

He would remember later that the first signs of trouble had been the sounds of breaking glass, but as he looked about the great room, he could find no disturbance. And then the multicolored shards began to rain down upon the crowd, slicing into faces and scalps as they fell. Some of the women began to scream, and Tristan saw Wigg turn around toward the crowd as if in a dream.

It was then that the prince lifted his eyes to the shattered domed ceiling of stained glass, and his mouth dropped open.

What he was seeing was unimaginable.

He watched the first one drop—no, *fly*—to the floor of the Great Hall, its dark, leathery wings snapping shut as it drew a great, curved sword from its scabbard and looked about the room with hate brimming in its eyes.

The creature stood motionless for a moment and then, jumping up onto the dais in one great leap, swung its sword with a speed Tristan had never seen before, cutting Frederick's head from his shoulders in one swipe. Frederick's severed head rolled across the dais and fell off the end, landing on the marble floor of the hall as his body crumpled into death. Shailiha screamed, the blood from her husband's wounds splat- tered down over her maternity gown. Already the thing had jumped to the floor of the Great Hall and begun wildly butchering the populace at random.

Tristan shoved Wigg aside, his hand automatically reaching for one of his knives, the blade spinning through the air even before he realized he had thrown it. The knife drove deeply into the back of the thing's head right below the shiny, winged helmet just as the creature was about to try to cut down one of the Guard. The creature fell forward, dead.

Tristan's first response was to run to his sister. He held her tightly in his arms as she shuddered and screamed in terror. By the time he turned back to the Great Hall the sight that greeted his eyes turned his insides to ice water.

Hundreds of the awful things were descending into the room and attacking at will. Several leapt up on the dais and ran toward the wizards. Tristan threw another dirk just as one of the monsters was about to swing at Slike with his awful, curved sword, and the knife plunged headlong into the thing's left eye. It screamed in pain and fell off the dais. But there were just too many of them—they seemed to outnumber the Royal Guard by at least ten to one. For every one of the winged attackers that went down, five or six of the Guard died with it and even more of the monsters were still pouring in through the gaping rent in the ceiling.

Tristan suddenly felt hands upon him from the rear. He turned quickly to kill another of the awful creatures, but found himself facing Wigg. The old one shouted at the top of his lungs into Tristan's face, his aquamarine eyes almost insane with the need to try to make the prince understand.

"Tristan! You and Shailiha *must* stay near me here at the altar! For the sake of everything you value and love, you both *must* stay by my side!"

Tristan tore his gaze away from the wizard long enough to see several of the winged barbarians starting to hack savagely into the row of the wizards of the Directorate, cutting them to pieces. First he saw Killius go down, his head severed from his body; then Egloff—the timid, likable scholar of the Tome—stood to resist the monster that had him by the robes, the point of its sword up against his throat. But before the prince could free himself from Wigg's powerful grip, the invader moved the handle of the sword somehow, and suddenly the point of the blade shot up and through the wizard's head and exited violently through the top of his skull, spraying bone and brain matter across the wall.

Tristan turned, his own eyes now bordering on insanity, and looked pleadingly at Wigg. The old one still stood where he was, screaming, beseeching the prince and his sister to come and stand near him once again at the altar. *The wizards,* Tristan raged silently. *Why aren't they using their powers to defend us?* And then the answer came to him as clearly as if Wigg had just spoken it. *The Paragon. The stone is in the water, and their powers have been taken away.*

Without thinking, Tristan started to reach into the chalice and remove the stone, assuming that if he did, the remaining wizards' powers would return and help them. But as soon as he reached for it he felt Wigg's stronger hands pulling him away, screaming something at him about how he must leave the stone where it was, and bring his sister to stand with him near the altar. Tristan looked into the old one's eyes with a mixture of frustration and horror. *Is he mad? Can't he see we're being butchered? Why isn't he at least trying to help us?*

Violently tearing himself away from Wigg for the second time, he turned to see the sickening fates of three more of the wizards. Slike was already dead, lying in a pool of his own blood at the foot of his throne. A horrible-looking type of silver wheel with teeth all along its edge was embedded in the side of his skull. Tretiak, the second most powerful of the Directorate, lay in a gaunt posture of death, half of his robed body off the edge of the dais, a dagger deep in his chest. Maaddar was a few feet from his throne, bravely trying to stand before the royal family as several more of the hideous killers began to move quickly toward them. Tristan's arm again took to his knives, three fast times in a row, and several of the monstrous things died in their tracks. But before the prince could do anything else, a shiny, silver disk careened through the air, narrowly missing his head. It slammed into the side of Maaddar's neck, cutting the carotid artery, and blood began to pump violently from the wound. Tristan watched in shock as the wheel kept on impossibly flying as if it had never struck the poor wizard, unbelievably arcing around to return to one of the attackers standing on the hall floor. The winged butcher in the shiny silver helmet plucked the bloody wheel out of the air as if it were second nature and turned to look directly at the prince.

And then the monster laughed at him.

Something in Tristan snapped. A combination of hate, determination, and fear flooded through him, and he screamed in rage at the grotesque thing that stood laughing before him.

The creature drew his sword and, with his free hand, beckoned Tristan to come to him.

Tristan went for his knives, not sure how many he had left, but knowing in his heart that he would keep throwing until they were either gone or he was dead. His arm moved like lightning as, one after the other, the silver dirks flew through the air toward the killer.

But the winged monster was too fast, and Tristan watched in abject horror as the winged, musclebound freak easily used his curved sword to deflect each of the knives as they came at him.

Again he laughed at the prince, and Tristan flew toward the edge of the dais in a rage.

Everything else had been blotted from his mind, even his family's safety and the presence of Wigg still standing at the altar, as he jumped from the dais and picked up a discarded Royal Guard broadsword, its handle covered in the blood of its owner. All he could see before him was the thing that had killed his friends, and even if he died trying, he would taste yet more blood this day.

Screaming insanely, he charged with his bloody sword held high and slashed with all of his strength at the taller, heavier monstrosity. But his opponent easily parried his blow, sending the prince flying. Tristan again attacked, this time swiping at both feet to cut the invader's legs from beneath him. But with surprising agility the thing jumped into the air, escaping Tristan's swing completely, and laughed yet again.

The prince backed off, watching the winged monster as the two of them circled each other in a centuries-old dance of death. Suddenly the sickening image of Frederick's head rolling off the dais and the dirk he had thrown at his brother-in-law's attacker tore through his mind. *Even if I die at this moment, at least I avenged Frederick.*

With every last ounce of his strength, Tristan lunged, sword slashing. But the creature simply stepped to the side and scooped him up in a chokehold from behind, and then applied a torturous elbow lock to the prince's sword arm.

He whispered directly into the prince's ear, with a voice that was both terrifying and taunting at the same time.

"You're no match for me, boy," the low, commanding voice said. "I am not supposed to kill you yet, as the mistress has changed my orders slightly. But she didn't say anything about not abusing you, and I have personal reasons for wanting to do so. Drop the weapon, or I shall see to it that your sword arm is broken slowly, and in more than one place."

Tristan was on his toes in indescribable pain, held in a vise lock from behind, the arm around his throat so tight that he could scarcely breathe. He knew that in a moment either his arm would break or his elbow would dislocate. He turned his head slightly and summoned his remaining breath.

"No!" he snarled through the unrelenting pain. "Not before I see your guts on the palace floor!"

Instead of the sound of his arm breaking, the sickening, diseased laugh once more drifted to his ears.

"Your supposedly endowed blood will not help you now, you worthless whelp. Besides, that's no way for a *king* to talk, do you think?" it said, mocking him.

Then, suddenly, he was spun around to face the thing and was struck in the face with such force that he almost went unconscious. He skidded to the floor a few feet away, landing in one of the many puddles of blood that had collected almost everywhere upon the marble floor. *The blood of my people,* he heard his mind whisper. *Don't black out. If you black out now you will never wake up again.* He staggered to one knee to face the monster as best he could, but before he knew it his attacker was upon him, this time striking him in the windpipe, bending him over in exquisite pain. Both his hands immediately went to his throat as he desperately tried to refill his lungs with air. He was choking to death, and he knew it.

The faceless beast in the shiny winged helmet reached down and took a handful of the prince's dark hair, wrenching Tristan's head violently up and back. Air rushed into Tristan's lungs.

"Don't worry, *Prince* Galland," the thing said menacingly, virtually spitting the words out into Tristan's face. "I won't allow you to choke to death. That would be far too easy. No, you will not die just now, but before this night is over you will beg me for death, and I will oblige you."

With unbelievable strength the attacker lifted Tristan by his throat with one arm, dragged him back to the dais on his toes, and literally threw him upon it as if he were a rag doll. Tristan landed hard on one side of his face, colliding into the uneven row of wizards' chairs as he fought to regain his breath and take stock of his surroundings.

Coughing and gasping, he managed to get up on all fours and look up to where his family had been standing before he had jumped down onto the floor of the hall.

They were alive. *Thank the Afterlife, they're still alive.*

King Nicholas was holding Morganna in his arms and speaking softly to her, apparently trying to give her hope. Wigg was standing next to them, a look of total loss upon his face such as Tristan had never before seen on any human being in his life.

And then he saw his sister.

Shailiha sat at her parents' feet in her now blood-soaked gown, pathetically holding the headless corpse of her husband, crying and talking to the dead body as if it could talk back. *She's lost her mind,* he thought.

Upon seeing Tristan back on the dais Nicholas quickly reached out to him, but one of the invaders backhanded him across the face almost immediately. The king fell backward, crashing down into his throne. Morganna, crying, reached down to help him up.

As his vision cleared and his senses slowly returned, Tristan could see that the royal family was no longer being attacked. Instead, a ring of the winged soldiers had formed around them, holding them in place and watching their every move. Suddenly, strong hands gripped him from behind, wrenched him to his feet, and roughly threw him back to the floor, inside the circle with his family.

Hearing screaming again, he turned his head to look out over the Great Hall.

The scene before his eyes made him start to vomit, and he put his head to the floor, forced just to let it happen.

Even with his head down, he could tell that the battle inside the hall itself was over, but he could hear fierce fighting going on through the open windows. Apparently there were more of the awful things outside the palace, and they were attacking the Royal Guard. Still on all fours, he looked down to the floor of the dais in shame. If the members of the Guard outside of the palace did no better than their comrades in this room, then all was lost. Indeed, even as he thought the words, it seemed that the sounds from around the windows were lessening already.

But he knew it was the scene in the hall itself that would be the most horrifying. He slowly stood and raised his face to look at it—to look at what they had done to his countrymen.

Men, women, and children had been slaughtered with no quarter. They lay everywhere in giant, spreading, dark-red pools of their own blood. Severed arms and legs were scattered crazily at random, as were the heads of many. He could see some of the strange silver wheels still protruding grotesquely from a number of them.

The methodical, winged killers were walking quietly among the wounded, kicking them and poking them harshly with their daggers. If any of the supposed dead moved or cried out, they were killed on the spot with the strange, curved swords.

But many of the visitors were still alive and unhurt, crying and screaming as the monsters walked in their midst, finishing off the wounded. Tristan estimated that about half of the civilians had been killed, along with every single member of the Royal Guard. The many shiny breastplates carrying the broadsword and lion were covered in blood.

They died well, he thought.

The citizens who remained alive had been forced to their knees, and now that the killing of the wounded was beginning to subside, some of the creatures had begun striking and abusing the survivors in order to make them quiet.

Finally, after at least an hour, the Great Hall once again became still, the many surviving citizens who had had the bad fortune to attend the ceremony still quietly on their knees in a small sea of Eutracian blood.

Instinctively, he thought to look for Evelyn and her parents, but finding any one person or persons in the bloody throng seemed impossible. After a few minutes of looking in the general area in which he had last seen them, he finally spotted Evelyn's blond hair.

She was lying in a pool of blood on the floor, her throat cut, her eyes frozen open and staring outward as if she were still gazing at him, even in death. Her parents lay nearby. Her father had been butchered with a sword, and her mother's head was all but off her shoulders and hanging down over her back, one of the horrible silver wheels embedded in the side of her neck.

Tristan looked away, back to the winged monstrosity that he had fought with—and lost.

Tristan's attacker seemed to be in charge, he noticed. The creature walked throughout the hall with the others, giving orders and occasionally killing one of the wounded himself. Then, as Tristan watched, the monster jumped on the dais with ease and pushed its way through the circle to stand before Tristan, Wigg, and the rest of the royal family.

Slowly reaching up, it removed the winged helmet and looked directly into Tristan's eyes.

It was a face the prince knew he would never forget: unkempt, shoulder-length black-and-gray hair; dark goatee; long, white scar; and impossibly dark, piercing eyes. The creatures seemed to be human, despite their wings and their overall advantage in size. The one who stood looking down into the prince's eyes with contempt was easily seven feet tall.

I will kill this creature one day, Tristan swore silently. *In the name of everything that I am, and all that I hold dear, I will kill him.*

The monster's gaze pulled back to take in the rest of the family and the wizard, and finally he spoke. "Sit down," he ordered, pointing to the row of bloody wizards' chairs that sadly were now empty. "First the wizard, then the prince, the king, the queen, and the princess, in that order," he said simply.

Looking around briefly at each other, they did as they were told. Tristan found himself seated between Wigg on his left, and his father on his right.

"My name is Kluge," the creature said, "and I am the commander of the Minions of Day and Night, the troops who have smashed your overrated Royal Guard. From now on your nation, and everything in it, belongs to someone else." The one called Kluge turned and walked a couple of paces to Nicholas' throne, which had been tipped over on its side in the melee. Putting one of his boots atop the nearest of the throne legs, he pushed down on it with his foot and disrespectfully righted the throne in one sudden, single movement. He confidently dropped himself down into it at an angle, his back against one of the arms and one of his long legs up and over the other.

He turned to address the troops that were still encircling the family. "You may remove your helmets," he said to them, "and rejoin your comrades on the floor of the hall. They may remove their helmets, as well. Please have patience. You will be able to begin taking your pleasures soon enough. Have someone send for Traax. And someone bring me something to eat." He smiled wickedly into the prince's face. "All of this killing has made me hungry."

As a group they all smartly knocked the heels of their boots together and left the dais. Tristan saw one of them go outside, presumably to fetch the warrior named Traax, as another of them walked to the great banquet table and began to tear the leg off one of the roasted turkeys. He returned to his commander with it quickly, like a dog that had been sent off to play fetch.

Kluge looked curiously at the food, smelled it discerningly, and then took a huge bite, chewing with his mouth open. He looked at Nicholas. "We do not have this where I come from," he said. Some juices ran down into his goatee. "I do believe I am going to enjoy myself here in your little kingdom." He gave a leering look up and down Queen Morganna's face and body as he continued to assault the turkey leg. "Yes, I shall enjoy *all* of the pleasures of your land," he added, leaving little to the imagination.

Tristan's reaction was immediate. He lunged out of his chair and went for Kluge's throat with both hands, but with a single swipe of his free arm the commander sent him sprawling backward to the floor, the prince's left cheek cut badly from the sharp points mounted on the back of the black leather gauntlets. Kluge threw the food to the floor and again picked Tristan up by the throat, this time tossing him back to the throne that he had occupied.

Nicholas stood up to face the enemy. "Why are you here?" he demanded in frustration. "What do you want?"

But the voice that answered did not come from Kluge. It was a woman's voice, smooth and silky, and it came from somewhere above them.

"The answer to that is really quite simple," the satiny voice said. "We want everything."

Tristan regained his composure long enough to look up to the broken stained-glass ceiling. What he saw would stay in his memories for the rest of his life.

Cradled in the outstretched arms of yet another of the winged warriors, her arms about his muscular neck, she was perhaps the most beautiful woman he had ever seen. Together they continued to descend through the huge break in the stained-glass ceiling. The flying creature then changed course, flying her twice about the boundaries of the Great Hall, allowing her to survey the ghastly scene below. Finally, at her command, the Minion warrior flew her to the dais, where he set her down as lightly as a feather. The silk of her black gown gently billowed up and around her, exposing first one milky-white thigh and then the other.

As she came even closer, Tristan could see that there was a symbol embroidered upon her gown. It appeared to be a five-pointed star, located over her left breast, and had been expertly worked in the palest of gold thread. The monster called Kluge went down on bended knee before her.

"Mistress, I live to serve," he said quietly.

"You may rise," the woman said.

Tristan now had the opportunity to look directly into her face, and despite the severity of the circumstances, what he saw almost took his breath away. Her dark, exotic, almond-shaped eyes seemed to give silent commands all of their own, and whenever the full, inviting red lips parted they revealed perfect, white teeth. He had never seen a woman's hair this long, or with such a luminous texture. It hung down her back like strands of the best black silk, ending just above her waist.

Tristan looked briefly to his left, at Wigg. The old one had yet to speak since their capture, and the prince was hoping for a word of reassurance. But Wigg was staring at the woman, his eyes hard and full of hate, his lips pulled back slightly in a kind of silent, vicious snarl.

He knows her, Tristan thought.

Wasting no time, she walked straight to the altar. As she picked up the chalice containing the Paragon and looked inside, her face radiated pure joy. Tristan could see Wigg stiffen. She reached slowly, almost lovingly into the chalice and withdrew the Paragon. For several moments she examined it as the the water of the Caves dripped onto the floor of the dais, twinkling impressively in the light of the room. And then, carefully placing the gold chain over her head, she lowered the stone into place around her neck.

For some inexplicable reason, wearing the stone was like a tonic to her. She smiled joyously, stretching her long, slender arms to the ceiling, arching her back like a cat. Taking a long, deep, single breath, she let it out in an almost sexual expression of relief.

She then immediately walked to where Wigg was sitting. Without speaking, she backhanded the old one with impossible speed. Wigg's head recoiled from the blow, and the wizard almost fell out of the throne. She reached down with one hand to grip his face and stretch his neck upward, forcing his eyes to meet hers.

"Wigg," she said almost gently, "Lead Wizard of the so-called Directorate of Wizards. Yes, it is I, Succiu. I'm sure you recognize me. After all, like you, I have not aged a single day in over three hundred years." She smiled. "We have returned, Old One. And now we have the stone—and even the unused Cave water in the other amphora. Everything that you once had is now ours. And this time we will not fail."

She cocked her head and looked pityingly at him. "Your powers have, of course, returned, just as mine have. That is to be expected. But I know you will not try anything foolish. Even *you* cannot believe you could defeat both me and the entire army I command. I suggest you simply cooperate for the time being, and listen to what I have to say. If you do not, it will only go worse for you and the prince."

Wigg strained to pull back, but still did not speak.

"You have no doubt noticed that all of the other wizards are dead." She smiled with great self-satisfaction as she continued to hold his face clamped in her hand, her eyes locked upon his. "But I left you and the royal family alive for a little bit longer, so that you might bear witness to what will be done here tonight."

She pushed his face back with what appeared to Tristan to be terrific force, and the wizard's head and neck smashed against the high-backed throne. Arms akimbo, head tilted slightly to one side, she stood as if she were trying to make up her mind about something.

"Yes, why not," she said finally. "You are wondering how it was that you could not detect my endowed blood before this, are you not?" she asked coyly. Tristan could see that this was a woman who enjoyed playing a deadly game of cat and mouse. "Just think," she continued nastily, "if you had been more observant, you might have been able to prevent all of this." She gloated as she waved her hands toward all of the dead bodies, terrified citizens, and thousands of winged warriors that filled the room before them. She pursed her lips in mock concern. "I know that *I* certainly wouldn't want any such personal shortcomings to prey upon my conscience for all of eternity. But then again, I wouldn't worry too much about it if I were you, because you really aren't going to live very much longer."

She took a step backward, running the index finger of one hand slowly across her lower lip. "So many questions, aren't there, Lead Wizard?" she said. "How did we get across the Sea of Whispers? How have we survived all of these years, and how is it that we have made the trip back? But the riddle you must be most curious about is no doubt the one concerning your own inferior abilities, and how it was that you could not detect my presence. Yes, that must be the question that most haunts you now. Very well, then. I shall show you."

She turned to Kluge. "Tell her that she may join us," she ordered.

Kluge walked across the length of the dais and disappeared briefly into the anteroom that was just off to one side. Momentarily he returned, with someone following behind him. Tristan looked up to see Natasha, the duchess of Ephyra, following him. As she walked over and stood shoulder to shoulder with the one who called herself Succiu, he detected in her a more commanding presence than he had ever seen before.

Then, suddenly, he understood. *Natasha is one of them,* he realized, the importance of it pounding through his brain. *She always has been.*

"That's right," Succiu said to Wigg. "She has been one of us since she was five, and she is now more than three centuries old, almost as old as you are. I believe you know her personally. She looks good for her age, don't you think? But there is more. She is a Visage Caster, which has allowed her to do her work here in secret while also disguising female endowed blood." She smiled again, exposing the beautiful teeth to the hushed room. "While you and the other wizards of the Directorate so pompously supposed that you could forever rule Eutracia, my Sister who now stands next to me after all of this time was making sure that this day of days would succeed, and succeed it has." She let out a calculated, demeaning laugh before continuing.

"But there is more, Old One," she said, gloating, as she continued to show her centuries-old prize off to him. "Natasha has even more secrets than that." She placed her face less than an inch away from the wizard's. "She is also that same little girl who was the first to decipher and read the Tome of the Paragon," she whispered triumphantly to him.

Tristan couldn't hear her words, but he saw that Wigg's eyes had gone wide, and tears had began to run down the old cheeks.

"You now more fully understand the implications of all of this, do you not?" she asked him smugly. "This means that the daughter of your beloved Faegan, probably the most powerful of all of you, was the one who helped the Coven in their cause." She once again reached down and gripped his face. "Yes, you ignorant old man—Faegan, the one you all revered so much, the one who was originally to have become Lead Wizard. I'm sure you must remember him," she said sarcastically. "You all assumed he died in the wars somehow, and you and the Directorate spent a great deal of time memorializing him, I believe. I am told that there is even one of your ridiculous marble monuments to him somewhere in the countryside, presumably where you thought he had met his untimely death."

She let go of his face, and Wigg's chin slumped down onto his chest. Not from pain, Tristan knew, but rather from defeat. It was the first time in his life he had ever seen the old one in such a state.

"There is just one more thing I will permit you to know before you die today, Lead Wizard," she said in a hushed tone. Tristan could barely hear her. "You wasted our time and energy in erecting a memorial to Faegan. Because he lives—in Shadowood, with his precious gnomes." She smiled wickedly. "And we've seen to it that he isn't quite the man he used to be."

Tristan saw a look of pure shock spread across Wigg's face, followed immediately by a calmer aspect of understanding. Tristan had no idea who Faegan was, but he could see the old one nod slightly, as if some long-standing question had been resolved in his mind. Wigg lifted his face back to Succiu and then to Natasha before he finally spoke.

"You black-hearted whores," he said quietly. "You used him, didn't you? He was the finest and the strongest of all of us, and besides his friendship with us there was only one thing in the world he cared about above all else: his daughter. So you took her and bent her to your will, and used his grief to keep a wizard of important power under your control." He gazed at Natasha. "The daughter of Faegan," he said sadly. "You have no idea what you have done."

"Very astute of you, Lead Wizard," Succiu said sarcastically, "but it is really much more complicated than that. However, I shall not bore you with all of the details, since you have so little time left and there is still so much to do this night."

She bent down one more time and looked deeply into his eyes. "Is this day tragic irony, or poetic justice?" she asked coyly. "You tell me."

Succiu turned with Natasha in tow and moved to face Tristan where he sat in the wizard's throne that had once belonged to Slike.

"Beautiful, isn't he?" Natasha commented. "And apparently so strong in spirit. Given the quality of his blood, I'm sure he could easily please my mistress if she is so disposed this evening. I had hoped that we could keep him alive for a little while, in order to indulge ourselves."

Had Succiu been looking at Kluge's face, she would have seen the jealousy starting to build there at the mention of Natasha's suggestion. The second mistress bent down slightly, touched one of her fingers to the blood on the side of Tristan's face, closed her eyes, and put the tip of that finger to her tongue.

"Such exquisite blood, my sweet prince," she said, her eyes still closed as if she were in the midst of some unknown rapture. "I have never known any like it. But then again, you wouldn't know about that, would you? There is still so much about you that remains unsaid, that now you shall never know."

She turned to Natasha. "Would I normally be predisposed to his services? Oh, yes, my dear, more than you know. But the quality of his blood makes him a mortal threat to us, and business before pleasure. Or, in this case, the lack of pleasure." She once again looked into the prince's eyes, and despite the situation he found it difficult not to be captivated by her.

Her right hand came down and began to trace circles on his groin. "A pity you must die this day before I could have experienced some of your many purported talents," she said almost sadly. Finally she turned to Kluge. "Leave the wizard and the prince for last, so that they may witness what is to become of their beloved but so fatally flawed realm this night," she said casually.

"Yes, Mistress," Kluge responded.

They will die, too, Tristan told himself, trying to hold back his rage. *No matter what becomes of me or what I must go through to do it, these two women shall die at my hands.*

The two sorceresses now stepped before the king and queen.

"Pathetic-looking specimens, aren't they?" Succiu said sarcastically, looking more intensely at the queen than at the king. "Hard to believe, isn't it, that these two common peasants, mere pretenders to the throne and the craft, could have collectively sired twins of such magnificent blood? But there you are." She bent down and looked into Nicholas' eyes. "I suppose I should thank you for siring them for our use." She smiled her wicked smile. "But I won't." She slapped Nicholas hard in the face, and Morganna's hand moved to cover his in comfort. Succiu looked at the queen. "Don't worry about what happens to any of them, my dear," she said almost kindly. She looked out to the waiting troops in the Great Hall. "By the time they are done with you, you will be past the point of caring about anything, anyway." She turned to her commander. "Do what you like with them. They are of no importance to us. Just make sure that in the end they are both dead."

She moved to stand in front of Shailiha, and Tristan saw a strange look come over both of the sorceresses' faces. They approached his sobbing sister quietly, almost reverently. And then they did the unimaginable.

They both bowed to her.

Succiu took one of Shailiha's hands in hers and caressed it gently. Shailiha pulled back, not out of revulsion or fear but rather in a kind of stark, unknowing confusion.

She's delusional, Tristan thought. *One more reason to kill them all.*

Succiu looked at Kluge and, without speaking, gestured to him to remove Frederick's body from the princess' feet and place it out of sight. When he obeyed, Shailiha howled painfully, reaching in vain for the departing headless corpse and then hugging her abdomen, swollen with child. Succiu looked down into her eyes, and Shailiha stilled. The second mistress then asked, "Are you all right, my Sister?"

The words hit Tristan like a thunderbolt. *Her Sister? What in the name of the Afterlife is she talking about?*

"Are you injured in any way?" Succiu asked gently. Shailiha, hazel eyes wide open but unseeing, managed to shake her head no. "Strange as it may seem to you now, we three have a great deal in common," the sorceress told her. "You, my Sister, are one of the reasons we have come."

Succiu gave an almost imperceptible nod to Kluge, who summoned several of his troops. They mounted the dais and put their helmets on. Succiu turned to address them directly.

"Escort her to the prearranged area as quickly as possible," she ordered sternly. "Take as many additional of you as you feel necessary to protect her safety. There still may be stragglers of the Royal Guard in the countryside." Her eyes lowered dangerously. "If any harm or abuse comes to this one in any way, I shall personally kill the warriors responsible."

Tristan reacted immediately, jumping up from his chair and trying desperately to reach his sister. But Kluge was suddenly in front of him, one hand reaching behind to grip the long hair at the back of Tristan's neck, the other holding a dagger at the prince's throat.

"You continue to try my patience, boy," he said venomously. "You have just guaranteed yourself and your wizard friend very slow deaths." With only the hand that gripped the prince's hair, he picked Tristan up and threw him the length of the dais, sending him crashing into the throne he had just left and knocking it sideways to the ground.

Tristan immediately felt strong hands on him, holding him down, and found himself looking into Wigg's face. "Stay close to me," the old one whispered. "It is the only possible way."

Tristan quickly looked back to Shailiha. Several of the troops were already escorting her into the anteroom, and then she was gone. He hung his head and let out a soft, animal-like moan.

Another of the Minion warriors jumped up on the dais and faced Kluge with a click of his heels. "You called for me, Lord?" he asked.

"Yes, Traax," Kluge said. "How goes the struggle on the outside?"

The one called Traax smiled broadly, obviously enjoying himself. "What struggle?" he replied sarcastically. "They were simply no match for us. Virtually all of the Guard has been killed, and I hope by dawn to have the heads of any of those who have managed to remain alive thus far. You may consider the situation completely under control." He clicked his heels once again and stepped back.

"You may now order the signal fires to be lighted," Succiu said to Kluge. "Our captains will surely want to join in the spoils of war. Remember your orders, Commander. As the First Mistress has said, if it moves, kill it. You have only two days in which to indulge yourselves. After that, anyone not with us I will gladly leave behind in this miserable place." She turned with curiosity to Natasha. "By the way," she asked coyly, "what has become of your useless husband of unendowed blood? I don't happen to see him about anywhere." Her tone made clear that she already knew his fate.

"Poor old Baldric?" Natasha gave a look of smug, false concern.

"Oh, he somehow was pushed up against a dreggan just as its point was released," she replied, looking at one of her nails.

Kluge removed his dreggan from its scabbard and pointed it at Tristan's face. "Do you mean like this?" he asked. He touched the hilt of the sword with his thumb, and the point of the blade shot viciously forward at least a foot, stopping less than an inch from the prince's right eye.

Tristan didn't flinch. Part of him was past caring. *If they want to kill me, they can,* he thought. *But somehow I will find a way to take this bastard with me.*

Kluge looked to King Nicholas. "Your Highness," he said, "I believe you shall be first." He motioned with his sword to two of the Minion warriors, who immediately went to the king and wrenched him from his throne. They hauled him to the altar of the Paragon and pinned his shoulders and head down upon it, forcing him to bend over at the waist. With an arm held painfully down on either side of the altar, Nicholas could barely turn his head to face Tristan and Wigg, but somehow he managed. He looked helplessly into the eyes of the Lead Wizard.

Then Kluge did an amazing thing. He handed Tristan his dreggan. As he did so, several of the other Minion warriors drew their swords and moved closer to the prince.

"Feel what a real sword is like, my prince," the commander said. "This is not one of your Eutracian broadsword toys."

Tristan took the sword from him, speechless. It was the heaviest, yet most finely balanced weapon he had ever held. *Is he insane?* Tristan thought. *He must know I will try to kill him with it, no matter what happens to me.* The sword seemed massive in his hands, its power overwhelming. But then he realized that whatever he tried, Succiu could certainly put an end to it almost before it had begun.

He stood there, not knowing what to do, the breath coming out of his lungs in fast, ragged anticipation of whatever was to happen next. His answer was quick in coming.

"I shall grant you a choice," Kluge said. "You may either behead the king right now, with one, swift, merciful swing, or you may stand aside and watch me take him apart slowly, piece by piece." The monster was clearly enjoying every word. "The choice is yours."

Tristan looked at Kluge dumbly, unthinking, unknowing. *Surely even he can't mean it!* But the reality of the situation came over him as he turned to look at the old wizard. Wigg lowered his eyes and then slowly brought them back to his king. Tristan also looked at his father, helpless upon the altar. *He would have me kill my own father.* His thoughts rushed through his mind like a torrent of grief. *Upon the altar of the Paragon.*

He looked at the awful killer that stood before him, the leader of the monsters that had butchered his people.

"No," he said simply. He had no other words.

Kluge reached out and grabbed him violently by the front of his leather vest, raising him up off the floor and to his face like some kind of dangling children's toy. Tristan, overcome with the horror of the moment, simply let it happen, the dreggan hanging loosely at his side.

"I don't think you understand, Your Highness," the murderer said, smiling. Tristan could both feel and smell the awful breath. Even the monster's breath smelled like death.

"Either you kill him now, or I shall do it myself, one inch at a time. While you, the wizard, and the queen all watch." He pulled Tristan even closer. "And it will go on for a very, very long time. Choose!" He let go, and Tristan fell hard to the floor on his knees. Getting awkwardly to his feet, the prince turned his face to his mother, silently pleading with her for a sign. But Morganna looked back at him helplessly, her eyes lost in abject fear.

While the prince was looking to his mother, Nicholas focused his gaze on Wigg. For a moment the old wizard made no expression, as if he were lost in time. But then, slowly, he closed his eyes and nodded to his king, fresh tears running down his weathered cheeks.

He wasn't simply answering the king's question. He was also saying good-bye.

Nicholas understood. "My son," he said gently.

Tristan faced his father, the dreggan still in his shaking hand.

"You must do it, Tristan," Nicholas said slowly. "It is the only way. You must trust in what I tell you now, and do it, no matter how impossible it seems."

Tristan stared at him, wild-eyed, without moving. Nothing was registering.

"You must spare your mother and myself the torture and humiliation of my dying slowly at his hands. And more than that, you must think of your subjects. There is so much we could not tell you, so much that we now never shall, but hear me when I say that you and your sister are the very future of endowed blood in Eutracia. And you must not force your subjects to see their king tortured."

Tristan looked blankly over the altar to the hundreds of citizens who were watching the horrible scene being played out. He turned his head and then looked down unseeingly at the sword in his hand as if it were some hideous yet beautiful creature from another world.

"My son," he heard his father's voice say from somewhere far away, "your mother and I brought you into this world with an act of love.

You must now take me from that same world with another different, but just as important, act of love."

Finally, no matter how inconceivable the concept, Tristan understood that he must obey his father, and his king.

As if in a dream, he saw himself move slowly to the altar as Kluge and the sorceresses grinned wickedly. He looked for the last time into his father's eyes, and bent over to kiss him on the lips.

"Good-bye, Father," he heard himself say, impossibly.

Tristan gripped the heavy sword in both hands and raised it high over his head.

I beg the Afterlife, let my aim be true, he heard a voice say. A voice that was distant, yet at the same time deep within himself.

Tristan brought the full weight of his strength down with the dreggan, cleanly cutting the king's head from his shoulders. Blood erupted everywhere as the head rolled off the altar and onto the floor. Morganna screamed and collapsed.

In a flash he was upon Kluge with everything he had left, the blade of the dreggan swinging through the air directly at the monster's head. But again the larger man was too fast for him, neatly avoiding the swing while at the same time slamming his fist hard into the prince's stomach. Tristan went down hard, retching, and then simply lay there, crying, until the vomit came once again. The dreggan skidded violently across the blood-soaked dais, landing beneath one of the thrones.

"Well done!" Kluge shouted. He kicked Tristan viciously in the ribs as the prince struggled to get up on all fours, rolling him a little way back down the dais, closer to Wigg. Kluge then looked to Traax.

"Bring me some chain, and a stout rod," he ordered. Walking over to the prince, he grabbed some of Tristan's hair and bent his head backward to face his own. "You just don't know how to give up, do you?"

The chain and steel rod arrived, and Kluge immediately busied himself with tying the prince's feet together, then pulling his hands behind his back and running the chain tightly around his wrists. With the heel of his boot, he viciously pushed the prince to the floor on his stomach. The commander of the Minions then ran the remaining length of chain from the prince's hands up to his neck and secured it around Tristan's throat tightly, bending him backward in a semicircle on his stomach, with his feet, head, and shoulders up off the floor. He then rather curiously put the rod partway through one of the links of the chain, about halfway between the prince's hands and head.

Kluge looked to his mistress for the order. Succiu smiled briefly, and then nodded.

Kluge turned the rod one full revolution clockwise, and the length of chain between the prince's feet and head tightened torturously. Tristan thought at first that he would suffocate, but realized that if he kept his feet and head high off the floor and therefore as close together as possible, he could manage very small breaths. The position was excruciatingly difficult to support, and whenever he relaxed, the air to his windpipe was immediately cut off. He felt warm fluid between his stomach and the floor, and if he could have, he would have vomited again.

He was lying in the spreading pool of his father's blood.

The father that I just murdered, he heard his inner voice accuse.

Tristan summoned up all of the breath he could muster and hoarsely whispered, "Kluge."

Curious, the Minion commander lowered his head to Tristan's face and smiled. "Yes, my prince?" he asked sarcastically.

Tristan strained his eyes up to the face of the man who had ordered the murder of his father.

"I will kill you one day," he whispered, and then he spat a mixture of blood and saliva directly into Kluge's face.

Kluge immediately stood up, enraged, and kicked him again in the ribs, so hard that Tristan rolled completely over his chains and ended up at Wigg's feet. This time he had heard one of his ribs break, and the fire in his side was excruciating. He felt one of Wigg's hands touch his shoulder in reassurance.

Wiping the blood and spittle from his face, Kluge placed the toe of one boot directly under Tristan's chin and violently raised up his face.

"Kill me one day? I don't think so," he said. "You don't have any days left, you worthless royal bastard."

Without looking up, he called to his second in command.

"Traax! Bring me a spare Minion dagger and a line of stout rope. We're going to have a little fun."

When Traax returned with the rope and the dagger, Kluge stepped to the altar. Laying them down on its marble surface, he picked up the headless body of Nicholas and threw it into the crowd of kneeling, weeping Eutracians.

"If they want their king so badly, then they can have him." He laughed as some of the startled citizens tried to get out of the way.

"Now bring me the heads of each of the dead wizards, of the so-called commander of the Guard, and of the dog who was their king," he told Traax simply as he picked up the dagger and the rope.

"Yes, my lord," Traax responded, and began to locate and bring to the altar each of the dead wizards' heads, and finally the heads of Nicholas and Frederick.

Lying on his side and looking through bloody, dazed eyes, Tristan watched in horror as Kluge placed one end of the rope through a ring at the handle end of the Minion dagger and knotted it there. He then placed the heads in a neat row on the altar; some had their eyes still open, staring into space as if watching from a distance.

"I think this room could use a bit of decoration, don't you?" he asked Traax, who was obviously puzzled at what his master had in mind.

"Er, yes, I mean of course, sir," the younger man replied, curiously stepping around the altar for a better view.

Tristan would never forget what the monster called Kluge did next.

Holding the dagger with the rope attached in his right hand, Kluge picked up the head of Slike and pushed the knife directly into the skull's right ear. Then, with a grunt, he turned the head over and banged the end of the dagger's handle on the altar until the blade had been pushed through the brain and out the other ear. He pulled the dagger through that ear as casually as if he were working on a needlepoint, the bloody rope still attached, until the rope was completely through the wizard's head.

Tristan turned his head away in tears. *The bastard is actually going to thread their heads on a rope!* Had his throat not been bound, he would surely have screamed with the pain of what he was seeing. *I beg the Afterlife, bring this madness to a stop!*

But it didn't stop. Kluge kept on happily working at it until all seven of the heads had been threaded onto the rope, including those of Nicholas and Frederick. He handed one end of the rope to Traax, and the two of them held it high, the heads swinging back and forth between them as they admired their prizes the way a fisherman might show off his string of freshly caught trout.

Kluge turned to Succiu for her approval.

"Where would you like it hung, Mistress?" he asked proudly. "Personally, I think it should go up somewhere in a position of prominence."

"Imaginative, isn't he?" Natasha said to Succiu, her arms folded across her breasts.

"Oh, more than you know, Sister," Succiu replied, without bothering to try to restrain the hunger in her voice. She touched the tip of her tongue to one corner of her mouth. "He has proven useful for an entire variety of needs."

Natasha smiled knowingly back at her.

"Have your warriors pound twin posts into the ground at opposite ends of the entranceway to the palace," Succiu said gleefully. "Then tie the rope between them and let it swing in the breeze as a message to all regarding what has happened here this night. Before we depart, take them down and mount one each to the prow of the first seven of our warships for the return visit home. Strip each of the bodies naked and hang them upside down for the vultures."

Kluge nodded to Traax, and the second in command walked out with the string of heads, followed by several of the warriors who began to collect the matching headless corpses.

Tristan once again felt the wizard's hand on his shoulder and tried to look up at the old one, but he could not. If Wigg was trying to tell him something, Tristan couldn't imagine what it was. Straining to stay in a position so as not to faint from lack of breath, he tried to remember what it was that Wigg had said to him at the height of the battle. Then the wizard's words slowly came back to him out of the gloom of those frantic moments.

"Tristan!" Wigg had shouted. *"You and Shailiha must stay with me here at the altar! For the sake of everything you value and love, you must both stay by my side!"* And Wigg had mysteriously stayed next to the altar the whole time, unmoving, until the battle was over and their captors had forced him into one of the thrones. But Tristan had not listened. He had joined the fight, ignoring the wizard's pleadings. A strange feeling began to creep into his mind as he struggled for every breath. *Had I done as the old one said, would things have been different? Why didn't he join us in the fight? And what is it he is trying to tell me now?*

But before he could think of any answers, Kluge's face was back, leering over him.

"My mistress has commanded that I leave you and the wizard for last," he said gloatingly as he looked into the prince's eyes. "And leave you two for last I shall. That leaves only one person on the dais left to deal with before I turn my undivided attention upon you." He turned his gaze to Morganna, who lay sobbing on the floor of the dais, and then looked out at the thousands of sweating, anxious warriors waiting in the Great Hall. "I'm sure my troops will enjoy her company very much," he said, his tongue protruding slightly between his teeth in anticipation. "There are certainly enough of them to keep her occupied for the full two days until we leave."

Kluge walked across the dais to Morganna, pulled her roughly to her feet, and slapped her hard across the mouth. Then he reached to the bodice of her gown and ripped it all the way to her waist, baring her chest.

Tristan went wild with hate, the disgust and aversion so deep within him that if Wigg had not been nearby to control him, he would surely have suffocated himself in the attempt to reach his defenseless mother. But Wigg had tightened the grip upon his shoulder with an iron hand, and no matter how hard the prince thrashed and strained against his bonds, between the chains and the old one's strength, he couldn't move.

Kluge picked Morganna up in both arms and buried his face between her breasts while she screamed and tried to beat him with her fists. He simply laughed at her as though her blows were nonexistent and carried her to the edge of the dais.

The crowd of soldiers hungrily moved nearer. As Kluge stood there with the queen in his arms, a hush fell over the room.

"Warriors of the Minions of Day and Night!" he shouted. "You have fought well, and many of you have fallen this day. To my survivors, I say that the time has come to reap the rewards of your victory. Though you have never before been allowed to take women without wings, I know you are as anxious to taste them as I. Therefore, you may do so now. Take any of them you wish, including the high-born ones in this very room. I order you to make their mates stand in lines and watch what real men can do to a woman. Should any of them resist you, cut them down on the spot." He looked into the hysterical blue eyes of the queen and then ran his tongue down her chest. "You may begin with this one." He laughed. "She still smells as sweet as a Minion virgin on a perfumed brothel bed. But do not kill her. Make sure when you are done with her that she is returned to me, so that I may show her why it is *I* who command the rest of *you*."

Tristan tried again with all of his strength to move, but Wigg still held him down.

Is the wizard mad? Does he expect me just to let it happen?

And then, without warning, Kluge lifted Morganna high over his head with both arms and threw her into the mob.

Tristan wanted to scream, but could not. He fought to move away from the old one's grip, but Wigg held him in place. He closed his eyes as he heard the cries of the women begin, and tried to tell himself that he could not distinguish the screams of his mother from those of the other women.

But he could.

Tristan closed his eyes to block out the sickening, screaming scene and began sobbing incoherently, not caring whether he lived or died. In his pain he did not notice when Wigg placed his feet beneath the prince's body, and his hands upon him, as well. Oddly, it seemed to the prince that the wizard was no longer trying to control his movements.

He was trying, for some reason, to stay as close to him as possible.

And then Kluge's hand was again in Tristan's hair, wrenching his eyes up to his.

"And now, you sniveling royal bastard," he said angrily, "it is time for you to die, as well."

Good, Tristan thought. *I have nothing to live for now. At least I will not have to see Wigg die, too.*

Tristan looked to the sorceresses to see if they were still there. Succiu and Natasha stood nearby, Succiu still wearing the Paragon, both of them grinning wickedly down at him.

Of course they will watch. It's what they do.

Kluge had another shiny dagger in his hand, and moved it to Tristan's right eye.

"I am going to cut you into pieces," Kluge said seriously, as a healer might describe a treatment to one of his patients. "I have been looking forward to this ever since I learned that you possessed endowed blood. And I know exactly which pieces you can live without for a long time, so I can afford to enjoy myself. For example, even though I want you to see what is happening to you, you don't need both eyes to do it." The shiny point of the dagger started to move to Tristan's right eye. Resigned to his fate, all he could do was try to close it.

And then things started to change.

Wherever Wigg was touching him, either with hands or feet, Tristan began to feel a strange kind of pain, a tingling sensation that started to overcome his entire body. He opened his eyes to see, and instead of finding the knife in his face he found himself looking into the hysterical eyes of Succiu as she frantically tried to push Kluge aside. And then his entire universe became bathed in a swirling vortex of brilliant azure, blotting out everything in his vision.

He felt as if he were about to begin turning over and over with the vortex as it encircled him. *Perhaps this is what death is like,* his mind said from somewhere far away. On and on the vortex came, the swirling circles ever growing in his eyes.

The last thing he remembered were Succiu's long red nails trying to dig at the skin of his face while her manic screams went on and on in the Great Hall.

CHAPTER

Nine

He woke with a convulsive start, his entire body jumping all at once as if he were suddenly waking from an awful dream. He was in a small, stone-lined room, lying upon the covers of a large bed, and he was still fully clothed. There was a small fire burning in the fireplace, and a table with food in one corner. Tristan raised himself up upon his elbows and shook his head, trying to understand where he was. Then he remembered. *What an awful dream,* his subconscious tried to tell him. *The winged creatures, my family, the wizards. All of the death and blood. What would make me imagine such a thing?*

It was then that he saw the chain and rod lying on the floor a little way from the bed. The chain and rod, his own dried blood still upon them, that the awful winged thing had used to bind him. The thing that had killed his family in his dream. And then, as he continued to look dumbly at the chain, the hideous reality of it all shot through him and he screamed in agony.

It was real! he thought, the torment of it tearing through his head and heart.

My family is dead.

And the killer's name is Kluge.

Wigg, standing a little distance away, calmly took two steps away from the wall, closer to the prince.

Tristan could see that Wigg's eyes were full of tears, but he didn't care. He looked with hatred upon the one who had done nothing to help his family in their time of need. He started to get up, determined to strike out at the old one. But then those sharp, aquamarine eyes narrowed, and Tristan felt something begin to close in around him. It wasn't painful, but he found that he couldn't move his hands or his feet: He was forced simply to lie still upon the bed. He looked up at the wizard.

"You've put a wizard's warp around me, haven't you?" he asked. "Your powers are back. What are you going to do now, you traitor? Watch as they kill me, too?"

"No, Tristan," Wigg said in a tired, sad voice. "The warp is for your own protection, and I will keep it in force as long as necessary in order that you may hear what it is that I have to say." Tristan's words had pierced Wigg's heart, but the wizard understood. Put in the prince's position, he would probably feel the same way.

Tristan lowered his face, and the tears came once again. "My family is dead, aren't they?" he asked, his voice a barely audible whisper.

"Yes, Tristan," Wigg said gently, walking to the bed and sitting down next to him. "Your father, mother, and Frederick are all dead. And all of the other wizards of the Directorate. But I believe Shailiha still lives."

Shailiha. He turned his face to the wizard in sudden realization. They had addressed her as their Sister, and had taken her away before they killed his parents.

"Why did they take only her and kill everyone else?"

"I'm not sure, Tristan," the old one said truthfully, "but I think they mean to keep her alive."

"Where are we?"

"In one of the farthest reaches of the Redoubt of the Directorate, below the palace. They will not find us here. I doubt they know the Redoubt exists. If we do not move we should be safe here for the two remaining days that the sorceresses and their army are in Eutracia. The Redoubt is deserted. Two weeks ago I ordered all of the consuls, their sons, and the entire Redoubt support staff into the countryside."

"Why?" Tristan's voice was still full of fury at the old one.

"Because the Directorate and your father feared that something might happen during the ceremony, and we wanted not only the consuls of endowed blood away from the palace, but the Redoubt itself empty," Wigg said calmly.

Tristan strained against the warp that held him, his eyes blazing with blind, unthinking hate.

"You *knew*?" he screamed incredulously. "You knew that something was going to happen and you let us walk right into it while you sent the others to safety?" He shook his head wildly back and forth with the sheer incomprehensibility of it all. "In the name of the Afterlife, *why?*"

"It was the appearances of the blood stalker and the screaming harpy that alerted us to the possibility of danger, especially when they both arrived so close to the ceremony. It had been centuries since we had seen either of their kind. At that time, those creatures had only one purpose, and that was to serve as tools of the Coven. We therefore had to admit the possibility that the Coven had survived, despite our banishment of them into the Sea of Whispers over three hundred years ago. And although we would be at our most vulnerable while the Paragon was in the water and the wizards were temporarily without their powers, it was still agreed by the Directorate that your coronation should take place at the appointed time. What your father said is true. For reasons you do not yet understand, you and your sister are the very future of endowed blood in Eutracia.

"The palace was still the safest place to hold the ceremony, considering its fortifications and the presence of the entire Royal Guard. And even given the possibility the Coven had somehow survived, we still couldn't fathom any way that they could do us harm." The Lead Wizard looked down at his hands again. "We knew we could be mistaken. The truly maddening part about it was that, even if we were wrong, there was nothing about it that we could change."

As only a wizard could, Wigg reached gently through the warp that surrounded the prince and lifted the medallion that hung around his neck, the one that Morganna had given him only a few days before. "This was to have been a gift to you from your parents after your coronation. It was their intent that it lay upon your chest, next to the Paragon, for as long as you were king. And then still hang around your neck long after *your* son took the throne."

Tristan looked sadly down at the medallion. He would wear it always—including the day he avenged his parents and Frederick, killing the ones called Succiu, Natasha, and Kluge. His rage at the old wizard was beginning to dissipate, but he still had many questions, and until he finally got the answers that he had been longing for all of his life, he decided he could trust no one, not even Wigg. Suddenly a realization dawned upon him.

"Natasha and Succiu are members of the Coven," he said slowly. "Who are the other two?"

"You mean, who are the other *three*," Wigg corrected.

"Three?"

"Yes," Wigg replied. "Three. Succiu is the second mistress of the Coven. I am not sure why Failee sent her here instead of coming herself. Perhaps Failee is dead. But Succiu was not the most powerful of them. Failee was."

"Failee?" Tristan asked.

"Yes. She is the one I was referring to that day in the woods when I told you there had been one who had mastered the Vagaries. That person is Failee. In addition to Failee and Succiu, there are two others of lesser, but still great power. One is named Vona, the other Zabarra. Together the four of them made up the Coven that was responsible for the Sorceresses' War. There were many other sorceresses, women who had rudimentary training in the craft, who joined their demented cause, but without Failee's knowledge of the Vagaries, most of these were cut down almost immediately. Even those brave enough to take up arms *against* her had little chance. And, conversely, there were endowed men who turned to Failee's cause. But as her use of the darker side deepened, so did her madness. She eventually came to see all men as a threat. And so these four sorceresses were the only ones who survived. Or so we thought. Obviously Natasha is also a sorceress, able to disguise her endowed blood. Until last night, even I had no knowledge of her existence."

"If your powers returned when theirs did, why didn't you try to fight them?" Tristan asked angrily. "I would have helped you all that I could have."

"That would have been quite useless," Wigg told him gently. "For I am only one. And not only were there two sorceresses present, but the Minions, as well. Saving you, your sister, and the stone were the goals, rather than dying, trying to seek revenge."

Wigg wiped a tear away from one cheek. "I don't know what we will find when we finally surface two days from now, but we have to wait until they are gone. No one single wizard can match their combined power as long as she wears the stone."

Tristan had begun to calm down, but his heart was still breaking desperately over the loss of his family. He closed his eyes and opened them again before he spoke to Wigg.

"Would you please remove the warp now?" he asked, almost apologetically. "I was wrong to doubt you, and I'm sorry. I promise I will not try to hurt you again."

"Very well." Wigg narrowed his eyes, and Tristan felt the pressure that had been holding him lessen, and then dissipate completely. He stood up and slowly walked to where the bloody chain and rod lay on the floor.

He held the chain up before Wigg. "Who are the winged ones?" he asked, his hand trembling with hate for the winged monstrosity who had done this to him, and the two sorceresses who had watched with pleasure. "I have never seen such creatures in my life."

"Nor have I," Wigg said. He pursed his lips as he thought. "I can only surmise that they are part of the population of wherever the sorceresses came from. Either way they are formidable opponents, and the Royal Guard is gone." He again looked down at his hands. "So many good men, and all of them destroyed in a single night."

"How did we get here?" Tristan asked suddenly as he looked around the room, the knuckles of his hands still white as he gripped the chain. "The last thing I remember was everything going strangely blue in the Great Hall just as Kluge was about to blind me, and then I saw Succiu coming for me in some kind of mad, screaming rage." He looked down at his clothes for a moment. "I know Kluge kicked in at least one of my ribs. And although I do hurt badly, there isn't as much pain from it as I would have expected, nor from any of the other things that were done to me." He shook his head slightly in puzzlement.

"Do you remember when I was pleading with you to bring Shailiha and stand next to me at the altar?" the old wizard asked. "It wasn't out of fear that I stood there, Tristan. It was out of duty. Duty to your father, the Directorate, and the nation as a whole."

"I don't understand."

"As I have told you, we knew that the potential for danger existed, but we didn't know exactly when or where, or if it was to come at all. But the most probable timing for any kind of trouble was obviously when the Paragon was in the water, and that meant during the abdication ceremony. After days of talking and planning beforehand, we finally agreed on a plan. Although risky and admittedly perhaps impossible to accomplish, it would hopefully save the life of yourself, your sister, and one of the wizards, so that eventually your training in the craft could take place as required. The plan also provided for retaining possession of the Paragon. The Coven now has Shailiha and the stone, so we were only partly successful, but at least you and I are alive."

"Why only Shailiha and me? Why not everyone?"

"We didn't know how many we could save, because such a thing had never been done before. It took the entire Directorate weeks to prepare the Achievement. Everyone agreed that you and your sister were the most important, and all of the others were willing to die for the two of you to live, including Frederick. But before the Achievement could be enacted, everyone except you and I had already been dealt with in one way or another."

"Frederick knew?" Tristan exclaimed.

"Everyone on the dais knew, Tristan, except for you and your sister. "We considered telling you, but given your impulsive nature of late, especially your unnerving habit of disappearing into the woods, we felt you might simply vanish, perhaps this time for good. And for you to leave your sister alone would have been unfair. She is your twin, and is more connected to your existence than you yet know." *The Chosen One shall come, but he will be preceded by another,* Wigg thought. *He still has no idea. How could he?*

"What of the consuls of the Redoubt?" Tristan asked. "Could you not have asked them to help us if necessary? Surely their combined powers might have been of some use."

There is still so much he does not yet understand, Wigg thought sadly. "We could not ask them to help us," he replied. "They were already gone."

"What do you mean?"

"Your father and the Directorate both agreed that the best use of the consuls was to send them out into the countryside, trying to kill as many of the blood stalkers and screaming harpies as possible, for we feared those creatures might be preying upon the citizenry, as well."

Tristan thought for a moment, and another, stark realization came to him. "Why didn't you enact the Achievement sooner, so that we all could have lived?" he suddenly cried out in pain. He was starting to come apart again, and the old one could see it. Wigg gently put an arm around the prince and held him close, as a father would a son.

"We couldn't, Tristan," Wigg said gently. "Such an Achievement had never been accomplished before, and we had no control over the timing. The best the entire Directorate as a whole could do was to tie the process to the life of the Paragon and ensure that the incantation would occur at some point during the evening of the coronation. And the reason I was begging you to bring your sister to me was because the Achievement was arranged in such a way that only those persons or objects that I was physically touching would be affected. Sadly, had everyone been able to touch me at the time of the Achievement's commencement, they would all be alive today."

Tristan buried his face in his hands, beginning to understand. But there was still so much he could not comprehend.

"What happened when the Achievement began?" he asked.

"Luckily, the last time Kluge kicked you, it sent you once again back near me," the old one said. "Do you remember feeling my feet beneath you and my hands upon your back? That was to make sure that there was a connection between us."

Tristan was still baffled. "But what really *happened*?" he asked.

Wigg allowed himself the beginnings of a small smile, the first that the prince had seen since waking up in this place. "We became invisible," the wizard said calmly.

Tristan's mouth fell open. "I don't believe you."

"Oh, it's true enough, all right," Wigg said, finally breaking out into a full-blown smile. "It was the only thing that the Directorate could think of that had any conceivable chance of working, and even then we had our doubts. Invisibility had never been accomplished before. But we knew the stakes were great, and we all gave it our best efforts. Putting this Achievement together was the reason that so little was seen of the wizards and your father those last few days before the ceremony."

"But I went unconscious," Tristan protested. "How did I get here? It couldn't have been so simple as you merely walking away with me. And how is it that you were not rendered unconscious, too?"

"I stayed conscious because of my training in the craft," the old one said simply. "And as for getting you here, what you haven't yet realized is, since the floor of the dais was also being touched by me—"

"It also became invisible!" Tristan exclaimed.

"That's correct," the old wizard said, reminding Tristan of his many days spent before the old one in class at the Wizards' Conservatory. "And because the floor was now invisible, I could slide us through it unseen. We discovered during the construction of this Achievement a very interesting phenomenon of the craft—namely that two invisible objects, unlike two normal objects, are able to share the same space at the same time. So we just went through it. When we were below the dais and I was no longer touching the floor that was now above us, it became solid again. The whole thing happened in the twinkle of an eye. So fast, in fact, that the outward appearance of the floor did not change to anyone standing upon it. To them, we simply vanished, while all the time we were just below their feet."

Tristan sat there stunned, the old one's arm still around him. "How did you get us here?" he asked.

"That is the most simple part of all," the wizard said. He got up from the bed and went to the table to pick up an apple. "I simply waited. You should have heard them, Tristan. They went berserk. As we had suspected, Succiu's first instinct was to think that we had somehow magically transported ourselves as far away from the palace as possible, and she sent her Minions immediately out into the city and countryside to turn it upside down looking for us. But all the while we were just below her feet. She wasn't able to detect my endowed blood because of the invisibility cloak. It seems to evade all forms of detection, somehow. Succiu ordered everyone out of the Great Hall, and several hours later, both of us still under the effects of the Achievement, I was able to carry you to the library where the gravitating chamber is, and bring you here. I induced a deep sleep upon you, and I worked on some of your wounds and injuries while you slept." He smiled slightly once again.

"In addition, as long as we remain in the Redoubt, neither Succiu nor Natasha will be able to detect our blood. That is the second part of the riddle of our disappearance. An accomplishment, indeed for the Directorate. We owe those five dead wizards very much, indeed."

Tristan felt ashamed at being alive. He thought back to some of his father's last words to him: *"There is so much we could not tell you, so much that we never shall, but hear me when I say that you and your sister are the very future of endowed blood in Eutracia."*

He broke down again and began sobbing before the wizard, his face buried in his hands. "I killed him, Wigg," he said, his eyes turning into tortured, wet slits of pain. "I killed my own father!" He shook his head dumbly. "And because of that, I should be dead, too."

He has been changed forever in a way that I can only imagine, Wigg thought as he put a hand on the prince's shoulder.

"Tristan," he began softly, "have you ever heard of the wizard's parable that says no man can wade into the same river twice?"

The prince looked up into the wizard's face with wet, bloodshot eyes. "No," he said simply. "What are you talking about?"

"A man can only wade into any river once," the old one said, "because the river is always moving, and therefore each time he approaches it, the river is different, as is the man. Thus, a man can never wade into the same river twice, because change is a constancy of nature. To embrace change is effortless. But to resist it is impossible, and goes against the natural order of the universe."

"How does all of that affect me?" Tristan asked.

"You have been changed today, just as were the river and the man who tried to cross it twice. You will never be the same, nor shall I. But that does not make any of it your fault."

"I will kill them, Wigg. On the name of everything I hold dear, I will kill them all."

"Your father looked to me for guidance, just before you brought down the sword," Wigg said, looking at his hands.

"What?"

"Your father looked to me for the answer, and I gave it to him. He nodded to me, and I knew he not only understood, but that he was also saying good-bye. Then he told you that you had to do it, no matter how impossible it seemed at the moment. I loved him, Tristan, just as I love you and your sister. And, as infeasible as it may seem to you now, what you did was right. Your only other choice was to watch him die. Horribly."

Tristan walked to the table and looked down at the food. He didn't think he would ever eat anything again.

"What about Shailiha?" he asked the old one. "What is it they want of her?"

"Although I am not entirely sure, I feel it must have something to do with the quality of her blood, and the fact that she is female. But you must obey me when I tell you that there is nothing that can be done for her right now. No power in the world that I know of is strong enough to wrest her away from a sorceress of the Coven who is wearing the stone. Remember, Natasha is now with Succiu, and the two of them can join their powers. No, Tristan, the best thing we can do to help Shailiha is to wait."

Wigg could see Tristan gnashing his teeth at the thought of Shailiha with the sorceresses. But in his heart the prince knew the old one was probably right. He turned and faced the wizard with deadly seriousness. He had waited for the answers long enough.

"You just alluded to the quality of her blood, just as so many people have also alluded to mine. Over the course of my entire life I have endured hushed whispers in the hallways of the palace, the fact that I was supposed to join the Directorate after my reign, and being constantly told that the many questions I have always had could only be answered after my coronation."

Tristan walked to the wizard and looked at him with the suddenly aged eyes of a man who had killed, a man who was ready to kill again for what he thought was right, and a man whose mind had been tortured in the extreme by forces that were out of his control. A deeply scarred man, to be sure, and now also a different man. Tristan would no longer be denied the answers to his questions, and Wigg knew it.

"I want some answers to all of this, Lead Wizard, and I want them now."

I can see the power in his eyes already, Wigg thought as he looked at the prince. *I will answer his questions this time. He deserves some answers, especially since we will probably soon die.*

"Sit down, Tristan," the old one said, "and I will explain to you the history of Eutracia, the one we did not teach you at school, and the secrets of the nature of your birth."

*I*n the meaningful silence that hung between them, the wood in the fireplace snapped and popped, and then one of the logs fell farther down into the grate, signaling the beginning of its blazing demise. Without speaking, Wigg walked to the hearth to place several more logs upon the flames. It would be a long night.

Suddenly Tristan had a thought. "How is it that the smoke going up the chimney does not give us away?" he asked. "Won't it be seen?"

Wigg finally let go a small smile. "There are no chimneys in the

Redoubt," he answered. "The smoke immediately burns away into nothingness. Only the heat and scent remain. Slike worked for weeks on the incantation, getting it just right."

The old one then turned and walked to the table. He picked up a bottle of red wine and poured himself a glass. Turning to the prince, he raised his glass questioningly, but Tristan shook his head.

"I thought that the wizards of the Directorate didn't drink spirits," the prince commented. "I have never seen you with a glass of wine or ale before."

Wigg looked at the prince for a rather long time before he responded. "There *is* no Directorate, Tristan," he said wistfully. "Unless you want to call it a Directorate of One. And if it is to be a Directorate of One, then I suppose I am bound to create my own rules from here on." He took a slow, thoughtful sip of the wine.

The prince looked down at his boots, suddenly ashamed. "I'm sorry for your loss, Wigg," he said. "I have been thinking only of myself, and I apologize. I know how much you loved them all, and you have lost as many dear ones this day as I have. I am also sorry for having doubted you during the attack. If I had listened to you then, Shailiha might be sitting here with us right now."

"Come and sit with me at the table," the old one said simply, "and I will answer some of the questions that have been troubling your mind for so long."

Tristan pulled up a chair at the table. Without further introduction, the wizard began his tale.

"Near the end of the war, the wizards were losing badly," Wigg began. "Many had been captured, killed, or turned into blood stalkers. The sorceresses were growing in number, and their ability to join their powers made them almost invulnerable. The wizards were the last hope for Eutracia, but were themselves slowly becoming extinct. The savagery of the sorceresses knew no limits. They also controlled most of the towns, and therefore most of the population west of Tammerland."

"How could they control such large areas?" Tristan asked.

"Up to two sorceresses were left in each town, sometimes accompanied by blood stalkers. Healthy human males of unendowed blood were forced into the ranks of their armies under the penalty of death or the threatened murder of their families. The four leaders were the most powerful and learned—they came to be called the mistresses of the Coven. They directed the war from migrating headquarters, usually just behind their ever-advancing eastern front, and took as their symbol the Pentangle, or five-pointed star. We never knew why they chose it, but it was said that it had to do with some arcane incantation of the Vagaries.

As town after town was swallowed up, their ranks increased, as did the collective abilities of their powers. Toward the end, most of the wizards had retreated and taken refuge in Tammerland. They knew in their hearts that the end had begun."

Tristan finally relented and poured himself a glass of wine. It felt warm and comforting as it went down, reminding him of how long it had been since he had last eaten.

"As the war dragged on," Wigg continued, "and the sorceresses and their troops came ever closer to Tammerland, food, especially fresh meat and fish, was becoming scarce. Eventually, out of desperation, small hunting parties were sent out into the Hartwick Woods. They were usually accompanied by a wizard for protection."

Wigg stood and walked over to stand before the fire, seemingly lost in thought. After a few moments, he turned back to the prince.

"It was one of those hunting parties that first discovered the Caves of the Paragon, and the falls that constantly tumble there into that dark, stone pool. The area was explored, and a chained jewel, a chalice, and a large book, among several other lesser objects, were found. Each of them, save the Paragon, was inscribed with a strange language never before seen in our land."

He walked back to the table and refilled his wineglass.

"The Paragon was found accidentally, and could have been easily missed," Wigg continued. "It was discovered hanging from its gold chain, suspended under the waterfall. As you know, if the stone is not worn by a suitable host it must be immersed in a sufficient quantity of the waters of the falls to retain its properties. Later on, we realized that the stone was hung in the waterfall to ensure a constant, fresh covering of water at all times, and therefore, its continued existence. Blessedly, when the wizard removed the stone from the Caves he had the presence of mind to fill the chalice with water and place the jewel inside it. Both the stone and the chalice were taken to Tammerland that same day. The wizard also removed all the other objects that were found nearby, knowing that the sorceresses' forces were near." He paused for a moment, his eyes far away. "That wizard was me.

"Once the items had been received by the wizards at the palace, it was generally agreed that the book, or the Tome, as we came to call it, was meant to explain the purposes and uses of the other items that were found," he continued. "Immediately the greatest of the wizard scholars, myself included, attempted to translate the book, but this proved almost impossible, since absolutely nothing of the language was known. As the sorceresses began to close in on Tammerland, time was running out, and despite the wizards' best efforts, little had been learned about the jewel or its secrets. Many wizards lost their lives making additional trips to the Caves to continually supply fresh water for the stone, but still we managed."

Wigg shook his head sadly. "Meanwhile, the citizenry inside the walls of Tammerland had begun to riot. Shortages of fresh food and water were beginning to cause crime and disease. Many of the citizens wanted to surrender to the sorceresses. The wizards rejected the idea and did the best they could to calm and control the population by peaceful means. But it was all starting to come apart."

"Were they still working on the book?" Tristan asked.

"Oh, yes," Wigg said, running his hand down the length of his face. "The jewel and the other items that had been recovered from the Caves were locked away in one of the library suites in the wizards' quarters of the palace. One day, one of the master wizards went there to examine some of the other items found in the Caves. Accompanying him was his precocious five-year-old daughter of endowed blood. The little girl was all the wizard had left, and she meant everything to him."

Wigg took another apple and began slicing it into pieces. "During his investigations, he began to hear his daughter chatting on endlessly to herself. When, at long last, he went to collect her and return to his quarters, what he saw there changed history."

"What did he see?" Tristan asked anxiously.

"His daughter was sitting in a very large chair, much too big for her, her feet dangling off the edge, not touching the floor. The huge Tome was in front of her, open to approximately the twentieth page. Her face was a mask. With glassy eyes and a monotonous tone, she continued to speak, completely ignoring his presence. Walking up to her and finally looking over the edge of the book, what he saw made his jaw drop."

"And that was?"

"She was reading the Tome, translating it into Eutracian. Around her neck hung the Paragon, still wet and dripping from the chalice water. The jewel had seemed to come even more alive. In the ensuing weeks, many things were learned from the child. She had seen the jewel submerged in the water, and her curiosity had enticed her to put it around her neck. After retrieving the stone from the funny red water and putting it around her neck, she was sure that she was as pretty as a princess. Looking around the room, she had spied the very large chair. Every princess should have a throne, she reasoned, so she hoisted herself up into it. The only object to play with on the facing table was a big old book, so she began to read to her pretend subjects from it. But upon seeing the first page, she had simply, uncontrollably, begun to read aloud, and the words that were written there came to her voice as if she had been reading them all of her life."

"A little girl?" Tristan asked incredulously.

"A little girl," the Lead Wizard replied. "A little, untrained girl saved our nation from the sorceresses."

"What became of her?" Tristan asked. "She must be some kind of national hero, yet I have never heard of her."

A very strange kind of half smile came to the old wizard's lips, and then he continued without directly responding to the prince's question. "Amazed, her father ran from the room for help. In the ensuing days it was learned that whoever of endowed blood wore the jewel around his or her neck became imbued with powers and abilities that even we wizards never thought possible. Included among these gifts was the immediate ability to read the ancient text and translate it into our native tongue. Eventually, the jewel was placed around the neck of her father, the most learned and talented of our wizards, and he began to recite the Tome from the first page as the Directorate's scribes recorded the first two of its three volumes. In the weeks that followed, the girl was allowed to continue to wear the stone, since it seemed that no one, not even the most powerful among us, was able to take it from around her neck. And because she liked it so much, she refused to do so for us. In the end we had no other choice than to let her recite the entire text, word for word, as her father wrote it down. Finally, among the many things we learned was that only the wearer of the stone could remove it from around his or her neck. And if the stone was not allowed to regenerate in between human hosts, it would kill the next wearer instantly." He paused for a moment, as if lost in time. "In the end, it was the knowledge gleaned from the Tome, combined with the use of the Paragon, that enabled us to win the war and banish the sorceresses. And then we decided, for reasons of security, that no one of endowed blood who had already been trained in the craft should ever again wear the stone."

Another question occurred to Tristan. "And why is it that the wizards lose their power when the stone is immersed in the water from the Caves?" he asked.

One corner of the old wizard's mouth came up. "Before I answer that, it is important that you first understand how the stone empowers endowed blood, for the answers to both questions are interlocked."

Wigg took the prince's right hand and held it palm up. "Don't worry," he said, seeing Tristan's questioning look. "This won't hurt." Wigg narrowed his eyes and looked at Tristan's hand.

Almost immediately Tristan felt a tickling sensation in the tip of his right index finger, and an azure glow began to surround his hand. He watched, spellbound, as a small cut began to open up and a single drop of dark-red blood plopped unceremoniously upon the tabletop. Then the aura began to dissipate.

"The truth of the matter is that the blood of an endowed person, any endowed person, is *alive*," Wigg continued. "Just as is the Paragon—each in its own way. True, our blood flows through our hearts and veins like that of any other creature or unendowed human, but in our case our blood literally has a life of its own. In this I mean that our blood is at least partially sentient, and definitely far different from that of other humans."

Tristan stared at the drop of his blood on the table, stunned at the wizard's words. Finally he found his voice. "But ours doesn't appear any different to me than anyone else's," he said skeptically.

"That's true." Wigg smiled. "However, this is not about how our blood *looks* but rather about how it *behaves*." Staring at one of his own fingertips, he opened up a small wound. A drop of his blood fell obediently onto the table next to Tristan's, identical in color and shape. But then something extraordinary happened.

The blood drop from Wigg's hand began to move.

Speechless, Tristan watched as the wizard's blood began to undulate, swimming to and fro across the tabletop as if looking for something. His mouth open, the prince could barely form the words. "Are you causing this?" he whispered, never taking his eyes from the blood drop as it continued to move hauntingly back and forth.

"No," Wigg told him with a broad smile. "As I said, our blood—that is, the blood of the endowed—has a life of its own."

"But why, then, is mine not moving also?" Tristan asked. The drop of his blood had lain motionless the entire time; it looked like it was starting to congeal. In contrast, the wizard's blood remained a vibrant red as it moved about.

"Oh, make no mistake," Wigg added. "Your blood is just as alive as mine. It does not show the same characteristics because it is still in its dormant phase."

"What do you mean?"

"That is to say, you have not yet been trained in the craft," the Lead Wizard said simply. "The day you were conceived you were blessed with such blood, but it has remained relatively quiet for all this time, as is always the case. Only when your training begins shall your blood come out of its dormant phase and start to become more active, much like a Eutracian butterfly emerging from a cocoon. Then and only then is it able to accept the power of the Paragon and become empowered. The more highly trained the wizard, the more alive and receptive is his blood. During training, the stone recognizes the infusion of the knowledge, seeking out and metaphysically joining with sentient blood, beginning to empower it. This relationship grows and strengthens as one's expertise and knowledge of the craft increases. The stone empowers both sides of the craft, Tristan. And contrary to what one might think, a practitioner needs neither to be touching the stone nor be in close proximity to it." Wigg paused and unceremoniously wiped the blood spots from the table with the sleeve of his robe.

"In essence, then, the stone is able to empower endowed blood because they are both alive, need one another, and are able to seek one another out on a metaphysical level," Wigg continued. "The Tome barely mentions this bond, but we believe that they are actually able, on some level, to communicate with each other. It is this, then, that makes us different from other human beings, and that enables us to perform the craft and execute things that other humans find to be so miraculous."

The old wizard stood and walked slowly to the far wall near the fireplace. Placing his hands on the marble, he found several dark spots in the smooth stone, closed his eyes, and then backed away. The entire fireplace began to pivot, rotating around to reveal light from another room beyond. Tristan heard a somehow familiar but not quite recognizable sound. "Follow me," Wigg said simply. In a moment, he was gone.

Tristan stood and rather gingerly approached the wide gap to the left side of the fireplace, then stepped through and into the room beyond.

Stunned, he simply remained standing in place, staring in wonder.

The room was large, larger than it needed to be, and the walls, floors, and ceiling were made of the finest black marble the prince had ever seen. Numerous chandeliers of oil lamps hung from the ceiling, their flames reflected in the shiny surfaces of the room. As was the case with each of the rooms Tristan had so far visited in the Redoubt, there were no windows. Several colorful, complexly patterned rugs adorned the floor, and the air had a wonderfully sweet, relaxing scent. No furniture filled the room. The far wall was its only focal point, and had but one use.

Tristan walked to it, coming to stand next to the wizard.

From an ebony spout in that wall, the thick, red waters of the Caves of the Paragon were spilling out into a deep trough that curved out from either side in a great semicircle. At each end of the trough, the water seemed to flow back into the wall, as if returning to the spout to repeat the cycle. The trough, too, was made of the finest black marble, and upon its ledges sat several gold and silver chalices of various sizes. Once again in the proximity of the water, Tristan began to feel its overpowering, intoxicating effects on his blood.

Wigg immediately noticed. "We will not stay here long," he said drily. He raised the infamous eyebrow. "We wouldn't want a reoccurrence of what happened in the Caves, now would we?"

The wizard picked up a very small chalice, about the size of his thumb, and carefully filled it with water from the trough.

"This room is known as the Well of the Redoubt," he said, "and it holds some of the water of the Caves of the Paragon. This water is pushed through the wall via the same type of hydraulic mechanism that powers the gravitating chamber, but that is not important. What is important is that during the war the wizards smuggled the water to this secret room little by little, as a safeguard against the day that the sorceresses might discover the Caves and bar us from them. We knew that if such an occurrence ever took place we would need sufficient water to continue our study of the craft, sustain the Paragon in between hosts, and hopefully achieve victory in the war."

The Lead Wizard could see that Tristan was growing dizzy. "It is time for us to leave," he ordered. Carrying the small chalice, he guided the prince back through the gap in the wall and rotated the fireplace to its original position. He helped Tristan sit down at the table and watched carefully as the younger man's eyes and demeanor began to return to normal.

"Why does the water affect me so?" Tristan asked thickly, running a hand back through his dark hair.

"A big question," Wigg replied, the corner of his mouth quirking up in a hint of a smile. "In fact, a vast section of the Tome is dedicated solely to the subject of the waters of the Caves." He placed the small chalice down on the tabletop. "One of the first things we learned was that the waters have many, many uses. Also, the water is never to be ingested, for the Tome makes specific reference to this fact. It is drinking the water that turns butterflies into the Fliers of the Field."

Tristan recalled how dangerously close he had come to drinking some of the water. He silently thanked the Afterlife, shuddering to think of what it might have done to him.

The look on the prince's face had not escaped the elderly wizard. He cleared his throat. "And third," he said finally, pointing an index finger up into the air, "is the fact that the water's power appears to have an indefinite life span. In addition, it will not evaporate, as will other liquids. Unless the Paragon is placed into it, causing it to become clear, it will retain its properties and powers forever. The water you saw in the Well of the Redoubt has not been replaced, except for what has been taken and used, for over three centuries. And the waters are very, very powerful indeed. For example, accelerating the healing process is usually a very slow, very difficult incantation to perform. However, allow me to demonstrate."

Wigg took Tristan's hand and poured a single drop of the water from the chalice over the wounded fingertip. Immediately an azure glow began to surround the finger. The effect was completely painless, and when the glow had dissipated the cut had been completely healed.

"A very small example of its abilities"—Wigg sniffed—"but impressive nonetheless. Even if I, as Lead Wizard, had myself accelerated the healing process in your finger it would have taken at least one full day to complete. This took only moments.

"But to answer your question about the wizards losing their power when the stone is immersed in the water," he went on. "The beings who left us the Paragon and the Tome needed a way to prepare the stone for its next host. This is necessary because, although the stone empowers all of those with endowed blood, the relationship it garners with its wearer is quite special, and unlike any other." Once again his bony right finger went into the air for emphasis, reminding the prince of all of Wigg's lectures he had attended at the conservatory. Just now he was beginning to wish he had paid closer attention.

"You see," Wigg added, "the waters have yet another intriguing property. They insulate the stone from the blood of the endowed. This form of insulation, or protection, if you will, forces the stone to lose its color, since its connection with the wearer—in fact, with anyone of endowed blood—is blocked. This allows the stone to return to a virgin state, which is necessary because the proximity of the stone to the blood of its wearers is so close that, in a metaphysical sense, they become virtually one. Therefore, to place the stone around the neck of another without removing the influence of the first wearer always results in the instantaneous death of the second person to take the stone. It is simply a case of it being too much for the new wearer's blood to bear, so to speak. For the lack of a better explanation, the stone must be 'weaned away' from its wearer, and subsequently prepared for its next host." Wigg paused and took another sip of wine as he collected his next thoughts.

"But this process," he continued, "although potentially dangerous to wizards because of the loss of their powers, is absolutely crucial to passing the Paragon from one person to the next. Presumably, the individuals from whom we inherited the stone and the Tome could not be sure we would eventually discover and make use of the time enchantments. They needed to ensure that we could pass the stone from one person of endowed blood to another." *And to help us wait three long centuries for the coming of the Chosen Ones,* he thought. "All of this knowledge and instruction that we have gleaned over the last three hundred years comes from the Tome, the great book of the Paragon." Wigg sat back in his chair and placed his hands into the opposite sleeves of his gray robe.

"There is still something I do not understand," Tristan said slowly, shaking his head. "You have often alluded to the fact that the wizards and sorceresses both had a modicum of power *before* finding the Paragon and the Tome. And when the stone is removed from its human host and being prepared for another, all those of endowed blood lose the use of their gifts. But when this happens, how is it that each of you cannot revert to your previous, albeit lower powers? Are they gone for some reason?"

Wigg sighed as the question dredged up painful memories. "Those were truly dark days, when we discovered the Paragon and the Tome, and made the decision forced upon us because of that event," Wigg said sadly. "It has long been the belief of some of us that the ones who left us the Tome and the stone were our ancestors—that we inherited our endowed blood from them, and that this, in turn, allowed us certain instinctual yet unsophisticated uses of the craft. Personally, I still cling to this hypothesis." He paused once again, thinking.

"But when Faegan first began translating the Tome, he was shocked at what he saw there," he finally continued. "It told us that if the finders of the Stone and the Tome decided to employ these items to augment their knowledge, then *all* those of endowed blood would immediately lose their previous, lower powers. Those lesser powers would vanish forever, never to return—to be forever replaced with the supposedly greater power of the stone and the higher knowledge gained by the reading of the text. This, they said in the Tome, was the reason they would not allow us to go back to our previous use of the craft. They wished us to reach far greater heights in our powers for the benefit of all mankind." Wigg paused for a moment, taking another sip of wine. "It wasn't that they simply wanted us to have the knowledge," he added. "They wanted us to use it for the purposes of good, fully aware of the differences between the Vigors and the Vagaries, never to risk perpetuating the evil of the Vagaries.

"You can easily imagine our dilemma," he went on to say. "If we chose this path, not only would we empower ourselves, but the sorceresses, as well. The seemingly endless debate that raged while the sorceress closed in on fortress Tammerland nearly caused us to lose the war. But in some ways our fear and hesitancy were indeed justified. In place of our previous, instinctual gifts would come an unknown to be embraced. The Tome described it as a unified whole, or 'group consciousness,' as the blood of all the endowed, wizard and sorceress alike, simultaneously gained the power of the stone. It is this group consciousness, for example, that allows one of endowed blood to detect that of another. But when the stone is being prepared for a new host, temporarily losing its

power, the group consciousness is broken, allowing none of us to connect with the gift in any way. Neither to our newfound knowledge, nor
to our powers of the past. We took this demand of the writers of the
Tome to be a leap of faith, if you will, and a test of our commitment. A
cleansing of the old, in favor of the promise of the new. It was to be, in
effect, their legacy to us. They also wrote that they hoped it would
more tightly bind their descendants of endowed blood together as a
whole, creating greater harmony and forestalling the strife that they
themselves were experiencing. Had we wizards found the Paragon and
the Tome before Failee began her revolt, the war might never have occurred, and our nation might have been able to exist in peace. But, as
we now know, that was not to be."

"But didn't the ones who wrote the Tome take a terrible chance in
hiding the stone and the Tome that way?" Tristan countered. "What if
you had never found them, or they had been found by the sorceresses
first?"

"Some mention is made in the Tome that they believed their way of
life was coming to an end due to their enemies, just as we thought ours
soon might. They took a great risk, but probably less so than if they had
not hidden them at all, and allowed the stone and Tome to be taken by
their enemies. Because the good derived from the Vigors is the equal to
the evil that can be gleaned from the Vagaries, they hoped the items
would be found by those who would perform the craft properly, for the
betterment of all."

"But if the Tome teaches of the Vigors and the Vagaries, what is
the third section about?" Tristan asked.

"The Prophecies," Wigg said, reaching out for another piece of apple. "The Vigors, the Vagaries, and the Prophecies. Each section is distinct from the other two in context and purpose, but all of them relate
to the stone itself."

Tristan's eyes narrowed as he sat there before the wizard, trying to
absorb everything he was hearing. "Wigg," he asked, "if the stone had
been placed around my neck yesterday, would I have been able to read
the Tome?"

The old wizard looked directly into the questioning, dark-blue eyes.
"Yes, Tristan," he said softly. "*Especially* you."

But before the prince could pursue how all of this impacted him, the
wizard purposely cut him off. "I still haven't answered the very first
question you asked me."

"Yes," Tristan said. "The little girl, the one who saved our country,
what happened to her?"

Wigg took a deep breath and stiffened a little, not even himself believing what he was about to say. "Succiu told us herself, just yesterday. The father of the little girl was the wizard Faegan, once my best friend. And his daughter, the one who saved Eutracia, is now Natasha, duchess of Ephyra."

Tristan sat staring at the wizard, speechless. He now remembered Succiu's words from yesterday, but at the time he hadn't understood what she was talking about, especially in his heated rage to kill her.

"What happened?" he whispered.

"He disappeared. He was the most talented of us all, and also commanded the power of Consummate Recollection. That is, from the time of his birth he had been able to recall instantly with perfect accuracy anything that he had seen, read, or heard. Anything at all, no matter how trivial. His disappearance was a huge loss to us, but the war was coming to its final climax, and no one could be spared to mount a search party at that time. Some of us thought that his daughter had run away, while others felt that the little girl had somehow died and Faegan had gone off and taken his own life in grief. There was also a rumor that he died in the fighting as it neared the city, but his body was never recovered. Either way, we could not worry about it. We simply didn't have the time. But Faegan was the finest and the most brilliant of us all, and I believe that had he remained with us, he would have been made Lead Wizard instead of myself."

"And now?" Tristan asked.

"Now, thanks to Succiu, we know that both Faegan and his daughter live. And, as I told her yesterday, I believe I know what happened. I am convinced that the Coven took his daughter from him just before the end of the war, and then threatened to kill her if he didn't help them."

"But if Faegan and Natasha both still live, then why wouldn't he use his powers to try to convince her to end her association with the sorceresses?" Tristan realized he knew little about the ways of wizards, especially one he had never met.

"He must believe her to be dead," Wigg said in a painful whisper. "Telling him such a thing would be typical of their cruelty. If they had told him she died, and then they had taught her to become a Visage Caster, he wouldn't be able to recognize her even if they were in the same carriage together."

Tristan's brow knitted together in curiosity. "What's a Visage Caster?"

"One of endowed blood who can change his or her appearance at will," Wigg said in a quiet voice, obviously lost in a different insight.

Something didn't make sense to the prince. "If the Tome of the Paragon was known only to the wizards and not to the Coven, then how did the mistresses learn of the existence of the Paragon, and teach themselves the Vagaries?" And then yet another question came to him. "Why didn't they win the war?"

"What do you mean?" the wizard asked, knowing full well what Tristan was going to say next.

"You say that this Failee is a master of the Vagaries, yet she had no access to the Tome. Therefore, since she was banished and she herself has never returned to Eutracia, she must have somehow learned the Vagaries while she was still here. So two questions remain. First, how did she acquire the knowledge, and second, since you say that the wizards only practiced the Vigors, then how did you overcome them in the war?"

"Very good," Wigg said, and he meant it. He took another sip of wine, then cut himself a piece of cheese.

"How can you eat at a time like this?" Tristan asked.

Wigg gave him another little smile. "A simple matter of survival," he said. He took a large bite.

"Anyway," he said, once again raising his imperious index finger to the prince, "the solution to your first question—namely, how did they learn the Vagaries—can have only one answer. Only the wizards had access to the Vagaries, and only one wizard was unaccounted for, and may have had a strong motive to help them."

"Faegan," Tristan said with finality.

"Yes," Wigg said. "The Directorate had always suspected him of it, but we were as equally sure that he was dead." He narrowed his eyes as he thought for a moment. "Succiu did herself no favors by telling me of his continued existence, but then again she was sure I was about to die, and couldn't resist the temptation to gloat. And as for your second question—that is, how is it that they did not win the war? The answer to that is really quite simple. They didn't have the time."

"What do you mean?"

"The war was finally turning in our favor, since we had gathered so much power from our discoveries in the Caves. Even if we assume Faegan supplied them with *all* of the knowledge of the Vigors and the Vagaries, they still didn't have the time to learn their use and defeat us, since we had acquired the information so much sooner than they. The craft is just like anything else in one respect, Tristan: I can tell you for days how to shoot a bow or slash with a sword, but until you have practiced it enough for yourself, you have no proficiency. And the longer you practice, the better you become."

Tristan sat trying to absorb all the information, then suddenly looked up at the old one. "Who, then, Lead Wizard, wrote the Tome, and left the Paragon in the Caves?"

So he has finally gotten around to asking that, the wizard thought. *The greatest of all the riddles.*

Wigg took another sip of wine, then looked down at the glass as he slowly began rolling it back and forth between his palms. He took a deep breath.

"Little is actually known of them, Tristan," he said. "Although they do identify themselves as the authors of the Tome. The authors say in their writings that the the Tome was left for us to study, and to put to the best use possible for mankind. This we thought we had done, by constructing the Directorate, the Redoubt, and the monarchy, and forbidding ourselves any further study of the Vagaries. They left the Tome and the Paragon there for us, we know not how long ago, as if they could no longer use it themselves and wanted it to be found by someone they could trust. And the Tolenka Mountains and the Sea of Whispers have effectively blocked any exploration past the reaches of what we have traditionally recognized as the boundaries of Eutracia, so the whole thing remains a riddle." He shrugged as he sipped his wine.

"What were they called?" Tristan asked.

"I thought you would never ask. They called themselves the Ones Who Came Before. Simple and to the point, don't you think?" Putting down his wineglass, Wigg placed his hands into the sleeves of his robes and sighed. "That is all the mention of them that there is, and no further light has been shed upon the subject since."

"Where is the Tome now located?" Tristan asked. He was surprised at himself for not having asked the question sooner.

"It is hidden in the Caves of the Paragon, in the tunnel you discovered when our warp pushed you back out of the way." Wigg sat back in his chair.

The Paragon, the Caves, and the Tome, Tristan thought. *The Vigors, Vagaries, and Prophecies. The three volumes of the Tome. The sum of the knowledge of the Ones Who Came Before.* It was then that the realization hit him like a thunderbolt. For as long as he had known the wizard, Wigg had never uttered a single word about the Prophecies. *The Prophecies,* he mused. *The third volume of the Tome. The volume of which no one ever speaks.*

And then a strange thing happened.

As he gave more and more thought to the Prophecies, he began to feel the endowed blood in his veins race even faster. He started to feel flushed and then slightly dizzy, the way he'd felt when he approached the Well of the Redoubt. It was frightening, yet at the same time it gave him a kind of euphoria that he had never experienced before.

The Lead Wizard sat across from the prince, watching the changes in him, his ancient, aquamarine eyes missing nothing. *He will ask me now,* the old one thought with a smile, *and I will tell him some of it. The Chosen One shall come, but he will be preceded by another. And the knowledge that he seeks he shall one day demand of the one who recovers the stone.*

"Wigg, tell me of the Prophecies," Tristan said, almost as if he were in a trance. "When I think of them, my heart and blood race, and the need to know increases tenfold." He bent over slightly and looked at the wizard in a dominating way that Wigg had never seen before. "I must know of the Prophecies. And somehow, within me, I know that you are the one who was ordained to tell me. And I think you know that, too. Speak."

It hadn't been a request. It had been a command.

Finally the day is here, the old wizard reflected. He looked at the prince he had known so long, aware that from this moment onward Tristan would be forever changed. "The Prophecies are about you, among other things," he said softly. "They speak of your birth, of the birth of your twin sister, and of the quality of your blood. They speak to who you are, why you were born, and how and why it is that you are different from others of endowed blood. The Prophecies are your story, Tristan—the story of the meaning of your existence, and the qualities that you possess that make you so special."

Tristan hadn't flinched. His face was a mask, a combination of need and hunger that radiated from him, just as it had on the day he discovered the Caves.

"Who am I?" he asked breathlessly.

"You are Prince Tristan, of the kingdom of Eutracia, son of Nicholas and Morganna of the House of Galland." *Make him work for it,* the wizard reminded himself. *It must not come too easily, or too soon.*

"Don't toy with me, wizard," Tristan said, with surprisingly little friendship in his voice. "Who do the *Prophecies* say I am?"

"The Chosen One." Wigg firmly held his ground in the contest of wills as he looked into the dark-blue eyes. "One of the earliest chapters of the Vigors says the Chosen One will come but he shall be preceded by another."

"There was another like me?"

"Not *was*, Tristan, *is*."

"Who is this man?" the prince asked, a look of danger in his eyes. "Do I have reason to fear him?"

"No, Tristan, you have no reason to fear this one."

"Then who is it?" he demanded. He inched his face closer to the wizard's.

Wigg looked compassionately at the man across from him whom he loved so much, wishing that the other one could be here now, as well.

"The other Chosen One is your sister, Shailiha."

Tristan sat wide-eyed, still staring at the wizard, hardly breathing. *Shailiha?*

"You must be wrong," he finally said, hoping with all his heart that the wizard was mistaken. *She's been through so much,* he thought, *and now she is with them.*

"Why must I be wrong?" the old wizard asked patiently.

"Because we're twins," he said adamantly, "at least that's what everyone always told us. And you said the other Chosen One preceded me, and was already here."

Wigg raised the infamous eyebrow, not really surprised that Tristan had not grasped it. "You and your sister *are* twins, Tristan," he said compassionately. "She preceded you into this world by eight minutes. I know. I was there."

Tristan sat back in his chair, stunned.

"You were there at our births?"

Wigg smiled. "Yes," he said, "as were all of the other wizards of the Directorate, and your father, as well."

"Why?"

"Because your coming had been foretold in the Tome, and the volumes were very clear about the fact that we should be there to witness your birth, and to train you and closely follow your progress from that day forward. That is why your father chose to join the Directorate—and ordained that you would one day join the Directorate, too, and be trained in the craft. Despite their great love for each other, Morganna agreed to an eventual death of old age, alone, while she watched you grow and your father continue to live, unchanged, under the influence of time enchantments once his training in the craft had begun. The queen was truly one of the most selfless people I have ever known."

And the one who recovers the stone, and any others of like power who practice the Vigors, shall witness his coming, so as to know that he is the One, Wigg remembered.

"The volumes were very explicit," Wigg continued. "They spoke of a blue aura that would surround the mother of the Chosen One at the time of your conception, and follow her until your birth. That is how we identified you, and knew who you were when you finally arrived in this world. After you and your sister were born, the aura around Morganna faded away." *And I never saw it again until I saw it on you, when you bathed in the water of the Caves,* the old one reminded himself.

"How is it that we are so special?" Tristan asked, his gaze unwavering.

It was a question that Wigg had been waiting thirty years to answer, but he had never expected to have to answer it in such catastrophic conditions. He removed one hand from the opposite sleeve of his robe, taking another sip of wine.

"It is because of your blood," he began. "The Tome tells of the One who will come, preceded by another, who will have endowed blood of a purity never before seen. It is also said that the purity of this blood will enable the Chosen One to lead us, and finally show us the way."

"Is the purity of my blood the reason that the waters have such an effect on me?" Tristan asked.

"We cannot be sure, but I have to believe that is so—even though your blood is still dormant, since you have not yet been trained. Such a thing has never been seen before."

Tristan's mind was taken back to Wigg's explanation of the Ones Who Came Before. "What do you mean, I am 'to show us the way'?" He looked down at his hands, rubbing them together gently in his confusion. "I as yet have no special talents, and despite the fact that I know my endowed blood runs through me with great power, I have no idea what you are talking about. What does 'the way' mean? The way to live? The way to practice the craft? The way to be able finally to travel past the natural boundaries that have always kept us geographically locked within our own country? I don't understand."

"We considered all of those possibilities," Wigg said, gazing back toward the fire. "But we never solved the riddle. The Tome says that it is you who must deliver the answer."

"How?"

"By reading the Prophecies yourself," Wigg answered simply. "The third and final volume of the Tome. The only one that to this day remains unread."

"But if the Prophecies contain the answer, and anyone of endowed blood could read the Tome, why is it that the Prophecies were not explored further for the answers?"

Wigg sighed and pursed his lips as he looked tiredly at the prince. *There is so much that I cannot tell him,* he thought. *So much that he must discover on his own. The entire Directorate and his father were going to help me in his quest, but now they, too, are all gone.* "The Prophecies forbade it, Tristan," he said. "The very last page of the Vagaries strictly prohibited the reading of the Prophecies, the third and final volume of the Tome, by anyone but you. A warning that we heeded. And because of this prohibition, they were not translated and written down by the scribes, as were the Vigors and the Vagaries. The writings of the Prophecies exist only in the Tome, in the Caves of the Paragon, and you were to have read them only after you had accepted both the life and death enchantments." Wigg paused, carefully selecting his next words. "That was to be the beginning of your training, setting you on the road to fulfilling your destiny as the Tome decrees. Namely, to be the first to eventually master, join, and effectively command the two opposite sides of the craft, namely the Vigors and the Vagaries."

Death enchantments, Tristan thought to himself. *The esoteric use of the craft that instantly produces the death of a wizard who breaks his vows, or attempts the practice of the Vagaries.* Suddenly, he made the connection.

"And the Afterlife," he said softly, almost reverently. "The Afterlife is mentioned in the Tome, isn't it, Lead Wizard?" He could tell by the look on Wigg's face that he had hit upon yet another truth. "If that is the case, then why is so little about it truly known?"

Wigg sighed, remembering that the man who sat before him would, if he lived, easily one day dwarf even the Lead Wizard himself in his use of the craft.

"Yes, the Afterlife is mentioned in the Tome," Wigg said, nodding slightly, "but there is truly very little about the Afterlife that we actually know. The Vigors make brief mention of an Afterlife, a compassionate place where the souls of the dead supposedly go. It also mentions an Underworld, an opposite place, just as the Vigors are the opposite of the Vagaries. There is a quote from the Vigors that states, 'And the practice of the Vagaries shall lead to the madness of other, lower worlds.' The wizards of the Directorate always took this to mean that there is an Underworld, just as there is an Afterlife."

Wigg paused for a painful moment, thinking of Failee and wondering how far her knowledge of the craft had progressed over the last three centuries. *Very far indeed,* he realized. *And now the other three with her apparently also have at least a modicum of understanding of the Vagaries as well. And are no doubt also at least partially mad.*

"Over the course of the last three hundred years, the occasional use of the word 'Afterlife' by the members of the Directorate came to be overheard by the general population, and was eventually adopted into our language as a natural part of our custom of speech, although no one outside of the Directorate ever had the slightest inkling of what it really meant," he continued. "We did not discourage its use because it seemed to guide their perceptions about death to a more peaceful, gentle conclusion. It seemed to provide hope both to those who were about to die, and to those who had lost loved ones. But the deeper meaning of both the Afterlife and the Underworld is contained only in the Prophecies, and, as I have said, only the Chosen One is to read them. So you see, it is both the Underworld *and* the Afterlife, the Vagaries *and* the Vigors, the dark *and* the light, that you alone are to come to eventually understand, join, and employ. Part, no doubt, of what the Ones Who Came Before meant when they said 'show us the way.' "

"And to do that, I must have the stone," Tristan said in a whisper, almost to himself.

"Yes," the old one said, his heart breaking. "And the stone is gone."

For several long moments the two of them sat in abject silence, the only sounds the wood as it crackled in the fireplace.

Tristan reached up to wipe away a solitary tear. He felt over-whelmed and awed by the circumstances of his existence. And there was another emotion sweeping through him.

Shame. The odd, often insurmountable weight that can come with being left alive, when others around you have perished.

From somewhere in the far reaches of his mind came the words that Nicholas had spoken that day when Tristan had been called to the meeting room deep within the Redoubt. *"I am truly sorry for all that you have been through,"* his father had said, *"and all that you may yet have to endure. But believe me when I say that every man in this room loves you, none more than myself, and that everything that has occurred in your life, indeed even the things that have not occurred, have all been for a reason."* Tristan hung his head as he sat there before the Lead Wizard. *And now they are all dead,* he thought. *Except Wigg.*

Tristan stood, walked around the table to stand before the wizard, and put his hands on the old one's shoulders. He had to know. She was the only family he had left.

"Why do they want her?" he asked, barely able to hold back his tears.

Wigg shook his head fatalistically. "I wish I knew," he said, the look of discouragement plain upon his ancient face. "We always knew that during the war they were desperate for a fifth sorceress, but we never knew why. But if Natasha is one of them, then why not just take her back with them as their fifth? Why would they need Shailiha, too? And now that they have someone of Shailiha's blood quality in their grasp, the future could be dark, indeed."

"They called her 'Sister,' " Tristan remembered, "and bowed to her. Why would they do that?"

"I don't know," Wigg said, truly perplexed. "And there is some-thing else that bothers me. How is it that they could know all of these things, and time their attack to the precise moment that the stone was in the chalice? For all of these years they have been far away from Eutracia. Even Succiu confirmed that fact." He drew his hand down his face in thought. "Of course it has to do with Natasha, but how?"

"Can the sorceresses communicate with each other in some way over long distances?" Tristan asked. "I don't just mean sensing the presence of other endowed blood, but actually sending and receiving thoughts? That would explain much."

Wigg narrowed his eyes. "Egloff would have been the one to answer that," he said thoughtfully. "I seem to remember some brief mention of it in the Tome. But we never pursued it as a practice because the true teaching of it was found only in the volume containing the Vagaries. To employ this particular art would go against our vows, and enact the death enchantments."

Then they truly have mastered the Vagaries, Wigg thought. *And now they are also in possession of the stone.*

The prince walked to a spot in front of the fireplace, his eyes lost to the dancing orange-and-red flames. He spoke to the wizard without turning around.

"I have to get her back, Wigg," he said softly, so softly that in order to understand him, the wizard had to use his powers to augment his hearing. "She's all that I have left of my family, and I can't let anyone or anything stop me." He turned back to gaze at the wizard with the same grim look of determination that had been on his face earlier that night. "Including you. If I must defy you this night, I will."

"We wait," the old one said firmly. "We can do nothing except harm ourselves or be captured again as long as they are still here. Maddening as it is, we must not surface until tomorrow night, when they are gone. You are untrained in the craft, and I am but one. Coming out to face them is exactly what they hope we shall do."

"And if, when they leave, they take her with them?" His eyes were glistening with hate and the pain of his frustration.

"Then we follow, and make our plans as we go. Succiu has already unwisely boasted that she and her army had somehow crossed the Sea of Whispers to get here, so we know in which direction to turn: east."

"And just how do *we* manage to cross it?" Tristan asked, the rage once again building inside him, leaving no small measure of hatred in his voice.

"We learn how," the wizard said, walking slowly toward Tristan as he spoke. "From the one person in all of Eutracia who may know."

"Faegan," Tristan said simply. "The rogue wizard."

"Yes," Wigg said, still carefully approaching him. "Tomorrow night we leave for Shadowood."

"Shadowood?" Tristan asked, momentarily confused, as he watched the wizard oddly tilt his head. "I have never heard of a place called—"

Wigg immediately reached out to catch Tristan as the prince fell heavily forward, lost in a coma-depth sleep induced by the old wizard.

Wigg carried him to the bed, then stood there looking down at him for a long time. Into the face of the Chosen One. *Regardless of the fate of Shailiha, your path will be a very difficult,* Wigg contemplated.

He extinguished the lamps, leaving the room shadowed in the half-light coming from the flickering orange-and-red embers of the fireplace. He sat down heavily at the lonely table, lost in his thoughts.

CHAPTER
Ten

S ucciu stood next to Natasha on the deck of her warship, sipping
the delicious red Eutracian wine and relishing her victory. It had
been over three hundred years since she had tasted either wine or personal success of such quality. She cast her eyes skyward, smiling. The
three red moons were up, and they were all full, bathing sea and coastline in their familiar, rose-tinted glow and reflecting beautifully off the
Paragon that now hung around her neck.

All their warships were moored close to her own, here in the curve of
the Cavalon Delta, as ordered. They were completely deserted, even their
Minion captains having gone ashore to take their share of the Eutracian
women and participate in the destruction of the beleagured nation. The
silent, dark, gently floating hulls were a grim reminder of their deadly
purpose amid all the beauty that was Eutracia. That had been Eutracia.

We have done it, Succiu exulted silently. *The princess and the stone are
ours, and after tonight and tomorrow there will be little left of this nation.*

The second mistress of the Coven turned her attention to the prow
of her ship, and to the head of King Nicholas, impaled upon it. The
seven other severed heads—those of Morganna, Frederick, and the wizards of the Directorate—had been similarly placed upon the prows of
seven selected ships that lay at anchor nearby. She turned to Natasha,
who was gazing intently at the coastline.

"It makes for quite a spectacular masthead, don't you think?" Succiu asked.

"Indeed," the other mistress said. "I sincerely hope that the vultures don't do it too much harm before we sail. I would like to have it still displayed there when we return home in triumph."

Succiu diverted her attention from the masthead to the shoreline of her former home. "Beautiful, isn't it?" she asked. "See how our work lights up the sky, my Sister?" The bright orange-and-yellow glow was reflected in the darkness of the nighttime sea.

It seemed that all of Eutracia was on fire.

Before them, the capital city of Tammerland was engulfed in an uncontrollable blaze. Other fires dotted the coastline, and she knew it would be only a matter of time before the cities had been razed, and the fires would go out. And all that would remain would be the dark gray soot of destruction, and the charred, foul scent of death.

Death by fire.

Some of the other, smaller fires were unique: Smaller and definitely better controlled, they seemed to burn endlessly, with a silent but gruesome intent all their own. Succiu knew that these would be the funeral pyres of the Minions, and the ceremonial burning of their fallen members would easily go on into the next day. It was their custom and their right, and the practice dictated that no dead Minion warrior should ever be left behind to be desecrated by the enemy.

Natasha sighed. "Failee will not be entirely pleased, you know," she said seriously. "The Lead Wizard and the prince still live. And despite your orders, Kluge has yet to bring us their heads. I assume that we still sail on tomorrow evening's tide, as per the First Mistress's orders." She paused, letting the import of her words sink in. "If we leave, and have not found them, what will you tell her?"

"I will gladly tell the First Mistress that it was her fault, and her fault alone," Succiu said defiantly, her lip in a sneer and her eyes narrowed. "What you do not know is that we all told her, repeatedly, that the recalling of certain of the stalkers and harpies before the invasion was madness. All it could have done was alert the wizards to our continued existence, and enable them to prepare for us. And that was exactly what happened. Now, despite the fact that we were basically successful in our quest, the two who escaped us were the two worst possible of those who could have survived."

"Why?"

Succiu took another sip of wine and turned to look into Natasha's eyes. " 'Why?' my Sister asks? I'll tell you why. Because Tristan and Shailiha are twins, and the prince's blood is the equal of, if not superior to, the blood of the princess. There has never been, nor will there probably ever be again, naturally occurring blood of such purity. And although he has not yet been trained in the craft, the prince has within him the power to perform such feats as have never before been seen. And Wigg was one of the most learned and powerful of the now dearly departed Directorate. As such, he was also one of their best teachers." She leaned against the rail of the ship and returned her gaze to the mesmerizing fires on the coastline. "So you see, my dear, if there was ever a combination that was a danger to the Coven and to what we are ultimately trying to accomplish, those two Eutracian bastards are it."

For a long moment they stood without speaking, interrupted only by the occasional, gentle slapping of the sea against the hull of their ship. It was finally Succiu who broke the silence.

"Have you had contact with her?" she asked Natasha.

"No, Second Mistress," Natasha answered. "I was instructed only to attempt to contact the First Mistress if there was a problem of great importance, or if the mission had failed completely. I did not immediately consider the escape of Tristan and Wigg to be a problem of such magnitude. But now that I better understand, if you wish me to try—"

"No," Succiu snapped. "There is no need to contact the First Mistress. We may yet be successful in capturing them. And even if we are not, they are still isolated here, in Eutracia, and have no way to cross the Sea of Whispers. If we must leave tomorrow night with our business unfinished, then so be it. I will take the responsibility of making the proper explanations to Failee."

Natasha smirked as she thought of what she would have liked to do with the prince had she been given the chance. "A pity," she said longingly, "since Tristan is still alive, that his reported talents could not have been put to better use."

Since she was in a more businesslike than contemplative mood, Succiu dismissed the comment. "Have the forty Eutracians been arranged?" she asked. "We must have them to ensure our safe trip home. Make sure that they are handpicked and brought to the warships without fail before we depart tomorrow night. They will be killed just before we reach the area of the Necrophagians, so that their bodies will still be fresh. I have no desire to displease the Eaters of the Dead on our return home."

"Yes, Mistress," Natasha responded dutifully. "All will be done as you order."

"There is just one more thing," Succiu said, throwing her long black hair over her left shoulder and away from the night breeze coming off the sea. "You realize, of course, that if the wizard and the prince are not found and killed, you will be staying behind, here in Eutracia, for as long as it takes to do so."

"I am fully prepared to do whatever is necessary to aid the cause," Natasha said plainly, although obviously disappointed.

"Feel honored, Sister," Succiu said. "You are the one who is best acquainted with the country, and you can disguise yourself by changing your appearance at will. We have taught you to cloak your endowed blood from Wigg, and you are protected by time enchantments, so time is of no importance. We will expect you to communicate your progress to us at regular intervals. If we do not hear from you, we shall consider you dead at the hands of the wizard. You must find and destroy both of them, no matter how long it takes. Don't worry. You will eventually see Parthalon."

Succiu raised a long, painted nail in front of Natasha's face as she continued. "But hear me well, Sister. It is imperative, if at all possible, to kill the wizard first. Despite the purity of the prince's blood he has not yet been trained in the craft, and poses a much smaller threat to your existence than does the Lead Wizard." She gave Natasha a knowing smile and a brief nod of her head. "Who knows?" she added. "Perhaps if you do indeed kill the wizard first, you may get your chance to taste the pleasures of the prince after all. Before you kill him, of course."

"Of course, Second Mistress," Natasha agreed, smiling back.

They both turned their attention back to the coastline, and to the fiery destruction that was their handiwork. For a long time they watched in silence as an entire civilization was systematically raped, burned, and murdered virtually out of existence.

Succiu finally grew tired of the spectacle and decided it was time for more important matters. "Shall we check on our passenger?" she asked with a smile.

"By all means, Sister, lead the way."

Succiu turned away from the bow of the ship and led Natasha back toward the gangway to the lower decks. Belowdecks the light changed dramatically, the narrow but ornately finished passageways bathed in the golden glow of the many oil sconces. Succiu finally stopped at a heavy mahogany door. "This is Sister Shailiha's room," she said, "and mine is just next door, where I can keep an eye on her during the voyage. I also brought several of my personal handmaidens from Parthalon to tend to her needs." Without further ceremony Succiu tilted her head, watched the door unlock itself, and then purposefully walked into the room.

Upon following her stress into the stateroom, Natasha's eyes fell upon a scene that was both sumptuous and chilling at the same time.

The room was grand, as beautiful as anything that she had seen on land in Eutracia, albeit smaller. The walls were of intricately carved mahogany, and rugs in a variety of patterns and colors covered much of the pink marble floor. Paintings and tapestries adorned the walls, and a magnificent oil lamp chandelier hung in the center of the room. Sofas, chairs, and tables had been strategically placed about, and in one corner was a very large, overstuffed, canopied bed with white silk sheets and pillows. The scent of freshly cut flowers filled the air. But the windows in the far wall were barred.

Then she heard a whimper.

Soft and low, it was a strange cross between crying and moaning. For a moment, as it wafted out onto the air of the room, Natasha could not detect the origin of the sound, but then Succiu walked over to stand before one of the sofas that had obviously been turned around and pulled before one of the barred windows on the far side of the room. Natasha followed—and found herself looking into the face of Shailiha.

The princess of Eutracia had been bathed, her hair washed and combed, and was now clothed in a magnificent maternity gown of the palest imaginable pink, with ornate white lace at both the neckline and the sleeves. Sewn into the left side of the bodice of the gown, radiating outward in the palest and finest of gold thread, was a Pentangle. The sign of the Coven.

Though Shailiha continued to moan softly, it was obvious that her eyes saw nothing as they stared out past the barred window at the burning coastline of her nation. Periodically she would clutch at her abdomen as if to remind herself of her unborn child, and then begin to cry again, rocking back and forth as she stared unseeing into the night.

Her mind is gone, Natasha thought. She turned to notice that several of Succiu's handmaidens had entered the room and were standing next to the beleaguered princess, watching her with concern.

Succiu turned to the first of the girls. "Has she eaten?" she asked.

"No, my mistress," the handmaiden replied. "She will touch neither food nor drink." She gestured to a table on the other side of the room that was heaped with sumptuous-looking food. "She continues to refuse all sustenance. Sometimes we are of the opinion that she cannot hear us when we speak to her, and other times we think that we can see a hint of comprehension. She has not spoken since her arrival."

"An unfortunate occurrence," Natasha said as she looked down on the princess. "Failee will not be pleased to learn that she has been damaged."

"It is of no concern," Succiu said easily, surprising Natasha with both her comment and her tone.

"How can that be?" Natasha asked. "Is her cooperation not absolutely necessary once you have returned to Parthalon?"

"Oh, yes, indeed it is." Succiu bent down to examine the princess' eyes. Shailiha clutched her abdomen and shrank farther back into the sofa. "But I am not disturbed by her condition. In fact, I welcome it, as I am sure Failee will, also. Consider this fact: If her mind and memory are already partly gone, will it not be even easier to turn her thoughts to ours, thereby making our job simpler?"

"I suppose so, Sister," Natasha said, rather confused. "But such things are beyond my ken, and should best be left to you and the First Mistress."

Succiu looked at Natasha and smiled. "Quite so," she said coldly.

Succiu reached out her hand to the princess, and Shailiha recoiled in terror and began to tremble. "I am not going to hurt you, my dear," Succiu said in the kindest of voices. "We are your friends, and we want to help you. You are one of us, and you have been through a difficult time. All we want to do is make you better."

Succiu was finally able to put her hand slowly upon Shailiha's head, and after a time, the princess began to settle down. Succiu closed her eyes and seemed to be concentrating. At last she opened them again and removed her hand from the princess. "She is able to speak, but refuses to," she said simply, "and her mind is undamaged except for the shock of the scene in the Great Hall. In addition there is some partial amnesia, but the unborn child that she carries is well."

"How long will she be like this?" Natasha asked.

Succiu lowered her voice so that only Natasha could hear her. "That is difficult to say," she whispered. "But the longer she is with us, and sees and hears no more talk or scenes of her previous life, the sooner she will come to accept the idea that she is one of us, and always has been."

So that is how they will get her to join us, Natasha thought. *By making her believe she was one of us all along.*

Succiu turned to the head handmaiden. "Light all of the oil lamps in this room, and then cover and lock each of the windows so that she cannot see outside," she said, her voice barely audible. "The longer she continues to gaze upon her lost homeland, the harder our job becomes. In addition, from this moment forward, there is to be absolutely no mention of why we came here or any reference whatsoever to this country or any of its inhabitants. To disobey this order is to invite a penalty of death."

She bent down again and looked into Shailiha's unseeing hazel eyes. "Our need for you is very great," she said quietly. "And you will soon come to understand that you are one of us, and you will worship the Pentangle as we do. You would never have achieved your ultimate potential without us, and we will see to it that your coming life, and the life of your child, will be one of great luxury and power."

Natasha watched as Succiu gently kissed the top of Shailiha's head. The princess simply sat there, lost somewhere inside herself, unmoving.

"Until the morning, my Sister," Succiu said meaningfully.

Then the Second Mistress led Natasha out of the room, leaving her handmaidens to their care of the newest mistress of the Coven.

Eleven

H*e has been sitting like that for hours,* Wigg thought, *and he probably will sit there longer still. And even though time is our enemy, after what he has been through I have no right to hurry him in this.*

Wigg stood quietly to one side of the graves, holding a lantern in one hand and the reins of the horses in the other. The lantern cast long and impossibly damp, eerie shadows across the ground around him. It was well past midnight, and it was still raining, just as it had been for the last three hours. He felt tired and dank, and the gray robes of his office stuck cold and clammy to his skin. Even the leaves of the trees drooped wetly down in the darkness as though possessed by their own sense of abject sadness.

Tristan sat on his heels in the wet grass of the royal cemetery, head bowed, before the row of freshly filled graves. His tears had finally stopped, but he had remained in this position for hours, his only movement the occasional fingering of the gold medallion around his neck. The medallion that held the broadsword and lion, of the House of Galland. The last gift given to him by his parents.

Wigg looked to the row of dirks in the quiver that had now been refilled, and to the curved, strangely beautiful sword of the Minions, which also hung across the prince's back in a tooled black scabbard.

Earlier that day they had cautiously crept their way through the subterranean levels of the Redoubt, wondering at every turn of the hallways whether they would encounter either the mistresses, or more warriors of the Minions. Blessedly, they had not. Wigg had insisted that the prince wear one of the robes of the consuls, so that he could use the hood to hide his face. Even if the Mistresses and the Minions had sailed on last night's tide as Succiu had said, Wigg felt it important that no one, not even the prince's subjects, be able to recognize them. They simply could not be delayed by any reason or person. The stakes were too high. Once on the surface they were sure to discover many disturbing scenes of atrocity, and it would be Wigg, especially, who would be begged to use his powers to ease the suffering of those they encountered. And despite the fact that it broke the old wizard's heart not to be able to help, he knew that his responsibilities lay elsewhere this day. He had carefully tucked his braided wizard's tail down into his robe and pulled the hood up over his head.

They had first gone to the kitchens of the Redoubt, where Wigg had selected provisions and Tristan had packed them into stringed leather bags that could be carried on horseback. Then they had gingerly made their way to the gravitating chamber and came back up into the library Wigg had shown Tristan that day when the prince had first learned of the Redoubt. Slowly and carefully they made their way back to the center of the palace, but nothing could have prepared them for what they were about to experience.

The scene that they encountered upon reaching the Great Hall was beyond belief.

Hundreds upon hundreds of their countrymen, civilians and Royal Guardsmen both, lay dead upon the floor. Not a single Minion corpse was among them. Severed limbs and heads lay about everywhere, and the marble floor of the hall was completely awash in the still partly liquid and partly viscid blood of the victims. Whenever the wind came up and blew hauntingly through the torn curtains and smashed stained-glass windows on either side of the room, the blood that had not already dried moved back and forth in sluggish little crimson waves of death.

The men, children, and soldiers had simply been murdered where they stood. But the women, even the elderly ones and the very young girls, lay naked everywhere, the remains of the Minion warriors' savage carnality evident upon each of their bodies and faces.

The bodies had already begun to stiffen, and their stench permeated the air.

And there was more.

On the walls of the Great Hall the Minions had painted, in blood, the Pentangle, the sign of the Coven. The numerous five-pointed stars stared back at the two guilty survivors with a kind of haughty and sneering victory, dominating the room in silent and enduring triumph as the redness ran down the walls in streaks.

Over the entire room hung the deafening, impenetrable silence of death, the only faint movement and sound coming from the torn, blood-stained curtains as they flapped haphazardly with the incoming breeze.

Wigg had wanted to leave immediately, but the prince shook his head and, instead, jumped up on the dais. *The dais, the killing ground of everyone I held dear,* he thought. He had walked to the white marble altar, still covered with the partly dried blood of Nicholas. *The altar upon which you murdered your own father,* he snarled at himself. Tristan touched a fingertip to a small spot of still-liquid blood and gently rubbed it between his fingers, blatantly crying aloud, and finally sank to his knees in pain. It was some time before he lifted his head once again.

It was then that he saw it.

The dreggan, in a black-tooled scabbard that Kluge had somehow left behind in the melee. Tristan recognized it immediately as the same sword he had used to kill his father. It lay innocently beneath one of the wizard's thrones. He approached it carefully, almost as if the inert sword could do him harm, and then finally reached beneath the seat and took it in his hand. He held it to the light for a time, mesmerized by its dangerous beauty. Despite everything that had happened, he was oddly not repulsed by the sword. He had never seen or held such a magnificent weapon in his life.

Tristan removed his robe. Then, gripping the scabbard with his left hand and the hilt with his right, he drew the blade. It rang loud and clear in the silence of the room, and it seemed a very long time before its mercenary song of death faded away into nothingness. The blood from Kluge's recent victims that had pooled in the bottom of the scabbard came out with the sword and began to run the length of the blade, dripping to the hilt, his hand, and finally to the floor.

Lowering the blade, he calmly walked to face one of the thrones. He pointed the curved, single-edged sword at the back of the chair, his index finger searching for and finding the little lever that he knew was there. Without hesitation he pushed it. The blade of the dreggan shot forward at least a foot, its point going all the way through the back of the chair and out the other side. He pushed the lever again, and in an instant the blade retracted to its previous position. Lowering the dreggan, Tristan stood looking at the awful, yet wondrous thing as if in thought. Then he placed the blade against his trouser leg and pulled it back, wiping it clean of the blood. He replaced the dreggan in its scabbard, then lifted the baldric over his head and put the sword behind his back, the strap across the front of his chest, the hilt rising behind his right shoulder, the curved and ever-widening blade reaching down his back to his left hip. He then readjusted the baldric so the handle of the sword reached fairly high and close to the side of his neck, so that he could easily grab either the dreggan or his throwing knives. He walked back to the altar and stood there silently for a moment, looking down at the place where his father had died.

I will kill him with this very sword. I swear by everything that I am, and everything that he has taken from me, the winged murderer will die at my hands.

He put his robe back on and jumped down from the dais to look into the infamous raised eyebrow of Wigg. But the look of grim determination upon the prince's face kept the old one silent. They each realized that there was no time to enter into an argument that the wizard would only lose.

Wigg turned and led them from the room.

After a brief stop at Tristan's living quarters to retrieve all the kasi, the gold coin of the realm, that they could carry, they went out to the palace smithy's shop, which was in an open area a little distance away from the castle. Wigg would have preferred to go to the stables first, so they could make a quick escape on horseback, if necessary, but Tristan had other ideas, and the wizard had no choice but to follow. Along the way they encountered not a single living soul. The blacksmith's shop was utterly deserted. While the wondering wizard watched, Tristan went to the wall behind the hearth and removed several stones, exposing a hole in the wall. Reaching in, he withdrew a black satin bag and laid it upon the ground. Wigg then realized what was in it.

Dirks.

More of the prince's steel throwing knives had obviously been hidden here against the day when the king might either have ordered Tristan to put them down for good, else ordered the smith not to make them anymore. The old one watched Tristan as he removed a dozen dirks from the bag. Quickly the prince placed them in the quiver that now lay against his back just to the right of the dreggan. Then he handed the bag to Wigg, and they continued on.

Tristan held his breath for what seemed the entire way to the royal stables. Besides Wigg and Shailiha, there was only one other living being in the world that he loved whom he hoped had not been killed.

Pilgrim.

As they approached the stables, they saw increasing numbers of corpses of livestock. All manner of cattle, pigs, horses, chickens—indeed, almost any living creature that one could imagine to be domesticated—had died in the same grisly fashion as their owners. They came upon more than one horse that could be seen trying to get up without a hoof or a leg, screaming insanely in pain as only a horse can, eyes wild with agony and fear. Wigg always stopped before these pitiful creatures, turning up his hands and closing his eyes, giving them a painless, humane, wizard's death.

As they walked through the gates and into the stables proper, Tristan started to become frantic. Dozens of dead horses lay all over the yard, including Shailiha's bay mare, but the longer he looked, the more hopeful he became that Pilgrim was not among them. "Any two horses will do," Wigg told him compassionately, hoping that the prince would give up the search so that they could be on their way. Time was critical. But Tristan was adamant, and Wigg could see the same look in his eyes that had been there when he had taken up the dreggan. "Pilgrim shall either be under me, or I shall know that he is dead," Tristan said sternly, and nothing more.

Wigg watched as the prince placed two fingers in his mouth and blew a loud, piercing whistle. The Lead Wizard winced. The last thing they needed to do was to attract attention to themselves, especially if the invaders had not all left. Again Tristan blew the whistle, the one that always brought the stallion running.

But there was nothing.

Tristan hung his head, and the tears once more began to come. *They have killed my horse, too,* he thought, rage boiling up in him again.

And then he heard it.

Soft and low, from somewhere in the nearby woods came a single, frightened snort. Tristan looked up, not daring to believe. He placed his fingers in his mouth and again whistled, and this time, after a few moments, he heard a whinny and the sound of a hoof pawing the ground nervously. Finally, several horses stepped from the woods into the clearing of the stable grounds upon frightened, shaking legs.

The one who led them out was Pilgrim.

The dappled gray stallion appeared to be uninjured, but there was a wildness in his eyes that the prince had never seen before. Several of the others had the same look in their eyes, as well as wounds that ranged from minor to serious.

Tristan walked slowly to his horse, talking to him gently. When he finally approached and tried to touch the stallion's face, Pilgrim reacted sharply, drawing his head back almost as if in pain. But as Tristan kept talking, the horse began to quiet down. At last the stallion rubbed the length of his face against Tristan's shoulder, almost knocking him down, and the prince knew Pilgrim was himself again.

Wigg and Tristan quickly examined the rest of the horses. Two were injured so badly that Wigg had to put them down, but the others looked as though they would be all right. Wigg saddled a black gelding, while the prince did the same to Pilgrim. After loading their mounts with the food and the bag of dirks, they secured the other horses in one of the paddocks, then left the stables.

Despite the urgency, they had agreed to take an unnecessarily long route through the city, veering away from the palace in order to remove suspicion of their association with it in case they happened upon anyone living.

The prince felt like a stranger in his own land as they rode through the city, clothed in a robe he was unaccustomed to, the hood drawn over his head so as to avoid being identified. "Steel your heart, Tristan," Wigg had said as they started down the streets. "Be surprised at nothing you see. Keep your head down, avoid attention, and whatever you do, don't stop to help, no matter how much you want to."

Tristan had always relished the chance to be away from the castle, mingling with the citizens whenever he could, but as they entered the outskirts of Tammerland the people he saw and the city he once knew had been so horribly changed that he could barely recognize either.

Virtually every building was on fire. The men of the city had apparently long since given up trying to quell the flames, and many of them simply stood in the streets before their homes or shops, sobbing. The fires were everywhere, making it difficult to walk the horses down the streets. There were many places where Pilgrim and Wigg's gelding simply refused to enter because of the flames, and they often had to resort to less-congested side streets or go around the flaming areas altogether.

Bodies were everywhere, both of the citizens and the Royal Guard. People had been dragged out of their homes in the dead of night and either killed on the spot, or raped and then killed. Body parts lay everywhere, and the imaginative nature of the Minions' carnage had apparently known no bounds. Everywhere they looked, heads and bodies were impaled on hooks and pikes. Internal organs had been torn away from their hosts. Packs of dogs wandered the streets, snarling and fighting amongst themselves, and some had begun to tear into the bloated corpses that had yet to be disemboweled.

At one of the street corners they came upon a pile of human bodies, naked, all women. They had all been abused, killed, and then thrown upon the heap as if the attackers had tried to see how many of them they could take in a single day, and make the pile of rotting bodies as high as possible.

Crippled horses and livestock ran, walked, and hobbled down the city streets in a daze, many of them bleeding to death as they went. Vast volumes of blood, both animal and human, ran down the streets and dripped from the burning buildings. It seemed to have washed almost everything in a drying, red-and-brown stain that Tristan knew would never leave this land, even when it could no longer be seen. The

Pentangles appeared, painted in blood, on almost every building. The arm and legs that had been used as fresh, flowing paintbrushes lay beneath the grotesque, red symbols.

But what struck Tristan as most horrible was the plight of the living.

Everywhere there was screaming. Women clutched to themselves the dead and bloody bodies of their loved ones. Men walked through the streets in a kind of trance, eyes wide open but unseeing, ears deaf, voices muted.

Some of the survivors were more rational, and Tristan was aghast when he heard what they were saying. "They're all dead!" a shopkeeper exclaimed. "And it is being said that the traitorous prince has taken the head of his own father! Now we all shall die!"

"What will become of us?" an old woman begged to the sky. She was sitting in the bloody dirt of the street, holding a dead lieutenant of the Guard in her lap—her son, perhaps. His eyes had been gouged out. "Who will protect us now?" she screamed to no one in particular.

The living may yet envy the dead, Tristan thought sadly. *And I am their prince, but am powerless to help.*

He lowered his face in shame, trying to neither see nor hear, and simply let Pilgrim follow Wigg's gelding at his own pace.

But his greatest disappointment of their ride was yet to come. Rounding a street corner, there came to his ears the sounds of broken glass, and more screaming.

The madness isn't over, he realized in disbelief. *Now we are doing it ourselves.*

Gangs of thugs, unfettered by law or reason, had begun roaming the darkening streets, taking whatever they wanted, killing those who got in the way. They were looting the shops that had somehow survived the fire. Many of them were drunk, waving stolen broadswords of the Guard as they went. Down the dark alleys that the prince and the wizard passed by, the screams of women could be heard, and more than once Tristan saw dirty, leering men lined up at the alley entrances, waiting their turn.

Tristan spurred Pilgrim to catch up to Wigg. Alongside the wizard, he chanced a sidelong glance at the ancient profile.

"We have to help!" he whispered. "I cannot simply ride by all of this as though it has no importance to me!"

"Look around you, Tristan," the old one whispered back. "Can't you see what is happening? Do you think that this is an isolated event? Don't be so naive. With the Royal Guard also went the last semblance of law and order. Look well, Tristan, and remember, for Eutracia and all that she once was is crumbling down around us."

"Despite that, I cannot merely stand by!"

"You can, and you will," Wigg snarled through gritted teeth. "Would you lose your life to save one woman when your sister is in danger, and the very future of your nation depends on what you do right now? Do you think that I would not like to extend my hand and stop the madness that I see before us?" Tristan had never seen such a look of angry frustration upon the old one's face. "If we are noticed, all could be lost. You must do as I say." Wigg turned his ancient, aquamarine eyes upon the prince, and Tristan could literally feel the wizard's power. Then Wigg said something that Tristan would never forget. Something that stabbed him through the heart.

"You are not yet as strong as you will eventually become. Do not doubt me here, again, as you did that day on the dais. This time I cannot save you from yourself."

Tristan did not speak.

I have hurt him, the old one realized. *But there is no other choice. The Chosen One must survive, no matter what the cost.*

It was then, just as they rounded another corner, that they first encountered the stench.

It was unlike anything that Tristan had ever smelled, and it hung visibly in the air in alternating black-and-beige layers with a kind of sickeningly sweet, yet repugnant flavor. There had been very little wind that day, and both the odor and the drifting particles that comprised it settled slowly, permeating everything it touched with its foulness. Then they entered an open field on the outskirts of the city, and heard the crackling of fire. Wigg instinctively knew what it was.

The Minions were burning their dead.

Hundreds of funeral pyres, glowing in the advancing night, lit up the sky for what seemed to be miles, the stench of the flaming corpses covering everything in a slowly settling dust of death.

As the last of the fires began to die in the gentle rain that had begun, the soft, deep rumble of thunder advanced across the ever-darkening sky. It seemed to Tristan that the entire world had begun to weep.

They rode on in the rain.

As their slow but deliberate circle began to take them back to the other side of the palace from which they had emerged, Tristan began to try to steel himself against what he knew he would encounter. He did not understand Succiu's mind as well as Wigg did, but he had little doubt that her orders would have been followed regarding the bodies of the wizards and the royal family. As they came closer to the palace entrance, Tristan began to look around for a horse-drawn cart. He had no illusions about being lucky enough to find one that was harnessed to a still–living horse, but if he could obtain one large enough he would use Pilgrim to pull it, and walk along beside.

He would need it to move the bodies.

When at last he found one and jumped down from his horse, he could feel the old one's eyes boring into the back of his head, as if to tell him that there was no time for this, and that they should leave. Tristan simply turned around, looking dead into the wizard's eyes.

"I know what you are thinking," he said, "and you're probably right. But I will not leave here until I have buried them. All of them. You can go on alone, if you want, but this is something I must do." There was no need for him to fight to maintain his determination. In this he would not be denied.

And so it was that they came full circle and approached the entranceway to the palace, and Tristan had to fight back the tears and the nausea when he was finally confronted with the sight that now lay before him.

It was almost midnight, and the dark, stormy sky gave no light. Other than the wizard and prince, the area was deserted. Torches had been lit to mark the spot of the spectacle, so that all those who passed would see it, day or night. Because they appeared not to consume themselves, Wigg assumed that the torches had been enchanted by either Succiu or Natasha.

Poles had been pounded into the ground, and the eight headless corpses were hung between them upside down by their ankles, naked. During the last two days, vultures and other birds of prey had picked away at their flesh. Some of the offal lay on the ground around them, rotting. The stench of death was very strong, wafting back and forth in the humid night air as they swung, silently, in the night wind, the wet rope above them creaking in between the soft rumblings of the storm.

From his horse Wigg looked up at the dusky edifice of the palace. Once this place had been full of gaiety, light, and love. It sat now, hulking and brooding in the night rain, looming over them like an enemy. The spires had all been relieved of their Eutracian royal flags and replaced, he noticed, with bright red flags that fluttered in the wind and rain. In the dark he could just make out the black Pentangle that appeared upon each one. The drawbridge was up, and the stone gargoyles that served as waterspouts high up on the edges of the roof were spewing rainwater from their mouths and back down to the earth. Dead soldiers of the Royal Guard lay everywhere, and the old one reminded himself that this had been the area of the worst fighting, as the terrible winged things had dropped onto the unsuspecting soldiers from above.

Tristan went to his knees before the bodies, sobbing. He stayed there for what seemed to be a long time before finally standing up.

Reaching over his left shoulder, he drew forth the dreggan with a single swift and determined stroke, and stood there listening to its now almost familiar ring slowly fade away into the night. Despite all of the damage that the awful thing had probably done in its lifetime, he found the sound it made in the air somehow reassuring.

For the first time this sword will be used for a compassionate purpose, and release some of its victims from their bondage, he told himself as he began to walk toward the poles.

From his horse, Wigg watched the prince as he strode toward the torches and the bodies, the dreggan firmly in his right hand. *Those torches will burn for weeks if we don't put them out,* the wizard thought. Then, suddenly, the old one sensed something. It wasn't quite like the feeling he got in the presence of unfamiliar endowed blood, but he could sense *something,* nonetheless.

He looked around in panic, but could find nothing amiss. There was no movement anywhere, except that of the prince, who continued to walk uncontested toward the lifeless bodies. Lightning tore across the sky. Wigg looked up just as it flashed, and for a split second the face of the castle was illuminated.

And then he knew.

The gargoyles! The large one in the center had never been there before.

"Tristan, come back!" he screamed against the rising noise of the storm. But the prince didn't hear him. A sickening revelation shot through the wizard's mind. *They knew we were still alive, and that the prince would want to come back to bury the bodies!*

Wigg stretched forth his hands to create a warp around Tristan and hold him in place, but it was too late. On his very next step Tristan had gone too far, and a red glow began to surround the area of the poles and the torches with the prince inside it. Tristan screamed, clutching his chest, and collapsed on the ground. Frantic, the old one tried to throw azure bolts of his own against the brightening circle of glowing red, but it was no use.

Their warp is in place, and I cannot penetrate it, he realized. *Succiu and Natasha have combined their powers to create it, and I alone cannot destroy it. They knew we would come back.*

The wizard tore his eyes from the prince long enough to look to the roof of the castle, and to the center gargoyle that crouched above the palace entryway.

To his horror, it began to move.

Slowly rising from its crouching stance upon both of its clawed feet, it stretched its muscles like a cat, and turning its head this way and that. Wigg watched, amazed, as the stone that encased it broke away from its body to reveal a dark green, scaly, winged creature with slanted yellow eyes, and sharp, equally yellow teeth. Small, useless-looking wings were upon its back. It stood upright on two powerful, bent legs, and its short but powerful arms ended in long, black talons. A curving, barbed tail led from the base of its pointy spine down to the ledge of the roof, and snaked back and forth in anticipation. It was at least the size of the prince, and it jumped off the ledge with ease, landing in the red-glowing circle just as Tristan was getting back to his feet.

And then, unbelievably, it spoke.

"I am a wiktor," it said venomously, yet somehow also casually. The creature's speech was perfect, almost eloquent, belying the horrific nature of its appearance. It pointed one of its talons at the prince. "And you shall not find me such easy prey as those ignorant blood stalkers or screaming harpies. I take great pleasure in what I do, and I am an expert craftsman. I am one of those whom the mistresses call upon when the task is to be very specific, and you must have great importance to them for one such as I to have been called forth and brought here to a foreign land."

Hissing loudly, it slowly began to circle Tristan, its tail twitching. Lightning scratched across the sky, highlighting the thing's grotesque features. Wigg sat nervously astride his horse, outside of the red-glowing perimeter, powerless to do anything but watch in dread.

Tristan lowered his eyes and pointed the dreggan at the thing's head, his momentary pain gone. "And just what is it you intend to do?" he asked. "Talk me to death?" He knew that this creature was in league with the Coven, and if he couldn't kill the sorceresses this night, then this horrible-looking thing would do. He relished the chance.

The thing called the wiktor smiled ominously, and Tristan saw green drool dripping down its face. "Your insolence will do you no good, mortal," it said calmly. "I intend to eat your heart. Doing so is my passion, and I enjoy human hearts above all else. They have a certain—how would you say?—consistency and sticky sweetness about them all their own. It has been a long time since I have had one, and from the looks of you, I don't think I shall be disappointed." It let out another long hiss, and tilted its head as it looked at the prince.

Tristan knew this was no game. In a flash he reached for one of his dirks and sent it hurtling toward the thing, aiming for the center of its chest. But as if in slow motion, the wiktor simply reached out at the last possible instant and plucked it from the air before it could strike him. It held the knife up to the yellow light of the torches that surrounded them and examined it carefully, leisurely, hissing again to itself as it did so, still tilting its head back and forth maddeningly.

"Ah, yes," it said, smiling, some of the green drool filming down over its yellow teeth. "Your beloved knives. The mistresses told me all about them. They're rather well made, aren't they? But, I fear, no use to you against me, dear prince. I shall keep them as a souvenir of your death." Hissing again, it sneeringly dropped the dirk into the dirt.

And then, without warning, it launched itself at Tristan, covering the ground between them in an instant, teeth and talons extended, the yellow, slanted eyes now mere slits in the thing's contorted face.

Tristan quickly drew the dreggan and spun completely around on one heel, just as Frederick had taught him, ending up alongside his adversary. But the wiktor was faster than anything the prince had ever seen, and it ducked below the deadly arc that Tristan cut sideways through the air. This was only the second time he had ever swung this blade in anger, and he immediately realized that its unusual length and width were slowing him down. *"Make every swing count,"* he heard Frederick's voice tell him from somewhere in the past, *"because you will tire, and each time you swing you will be just that much weaker than the time before. When the adversary is faster or stronger, time is nothing but an enemy."*

Again the wiktor rushed him, and again Tristan struck out with the sword, only to find that he had missed. Time after time the result was the same, and while the seeds of exhaustion began to grow in his aching muscles, the thing's talons were coming ever closer to ripping into Tristan's bare chest. Then the realization struck him. *I'm playing his game,* he thought. *The wiktor wants to tire me first, to draw me out, so that he can toy with me before he takes my heart.*

And then he knew what to do. But it meant that the wiktor's desire to take his heart must overshadow the thing's fighting instincts. He must tempt it to attack quickly, out of hunger, without thinking it through.

To Wigg's terror, Tristan dropped the dreggan into the dirt and stood before the hideous thing in the red glow of the warp. He put his hands over his head in surrender, elbows high, and looked down at his boots in dejection.

"I cannot defeat you," he panted breathlessly. "I can see that now. If I let you take my heart without a struggle, will you give me your word that you will let the wizard live? He is old, and his powers are failing. It is all I ask." Dropping to his knees, he unlaced the front of his leather vest and pulled it open, his gold medallion glinting in the ghostly red light of the warp.

The wiktor tilted its head, smiling, and Tristan could see that its hunger was growing. The yellow eyes stared back at him wickedly.

"They told me that you would present more of a challenge," it hissed, "but apparently even the mistresses can be wrong." A pink, forked tongue darted out of the thing's mouth and licked some of the green drool away from its face. "Prepare yourself," it said. "I accept your offer."

Tristan nodded resignedly and bowed his head slightly, just enough to give the impression of cowardice, as if he did not want to be able to see the wiktor when it reached inside him and tore out his heart.

I beg the Afterlife, he thought, *help me wait until the last instant.*

And then the thing came. Wigg watched in abject horror as the awful creature crossed the ground in a flash, talons extended toward the prince's heart.

"*Wait,*" Tristan heard Frederick say, as the thing loomed up. "*Wait, wait . . . now!*"

At the last possible second, Tristan raised his right hand behind him and grasped one of the dirks. In a flash he held it forward with both hands as the thing ran at him, talons first, and they rolled over and over in the dirt and the mud. Wigg lost track of them for a moment in the red glow, and then, finally, the aura started to dissipate and he saw Tristan astride the wiktor, pushing the knife farther into the thing's chest. Sensing that he could now penetrate the fading glow, the wizard ran as fast as he could to stand next to the prince.

Tristan stood, exhausted, looking down as green-and-yellow fluids started to ooze from the thing's fissured chest. He picked up the dreggan, and this time it felt genuinely good in his hand. And then the Coven's servant did something unexpected.

The dying wiktor smiled.

"I will give the Coven your regards, Prince." It coughed, sending some of the fluid from its mouth spraying into the air and down on the scaly green body. "We will see each other again, mortal," it hissed. "And next time I shall win."

Wigg started to raise his hand, presumably to finish it off, but Tristan gripped the old one's wrist with a strength that Wigg had never felt in him before.

Tristan placed the tip of the dreggan between the wiktor's eyes as the beast continued its sick smile. He leaned over the thing, looking directly into the slanted, yellow eyes.

"I don't think so," he said in a whisper. He touched the lever on the hilt of the dreggan, and the blade plunged forward, instantly cleaving the monster's head in two.

Inexplicably, the thunder and lightning started up anew, seeming to scream out of the sky to the very spot the wizard and prince were standing over the dead wiktor. The lightning came in huge, strong, brilliant scratches, tearing endlessly across the sky, the wind whirling around them and picking up debris, flinging it everywhere at once. Finally the storm subsided, and quiet once again reigned.

Tristan stood there for a long moment, gazing at the dead creature, and then he held the dreggan in the air and looked at it, too, for a long time. Finally he ran the blade in the crook of his elbow between his biceps and his forearm to clean it, then slid it back into the scabbard.

They cut the bodies down and loaded them into the cart. Tristan took special care to load and cover his mother's body first, using capes that had belonged to the dead members of the Royal Guard. Then followed the bodies of the men, also covered in the same fashion. Somehow the black coloring of the capes was more than fitting.

Before they left, Tristan quietly but sternly cut a limb from a nearby tree, cut off the branches, and sharpened each end. He pushed the limb deep into the earth beneath where the bodies had hung, and impaled the wiktor's smashed head upon it, leaving the thing's body on the ground nearby. If any of the Coven or their Minions had been left behind, he wanted them to know what had happened to their servant, and who had done it.

He turned and gave the old wizard a long look. Although there would be much to say about what had happened here, Tristan was in no mood to talk about it now.

There was more important work to be done.

They buried the bodies in the royal cemetery, taking the precaution to place them some distance away from the others, without markers, so that there might be less chance of tampering with them. It was these eight graves that the old wizard now stood over in the rain in the middle of the night, watching his prince as he grieved.

He has not moved or spoken for hours, Wigg thought. *He has been through so much. If he doesn't come back to me soon, I fear he may never do so.*

And then the prince moved.

Wigg watched, perplexed, as Tristan removed one of the dirks from his quiver, still kneeling before the graves, the medallion dangling from his neck, and began to speak.

"True peace of mind comes only when my heart and mind are aligned with true principles and values," he said quietly as he cried. "I shall forsake not, to the loss of all material things, my honor and integrity. I shall protect the Paragon above all else, but take no life except in urgent defense of self and others, or without fair warning. I swear to rule always with wisdom and compassion." He bowed his head.

The oath of succession, the old one thought. *The oath that he never wanted to take, he now takes upon himself willingly.* Wigg wiped a tear from his eye. *He is no longer my prince. He is now my king.*

The old wizard watched as Tristan took the razor-sharp dirk and drew a cut across each of his palms. Quickly he replaced the dirk in the quiver, then bent over farther and made a fist with each of his hands, squeezing his blood over each of the eight mounds.

"I swear to you on all that I am, and all that I ever may be, that I will bring my sister and her unborn child back to this land," he said, trembling, continuing to squeeze his endowed blood out of his palms and onto the soil. "And that when I do, I will accept the role that you had planned for me, and do the best that I know how."

Tristan finally stood, the tears still coming as he faced the blood-topped graves.

"Good-bye," Wigg heard him say softly to the fresh, wet mounds of earth.

Tristan turned and looked into the Lead Wizard's eyes.

"And so it begins," he said quietly.

They walked their horses out of the cemetery and started toward the northeast, to Shadowood.

PART IV

Journey to Shadowood

CHAPTER

Twelve

The two who remain shall seek the one who abandoned their cause, and find him se-
cluded, and alone in his use of the craft. And the Chosen One shall take up three
weapons of his choice and slay many before reading the Prophecies and coming to the
light . . .
—PAGE 1282, CHAPTER ONE OF THE VAGARIES OF THE TOME

For the next three days they kept to the main road leading north from the city. The dirt road was choked with refugees.

When they left the city, Tristan had noticed an equal if not greater-sized group heading south. *They want to live anywhere but Tammerland,* he reflected. *And I can't say that I blame them.* Most of the ones on the north road were probably trying to reach either Ilendium or Tanglewood, the two largest cities north of Tammerland. He ruefully wondered how many of them would still want to live in Ephyra if they knew the truth about its "duchess." Those heading south would be trying to reach either Florian's Glade or the coastal city of Warwick Watch.

The going was agonizingly slow, since the road was so crowded. It was seldom that they could gallop their horses, and the travel was made even more tedious because their conversation was so limited. A single slip of the tongue could reveal everything, and they could not chance that, so they talked little. Wigg kept his wizard's tail tucked down into his robe, and Tristan had removed the dreggan, covered it with a cape of the Royal Guard, and tied it across the back of his saddle. The robe that Wigg insisted he still wear was scratchy and hot, and the road dust irritated their noses and throats as they went along. It seemed that from everywhere came the sounds of wailing and lament from their fellow travelers, who had lost so much and were still no doubt in shock.

Each night they made camp far enough away from the road that they could talk about what to do next. Tristan enjoyed sleeping in the grass under the stars, but the old wizard complained about wanting a bed and a hot meal. It was decided that they would try to spend the next night at an inn two days south of the fork in this road. The northern branch went to Ilendium, the eastern branch to Malvina Watch. But after that there would be no road to take them were they needed to go, Wigg said, and they would have to strike out over the countryside. If there wasn't enough food for the journey, then Tristan would hunt it. He smiled one of his now-rare smiles at the thought of the old one eating rabbit over a campfire spit instead of being served roast duckling in the castle.

It was early evening of the fourth day when they found themselves standing before the inn. The Rogue's Roost was one of the largest hostels in the country, situated as it was on the main thoroughfare between the northern cities and Tammerland. They gave their horses to the stable boy and paid him well after he told them that the stable, like the inn itself, was very full. Tristan demanded extra oats and a good brushing for both horses.

The prince, carrying the concealed dreggan and the remainder of their food in the leather bags, was about to enter the inn when Wigg grabbed him by the arm, holding him back. "Be careful," the old one said. "The Royal Guard is no more, and this place has long been known as a favorite spot for drunkards and thieves to lay over and rest, even when the Guard was active. Speak little, and let me do the talking when it comes to getting a room. We must stay as low-profile as possible." Saying no more, the old one opened the door to the inn and beckoned the prince through.

The lobby, if one could call it that, was very large and served as a combination of tavern, meeting place, and eatery. Along one wall a large fireplace stood, its orange glow dancing about in the dim half-light of the room. The floor was full of tables, most of them filled with men of varying description, almost all of whom seemed sullen and distrustful. Many of them looked up quickly at the two robed figures who had just entered the room, and did not take their eyes off them for what seemed to be a very long time. Some of the men were drunk, and others were playing at cards or board games. The only women Tristan could see in the room were several barmaids who did their best to keep up with the loud, abusive demands of the patrons. Occasionally the men would grab at the women, and sometimes it was all the girls could do to break away from their advances. Any men who were staying here with their wives were probably keeping them upstairs, locked in their rooms, Tristan thought. He didn't know how long he could watch without doing something. The muscles in his jaw clenched as he followed the wizard to the desk at the far end of the room, knowing that Wigg was silently screaming at him to use self-restraint—something he was in very short supply of.

The innkeeper was a fat, greasy man with little pig's eyes. He looked up sullenly at the two of them as if they didn't matter.

"A room, with two beds," Wigg said politely, "and food and drink for tonight and tomorrow morning."

"We're full," the pig-man said. "Go away."

Wigg produced the bag of kisa and threw several of them on the countertop. As expected, the ring of the gold coins bought a measure of silence from the room.

"Inns are never full when the price is right," Wigg said casually. "How much?"

Pig-man cracked a slight smile, and Tristan guessed that the fellow had never seen that many gold coins in one place in his life.

"Who are you?" The innkeeper grunted. "You don't look like the usual type I get in here."

"We're refugees," Wigg said in a friendly tone, "just like everybody else. And we need a place to stay." He opened the bag a little wider.

"Six kisa," Pig-man said quickly. "The meal tonight is fresh mutton with vegetables." He turned and reached under the countertop, producing a key. "The room at the top of the stairs. When you come back down I will send one of the maids to your table."

Wigg produced three more kisa and placed them on the countertop. As they were turning to go up the stairs, Pig-man spoke again. "I have other things to sell that you may want," he said lewdly as he quickly scooped up the coins.

"Such as?" Wigg asked.

"The road from Tammerland is long and hot, and there are few diversions. Two men such as yourselves could possibly welcome some entertainment." The little pig eyes looked sure that more kisa would be coming their way tonight. He spread his hands flat upon the counter and smiled.

Tristan knew exactly what the man was talking about. "You sell the barmaids, don't you?" he asked, no small amount of anger in his voice.

"Indeed I do"—Pig-man leered—"whether they want to be sold or not. Refugees from the city, nice and fresh, they are. Since all the trouble in Tammerland, there's nowhere for them to go from here, and no way to get there on their own. Law of supply and demand, I say. They're mine to do with as I please. For just a few more kisa each you can have your pick, and be assured that they will be sent to your room." He leaned forward to the point that Tristan could smell the ale on his stale breath. "And if they don't do *everything* you want, I'll see to it that they are whipped, good and proper."

To Wigg's horror, Tristan reached over the counter, grabbed the innkeeper's dirty shirt, and pulled him halfway across the countertop. The wounds of his family's deaths were still too fresh, and he was reacting without thinking. "Don't you know that's illegal?" the prince snarled. "You could get into a lot of trouble for this."

Unperturbed, Pig-man looked squarely into the prince's eyes. "There *are* no laws anymore, boy," he said, pleased with himself. "Since the trouble down in Tammerland, I hear the Royal Guard are all dead, and the Directorate and even the royal family, too. So who's going to stop me, huh? Now, do you want the women or not?"

"No," Tristan said simply. He pushed the innkeeper back behind the dirty counter and grabbed the key.

After depositing the food and Tristan's dreggan in their room, they went back downstairs and took a small table in one corner, as far away from the others as possible, so that they might talk. Wigg was beside himself with fury.

"That was a very foolish thing to do," the old one said curtly. "If you keep drawing attention to us this way, we will never get to Shadowood."

Tristan looked across the room at the innkeeper, wishing he had done more, but he knew that the old one was right. "I just can't stand back and let all of this happen," he said angrily. "I already feel responsible for it all, and watching our people suffer in so many ways only makes it worse."

Wigg was about to respond when suddenly he lowered his head and cleared his throat, tilting his face slightly. Tristan looked up to see one of the barmaids approaching.

He found himself looking up into the face of one of the most beautiful women he had ever seen. She was tall and shapely, with expressive green eyes and long, curling red hair that caught highlights from the fireplace. She wore a simple peasant's dress, over which was a torn and stained apron. In her hands she held a tray of empty tankards. She looked to be about twenty-five years old.

And she was scared to death.

Clumsily, she asked, "What would you like to drink? I'm afraid that there is only wine or ale, but the red wine is fairly good, if you like that kind of thing." She stood there nervously, not seeming to know what to say next, as if she had never done this work before. She awkwardly shifted her weight from one foot to the other as she waited. The fear was apparent in her eyes, and despite the wizard's warnings Tristan found himself wanting to know more.

"Red wine will be fine," he said gently. "What is your name?"

"Lillith, of the House of Alvin," she said quietly, as though she couldn't understand why anyone would want to know. "My father was a friend of the king, before he died. Both of my parents and my brother were slaughtered in the massacre at Tammerland, and I left the city in a panic, trying to get to relatives in Ephyra." She gave a quick, scared little look toward the innkeeper before continuing. "I only arrived yesterday." She looked at each of them in turn, with a fear that Tristan had seen far too much of in recent days. She lowered her head, and a tear started to come. "Why do you ask?" She paused for a moment, biting her lower lip. "Are you going to buy me for tonight?" Her expression was one of genuine terror. "Is that why you need to know my name?"

"No, my child," Wigg said gently. "No harm will come to you from us."

She seemed to relax a little.

"Why don't you leave?" Tristan asked.

"How?" she said, crying a little bit. "I came here just as you did, with very little, trying to escape all the madness of my home, looking only for a room. And when he saw me, he took all of my money and clothes, and gave me these to wear. He watches us all day, and locks us up at night. He said that I was now his to do with as he wished, that I had to work for him, and that he would sell me if he chose to." She shook her head in pain. "And he said this morning that if no one bought me tonight, he would take me himself, to break me in."

Suddenly, from across the room, a particularly dirty one of the drunkards called out to her. "You little Tammerland bitch!" he shouted. "If you don't bring me my ale soon, instead of me paying you, you will be paying me!" He made a circle between his left index finger and thumb, and lasciviously ran his other index finger back and forth inside of it. He laughed while several of his friends slapped him on the back.

In a flash, she was gone.

Tristan put his face in his hands. "Have we really come to this?" he asked.

"Yes, we have, Tristan," the old one said. "And you must accept the fact that such things are now the way of our world, and that if you try to intervene in each problem that you see, we will actually end up helping no one. You must think of your sister. First, last, and always."

Tristan knew that the old one was trying to turn the subject away from the plight of Lillith the barmaid. And it worked. Tristan found himself once again preoccupied with Shailiha.

He looked into the Lead Wizard's eyes as they stared out at him from under the hood of his robe. "How is it that I have never heard of a place called Shadowood?" he asked simply.

Wigg took a long breath in through his nose and looked around the room before responding. "No one outside of the Directorate, not even your father, knew of Shadowood," he began in a low voice.

He paused as he saw Lillith returning with two glasses of red wine. She placed the glasses on the table and looked briefly into Tristan's eyes. Watching her walk away, the prince found it hard to drag his mind back to what Wigg was saying.

"Shadowood was created by the wizards, Faegan included, near the end of the war, at the time when we thought that all might be lost—just before we found the Paragon. It was created as a peaceful hiding place for the wizards, if necessary, so that male endowed blood would not become extinct. It is surrounded on all sides by a great canyon; the easterly side is very close to the Sea of Whispers." The old wizard pursed his lips. "I was greatly disturbed to hear Succiu make mention of it. That can only mean that the Coven has somehow discovered its existence." He sat back in his chair.

Tristan took a sip of the wine, thinking. "But there is no such canyon," he said. "I'm sure I would have heard of it if there had been."

"Oh, the canyon exists, all right," the old one said, smiling, "and was one of our greatest achievements. Truth be known, it cannot be seen. Still, it exists."

"I thought you said that until that day upon the dais, invisibility had never been achieved."

"It hadn't. This is different."

"What so you mean?"

Wigg sighed. *There is so much to teach him,* he thought. *And I am the only one left in the entire nation who can do it.* "It can be seen only by those of highly trained endowed blood. And just having the right blood and being trained in the craft does not mean that one can automatically see it. One must be trained in *how* to see it. Even you and you sister, despite your blood quality, would not be able to see it until you were taught to. That is not the same thing as invisibility. True invisibility is a much harder concept to achieve."

Tristan wasn't sure he understood the subtlety, but he was too interested in his next question to debate the point. "So what happens if an untrained person, or even one of unendowed blood comes upon it? What do they see?"

"They see exactly what we planned to have them see: a forest."

Tristan scratched his head as he took another sip of wine. Then he looked up at the old wizard. "And what happens if they continue to walk into this so-called forest?"

"Once they have walked far enough, when they put their next foot down upon what they think will be firm ground, they fall to their death." Wigg spoke as if none of this bothered him at all. "Anyone behind them who was watching simply thinks that the person ahead of them has somehow been swallowed up by the earth." A small smile crossed his face. "A human being suddenly sucked up by the earth, his horses and oxen not suffering the same fate, tends to add to the legend and keep people away, as you might well imagine."

Tristan was aghast. "Are you saying that innocent people can die by simply going there, just so you can protect a piece of ground?"

"Try not to be too harsh on us," the old one said, meeting the prince's stare. "We were virtually sure at that time that we would lose the war, and this was the best spell that we could invoke. Remember, we had not yet discovered the Paragon, and knew far less about the craft than we do now. The canyon around Shadowood seemed to be a good answer, since if the Coven had indeed won and enslaved the nation as they intended, then anyone who came our way was a potential enemy."

"So how do we get across?"

"There is a bridge, of course."

Tristan shook his head. This was all starting to sound like a bad dream. "A bridge? A simple bridge? Why don't we just fly across on some of your blue lightning bolts?" he asked sarcastically.

Despite the jab, Wigg was glad to see the prince's true personality beginning to return. Although he would have never told him so, Wigg had actually begun to miss Tristan's flippant remarks. Nonetheless, he gave the prince a rather deprecating look and was about to respond in kind when Lillith returned with their dinner. She put large plates of steaming mutton down before each of them, and a bowl of vegetables between them. When Tristan reached for his wineglass, his hand touched hers, and he looked up into her green eyes. She looked down, frightened, and quickly walked away. Tristan followed her with his eyes.

Wigg took a forkful of the mutton, placed it in his mouth, and chewed without speaking. Reaching for a sip of wine, he added drily, "It isn't that simple. The bridge has a guard. At least it did three hundred years ago. And if Faegan lives there, I would be willing to bet that the guard is still in place."

Tristan dug into his meat, suddenly surprised at how hungry he had become. Without looking up he asked, "So do we have to fight this guard to get across? I suppose he is some great, lumbering, three-hundred-year-old brute of a man."

Wigg pursed his lips and sighed. "The guard is a gnome," he said simply.

Tristan's fork stopped halfway to his mouth. "A *gnome?*" he asked. "What in the name of the Afterlife is a gnome?"

"To put it simply, a gnome is a little person. They tend to live to be very old, and are fiercely loyal to those whom they serve. I'm not surprised you never heard of them. In fact, I'm glad of it. That means they are all still in Shadowood." He served himself some vegetables.

"I don't understand."

Wigg smiled. "There's no way that you could. Gnomes have been in Eutracia for as long as we have. But before the war, some men found it to be great sport to hunt them down and kill them, and sometimes take the opportunity to rape their women. These poachers came to be known as gnome hunters. This was all before the creation of the monarchy and the Royal Guard. Because of the gnome hunters it took the wizards a long time to finally earn the gnomes' trust, and to enlist their help in our cause against the Coven. In return for guarding Shadowood, they were given the benefits of time enchantments and a safe place in which to live, free of the hunters. Ironically, the only wizard to live there now is Faegan, presumably the one who aided the Coven during the war."

Tristan sat back in his chair, spellbound. *Shadowood, Faegan, a giant canyon that cannot be seen, and a bridge guarded by something called a gnome.* He shook his head. "Is there anything else?" he asked, almost afraid to hear the answer.

"Oh, yes," the wizard said between bites. "The gnome might not let us cross."

"Why not? You're the Lead Wizard, aren't you?"

"Of course I am," Wigg said testily, brushing away the comment with his free hand as if it were a nuisance. "But even the Lead Wizard must prove his identity before being given permission to cross the bridge. Another safeguard."

"And just how do we manage that?"

"Actually," Wigg said, "for me it is extremely simple. You see, I have been specially trained to see it—another safeguard against the Coven. But as for you, with no training in the craft whatsoever, well, that will be a different matter. We will cross that bridge when we come to it, as they say."

Tristan decided to change the subject. "Wigg, what is a wiktor?"

Wigg sighed and took another sip of his wine. "I truly do not know. But I am certainly glad that you killed it."

"But it said that it had been awakened to come after me here, in a *foreign* land. Where, then, did it come from?"

"I don't know. Presumably from wherever the sorceresses were."

"The deaths of both the harpy and the wiktor were followed by thunder and lightning such as I have never seen," Tristan recalled. "I cannot remember such a thing ever happening on a clear day or night, and yet now, in such a short time, I have seen it twice. They must be related, but how?"

And I had not seen it myself for over three hundred years, Wigg thought. "Do you remember that day in the woods when I showed you what the Vigors and the Vagaries actually looked like—the two glowing, revolving orbs?" he asked.

"Of course," the prince answered. He would never forget that sight, no matter how long he lived. When he had first seen those orbs, they had made an indelible impression on his soul, as well as sending his endowed blood screaming through his veins. And now, after learning so much about himself from the wizard, he felt he was closer to knowing why.

Wigg took another forkful of the mutton. "Do you remember the darkness of the Vagaries—how the light shot back and forth inside the orb as if it were straining to break free of its prison? Well, the sorceresses practice the Vagaries, and the creatures they control—such as the stalker, harpy, and wiktor—are most certainly results of their incantations. Therefore, these creatures are all very closely associated with that discipline. I believe that the sorceresses and their servants are in fact so intertwined with the discipline of the Vagaries that when one or more of them dies it creates a tiny rent in the fabric of the Vagaries, in the actual substance of the orb itself, and therefore allows a diminutive amount of light and energy to escape, resulting in the disturbances we see in the skies." He pursed his lips for a moment, thinking.

"Just imagine," he said slowly, "the amount of power and destruction that would occur should a truly large rent in the Vagaries ever be opened. The result would be catastrophic. And still I believe it would be nothing compared to the uncontrolled, improper combination of both the Vigors and Vagaries together, should they ever be sufficiently ruptured at the same time." He sat back in his chair for a moment. "Another of the more famous wizards' conundrums, Tristan. The fact that the craft is infinitely powerful. Just as it is also infinitely fragile."

The prince's mind was once again taken back to the day he killed the wiktor. "Before it died, the wiktor said that we would meet again, even though it knew it was soon to be dead. Why would it say such a thing?"

Wigg smiled quietly into Tristan's eyes. "Because there is truly a difference between being killed and being dead," he said quietly. *And the practice of the Vagaries shall lead to the madness of other, lower worlds.* He could hear the text of the Vigors repeating it to him as if he had read it only yesterday.

Wigg was about to speak again when Lillith returned to their table. She gave Tristan a kind but still frightened look as she began to clear away the dishes. Tristan was about to speak to her when, seemingly from nowhere, two dirty, hairy arms snaked around her waist from behind. She jumped, dropping the dishes on the floor, breaking them. Tristan immediately stood up to see the man standing directly behind her, holding her firmly in a bear hug, wetly lick the side of her face as she tried to pull away.

"The innkeeper told me that no one has bought you yet," he said, smelling her hair and moving one of his dirty, gnarled hands closer to her breasts. "I told him I didn't care how much it cost. Tonight you're mine."

Tristan's reaction was immediate. To Wigg's horror, the prince stood up and tore off his robe. He quickly stepped behind the man, pulled one of his dirks from his quiver, and reached around to put an arm around the man's throat. With the other arm he placed the blade squarely between the man's legs. Tristan raised the blade a fraction until he could hear the knife begin to cut through the man's trousers. Lillith's attacker froze. The room became deathly quiet.

"She's already spoken for," Tristan whispered into the man's ear from behind. "And unless you want me to cut them off and have her feed them to her next customer, I suggest you let her go." He raised the blade yet another fraction, and he could feel the knife's edge resting against the roundness of the man's left testicle.

The man let her go, and she slumped forward. Wigg caught her as she fell, and helped her into Tristan's chair. Tristan turned the man around to face him. He had a sunken, sallow face and long hair, and was missing several of his teeth.

Tristan looked him dead in the eyes and raised his dirk up to the man's face. "Go away," he said softly.

"No. She's mine." The man stood there, defiant, despite the knife in his face.

In a flash, Tristan moved the blade even closer to his face, placing its tip against the man's lower eyelid. A small sliver of blood started to walk the length of the blade.

"If you don't leave now, the least you will lose is your eye," Tristan growled. He could feel the endowed blood in his veins running even faster now, as if begging him to avenge so many of the wrongs he had seen. *Just give me one more reason,* he snarled silently. He looked down at the man's groin. "And if you continue to resist me, you will lose it all, I promise you."

As quickly as he had appeared, the man turned and ran out of the room.

Without giving Wigg the chance to speak to him, Tristan marched across the room, the dirk still in his hand, and looked into Pig-man's eyes. He pointed to Lillith. "I choose her," he said to the innkeeper. "How much?" The look on his face was not to be denied.

Even so, the innkeeper decided to play his usual game. He licked his lips with greed. "Let's see," he began sarcastically. "Considering the fact that you are intent on driving away my customers, and, as far as I know, she is still a virgin, I think the price will be very high, indeed." He spread his hands wide and flat upon the surface of the countertop, taking his time with his thoughts.

Tristan had endured enough.

In the twinkle of an eye, the prince raised the dirk high above his head, and without even looking brought it down into the countertop with all of his strength—exactly between the first and second fingers of Pig-man's right hand.

"I said how much, you bastard?"

"S–s-six kisa," the innkeeper stammered, pulling his hand away from the dirk.

Tristan reached into his trousers and pulled out ten. He threw them on the counter with a loud clang. No one in the room moved.

Leaving the knife embedded into the counter, he reached out and pulled Pig-man across the counter to him. He then took up the knife and held it before the innkeeper's face.

"The four extra are for another room," he said into the little eyes. He dropped Pig-man on the bar and walked around to join him. "Which is your best room?"

The innkeeper held up a key on a gold chain. Tristan took it in his hand and walked back to the table.

Wigg sat there staring at him as if he were from another world, angry beyond belief. The girl named Lillith sat in Tristan's chair, stunned and more than a little frightened. "Does this mean I must go upstairs with you now?" she asked, obviously trying to keep the fear out of her voice.

"No," Tristan whispered urgently. "This means that were are leaving, just as soon as we can get upstairs, collect our things, and go out one of the windows. I rented the extra room only for appearances. You wanted to get out of here, didn't you? Well, here's your chance." Aghast, she looked at him as if he were out of his mind.

Wigg stood and looked Tristan in the face. "Are you mad?" he asked in a low voice. "I agree that after that little scene of yours we will certainly be leaving, but we simply cannot take her with us!"

"Both you and she come with me right now," Tristan demanded. He inched his face closer to the wizard's. "I have seen enough pain and violence to last a thousand lifetimes, much of it my own fault, and I have done nothing to help my countrymen other than to stand by and take orders from you. She goes with us, or she and I go and you stay here alone." He looked around the room briefly. Some of the other men had stood up from their chairs and were talking angrily among themselves, and it was plain to everyone that the three of them were the unfortunate topic of conversation.

Wigg looked into the eyes of the man that he loved so much and knew that Tristan would not be denied. Finally he smiled. "Very well. We go. All of us."

Tristan turned, the dirk still in his hand, and led the two of them across the floor to the stairs. With each step up he felt every angry eye in the room on his back.

They would have to move quickly.

Leaving the inn actually proved easier than Tristan had first thought. After collecting the bags of food and Tristan's dreggan, Wigg opened a window on the far side of the room. Beneath lay a shallow pitched roof, presumably over the inn's kitchen. It was directly across from the stables. They slid down the roof one by one, finally jumping to the ground, Tristan catching Lillith as she came down into his arms. He stood there holding her for a few moments longer than Wigg would have liked. Despite her obvious fear she managed to give him a smile, and he gave her a quick grin of encouragement back.

Tristan immediately ran into the stables to roust the stable boy and helped him saddle their two horses. At a word from Tristan, the stable boy produced a roan mare, complete with saddle and bridle. They galloped out of the stable yard and down the moonlit road, trying to put as much distance between them and the inn as possible. Occasionally Tristan looked over at Lillith to make sure she was all right and wasn't having any trouble keeping up. The mare she was on was almost as fast as Pilgrim, and to his relief he saw that Lillith was an excellent rider. Once, she looked back and smiled, apparently happy to be away, her long red hair flowing behind her in the wind.

Wigg finally raised his hand and slowed his gelding, and the three of them stopped. The Lead Wizard closed his eyes for a moment—Tristan guessed that the old one was using his mind to search the area for pursuers. Tristan was careful not to speak, aware that there were many things that must be kept strictly between himself and Wigg for as long as the young woman was with them.

After Wigg declared them safe for the time being, they walked the horses over to a small rise by a nearby stream, and Tristan and Lillith slept there in the grass that night, side by side. Wigg settled himself closer to the road, alone, saying he should be the one to stand watch. Tristan knew why: Wigg would be able to detect anyone coming long before Tristan ever could and, provided the girl did not see it, the old one could use his powers to deal with any problems. The Lead Wizard could go without sleep for days if he had to.

The prince was glad to be outdoors, under the stars again, and he and Lillith talked for what seemed a long time before they fell asleep, despite how tired they were. When she had asked Tristan and Wigg their names as part of thanking them for taking her away from the inn, they had both given her their true first names, but Tristan had of course not mentioned the name of his family house. Lillith apparently had no clue who they really were, but as a precaution the old one had kept his wizard's tail neatly tucked down into his robe, and Tristan had not unwrapped the dreggan.

They told her that Wigg was a blacksmith and Tristan his apprentice; that, like her, they were on their way north to escape the massacre at Tammerland. They had not been able to bring any of their tools, and would sadly have to start in business all over again in one of the northern cities.

For her part, Lillith explained that she was the daughter of one of the tax collectors of the outer reaches of Tammerland, and that it was in that way that her father, Agamedes of the House of Alvin, had known the king. She was a schoolteacher, as her late mother had been, and enjoyed her time with the children, especially the younger ones. Her brother, Chauncey, had been a lieutenant in the Royal Guard. Their home had been burned to the ground by the terrible creatures with wings, and when she had seen the bodies of her father and brother she had panicked, gathering up all her money and setting out on her horse for the north, just as so many others had done. The innkeeper had stolen all of her money and sold her horse the first day.

At the end of her tale, she broke into tears, and Tristan held her for a long time in the moonlight, knowing that despite how much she attracted him, they would have to part company on the day after tomorrow when they reached the fork in the road that led to Ephyra. That was where Tristan and Wigg would have to set out cross-country to reach Shadowood.

Despite the short time in which he had known Lillith, he already knew in his heart that he would miss her. She was beautiful, intelligent, and kind, and she had a rare sort of quiet bravery. The only other women he had ever known with such a quality had been his mother and his sister, and he lamented the fact that he could not introduce Lillith to them. He would have enjoyed that very much. It then occurred to him that the woman sitting next to him in the dew-laden grass was one of the few people he had met in his entire life who did not know him as the prince of Eutracia. But Lillith seemed to like him despite the fact that, as far as she knew, he was just a simple blacksmith. Somehow, that meant a great deal to him. Before they fell asleep, she leaned forward to give him a tentative kiss on the cheek, once again thanking him for his kindness back at the inn. He covered her with his saddle blanket and lay awake under the stars for some time, sorting out his feelings, before he, too, fell asleep.

The next day was slow going again, the road north still full of refugees. Wigg took the lead, apparently lost in scholarly thoughts, while Tristan and Lillith rode side by side behind him, talking and sharing their food. During the occasional moments of silence, Tristan tried not to look at the other people on the road for fear that someone would recognize him. He had no robe to pull up over his head, having left it on the floor of the inn when they had gone upstairs in such a hurry. Luckily, no one seemed to recognize him or the old wizard.

Many of the people on the road with them were in a very sorry state. A large number were bandaged and bloody, and limped along as best they could. Tristan reminded himself that until the Coven and the Minions had come, Eutracia had been at peace for over three centuries. *These people have never seen death and destruction on a scale such as this,* he said to himself. *They are still in shock, simply going north to where they think they might find some safety. Anything to get out of the death and stink of Tammerland.*

Most of the throng going up the road were on foot, because the Minions had slaughtered so much of the livestock. There were simply very few horses to ride, or oxen to pull the carts. Therefore, most of these wretched souls had been forced to abandon the vast majority of their possessions, taking with them only what they could carry. Food and water were in short supply, and it occurred to Tristan that fights and small riots might break out among them, as the hunger and thirst be-came worse. He silently blessed the knives that lay across his back, and his ability to hunt with them.

As dusk began to fall the three of them again went off the road and away from the crush of humanity to make their camp. They had been traveling alongside the same meandering stream all day, and they found a small clearing just above its banks where they could sleep. Tristan killed a pair of rabbits, which made a sufficient meal when combined with some of the vegetables they still had left in the leather bags.

The night was warm, the sky full of a thousand stars. The fire cast flickering, ephemeral patterns of shadow and light upon the three of them as they sat on the ground beside its warmth, knowing that tomorrow they would part.

Wigg turned to look at Lillith. "It has been a pleasure to know you, miss," he said, smiling. He then looked briefly at the prince. "I am sure that I speak for both Tristan and myself when I say that I wish our meeting could have come under different circumstances." He handed her a rather large handful of gold kisa from the bag that he kept at his side. "Please take these, with our compliments. And keep the horse, too. You will need a good horse underneath you as you continue to travel to Ephyra. I wish we could do more, but in the morning we must take our leave of you. Our business lies in a different direction." In the firelight Tristan could see that Lillith's eyes were watery, and she leaned over and gave the old one an affectionate hug. Tristan believed that even the crusty old wizard had come to genuinely like her, as well.

"Thank you, Wigg," she said, her voice cracking slightly. "I shall never forget you."

The old one stood, clearing his throat as if slightly embarrassed, and gathered his robes about him. He looked down at Tristan. "I will be on watch again, up over that rise, nearer to the road for the night. I don't believe there is anyone following us, but it always pays to be sure. I will see you both in the morning. Sleep well." He turned and walked up over the knoll and out of sight.

"Such a wonderful old man," Lillith said affectionately. "I'm sure if someone had the time, there are a great many stories that he could tell them. But sometimes he acts as if he has the entire weight of the world upon his shoulders."

If you only knew, Tristan thought to himself. "I owe him more than I could ever repay," he said simply as he watched the fire play with the highlights in her red hair.

They sat in silence for a moment, looking into the hypnotic, dancing flames of the fire. The nighttime murmurs of the woodland creatures had begun all around them, sending out soft, reassuring sounds, mixing with the occasional crackling of the fire. Lillith looked up at the stars.

"When I was a little girl, my father told me something about the stars that I never forgot," she said, as if from somewhere far away. "He told me that the night sky was a dark blanket the spirits of the Afterlife threw over us at the end of each day, to help keep us warm. And that the stars in the sky weren't really stars at all, but tiny holes that they had poked in the blanket, letting little beams of light through. That way the spirits could watch over us during the night, just as they did during the daytime. And that when we saw the stars at night we could sleep in peace, because the spirits were protecting us then, too." She looked into his eyes.

Tristan smiled at her, thinking about what a wonderful story that was. He would try to remember it for his children, if and when the time ever came. *If I survive all of this,* he thought. As he looked across the short space between them and into her green eyes, he allowed himself the impossible luxury of wondering what it would have been like to have fathered children with this woman. Overtaken by the moment, he gently reached his hand out to her, placing it behind her head, and kissed her deeply on the lips. She responded in kind, and a passion began to overtake him that seemed more real, more meaningful, than any he had ever known.

She looked at him with a half-mischievous, half-hungry look. Standing up, she slowly pulled the peasant's dress off over her shoulders, dropped it to her feet, and kicked it away. Her body was magnificent, and seemed to shimmer before him in the light of the full moon. Hungrily, he pulled her to him. But she only smiled and placed her right index finger to the point of his chin, gently pushing him away.

"I have a better idea." She laughed. "This afternoon I saw a deeper pool of water a little downstream. Let's swim."

Before he could find a reason to protest, she was gone, running up the bank of the river and diving into the moonlit pool about fifty yards from where he stood.

Two can play at this game, he thought happily, quickly disrobing and chasing after her. He dove headfirst into the water, wondering where she had gone, and got his bearings. The night was clear and warm, and the light of the full moons ran across the pool in a shimmering translucent path, broken only by the ripples he had made when he entered the water. Still he did not see her.

Suddenly, she surfaced noisily right next to him, laughing, and put her arms around him. Her mouth came down on his, and he could feel her wet, supple body against him. He immediately became aroused. He held her to him for some time, taking the wet ropes of her thick hair in his hands, bending her gently over backward under him, never wanting to let her go. Laughing again, she pushed herself away and was gone, and the game continued. For a long time their naked bodies flirted with each other in the warm, wet darkness of the pool, and Tristan found it intoxicating. His need for her grew even more.

They finally emerged from the water and walked arm in arm back up the bank of the river to where they had dropped their clothes. Tristan bent over to pick her dress up for her, but she stopped him and put two fingers against his lips to indicate silence. She took her dress from him and then picked up his clothes, as well. Laying them down in the dewy night's grass of the riverbank, she looked at him in a way that he had not seen from her before. As if seeming to have made up her mind, she gave him another long, slow kiss. But the moonlight on her beautiful face showed some of the fear that still lingered there as she released his lips and began to speak. She stepped even closer, putting her arms around him.

"I have never been with a man," she said quietly, as though not knowing how to begin. "I was scared to death that the awful innkeeper was going to rape me, and then you and Wigg came along. I know that we must leave each other tomorrow, and I am saddened because of that. I hope that you will never forget me."

He was about to speak again when she reached out hesitantly to touch his groin, and Tristan felt a searing heat go through him that he had never experienced before. He suddenly wanted this woman more than any other he had ever known.

"I want you to be my first," she said, lowering her eyes as if in shame. With her face still lowered, she said, "You are handsome and strong, and I know in my heart that you will not hurt me. Please be my first, Tristan, and give me something to remember you by always."

She placed her hand upon his bare chest and gently pushed him down onto his back on the ragged, rather sad little pile of clothes. Slowly, lovingly, she lowered herself down upon him as lightly as a butterfly.

"Close your eyes, my love," she said gently as she began to undulate her body over his.

Tristan did as she asked, and just let it happen. The warm night air seemed somehow to gather around them, as if they were the only two people in the world. *This must be what it's like,* he thought, *to be with someone that you truly love.*

His eyes still closed, he felt her lower her face down to his, and she reached out tenderly to put her arms around him, still moving her hips on him erotically.

"By the way," he heard a female voice say from somewhere, "this isn't my first time. And if our child is a girl, I will teach her everything I know. But if the bastard is a boy, my sweet prince, I will kill him with my own hands."

The voice was no longer Lillith's, but still somehow familiar. He snapped his eyes open. Lillith's face was gone.

He was looking directly into the eyes of Natasha, duchess of Ephyra.

Mistress of the Coven.

Instinctively he recoiled, desire replaced with sheer hatred. He tried to move his arms and legs to throw her off him, but he couldn't.

He was frozen to the ground beneath her as she looked down at him with a wicked, hungry grin.

"What have you done with Lillith?" he demanded, still not understanding. He tried to turn his head away from her face, but he could not move.

She smiled viciously. "There never was a Lillith, you fool." She laughed. "Although I suppose I could let you see her one last time before you die."

Tristan looked into her eyes as waves began to swim across his vision. Natasha's face actually looked as if it were beginning to melt, to decompose. And then, as soon as it had blended itself away into nothingness, the waves came back again, and the smiling, loving face of Lillith, complete with green eyes and long, red hair, began to appear. *This can't be happening,* he thought. *I must be going mad.*

And then he remembered. What was it Wigg had called Natasha? *A Visage Caster. Able to change her appearance at will.* He simply stared, speechless, up into the face of Lillith, the one he had once thought he could come to love, as the brown hair and eyes of the mistress of the Coven once again slowly began to reappear. She continued the slow act of coitus with him, keeping him aroused, somehow controlling that part of his anatomy, as well. She smiled.

"You bitch!" he screamed at the top of his lungs. "What have you done with my sister?"

Natasha reached out and backhanded him hard across the face, and then lifted her hand to her eyes. "Now look what you've made me do," she whimpered sarcastically. "I've broken a nail." She narrowed her eyes to stare at the finger, and Tristan watched as the long, painted nail repaired itself. She struck him viciously again across the face, all the while her hips moving back and forth suggestively.

"Don't concern yourself with your sister," she said coyly, looking into his eyes. "You will never be seeing her again, anyway. She is one of us, now, and is probably already halfway across the Sea of Whispers. Don't worry—she will receive the best of care. By the way, that was a very good trick the Lead Wizard pulled that day on the dais. We looked everywhere for you, and you were simply gone. But we know where you are now, don't we? And don't bother screaming for the old wizard. I've arranged it so that we can't be heard by anyone, even him."

"You have been with us since that first day at the inn," he said, almost to himself. "You have been with us for the last two days!"

"Ah, you're finally catching on," she said nastily. "We knew that the two of you would probably head immediately for Shadowood. It was the only logical assumption, given the fact that the Lead Wizard had been told of the continued existence of his old friend, my dear father. So I simply hurried to the inn ahead of you while you took your time visiting the corpses of your family and friends, as we knew you would do." She looked down at him, her eyes narrowing with pleasure. "By the way, how did you manage to kill a wiktor?" she asked curiously. "I do believe that you're the first one ever to do so. But it doesn't actually matter. It really isn't dead, you know."

"I enjoyed killing it," he snarled, "just as I am going to enjoy killing all of you."

"You overestimate yourself, my prince," she said, drawing her fingers across his face and down to one of his nipples. She began to make little circles around it with the long, red nail. "And, by the way, I want to thank you for your gallantry back at the inn, but it wasn't really necessary. I didn't need a hero. I could have killed every one of those ignorant, unendowed bastards with a single thought." She bent down and licked the side of his face lasciviously. "And your bringing me with you was more than I could have hoped for."

In addition to the rage he felt, a new emotion had begun to creep into Tristan's mind: shame. *Wigg told me repeatedly not to become involved in the things that I saw,* he thought. *Now my brashness has killed us both.*

"If you're going to kill me, then why don't you just do it and get it over with?" he said sarcastically. "All I ever hear out of you and Succiu is a lot of talk."

She closed the distance slightly between their faces, and he could see the endowed anger flashing in her lustrous brown eyes. He thought of that day back at the castle when she had spoken with him, and then licked her lips and walked away. *She has more in mind than just my death,* he thought, *and somehow I know what it is. And even if she kills me, I have to fight to keep her from getting it.*

"Oh, die you shall," she said. "Make no mistake of it. And the old wizard, too. But not before you and I finish our business. I shall take three prizes from here with me today. The head of the crown prince of Eutracia, and also that of the Lead Wizard of the Directorate. I shall dip them in wax to preserve them for the trip to my new home, across the sea."

"And the third prize?" Tristan asked. In his heart he already knew what it was. But something inside him wanted to hear her say it.

"Our child, of course," she said, her eyes glistening. "The child that you are about to give me, the one that will grow in my womb as I travel back across the sea, my work here finally complete. Just imagine: your blood mingled with my own, in the firstborn child of the Chosen One. And I shall be the one to carry it."

Without speaking further, she shuddered, as if she had now been consumed by the act of merely saying the words. She closed her eyes and began to rape him in earnest.

Tristan tried as hard as he could to escape, but he was still frozen in place, with the earth at his back. Natasha began to groan, as if slowly starting to build to her own climax. Her mouth was open, and her tongue was beginning to lick the area around her lips in ecstasy.

I have to fight this, he screamed silently. *Fight it as hard as I can. Even if she kills me, I cannot allow her to bear a child of my blood and do as they will with it.*

Natasha began to move even harder over him now, and Tristan knew he was losing himself to her. Somehow she had control over his sexuality, and he knew that it was only a matter of time before he gave her what she wanted. He tried to fight back the waves of desire as best he could, but every time she moved and shuddered and groaned it sent another bolt of ecstasy coursing through him and he could feel his endowed blood screaming through his veins, as if telling him that it was all right, to let go. Her groans had turned to wanton screaming now, and he knew he was in the grip of something he couldn't control.

He began to feel the familiar, needful waves of inevitability begin in his groin as she looked into his eyes. It would only be seconds, now.

And then he saw it.

At first it looked like some kind of blue blur in the night sky, but then it began to coalesce and take more distinct form. A flowing, moving line of azure light had silently snaked its way around behind the mistress, and one end of it seemed to dance and play in the night air behind her and just over her head, the other end continuing away and out of his line of vision. At first Tristan thought that it must have been the work of Natasha. But as he continued to watch it take its final shape, he realized that she was oblivious to its presence.

It was a rope: a rope of blue azure light that danced on its own in the night air. And it was made of pure energy. Tristan watched, speechless, as the free end of the floating rope began to curl around into a knot and move closer to Natasha.

It was a hangman's noose, and it quietly slipped itself around the mistress's throat.

But by now Tristan's own time had come, and just as he could hold himself back no longer and the inevitable began, the noose tightened itself around Natasha's neck. With a single, savage yank, it pulled her off the prince and over onto her back, near the river's edge.

Natasha's scream was cut off. Her eyes opened in terror and she tried to put her hands around the rope to free herself, but the azure energy was too strong, and she was beginning to weaken from lack of oxygen.

As she struggled in the wet grass of the riverbank, the glowing azure hangman's noose began to pull her toward the river.

Tristan found that he was able to move again. He immediately reached back to his pile of clothes and picked up one of his dirks. He didn't know anything about the azure rope or how it worked, but he was determined to help kill the monster that had murdered his family. He ran naked and screaming, his dirk held high, toward the mistress as the rope of energy dragged her, headfirst, into the river.

The water all around Natasha began to roil and steam as the mistress thrashed around in the river. Tristan finally reached her and, with a quick slash of his knife, cut her throat from ear to ear, just above the line of the rope. He grabbed her head and pushed her under the water with all his might, holding her there until the bubbles stopped and there was no longer any movement.

The azure rope of energy and the hangman's noose that it had created emerged from the river and vanished into the night as quickly as they had come.

Panting, Tristan grabbed the mistress's corpse by the hair and dragged it up onto the edge of the riverbank. Her eyes were still open, and in the moonlight he could see the bluish cast coming to her skin. Then he turned and scrambled up the riverbank, to kneel before his belongings. He unwrapped the dreggan and took it back down to where the corpse lay.

Natasha looked almost peaceful, almost innocent, as she lay there in the dim light. Tristan pulled the dreggan from its scabbard and listened to the sword's song fade away on the night breeze. Holding the dreggan in his right hand, he pushed the lever in the hilt, and with a resounding clang of highly tempered steel, the blade shot out an extra foot.

With both hands he raised the dreggan high over his head and stared down at the corpse of the one who had just tried to kill him—kill him and take his firstborn child. The blade glinted in the moonlight.

"As I have sworn to do," he declared. He brought the blade down with all his might, severing the head from the body.

Immediately the thunder and lightning started. The lightning tore across the night sky in patterns he had never seen before and continued unabated with such rapidity that the entire landscape was illuminated as if it were daytime. And the thunder, the loudest he had ever heard, was deafening, rolling across the landscape as if it had the power to mow down everything in its path. The wind blew and howled, picking up leaves and twigs from all over the area, blowing them around in a maelstrom of dirt and debris. He stood there, naked before it all, holding his sword in one hand as it finally dissipated, and then ended.

Tristan reached down and threw the severed head, and then the body itself, into the river. He watched in the moonlight as the rapids carried them away.

Exhausted, he walked back up the riverbank, but very suddenly brought his dreggan up once again. There was a shadowy figure a little higher up, sitting on the ground before him. He approached carefully, without speaking, and then calmly lowered his sword.

It was Wigg.

Tristan dressed quickly and went to the old one. Wigg didn't look up. The prince sat in the grass of the riverbank next to the Lead Wizard for some time, both of them looking at the river as it passed by in the moonlight.

"The azure rope was yours, wasn't it?" Tristan asked finally, already knowing the answer. He did not turn to look the wizard in the face. "Thank you, once again, for saving my life."

"You're welcome," the old one said simply. "I had my suspicions about her from the first time she approached our table, as Lillith, back at the inn," he said casually.

"You *knew*?"

"Not for a certainty," Wigg said as he picked at the hem of his robe. "When she first came to our table I could detect a faint aura about her, but there was no way of telling whether she was Natasha, or simply an innocent of endowed blood. As you may remember, Natasha had been taught by the Coven to disguise her endowed blood, but it is a terrible strain on one's powers to do so for as prolonged a period as she did, and I could occasionally detect brief evidences of it. Still, I couldn't be sure. That's why I took each of the night watches. So that I could be there for you, if need be."

Tristan thought to himself for a few moments, and then said, "That's why she didn't kill me right away, isn't it?"

"What do you mean?"

"She wanted my firstborn child, just like they want Shailiha and her unborn. She almost got it."

"Yes," Wigg said slowly. "Do you remember when I told you about the history of Eutracia, that for some reason near the end of the war the Coven spent a great deal of time trying to produce a special girl child of endowed blood? Sorceresses can control their conception, Tristan. It was obvious that Natasha had plans for your firstborn, provided it was a girl."

"If that is so important to them, then why didn't one of them take me that day up on the dais, when everyone was killed? Instead, they were willing to let Kluge butcher me."

Wigg thought for a moment. "Probably because they were under orders from Failee to return as soon as possible with the stone, and to make sure that we both were dead. But once we had escaped, things were different and they were free to indulge themselves. But I cannot be absolutely sure."

His training in the craft must begin soon, the old one thought. *But first we must find Shailiha and the stone, and we will probably die doing it. And even if we do accomplish the impossible, the Chosen One must still first read the Prophecies before his training begins.*

Tristan sat next to the old one for a long time without speaking. Despite the fact that Natasha was dead, there had been much more to her presence than he understood. It was about Lillith. He knew in his heart that she had never existed, but it was the possibility of such a woman that now consumed his mind. Lillith had given the appearance of a woman who could care about him without knowing who he was or what he could give her because of his station in life, and he had never known that before. And he had, despite the short time he had been in her presence, thought that he might have felt the beginnings of true love.

But Lillith had only been a phantom. And now she was gone forever.

"Despite the brief time in which I 'knew' her, I thought she might be the one," Tristan said sadly, to no one in particular. The night breeze came again to them from off the river. *No man can cross the same river twice,* he mused.

"I know," the old one said, turning to him. "Someday you will find your Lillith, but first you must find your sister."

The Lead Wizard stood and, without speaking further, walked back up to take his place on watch, closer to the road. Tomorrow, Tristan knew, they would head overland to Shadowood, and to whatever awaited them there.

He sat there until dawn, trying to sort out what had happened to him and wondering if there would ever be such a woman, a real woman, as Lillith in his life.

CHAPTER

Thirteen

Shailiha turned in her bed slowly, half asleep, and automatically cushioned the heaviness of her unborn child with one hand as she came to lie on her side on the silk sheets. The room was dark, and she didn't bother to open her eyes. Her child would be special, her Sisters had told her, and it was important to take the best of care with her pregnancy. She sighed slowly, her eyes still shut, and tried to remember—remember for herself all of the things that they had told her had happened, all of the things that they had said were so understandable for her to forget.

She had been in this land that they called Parthalon for two weeks now, and aside from the voyage across the ocean, she could remember virtually nothing of her life that had come before. Even large parts of the trip across the ocean with Sister Succiu were still a blank to her. Flashes of what seemed to be another, previous life would suddenly cross her mind at times when she would least expect it, both scaring and intriguing her at the same time. And when she tried to tell her Sisters of what she remembered, they just scolded her pleasantly, telling her that these images were not correct, that they should be forgotten. They said that these brief flashes were false memories, that would eventually go away, and that they would tell her all about what her previous life had really been like. Hysterical amnesia, they called it, and given what she had been through, her condition was not unusual.

But she wasn't sure.

Sometimes, especially in her dreams, she would see faces that were somehow familiar, and places that she had not as yet visited here in

Parthalon. But there were no names to go with the faces, and that troubled her. There was a kindly man with a jewel around his neck, a woman with beautiful blond hair, a man of about her age with dark hair whom she found to be very handsome, and in particular, another man with a brown beard who seemed to be reaching out for her swollen stomach and calling out to her every time she dreamed of him. There were also a number of odd-looking older men, all in robes, with funny tails of braided hair that ran down the backs of their necks. In the slow-moving, ephemeral cloudiness of her dreams she would try to speak to all of them. But they never spoke back, except for the man with the brown beard. And when he did, no sound came out of his mouth. Every time she came physically close to them in one of her dreams, she awakened, only to find herself back here, in the palace with her Sisters. *I know these people of my dreams,* she would often think to herself. *But they must simply be my imagination, because my Sisters tell me so.*

She had been forced to learn her Sisters' names all over again, and they had teased her and laughed at her politely when she got them wrong. They said it sounded so strange for one they had known so long to mix up their names. Failee, Succiu, Zabarra, and Vona. They were all her Sisters, they said, in both blood and bond, and they told her that she and Succiu had just returned from a great quest, during which her husband had been killed by the butchers that lived across the sea. She and Succiu had barely escaped with their lives. The tragic loss was what had caused her to forget all that had come before. But her Sisters would always be there to help her remember, they said, and slowly, carefully, they would tell her the true story of her life.

They were about to embark upon a great undertaking, they told her, and each of them would be required to do her part. Shailiha wasn't sure she understood it all, but she knew in her heart that she would do her best to help them, because they were her Sisters and she had grown to love them. Failee also told her that if her strange dreams did not stop soon, other dreams would come. Bad ones. Shailiha did her best not to think about that, and instead tried to concentrate on what her wonderful Sisters were trying to help her remember.

Her life here with them at the palace was certainly luxurious enough, and she had very little to do except try to get better. Rest and heal your mind, they had said, and above all make sure you take care of your unborn. Her private quarters were magnificent, with several connecting rooms at her disposal. She was personally cared for to an extent that was almost embarrassing, with dozens of maidservants to satisfy her every whim. Each morning when she rose at her leisure they would bathe her and brush her hair, and then dress her in any of the magnificent maternity gowns that lined her wardrobe for almost as far as the eye could see. She took each of her meals with her Sisters and, sometimes, Succiu's little hunchback, Geldon. They happily spent most of that time telling her of her past life, trying to help her remember. Sometimes they laughed and giggled like schoolgirls when they talked about some of the things she had done when she was young. And despite the fact that she hadn't yet remembered any of the incidents they kept reminding her of, with every passing day she felt more sure that she would.

Failee, the oldest of the five Sisters, always seemed to be especially kind. Every few days she would come to Shailiha's room and ask her how she was feeling. She would also place her hand on Shailiha's abdomen and close her eyes, as if lost in thought. Each time this had happened, Failee told her that her child was well, and the birth would be soon.

But she still dreamed of the others. Not as often as at first, but sometimes they came, like silent ghosts, to visit her mind. She would just have to be patient and wait until they were no more, just as her Sisters had told her would happen.

She was thinking about all this, in the dark of her bedroom, when she first heard the tiny scratching sounds, combined with little, nondescript squeaking noises. Even though her eyes were still closed, she could tell that the darkness of her bedroom was giving way to the light of day. The noise must be one of her maidservants arriving to bathe her as usual, she thought. *I must have slept unusually well, because the night seemed so short.* Gently rubbing her eyes, she sat up in bed, then looked around.

What she saw made her want to scream, but she couldn't find her voice.

This isn't my bedroom, she thought in confusion. *And it is not dawn, and I am alone.*

Shailiha immediately sat up straighter, instinctively holding one hand over her abdomen. Her bedroom was gone, and in its place was a small, stone-walled room, in the center of which sat her bed. There seemed to be no doors or windows. The light that she had mistaken for the break of dawn was in fact coming from wall sconces; the flames gave the room a kind of frightening, golden tone that seemed to mix with the grayness of the stones, creating sharp-edged shadows in their nooks and crevices. The floor and the ceiling of the tiny room were the same stone as the walls.

Then she noticed the stench.

Fetid and pungent, it smelled of human fecal matter and seemed to waft back and forth across the stone room in a sickening, gray cloud. She placed her hands to her face, thinking she might vomit. And then she saw why there was such an awful smell.

Something was oozing from the walls. A brown, murky slime, it trickled down to the floor from an ever-growing number of places between the stones. The more of it that appeared, the more horrible became the smell. She wanted to scream, but found that instead all she could do was vomit. *This can't be happening!* she shrieked silently as the warm, wet contents of her stomach ran down her negligee. *This simply isn't real!* She screamed aloud at the top of her lungs. But no one answered. And the strange scratching and squeaking noises grew louder.

Rats.

The slime had stopped dripping from the walls and had pooled sickeningly in dark puddles on the stone floor of the room. And now, coming from the same holes, were rats.

They poured out of the crevices in all four walls and began milling about on the floor around her bed. They were the largest she had ever seem, some as big as kittens, and they sniffed everything in their path as they ran over each other, through the mire on the floor, and began testing the bottoms of the bedsheets with their longish, pointed teeth.

Their squeaking and screeching became a cacophony of hunger, as countless more of them poured into the room.

Shailiha screamed again and thought that she might pass out, but the awful sounds of the squealing rats somehow kept her conscious. In only a few moments they would begin to climb the sheets. Her bed began to shake with the sheer numbers of them around the bottom of it.

Horrified, she realized it wasn't the rats that were shaking the bed. The bed was moving on its own. And it was somehow lowering itself into the floor.

Crying hysterically, Shailiha scrambled frantically up on all fours and looked around the room while the bed slowly went lower and lower. The most aggressive rats had begun to clamber up on the sides of the bedsheets as the silk bedding flattened out on the floor and washed into the dark brown slime.

As if with a life of its own, the ooze crept up over the side of the bed, and Shailiha slipped in the awful mire as it closed on around her. Clutching her abdomen, she fell facedown on the sheets.

The last thing she remembered before passing out were the approaching rats as they began to chew on her fingers.

"And I say once again to you that if the blood stalkers and screaming harpies had never been released, the prince and the Lead Wizard would be dead today!" Succiu exclaimed as Vona and Zabarra looked on aghast, neither of them ever having seen her address Failee so angrily. "We repeatedly warned you about the dangers of recalling them when we first planned the attack. If the old one and the Directorate had not been alerted to the presence of your now-useless creatures from the distant past, we could have finished our job that day on the dais properly. But instead, because of your unnecessary need for revenge, now we must contend with the fact that Wigg and Tristan are both still alive, and probably trying to make their way to Shadowood."

Succiu glared at each of the women at the table in turn, and then down to Geldon, who was, as usual, at her feet, chained to the iron ring in the marble floor of the chamber. He tried to look away. He had never before seen her this angry, and he didn't wish to draw any more attention to himself than was necessary. As it was, he was sure that at least one poor slave from the Stables would pay for her foul mood before the night was over.

The four mistresses of the Coven had been sitting at the five-pointed table in the chamber for over an hour now, and despite Succiu's criticisms, Failee seemed almost happily unconcerned. The First Mistress had uncharacteristically listened patiently, almost politely, as Succiu had arrogantly gone on and on, blaming Failee for their Eutracian mission's having not been completely successful. But now the dwarf could see that Failee had begun to tire of Succiu's faultfinding, and he lowered his head in anticipation of what was to come next. Nonetheless, Succiu pressed her argument.

"Even the wiktor that Sister Natasha and I arranged to intercept the prince and the wizard at the palace gates has presumably been killed," she continued, driving home her point. "No one has accomplished that before. And, worse yet, there has been no contact from Natasha. We have no choice but to assume that she is lost, too." The second mistress looked down at her nails for a moment, remembering the fatalistic look on Tristan's face when Kluge had chained him. Her demeanor changed to one of inward, rather than outward, concern. "We have seriously underestimated the Chosen One," she said, almost softly, "and we must now take pains to be sure that neither he nor the wizard can interfere in our undertakings. To fail to dispose of them could mean the loss of everything."

Failee let out a long, almost bored sigh, rose from the table, and walked slowly to the fireplace at the opposite side of the room. It was early evening, and the flames danced merrily outward from the hearth, adding to the warmth created by the wall sconces and chandeliers that burned so brightly. The First Mistress ran a hand through her long gray-and-black hair, knowing that her Sisters were disturbed, yet at the same time certain that they had no reason to be. But the veiled spell that she had been solely supporting since Shailiha's arrival now weighed heavily upon her powers, and she had little time or patience for those who were not sufficiently trained in the Vagaries to grasp what it was she was trying to do. She looked down at the red stone that hung around her neck and fingered it lovingly. It was time that they learned. She turned back to the table.

"Trust in me when I tell you that none of what you say is of any consequence, my Sisters," Failee said, as though she were addressing a roomful of impressionable schoolchildren. "True, the Chosen One and Wigg are alive, but what does it matter? They don't know how to cross the Sea of Whispers, and the entire Royal Guard is dead. Even if they do manage to reach Faegan, which is doubtful because of his ever-protective gnomes, the crippled old wizard will be of little help to them . . ." Her words trailed off as she smiled briefly. "And he does not have the means to travel about quickly, not after what we did to his legs. We only allowed him to live out of deference to Natasha. And now that she may be gone, as you say, we will eventually take measures to rid the world of him, too. But not just yet. There are more important things to do. And if we succeed, then neither Tristan, nor Wigg, nor even Faegan will matter." Her hazel eyes gleamed with certainty.

The three seated Sisters looked at Failee in wonder. Despite their deep feelings about her misguided use of the blood stalkers and screaming harpies, none of them could doubt her overall brilliance and power, or her position as their superior. *She has more mastery than the rest of us put together,* Succiu thought. *And it now seems even more so, ever since she placed the Paragon around her neck.* Succui relaxed a little. *She is probably right. She always is. Nothing can stop us now.*

Failee looked at Vona as the firelight danced off the younger sorceress' red hair, showing up the emerald Pentangle on the gold chain around her neck. "Did you bring Sister Shailiha to the chamber as I asked?"

"Yes, First Mistress," Vona said. "She sits in a chair in the hallway, as you ordered. But I have never seen her so disturbed. She asked to see you right away this morning, just after she awoke, screaming something about a horrible dream. She has refused to eat all day, and has done nothing but cry and babble hysterically to herself about her equally 'horrible' bedroom. But we examined her room, and it is unchanged from when her handmaidens saw her off to sleep last night. It is all very confusing. She is even more disturbed now than when I first saw her as she disembarked the ship from Eutracia. Something has happened to her, and I fear for her sanity."

And had I not healed her hands of the rat bites of last night, you would be even more alarmed, Failee thought. It was time she told them what was really happening to Shailiha.

She walked back toward the table, but remained standing above the other mistresses.

"Since her arrival here in Parthalon, Sister Shailiha has been subordinate to my personal ministrations—that is, she has been under a spell of my doing, and my doing alone. I tell you this now because her mental state will, from this point on, either deteriorate into abject madness, or she will willingly become one of us. Either way, we will still have her child. If the princess survives, she will, given the nature of her blood, clearly become the most powerful of us. When this occurs and her training in both the Vigors and the Vagaries is complete, I shall gladly give over to her my position as First Mistress. Given the fact that the spell I describe is of the Vagaries, and she has no prior teaching in the craft, I have no doubt that it shall be the darker side of the craft she will come to love." She waited for a moment, watching the surprised faces of her Sisters as her unexpected words sunk in.

"Each of you already knows why she has been brought here, so I shan't waste time with another explanation of it. Because of your limited knowledge of the Vagaries, what you don't know is that, in order for us to be successful, Shailiha must *want* to help us. Completely and without reservation. And to do that, she must be made to forget her previous life totally. Soon after she arrived I could see what a difficult task it would be to try simply to talk her out of her previous experiences, and try to replace them with those of our own creation. The bonds to her former world are just too strong. I should have known that, despite the trauma she has undergone, the strength of her endowed blood would not permit her mind simply to reject her true subconscious. Therefore, a way had to be found in which she would come to us *willingly*, and join us as our fifth Sister out of a desire that was seemingly born in her very soul. She must become the fifth sorceress. The fifth sorceress that we have needed for so long, needed even during the war with the wizards in Eutracia."

She looked down at the fifth throne by the five-pointed table, the one that had been empty since its construction, and felt once again the centuries-old yearning to have it filled. "And in only a month, not only shall we have our fifth Sister, but her baby daughter as well. The first-born female child of one of the Chosen Ones." Failee's eyes gleamed, and the others could see the intensity of her commitment as she spoke. "She shall either survive it and become one of us, her previous life wiped from her memory forever, or she will have perished from the stark madness that failing to withstand this spell invariably produces. There is no middle ground."

Succiu looked up at Failee with guarded curiosity. Her mood toward the First Mistress had calmed, but only marginally. "And, pray tell, just what is this spell that you have invoked upon her? It seems, at least to me, that the only change in her mental state has been one of deterioration. How is it, then, that such a thing can help?"

Failee sat back down on her throne, smiled, spread her hands flat upon the dark, intricately carved wooden table, and looked into the faces of her Sisters. *Even as powerful as they are, without further training in the Vagaries they are still as children,* she thought. "We shall accomplish our ends by inducing her to dispel her memories because she *wants* to. She will do the work of joining us herself." She leaned back in her throne with a sense of accomplishment and control. "I am not surprised that none of you have heard of this spell, since I am the only one among us who is completely proficient in the Vagaries. Very simply, it is known as the Spell of the Chimeran Agonies."

Noting the silent, intense looks of curiosity upon their faces, she continued. "Very simply put, the Chimeran Agonies induce people to change willingly almost any aspect of their behavior, in order to escape what become increasingly hideous dreams, or, should I say, what they *perceive* to be dreams."

Succiu's curiosity had become intense, to say the least, but she was lost in the First Mistress' logic. "I don't understand," she said.

"Two days ago, when I realized that she wasn't going to let go of her memories without 'guidance,' I approached Shailiha and told her that whenever she has a memory of her so-called previous life, no matter how brief, she is immediately to come and tell me. Then, that evening when she goes to sleep, I invoke an even deeper slumber upon her mind. A trance. A trance so deep that she can be easily moved from one room to another without waking. In this room await a great many unpleasant experiences for her."

Her eyes narrowed. "Last night I conjured human excrement and starving rats that came out from the stone walls of the room with no means of escape for her. I let her slip into the excrement, and also let the rats chew upon her fingers for a time before she passed out. It was necessary that I heal her hands before taking her back to her real bedroom, or she would have known immediately that the experience was genuine, and not a dream. Subsequent experiences will be even more unpleasant. When she invariably faints from the trauma, the sleep trance is once again placed upon her, and she is bathed, and dressed once again in clean, identical sleep clothing. She is then moved back into her own room and allowed to wake up on her own. The result is that she believes she has had a nightmare, but one far more real and terrifying than she can ever remember. Done correctly and often enough, it can literally shatter an otherwise healthy mind. And the victim, waking up in her own bed, detects no interference whatsoever from another person or persons. She will believe it is all of her own doing, that she is going mad, and she will become willing to try anything suggested to her to end the torment."

Succiu was impressed. She could see how the fear of the reoccurrence of such "dreams" could cause madness, even in one of endowed blood. But she was still at a loss to understand how all of this could help them. Looking into the faces of Zabarra and Vona, she could see that they, too, did not fully understand.

Zabarra, playfully toying with one of her blond ringlets as always, was the first to ask. "How is it, First Mistress," she asked, "that all of this, despite however effective it might be, helps us to make her forget her past? I fail to see the connection."

"She will force the memories from her subconscious as a matter of her own survival," Failee said simply. "And she has the ability, although she doesn't yet know it, to accomplish this because of the unusually high purity of her blood. But she must *want* to do it, and there is no time like the present to make it so. And by the way, when I tell her the obvious lie that each of us has also been through her current torment, do not contradict me." She turned toward Vona. "Please escort Sister Shailiha into the room."

Vona rose, left the room, and was gone for a moment. Geldon, still at Succui's feet and still not wanting to attract anyone's attention, quietly shifted his weight on the unforgiving marble floor. Succiu's mood seemed to have improved, but he knew from experience that it was only a matter of time before something would make her mean again. Even so, his curious ears hadn't missed a word.

Vona then reentered the room, with a very distraught-looking Shailiha following her. Upon seeing Failee, Shailiha's reaction was immediate. She rushed to the First Mistress and fell to the marble floor at her feet, sobbing uncontrollably, the blue silk of her maternity robes rustling gently as she ran. Failee looked quickly to the faces of the other women at the table in a tacit command of silence, and then reached down to raise the princess' face slowly up to her own. Shailiha's cheeks were covered with tears, and her eyes held the crazed, terrified fear of a cornered animal that seemed to be struggling for its sanity.

"My dear Sister, whatever is so wrong?" Failee asked innocently. "Why do you cry so?" Using her handkerchief, she wiped the tears from Shailiha's face.

"It was the dream!" Shailiha said wildly, looking around the room for agreement from her Sisters, as though having collected their mutual understanding would somehow alleviate her pain. "Last night. It was hideous. There was something coming out of the walls that made me vomit, and then there were rats, hundreds of them, that began to chew on my hands and feet. I was in a small stone room that I had never seen before, and there was no way out." She paused, placing a hand upon her abdomen, before continuing. "Had it not been for my unborn child, I should have wanted to die." She buried her face into Failee's hands.

"Dreams can sometimes seem very real, Sister," Failee said. "Especially when the person is of endowed blood."

"But this wasn't a dream!" Shailiha shrieked. "It was real! I know it! I was *there*, in that little room, awake, and the rats were all around me!"

Failee gently picked up each of Shailiha's hands and examined the ends of her fingers. "But there are no bite marks, my child," she said soothingly. "If, as you say, the episode was real, and you were bitten so many times, would you indeed not have the marks to prove it? No, this was a dream, Shailiha. But, I am afraid, not an ordinary one." A look of great concern began to cross the sorceress' face as she stared down at the terrified princess. "For some time we have been afraid that this might happen."

"What do you mean?"

"When you and Succiu returned from your quest, I told you that if the memories did not stop, these bad dreams would come. And yesterday you had memories, did you not, of your recent quest with Sister Succiu?"

"Yes."

"And, as I asked you, you immediately came to me to describe them, saying that you had remembered once again the large man with the great brown beard, among others. The man who always tries to touch your unborn child and speak to you, although you never hear what it is he is trying to say. Is that not also true?"

"Yes."

"These horrible dreams are your punishment for allowing these false memories to crowd into your mind, my child. That is the reason the nightmares come to you. When the memories stop, the nightmares will also stop."

"I still don't understand."

Failee took Shailiha's face in her hands. "You know in your heart that you have always lived here, don't you?" she asked.

"Yes, I suppose so."

"And that we are your Sisters, and have always been?"

Shailiha looked at the other faces around the table and tentatively bit her lip. "I have come to believe what you have told me, yes," she said quietly.

"Then you must also believe me now when I tell you that your memories are nothing more than the bad remembrances of the journey you made with Succiu," the First Mistress said gently. "The quest that I sent the two of you on to recover the stone that now hangs around my neck. The quest during which you tragically lost your husband to the murderers across the sea. If you do not cast off these memories, the dreams will keep coming, each one more hideous than the last, until you go mad."

"How do I rid myself of these memories that plague me so?" The fear and need to know were abjectly apparent upon Shailiha's face, and in her voice.

"You must use your endowed blood, Shailiha. Whenever one of these memories encroaches upon your mind, you must use your endowed blood to cast it off."

"How?"

"By focusing upon your life here with us, and concentrating upon the truths that we have been telling you. And by rejecting these false memories as harmful to both you and your unborn child. Done correctly, this will banish not only the unwanted remembrances, but any memories of ever having had them. All your mind will know and ever remember will be your life here with us, and the truths and training that we shall give you."

Shailiha looked up into Failee's eyes, genuinely glad to have such a loving and caring Sister. "I will do my best," she said, her tears beginning to subside.

"I know you will, my dear," Failee said. "But there is something you must promise me if you are to succeed in this."

"Anything."

"Whenever you experience these memories, no matter how brief, you must, after trying to cast them off, come to me and tell me of them immediately. No matter the time or the circumstances. It is only by knowing when they have occurred that I can help you to see reality for what it truly is, and better prepare you for the next time. Each of your Sisters, including myself, has been through this, and it is only our Sisterhood and our common blood that has seen us through in the past. Your especially endowed blood is not only your savior from this torment, but partly the cause of it, as well. But once you have succeeded your training can begin, and you can take your rightful place, here at our table."

Failee glanced meaningfully at the empty throne, and Shailiha's eyes followed. Then, to Failee's delight Shailiha cast her gaze upon the Paragon that hung around the First Mistress' neck. The younger woman's eyes began to brighten and glow, the first spark of an ages-old hunger now evident in the young princess for the first time.

Shailiha returned her gaze to her loving, older Sister. "I will do my best, Sister," she said dutifully.

"I know you will, child," Failee said. "I know."

CHAPTER

Fourteen

I t was raining and nearly midnight by the time Geldon left the Recluse, and the strap of the leather bag that he carried hidden beneath
his cloak weighed heavily upon the ever-painful hump in his back.
The rain came down in large, cold, splattering drops, and the dark sky
was starless, barren of moon and breeze. The fiery torches that lined the
parapets on either side of the drawbridge hissed and flickered in the
dark, showing off the rain-slickened walls and cobblestoned gangway.
Winged Minion guards stood at attention on either side as still as stone
statues.

It was important that he leave as quickly as he could.

The second mistress had surprised him when, at the conclusion of
the meeting in the chamber, she had told him that she wished him to go
into the countryside and procure additional slaves for the Stables. Such
errands were the only times he was allowed to leave the Recluse alone.
He smiled inwardly. *Her timing could not have been more perfect,* he thought
to himself.

Waddling down the many elaborate halls of the Recluse he had encountered the usual Minion guards, who gave him the customary wink
and nod. They were quite used to the nocturnal comings and goings of
the humpbacked dwarf. *Succiu's pimp,* he thought wryly. He returned
their leering smiles in kind, knowing that they were all-too-familiar
with his job of procurement for the Stables—the job with which the
second mistress had burdened him for more than three centuries.

He had, of course, often considered trying to escape; the many times she sent him forth from the Recluse to do her bidding always provided an enticing opportunity to do so. But upon reflection he had never taken the chance, knowing that the relentless Succiu, given her many talents and having the legions of the Minions at her disposal, would eventually find him no matter how long it took. She would take very seriously the personal embarrassment of losing her slave. He shuddered, thinking of what she would do to him for such a transgression, knowing in his heart that the punishment he had been forced to administer to the slave named Stephan would pale in comparison.

Nonetheless, if his own punishment had been the only ramification, he still might have attempted it. But Succiu had also warned him that if he ever forced her to employ the Minions to find him, the winged ones would be granted great latitude in butchering the members of the Parthalonian citizenry as they searched. *None of my fellow citizens should have to die because of me,* he thought. And so, despite the almost overwhelming temptation to flee, he always returned.

Oftentimes he thought back on that night in the Ghetto of the Shunned, when she had first found him and bestowed upon him her time enchantments. Without them he would surely be dead now, and sometimes he wondered if it wouldn't have been better had she simply killed him, there on the spot. For the millionth time his pudgy, greasy fingers felt the jeweled, iron collar that ran around his neck. He thought of the things that she had forced him to do to some of his countrymen over the last three centuries, and of the sexuality that she had taken from him and never given back.

Someday, he thought.

Because he was a frequent visitor to the Recluse horse barns, the few stable hands who were about at that hour took little notice except to smile rudely among themselves and point at him. No one outside of the castle proper knew anything about the "other" stables, the slavery Stables, so he knew that they couldn't be laughing at him about that. No, it was his appearance that would childishly amuse them so. But when he gave them a hard look they immediately turned away, as he knew they would. None of them wished to incur Succiu's wrath, not even indirectly, through her slave.

He pushed the horse hard through the rain for the next two hours, flying down the south road, seeing virtually no one along the way. He knew that the closer he came to his destination, the fewer people he would see. Especially at this time of the night. Then, finally, he saw it: the once-proud city that the sorceresses had taken as their own. Over three centuries ago they had murdered the inhabitants of the city, built a wall and moat around it, and then used it as a dumping ground for sick and criminal citizens, and anyone else who displeased them. Many went in, but no one had ever come out. Except him.

He had arrived at his previous home, the Ghetto of the Shunned.

He tied the horse to a watering trough outside the high, massive walls, and untied the leather bag from the saddle. It hurt his back again when he slung it over his shoulder, but that couldn't be helped.

Geldon was without question the only living person in Parthalon who went in and out of the Ghetto at will. There was no one in the nation who would venture inside willingly, and anyone inside who knew how to get out would certainly already have done so long ago. A little smile came to his crooked mouth. He was the only one who knew how to get in and out unnoticed, and it made him feel special tonight. It always did, and he enjoyed the irony of it all.

He stood looking for a moment at the incredibly high stone walls that surrounded the Ghetto, and the wide, deep, filthy water of the moat that surrounded it as he screwed up his courage. Geldon had purposely come to this lonely spot, on the opposite side of the city from the front gates that were always guarded by the Minions. He walked the necessary thirty-eight paces to the right of the watering trough and once again looked down onto the still, murky water. Every time he tried to enter the Ghetto secretly, rather than through the front gates, there was a good chance he would not survive the attempt, and tonight was even worse because of the weight and clumsiness of the bag that he had to take inside with him. But there was no other way. It had to be done. He could not allow the Minion guards to see him with his bag, which meant he would have to leave the same way, and gather his slaves for Succiu from somewhere else.

He walked to the edge of the moat and secured the bag around his chest and back as tightly as he could. He then filled his lungs with air, breathing in and out rapidly several times. On the final breath he held it for all he was worth, closed his eyes, and dove into the filth of the moat, swimming his way to the bottom.

The squalid water was warm, thick, and dirty, and he didn't dare open his eyes. *Start counting,* he reminded himself. *Start counting and find the grate.*

He swam, his eyes still closed and his lungs on fire, counting the strokes until he had completed thirty-two of them, and began to feel for the far wall of the castle that descended into the slimy water. Finally, he found it. He then felt along the submerged moat wall to the right until he came to the rusted iron bars of a grate. Blindly, his lungs running out of oxygen, he pulled at the grate and took it away from the wall, laying it aside upon the muddy floor of the moat. Clutching the bag, he squeezed through the opening and entered the underwater tunnel on the other side. He swam as fast as he could, knowing he was close to passing out. With a last great push he surfaced in a stone room without light, gasping for air to fill his lungs.

He had reentered the Ghetto.

Climbing out of the filthy, freezing water, he lay there on the cold stone floor, gathering his breath and his thoughts. Seeing the room again, his mind drifted back to the time when he had first found this inconspicuous place. Apparently it had been meant for the disposal of refuse out through the lower castle wall. Curious, he had taken the first dive into the submerged tunnel only to find a grate at the other end. It had taken him many such swims to loosen the grate, but eventually he had succeeded. Then, the very night when he was to have made his final escape, Succiu had found him.

Checking the leather bag, he was pleased to see that it had not ripped or otherwise come apart; its contents were no doubt soaked, but secure. He stood, dripping wet and still out of breath, and walked up the short flight of stone steps and out onto a side street.

Clinging closely to the sides of the buildings like a shadow, he went down the first few streets by memory. Macabre, makeshift fires burning here and there at some of the street corners provided the only nighttime illumination, any oil for the street lamps having been exhausted centuries ago. All of the storefronts had long since been looted, and not a bit of intact glass could be seen anywhere. He knew that marauding bands of men sometimes walked these streets by night taking anything and anyone they saw, including the few Ghetto whores who were brave or foolish enough to ply their trade at this hour. There was no law here other than the law of personal survival. It saddened him to realize that, by now, many generations of people had been born, lived, and died here over the last three centuries without ever having seen the outside world. There was no real hierarchy here, no government, no social order. Just human beings reduced to living like animals. Once he had been one of them. Despite how much he hated living in the Recluse as a slave, it was infinitely more appealing than being locked in this nightmare of lost souls.

He finally reached the first of his two destinations. It was a small, narrow nondescript alley that ran into a dead end. Walking to the end of it, he brushed aside some dirt from the floor of the alleyway to reveal a large, flat stone. He dug beneath one edge of the stone with his fingernails, then lifted it to reveal a wooden box. Removing the top of the box, he took out the two items that would help guarantee his safety this night. The first was a dagger, which he concealed in his right boot. The second was a piece of clothing, one that would give him a wide berth through the city, ensuring that no one would bother him.

The yellow robe of a Parthalonian leper.

The robe had come from the dead body of a diseased child. The dwarf had recognized its usefulness right away and had done menial services for the grief-stricken mother in order to pay for it. Now it proved invaluable each time he came here, for it offered him two things that he badly needed in order to move about at will: anonymity and solitude. He left the alley and continued on to where the lepers lived.

He saw a few of them along the way, their yellow robes easily seen in the light of the three red moons that had decided to peek out from behind the slowly parting, vaporous clouds. These poor souls invariably walked hunched over, and he knew that this was because of a mixture of illness and shame. He felt sorry for them, but there was nothing he could do to help them, either. *Perhaps one day,* he thought.

After passing through several streets he finally reached a two-story building in disrepair. The structure looked as if it had been abandoned for decades, and it had always suited his purposes perfectly. He entered and began to creep silently up the stairs to the second floor, listening for the familiar sounds that would tell him that all was well and as he had left it.

In the room at the very top of the stairs, he was joyously greeted by a younger man, also in a yellow leper's robe.

"I almost thought you dead!" the other man exclaimed, obviously glad to see the hunchbacked dwarf alive and well. "I thought for a time that something must have happened, that Succiu might have finally lost her temper with you and done something terrible."

"I know, Ian," Geldon said tiredly. "So much has happened in the last month that I scarcely know where to begin. I shall tell you about it all when time permits." He looked at the face of the blond-haired, blue-eyed young man, who once had been healthy and attractive, before the ravages of his disease had taken their awful toll. Ian was no more than thirty years old but it was impossible to guess at his age now, hunched over as he was, and covered with sores and decaying skin. *Still, he keeps his spirits up,* Geldon thought. *A lesson to us all.*

When Geldon had first met Ian, the younger man's leprosy had hardly been noticeable. But now it appeared to the dwarf that his friend with the insatiable curiosity and the keen interest in what transpired outside the city walls had little time to live.

"How are they?" Geldon asked, still listening to the soft, gentle sounds coming from the far wall of the shabby, little room.

"They're just fine," Ian said proudly. "The entire lot of them. And they miss you."

Geldon turned to look. The far wall was covered from floor to ceiling with small cubicles. This had been his life's work ever since he had met Ian, and they had come upon the idea together.

In each of the cubicles was a pigeon.

Most of them were gray, a few all white or black. They cooed and pranced as best they could in their limited surroundings, and even Geldon had to agree that they seemed to become more excited as he drew nearer to them. Ian oversaw the care and training, and Geldon supplied the food.

Geldon swung the heavy, water-soaked bag down off his aching back and onto the floor.

"Corn?" Ian asked hopefully.

"Yes," Geldon said simply. "Stolen from the Recluse kitchens. I thought the stuff was going to drown me this time as I came through the grate."

Without further fanfare the dwarf went to a meager writing table at the far side of the room and pulled up the chair. Taking a candle down from the wall he dripped some of the hot wax onto the desk, and then set the base of the candle into it. He reached into the desk drawer and produced a small scroll of parchment, a quill pen, and an ink bottle. And then he nervously began to write.

The hunchbacked dwarf sat there for a long time, trying his best to convey what was most important, completely unsure of his spelling yet hoping that his reader would understand. When he finally finished, he rolled the parchment up into a very small scroll, sealed it with wax, and tied an oilskin around it to keep out the rain.

He looked over at Ian. "Bring me one of the larger males," he said.

Ian looked across the cages of birds and finally found the one he wanted—the gray male whose sense of direction never wrong. He removed the bird carefully from the cage and handed it to Geldon.

"I agree," the dwarf said, looking the bird over. Geldon carefully tied the scroll around the bird's leg and handed it back to Ian. He then reached up on a shelf and brought forth a small, wooden, cylindrical object on a string, which he tied carefully around the bird's breast. It was a whistle. It would make a noise as the pigeon flew through the air, keeping the hawks away.

With a nod to Ian, Geldon took the bird out another door and onto a small balcony. The dwarf looked to the stars, thinking about the weather, the distance, and the danger. Finally, with Ian watching, he gently kissed the soft gray bird on the top of its head, and released it into the dark sky. It flew away immediately, then returned and made a large circle around the roof of the building as if saying good-bye before it turned away to its destination. It was headed to Eutracia. To Shadowood.

And finally to the wizard named Faegan.

CHAPTER

Fifteen

"Stop straining your eyes. The *harder* you look, the *less* you will see."

Tristan sat on Pilgrim in the hot afternoon sun, the long, golden stalks of wheat waving gently in the breeze all around him. For two hours he had been futilely attempting to put into action what the old wizard was trying to tell him. But the more the prince looked, somehow the less he saw. It was maddening, like trying to learn something by not learning it at all. He had been staring at the spot that Wigg had told him to, but still he could not see the canyon and bridge that the old one said was right in front of them. All he could see was what he first saw when they had entered the field of wheat—namely, a pine forest that began at the far end and seemed to run on into the hills forever, presumably ending at the coastline of the Sea of Whispers. Frankly, if anyone but Wigg had been telling him this, Tristan would have thought him mad.

Since the incident by the river, they had been traveling without the aid of roads, living off the land, journeying ever northeast. They had spoken little of Natasha, and even less of the one Tristan had known as Lillith. What was there to say? But despite the fact that the mistress of the Coven and daughter of Faegan was dead, the prince still could not get the other woman, the beautiful young woman he had supposedly rescued from the tavern, out of his mind. *Perhaps that was part of the problem,* he thought.

Wigg had sensed this, also. Therefore, during the last week or so the old wizard had decided to spend every waking moment trying to prepare the prince to see the canyon and bridge. He had imparted into Tristan as much training in this particular technique as he could, given the very short time frame in which they had to work. It typically took months for one of endowed blood to learn to see the entrance to Shadowood. Despite that, Wigg had hoped that the high quality of Tristan's blood would shorten the process. But there was really no way to know—not until they were actually faced with it.

Wigg could see both the canyon and the bridge clearly, and was pleased to find that they were just as he remembered them. But until Tristan learned to see them, the prince would not be admitted into Shadowood.

Wigg got down off his horse, walked over to where Tristan and Pilgrim were standing, and took the reins from the prince, hoping that one less distraction would help him concentrate. "What do you see?" the old one asked gently.

Tristan looked at the pine woods again, trying to let go of the image with his eyes just as the wizard had been telling him, and instead trying see what his *blood* knew was there. *Heed your blood, not your eyes,* Wigg had kept telling him. *Don't fight to see the image, but let it simply come to you, instead. Look for it with your heart. And listen to your blood.*

Tristan had seen the pines shimmer once or twice, and he knew that it wasn't the heat that made them appear that way. It was his gift. But for the last hour nothing else had happened, and he was beginning to tire.

He must believe, Wigg thought. *His will is stronger than any of the others I have trained, and he needs proof.*

Handing the reins back to the prince, the wizard began to walk away. Tristan watched as the old one strode oddly about the wheat field, apparently looking for something. Wigg finally bent over and picked up a rather large rock from the ground. Seemingly satisfied, he carried it back and placed it on the ground at Pilgrim's feet. He looked up at the prince.

"I want you to stop trying to see the canyon, and watch this instead," the old one said without any further explanation. He pointed to the rock, and it slowly began to revolve and lift itself off the ground, ever higher in the air, until it was about the same height as the prince's head. Wigg then pointed to the rock, and it slowly began to pass through the air, toward the place where the pine forest started to run down onto the field. He dropped his arm, and the rock sat still in midair, motionless except for the continuous revolutions it made. The old one then clapped his hands, and the rock fell to the earth. Except it didn't land on the ground, as Tristan would have expected.

The earth swallowed it up, and it was gone. It had fallen into the canyon—the one Tristan couldn't see but now knew for a certainty was there.

"Close your eyes," Wigg said calmly.

Tristan did as the old one ordered. No longer able to see the field or the woods, he focused instead on the warmth of the sun, the breeze that came and went across his face, and the rustling sounds of the wheat swaying gently back and forth in the wind.

"Open your eyes," he finally heard the old one say.

The prince opened his eyes to a magnificent view.

The pine forest was gone. In its place lay a canyon at least several hundred feet across; it stretched to either side as far as his eyes could see. The jagged and sheer walls descended straight down into a pitch-black nothingness that appeared to have no bottom. A bridge made of wooden floorboards and rope rails spanned the great, yawning gash in the earth. It swung gently back and forth in the breeze, making a creaking noise that Tristan could now hear but had been unable to detect before. And he could feel the presence of the endowed blood in his veins with new vigor, almost as if for the first time.

But it was the forest on the other side of the canyon that mesmerized him so. Huge, gnarled tree trunks, their roots exposed and seemingly grasping for ever more soil, lined the far side of the canyon, their branches so large that they almost completely blocked out the sun. The forest floor was covered with the thickest moss he had ever seen, and here again he saw the same gigantic trillium blossoms he had seen that day in the forest near the Caves of the Paragon. In fact, so much of the scene was reminiscent of the area that surrounded the Caves that he had to force himself to believe he was not back in that place he had discovered only a few months ago. A few lifetimes ago, it seemed now. Somehow, it was like going home.

He was looking at the place called Shadowood, the creation of the Directorate of Wizards as a sanctuary for those of endowed blood—and still, after all these years, the refuge of Faegan, the one Wigg referred to as "the rogue."

It was then that Tristan first saw the gnome. He had seemingly appeared from nowhere, and was standing rather defiantly next to the bridge where it met the other side of the canyon.

He was only about as high as the prince's waist, perhaps even somewhat shorter, but otherwise he seemed to be mostly human. He had red hair shot through with gray, and a scruffy, identically colored beard covered his face. The dark, beady eyes sat above a rather large, turned-up nose. He wore blue bibs over a bright red shirt, scruffy knee boots with upturned ends, and a strange, lopsided black cap that dangled down to one side.

From seemingly nowhere the gnome produced a chair and an over-sized jug of ale. He sat in the chair and took a long draught of the ale, and then proceeded to light the corncob pipe that Tristan now noticed sticking out from between his teeth. The gnome still had not spoken to them and seemed to be settling in for some time, as if he had all the time in the world and didn't really care whether the two of them could really see him or not.

Tristan couldn't believe he was finally looking at one of these secretive, hermitlike little people. He could feel his endowed blood tingling with what he could only describe as a great sense of distrust.

It was Wigg who spoke first.

"I am of endowed blood, and can see the canyon and you quite clearly. I demand the right to cross," the old one called.

The gnome took another leisurely swig of ale before responding. Finally, he replied. "I saw your trick with the rock, and I wasn't that impressed," he shouted across the chasm. "I am Shannon the Small, and I am the keeper of the bridge. What is your business here?" He took a long draw on the pipe, slowly sending the smoke out into the air from his nostrils.

"We have come to see Faegan," Wigg said simply.

At the mention of the wizard's name the little gnome sat up straighter in his chair and narrowed his eyes. "*Master* Faegan to you," he called back rather sarcastically. "The master sees no one. But when I return to his presence, who shall I say tried unsuccessfully to cross the canyon this day?"

"I am Wigg, Lead Wizard of the Directorate of Wizards, and this is Tristan of the House of Galland, prince of Eutracia," Wigg said. "I strongly suggest you let us cross."

Upon hearing the names, the gnome narrowed his eyes even farther, pursed his lips, and then tapped the embers of the pipe out against the heel of his boot. Standing from his chair, he walked to the edge of the canyon, presumably to get a better look at them. He stared back and forth between the wizard and the prince for a while before answering.

"I am to see that no one crosses. Not since the unpleasantness in Tammerland. Go away and leave us alone."

"Why can't we simply cross the bridge anyway, and go on to Shado-wood?" Tristan asked Wigg. "I haven't come this far just to be told by such a small man that this is where it all ends for us." His thoughts went to Natasha, and what she had said to him about his sister: *You'll never be seeing her again . . . She is one of us now . . . She will receive the best of care.* The dead sorceress' words played out often in his mind, sometimes becoming almost sickeningly confused with the kinder, more loving words that had come from the one named Lillith. But there had been no Lillith, only Natasha, he reminded himself. And that knowledge only made his blood course harder with the need to find his sister. He would allow no one to deny him in his attempt to bring her back—especially one so small as this arrogant gnome.

"You don't understand," Wigg said quietly. "Even if we cross the bridge and overpower him we will still need his permission, or Faegan will sense an unauthorized crossing. He would then most certainly go into hiding, especially considering everything that has transpired in the last few days. And without Faegan we would be right back where we started, only worse. There are a thousand places for him to hide in Shadowood alone. I'm sorry, Tristan, but we must have the permission of the gnome to cross. We would enter Shadowood, but we would lose track of Faegan forever."

Tristan couldn't believe his ears. He couldn't conceive of the Lead Wizard of the Directorate needing permission from an unendowed gnome in order to continue their journey. He looked back across the canyon to where Shannon the Small was still sitting, watching their obvious frustration with self-satisfied amusement.

"How do you know all of this?" Tristan asked.

"As I told you," the old one said, looking back at the gnome, "I was involved in the creation of the canyon." He pursed his lips, then ran a hand down his long, gnarled face.

Tristan had suddenly had enough. He would get the gnome's permission one way or another. But no sooner had he taken his first step forward when he felt Wigg's hand on his elbow, holding him back. The wizard put his lips close to the prince's ear. "If you are going to pet a stray dog with your left hand, make sure you have a rock in your right," he whispered. Tristan smiled and nodded. "Although they have no gifted powers, you may find him to be very strong and quick, especially when angry," the old one added. "Remember, we still need his official permission to cross."

Without looking at the wizard, the prince reached over his left shoulder and pulled the dreggan free of its scabbard. It rang loud and clear out over the deep canyon, the sound seeming never to want to fade away. The idea of using a weapon like this against one so small went against his better nature, but if it had to be, it had to be. Nothing was going to keep him from his sister. He began to cross the bridge.

Unexpectedly, the gnome darted across the bridge toward the prince as fast as his little legs would carry him. Tristan hesitated to raise the dreggan, not really wanting to use it, and that was his mistake. With a great leap, Shannon the Small closed the gap between them in an instant and wrapped his arms and legs around one of the prince's legs, holding on for dear life. The bridge swayed wildly in the air. Tristan's laugh died in his throat when he felt an intense, searing pain in his thigh. He looked down in horror to see that the gnome had sunk his teeth into his leg and wasn't about to let go. Shannon the Small was actually growling and shaking his head back and forth as he bit into the prince, just like a mad dog would. The pain was excruciating. Blood began to trail from the wound, dripping down toward Tristan's knee in winding rivulets of red.

Tristan instinctively reached down to grab some of the gnome's hair and pull him away from the injured leg, then stopped himself. If he pulled on Shannon the Small's head and somehow actually managed to pull it loose from his leg, the gnome might take part of his thigh muscle with him in his small, unbelievably powerful little teeth. The pain increased as the little man hung onto the prince's leg for dear life, and the blood was coming faster now.

Out of desperation, the prince looked to his sword, still held in his right hand. But something told him that he should not kill the gnome, no matter how appetizing the possibility seemed. Instead of slashing at the little man to kill him, Tristan raised the dreggan and brought its hilt down hard on the top of the gnome's head. Shannon the Small seemed dazed for a moment, but then, growling louder, he bit into the prince's thigh even deeper. Tristan brought the hilt of the dreggan down on the gnome's head again, this time much harder. The little assailant collapsed, unconscious, on the floorboards of the bridge.

Gasping for breath, Tristan looked down to see Shannon the Small's face and mouth covered with his blood. A gaping wound of about four inches across lay lengthwise in the prince's leg, beneath the torn trousers. Wigg had been right about petting stray dogs, he thought.

Tristan turned to look at Wigg, who had walked the horses nearer to the edge of the canyon where the bridge ended. "I suggest you revive him," the old one said dryly. "In case you have forgotten, we still need his permission to cross the bridge, and it should be interesting to see how you manage to get it, now that the two of you are such close friends." The old wizard again frowned his disapproval, folded his hands across his chest, and waited imperiously.

At this point Tristan didn't care what Wigg thought about it. He smirked back at the Lead Wizard. "I don't see *you* out here with *your* leg bleeding," he retorted.

His chest still heaving and blood still coming from his leg, the prince looked down at the unconscious body of the gnome. A smile began to creep across the prince's face as he looked down at the small, inert body. He had to admit that Shannon the Small was tenacious, if nothing else. He turned back to the wizard. "Throw me the smaller of the two water bottles," he said. Wigg complied, making sure when he tossed it to the prince that it did not go over the side of the bridge.

Tristan reached down and turned the unconscious gnome face-down. Then he lowered his dreggan and carefully hooked the point of the sword under enough of the gnome's clothing to be able to pick him up using only the sword itself. With a groan, Tristan lifted the gnome up off the floor of the bridge by the point of the sword and dangled him over the rope railing. He then gingerly picked up the water bottle and pried off the cap with his thumb. Shaking the water bottle, he sprayed water into the gnome's face.

It proved to be very effective.

Upon opening his eyes and realizing his situation, Shannon the Small started screaming and waving his arms. At first he wriggled wildly, trying to free himself, but quickly realized the folly in that particular strategy. Finally he covered his eyes with his little hands and managed to remain still over the great depths of the canyon—or as still as he could, considering that he was shaking with fear.

"Let me go," he said venomously. "I am the keeper of the bridge, and if anything happens to me, you will have to answer to Master Faegan!"

"Then perhaps I should just drop you right now, since seeing your master is why we came here in the first place," Tristan said calmly. He turned the sword about, swinging the gnome in the breeze. Shannon the Small swayed upon the point of the dreggan as if he were a mario-nette. "Grant us permission to cross and I shall let you live."

"No!" The words came out from the little mouth in a peculiar combination of stubbornness and fear.

Tristan let the point of the sword droop just a little. "You know," he said drily, "you're quite heavy for such a little fellow. I really don't know how much longer I can keep this up." He let the dreggan suddenly drop a good half a foot, and then pressed the lever in the hilt of the sword. With a loud metallic clang, the blade immediately shot forward a foot into the air over the cavern, taking the gnome with it. Shannon the Small was swinging back and forth even harder now, the collar of his shirt up around his ears.

Finally, the gnome relented. "You may cross," he said in a barely au-dible whisper.

"I can't hear you," Tristan said sarcastically.

"You may cross!" the gnome screamed. "Just put me back on the bridge!"

Tristan hoisted the little body back up over the rope railings and twisted the sword in the air, dropping the gnome on the floorboards.

Shannon the Small stood up shakily and looked into Tristan's face. "Would you really have killed me?" he asked meekly.

"That depends," Tristan said, knowing in his heart he probably never could have killed one so small. Nonetheless, he still needed to keep the upper hand. "We have important business with your master, and nothing can stop us, not even you." He pushed the point of the dreggan toward the gnome and motioned toward the other side of the canyon. "Let's get off this bridge," he said. He retracted the blade and slid the dreggan back into its scabbard behind his right shoulder.

As Shannon the Small turned to walk off the bridge, Tristan motioned to Wigg to follow them with the horses. Despite the fact that the canyon was so deep, the horses came along peacefully. It was only later that Tristan realized the obvious: The horses weren't frightened because they were unable to see either the bridge or the yawning expanse beneath them.

Once safely on the other side, Tristan sat down in the gnome's chair and Wigg attended to his wound. After washing it, the old one closed his eyes and clasped his hands before himself. Tristan could feel the burn of the gash start to diminish, and he watched as the wound closed itself. The pain was gradually replaced by a tingling, almost itching sensation. He told the old one as much.

"What you're feeling is the healing process, which I have accelerated," the wizard said. "It will take time, but eventually you will be fine."

Tristan sighed. He was tired, and he was thirsty. He grabbed for the gnome's ale jug and started to take a sip when the little one gave him a nasty glance and started to try to take it away. But a quick look from Tristan stopped Shannon the Small in his tracks. Apparently the experience of being dangled over the bridge was still fresh on his mind. Tristan took a long drink of ale and wiped his mouth. He looked up at Wigg. "We need to be going," he said. "Time is something we don't have enough of."

The prince stood up gingerly on his injured leg and was about to mount Pilgrim when he felt something tug gently at the back of his leather vest. Turning, he saw the gnome standing behind him, head down. "What is it now?" Tristan asked rather impatiently.

"I'm sorry about your leg," the gnome said sheepishly. "I didn't know what else to do." He was wringing his hands as he spoke. "Take me with you," he then said suddenly. "Please."

"Why should we?" Tristan asked. "You made it almost impossible for us to cross the bridge, and then wounded me in the leg. I don't trust you. You haven't made a particularly good first impression as a representative of your race." He looked down into the small, beseeching eyes with a commanding hardness that he was beginning to find difficult to sustain. He was finding that he was actually beginning to like Shannon the Small.

"I can take you to Master Faegan," the gnome said. "It will save you time."

"Why would you want to take us to him, when for the entire day you have done nothing but try to keep us from him?" Wigg asked, already astride his horse. Tristan could see that the old one's eyes were genuinely full of mistrust.

"Because you are the first ones to cross the bridge in all of the time since he has been here," Shannon said. "And if I take you to him, rather than simply let you go on your own . . ."

"It will look better for you in the eyes of your master," Tristan said, raising an eyebrow and completing the sentence in a way that wasn't exactly what Shannon the Small had in mind. The prince smiled at the little gnome for the first time, then looked at Wigg. "Is it true?" he asked. "Will it really save us time if we take him along?"

"Probably," the old one said grudgingly. "As you know, I can detect others of endowed blood, and that was to be our method of finding him. But Faegan was the most talented of us all, and if he doesn't want to be found I doubt that there is anything that even I could do about it. But it's going to be your responsibility to watch the gnome. I don't trust them, and I never have." He shook his head derisively.

Tristan looked down to see Shannon the Small beaming from ear to ear. "Well don't just stand there," the prince said with a gruffness that even he could tell was becoming ineffective. "Get your things and climb up."

The little gnome ran happily to gather up his pipe and his jug. Returning, he watched Tristan mount his horse.

"By the way," Tristan said, "his name is Pilgrim." He held his hand down to the little one and hoisted him up on the saddle in front of him.

Shannon the Small then pointed gleefully to an entrance in the thickest part of the domain of Shadowood, and Pilgrim began to step gingerly into the dark heart of the forest.

*A*lthough the next day's sun was bright and the weather warm, the prince, wizard, and gnome traveled through Shadowood in comparative darkness and cold, due to the dense foliage of the trees surrounding them. Here, as had been the case that day in the Hartwick Woods, the prince felt as if he had suddenly entered a place of otherworldliness, as if the three of them somehow did not belong in this foreboding but still beautiful forest.

Wigg refused to speak to Shannon, and it appeared to the prince that this arrangement was equally acceptable to the gnome. *I wonder what the basis for this mutual mistrust is,* the prince wondered as he and Shannon sat upon Pilgrim, leading the way through the ever-thickening woods. *Whatever it is, it has a very long history.*

Suddenly Tristan could feel the gnome seated behind him begin to stiffen, and as he looked ahead, he thought he could see why. There was a small clearing just in front of them, and the heavy, sickening odor emanating from it clearly carried the message that this was a place of death, and of the unattended dead.

"Go around it, whatever it is," Shannon said quickly. "We do not need to see it. Besides, Master Faegan awaits us."

It was precisely the gnome's insistence that made Tristan stop his horse, determined to investigate. He had known the wizard much longer than he had known the gnome, and if Wigg had his doubts about Shannon, then perhaps he should, too.

Swinging one leg over the pommel of his saddle, he slipped quickly to the ground, then reached over his right shoulder and withdrew the dreggan. He looked back up at the angry-faced gnome.

"You'll soon find that I don't take orders very well," he said sternly. "But then again, I would have thought that you might have learned that rather valuable lesson back at the bridge." Tristan looked back to Wigg, indicating that he should dismount and follow him. "And by the way," he added, "don't get any sudden ideas about stealing our horses." He narrowed his eyes and smiled ruefully. "Neither Pilgrim nor I would appreciate it." Without waiting for a response, he walked carefully into the clearing.

The scene before him was staggering. Some kind of barbaric massacre had taken place here. He began to try to count the bodies, but found that they were in so many pieces that counting them accurately was impossible. But from what he could determine, some kind of battle—no, make that slaughter—had taken place here. The ground was covered with a great deal of blood. Body parts lay strewn across the clearing in a random pattern of bloody, sudden death. He placed his cupped hand over his nose and mouth to block the stench as best he could. Busy flies and maggots had been at their grisly work here for some time. Then he realized that each of the mangled bodies and body parts were unusually small.

These victims were gnomes, he suddenly realized. *And someone or something has ripped them apart.*

He noticed two other anomalies: In a great many places he could see bones that had been completely stripped of their flesh, as they lay gleaming in the sun that shone into the clearing. *Carrion would not have polished these bones so,* he thought. *They positively shine.* And secondly, he could see no heads.

Sensing Wigg come up behind him, he turned around. "Can you possibly explain this?" he asked. Wigg raised the infamous eyebrow and slowly walked about the clearing, occasionally bending over to examine the remains more closely, apparently oblivious to the stench.

"Gnomes," he said simply. "A number of Faegan's gnomes were killed here, and by the looks of it, they died very badly. Literally ripped to pieces, I would say." He looked around a bit more before once again addressing the prince. "And did you notice that there are no heads?" he asked. "Strange. I am no great fan of the gnomes, but this is truly a tragedy."

"Yes," Tristan answered. "It doesn't make any sense."

"Perhaps not to us," Wigg said slowly. He looked back to where Shannon was obediently but angrily still sitting atop Pilgrim. "But the gnome may know more than he is telling. They usually do."

They walked back to the horses, and Wigg looked up into Shannon's face with a glance that could have frozen water. "What happened here?" he demanded.

"If you don't know, *Lead Wizard,* then someone as unenlightened as myself certainly couldn't figure it out for you, now could they?" Shannon answered sarcastically. "If you're really interested, I suggest you ask Master Faegan when you see him. But standing here in this glade all day pondering over dead bodies isn't going to get us there, now is it?" As if he had had quite enough of the wizard for one day and could simply dismiss him at his leisure, the gnome raised himself up haughtily in the saddle and turned his face the other way.

That was a mistake, the prince thought with an inward smile.

Tristan knew that Wigg was angry, but what he saw next quite frankly surprised him. The wizard reached up and yanked the gnome from the horse, using the endowed strength of his arms to hold Shannon in midair. The look in the Lead Wizard's eyes said that he wanted answers, and he wanted them now.

Wigg glared at the gnome. "Faegan isn't here, and frankly, I'm starting to wonder whether you truly know his location at all! I will ask you one more time, and one more time only," Wigg thundered, swinging the gnome back and forth slightly in his endowed, iron grip. "What happened here?"

Tristan smiled to himself. He was not sure that the wizard would win this contest of wills. Wigg's vows prevented him from unnecessarily harming the gnome, and Tristan knew that Wigg would never do such a thing, anyway. But the prospect of wondering who would win this was becoming amusing, despite the circumstances.

"Except for Master Faegan, I hate wizards, and I hate magic, and above all I hate you! And nothing you can do to me will make me tell. Besides, if you truly do not already know, which I doubt, then I don't care if you ever find out!"

Finally realizing that this had become nothing but a waste of time, Wigg unceremoniously dropped the gnome into the dirt at his feet. Quick as a flash, Shannon bounded back up and kicked Wigg in the shin—hard. Wigg let out a yelp and jumped to one foot, almost falling down.

Tristan couldn't help it: he burst out laughing.

"And let that be a lesson to you!" Shannon scowled as he walked away in disgust toward the horses and the ever-tempting ale jug.

"We had better get back there before he drinks all the rest of that stuff and becomes drunk again," Tristan said, still laughing. "We truly do not need a guide who is both obstinate *and* inebriated. The Afterlife only knows, he'll probably steal the horses, too!"

Wigg rubbed his shin and scowled back at the prince, placing his foot gingerly back down upon the ground. He cast another angry look back at the carnage in the clearing. "I still don't know who caused this, but at this particular moment, I'm not altogether sure I disapprove!" He rubbed his sore leg again. "I told you I hated gnomes!" he said grumpily as he started to walk away, his braided tail of gray hair swinging crazily back and forth as it matched his limping gait.

Tristan started laughing out loud again as he began to follow the limping Lead Wizard of the Directorate back to the horses. He then watched as the imperious, ale-swilling little gnome clambered atop a stump to hoist himself onto Pilgrim's back, looking for all the world as if he, not Tristan, was now the owner of the stallion.

But the prince couldn't shake the nagging thought that continued to run through his mind. *What happened here was no accident, and Shadowood was supposed to be a place of peace.* He shook his head. *That obviously is no longer true.*

CHAPTER

Sixteen

K luge looked down at the dead body that was impaled on his dreggan, and then to the pool of crimson blood that was beginning to spread across the ground beneath it. *I wish it were the endowed blood of that Eutracian royal bastard,* he thought. Raising his right boot, he negligently pushed the corpse off his sword and onto the earth. His opponent had fought well, but had obviously been no match for the commander of the Minions of Day and Night. He doubted in his heart that any of them were. *One day the corpse at my feet shall be the prince of Eutracia,* he thought. *Until he is dead, my mission remains unfulfilled, and Succiu will never be mine.*

He glared at Traax, who was standing nearby, watching. "Get me another one to play with," he said, pointing to the body on the ground. "This one is broken."

Traax bowed. "Yes, sir," he said simply, and began walking across the courtyard of the compound to select another opponent for the commander. Another warrior of the Minions who would no doubt die at the hands of his leader. An honor, many of them said.

As he waited, Kluge ran a hand through his sweaty, gray-and-black hair, pulling it off his shoulders and tying it behind his neck so that it fell straight down his back between his dark, leathery wings. He looked up into the clear Parthalonian sky and idly wondered what the weather was like today in Eutracia. Eutracia, where the Lead Wizard and Prince Tristan still lived—the prizes who had escaped that day in the Great Hall of the palace in Tammerland. The men of endowed blood he so badly wanted to kill.

Kluge looked down from the rise upon which he was standing and observed the training that was relentlessly going on below him. He was in the largest of the Minion compounds, the one nearest to the Recluse, and he had designated this to be a special training day, one in which he always participated personally. He enjoyed these days above all others, when he was allowed to kill his own troops.

After the inception of the Minions of Day and Night, long before Kluge's time, there had come upon the Coven a problem in the training of the warriors. Because the kingdom of Parthalon had never had a standing army, the science of war was unknown to them and there was no one with whom the warriors could effectively train. Every time any meaningful battle practice had been attempted against the population, it had simply been a slaughter and had served no purpose. The Coven had not cared, of course, whether the citizens of the population died. Their only concern had been that no realistic training to the death could be had, training that the Coven knew would be essential one day in their attack upon Eutracia.

The Coven had therefore not only ordered the Minions to train among themselves but to occasionally practice their arts to the death. To the sorceresses' delight, the Minions had immediately agreed to this command. Despite the obvious disadvantage of the loss of their own troops, the resulting carnage not only provided actual battle experience, but also weeded out the less skilled of the warriors. Some of those who survived were promoted to the officers' ranks, and those who were wounded beyond battle service were assigned other tasks, as best as their various handicaps would allow. The dead were honored as heroes and burned in huge funeral pyres that lit up the night sky for hours. Kluge looked down to the leaded glove on his right hand, the one that both threw and caught the returning wheel, the other great weapon of the Minions. Smiling, he was reminded that the bloodstains upon it came from a combination of Parthalonian and Eutracian victims.

He turned to see Traax following another warrior up the rise to where he stood. There were two reasons why Kluge always did his own practice upon elevated ground. First, so he could more easily follow the progress of his warriors as they fought to the death. And second, so that they could see *him* train. He took pleasure in making sure that each of them knew that he was the best. Tradition said that whichever Minion warrior could kill him during such training would, provided the sorceresses approved, assume his rank and automatically become their unquestioned leader. The policy had been put in place by the Coven long ago, in order to assure there would be no lack of opponents eager to train in this way with their leader, and to dispose efficiently of a leader whose prime had passed.

The warrior that Traax was bringing to him appeared fit and strong, and had both the look in his eyes and the scars upon his body of one who had lived through a great many such contests. As Kluge glanced again down into the training yards where thousands of his best continued to fight, he also noticed that many of them had stopped their individual battles to look up to where he was standing. He had always taught them to be ready for anything, to trust no one, and to be ready at a moment's notice. He silently decided to reinforce that concept.

As Traax and the other approached, Kluge waited until they were at least one hundred paces from him before he turned his back to them, something he had always taught his warriors not to do. He hoped a great number of them were watching.

Slowly, imperceptibly, he reached across his body with his right hand to remove the returning wheel from his belt. He knew that his opponent had not yet drawn his dreggan—he would have heard its distinctive ring. *His final, fatal blunder,* Kluge thought. *I always taught them to arm themselves the moment they were in sight of the enemy. Not doing so will be the mistake of his life.*

Kluge turned back toward his opponent with a speed that few of the men in the yard had ever seen. The returning wheel was already spinning through the air, a silver, spherical blur. Its razor-sharp teeth buried themselves in the man's throat just above his larynx, kept on tearing, and then exited the back of his neck as his head began to fall clumsily, held to the shoulders by only the briefest of pink connective tissue. The body crumpled to the ground as though the legs had just been amputated. The warrior's wings began to jerk reflexively back and forth upon the ground as his blood covered the ground around him.

Without even looking up from the dying man, Kluge reached his right hand back into the air and automatically caught the returning wheel in the bloodstained, padded glove. He hung the deadly sphere back on his belt, then walked over to the fallen warrior and removed the man's dreggan from its scabbard.

He placed the tip of the dreggan against the warrior's chest and pressed the button on the hilt that would release the remaining length of the blade, ending the fallen fighter's existence. The wings still flapped pitifully against the blood-soaked ground like those of a damaged bird that had fallen to earth, unable to lift itself.

He looked down at the crowd of men who had gathered closer to the spectacle, pursed his lips, and then lifted his sword. He retracted the blade and replaced it into the scabbard.

"Leave the body here," he said casually to Traax. He noticed that his second in command had been splattered with the blood of the fallen man. Kluge gestured to the troops below. "Make sure they get a good look at what happens to those who take their enemies for granted."

Just as he was about to turn away he heard the sound of someone clapping in praise, and a female voice called out to him.

"Well done, Commander," Succiu said from a place on the hill a short distance above him. She was dressed in a white silk gown, with touches of the darkest blue here and there in her jewelry and her shoes. Tiny droplets of blood from Kluge's victim had spattered her dress, and the wind gently blew her long, lustrous hair in slow, dark, undulating waves. Her slave, the little hunchbacked dwarf named Geldon, was abjectly sitting beside her in the dirt as she held the jeweled leash that ran to his iron collar. In her other hand she casually twirled a white parasol, also trimmed in dark blue, open to the sun. She looked dressed to attend a great ball, rather than the struggles of men killing each other in the dirt below her. But he knew her tastes well, and was not surprised.

It had been several days since he had seen her, and despite how well he knew every curve of her body and face he nonetheless drew an instinctively sharp breath at this sudden appearance of her beauty. With her unexpected arrival had also come the twin, bitter remembrances of both how she could never be his and how she had gazed upon the prince of Eutracia, the male of endowed blood, that day in the great hall at Tammerland. Warrior emotion rushed through his veins, fed by his intense, visceral hatred of Tristan. *The so-called Chosen One,* he spat silently.

"I see that the Minion custom of succession by death is still in place," Succiu said, smiling at him. She carefully touched the tip of her right index finger to one of the blood spots on her gown and daintily placed it on her tongue.

Kluge and Traax each immediately went down on one knee. "I live to serve," they said in unison.

Succiu was busy studying one of her nails. "You may rise." She sighed.

Kluge's eyes narrowed as he reexamined the little dwarf at her side. *Must she take him everywhere she goes?* he wondered. He took in the contemptuous sneer that lay deep in the hunchback's eyes as he watched the pudgy little fingers anxiously feel the jeweled collar around his neck. *Someday she may regret enslaving him,* Kluge mused. *Still, in some ways I envy the dwarf who is constantly at her side.*

Succiu looked at Kluge, her expression businesslike. "My conversation is for your ears only, Commander," she ordered. "Traax, you are dismissed."

With a quick bow, Traax started off down the hill. But Kluge called out to him, and he stopped and turned. "Yes, my lord?" he asked.

The Minion commander looked down the hill to where the warriors had resumed their practice. "Begin counting dead bodies," he ordered. "When you have reached two hundred, stop the training. That is all we can afford for one session of such combat. I shall join you later."

"Yes, my lord," Traax said. He turned and began walking back down into the courtyard.

With the departure of Traax, Succiu frowned slightly, her brow furrowed with thought. "Walk with me," she finally murmured, and turned with the jeweled leash in her hand. She began strolling along the ridge of the hill and away from the courtyard. The dwarf waddled hurriedly beside her.

After apparently walking as far as she wished to, she turned to him, and Geldon automatically sat down in the grass at her feet. "What I have to say to you is to be kept strictly between the two of us," she said strongly, her dark, almond-shaped eyes boring into his. "If I hear that any of our conversation has been intimated to anyone else, you will curse the day you were born. Do you understand?"

"Permission to speak freely?" Kluge asked. It was rare that he requested this privilege from her, but given her tone he decided he wanted the freedom to express himself.

"Yes."

"I will, of course, honor whatever wishes my mistress has of me, as I have always done. However, do you think it wise that there be another pair of ears present?" He cast his eyes down to the dwarf, so that Succiu would not miss his meaning.

"There is no cause for worry," the second mistress said, laughing lightly. "Geldon has been with me for more than three hundred years, and has heard things of far greater importance than those of which I am about to speak. He is usually with me because he amuses me, and performs some rather indispensable tasks."

The little dwarf suddenly jumped to his feet, thrusting his jaw out at Kluge. "I'm important, too!" he hollered indignantly, making wise use of the rare chance to prove his false loyalty to Succiu. "I was here almost three hundred years before you were even born! Whatever my mistress says to you, she can say to me!"

Succui's reaction was immediate. She backhanded the little hunchback for all she was worth, sending him to his knees, and he went rolling partway downhill until the leash brought him to an abrupt stop, almost breaking his neck. "I gave the commander permission to speak freely, but I do not remember giving you the same privilege, little man," she sneered. When Geldon finally managed to get up on all fours, she dropped the leash. Kluge watched her extend her right hand in the air toward the little dwarf, and suddenly Geldon began to cough.

Succiu was tightening his collar.

"No matter how many times I punish you, you just never seem to learn," she purred in obvious enjoyment. The dwarf's eyes were practically bulging out of their sockets, and Kluge could actually see a bluish tinge beginning to show in the little man's face.

Succiu turned her head slightly and pursed her lips as she continued to torture the dwarf. "He makes such a fascinating little toy, don't you think?" she asked happily. "And, as you can see, his collar serves more purposes than one."

It made no real difference to Kluge, but he was sure that the dwarf was about to die. Then, just at the last instant, Succiu again raised her hand, and the collar returned to its normal size. *She has done this often,* Kluge realized. *She knows just how far she can take him. Just as she knows how far she can take me when she commands me to lie with her.*

Coughing and gagging, the dwarf stood up and trudged back up the hill to sit once again at the feet of his mistress, almost as if nothing had happened.

Succiu twirled her parasol, her expression lighter now, as if the punishment of Geldon had been a tonic for her. "Now then, Commander," she began, "the reason for my visit. Put very simply, I want you to double the Minion guard near the vicinity of the Recluse."

"Of course, Mistress," he said automatically. "But is there some threat of which I should be told? I am aware of no immediate danger in the countryside."

"It is not Parthalon that concerns me," she said, frowning again. "It is Eutracia. Despite the overall success of our campaign, our mission was not completely fulfilled. The Lead Wizard and the Chosen One still live, and I believe they will try to do everything in their power to cross the Sea of Whispers and come for Sister Shailiha. Amazingly, they have apparently eluded several of the traps that I laid in Eutracia before we left. I fear I may have underestimated them both. Wigg doesn't know how to cross the sea, and neither does Faegan. Indeed, they have neither seen nor spoken to each other for over three hundred years. But I believe Wigg will try to find him, and when he does it should make for a very interesting reunion. And Failee seems somehow quite unconcerned about all of these possibilities." She paused, looking away momentarily. Uncharacteristically, almost to herself, she added, "Sometimes I do not agree with all of her decisions . . ."

She gazed off into the distance as if thinking about something else. Finally, she seemed to return to the present. "In any event, the other mistresses do not know that I am taking this precaution, and no one is to know other than you and me. Failee seems to think that there is no danger, that even Wigg and Faegan put together cannot cross the sea. She is probably right. But *my* blood tells me that they will try. You may get your chance to kill the Chosen One, after all."

Kluge's blood raced with the prospect of killing the prince of Eutracia, especially here, on his own soil. That royal, sniveling bastard would not escape him again, he thought. *I shall kill you in front of the second mistress, endowed blood or not, and prove to her which of us is the better man.*

The white-and-blue parasol twirled in what was fast becoming the late-afternoon sun. Succiu's mischievous mood had returned. "I can see by the look in your eyes that you are excited about the prospect of killing Prince Tristan," she said. "Fine and well. But hear me: He is not to die until I am done with him. When he is found he is to be taken alive and brought to me. There is to be no deviation from this order, or you will precede him into the Afterlife, where the two of you can finally take all of eternity, if you choose, to prove who is the best." She took a moment to smile at that thought before continuing. "I do not care what happens to the Lead Wizard, provided he dies. Make it as fast or as slow as you care to. But the prince is mine."

"Yes, Mistress," Kluge said, smiling slightly. "It shall all be as you order."

"Very good." She looked down at the dwarf. "Up," she said to him as if she were talking to her dog. "There is just enough time upon our return to the Recluse for you to pick out a worthy slave from the Stables for my use this evening." She looked cattily at Kluge. "I told you he had his uses."

She turned and began to walk away, the little dwarf waddling as fast as he could to keep up with her.

$\mathcal{A}$s Kluge turned and walked down the hill to join Traax, his mind still clung tenaciously to the image of the second mistress' unexpected appearance. The frustration was always the same, and fueled the flames of the other, equally burning desire in his heart: to eventually find and kill the one man in the entire world who truly appeared to fascinate her.

The Chosen One.

In truth there was little he could do about either emotion just now. But Succiu's nearness—her scent and her dark, enticing eyes—never failed to fuel the animal instinct in him. And since she had made no mention of needing him for "other duties" tonight, his only recourse would be to visit the brothels.

Which he intended to do soon.

He walked with Traax to one of the funeral pyres that were always built prior to training to the death. They watched a warrior gently touch a torch to the dry twigs and leaves at the bottom. Almost immediately the base of the great stack of corpses jumped into flames. The clothing of the dead fueled the flames higher still, and the familiar stench and dark, sooty haze of burning flesh started to cling to the air. Kluge casually turned to look at the other three pyres. The orange-and-red flames would light up the sky into the coming night and continue on for hours as they fed upon their victims.

"You stopped the fighting at two hundred dead, and collected their dreggans and returning wheels for new trainees?" he asked his second in command.

"Yes, my lord," Traax answered. "Just as is the usual custom."

"How many wounded?"

"Four hundred and fifty. Two hundred of whom will no longer be able to fight."

Kluge did not speak, for there was no need. These losses were quite acceptable for a full day of such training to the death, and both he and Traax knew it.

"But there is something else of which my lord must be advised," Traax said almost quietly.

Kluge stopped in midstride and turned his head. "And that is?"

"There is to be a Kachinaar starting soon in the Hall of Fallen Heroes. All is prepared. But I refused to let the warrior's vigil begin without your permission, and hopefully also your attendance."

Kluge glared intently into Traax's eyes with a ferocity that was more feigned than real, designed to make sure that clear, flashing master/slave signals passed between them just the same. *He learns quickly,* Kluge thought, *and reminds me of myself. In the future I must remember not to let his ambition go too far.*

"And who ordered this?" he demanded.

"I did, my lord," Traax said, lowering his head slightly in submission. "The need was clear."

"The crime?"

"Failure to finish off quickly one of his adversaries in today's training. It appears the two of them knew each other, and the warrior in question hesitated for a split second before doing his duty. He killed him eventually, of course, but the supervising officer thought his actions to be too slow, and brought it to my attention."

"And were his actions too slow?" Kluge asked.

Traax allowed himself a wicked leer. "Does it really matter?"

Kluge grinned back knowingly. "No," he said simply. "But go to the Kachinaar. I shall be there shortly. And call for Arial. I wish her to be present there for me."

"Yes, my lord." Traax smiled. "It shall be as you command." He immediately walked away, heading deeper into the heart of the Minion compound.

As Kluge slowly walked past the various Minion buildings, he looked around, in awe, as always, of the complexities of the Minion fortifications and all that it took to make them run smoothly. The sorceresses had indeed planned well.

This particular fortification housed at least one hundred thousand Minions, in addition to everything that was needed to run a city of that size effectively. There were granaries, kitchens, nurseries and healing areas, gathering areas for entertainment, and a great slaughterhouse. The list of required facilities went on and on. And in addition to all of these came the requirements for running and maintaining a battle force, such as armorers, fletchers and bow makers, barracks for the troops, training grounds, stables, blacksmiths, and specially trained healers for the wounded. He knew every one of the buildings in each of the three compounds in Parthalon, for it was his job to oversee them all. His reason for being in this particular stronghold today was the fact a training session to the death had been scheduled and he never missed one, no matter which of the compounds it took place in.

As he continued to walk though the busy streets among his own kind, his warrior's eyes took in the high, rough-hewn, foreboding walls that completely surrounded the fortress. With armed Minion warriors patrolling their tops, the ramparts were obviously intended to scare away the curious of the population should any of them actually be so foolhardy as to approach, and in his lifetime he had never heard of a single such case. But he also knew that if any of the Parthalonian citizens were ever to set foot somehow inside one of these fortresses, they would be shocked—because instead of the harsh and primitive conditions they would expect to find within these rough walls, what they would see was a city of luxury.

Each of the buildings was made of the finest marble, and their interiors were no less splendid. The many intersecting and winding streets were paved with shiny black granite bricks, and the oil sconces at each of the street corners were starting to be lit, giving the city a spectacularly soft, burnished glow. The brothels, barracks, and birthing houses especially, he knew, were almost overdone in their great luxury. Each Minion combat warrior had the very best of food, wine, and training. And, of course, the most beautiful of the very willing, talented whores of the brothels.

It was wise of the Coven to afford the Minions such luxury, he mused for the thousandth time. Kluge was under no illusions as to why the mistresses allowed him and his kind such lavishness. He knew that it was designed to keep his men happy and therefore less likely to revolt. A force such as the Minions would be potent indeed, even against the magic of the Coven, should the warriors become restless. He closed his eyes for a moment, luxuriating in the memories of various experiences that being their commander had afforded him and him alone. *Yes.* He smiled to himself. *It is this life that keeps them content. That—and the fact that they know nothing better, such as the glories of the interior of the Recluse or what it is truly like to lie with a sorceress such as Succiu.*

As he turned the corner to approach the massive Hall of Fallen Heroes, he was again reminded of his utmost duty to the Coven, aside from protecting them and controlling the citizenry. This second-most important of his tasks was to oversee constantly the increase in the numbers of the Minions, especially the combat troops. And so the luxurious brothels that constantly fed the birthing houses were also a critical part of his responsibilities. They had been here long before him, and would probably be here long after he was dead. He smirked to himself knowingly. The Coven had never granted the benefits of the time enchantments to the Minions except for briefly accelerating the aging process during childhood, and then also temporarily decelerating it later in life so as to be able to widen the window of opportunity to produce yet more Minion children. But in the end every Minion eventually died of battle, disease, or old age.

To this day Failee could still sometimes be seen walking through the fortresses, commanding certain members of the population to gather together upon bended knee for her application of the incantations. She would sometimes walk through the luxurious brothels, as well, placing her hand upon the abdomen of each of the women there, determining which of them might already be pregnant. Such women would be taken immediately to the best of quarters, so that Failee's enchantments of acceleration might be placed upon them to speed their gestation. It was an eerie sight, even to Kluge's hardened mind, to see the First Mistress plying the craft in this way.

He paused, thinking, wondering just how many more warriors the Coven would desire now that they had accomplished their mission in Eutracia. Would there be other such conquests? He surely hoped so, and the thought of yet more campaigns of sudden, violent death caused him to grip the hilt of his dreggan tightly, his knuckles turning white with anticipation.

The Hall of Fallen Heroes was gigantic in size, and the sorceresses had seen that it was the utmost in luxury—second only, perhaps, to the Recluse itself. It was constructed of unusually fine, blanched marble with variegated indigo streaks, the facade trimmed in the palest of gold. Dozens of blanched-marble columns reached to either side of the magnificent portico, their white-and-indigo variegated lengths stretching to support the great gilt-edged, tiled roof. The steps in front of the building were of the finest black granite, and the sun glinted off them as he began the rather long climb. Finally reaching the huge double doors, he walked through and into the hall.

The scene before him was as amazing as always, and he drank in the sights, smells, and sounds of this place as if he were a drowning man in need of air to breathe.

The Hall of Fallen Heroes had always been meant as a place of revelry rather than of quiet. Today was no exception, as the feasting and celebration that traditionally followed a day of training to the death was always particularly rowdy and ostentatious. But what made today's orgy of food, wine, and carnality particularly intriguing was the fact that there was about to be a Kachinaar.

Hundreds of his warriors, mostly his officers, filled the room at long banquet tables eating and drinking their fill, laughing and slapping each other on the back between their dark, leathery wings. Many of them were already seriously drunk and telling stories of how they had been fortunate enough to kill and once again survive the day. Taking small, tentative steps—all their bound feet could manage—the Minion women brought them ever more food and jugs of wine and ale.

Occasionally a man would reach out to touch or grab a woman, leaving little of his intentions to the imagination. The willing girls almost always fell easily into the warriors' arms. More often than not, outright copulation would rigorously begin in front of everyone, either on the floor or on the banquet tables themselves, amid the food and drink. Leering crowds of men and women alike shouted lustful cheers of support. Under normal circumstances these indulgences of the flesh would continue well into dawn. But today there was to be a Kachinaar.

The Minion commander looked around for his second in command. When Traax saw his superior he jumped up from his chair, spilling to the floor both his goblet of wine and the naked woman in his lap. Immediately, he screamed his warriors to attention, and they, too, quickly jumped to their feet. A riot of plates, dishes, food, wine, and chairs crashed, slipped, and slopped noisily to the floor. The hall became as quiet as a tomb.

Suddenly, all at once, the air was filled with the sound of silver-studded boot heels clicking together in unison. Then silence reigned once again for what seemed an eternity as the commander of the Minions of Day and Night looked out across the hall.

"You have done well this day," Kluge began, shouting in his deep, strong voice. "And to those of you who have fought and survived, I grant this day of feasting and celebration!" Cheers went up all around the room, and the carnival of indulgences began anew. Kluge motioned for Traax to join him.

"Yes, my lord?" the younger man asked.

"The Kachinaar is ready?" Kluge asked.

"Yes, all is prepared. It is to take place in the usual area."

Kluge's eyes narrowed. "And Arial, is she here?"

"She has been summoned, my lord, and awaits you. She seems eager."

"Very well," Kluge answered. He and Traax began to make their way through the loud, almost insane revelry to stand before a very special area of the room.

The Kachinaar had been Kluge's concept from the first, and he was quite proud of it. Early in his career as the commander of the Minions he had realized the need for maintaining order in a way that would produce the greatest respect, the greatest fear of his leadership throughout the ranks. Simply striking down warriors who transgressed had always been the way of it before, but as the ranks grew it became apparent to Kluge that another, more effective method needed to be found. His warrior's mind had no time or patience for the niceties of asking questions or conducting trials. And so he had devised a cleaner, quicker way to deal with the problem. He had invented the Kachinaar, or the warrior's vigil, as it came to be known by the troops.

The concept behind it was blindingly effective and simple. Any warrior accused by any of his fellows of a transgression, no matter how small, could be brought before the Kachinaar. The final decision to proceed was always left to Kluge or Traax. It mattered not a whit whether the man or woman was guilty or innocent, only that he or she had been accused. Indeed, Kluge was well aware of several of his men, officers included, who were quite guilty and had nonetheless survived the vigil, only to be fully reinstated to their places in the ranks. But those transgressors who were lucky enough to survive the Kachinaar would never again go astray.

If the accused survived he was deemed innocent. And if he perished he was guilty, the punishment having already been carried out—in the process sending yet another warning of obedience through the ranks.

Today's Kachinaar was ready to begin. There was a deep marble pit in the floor of the hall, and suspended over it was the accused warrior. Ropes stretched from his wrists to brackets on the wall at either side. He dangled there helplessly, his wings no good to him now. He looked at

Kluge but did not speak, for he knew it would be taken as a sign of weakness and would not help him in any event, for warriors of the Kachinaar who begged for mercy or tried to explain their supposed transgressions were always always killed. Slowly and methodically. The Kachinaar was not meant to be a forum for explanations, and Kluge would not have it as such.

Kluge walked over to the edge of the pit and looked down on the three Parthalonian wolves trapped at the bottom. They had been taken from the countryside and starved almost to death. Now they snarled up at Kluge with bared teeth, their eyes glowing with the prospect of the meal that hung so temptingly above them. The floor around them was littered with the clothing and polished bones of Minion warriors. And then Kluge noticed something else, an enhancement no doubt introduced by Traax, and was momentarily perplexed.

Each of the wolves was wearing a silver-spiked collar. Suddenly, Kluge grasped the reasoning. The collars were to prevent the wolves, starving and half mad as they were, from eating each other.

He smiled to his second in command. "Shall we begin?"

"By all means, my lord," Traax answered.

Five Minion warriors were called forth, and a blindfold was produced. The warrior hanging in the ropes knew precisely what was about to happen, for he had witnessed it himself several times before. Each of the warriors would be blindfolded, and would take a turn throwing his returning wheel at the ropes. If the ropes were cut, the warrior would die and was therefore guilty, his punishment already inflicted. But if they missed or cut only one of the ropes, the warrior would be deemed innocent and returned to his unit. The room became hushed, and the crowd pressed in toward the pit.

The first Minion warrior came forward and took the blindfold. Grasping his returning wheel, he threw it in the direction of the ropes. The crowd held its breath.

The wheel sliced through one side of the rope, leaving it shredded but still holding the weight of the warrior. He dangled there above the pit just a little lower than before, closer to the snarling, hungry wolves at the bottom.

Kluge glanced to the rear of the hall to be sure that one of his men would be catching the wheels as they started to come around again. Satisfied, he returned his gaze to the scene before him.

The next three warriors had little luck, their wheels missing amid catcalls from the crowd. The warrior hanging in the ropes looked intently at Kluge, knowing that his fate would soon be sealed.

The fifth warrior to take the blindfold threw his wheel with great

force, and it spun unerringly toward the as–yet–unharmed rope, slicing it cleanly in half. Great hollers and yells of congratulations erupted
among the crowd as the warrior hung between life and death from the
shreds of a single frayed rope. The circling, half-mad wolves could be
heard demanding their reward.

As was always Kachinaar custom, if the warrior had survived five of
whatever the particular ritual called for, Kluge was given the opportunity to try his hand, thereby settling the issue. Smiling, Kluge placed the
blindfold over his eyes and took the returning wheel from the hook on
his broad leather belt.

There were many experts of the returning wheel among the Minions, but even the graybeards among them had always said that there had
never been one to match Kluge. He had been given the title of wheelmaster by his previous teacher, who had also been a wheelmaster before
him, and there were currently only three living warriors to have earned
that title among the entire Minion population. Kluge was the best of
the three.

But such a throw would be impossible even for Kluge, many of the
warriors thought.

The room became as still as death. The warrior hanging from the
shredded rope closed his eyes.

Kluge paused for a moment. He tilted his head slightly as if trying
to anticipate the angle, and then immediately loosed the wheel with a
strong, sure whip of his right arm.

The revolving, silver blur raced toward the warrior hanging by the
single shred of rope. The wheel sliced cleanly through the rope as if it
weren't there. The warrior tumbled sickeningly into the pit as Kluge
reached up and removed his blindfold.

The crowd pushed forward to lean over the pit as the wolves tore
into the screaming warrior, stripping the flesh from his body, the sounds
of the riot of carnage and blood rising to fill the hall. Kluge turned to
Traax. "Guilty it is!" he shouted happily over the din.

Traax returned the wicked smile. "So it would seem."

Kluge began to walk back to the front of the hall, but stopped
when he heard a woman's voice call out his name. He turned to see
Arial, the whore he had ordered Traax to summon, standing before
him, and he drank in her beauty in much the way he always did that of
the second mistress.

Because they were so similar.

Arial stood confidently before Kluge, staring at him with her large,
dark eyes. The long, straight black hair that flowed down her back and
the shapely curves of her body took him back to that afternoon, when
he had seen Succiu upon the hill.

And to when she had left, leaving him hungry for her.

"You called for me, my lord?" Arial asked, smiling. She knew full well why she was here, and she was eager to be with him, as always. She knew his tastes, and enjoyed indulging the commander in them.

Without speaking, Kluge violently used his right arm to wipe away the food and drink from a large section of one of the banquet tables, then lowered Arial beneath him.

CHAPTER
Seventeen

Shailiha lay in her bed in her sumptuous quarters, the lights in the room still ablaze. She was frantically hoping that keeping them lit would help to prevent her from falling asleep. But it was well past midnight, and her eyelids were becoming heavier by the minute, as if a blanket of luxurious, inevitable sleep were being drawn over her. She looked down at her swollen abdomen and gently caressed the silk of her pink maternity gown. *I will give birth very soon,* she thought.

Yet another flood of exhaustion tried to engulf her consciousness. She could feel it roll over her mind like an unstoppable wave. She fought back tears, but it was no use. She was soon crying openly, and trembling inside as though her panicked shaking would never stop. She was terrified of the coming night, and she could see no way through it except to stay awake—stay awake against what she feared might appear in her dreams.

For that afternoon she had experienced another of her memories.

It had been many days since such thoughts had come to her. She had been in the conservatory with Succiu and Vona when the strangers had walked back into her mind.

First had come an old man with a gray robe and a funny, woven braid of hair that fell down the back of his neck. Then, out of the fog, had come another, younger man. He was tall and had dark hair, and seemed to be trying to call out to her, beseechingly. But she had been unable to hear him, his mouth working as if in slow motion, his words lost to the cool, dense fog that surrounded him. She had noticed a medallion hanging around his neck. Made of gold, it carried the impressions of a lion and a broadsword, images she recognized, although the significance of them meant nothing to her. Then, suddenly, just as soon as the two men had appeared, they were gone. And she had collapsed into tears. Succiu had ushered her into Failee's chambers immediately.

The First Mistress of the Coven had embraced her lovingly, holding her until the crying had stopped. They had talked for a long time. Shailiha had felt abject shame in having to come to see her, despite the fact that she had been strictly ordered to do so. Sensing this, the First Mistress had insisted that one of the four other Sisters be in Shailiha's presence at all times, just to be sure that she would be brought to her if indeed such an occurrence transpired.

Shailiha lay in her sumptuous bed, breathing heavily, her eyelids closing fully now and again, her head sometimes tilting off to one side on the dark-blue silk pillow, her shiny, blond hair spilling off it and onto the sheets. The bed felt so soft and comforting. *Stay awake,* her mind called out to her from nowhere. *The bed is your enemy tonight. Stay awake or you will have to endure it all again.*

She tried to remember some of the things Failee had told her. Perhaps that would help to keep her alert. *"These horrible dreams are your punishment for allowing such false memories to crowd into your mind,"* the First Mistress had said. *"You must use your endowed blood to cast them off . . . If you do not cast off the memories, these dreams will keep coming, each one more hideous than the last, until you go mad."*

She whimpered and bit her lip, praying that she could stay awake just this one night, and be allowed to remain in peace. Trembling, she pulled the silk sheet up over her head, just like she had done as a child here in the Recluse. Just the same way her Sisters had told her had been her habit when she was growing up. Somehow the greater degree of darkness given by the sheet and the counterfeit sense of being protected from the room finally began to relax her. And as the next wave of slumber came to her seemingly from somewhere far away, she closed her eyes and had no choice but to surrender to its indulgent, irresistible peace.

She awakened lazily and stretched luxuriously in the bed before reaching down to scratch the bite that some insect had left on her arm. Opening her eyes, she looked down at it.

It was a boil, and it was bleeding.

The itching was quickly becoming unbearable, and Shailiha scratched at it even harder. But as she did so the sore opened wide and began to bleed freely, the bright-red blood running onto the silk sheets. Her hands covered in her own blood, she turned to run from the bed and wash herself. But she froze when she looked up at the room. The walls were of stone, and the oil sconces were not the ones she was accustomed to. She began to scream.

Somehow she had returned once again to the room of her nightmares.

She was beginning to itch everywhere. Crying and babbling incoherently, she lifted the hem of her maternity gown to look at her body.

What she saw made her retch. Sores and boils were beginning to develop—first as small, rose-colored spots—and then almost immediately opening up to bleed and fester. There were dozens of them all over her body, and still more were forming before her eyes.

Screaming hysterically, she looked to see that the bed was covered in blood. Still screaming, she started to climb off the bed to go find help, then realized that, once again, she was in a tiny room with no windows and no doors.

She was alone, she was bleeding to death, and there was nothing she could do to stop it.

Even more sores were appearing, and she raised her hands to her face in horror to see her palms covered in lesions. An exploratory touch with a finger told her that her entire face was now festering, as well. The blood from the sores on her forehead began to run, warmly and redly, into her eyes.

She began to vomit in earnest, spewing the contents of her stomach down her gown and over the sides of her protruding abdomen, to mix with the blood on the bed. She screamed again, her wail ending in a barely audible sob. The itching had turned into an indescribable pain.

She got up on all fours and clawed at the bloody sheets in desperation. "I have done nothing to deserve this!" she screamed aloud, knowing in her heart that no one could hear her. "Please, I beg you, for the life of my child, leave me alone!"

And then the bed began to spin.

It moved slowly at first, turning around and around in the little room like a child's spinning top. But soon it began to gather speed, and she found herself lying back down in the blood and vomit and holding on for all she was worth to keep from flying off as the bed went round and round ever faster, like a whirling dervish. Blood sprayed the walls and began to drip sickeningly onto the floor.

Above her, the stone ceiling spun, her blood covering it, as well, mixing frantically with the dark gray of the stones in a dizzying pin-wheel of her own gore.

The last thing she thought of was *them*. Not of herself, or even of her unborn child this time, but of *them*. The ones who kept coming to her in her memories. *They were the cause of this.* Just before everything went dark, she knew that she hated them, all of them, and she wanted them dead. Real or not.

Eighteen

Tristan lay on his back on the deep, mossy forest floor of Shado-wood, his head and shoulders propped up on the saddle that served as his pillow. From all around him came the sounds of the night-time forest, familiar yet also somehow foreign here in this place. Shado-wood. A place that he had never known existed. Despite his love of the outdoors, this forest gave him not only a measure of familiarity, but an underlying feeling of dread, as well.

He looked up into the night sky, full of the bright pinpricks of stars, and watched the wisps of smoke, dark and pungent, rise from the happily burning campfire in the center of the clearing. The ribbons of smoke spiraled ever upward as if trying to reach those twinkling, astral bodies suspended so high above them, only to vaporize in the chill of the night breeze. Spiritlike shadows, randomly created by the flicker-ing firelight, danced back and forth among the trees surrounding the clearing like teasing, long-waisted maidens of the court at Tammer-land, beckoning him to come dance with them in their loneliness. But there was no longer a court at Tammerland. And there were no more great balls at which to dance. He sadly wondered if there ever would be again.

He looked over at the two figures lying asleep near the fire. *Quite a pair of traveling companions,* he thought. The irascible old wizard and the equally ancient and abrasive gnome. The two had distrusted each other from the beginning. Tristan and Wigg had been traveling for two days now with the little one as their guide, and Shannon the Small had promised them that tomorrow they would finally meet Faegan. The gnome had gone off to sleep drunk, as he had done on each of the two previous nights, but not before haranguing them for over an hour about his supposedly vaunted relationship with Faegan. "*Master* Faegan to you," as he was so fond of saying. Tristan smiled as he looked at the little man lying there in his bibs, upturned boots, and black cap, snoring loudly from the influence of the ale. He then looked down to his right thigh, the one that Shannon had bitten. It had all but completely healed, and despite the wound, over the course of the last two days the prince had come to like Shannon the Small. Wigg had not.

Unable to sleep, Tristan reached behind his right shoulder and pulled out one of his dirks. He held it up to the orange light of the campfire, admiring its blade and the skill with which the palace blacksmith had fashioned it. He had very much liked the congenial smith, and had wondered on more than one occasion what the gnarled old man would have thought of the dreggan that now lay peacefully in its curved, black, tooled scabbard in the moss at the prince's side. But the smith was dead now, too, as were so many of the ones Tristan had loved. *I killed several of the winged monsters with these very knives,* he reflected. *Of that much, at least, I can be proud. And so could the smith.*

Reaching over near the fire, Tristan snatched up a fallen branch and began to whittle it with his dirk. Upon the very first stroke the knife glanced over a bump on the limb and slipped off, slicing slightly into his left index finger. He scowled. After handling the knives for so many years he had certainly had his share of nicks and cuts, and he absentmindedly put his finger into his mouth to clean the wound. Then he took it back out and examined it in the light of the campfire, watching as the bright red blood dripped slowly from the cut.

Narrowing his eyes, he rubbed a few of the drops between the finger and thumb of his other hand, feeling the warmth of the blood, examining its color and texture, almost as if he were seeing it for the first time. *This is what it's all about,* he thought to himself. *All of this death, and magic, and insanity.* For some reason that neither he nor the wizard understood, the Coven had taken his sister. And it was all about blood. He suddenly realized that it was really a question of who had it, and who did not. And it was also a question of what they chose to do with their power once they had harnessed it, sometimes making a life-altering choice between the Vigors or the Vagaries. He understood that endowed was more powerful than unendowed, that Wigg's blood was more powerful than that of the consuls of the Redoubt, that Shailiha's blood was more powerful than Wigg's, and that his was supposedly the most powerful of all. He shook his head.

Mine, he thought.

Still looking at the red fluid between his fingers, watching the fire-light glance off it in the night, he scowled to himself. *What a wonderful vessel the fates chose into which to pour the purest of all blood,* he thought. *The man who was too selfish to want to become king.*

Tristan's mind began to wander farther still as he looked at the inert body of the old wizard who lay sleeping near the fire. *Is the old one really asleep?* he wondered. Tristan was well aware that Wigg could go for days without sleep, if necessary. He also realized how little he knew about the wizard, despite the fact that he had known the old one all his life. Over the last three days Tristan had often tried to imagine what this journey must be like for Wigg. To finally come face-to-face with Fae-gan, the wizard suspected of helping the Coven during the war. Tristan assumed that Wigg must hate him, despite the fact that the old one had never said as much. The prince also wondered what it was that Faegan had done to help the sorceresses, and for how long—and, above all, why he had done it. Was it only because he feared for his daughter, or had there been more? Tristan couldn't even begin to imagine what Wigg's reaction would be to seeing Faegan after all these years.

Wigg had been the wizard who first discovered the Tome of the Paragon, Tristan mused. *The great book that still resided safely deep within the Caves of the Paragon, vastly important, but useless without the stone. Wigg had also been the one to discover the Paragon itself, the jewel now in the hands of the Coven, along with Shailiha. And it had been Faegan's daughter, Natasha, who first de-ciphered and read the Tome at the tender age of five years old. Faegan's daughter, taken by the Coven, and raised to be one of them. Was that what was going to happen to Shailiha?*

He thought of Natasha, the one he also knew as Lillith, and how she had tried first to rape, and then to kill him. *What, I wonder, was her real name, the one Faegan gave to her at birth?* he asked himself. Then his mind suddenly turned to yet another thought. *Will Wigg tell him how she died? But to tell him that, Wigg will first have to tell him that his daughter was alive all these years—only to tell him that she is once again dead. How long has Faegan assumed her to be dead? Will Wigg mention her at all?*

His mind became a whirl of questions, each one bringing forth even more questions, yet never the answers to them. Was Faegan really as powerful as Wigg said? Wigg had said that Faegan commanded some-thing called the power of Consummate Recollection, that he quite lit-erally never forgot anything that he had ever seen, heard, or read, and could recall as much of it as he cared to at will, with perfect accuracy. Could such a thing be true?

Tristan turned to look once more at the campfire's shadow dancers, flickering between the trees as if they could speak and might answer for him the questions that careened through his mind. *If Faegan aided the Coven once, how do we know he won't do it again? Did he know about the attack on Eutracia?* His mind began to reel as he sat there in the night, in the wonderfully strange forest.

He thought of Shailiha, wondering where she was and what was happening to her. *Even Wigg does not know,* he thought. *But I have a suspicion the one called Faegan does.* His grip tightened on the handle of the knife.

He threw another log on the fire. The blaze hissed and popped angrily at the disturbance, as if trying to reject the very fuel that it needed to sustain its life. He looked up at the giant trees in the darkness, their huge branches waving overhead in the night breeze like waves rushing toward a distant shore.

Suddenly, he was reminded of something Wigg had said to him just before they entered the forest of Shadowood two days ago. *"Heed my words, Tristan,"* he had said, the infamous right eyebrow rising high into the furrows of his forehead. *"This is a place where reality is the intruder, not illusion. Stay close to me, and be surprised at nothing that you see."*

As if Wigg had just now uttered those same words, Tristan froze, amazed at what he saw before him.

He thought his eyes must be playing tricks on him. His muscles started to coil, his dark eyes staring in amazement as the thing came closer, drip by drip, glowing a bright green in the dark of the night. Instinctively he knew he should not move or cry out, but it would soon be upon him if he took no action.

He replaced the dirk and silently reached for the dreggan at his side. Standing slowly, he took two paces to one side as the green fluid pooled in the depression he had left in the soft grass. His eyes searched the branches overhead, but could see nothing. Then, as he glanced back down to the wizard and the gnome, his blood froze in his veins.

A solid stream of the fluorescent fluid had begun, almost as if it had a life of its own, to slither toward the fire.

Meanwhile, an impossibly bright line of the green fluid was descending from another tree, snaking its menacing way down to touch the floor of the forest. Instinctively, Tristan stepped around behind his tree to hide himself as best he could.

It was then, from behind the great tree, that the prince saw the first of them.

It was an apparently human form—long, lean, and muscular—and it was slowly sliding down the rope of fluid, hand under hand, cautiously pausing now and then in its descent to take stock of the scene. When it stopped halfway down, the prince was able to finally discern its appearance in the flames of the campfire.

What he saw would remain lodged in his mind forever.

It was naked and hairless, its skin a smooth, shiny, dark brown. As it turned slowly in midair upon the glimmering rope of fluid, its face finally came into view.

Except there was no real face. Only eyes, and a slit for a mouth.

There was no nose, no brow, no ears. It reminded Tristan of the many marble statues in Eutracia that had been standing in the elements for centuries, their features worn away by the ravages of time. The creature had arms and legs but, as far as Tristan could see, no genitalia. Its eyes were its most arresting feature.

The bright green eyes were the same color as the fluid rope it was slithering down. No irises, no pupils, no whites showed. It was as if the sockets were filled with the same ominous green light that came from the fluid, and that haunting illumination shone out like twin beacons slicing through the night. They glowed brightly against the smooth, dark brown of its skin. More of the bright-green fluid could now be seen trailing from its mouth, dripping slowly down onto the smooth, brown, muscular body.

Then, as it raised one of its hands for a better grip, the breath rushed out of the prince.

The creature's fingers, toes, and underarms were webbed.

It dropped soundlessly the rest of the way to the forest floor, landing warily in a crouch and casting the light from its eyes about the clearing. Even more of the bright green fluid began to run from its mouth as it looked over at the sleeping wizard and gnome. Standing there in the glow from the campfire, bathing both of Tristan's defenseless friends in the eerie glow of its vision, it menacingly held its hands and arms slightly away from its sides as it crouched upon the grass.

It seemed to be death incarnate.

To the prince's horror, another of the fluid ropes began descending from the trees above and down into the campsite. And then another.

Tristan watched, the dreggan tight in his hand, as two more of the things, identical to the first, landed silently upon the forest floor. The first one began to creep softly in the direction of Shannon as the other two stood by, turning their glowing eyes this way and that, apparently searching for anyone else who might be near.

In the dim light of the fire, the prince watched in horror as the thing bent over Shannon's face and began to open its mouth.

Now! Tristan screamed silently. *You must do it now!*

He quickly stepped from behind the tree and in one fluid movement tossed the heavy dreggan from his right hand to his left. Immediately his free hand found one of his dirks, and almost before he knew it the silver blade was wheeling its way toward the creature nearest the gnome.

As the razor-sharp dirk buried itself sickeningly in the right temple of the thing's head, the creature let out an ear-splitting scream and immediately recoiled, bright-green fluid spurting from its head and mouth. It fell to the forest floor, dead, the strange light from its eyes dimming into final nothingness.

"Wigg, Shannon, get up! Now!" Tristan screamed as he watched another of the things approach the gnome. But apparently the death scream of the first had awakened them both, for the gnome and the wizard were suddenly on their feet, sleep still apparent in their faces, trying to grasp the hideous nature of the emergency.

The second of the awful creatures laughed at Shannon, a terrifying, insane laugh that shot through the woods and seemed to go on forever.

But Shannon was quick to react. He rolled quickly across the grass, landing near the wizard, just missing the oncoming stream of green fluid that shot from the mouth of the nearest creature. Now the two creatures were standing between the wizard and the gnome on one side, and the prince on the other. They looked confused as the glow from their eyes crazily flashed from one side to the other.

"Don't let the fluid touch you!" Shannon screamed. "Whatever you do, don't let it touch you!"

The larger of the two remaining nightmares whirled toward Tristan and opened its mouth. Almost immediately a bright-green stream of the ominous fluid flew through the air toward the prince.

But it wasn't fast enough. Wigg raised one of his hands, and a bright-azure bolt of light shot toward Tristan, arriving just before the fluid. Wigg's azure bolt instantly turned itself into a wall of glistening blue, shielding the prince. The green fluid struck the blue wall dead center and fell drippingly to the floor of the forest, hissing as it went, coalescing into yet another pool.

Wigg wasted no time. With a wave of his hand, the azure wall became a magnificent sword, hanging in the air. With lightning speed, the sword tore across the clearing and sliced the creature's head cleanly from its body. The creature fell to the ground, its mouth still working grotesquely in the severed head in an autonomic spasm of death.

That leaves just one, Tristan noted wildly. *And it belongs to me.*

But it was not to be. The last of the hideous things, apparently cognizant of its situation, instead turned its head and opened its mouth in a completely different direction, aiming up into the treetops.

A solid stream of the awful fluid shot high into the trees. Then the creature closed its mouth, seeming to bite down on the string of fluid and cut it in two. With amazing speed, it took hold of the rope of fluid and, with a single, powerful jump, swung itself up and away, into the darkness and safety of the limbs above, pulling the fluid rope up after it. The trees began to rustle hauntingly, one after the next, as it apparently leapt nimbly from limb to limb. Bright-green fluid dripped down sporadically, leaving an eerie trail in the darkness of the forest as the thing ran through the tops of the trees as quickly as any man could ever have run across the ground. And then, finally, just as Tristan thought all would be quiet, from far away came another of the insane, blood-chilling laughs, resounding through Shadowood.

And then it was gone.

Tristan stood there, his chest heaving, in complete disbelief. He immediately ran to the wizard and the gnome.

They both seemed unhurt, but Wigg's amazed expression was quickly turning into anger as he stood there in the firelight, glaring at Shannon. As for the gnome, he was shaking uncontrollably from fear, and quickly waddled over to where the jug of ale lay next to the fire. As if he hadn't a moment to lose, he put the jug to his lips and took a huge gulp, followed by another, and then yet another. Tristan was about to reprimand him for drinking again, but given the nature of the situation, decided to let the little one have his fill for a while.

"I told you never to trust the gnomes!" Wigg shouted at Tristan, obviously upset. "I told you not to bring him along! And whatever those things were, Shannon had to know about it! He's lived here for three centuries! And he didn't say a word about this possibility!" He glared back at the gnome, who was greedily drinking. "I would say you have some explaining to do!"

Despite the fact that they had all just nearly been killed, Tristan had to smile at what came next. Without hesitation, the gnome wiped his mouth with his sleeve. Looking into the jug and seeing that there were only a few gulps left, he carefully set it down. At the same time, he reached down to grasp a rock, which he promptly launched at Wigg's head. The wizard stepped neatly aside, avoiding the rock as it tore through the air, but the tone between these two had once again definitely been set.

"You pompous old bastard!" Shannon yelled. "How dare you! You know what those hideous things are as well as I do!"

"What are you talking about?" Wigg shouted back, clearly beside himself. "I've never seen anything like them in my life!"

"You know full well what they are," Shannon said. His voice had now become softer, but the anger in his eyes was no less apparent. "You created them," he whispered nastily.

Wigg just stood there and stared at the gnome as if he were from another world. He narrowed his eyes at Shannon. "What do you mean?"

"Don't joust with me, Lead Wizard," Shannon said defiantly. "Those
things were vomited into existence by you and the rest of your beloved
Directorate, near the end of the Sorceresses' War, when you all so efficiently created Shadowood." The gnome lowered his eyes, some of his
anger now replaced with sadness. "And they have been plaguing our
kind for the last three centuries. Even Master Faegan, the great one, is
only of limited use in protecting us from them. It was your rush to protect your beloved magic, three hundred years ago, that brought these
monsters forth."

Wigg looked as if someone had just slapped him across the face. His
mouth was open, but no words came. A look of great pain came across
his tanned, creased face.

"What are they called?" Tristan interrupted.

"Berserkers," Shannon answered.

"What?" Tristan exclaimed.

"We call them berserkers because of the vicious way they attack us
and the awful, insane laughter they inflict upon their prey just before a
kill," Shannon said. He looked at the corpses in the grass. "I believe you
can now appreciate the name we gave them, after having seen them for
yourself."

Wigg took a step closer to the gnome, the anger completely gone
from his face. "They were once gnome hunters, weren't they?" he asked
quietly.

"Yes," Shannon said. "The same humans of your kind who once
slaughtered us and took our women. It seems that when your transformation of Shadowood took place, you effectively protected all of the
gnomes living here at the time, but quite forgot about whatever gnome
hunters were also here. They were transformed into what you see lying
dead before you. You and your precious magic created the creatures you
just had the unfortunate opportunity to encounter." He paused, as if in
sorrow. "The scene of the massacre we saw two days ago was the work
of berserkers."

Wigg literally hung his head in shame, a rare sight indeed. "Why
has Faegan not been able to rid Shadowood of them?" he asked quietly.

"Even Master Faegan has his limits," Shannon said. "And when you
finally come face-to-face with him, you will understand why."

Tristan walked over to the body of the berserker he had killed. The
fluid that had pooled next to it in the grass still glowed. "What is this
substance that comes from their mouths?" he asked. "It is deadly?"

"Yes, but not in the way you might think," Shannon replied. "They live in the branches, and hunt only at night. The fluid is used to help them traverse the trees. But they also use it to injure their prey. If it touches your skin, the affected area will quickly begin to wither and bleed. If the attacking party is small, the Berserkers follow the wounded, waiting for them to become weak and helpless. Then they gather around him with their insane laughter and tear him apart, limb from limb. But a large attacking party will kill the prey on the spot, covering it with large quantities of the fluid."

"But why are they so intent on killing the gnomes?"

"They need us for sustenance," Shannon said angrily. "They eat us—while we are still alive." He looked carefully at Tristan.

"After they have eaten their fill, they take the heads, skin them, and remove and eat the brain. They then polish the bare skull to a high gleam," Shannon continued. "They store these trophies in the branches of the trees in which they live. We believe that there is some sort of hierarchy to their existence, that the one with the most skulls is the leader, but there really is no way for us to know. If we come upon a collection of skulls in our travels, we try to steal them back for burial later." He gave Wigg a hard look. "Many of my closest friends have died while trying to perform this act of kindness."

Tristan thought to himself for a moment. "This is why you were so difficult with us back at the bridge, is it not?"

"Yes," Shannon replied. "While it is my duty to Master Faegan to protect the bridge, I also have no use for anyone, other than him, who indulges in the craft."

"And the massacre we came upon two days ago, why did you not tell us of them then?" Wigg asked.

Shannon turned to the wizard. "I did not mention it because I saw no look of guilt upon your face, only curiosity. Had you, as one of the creators of this madness, seemed more contrite I would have discussed it. As it was, I felt it best to say nothing."

"We thought we were doing the right thing," Wigg said apologetically. "We knew we had perfected the incantation for the protection of the gnomes, and we were fairly sure that the transformation would kill the gnome hunters." He sighed greatly, pursing his lips. "I am truly sorry, Shannon," he said. "And I will do everything in my power to correct this when we reach Faegan,"

"*Master* Faegan to you," the little gnome added imperiously.

Wigg smiled slightly for the first time. "*Master* Faegan," he agreed.

Although dawn was still several hours away, Tristan doubted that any of them would be getting very much more sleep that night. Shannon went to retrieve the ale jug, and Wigg sat down next to the fire, lost in thought.

Tristan sat down as well, still astounded at what he had just heard. Pulling his knees up against the chill of the night, he began the rather long wait for the first prisms of dawn.

⚬⚬⚬━╋━━

*T*he prince of Eutracia shifted in his saddle as Pilgrim half walked, half trotted up a little wooded knoll. He and Wigg had been traveling for the last two hours in relative silence, following as the gnome led the way on foot through the dense forest of Shadowood. Despite his lack of sleep, Tristan was not tired, too excited at the prospect of finally meeting Faegan and, he hoped, coming one step closer to finding Shailiha.

Looking around at the forest, he continued to marvel at the similarity it held to the Hartwick Woods, especially the area in which he had discovered the Caves of the Paragon. The same lush and colorful ground foliage grew here, as did the huge, gnarled trees that until now he had never before seen in any other part of the kingdom. The branches overhead were just as thick and dense as those surrounding the Caves, and the air brought back to his nostrils the same sweet, light scents that he had first detected before finding the wall that led him tumbling down into the earth. Once again his overactive mind sought out the similarities, trying to connect the possibilities of such coincidences. *Wigg has said that Shadowood was created by the Directorate just before the end of the war, as a refuge for endowed blood,* he thought. *Could the Hartwick Woods be the same kind of thing? Did the Directorate create that place, as well?*

Looking ahead, Tristan thought that he could discern some brighter light at what finally appeared to be the edge of the forest. Pressing his heels to Pilgrim's sides, he sped up to follow Wigg and Shannon as they finally exited the woods.

What Tristan saw beyond the trees took his breath away.

He was looking down onto a wide plain of grasses and wildflowers that seemed to stretch off to his left, to the west, forever. To the east was the Sea of Whispers, the great uncrossable ocean. With the crashing of waves upon the jagged rocks of the coast, it came ever rolling into the land, angrily attacking over and over with dark, frothy arms, only to tentatively retreat, regroup, and roll in again.

Straight ahead lay a ridge of low mountains, at the bottom of which was the most beautiful lake he had ever seen. Tranquil, deep, and dark blue, the water gently swayed back and forth to a rhythm of its own, seemingly unaffected by the breezes that were blowing over it. At the far end of the lake was a very high waterfall. Jutting out from the ridge, it billowed its contents out and down the amazing height as if nature had intentionally commanded all of the beauty and grace in her power to this one spot. The endowed blood in his veins ran quicker the longer he looked at it, and he somehow knew, without a doubt, that the waterfall was their destination.

Tristan and Wigg watched from their horses as the excited little gnome in the red shirt and blue bibs started to jump up and down with glee.

"I told you!" he exclaimed happily. "I told you we would get here! My master awaits on the other side of the falls." Over the last two days, Shannon apparently had come to regard Tristan and Wigg as trophies to be shown off to his master, rather than as the imposing Lead Wizard of the Directorate and the prince of Eutracia who had come to find Faegan. He rubbed his hands together anxiously, and instinctively reached up for the jug of ale that was tied to the back of Tristan's saddle. It had been their practice not to let the ale-loving gnome near his swill while guiding them through the forest, letting him drink it only at night around the campfire. They had no need of a drunken guide. But knowing that the jug was almost empty, Tristan decided to let the little one have one final, congratulatory swig of the potent, dark brew, despite the glower on Wigg's face, and handed down the jug.

"It won't be long now," Shannon said, wiping his mouth on his sleeve, at the same time nodding his thanks to the prince. Tristan simply sat atop his horse and smiled. On the pretense of wanting a drink himself, he reclaimed the jug from the little one, retying it to his saddle after a quick swallow. Finally the three of them started around the western edge of the lake, and on toward the falls.

It was then that Tristan saw them.

When the first slash of color came swooping out of nowhere to career before their eyes, Pilgrim began to dance about nervously. Tristan instinctively unsheathed the dreggan, touching the button on the hilt of the great sword and sending the tip of the blade shooting out angrily. Then, at the same time he realized he didn't need it, he heard the old wizard speak his first words of the day. "If you can cut one of them down in midair, you will be the first ever to to do so, Chosen One or not," the old one said calmly, pursing his lips. "The Directorate brought them here, over three hundred years ago, for their protection. I shouldn't like to think that the prince of Eutracia had become responsible for their demise."

Smiling and chagrined, Tristan replaced the dreggan in its scabbard. He spoke gently to Pilgrim and stroked the horse's neck as the riotous flashes of color continued to dart and swerve around them.

For the second time in his life he was watching the Fliers of the Fields.

Except this time there were hundreds of them.

The huge, multicolored butterflies swooped and darted back and forth across the afternoon sky with amazing speed, teasing the horses and their riders, zigzagging in and out of the forest behind them at will.

Wigg turned in his saddle and stretched out one of his gnarled hands. In a moment, a violet-and-yellow flier came to rest upon the old one's forearm, settling down and remaining very still save for the gentle opening and closing its long, diaphanous wings. Tristan's mouth fell open. He had no idea that there had ever been any kind of bond between the fliers and human beings.

"When we realized that the fliers had been changed by the waters of the Paragon," the wizard continued, "not only did we feel responsible for their welfare, but we knew that we needed to find a place to hide them, lest the curious come looking for them and discover all of the same things that you did that day. But despite our best efforts to keep their existence a secret, the rumors of their existence still persist."

"Why didn't you tell me all of this that day in the Redoubt?" He remembered all of the pain that he had felt that afternoon in his meeting with the Directorate and his father. How none of the things that they had told him had made any sense. And how angry he had become. He looked directly into the wizard's penetrating aquamarine eyes. "It would have helped me to know that there were at least other fliers that were still alive."

Wigg sighed and lifted his arm, and as if by silent order, the giant violet-and-yellow butterfly once again took to the air. "We couldn't, Tristan," he said simply, "no matter how much we wanted to. The coronation ceremony was only a month away, and in your state of mind at the time, we couldn't take the chance of you wanting to come here to prove it to yourself. You would never have made it across the canyon alone."

The old one looked with genuine love into the dark-blue eyes of the man who had so quickly, so painfully, come to so many realizations. "Your father told you that day that everything that was done, indeed even everything that was *not* done, as well, had a reason. I hope you are beginning to understand."

Tristan lifted his eyes from the wizard's gaze long enough to see that the little gnome was trotting happily around the edge of the lake to the left, through the tall grasses and wildflowers of the pastures.

"We had better hurry up and follow him," Wigg said. "I suppose it's actually possible that we could lose him in all this high grass." He pushed his tongue against the inside of one cheek. "And what a shame *that* would be," he added caustically.

They soon caught up to Shannon and followed him around the lake to a spot very near the rushing water of the falls. Tristan had never seen anything like it, even in the caves of the Paragon. It was the highest waterfall he had ever seen, and the roaring sound that it made as it poured its flowing, almost crystalline contents out and down into the indigo lake was deafening. The spray brought to his nostrils the sweet, familiar smell of morning rain. He watched Shannon and Wigg exchange a few words, and then the gnome inexplicably stepped behind the falls and disappeared.

Confused, the prince trotted Pilgrim up to stand next to Wigg's horse, making sure he was close enough to the old one to be sure they could converse amid all of the noise. Both horses had begun to dance about in their nervousness at being so close to the rushing water. Tristan reached up to stroke Pilgrim's neck as he leaned over to shout into the old one's ear.

"Where did he go? How could Shannon just disappear like that?"

"He didn't," Wigg said calmly. Still looking straight ahead at the place where Shannon had slipped away behind the falls, he added, "Dismount. We walk in from here. Make sure and hold the reins very tightly." Wigg got down off his gelding and curiously passed his hand over each of Pilgrim's eyes. Immediately the stallion began to grow calmer, more docile. The wizard then accomplished the same feat with his own mount and began to walk behind the falls, leading his horse, beckoning Tristan to follow. Before Tristan knew it, Wigg, too, had vanished.

Holding the reins tightly, Tristan tentatively stepped behind the rushing water, not knowing what to expect, a trusting and subdued Pilgrim following him obediently. It took a few moments for his eyes to become accustomed to the darkness, but once they had, what he saw made him stop in his tracks.

The three of them were standing in a tunnel carved out of the rock. It seemed to go on for rather a long way, and he could not immediately discern any light coming from the opposite end. The only illumination was the sunlight that filtered in from behind the rushing water as it flowed down past the entrance. The dark gray walls were slick and glistening, and the sounds from the falls were muffled. The floor of the tunnel was flooded with dark, murky water.

Tristan waded forward a few steps to stand side by side with Wigg. The water was about two feet deep. "Where are we?" he asked anxiously.

"This tunnel was fashioned by the wizards just before the end of the war, as the final obstacle to reaching the settlement that exists on the other side of Shadowood," Wigg said almost absently as he glanced around at the walls and floor of the dark, empty cylinder in which they stood. Tristan guessed that the wizard, who no doubt had been one of the chief engineers of its construction, was examining the tunnel for signs of decay and stress. "I have not been here for more than three hundred years," Wigg said quietly, to no one in particular.

Tristan and Shannon watched as Wigg raised his hands above his head and closed his eyes. The tunnel began to fill with green light, and Tristan looked up to see that the entire length of the tunnel roof was lined by glowing stones. They were jagged and sharp, crystalline, and they glowed more and more brightly until, when Wigg finally dropped his hands back to his sides, the tunnel was shimmering in sage-colored light. Wigg smiled, the first grin that Tristan had seen on his face in days.

"These are called radiance stones," he said simply. "We created them, and then brought them here over three hundred years ago, just as we were completing the tunnel. I am immensely glad to see that they are still just as powerful as the day we first activated them."

Tristan moved forward a couple of paces, hoping to get a better look at some of the radiance stones, but his knee bumped into something in the murky water. He glanced down, only to jump back immediately, drawing his dreggan. The now-familiar clang of the blade as it leaped out the extra foot resounded down the length of the dark tunnel and echoed hollowly off its barren walls.

He was standing over a skeleton.

It was the full skeleton of a man, or at least he assumed it to have been a man, because of its size. The skull looked up at him with empty, yet somehow smirking eye sockets from just below the surface of the water, as if taunting him, laughing at him for being afraid. The bones were of the purest white; they seemed to shimmer in the light of the radiance stones.

He looked around in the strange, pale-green light of the tunnel to find that the dank water in which they were standing was quite full of them. The various bones had been polished clean by the ever-moving water, and lay at impossible angles in the tunnel, sometimes missing limbs, sometimes not. It was Shannon who first broke the silence—with his laughter.

"The prince frightens easily, does he not, considering that these poor fellows cannot fight back?" He laughed, holding his stomach, at the same time craftily eyeing the ale jug that was still attached to the prince's saddle. "Don't worry, my prince." He snickered. "None of them can harm you. I would have thought that the old wizard might have told you about them before we entered the tunnel." He continued to grin at the prince, enjoying the moment.

"I would have thought so, as well," Tristan said, eyeing Wigg as he returned the dreggan to its scabbard. He reached down and plucked one of the skeletons from the water, examining it for a cause of death. Unsatisfied, he dropped it back into the wet darkness that was the floor of the tunnel and looked at Wigg. "How did they get here?" he demanded. "What happened to them?"

Wigg took a long breath in through his nose and pursed his lips before answering. He clasped his hands in front of himself. "As to *who* they are, I really couldn't say," he explained. "But if they are *what* we expected them to be when we built in the tunnel's safeguards three hundred years ago, I imagine they are the usual rabble that was so prevalent in those times: grave robbers, looters, common criminals, and gnome hunters."

At the mention of gnome hunters, Tristan watched the smile vanish from Shannon's face.

"The gnome hunters were most active near the end of the war, when there was very little control left over society," Wigg went on. "This passageway is the last defense before entering Shadowood proper, and if anyone of unendowed blood or without the benefit of time enchantments enters this tunnel, they are recognized by the incantations we left behind, and immediately killed. Only gnomes are exempt." Wigg looked down at the skeletons. "If these are gnome hunters, they were killed before the transformation of Shadowood, since their skeletons are still human. Obviously, a great many of them tried to get past and failed. I am glad to see that this trap, too, works as well as the day we left it here."

As his eyes grew more adjusted to the light, Tristan could make out the skeletons of larger creatures that lay in the same watery graves as the remains of the humans. He saw the unmistakable skull and jaw of a horse, and then another, and then yet another. *Beasts of burden for criminals and robbers,* he thought. He stared incredulously at the sight before him. *It's like a ghastly, flooded cemetery with the lids of all the coffins removed.*

Tristan looked back up at Wigg. "What killed them all?"

"Oh, they drowned," the wizard said nonchalantly.

"How?"

"When the wrong person enters the tunnel, it immediately begins to fill with water from the falls. At such a fast rate, I might add, that escape is impossible," Wigg explained. "We thought it rather a good idea at the time, since these falls had been known to have been here for centuries, and had never run dry."

"How did they ever get this far?" Tristan asked.

"What do you mean?"

"How did they get across the canyon to reach this far?"

Wigg smiled. *He is beginning to think like the Chosen One.* "If you remember, I said that the tunnel was created near the end of the war, as a precaution. At that time, the canyon had not yet been created. Each of these skeletons came to rest here long before the canyon or bridge existed."

"Does this place have a name?" Tristan asked. Whether it had a name or not, he would not soon forget it, he told himself.

"Not that I'm aware of," Wigg murmured.

"The Tunnel of Bones," Shannon quietly interjected. His voice sounded small and far away, as though some of the bravado of before had left him. "That's what we started to call it after the skeletons began to pile up in here. Somehow, the name just stuck."

Wigg nodded thoughtfully. "The Tunnel of Bones it is," he said. He looked at poor little Shannon, who was almost up to his neck in the cold, dank water.

"By the way," the old wizard asked of the gnome. "How is it that you can traverse this tunnel without being of endowed blood?"

"One does not have to be of endowed blood, provided he has a brave heart," Shannon answered, puffing out his chest. "I wade in the water in the dark, sometimes up to my chin, parting the bones as I go. It is not pleasant, but it is necessary. For Master Faegan, I would do anything."

Wigg pursed his lips in thought. "Pick him up and put him on your horse, Tristan," he said finally. "I'll see what I can do to make this passage a little easier."

Smiling, the prince reached down and hoisted the little gnome up into the saddle. When Shannon immediately began to eye the ale jug, Tristan shook his head and waggled a finger back and forth.

Tristan then watched curiously as Wigg waded several steps back down the length of the Tunnel of Bones from which they had come. The wizard raised his hands in the air and bowed his head. At once, the skeletons, human and beast alike, began to move.

They were crawling out of the water and wading slowly toward the sides of the tunnel.

Tristan stared at them, astonished. *This can't be happening. They have all been dead for hundreds of years.*

Like some kind of macabre army of the dead, they looked about with empty, unseeing eye sockets and then walked to the edges of the tunnel walls, where they stood in long, silent lines that seemed stretch on forever. They looked like something from a bizarre nightmare as the water dripped from their bones, the pale-green light illuminating their stark whiteness against the dark walls behind them. Even though they had perished hundreds of years ago, Tristan could almost smell the death in the air.

Their path now clear, Wigg turned around to look at the speechless prince and gnome, raising the familiar eyebrow as if he were displeased with them for some reason. "Don't you think it time we left?" he asked. Without waiting for a response, he collected the reins to his horse and began to lead the way down the tunnel.

They waded through the Tunnel of Bones for a good hour, the silent, white sentinels of the dead never moving from their positions against the walls as the three of them passed by. They walked in silence, even Shannon the Small's voice having been repressed by the sight before him. It was almost like passing through an honor guard of death, the pale-green light pointing up both the stark whiteness and murky shadows at once, the sound of the water dripping from the bones into the darkness of the tunnel strangely loud in the silence. There must have been hundreds of them.

Finally, blessedly, Wigg stopped at what appeared to be the far end of the tunnel. The entrance was blocked by a large, round stone, but from around the edges Tristan could see shafts of natural sunlight here and there, pricking their way through from the outside.

Wigg turned around and silently motioned for Tristan and Shannon to step behind him, their backs to the circular rock that blocked the tunnel. Then he stretched his arms out straight ahead, pointing down the tunnel, and closed his eyes. Almost immediately the skeletons began falling back into the dirty water of the passageway, bobbing oddly, almost as if they had just been freshly killed. One by one they fell, all the way down the dark tunnel, until their tumblings could only be heard and no longer seen.

When the splashing stopped, Wigg turned his attention back to the circular stone door. It was as if he were looking for something in particular. At last he cast his aquamarine eyes up toward the gnome, still perched atop Tristan's horse. "I assume, since you come and go through here often, that you know where the lever is," he said without pretense. "I can only imagine that it has been moved in the interest of security at least once over the course of the last three centuries. The Faegan I knew would have insisted upon it."

"Of course," Shannon said confidently. It was obvious that the gnome enjoyed the fact that the wizard was now, finally, asking for his help. "It was moved from its original position to there, where I could more easily reach it." He pointed to a dark, square spot on the wall down near the surface of the water. "The panel can be slid away either manually or by the use of the craft. The lever you seek is behind it."

Wigg pointed two of his long, ancient fingers at the dark spot, and the square retreated back into the wall and slid to one side. Peering into the resulting hole, Tristan could see a rather long stone lever that seemed to be hewn into the rock. He raised his eyebrows questioningly at Wigg.

"Not everything is better left to the devices of magic, Tristan," Wigg said as if he were still reciting one of his lectures back at the Wizards' Conservatory in Tammerland. "As I told you, gnomes are not gifted with the craft. Therefore, Shannon had to be given some way to move the stone manually." He thought to himself for a moment before speaking again. Finally, he said, "Would you care to do the honors?"

Tristan breathed in sharply, eyes widening. Then he handed the reins to Shannon, waded over to the lever in the wall, and looked up at Wigg.

The old wizard gazed deeply, seriously, into Tristan's eyes. "What you are about to see, you are to tell to *no* one," he said, scowling slightly and looking down his nose for emphasis. "Too many lives are at stake."

"I understand," Tristan said. He pulled up on the lever, and the great stone blocking the end of the tunnel began to roll away to the right, allowing some of the water on the tunnel floor to begin to gush out. Squinting into the bright afternoon sun, Wigg and Tristan led their horses out and remounted, Tristan settling in front of Shannon on Pilgrim's back.

As his eyes began to adjust to the brightness, Tristan looked down the long, gradual grassy slope upon which they were standing. At the bottom of the slope he could see a great many huge, gnarled trees, like those they had seen that morning. But at last he looked upward, at the branches of the trees, and he understood. The gnomes lived above ground, in the trees.

There were literally hundreds of tree houses. They were fashioned of the same kind of wood as the trees they were built in, and most of them had bridges that connected them to each other, not unlike the bridge over the canyon. There were windows, balconies, porches, and chimneys, and if the houses had been upon the ground instead of in the trees, no one would have given them a second glance, except, of course, for their smaller proportions, scaled to gnomes. Curiously, each of the houses had a large, flat platform constructed both above and beneath it that completely encircled both the house and the tree in which it was built. As they approached more closely, Tristan realized that something didn't seem right about these woods.

Then it hit him. *There is no one here! Their city in the trees is deserted.*

Suddenly a group of gnomes, all male, rounded the corner of the village on foot, brandishing weapons such as longbows, crossbows, and spears. There must have been at least two hundred of them, and Tristan could see that they were both angry and afraid. *From what Shannon has told us, none of these little people have seen any man but Faegan for over three hundred years,* Tristan reflected. *They probably think we are gnome hunters, come to kill them and take their women.*

Reflexively, he pulled his dreggan from its scabbard, and just as quickly he saw Wigg turn toward him with a look that spoke volumes.

"Put that away, right now," the wizard said through clenched teeth, "unless you want to lose Faegan forever. Besides, the gnomes may be small, but they can fight like lions. We would be forced to kill a great number of them before they finally backed off. We are here to see Faegan, not to start another war. There is a much better way to handle this."

The wizard looked at Shannon, who was still sitting on Pilgrim, just behind Tristan. "Go to them," he ordered the gnome. *"Now."* He stiffened a little in his saddle as he contemplated his next words. "Make them understand that you brought us here to see their master, nothing more. I do not wish to cause any harm to them, but if I have to, I shall." He looked down the hill to see that the gnomes had begun to approach within longbow range. Wigg pushed his tongue against the inside of one of his cheeks, then let out a long breath as he scowled at the gnome. "I suggest you go *now!*"

Shannon jumped to the ground and began running toward his fellows as fast as his little legs could carry him. They began to crowd around him, shouting in strange, scratchy voices and pointing excitedly at Tristan and Wigg. Shannon was hopping around in desperation, obviously trying to make them understand that they had much more to lose by fighting the Lead Wizard and the prince than they did by letting them pass. After several minutes of commotion, they finally settled down and allowed Shannon to walk back up the slope to Tristan and Wigg.

The little gnome stuck his thumbs in his bibs and pushed them outward with pride. "I have arranged safe passage for you to see Master Faegan," he said, fairly bursting with himself. He waved a cautionary finger into the two faces that looked down on him from their horses. "It's a good thing for you that I was here, or else you would have tasted their wrath. No one has successfully visited here for over three centuries." He looked at the ale jug that was tied to the back of Tristan's saddle. "I need a drink," he said commandingly.

Wigg glanced at the gnome with a combination of disbelief and rather undisguised contempt. "Yes," the old one said slowly, as he scratched the back of his neck. "I don't know *how* we could ever have done it without you." He glanced at Tristan, his infamous left eyebrow raised. The prince smiled knowingly back in return. Wigg looked at the prideful little gnome. "You may lead us through the village, Your Highness," the old one said.

Oblivious to the wizard's sarcasm, Shannon began to lead them down the hill.

As the crowd of angry gnomes parted to allow them entrance to the village, Tristan had a chance to study the tree houses more closely. They were really quite extraordinary, each one unique in its craftsmanship, and looked to be as sturdily built as anything he had seen upon the ground. And then he began to see the gnomes' wives and children as they popped their heads out of windows and emerged onto balconies to watch the strangely dressed giants riding past their homes. Occasionally he caught the scent of a freshly baked loaf of bread, or a pie that was resting on an open windowsill.

Tristan once again looked at the platforms that had been built above and below each of the houses, and understanding dawned. *The platforms are a guard against the berserkers,* he realized.

Tristan looked down to the gnome. "Shannon," he asked, "is there a name for this place?"

"Of course," the little one said. "It is called Tree Town. Simple and to the point, don't you think?"

Tree Town, Tristan thought. *Where we will finally find Faegan and, hopefully, the answers to so many of our questions.*

Shannon stopped at last in front of the largest tree the prince had ever seen. It would have taken Pilgrim at least fifty steps to walk its circumference. The branches reached endlessly into the cool air of the coming night, and ensconced in them was by far the largest tree house he had seen that day. It was several stories high, built of very dark wood, and seemed to go on forever Soft, yellow light glowed in the many windows, and several of the chimneys were smoking. The gentle, sweet sounds of a violin began to waft out of the house, floating down to their ears.

It was like looking into a dream.

This is where he lives, Tristan said to himself. He felt a sudden rush of endowed blood through his veins. *I know he is here. I can feel it.*

Uncharacteristically quiet, Shannon the Small beckoned them closer to the trunk of the great tree. "My master awaits you," he said reverently. "He will know you are here."

Suddenly a section of the tree trunk began to pivot open. Larger and larger the opening became, until it was the size of a doorway. Shannon pointed. "This way," he said simply, and he walked inside, into the darkness.

Tristan touched Wigg on the arm before the old one could enter the great tree. "Do you sense him? Is he here?"

Wigg took a deep breath and closed his eyes before responding. "There is someone here of endowed blood," he said cautiously. He looked into Tristan's eyes. "Someone with a *very* long lifeline."

They stepped into the tree next to the gnome, and the trunk closed and sealed itself behind them.

Nineteen

The rising breeze billowed softly through the open window of Shailiha's quarters, admitting with it the promise of a beautiful morning, along with the scent of the bugaylea trees that had just come to bloom in her private garden. Dawn light poured generously into the chamber and twinkled on the mirrors and decorative pieces in the sumptuous room. But the beauty of the room belied the seriousness of what was taking place inside it. Normally the princess would have awakened to find great joy in such a morning, here, in Parthalon, with her Sisters. But today it was not to be.

For today Shailiha did not awaken.

When her handmaidens discovered her writhing in her bed, screaming, they found they could not bring her to consciousness. Without delay, they sent one of them running to Failee. The First Mistress had come immediately, and had also summoned the other mistresses of the Coven to join her at Shailiha's bedside. For the last hour they had been standing around the princess' bed in relative silence, the only communication between them the blatant, castigating glances from Succiu to her lead mistress. With a wave of the hand, Failee finally dismissed the weeping handmaidens from the room.

Failee at first feared that Shailiha had not been able to withstand the intensity of the Chimeran Agony she had placed on the young woman the previous night. When the First Mistress had had the inert princess moved from the small stone room, bathed, dressed in her original clothing, and placed back in her own bed, she had not been concerned. But the princess' inability to wake up the following morning was a sign, and she knew that Shailiha was now at the crossroads of her sanity.

Without yet having completely forgotten her memories. Without yet having completely become one of them.

Failee extended her right hand and placed it on Shailiha's abdomen, closed her eyes for a moment, and then opened them again. Immediately the princess began to calm, and although her eyes did not open she stopped writhing and calling out the names that she had been screaming all morning.

The names of her family in Eutracia.

"Her unborn is well, and shall be delivered soon," Failee said in a quiet voice. "At the very least, we shall gain that much. And Sister Shailiha is also well, in the physical sense." She looked up into each pair of the other six eyes in turn, so that the woman standing before her would not miss her meaning. "Her psyche, however, namely that which makes her who and what she is, is damaged. Perhaps beyond repair. She may never come back to us. At least not in the way that we would like. If she does not find her way out of her memories, she may remain like she is now for all time, and quite useless to us." The First Mistress turned decisively from the bed and walked to one of the windows, lost in her thoughts.

It was Succiu who took the lead in criticizing her. "First the blood stalkers, and then the screaming harpies, both alerting the Directorate to the possibility of our existence! And now this!" she exclaimed with fire in her eyes. She glared at the First Mistress' back as Failee continued to gaze peacefully out the window. "Have you lost your mind? Does your hatred of Wigg so completely blind you to what is happening to Sister Shailiha? Need I remind you that it is paramount we have her able to help us in our plans? If Shailiha dies, we will be forced to wait until her daughter gains the maturity to understand our cause and can be fully trained in the craft. And what of her daughter's blood? What if it is not equal to that of her mother, eh? Do you not remember that Frederick, her husband, was of unendowed blood? Had you considered that when you began these Agonies of yours? How can you take this so calmly?" Frustrated and seething, Succiu stood her ground in a rare display of disrespect, her knuckles white, her eyes angry slits.

Despite all of their knowledge and power, my other Sisters are still as children compared to me, Failee thought serenely, still looking out the window. *Only a complete study of the Vagaries can bring one to the place of enlightenment that I have found, and therefore to the understanding that I now alone possess. They must follow me, as they always have. They have no choice. They never will.*

She turned calmly to face Succiu. "Of course I took that into consideration. The fact of the matter is that Sister Shailiha is now, finally, in precisely the mental state I need to invoke the last of the Chimeran Agonies. That is, she is now on the cusp of madness. The last of the Agonies will occur tonight, whether she regains consciousness or not. We cannot afford to wait. Her mind, because of the quality of the endowed blood that flows through her, still tenaciously grips the distant memories of her previous life. But this time there is a difference. She now believes that her memories are the true cause of her Agonies. Therefore Shailiha is finally ready to make the last leap away from her past life, and into a life with us." Failee smiled slowly. "She finally, truly, wants her memories dead. Her memories shall die tonight, or she will. In any event, we will still have the child. And I believe there is little question that the child will be endowed, given the unprecedented quality of Shailiha's blood. If she begins to die I will induce labor, and her daughter will be born and will know nothing *except* us. Either way, success will be ours." She returned to the bedside.

Succiu was still angry, as were Vona and Zabarra, but she was also intrigued with what Failee was saying. She arched an eyebrow at the First Mistress. "And just how is it that she will now succeed in finally killing off these memories of hers?" she asked. "What will be different about it this time?"

"She can only withstand one more such experience. To make her successful, we must be sure that the final Chimeran Agony threatens to take from her that which she cherishes most: namely, her unborn child. And whoever threatens her unborn will be the recipient of both her hatred and her untapped powers."

Succiu thought for a moment in silence, beginning to understand. "And just who will it be who threatens her unborn in her next 'dream'?" she asked, smiling for the first time that morning. She thought she already knew the answer.

"Why, my dear Sister," Failee replied, "her attackers will of course be the very memories she wants to destroy."

Shailiha turned in the silk sheets of her bed, and her eyes opened partway. The morning sunlight had been replaced with the dusky, violet hues of early evening, and a distinct coolness had begun to waft into the room through the still-open windows. The night sounds of the tree frogs and nesting birds had begun, and the air had the hint of scent that always preceded a night rain. Someone had already lit the oil sconces on the walls, and their light was gradually taking over the room.

But Shailiha saw nothing except what was being created in her mind; she neither heard nor smelled anything other than the creations of the visions that tormented her.

And they went on and on in her bedroom, her prison, her mind.

She had been like this for the entire day, and had taken no food or water. Her handmaidens had been by her side the entire time, to see that she didn't harm herself. Failee had been in every hour to check on her, and to make sure that her condition had not worsened. If Shailiha began to die, the First Mistress needed to be ready to induce labor and take the child. Failee had considered commencing the last of the Chimeran Agonies immediately but changed her mind, remembering that the Vagaries promised a more effective resolution if the spell was cast at night. And so they had all waited for the coming night, hoping that the princess did not perish from her torment before Failee could once again use the craft.

Shailiha opened her hazel eyes once more, but instead of seeing the beauty of her bedroom, she saw only images of horror and confusion. People, places, and things flew by in an incoherent pattern. Some of the people tried to speak to her, but she could hear nothing. An older man with a gray beard and dark blue robes, an oddly shaped stone hanging around his neck, accompanied a woman of great beauty, with hair like Shailiha's own. Another old man, this one with a stern face and a funny braid of hair down the back of his neck, came and went repeatedly, simply walking by in his gray robes as if she did not exist. Then another younger and much more handsome man came near, dressed in a black vest and knee boots, who looked quizzically through the fog at her. She tried to run to him but found herself unable to move. She then saw another man, large, with a great brown beard, who simply looked at her and cried. He cried for a very long time, until suddenly his head fell away from his body in a great sheet of blood. She screamed frantically and tried to reach him, but he was already dead.

And then had come the pretty women.

First the older one with the gray-streaked hair, and then the beautiful, exotic-looking one with the silken black hair that reached to her waist. After them had come the blond and the redhead, each of them dressed in amazingly beautiful gowns, calling to her to join them. Join them and be happy. Join them and bring her unborn child, and live with them in a huge castle. As Sisters.

Looking out into the fog but now seeing no one, she clutched at her abdomen and sadly, quietly, began to call out names. Names that came from nowhere, and went to the same nonexistent place. Names that had no meaning to her.

Then everything began to spin again, and she saw nothing.

*I*t was the sharp, pulling pain in her left shoulder that woke her again. She had tried to turn over in her sleep but had been unable to do so. There was something unusually hard and unyielding at her back. She opened her eyes and immediately let out a scream that never wanted to end.

She was back in the little stone room again, except this time things were different.

This time she couldn't get up, and the bed she was lying on was made of stone.

She raised her head as best as she could and found that her hands were secured to the great stone with iron rings. Looking down the length of her blue silk sleeping gown, she realized that her feet were flat upon the bed. Her knees were up and apart, and iron rings ran around her ankles and secured them to the surface of the stone. Her bedclothes had tumbled down the lengths of her thighs and collected in her lap. She felt horribly naked, exposed. And then the realization came to her. This was not a bed. Beds weren't made of stone.

The very large stone on which she lay was the same size as her bed. It sat directly in the center of the small room. Yet everything else about the chamber was as she had remembered it. The stone walls and ceiling, the absence of a door, and the oil sconces on the walls were all just the same as before. But unlike before, the room was dead silent, as still as a tomb. *Nothing is happening to me,* she realized. The conversely bizarre nature of that thought made her tremble with the panic that already had her in its grip. And she was becoming cold.

Water vapor was condensing in the air each time she let out a breath. Still, there was no movement, no sound. She lay very still with her eyes wide, terrorized and afraid to move, as if the slightest bit of motion might bring forth something even more terrible.

And then she heard them.

Soft at first, it almost sounded like music. But then the sounds grew closer and more recognizable. *It isn't music. It's voices!* And they were becoming louder.

Slowly, five hooded figures appeared. At first all she could see was the outline of their black robes as they materialized, the cowls hiding their faces. And then they were suddenly standing a short distance from the end of the stone altar, looking at her, their hands folded in front of them as they moaned and wailed, the foglike vapor streaming from their mouths.

It wasn't until they raised their faces in unison to look upon her that she screamed again.

The faces were identical, each of them out of some kind of nightmare. They were long and pale green, the eyes mere sockets in the heads, the skin surrounding them decayed and falling off in places. The mouths were wide and angular, with black teeth and dripping drool. Their smiles were monstrous as they came closer to the foot of the altar, nearer her feet, nearer to her nakedness.

She began screaming at them in earnest, crying wildly, tears streaming down her face. Terrified of what they might do next, she was straining so violently at the unforgiving iron rings around her wrists and ankles that she knew she was starting to bleed. And still the hooded figures came.

"Go away!" she begged, bucking against the harsh stone of the altar. "I have nothing that you could want!" She laid her head back against the cold stone, on the verge of giving up. Then, faintly, she whimpered, "Please, please let me live." At the very edge of madness, she closed her eyes in resignation knowing she was powerless to stop whatever was about to happen.

She could feel their hands and fingers on her, touching and stroking her inner thighs as they gathered around the altar, grinning and moaning in quiet, almost murmured tones. And then the fingers of one of them began to probe her, painfully violating her. She tried to close her legs, but the iron rings held her fast, and all she could do was scream and strain against the altar. And then she knew.

They're here to take my child. My unborn child. She could feel the drool that ran from the five gaping mouths dripping sickeningly upon her thighs and groin, and knew she was about to vomit.

Her mind on the very cusp of madness, she let out a long, final scream of agony.

And that was when everything changed.

Suddenly things were clear, and she was amazingly unafraid. She stopped resisting, and the irises of her hazel eyes receded deeply up under her eyelids. She suddenly felt something cold and hard in her right hand and, looking over at it, saw that she was holding one of the long, curved swords that she had seen the winged protectors of her Sisters carry in and around the castle. Her ankles and hands were free of the iron rings, which had vanished. She looked calmly up into the faces of her attackers.

Their faces had changed. They were now faces that she had seen before—faces she hated with all her heart and soul.

One had become the older man with the gray beard and strange stone about his neck. Another had become the elderly man with the gray tail of hair down the back of his neck, and yet another was the beautiful woman with the hair like her own. The fourth one had be-

come the man with the great brown beard and hair that was thinning at
the temples, and the last was the handsome young man in the black vest,
with a strange-looking gold medallion around his neck. And they were
trying to take her child.

The figure with his hands inside her was the one with the gray tail
of hair, and he died first.

As she jumped to her feet upon the altar, she swung the heavy
sword with confidence, as if she had been doing it all of her life. The
old one's head rolled off his body and landed on the cold stone floor, his
hands and body vaporizing. Then came the man with the brown beard.
He died the same way, as did then the woman with the blond hair and
blue eyes. But the man with the gray beard and the stone around his
neck was trying to penetrate her, reaching up to put his hands where
the hands of the old one had once been. Shailiha cut his extended arm
off first, then swung for his neck, his head rolling bloodlessly, almost
gracefully, to the floor as had the others.

And then the only one left was the handsome young man. He was
not trying to reach up to her as the others had been, but rather was
looking up at her strangely, as if he knew her. He was crying.

Pausing, she calmly looked down at the medallion around his neck.
Neither the sword nor the lion, engraved in the twinkling gold, meant
anything to her. Raising her face back up to his, she slowly pointed
the dreggan at him and smiled, as if to calm his fears.

Something told her to press the lever on the sword hilt, and the
blade obediently launched itself out another foot, shooting through the
young man's throat and exiting the back of his neck. He crumpled to
the ground bloodlessly and vaporized, the medallion that had been
around his neck falling to the floor. Sneering, she dropped the sword to
the floor with a noisy clang that echoed sharply off the walls of the oily
stone room. Involuntarily, her eyes closed.

Immediately her mind swirled with a golden, intense, serene peace.
It engulfed all of her senses and cascaded through her body in an ecstatic ripple of light and understanding as she raised her arms to the ceiling
in newfound rapture. She stood that way for a long time, finally opening her eyes and looking around, as if seeing the room, her life, and herself for the first time.

Shailiha climbed down from the strange stone altar in the middle
of the room, wondering why she was here, and not with the Sisters
she loved so much. Looking around the room, she saw that a doorway
had materialized, through which came the warm, golden light of the
Recluse oil lamps, leading upward to the living quarters.

As she began to walk out, her foot struck something, and she bent
over to see what was there. It was a gold medallion. She picked it up,

and it twinkled in the light of the room as she held it before her face. She saw that it held the images of both a lion and a broadsword. It was pretty, so she placed it around her neck and tucked it beneath the blue silk bodice of her sleeping gown.

She walked confidently to the door, remembering nothing of what had happened in the room, and caring even less. No memories existed for her other than those of living here in the Recluse with her Sisters. She would gladly kill anyone or anything that endangered them.

She walked confidently out of the room and into the light. Shailiha was no longer the princess of Eutracia. She was now a mistress of the Coven.

The long-awaited fifth sorceress.

Twenty

Shannon led the party of three up a ramp that snaked its way ever upward and around, inside the hollow body of the great old tree. The ramp, surprisingly, was made of blue Ephyran marble. Oil lamps mounted on the carved wooden walls gave off an eerie, shadowy light, and the air smelled of musty, dried wood. Finally they exited another door at the top of the ramp and found themselves looking into the living quarters of the wizard named Faegan. Without looking at Wigg, Tristan could feel the tension in the old one's body.

"Wait here," Shannon said simply. "I will see whether Master Faegan will admit you now." He turned on his heel and waddled away, down one of the halls that stretched off to the right.

The room they were standing in was some kind of atrium, filled with unfamiliar plants of all descriptions and sizes. The walls and ceiling were made of glass, and when Tristan looked up he could see the stars, surrounded by the now-inky blue of night. The floors were of highly polished mahogany, and the air was perfumed with a blend of scents from the plants. Occasionally a gnome would come in and tend one or two of the plants, completely ignoring the two visitors.

Wigg walked slowly over to a potted tree and began to examine it closely. He rubbed several of its leaves, leaned in to smell them, and studied the twigs carefully. He turned to the prince. "I have not seen these plants for over three hundred years," he said, putting a finger to his lips in thought. "I had assumed them all to be extinct. Near the end of the war the Coven burned all of the fields that contained them, so as to keep them from us. These are herbs, petals, and roots that are used in especially high disciplines of the craft, and some of them have value beyond measure. We have not been able to use them in all this time." He took several steps back, obviously impressed, an emotion that was not often seen upon the face of the Lead Wizard. "Cat's claw, sneezeweed, romainia, tulip of rokhana, and even sandalwood." He pursed his lips. "It makes me wonder what else he has here in this place." Concern lingered on his face.

Shannon returned and made a great show of removing the ever-present pipe from between his teeth. "The master will see you now," he said imperiously. "He has instructed me to bring you to the music room."

Tristan gave Wigg a quick, questioning glance as the two of them began to follow the gnome down one of the halls of highly polished wood.

"It would be best to let me do the talking," the wizard told Tristan seriously. "I have known this man for a long time, although I must admit that nothing I see or hear this day will surprise me."

As they walked along, Tristan began to hear the low, sad strains of a violin. The rich tones grew louder as the men neared the end of the hallway. At last they entered another room, and Tristan of the House of Galland was offered his first glimpse of Faegan, the rogue wizard.

He was not at all what the prince had expected.

A rough-hewn chair on wheels sat on a highly patterned woven rug in the middle of the large, expansive room, its back to the doorway, its violin-playing occupant facing the burning fireplace. Long, gray hair covered the shoulders of the simple black robe, almost touching the back of the invalid chair. A sudden, cruel memory of Succiu's words came to Tristan from out of the past, words she had spoken to Wigg upon the dais of the Great Hall, the day the prince's family and the Directorate of Wizards had all died. Tristan had not understood those words at the time. *"You wasted your time and energy in erecting a memorial to Faegan, because he lives,"* she had hissed. *"In Shadowood, with his precious gnomes. And we've seen to it that he isn't quite the man he used to be."* Now Tristan realized what she had meant. The Coven had destroyed his legs.

A dark-blue cat with a silver chain around its neck sat patiently on the floor next to the man in the chair and stared at the visitors, unperturbed. *But there is no such thing as a dark-blue cat,* Tristan thought. He slowly took his eyes off the animal and took in the room around him.

The wizard in the chair may have looked shabby, but the room was sumptuous. Musical instruments lined the walls, tomes and sheet music filled the bookcases and littered the tabletops. Oil chandeliers gave the room a pleasant, welcoming glow, and a hint of jasmine combined with the musty smell of old memories filled the air. A small table stood near the chair, holding a crystal goblet half filled with red wine. Tristan took another tentative step forward to stand next to Wigg.

And then the music stopped, the violin came down, and the wizard turned his chair around to face them.

Tristan had never believed he would see a pair of eyes more intense—or more beautiful—than Wigg's. But he had been wrong. Faegan's eyes were even more amazing.

Large and heavily hooded, they stared back at Tristan with absolute candor and calmness. A calmness born of power. The gray irises were huge, flecked with strange green motes that made the eyes look rather like continuously turning kaleidoscopes. Over the eyes rested long, arched brows; the gray hair was rather raggedly parted down the middle and fell over his shoulders. A large, hawklike nose hung over a long, thin-lipped mouth. The strong jaw commanded respect.

Tristan felt the silence in the room thicken as Faegan turned his gaze to Wigg.

"I have brought with me Tristan of the House of Galland, Prince of Eutracia," Wigg said carefully. The Lead Wizard let his words hang in the air for a moment before continuing. "He is the Chosen One for whom we have waited so long."

"Come to me," Faegan told the prince.

Tristan began to take a step toward the wizard when Wigg reached out a hand to stop him.

"I understand your concern, Wigg," Faegan said. "It has indeed been a long time, and there is a great deal that needs to be said. But surely you must know I would not hurt him for all the world. Is he not the one for whom we have waited so long?" He held his hand out to the prince.

Wigg's hand dropped to his side, and Tristan walked to the wizard in the chair.

"Bend over and look into my eyes," Faegan commanded. Tristan did as he was told, and almost immediately became lost in the swirling green motes. It was like being caught in a bottomless whirlpool of color. The wizard held his gaze for what felt like a long time.

"You may rise, Tristan," Faegan said. He looked at Wigg. "You have seen the azure aura about him with your own eyes?"

"Yes," Wigg answered curtly.

"And you were also there at his birth, as the Prophecies describe?"

"Yes."

"Other than the occasion of his birth, when was it that you first saw the aura?" Faegan's attention was completely on Wigg now, and Tristan could see that his questions were not to be denied. There was an unmistakable aura of power in this crippled wizard that seemed to command everyone and everything in his presence.

"The same day that he discovered the Caves of the Paragon," Wigg answered. "Just after I killed a blood stalker."

At the mention of the blood stalker, Faegan narrowed his eyes and tilted his head slightly, letting out a small sigh.

"It was Phillius," Wigg added. "I identified him from the birthmark on his forearm. I burned the body and returned the battle axe to be interred in the wizards' crypt. There was also a screaming harpy, attacking the palace courtyard. I killed her, too, with a wizard's cage."

Faegan looked down at the useless feet covered by the black robe and then turned his wheelchair around to face the open glass doors of a balcony. He wheeled himself out onto it and sat there silently, looking at the trees.

Despite the fact that this wizard had supposedly been a traitor and was, at the very least, partly responsible for the abduction of his sister and the destruction of his family, Tristan began to feel a certain compassion for the old man. The prince began to take a step forward to join Faegan on the balcony when Wigg stopped him, shaking his head.

Faegan finally broke the silence. "Shannon, you may leave us now," he said quietly.

Tristan had completely forgotten the little man was still there. Now he turned to watch the gnome obediently leave the room and walk back down the hall from which they had come.

"So the Chosen One discovered the Caves on his own, before the coronation?" Faegan asked, his face still toward the crashing sea.

"Yes," Wigg answered.

"Interesting." Faegan sighed. "And the Tome—the three volumes are still intact, still safe, the wizard's warp effectively guarding the entrance to the tunnel near the falls?"

"Yes," Wigg replied. "The prince got his first taste of a warp when he tried to enter the tunnel." By his tone it was apparent that the Lead Wizard was tiring of answering questions and was eager to ask a few of his own.

"I therefore assume, given the nature of everything that has happened, that you have informed Tristan his training cannot begin until he reads the Prophecies, and that he cannot do that without the stone?" the crippled wizard asked. Faegan seemed particularly interested in the answer to this question. He abruptly turned his chair around to face them. "I can easily discern the hunger for knowledge in his eyes, Wigg," he added. "More so than anyone of endowed blood that I have ever seen. But then again, it's what we expected, is it not?"

"Tristan has been informed of the nature of his responsibilities, his potential power, and his impending training," Wigg said impatiently. He glared menacingly at the older wizard with an intensity that Tristan believed could scorch the very air that surrounded them.

"You may say what is on your mind, Wigg," Faegan said gently. "I am reasonably sure I know what it is."

Wigg took a step forward and pointed a long, bony finger at the seated man. "I should kill you where you stand," he snarled, the words barely a whisper. The threat came out like venom from the mouth of an angry viper. "Or in your case, where you sit."

Tristan watched the crippled wizard's face for a reaction to the insulting reference to his disability. There was none.

"Foolishness was never one of your traits, Wigg," Faegan said serenely, shaking his head. "I do not recommend you take it up now. I could kill you with a single thought, and you know it. You, however, cannot do the same to me." He wheeled himself to the small table, lifted the wineglass to his lips, and swallowed slowly. "The ironic truth is that I am not your enemy, and we desperately need each other now, if there is to be any hope of putting things right. There is still a great deal that you do not know, Lead Wizard, and there is little, if any, time left in which to act."

Faegan looked down at the dark-blue cat and motioned with his index finger. Immediately the cat jumped up into his lap.

Tristan thought that he could see some softening in Wigg's face. A memory, perhaps. But it was not so touching that Wigg was ready to trust Faegan again—least of all with their lives.

Wigg pointed to the cat in Faegan's lap. "Nicodemus, I presume?"

"Your memory is still as sharp as ever," Faegan replied, smiling for the first time. "Proof that time enchantments can work well on animals, also."

Tristan had suddenly had quite enough of all of this useless conversation. He took two steps closer to the chair-bound wizard and looked deeply into the strange gray eyes. The gold medallion around his neck fell forward, twinkling brightly in the light of the fireplace.

"My family and the Directorate have been murdered, the only sibling I shall ever have is with the Coven, the nation that I love lies in tatters, and you are busy being coy with your secrets," he said firmly. "I want some answers, and I want them now! I am only interested in what became of my sister and the part you may or may not have played in it." He turned around and gave Wigg a hard look, putting the Lead Wizard also on notice before returning his gaze to Faegan. "It seems all the two of you want to do is discuss three-hundred-year-old cats!" He could feel his endowed blood rising in his veins, and he silently vowed to get his answers, or die trying. He had come too far to be stopped by yet another arcane relic from the distant past, no matter how powerful this wizard was purported to be.

As if Tristan did not exist, Faegan turned to Wigg. His response was unexpected. "I'm sure you were intrigued with the plants in my atrium. I have something to show you," he said wryly. One corner of his thin-lipped mouth mischievously turned up into a smile, and something about that grin told Tristan that there would be more smiles from the wizard before their time here was over. "I believe it will surprise you," Faegan continued. "True, there is much yet to talk about this night, but please do me the honor of indulging the ego of a lonely, eccentric old wizard who rarely has the opportunity to receive guests."

Without waiting for an answer, Faegan began wheeling himself toward another of the many highly polished wooden hallways, Nicodemus still in his lap.

Tristan started to ask Wigg a question, but before he could speak the Lead Wizard shook his head and replied. "Yes," Wigg said, pushing his tongue against the inside of his cheek in frustration, "this is indeed how he always was. Maddening, isn't it? Because his power was so much greater than that of the rest of us, we were always obliged to follow his lead, including trying to keep up with his amazing mind as it careened off in various directions. He was famous for it. And now, to this day, except for being in that chair, it seems nothing about him has really changed." The old one sighed resignedly. "I suppose we must follow him, but stay behind me, and be careful. His motives are still unclear to me."

The hallways seemed never-ending, reminding the prince of the sheer size of this mansion in the trees. Once again the oil lamps of the passageways gave off their soft, translucent hues, and the clean, luxurious scent of the highly polished wooden floors and walls permeated Tristan's nostrils. Finally, after what seemed an interminable walk, Faegan stopped before a pair of large double doors. He pointed one of his long, angular fingers at the doors, and they dutifully opened. The old wizard beckoned for Wigg and Tristan to follow him through.

What Tristan saw below him took his breath away.

The three of them were standing on a brass-railed balcony, overlooking a lush garden of the most wildly colored plants and trees Tristan had ever seen. The soft, grassy floor was at least fifty feet below them, and it stretched on for hundreds of feet in each direction. The walls and ceilings were made of glass, and the prince could see the evening stars and the three red Eutracian moons through the shiny, transparent ceiling above them. The atmosphere was warm and humid; the sights and smells of the incredible gardens below him were absolutely overpowering. *I have been here before,* he thought. *Or at least someplace just like it.* And then it hit him. *The Hartwick Woods. The amazing area that surrounds the entrance to the Caves. It's just like being back there again.* Totally overwhelmed, he simply had to ask.

"Faegan, what *is* this place?" the prince asked. "I feel that I have been here before."

"In some ways, you have," the old wizard replied as he stroked the head of his cat, his impish grin beginning to resurface. "This is my private atrium, in which are kept the most exotic of all of the plants and trees that we wizards once used in the practice of the craft. And yes, many of those you see before you also exist in the Hartwick Woods, but not the truly rare and valuable ones." His face began to darken again. "Those same fragile plants that the Coven supposedly destroyed during the war I have been able, over the course of the last three centuries, not only to recultivate but to cause to flourish here, under my care." Faegan glanced out over the scene below him. "Their value is beyond description."

It was then that Tristan noticed the anomaly. In the center of the garden was a clearing, and in the clearing was a circular floor of brightly polished lavender marble, shot through with streaks of indigo. But that was where the similarity to any other floor the prince had ever seen ended. All around the circumference of the circular marble floor were additional pieces of marble, such as would make up the spokes of a wagon wheel. At the top of each of the spaces, inlaid into the marble, were the letters of the Eutracian alphabet, in a very antiquated and flourishing script. Each one had its own space, and as the prince looked farther he could see that they began at the top of the great wheel with the letter *A* and continued around in a clockwise direction, in alphabetical order, the *Z* finally in place just to the left of the *A*.

It was Wigg who broke the silence and asked the obvious question, the infamous eyebrow arching higher than ever. "And just what, pray tell, does a marble schoolchild's alphabet have to do with growing the plants of the craft?" he asked. Tristan noticed that Wigg's tone had become unusually harsh, and for a brief moment he wondered why. But suddenly his mind was taken up with Faegan's response.

"I needed some help," the elder wizard replied, still calmly stroking the purring Nicodemus. "I may be Faegan," he added imperiously, "but after all, I'm still in a wheelchair."

"Explain," Wigg demanded.

"Why don't I just show you both, instead?" Faegan said, smiling again. "I believe you will be much more impressed with the display than with only the spoken word."

At this Faegan raised his hands and closed his eyes. Immediately one of the glass sections of the ceiling began to hinge up and away, opening the garden to the sky. The cool night breeze began to waft into the great room, carrying the scents of the plants ever farther up to the three of them on the balcony.

Faegan turned to Wigg, his countenance more serious than before.

"Observe, Lead Wizard," he said calmly. "Behold our friends once again."

Almost immediately the giant butterflies called the Fliers of the Fields began to pour in through the opening in the roof, so many in fact that at first Tristan thought they would collide with each other, even though previous experience told him that they never would.

There were hundreds of them. They swooped and darted, careened and wheeled through the air of the atrium, some of them occasionally landing on the plants. A small squadron of the most colorful and vibrant of them came to rest on another brass rail that was attached to a nearby glass wall, not too far from where the three men were observing them.

They were magnificent.

"Ask them a question," Faegan said to Wigg, as if such an incredible demand were an everyday occurrence.

Wigg's mouth fell partly open with shock, a look that Tristan had seen only a few times in his life on the face of the Lead Wizard.

"Wha—what?" Wigg whispered, his voice suddenly seeming ragged and small.

"As I said," Faegan ordered imperiously, looking up at Wigg. "Ask them a question."

"Are you mad?" Wigg retorted. "I will not talk to butterflies! Such a thing is not possible, even for you!" In defiance, he placed each of his hands into the opposite sleeve of his robe and hardened his jaw.

"Simply because you have been Lead Wizard for the last three centuries does not preclude you from learning something, *especially* from me," Faegan said, his eyes narrowing at Wigg. Tristan was awestruck. He had never heard anyone speak to Wigg that way, not even his father, the king. "Now, as I said, ask them a question," Faegan continued. "And kindly address those fliers that sit on the brass rail beside us."

Wigg was obviously furious—so much so that Tristan thought he might soon see steam rising from the top of the Lead Wizard's head. Finally, and with apparently great effort upon his part, Wigg seemed to gain greater control over himself. He turned to face the fliers sitting quietly on the rail.

"What is the name of your master?" Wigg asked them sarcastically, still apparently not believing that he was actually doing such a childish thing.

What Tristan saw next would remain lodged in his memories forever.

Immediately one of the fliers took off in the direction of the floor, gracefully soaring down toward the marble area until it had neatly landed upon the letter *F.* Holding his breath, the prince watched in awe as the remaining fliers took off from their perches, each of them landing upon a letter engraved in the circular floor until they had, in turn, landed upon one of the letters, two of them now side by side upon one of them. Tristan followed the order in which they landed.

F–A–E–G–A–N.

Such a thing is not possible! Tristan stared in disbelief. *It simply cannot be.*

But the fliers continued to sit quietly upon the marble floor, their diaphanous, colorful wings slowly opening and closing as if in anticipation of the next question.

Faegan wasted no time in pouring salt into Wigg's fresh wounds. "Still don't believe me, Lead Wizard?" he asked gloatingly. "You certainly haven't changed much in the last three centuries, have you? Still as stubborn as a Eutracian mule. Would you like to try another question, just to make sure? Or can't you get your mouth to work?"

They're behaving like two novices competing at the Wizards' Conservatory, Tristan thought. *So this is what is was like between them three hundred years ago. And this is why Wigg is so angry. It's jealousy! An emotion I doubt he has had to deal with for over three hundred years, since there was no other wizard superior to him in his use of the craft.* Tristan smiled to himself.

Until now.

Wigg just stood there, seemingly frozen in time, as if the scene below him was simply not registering in his brain. Quickly he turned back to Faegan.

"Is it true?" he demanded. Tristan thought he could see an angry vein beginning to throb in the Lead Wizard's forehead. "Did you truly find the key to communicating with the animal world?"

"If you're asking me whether I can talk to the animals, the answer is decidedly no." Faegan sniffed. "At least not yet. But with the fliers I have achieved a rudimentary level of correspondence." He smiled again. "Go ahead, skeptic. Ask another question of them. Ask as many as you like. Prove it to *yourself.*"

This time Wigg needed no coaxing, his curiosity having at least temporarily won out over his contest of wills with Faegan. He leaned over the rail slightly and shouted, "Please, fliers, tell me the name of the stone that controls the power of magic!"

Immediately the giant butterflies that were perched upon the letters took to the air, fluttered their colorful, diaphanous wings, then began to descend once again—this time upon some different letters. Tristan watched, carefully noting the order in which they landed. And then he stared in awe at the circular floor, his mouth open in amazement.

P-A-R-A-G-O-N.

"How?" Wigg demanded. "How did you do it? The entire Directorate tried for over three hundred years to accomplish such a thing, and even then we were unsuccessful. You could never have accomplished this on your own! It has to be a trick!"

"No trick, Lead Wizard," Faegan gloated. "That is why I made you ask your own questions, so that you could be sure." He put a finger to his lips and seemed to ponder a thought, with a new twinkle now in his eyes and the playful smile returning. "If, however, you still require proof, I'm sure something can be arranged." Looking up directly at Tristan, he added, "Perhaps we should take some of the starch out of his attitude."

The wizard in the chair closed his eyes, and several of the fliers that had been circling the room quickly soared up to hover in a riotous pattern of color over the top of Wigg's head. Using their slender legs to grasp the wizard's braided tail of gray hair, several of the fliers suddenly began to bounce it up and down in the air, while one of the others perched atop Wigg's head and began prancing about in the general area of his widow's peak as if doing some kind of dance. Others began to hover around Wigg's feet and beat their wings harder, causing the hem of his robe to billow and rise, showing the wizard's bony legs and leaving little else to the imagination. Tristan tried hard not to laugh, but it was quite impossible. He soon found himself roaring at the spectacle and doubled over with tears in his eyes, despite the castigating look on the Lead Wizard's scarlet face. The butterflies around Wigg's feet were beating their wings so quickly that the prince could feel the breeze. He thought Wigg was literally about to come apart with rage, while Faegan simply sat in his chair and continued his maddening smile.

Another schoolboy prank, Tristan realized. *These two must have been incredibly difficult for their teachers, despite all of their arrogant posturing in their old age.* They reminded him of the endowed children he had seen in the nursery of the Redoubt of the Directorate. *Except those children had been better behaved.*

"Enough!" Wigg finally shouted. "I believe you!"

"Are you sure?" Faegan asked, delighting in the scene being created by his obedient butterflies. "Are you sure you wouldn't like to argue with me some more? The fliers can keep this up all day, you know." A quick glance to Tristan was followed by a conspiratorial wink.

"No, no, you fool!" Wigg shouted. "Just get them off me!"

"Very well," Faegan answered reluctantly. He lowered his head, and the fliers that were torturing Wigg dutifully rejoined the others circling the atrium.

"But what do the fliers have to do with the garden?" Tristan asked, finally managing to overcome his laughter as Wigg angrily began smoothing out the hem of his robe.

"Ah," Faegan replied. "Leave it to the Chosen One to bring us finally to the heart of the question. I needed the fliers to be my legs, to travel away from this mansion and bring back the pollen, seeds, and spores I required to produce the plants and trees that you see here. It took them over a hundred years to gather it all. Without the fliers, none of what you see here in this room would exist."

The prince could clearly remember his own time in the Caves, and how the fliers had been there with him, drinking the water from the stone pool. But then a different question began tugging at the back of his mind. "Why not just use the gnomes to collect what you needed?" he asked. "Surely they would have been easier to communicate with than the butterflies." *Communicate with the butterflies.* He shook his head at the seeming absurdity of the thought.

"For the simple reason that the fliers cannot speak. You see, I feared that if the Coven ever returned, the information could be easily tortured from the gnomes." He smiled. "But not from the butterflies."

The unexpected mention of the Coven brought Tristan's mind back to the true problem at hand, and he suddenly felt guilty for having spent so much time watching the fliers and listening to the two ancient wizards trying to insult each other. He looked hard at the wizard in the chair.

"Faegan, as I told you before, I need answers about my sister, and I need them now." He glowered, his face grown cold and hard.

The answer surprised him.

"Have you eaten?"

Tristan stared incredulously at the old wizard. "What possible difference could that make?"

"I took the liberty of having a dinner prepared when I knew the two of you were getting close to me. It is about to be served in the dining room, and I am hungry. The two of you shall join me."

Tristan scowled. "And if we don't?"

"Then the two of you shall remain both hungry *and* unenlightened, I'm afraid," Faegan said simply. "Besides, you really don't have a choice. You can either dine with me, or I will instruct Shannon to show you the way out." He smiled up impishly at the pair of them. "I am reasonably sure that since you took such pains to come all this way, you will not leave, your questions unanswered, simply because I have offered you a meal." Without further comment, he wheeled around and headed back into the room, laughing softly as he went.

Tristan looked incredulously at Wigg, who merely raised a frustrated eyebrow. Then the Lead Wizard sighed, some of his anger apparently having dissipated. "I know he can be infuriating, but he's also right," he whispered. "And just now we really *don't* have a choice."

Tristan looked out at the exotic garden spread out below him, and at the giant butterflies that had begun silently, effortlessly, to sail back out the opening in the glass ceiling. Finally he turned and joined Wigg as they followed the rough-hewn wooden wheelchair and the snickering rogue wizard.

Faegan's large dining room was paneled in rich, dark mahogany with wainscoting on the walls. Patterned rugs adorned the floor, and a huge oil chandelier hung from the center of the ceiling. Directly below it sat a highly polished table large enough to seat ten. The table was set for three with excellent crystal and flatware, and the air was full of several wonderful but different scents that drifted in through a door that the prince assumed led to an adjoining kitchen. The ceiling was glass, and Tristan looked up to see that the stars were now fully visible, the night having completely overtaken Shadowood.

Looking again at the wizard in the wheelchair, Tristan felt a strange mixture of sadness and compassion trying to wash over his distrust. The luxury and size of the room belied the emptiness of the wizard's life, and spoke little of the many sad and lonely nights that the solitary Faegan would have sat here and eaten in silence, left to his thoughts of his personal betrayal of the Directorate and the loss of his daughter.

The kitchen door opened suddenly, and three gnome women wearing little white chef's aprons blew in, chatting noisily to one another. They carried a tureen of soup, a large silver platter of vegetables and potatoes, and another, much larger platter on which were piled three roasted Eutracian pheasants, complete with stuffing.

As the women laid the trays down and began to serve, Tristan was able to get his first good look at them. The female gnomes looked very much like the males both in their faces and in their broad and stout, rather than curved and sensual bodies. They seemed to be very hard workers, and were clearly devoutly loyal to their master. Tristan realized that he was coming to like and respect the gnomes very much. *One could have worse friends,* he reflected. He removed the dreggan and its baldric, hanging it over the high-backed chair so that the handle of the sword could be reached in an instant, and sat down. From his place at the head of the table, Faegan gave the dreggan a sidelong glance and pursed his lips in a gesture of curiosity.

"The sword that killed your father, I have been told," he said with a measure of sympathy in his raspy voice. "I can understand why you carry it, and I have also heard that you have already had occasion to use it. But understand me well, young man, when I tell you that one day soon you will find such weapons as crude and unnecessary as they now seem to you to be important and useful." He reached for his goblet of red wine and took a sip.

"*. . . I have also heard that you have already had occasion to use it.*" His words echoed in Tristan's mind. How could Faegan know? Was he referring to Natasha, or to the wiktor that had attacked Tristan in the palace entranceway?

"I want to know about Shailiha," Tristan suddenly demanded, ignoring his food. "You seem to have a great many answers about a great many things, and I demand to be told."

"No." Wigg had surprisingly but simply said the single word from the other side of the table. "First he and I have some unfinished business." The Lead Wizard looked at Faegan.

"You and I have known each other for a very long time. I need to know. Now, before anything else is said." Wigg glared hard at the wizard in the black robe. "Did you betray us?" The question hung heavily in the air like a sword over all three of their heads.

Faegan put down his wineglass and stared sadly into Wigg's eyes. "Yes," he said quietly. "But not for the reasons that you think, nor to the extent you certainly believe." He closed his eyes in pain. "They had Emily."

Emily, Tristan mused. *Natasha, the duchess of Ephyra. Lillith. Her real name was Emily.*

"We assumed as much," Wigg snarled. "But the threatened loss of one family member does not justify helping the Coven, no matter how much you loved her! I swear to the Afterlife, if I could, I would kill you right now with my bare hands!" Tristan had never in his life seen the Lead Wizard so angry. The vein in Wigg's right temple had begun to beat furiously again, his endowed blood racing.

"You don't understand," Faegan said. "It wasn't because of Emily that they received my help."

"Explain."

"Shortly after Emily learned how to read the Tome by putting the stone around her neck, the Coven recognized her potential value to them and abducted her. To this day I do not know how. They knew that I had the gift of Consummate Recollection. I received a parchment with a lock of her hair three days later, telling me to read the complete

Tome and then come to them, or they would send parts of my daughter back to me, one day at a time." Faegan looked down at his dinner plate. "It was signed by Failee."

Wigg looked as though he had just been slapped across the face. "And what then did you do?"

"Nothing. I sent the parchment back, telling her that they could kill my daughter if they chose to, but that I would never help them."

Wigg sat back in his chair, his eyes narrowed. "Why didn't you tell us? We could have helped."

Faegan raised his head back up, the once-haughty eyes on the verge of tears. "And do what, Wigg? I know that Tretiak, Slike, Killius, and the others would have given me their very lives if necessary, but to what end? The Coven was winning the war, our only chance was the immediate use of the Tome and the stone, and time was running out. Despite my personal feelings, it would have been an egregious waste of time and energy. My Emily died, but in the end the sorceresses lost the struggle. All I have left of her is that single lock of hair."

Wigg sat quietly for a moment, digesting what he had just heard. "But you *disappeared*," he said finally. "No one ever knew where or why. You were just suddenly gone. And immediately after you vanished, the Coven became inexplicably more powerful. We very nearly did not prevail, and many of us in the newly formed Directorate quietly assumed that it was because of your defection." He looked away for a moment, lost in time. "The sorceresses were banished to the Sea of Whispers. I know. I did it myself."

Faegan reached out and placed his hand on Wigg's arm. "We both made terrible mistakes," he said. "Banishing the sorceresses, instead of killing them, was yours." He paused for a moment, and a look of remorse shadowed his face. "Shannon told me of your experience with the berserkers. You have your regrets; I have mine. And now, it seems, we have mutual decisions about our creation of Shadowood to be sorry for."

Wigg looked as if he was about to become ill. He stood and walked to one of the open leaded-glass windows. He stood there for some time, looking out at the trees, then turned back to face Faegan.

"How was it, then, that you betrayed us?"

"I did not go to them, as you all have suspected for so long. I was taken."

"How could they just take you?" Tristan interjected skeptically. "I thought you were the most powerful of all of the wizards."

"I was," Faegan replied. "But did Wigg not tell you? By that time, the sorceresses had learned to join their powers. Even I could not withstand the joint strength of their collected abilities."

"How did it happen?" Wigg asked.

"It was foolish of me, I know, but I was making a solitary visit back to the Caves to search for any more clues or artifacts that might help us accelerate our understanding of the Tome. I thought if I went alone I could go there and back much more quickly and quietly. Four of the lesser sorceresses came upon me and captured me. Because I was wearing a wizard's robe, they took me straight to Failee." He hung his head in shame. "She cackled aloud at seeing me, and said that I would recite to them everything I had read in the Tome, or they would kill Emily before my eyes."

"What happened?"

"They shackled me to a chair in the town square of the city of Florian's Glade. It had already been in their hands for some time, controlled by an army of blood stalkers. They brought Emily out before me, and once again threatened to kill her."

"What did you do?" Wigg asked.

"I beckoned Failee to come closer, and spit into her face. I then looked up into the eyes of my only child and said good-bye. Vona dragged her by her hair into one of the houses and slowly cut her throat. She walked back out with a bloody knife and more handfuls of my daughter's hair and threw them into my face, laughing. I still hear Emily's screams in my sleep."

Wigg turned to Tristan and gave him a hard look. The prince immediately understood. *We will probably never know who it was Vona killed that day,* he thought, *but it wasn't Emily.*

"What happened then?" Wigg asked gently.

"They tortured me for the information."

"How?"

"Look at me, Wigg," Faegan said, raising his hands slightly in a gesture of disbelief. "Can't you imagine?"

Wigg touched Faegan's shoulder with a gentleness that the prince had not seen in him for some time. "And was it then that you told them?"

"No," Faegan said proudly. "I did not. The torture went on for weeks as they slowly crippled me, starting at each of my toes. The used fire, spells, and incantations. Virtually everything I had ever known or learned, they tried upon me. But still I did not talk. Somehow most of my blood and training held out against them, and they failed."

Wigg closed his eyes and sighed. *So much pain and death,* he thought. *And now, over three hundred years later, I am still learning of their crimes.*

"How was it, then, that they finally broke you?"

"Failee had succeeded in pushing past one small fraction of my mental block that had slipped during the worst of the torture. It had to do with the Vagaries. A very obscure but ultimately useful passage. From it she learned a technique of mental torture that is irresistible. It has to do with dreams, and the complete reversal of a person's logic and allegiances. Used properly, no one can resist it, not even a wizard with blood as pure as mine. With its use, I eventually gave over to them some of what I had read in the Tome, and, as you said, they subsequently became much stronger, and almost beat you. They kept me prisoner until the end of the war, until things became desperate for them. By that time I was so weak from torture that I was incoherent, and my legs were unable to function. I was so near death that they no longer considered me a threat, and they simply left me to die. But I regained consciousness and used the craft to fashion this chair you now see me in. I knew my only hope was to try to get to Shadowood. Finally, the gnomes found me and took me in. Slowly I was able to regain my health. In return, when I was well I promised to live here among them and give them my protection as best I could."

He looked at Tristan. "The form of mental torture they used on me is called the Chimeran Agonies." He paused, letting the prince contemplate what he had just heard, knowing that what he was about to tell Tristan would be one of the most painful experiences of the prince's life. He put one hand on Tristan's shoulder. "It is what they are torturing your sister with as we speak."

Tristan sat back in his chair, stunned. *They are torturing Shailiha,* his mind roared at him. *And I am sitting here, having dinner with a madman.*

Tristan's reaction was immediate. He reached behind his back and in a flash had one of his dirks in his right hand. He stood and grabbed Faegan by the robe, yanking the eccentric wizard toward him. "How could you possibly know such a thing?" he demanded. "Besides, why would they torture her? They treated her like a queen that day upon the dais! Succiu even called her Sister, and bowed to her! I saw it with my own eyes! You don't know what you're talking about!" He moved the razor-sharp dirk to within an inch of the wizard's right eye.

As Faegan looked calmly up into the dark-blue eyes of the Chosen One, one corner of his mouth turned up. "You don't really think you can harm me with that toy, do you?" he asked. When Tristan refused to give any ground, Faegan looked over at Wigg. The Lead Wizard spoke directly to the prince.

"Put the knife down, Tristan," Wigg said calmly. "This must be done his way. He has all of the answers, and so far we have no reason not to believe him. We must hear him out." When Tristan did not relent, Wigg raised the usual eyebrow at the prince. "It would be much easier to do all of this with you still alive, don't you think?"

As much angry with himself as he was at Faegan, the prince reluctantly replaced the dirk in the quiver and sat down. "I think it's about time you told me where my sister is, and what's happening to her," he said menacingly. "I have waited for your story as long as I care to."

Faegan sighed, and decided to begin at the beginning. "Your sister is in Parthalon, the kingdom across the Sea of Whispers that is ruled by the Coven. I have long believed that the two nations at one time shared a common heritage because of the same basic similarities in language and customs, but as yet there is no way to be sure. Shailiha and the Paragon were taken there because of a great plan the Coven has in store, one that Failee garnered from my recitation of the Vagaries to her. The incantation they are planning calls for five sorceresses of highly endowed blood. There is no naturally occurring endowed blood in Parthalon. Therefore, if any of them were to mate with the local males to produce a female child to raise, the blood quality would not be high enough for their needs. That is why they came here. To take both the stone and Shailiha. They are using the Chimeran Agonies I described to turn her into one of them."

And those of the Pentangle, the ones who practice the Vagaries, shall require the female of the Chosen Ones, and shall bend her to their purpose, Faegan thought. The quote from the Vagaries rang as clearly in his mind today as it had three hundred years ago when he had first read it. "They are turning your sister into the fifth sorceress, and after the incantation she will not only be one of them, she will also willingly be their leader."

Tristan and Wigg sat staring at each other from opposite sides of the table, speechless. The silence hung in the room for what seemed a long time. Finally, Wigg was the first to break the stillness.

"So there *is* a land across the sea?" the Lead Wizard asked incredulously. He looked at Tristan. "We had long suspected it. We even sent numerous sailing expeditions out to try to cross the ocean, but few ever returned. The farthest anyone went and lived to tell about it was fifteen days of sailing." He looked hard at Faegan. "How do you know such things, unless you have had contact with the sorceresses when they were last here?"

"There is one in Parthalon who is loyal to me. He sends me messages."

Tristan sat there in his chair, still stunned. Slowly getting hold of himself he finally asked, "How do you receive his messages? Are you able to join with his mind as we believe the Coven can? And how does he supposedly know of the intimate lives of the mistresses?"

"I am not telepathic to that extent," Faegan said. "I do have a modicum of telepathic ability, but I cannot completely join to a mind that I have not prepared, let alone never met. However, if I had chosen to study that aspect of the craft I am sure I could accomplish it, and I am familiar with lesser derivations, although some of them are practices of the Vagaries. Remember, I never took the wizards' vows or accepted the death enchantments—Failee captured me before they had been introduced. Therefore, not only have I read the complete volume of the Vagaries, but I could, if I chose to, also practice them." He smiled coyly for a brief moment. "I would not, however, enjoy the side effects should I practice them mistakenly, as has the Coven. No, Tristan. In this case the answer is much more simple. My friend across the sea sends me handwritten parchments, tied to the legs of pigeons. These birds are extremely swift and hardy. One can usually traverse the Sea of Whispers in several days of nonstop flight. I read the message, write to him, and send the bird back after it has had sufficient rest." He paused, taking a sip of wine.

"I don't understand," Tristan countered. "How is it that these birds can do such a thing, especially in several days? It seems impossible."

"Indeed," Wigg replied drily.

"After nearly three centuries of trying, I was unable to cure my legs," Faegan answered. "I have long known that my usefulness would be forever limited. But when I heard of the return of the Sorceresses, I knew I had to try, in whatever fashion I could, to make a contribution to their downfall. Somehow I needed to gain all of the knowledge I could about them, and their impossible, unexpected return. And then an idea came to me. Although no one had ever before been able to cross the Sea of Whispers, it seemed to me that the only place the Sorceresses could have come from was across that same sea. So I ordered the gnomes to capture a group of Eutracian pigeons and bring them here to my house in the trees."

"You enchanted these birds?" Wigg asked skeptically, the infamous eyebrow arched.

"True," Faegan answered, a smile finally coming to his lips. "As a result they are imaginably swift, and can cross the Sea in matter of days, never stopping. Not forever, of course—eventually their hearts would give out. But the spell sustaining is sufficient for our needs. At first they were simply enchanted to fly east until flying over land or dying in the attempt. It took many birds and many convolutions of the spell before the first of them finally returned to me with proof that it had struck land. It was at that point I began to tie notes to their legs. Naturally I was extremely careful not to reveal where the notes came from, in case they fell into the hands of the Coven. Luckily, they did not. You can imagine my joy at finally seeing one of them return with a note from someone across the sea—someone who is also an enemy of the sorceresses. We have been conversing ever since."

"Does this supposed person from across the sea have a name?" Wigg asked.

"Geldon. He bravely continues to correspond with me, despite the risk. He contends he does not mind dying, if his efforts will have helped defeat the Sorceresses—he hates them that much."

"And just who is this Geldon in the social order of Parthalon to be so well informed?"

"He is a Parthalonian dwarfed hunchback upon whom Succiu has granted time enchantments. He is almost as old as you and I are. He is also Succiu's slave. He wears a jeweled collar around his neck that is attached to a chain leash. She forces him to help her practice some of her more exotic hobbies. Fortunately, she makes the mistake of taking him with her almost everywhere she goes. He hears much, and risks his life every time he sends a bird to me. His enforced loneliness and hatred of the Coven is so great that he began taking the chance of randomly sending out birds with messages, simply letting them go in the air, not knowing where they would end up or that there was even a nation called Eutracia. I believe at first he was only trying to find a kindred spirit in Parthalon to talk to, someone to sympathize with. Imagine his great surprise when the bird returned from me. We have been 'conversing' ever since."

"And as for trusting him, I did not at first, of course," he finally continued. "Until the attack upon Eutracia, I kept my return messages to him rather cryptic, saying little. It wasn't until Succiu and her Minions had come and gone that I began to realize I must take the chance of confiding in him in earnest. This sounds contradictory, I know. He could have been lying. But at this point, I felt there was much less to lose by being forthright—and more to gain if he were indeed genuine. A gamble, assuredly. But then again, so many things in life are. I am still not entirely sure that he can be trusted. But given the severity of our situation, what other choice could there be? If anything he said was true, even the slightest scrap, I needed to know what it was." Pausing again, he narrowed his eyes in thought. "Even the greatest of wheels sometimes revolve about the smallest of hubs," he added quietly.

Wigg leaned forward over the highly polished dining table. "Did Geldon know of the impending attack upon Eutracia?" he asked bluntly.

"Yes, he did."

"Then why didn't your loyal letter writer warn you?" Tristan asked skeptically. "I thought the two of you were the best of friends."

"He couldn't. During the period between which he first heard of the plan and the actual attack, the atmosphere at the Recluse was very tense. Succiu kept him with her almost every second. She never sent him out of the Recluse, so he had no chance to send a note to me. I didn't hear from him during a period of almost three months, and at first I thought him discovered, and dead. Then after the attack he contacted me with a note of great sympathy. He lives each day with the knowledge that he might have been able to warn us, but could not. And each day his hatred of the Coven grows. He cannot write to me simply because he would like to. He must first be sent out of the Recluse by Succiu in order to do it without detection."

"How convenient." Wigg sniffed.

"And just why does he supposedly hate the Coven?" Tristan asked.

"As I said, Succiu discovered him and made him her slave. At the same time she placed a Blood Pox upon him, and took away his reproductive powers. She spends a portion of each day laughing at him because of it, and embarrassing him in front of whomever she comes across."

That would be like her, Wigg thought. He scowled and rubbed the back of his neck. "So where did she supposedly find this Geldon?"

"In the Ghetto of the Shunned."

"The *what*?"

"The Ghetto of the Shunned. It's a walled city two hours' ride south from the Recluse. The Coven needed a place to put their so-called 'undesirables' while they were subjugating the nation, so they loosed a disease upon the entire population of a nearby city, murdering them. It's one of the reasons they were able to enslave the nation without the immediate need for any allies. The resulting walled, empty remains of the city suited their needs perfectly. Their enemies are confined there rather than killed outright because it is said that unending relegation to the Ghetto is worse than death, and therefore a greater means of control. It exists to this day, and confines almost two hundred thousand lost souls. There is only one commonly known way in: the front gates, which are controlled by the sorceresses and guarded by the Minions. But, unknown to them all there is a secret way in and out, and Geldon was the one to discover it. Only he and one other know of its existence. The Ghetto is also where he keeps his birds." Faegan paused, thinking it over. "A perfect location, really. The last place anyone would want to go looking, even if he could."

Wigg raised his wineglass and looked into the crimson liquid as it twinkled through the crystal. *It looks just like blood—endowed blood. The cause of it all,* he thought, unknowingly echoing Tristan's private thoughts by the campfire of two nights earlier. He narrowed his eyes as he formulated his next words.

"An unknown country across the sea, butterflies that can spell, a supposedly disloyal slave who sends you notes tied to birds, your life here in the trees among the gnomes, and your story of your 'dream' torture at the hands of the Coven. All very interesting." The obviously skeptical Lead Wizard continued to examine the wine as the glass twirled slowly between his fingertips. "There is, however, the greater remaining question. The one you have still to answer."

Tristan leaned forward intently, waiting.

"Exactly why did they take Shailiha?" Wigg finally asked. He returned his gaze to Faegan. "Why do they need her to be their fifth sorceress?"

The crippled wizard's face darkened as he set down his fork and looked first to Tristan, and then back to Wigg. "They plan to invoke the Blood Communion." Faegan sat back in his wheelchair as if a great burden had just been placed upon him, and his eyes grew shiny.

Tristan had no idea what Faegan was talking about, and he could tell by the look on Wigg's face that the Lead Wizard did not, either. But the mere sound of it all sent a shiver through him, one that he couldn't quite explain. "Please tell us about it," he said.

Faegan sighed heavily and wiped his face with his hands, as if he were suddenly very tired. "The Coven will gather in a specific place, the location of which is probably somewhere in the depths of the Recluse. Shailiha, unfortunately, will by then probably be one of them, although still untrained in the craft. She need not be trained for this purpose. They only need her blood, not her talents, and then they can take all eternity to train her if they so choose, as they undoubtedly will. The sorceresses will all be around the Pentangle, their chosen symbol as illustrated in the volume of the Vagaries. I'm sure you have seen it embroidered upon their clothing. In the center sits a white marble altar, upon which rests the goblet that was taken that day in the attack on Eutracia—the same goblet that Wigg found in the Caves, along with the stone. A small amount of blood is taken from each of them, about one-fifth of the total volume of the goblet. Their blood is then mixed, and the goblet filled with it. The Paragon is then hung by its chain directly over the center of the Pentangle. The Vagaries tell us that when all is finally in place, a stream of light from the night sky descends and strikes the Paragon, called down by the very act of having five such highly endowed people standing upon the points of the Pentangle. This light is refracted through the stone, much like a prism, separating into individual beams of colored essence. Each colored shaft of light descends into the blood in the goblet. The five then take turns drinking from it. At this point, the Paragon has united and empowered their blood. All five are as one, sharing the potency of Shailiha's blood, though alone, none of them will ever command the raw power that she does." Faegan paused, running a worried hand down the length of his hawklike face. He closed his eyes before continuing. "Still," he said quietly, "this is nothing but preparation for what is yet to come."

Tristan looked at Wigg, speechless. *This is insane,* he shrieked silently. *Shailiha would never do such a thing.* He looked at Wigg for a comforting gesture or kind word, but none came. The Lead Wizard's face had become as hard as granite.

"And what is it that is yet to come?" Wigg demanded.

Faegan stiffened, his eyes still closed. "The Reckoning," he said simply. "It immediately and irrevocably follows the Blood Communion. It is the supreme, undeniable control of all things—people, creatures of the land, sea, and sky; even the weather. Both Eutracia and Parthalon will no longer exist as we now know them but as mere possessions of the Coven, populated by mindless, wandering slaves who were once the citizens of those lands. With the stone and the princess, and the knowledge that Failee tortured from me, they can literally possess the world, and the minds of everyone and everything in it. They will only need to *think* a thing for it to happen. I don't believe I need to describe what life would be like under their complete control." Faegan opened his eyes, and Tristan once again found himself adrift in that deep, impenetrable grayness.

The room had become as silent as death, the only sounds the gentle rustling of the curtains against the open window frames and the soft, endless rush of the ocean beyond.

Wigg lowered his head in frustration and rubbed his brow with his fingertips, as if trying to force himself to understand better. He gave a deep sigh and then said, "You mentioned earlier that you gave Failee only *some* of the information contained in the Vagaries. Does that mean that she is not in possession of all of it?"

"That is correct."

"How is it that you were able to keep any part of the Vagaries from her, if the Chimeran Agonies, as you say, are irresistible, even for someone of your quality blood?"

"I was able to shield part of my mind from her through a supreme effort of will. To this day I am not sure how I accomplished it. My family was dead, and at that point in my life I had nothing more to lose. It ultimately came down to who could last the longest. The Chimeran Agonies worked on me, but not to the extent that Failee believes. Her knowledge of the spell was only fragmentary, and when it was applied to me it was only partially effective and I was able to withhold much of the Tome from her. There is a good chance that to this day she still does not realize this."

"But this is a good thing, is it not?" Tristan quickly asked, sensing the first ray of hope since this frightening conversation had begun. "If the Coven is only in partial possession of the Vagaries, perhaps there are other parts of it that we can use against them, parts unknown to them. Parts that they have no knowledge of how to stop."

Faegan looked sadly into Tristan's eyes. "If only that were the case," he said quietly. "Actually, I fear that by withholding some of the Vagaries from her, I may have created an even worse dilemma than we first thought."

Tristan's heart sank, and when he saw the devastating look that crossed Wigg's face, his heart sank farther still. *How could keeping such powerful information from the Coven possibly be injurious to us?* he wondered.

"I can see by the look on your face you can now imagine the scope of the problem, Wigg," Faegan said. "Would you like to tell the prince, or shall I?"

"No," Wigg said. "We wish to hear it from you."

Faegan sighed. "Just as the technique of the Chimeran Agonies was only partially imparted to Failee, so were the parts of the Vagaries that I had read, because I was able to shield my mind from her for a time. She believes she has all of the information but does not, and she will therefore most certainly be forced to make disastrous mistakes in their application. The Blood Communion may be correctly performed, because she was given all of it. But the Reckoning itself will be another matter. The information she has regarding the Reckoning is fragmentary at best. Therefore the odds are overwhelming that she will conduct it incorrectly."

Tristan felt another shiver go up his spine, and it wasn't because of the cool night breeze that blew in through the window. He almost dared not ask the painfully obvious question. "And if the Reckoning is not performed perfectly?" he asked tentatively. "What happens then?"

"Then the world as we know it will cease to exist. Completely and irreversibly. The incorrect application of the Reckoning, due to the combination of the Vigors and the Vagaries, will result in the complete and total destruction of the entire world, and everything and everyone in it. This is why the Vigors and the Vagaries are housed in *separate* volumes of the Tome. The combination of their knowledge and their use was only to reside in the mind and heart of one person, the Chosen One. You, Tristan. As the Ones Who Came Before intended it to be. But if the Vigors and the Vagaries clash in combined or even simultaneous use by anyone but you, the result is cataclysmic. And she will doubtless attempt to combine them, because her knowledge is limited." He paused to look into each of their faces in turn. "It is no longer just a struggle to save Shailiha. It is now also a struggle to save our world."

"I have learned from Wigg that combining the two schools of the craft would have a disastrous effect," Tristan said. "And after witnessing the orbs myself I can understand that. But how can you be so sure that what Failee intends to do would mean the end of the world? I cannot conceive of any reaction that powerful."

Faegan turned his attention to the Lead Wizard. "So you have shown the two sides of magic to the prince?" he asked simply. "Not simply their effects, but what the orbs of the Vigors and Vagaries actually look like?"

"Yes," Wigg answered.

"Then, Tristan, you must think back to the actual appearances of the orbs. Do you remember the lightninglike strikes of energy that shot to and fro inside each of them as if trying to escape? In order for Failee to invoke her ritual, she'll need to call forth so much magic from each of the orbs that she will create a massive tear in each of them such as has never been seen. This phenomenon alone would be bad enough, I assure you. But then not only will she call forth these gigantic amounts of energy from both sides, but she will join them—something only the Chosen is to do, as foretold in the Prophecies. Believe me, both of you, when I say that if she succeeds, she will then immediately fail. And when she does, there will truly be *nothing* left. Not even the Vigors or the Vagaries themselves. Just emptiness, with no hope whatsoever of redemption."

A deathly pall came over the room. Finally Wigg broke the silence.

"But surely Failee herself knows that combining the two sides of the craft will result in this calamity," he interjected. "She is, after all, very skilled and immensely knowledgeable. And yet you believe she will try, risking such a disaster?"

"Of course," Faegan said softly. "If she were not intent upon trying the incantation she would not have risked everything to cross the Sea of Whispers to abduct Shailiha, her fifth sorceress. She would not have needed her. Never, never forget the fact that she is quite mad. Her practice of the Vagaries has taken her insanity to the very edge, and it is my opinion that she now lives in a world unto herself, in complete denial of the possible consequences, and considers herself to be infallible."

"And the other sorceresses do not know of the risks?" Wigg asked.

"Probably not," Faegan said, narrowing his eyes. "Remember, their expertise in the Vagaries is far less than Failee's. They trust her, and believe what she teaches them. They are most probably not aware of the fact that she will be forced to combine the two sides of the craft. In addition, their own, lesser practice of the Vagaries has started to lead them down the road to dementia as well, which to a certain degree makes them more willing followers." He paused for a moment, as if lost in thought. "A true case of the blind leading the blind," he whispered, almost to himself. "It is also the reason for their bizarre sexual needs."

Tristan was immediately taken back to the night on the banks of the river, when the one he knew as Lillith had suddenly become Natasha, and tried to rape him. "What do you mean?" he asked Faegan.

"Their dementia has tricked them into believing that those sexual acts of depravity they are so well known for actually increase their power—that the craft itself is calling them to do these things. During the use of some arcane teaching of the Vagaries, Failee may have felt something akin to this sexual enhancement of her power, as may have the others. For the practice of the Vagaries can, when strong enough, actually feel that way in some respects—a sense of total ecstasy. I know, for I have felt it myself. The volume of the Vagaries makes brief mention of it. But now her madness strengthens the belief that the craft demands these acts. Even Succiu and the others, schooled in the basics of the Vagaries under Failee's misguided teaching, also believe it to be true. Thus the need for the Stables." He looked sadly at Tristan for a moment, knowing that he was about to add greatly to the prince's pain. "And Shailiha, once trained by Failee, will no doubt also be prone to these sexual depravities and may ultimately become the most wicked of them all, due to the purity of her blood." He sat back in his chair, resigned to the fact that Tristan would probably fight him on this point, and not want to believe.

Tristan stared at him, stunned. Then he slammed his fist down on the table with all his strength. "I don't believe you!" he shouted. "How could you be sure of all of this, anyway? At least part of what we are talking about happened over three hundred years ago! How can you possibly be so sure?"

"You are forgetting something, my young friend," the rogue wizard replied calmly. "I have the gift of Consummate Recollection. Every single thing I have ever seen, heard, learned, or read is automatically and flawlessly ensconced in my mind, and can be retrieved at any time of my choosing. Sometimes it is more of a curse than a blessing, I assure you. Few wizards are born with the gift. I am one of those wizards. And I was there when the first feelings of ecstasy came upon Failee. It was when I was still their prisoner, and her experience in this resulted eventually in the sexual depravities of that war that Wigg may have told you about. They carry this sickness with them to this day, except it is now much worse." He looked to the Lead Wizard knowingly, and then continued.

"After my daughter, Emily, first put the stone around her neck at the age of five and began reading the Tome, I was, because of my gift, the one selected by the other wizards to read it first. With the rest of the Directorate dead, Wigg and I remain the only two persons in the world to have read both the Vigors and the Vagaries. Of course, neither of us have read the third volume, the Prophecies, but certain sections of the first two volumes deal in some small ways with what will happen in the future. That is how Wigg, myself, and the others knew beforehand of your coming, and of how and when you were to be trained." Faegan looked hard into the prince's eyes, the strange green motes once again swimming in Tristan's vision. "As distasteful as it may seem to you now, believe that what I have told you is the truth."

Tristan, feeling completely beaten and alone, stood from his chair and walked on trembling legs the short distance across the room to stand looking out the window. *My sister, my only remaining family, is somewhere across the sea,* he thought to himself, *and I have no way to get there, and no training in the craft with which to fight for her life, even if I could.* He lowered his head in silence, and then a thought came to him. He turned back to Faegan.

"There is something that has always bothered me, and I feel that now is the time to ask it. If Emily was of your blood, and your blood is of such high quality, then why did the Coven not simply keep her and train her as one of their own, rather than kill her? Why wait three hundred years for the birth of Shailiha?" The prince immediately saw the look of fury that crossed Wigg's face, but he didn't care.

"I was married to a woman of unendowed blood, Tristan. Her name was Jessica, and Emily was our only child. Emily's endowed blood was of good quality, but not of sufficient worth to accomplish what the Coven had planned. So they simply used her for what they could. Emily was a wonderful child. Happy and intelligent. I would have endowed her with time enchantments, just as you shall one day be. Perhaps the two of you would have met one day. You would have liked her."

Tristan glared across the table at Wigg and finally walked back over and sat down. "Are you going to do it, or shall I?" he asked.

Wigg glowered at him. "I don't think that this is the time to—"

"But I do!" Tristan interrupted. He had had enough of secrets, riddles, and games. "The fact is I *did* know your daughter," he said gently but firmly to the crippled wizard. "She had stayed alive for all of these years, living in secret as the duchess of Ephyra, among other things. She had also become a Visage Caster, and her identity was never truly known until that day on the dais when my entire family died. She was not killed by the Coven in Florian's Glade as they led you to believe. Someone else died that day, instead. She was one of them. I am sorry to have to tell you of this, but my sister's life hangs in the balance."

The prince sat back heavily in his chair, not proud of the pain he had just caused the already crippled wizard, but glad that the truth was finally out. He looked across the table at Wigg and countered the disapproving stare with an equally defiant one of his own. He opened his palms and held them both up, revealing the freshly healed scars that had been created that night on his knees in the rain when he had dripped his own blood over the graves of his family and the Directorate, swearing vengeance against the ones who had taken their lives.

"I have sworn with my blood to bring my sister home, and so I shall, one way or another," he said menacingly. He looked at Faegan before speaking again. "Each of us has his own scars. I have mine, Wigg has his, and you have yours. I am sorry to have been the one to tell you this, and add to them."

Faegan's face had become ashen. He looked to Wigg, then to the prince, and then back to Wigg again, all the while his mouth working soundlessly up and down. He was obviously in shock. At last, he spoke to Wigg.

"Emily—Emily has been alive all of this time?" he stammered.

Wigg glared at Tristan, hoping that the prince would keep quiet and at least let him finish the story in his own way. "Yes," he said gently. "But she is no longer alive."

"She was one of the Coven?" Faegan asked, staring out into the space over the table, looking at nothing. "For all of these years, living here and waiting for their return?"

"That's right. We knew her as Duchess Natasha, of the house of Minaar. Wife of Baldric, duke of Ephyra. I believe the marriage was her means of making sure she would be accepted at court and have access to the coronation ceremonies. She killed her own husband on the day of the attack."

"Tristan said she was also a Visage Caster. She was undoubtedly trained by the sorceresses to employ that power," Faegan said weakly, as if to himself.

"Yes," Wigg answered. "She surely held many different stations, titles, and husbands during the three hundred years since her birth, apparently changing her appearance and moving on whenever it started to become apparent to those around her that she did not age, or ever become ill. She also knew when the attack was to start, and I believe she had some type of telepathic link to Failee, indicating the precise moment when the stone was in the water and all of the wizards of the Directorate would be without their powers. It was very well thought out. It was just then that the winged killers descended through the stained-glass roof of the Great Hall, and our world as we knew it was forever changed."

"The Minions of Day and Night," Faegan said weakly, a lone tear tracing its way down his cheek toward his long, gray beard. "Kluge. And Traax, his second in command. The taskmasters the Coven uses for their dirty work. Geldon tells me in his notes that they number in the hundreds of thousands."

At the mention of Kluge's name, Tristan's hands curled tighter around the arms of his chair until his knuckles were white. *I will kill that hideous thing one day,* he again swore to himself. *And as many of the others like him as I can before they finally strike me down.*

"What are these creatures?" Wigg asked. "Do you know? Are they indigenous to Parthalon? I had never seen anything like them before."

"I truly do not know, but they are a fighting force of unparalleled efficiency. It is said in Parthalon that rather than face one of the Minions in battle, most men simply cut their own throats, instead. Geldon has also written me that the Minions even train to the death among themselves, because there is no one else of sufficient caliber with whom they can compete. I get my information from the gnomes. They are very stealthy. They listen at windows or hide in the thick foliage of trees that overhang the roads, gleaning everything they can. As far as I know, they are never seen. It was one of those in the trees who first heard of the attack on Tammerland, as the many refugees came pouring down the road. My elder of the gnomes, Michael the Meager, informed me that the Minions swept through the Royal Guard like a plague of locusts through a wheat field."

"And how is it that the gnomes choose to stay in a place where the Berserkers threaten their existence?" Wigg asked. "One would think they would leave."

"And go where?" Faegan countered. "Remember, they were once hunted for sport. Which would you think was the better choice, eh? To be hunted by an entire population, or to live here with the relatively few Berserkers, hopefully protected by a wizard?"

The crippled wizard had begun to regain his composure. He looked at Wigg, and Tristan knew that the most difficult of questions regarding Emily was about to be asked.

"How did she die?" Faegan asked simply. "Do you know?"

"Yes," Wigg said hesitantly. "I do know how she died. It was at my hand. Mine and the prince's. Emily, the one we knew as Natasha, had stationed herself at a tavern and taken a new identity. We thought we were helping an innocent young woman escape a difficult situation, but later discovered that she was only waiting to find the right place in which to kill us without raising suspicion." He paused, wondering how far he should go with all of this, finally deciding to press on. "She was trying to rape Tristan and take her unborn conception back to Parthalon when I killed her with a wizard's noose."

For a long moment Faegan stared out into space. "You said that the prince also played a part," he whispered eventually. "Tristan, what was it that you did?" He turned, and his gray eyes seemed to be looking into the prince's very soul. Tristan had the impression that Faegan was asking not only to learn about the death of his daughter, but for another reason, as well. But the prince had no idea what that reason might be.

"During Wigg's application of the noose she continued to struggle, and I knew that the only answer was for her to die. I finished her with my dreggan," Tristan said simply. He felt sorry for Faegan, but at the same time was not ashamed of what he had done. The woman had been partly responsible for the slaughter of his entire family, and he would kill her again in an instant, if necessary. Faegan or no Faegan.

Faegan cast his gray eyes up to the dreggan and baldric that hung over the back of the prince's chair. "Is this the sword?"

"Yes."

"The same one that killed your father?"

"Yes."

"And the same one you hope to use to kill the Coven and Kluge?"

"Yes."

Faegan lowered his head and closed his eyes as if lost in time for a moment. Without opening them again, he began to speak. " *'And the Chosen One shall take up three weapons of his choice and slay many before reading the Prophecies and coming to the light,'* " he said.

"A quote from the Vagaries?" Wigg asked, puzzled.

"Yes," Faegan said, looking at the dreggan as it hung peacefully behind the prince. "I can only assume that the second weapon mentioned is the collection of knives that hangs behind his right shoulder. But as to what the third one shall be, only time will tell. The Vagaries make occasional mention of many things that will come to pass. But only the Prophecies will tell Tristan the course of action he is to take. And only he is to read them."

Faegan took both of the prince's hands in his and looked at the angry red scars on his palms for what seemed to be a long time. "It is true, each of us carries his own kinds of scars. You, I am afraid, will be subject to a great many more before it is your turn to rest. As regards my daughter, the one you knew as Natasha, I forgive both you and Wigg for what you did. It was necessary, and in truth, despite how much I loved my Emily, Natasha was as far removed from me as any of the sorceresses could have been. I prefer to believe that the Emily I knew died that day in Florian's Glade, despite what I now know to be the truth."

Tristan was about to speak when one of the gnomes knocked on the door of the hallway from which they had entered the room.

"Yes, Michael?" Faegan asked.

Michael the Meager, the gnome elder, was about the same size as Shannon the Small, but appeared to be much older. Bald and rotund, he

stood at the door holding a strange box with several holes in it. His face
was intelligent, his manner sincere.

"Begging your pardon, Master," he began, "but another has just
come. We thought you would want to see it right away." After a nod
from Faegan, Michael the Meager walked the box into the room and set
it on the table in front of the crippled wizard. Tristan shot a quick,
questioning look at Wigg, but it was evident the Lead Wizard was also
puzzled about the strange container that lay on the table between them.

Faegan indicated to Michael to proceed. The gnome opened the
top of the box, reached in, and produced a sleek-looking gray bird. Its
wings were long and tapered, and it seemed to be quite content in the
hands of the gnome, as if well accustomed to being handled. He automatically looked to the bird's leg and saw that a scroll of oilcloth was
wrapped around it; also, a cylindrical object had been tied around the
bird's breast with a leather string. *One of Faegan's enchanted pigeons,* Tristan realized. *A note from Geldon.*

As if reading his mind, Faegan looked at Tristan and said, "Yes, it is
what you think. The whistle tied to the bird makes a sound as it wings
through the air to us, keeping flying predators away." He looked down
at the pigeon and gave it an unexpected, short kiss on the top of its
head. "This is the fastest of them," he said seriously. "The message must
be important for Geldon to have risked this particular bird."

Faegan untied the oilcloth from the pigeon's leg and unwrapped it
to reveal the parchment hidden inside. It was rolled into a scroll, and red
sealing wax rejoined the end of the note to itself. Faegan quickly broke
the wax seal, unrolled the note, and began to read.

Hungry for a word, a scrap of information, anything that he might
learn about his sister, Tristan tried hard to decipher the look in the crippled wizard's eyes. But as he did so, his heart sank. He watched Faegan's
hopeful expression change rapidly to one of extreme worry and concern. Faegan then raised his eyes from the note and looked at the
prince. "I think you had best read this for yourself," he said sadly.

Tristan eagerly snatched the note from the hands of the wizard and
barely noted the odd, rather exotic handwriting as his eyes tore across
the page:

Master Faegan,

*I wish with all of my heart that there was some other way to inform you
of this, but what we have feared most has come to pass. Princess Shailiha has
finally been turned. The last of the three Chimeran Agonies have successfully
rid her of her past life, and she now believes herself to be one of the Coven. In
fact, in many ways she has quickly become the worst of them all. To the delight*

of the others, she has already committed several acts of voluntary depravity. Her hunger knows no bounds in its quest for both the Blood Communion and the Reckoning, and her thirst for her training to begin as a sorceress is without equal. Mention is often made of her soon becoming their leader. Her unborn could come at any time, another innocent of endowed blood for the sorceresses to corrupt.

You told me that once there was a fifth sorceress, Failee would need nine days to mentally prepare for the Communion. I can only assume that at least three have passed since the releasing of this bird. That leaves only six. Time is of the essence.

As you have told me, the possibility is great that instead of being performed correctly, the Reckoning may be compromised and the entire world may perish. After three hundred years of slavery, I must confess that sometimes I do not know which of the two outcomes I would prefer.

I await your word. Whatever you choose to do, Master, it must be soon.

Geldon

Speechless, Tristan dropped the note to the table in front of Wigg and rose from his chair, once again walking to the open balcony doors that faced the Sea of Whispers. *Shailiha is a sorceress of the Coven,* he thought in disbelief. *All is lost. Even if we could get to her, there is no way to stop what she is doing, or what she has become. Once I thought that if I went to her and she was at least still one of us, we would have a chance. But not now. Her torture began the instant she watched her husband murdered on that dais. And although she does not know it, her torture will now continue for all of eternity.* He wiped a tear away from one eye. *Only six days left. No one other than the sorceresses has ever sailed farther than fifteen days into that sea. And even worse, we have no way of knowing how long the complete journey takes.*

The sound of Wigg's commanding voice brought Tristan's mind back into the dining room. He turned to see that the Lead Wizard had apparently read the note and was handing it back to Faegan. "What is it that Failee must do to prepare herself for the Blood Communion?" Wigg asked. "Geldon's note speaks of nine days."

Scowling, Faegan worriedly rubbed his hands together. "She will go into virtual seclusion, except for making a daily visit to the place in the Recluse where the Blood Communion is to take place. It is she who must call the light from the sky that passes through the stone, thus beginning the process. The preparation of the incantation is very complex, and demands total concentration for that number of days before she is able to call forth the light." He looked over at Tristan.

"I tend to forget that the only members of the Coven you have actually seen are Succiu and my daughter Emily, or as you knew her, Natasha. I know you have witnessed some of the evil that they are capable of. But make no mistake, even though you are the Chosen One. Despite what you have seen from Succiu, she is nothing compared to Failee. Not only is Failee the most powerful of them because of her mastery of the Vagaries, but she is also quite mad, and is largely the cause of all of this. Without her, there would have been no Coven, and no other sorceresses to follow her." At these words, Wigg's countenance became quite dark, and Tristan made a mental note to ask the usually secretive Lead Wizard to tell him more about the history of the Coven one day. *That is,* he reflected, *if we have many more days left.*

Wigg stood, walked to the window where the prince was standing, and put an affectionate hand on Tristan's shoulder. "I see no way to continue," he said quietly. "I know this is not what you wanted to hear, but it is in Shadowood that our journey apparently ends. The Sea of Whispers is probably much more than fifteen days' sail, even if we knew the secret to getting across. And we don't. I fear, without help, that we have failed. I can see no way to get to Shailiha, and that is obviously what must be done." Tears were starting to come to his eyes. "I have failed you, Tristan. And your father. Please forgive me, but I see no way that our quest can be accomplished."

"You were always too much of a pragmatist, Wigg," Faegan suddenly said from his chair at the end of the table. The strange, dark-blue cat was once again in his lap. "That is why I became the more powerful of the two of us. Sometimes you just have to let your imagination flow." He smiled at them both as he stroked the contented cat.

"What are you trying to say?" Wigg asked, his infamous left eyebrow arched.

"I can send you to Parthalon. Both of you. Immediately. And I suggest you let me, because each second that ticks by is one more second closer to the Communion."

"What are you talking about?" Tristan demanded. He walked back over and sat down. Wigg followed. "If there is a way to get to Parthalon, I suggest you tell us right now."

Faegan relaxed and took a deep breath. "Listen carefully, both of you, to what I am about to say. There is a portal that can be summoned, but only by me. Even Failee does not know of it. Remember when I said that she does not possess all of the teachings of the Vagaries?" He sat back in his chair, still holding Nicodemus. "This portal I refer to is just that—part of the teachings she still knows nothing of. Had she suspected such a thing could exist, I would have been dead hundreds of years ago." He smiled. "By the way, it is also the reason that Nicodemus is blue. Think to yourself, Tristan," he asked, pursing his lips. "Have you ever seen a *blue* cat before?"

"What in the name of the Afterlife are you talking about?" Tristan snarled. "You talk the way a drunkard walks—in every direction save the one in which he should truly be going! And as far as your cat is concerned, I doubt that very little could surprise me anymore. Certainly nothing that involves a wizard."

Faegan raised an eyebrow at Wigg. "Stubborn, isn't he?"

"More than you could ever know," Wigg returned. "But if there truly is a quicker way to Parthalon, we must know of it now."

Faegan smiled. "Very well. Tristan, I'm sure you remember me speaking of an aura that surrounded you at your birth. What color did I say it was?"

"Azure."

"When Wigg killed the screaming harpy that day in the palace courtyard, what color was the wizard's cage that he employed?"

"Again, azure."

"And when Wigg was forced to kill Emily, what was the color of the wizard's noose?"

Tristan narrowed his eyes. "Azure, of course. What of it?"

Beginning to catch on, Wigg entered into the questioning. "That day on the mountain, when you first discovered the Caves and I killed the blood stalker, night fell and I used a powder to illuminate our way back down. What color did the path become?"

Tristan frowned. "Azure, of course. You know that as well as I," he said.

"And what does that tell you?" Faegan asked.

"What I have always known. That when a wizard employs the gift, an azure color is created."

"Not quite," Faegan corrected. "Have you seen Wigg or any of the others of the Directorate use their power and not create this color?"

"Yes."

"Then your answer needs to be modified."

Tristan thought for a moment, and then suddenly looked at them both. "When a wizard employs a great abundance of his power, or the action he is attempting to undertake is particularly difficult, the azure glow is created in one form or another. But if the action taken is relatively easy to perform, then it is not."

"Well done," Faegan said. "And what does this tell you about Nicodemus in relation to the portal I have mentioned?"

Momentarily confused, Tristan sat back in his chair, wondering. He had never seen a blue cat before, but this line of reasoning was maddening. He looked up at the smiling, crippled wizard and wanted to wrap his hands around his throat, forcing the answers out of him. A quick glance at Wigg told him that he was to do this Faegan's way. Realizing he had no choice, Tristan grudgingly resolved to play the wizard's game. Then, suddenly, the answer came to him.

"You sent him through!" Tristan exclaimed. "The cat has been to Parthalon and back! That is the only thing that could explain his color! But why did he stay that way?"

"Excellent," Faegan said happily. "But the truth is I have no idea why he changed color. Perhaps it was because the cat is a less intelligent being, or because he obviously has no endowed blood. Either way, he has stayed that way."

"Why did you do it?" Tristan asked.

"To be sure that the portal worked, of course," Faegan said. "Then I would open it again, and Geldon would put Nicodemus back through from the other side, with a note confirming that the transference had indeed happened, proving Nicodemus had not simply been wandering about somewhere in between."

"Tell me more about the portal," Wigg asked cautiously, taking another sip of wine. "The Directorate tried long and hard to find such a way to travel, especially during the war, but we were never successful. How does it work?"

Faegan smiled. "I open the portal, you walk in, and in a matter of seconds, you are there."

"That's impossible!" Tristan objected. "Traveling across the Sea of Whispers is the only way to Parthalon, if such a place even exists. No one can travel that distance in a matter of seconds! You're insane." But Faegan just continued to smile.

Wigg put a finger to his lips in thought, now obviously intrigued. "You still haven't answered my question," he said to Faegan politely. "How does the portal work?"

The crippled wizard picked up his cloth napkin and laid it flat upon the dining room table. Pointing one of his long fingers at the center of the left half of the napkin, he burned a small hole in it. He then pointed to the center of the right half, doing the same thing.

He indicated the hole on the left. "This hole represents Shadowood," he said. Then gesturing to the hole on the right side, he added, "This hole represents Parthalon." He then picked the napkin up at each end and held it out stretched out flat, parallel to the table. "The way the portal works is by temporarily compressing the space between the two places." He brought the ends of the napkin together until they touched, the folded center of it dropping in the middle toward the table. The holes were up against each other and could be seen through. "Once this has been accomplished, all one has to do is walk through to the other side and arrive at his destination." He let go with one hand and unceremoniously poked a finger through the two holes. "A distance of hundreds of leagues crossed with only a few steps, proving that the shortest distance between two points is not a straight line, but rather, no distance at all." He smiled while scratching one corner of his mouth. "If you don't believe me, ask Nicodemus." He opened the napkin and put it back down flat on the table as it had been before he started, then stared at them as though he had just discussed something as simple as what he had eaten for breakfast that morning.

Tristan looked up to see Wigg looking spellbound. "Amazing," the Lead Wizard said quietly, his gaze transfixed by the sight of the burned napkin that lay before him. "We had been working on the problem, but this solution never occurred to us. Closing the distance between two points by *eliminating* the space between them, rather than *crossing* the distance itself. Ingenious."

"As I said, Wigg, you were always too pragmatic."

Tristan stared at the two of them, stunned. "Do you actually propose to have the three of us go through this portal?" he asked.

"Two," Faegan said calmly. "And the sooner the better."

"Then perhaps you could be so good as to tell us where it comes out on the other end, how we are supposed to know where to go, and what to do once we get there?" The prince defiantly sat back in his chair and crossed his arms. "And I take it you will not be accompanying us?"

"No," Faegan said, serious now. "I cannot."

"And why not?" Tristan was becoming more suspicious by the second.

"There are two reasons. First, if I were to go with you, who would then reopen the portal on this side for our return? I can only hold the portal open for an hour or so at a time, and I have never had the strength to do so more than once a day. We must have a prearranged time each day that I will open the portal, so that you can be in a position to return if you are able. And second, look down at my legs, Tristan. Have you forgotten? Even I have been unable to undo the damage that the Coven caused, despite over three hundred years of trying. You and Wigg pushing me around Parthalon in this chair isn't going to prove to be much of an advantage."

"But your powers would be invaluable to us there. You are supposedly even more powerful than Wigg."

"Faegan and I wouldn't be able to use our powers, anyway," Wigg said from across the table. "At least not right away."

"Why not?"

"Because Failee would sense our presence. As it is, my powers will be strained to the utmost to conceal our endowed blood from her while we are there. I must not use the craft in an obvious way until the very instant that it is needed to stop the Communion. That much is apparent. No, Faegan is right. He belongs here."

"You're the Lead Wizard—why can't you open the portal for us on the other side, whenever we may need it?" Tristan asked Wigg.

Faegan smiled slightly. "This incantation took me ten years to perfect, Tristan. Ten difficult years. And despite how talented I know Wigg to be, it would take me at least fifteen days just to teach the formulations to him, plus another two or three months of practice for him to perfect the technique. You read Geldon's note. He estimates we have only six days left." His amazing eyes slowly became sad once again. "We simply don't have that kind of time."

Wigg raised an understanding eyebrow at the prince before again addressing Faegan. "And just where in Parthalon would you be sending us?"

"The only place that makes sense. The Ghetto of the Shunned— the only place the Minions do not bother to enter. You will be safe there until Geldon can get to you and take you to the Recluse. If Geldon is unable to be there at the moment of your arrival, one named Ian will be. He is trusted, and helps Geldon tend to the birds. He will help hide you until Geldon can arrive."

"How will Geldon know that we are coming?" Wigg asked cautiously. "If we go now, as you say we should, we will arrive well before any note to him could be received."

"He already expects your arrival."

Wigg's eyebrow arched. "Sure of yourself, weren't you?" he asked.

Faegan smiled compassionately. "Even though you gained Shannon's permission to cross, I could detect the unusually violent moving of the bridge. And since all the others of the Directorate were killed, I knew that the only one who could be crossing was you, Lead Wizard. I immediately sent the fastest of my birds to Parthalon."

"And once we get there?" Tristan asked. "How do we stop the Communion?"

"Failee needs two things to ensure the Communion: First, the Paragon. And second, the fifth sorceress, Princess Shailiha. Return the stone and the princess to Eutracia and you will have thwarted her, at least for the time being." Faegan gave Wigg a cryptic look. "But finding a way to kill the four original sorceresses would be the optimum choice, ensuring no further such attempts," he added.

"Killing the sorceresses sounds impossible," Tristan said glumly. "Especially when they can combine their powers, and Wigg will be the only one able to employ the craft against them."

"If you can manage it, be close to them during the commencement of the Communion," Faegan told them. "During the Communion, while the stone is refracting its light into the blood, Wigg and the sorceresses will be powerless, because the stone will be without its color. Just as the wizards of the Directorate were powerless during the coronation ceremony while the stone was in the water. That is the only time that you should even conceive of striking against them. This narrow opportunity will be your greatest weapon, but you will only have the chance to use it once. If you successfully stop the Communion, then the Reckoning cannot follow."

The fire in the fireplace had begun to die out, and the room had gradually begun to darken and chill. They had been talking a long time. Faegan narrowed his eyes, and a log from the pile near the hearth levitated and floated over to land upon the fire. Almost immediately, the room started to lighten and warm again.

"There are a few more things that need to be said," Faegan began. "Unpleasant things, but you both need to hear them nonetheless. First, there are dangerous creatures other than the Minions that roam Parthalon, creatures spawned by the Coven. I do not know their exact nature, but Geldon has alluded to them a few times in his notes. They are apparently used to help retain control over the population by inspiring terror. You must be very careful, or you may not reach the Recluse at all."

The crippled old wizard then gave Tristan a hard look, which began to soften slightly as he started to speak. "You have been out of touch with the news of Eutracia for several weeks. My gnomes bring me back all kinds of gossip and news, some trustworthy, some not. However, something has happened that, unfortunately, I believe." He sighed, rubbing his face with his hands as though not wanting to continue. "Tristan, when you get back home, *if* you get back home, there will probably be a price on your head. You will likely be the most highly sought-after criminal in all of Eutracia."

Tristan felt the blood draining from his face even though his heart was racing as fast as it ever had in his life. He stared at the old wizard, his mouth hanging open. "Why?" he asked breathlessly. He couldn't believe what he had just heard.

"For the murder of your father, the king of Eutracia."

"But I was forced to kill him!" Tristan objected in horror. Memories of that awful day flooded his mind. "If I had not killed him quickly, Kluge would have tortured him to death! Both my father and the Lead Wizard ordered me to do so!" The image of his father being held down upon the altar of the Paragon by two of Kluge's winged monsters floated mercilessly before his eyes. Then had come the descent of the blade, and everything Tristan had known and loved had irrevocably changed. Tears welled in his eyes, and he brushed them angrily away. This simply couldn't be happening.

"There were witnesses in the Great Hall! How could they think me responsible?" he shouted.

"Hundreds of people saw you take a dreggan and apparently willingly kill your father. There was a great deal of noise and confusion in the room. Very few of them probably heard your father or Wigg. All they saw was you killing him, and you and Wigg watching what was done to your mother and the others. And then, despite your harsh treatment by the Minions, you and Wigg both somehow seemed to escape. I believe the story has been enhanced by the sorceresses, and by the Minions as they raped their way through Eutracia. And I believe the price on your head is being provided by the Coven, as well, along with payment to many of the witnesses to spread lies about what really happened. It would be yet another clever way for them to help ensure your death, since they weren't able to accomplish it on their own before they sailed."

Tristan sat in his chair like a broken doll, speechless. *There is simply no end to the insanity!*

Seeing the prince's grief, Wigg took up the conversation with the crippled wizard. "What else do you need to tell us?" he asked.

"You and I both know that the odds on your being able to stop the Communion or destroy the four sorceresses are not good." Faegan turned his gray eyes directly on Tristan. "If you are unable to stop the Communion, kill the sorceresses, or remove the princess or the stone from the Recluse, you must, at the very least, kill Shailiha. Even if it comes at the cost of your own lives." He sat back in his chair, exhausted at what he had just spoken aloud.

At the mention of his sister's name, Tristan's mind snapped back to reality, leaving behind the visions of his father on the altar of the Paragon. "You would have me kill my own sister?" he whispered. He stared back at Faegan in utter disbelief. "It is true," he said then, his eyes narrowing. "You are mad. Or you are in league with the Coven and are trying to use me as your agent. Either way, it won't work."

"Tristan, you must listen to me," Faegan said. There was a pleading in his voice now that neither Wigg nor the prince had heard before. "If you are unsuccessful in the undertakings I have described, Shailiha must die for two reasons. First, she may be the *only* one you can kill, since she is the only one who is untrained in the craft. And second, she is pregnant, so killing only one of the other sorceresses will still eventually leave five, as according to Geldon, her baby will be a girl. If that proves true, in only a few short years we will be right back in the same position we are now."

Tristan stared dumbly down at the highly polished table, lost in his thoughts. He understood what the wizard was telling him, but he just couldn't believe it. Nothing in this world could make him harm his sister.

"I know how you feel, Tristan," Faegan said. "We have all lost loved ones to the Coven. But you must trust me when I tell you that Shailiha is no longer your sister. She belongs to them now, heart and soul. And you must treat her just as you would any of the other four, no matter how difficult."

Silence reigned for a long moment in the dining room. Wigg finally was the one to speak. "How do we return, if we are lucky enough to be able to do so?" he asked. "How will you know when we are ready?"

"There are approximately six days left until the day of the Communion. I will open the portal each of the five days before, in case you need to escape Parthalon sooner than predicted. Each day, starting with tomorrow, I shall open the portal for one hour, beginning at high noon in Parthalon. That is as much time as my powers will allow. Because Parthalon is so much farther to the east, this time of day will be earlier for me. You must rely on Geldon to help you with that part of it. I will try to hold the portal open for several more days after the sixth, as well. But there will probably be no need for it."

"Why not?" Tristan asked.

"Because by then, one of three things will have happened. Either you will have returned, or the Communion and Reckoning will have taken place and we all will be slaves to the Coven. Or the third, most likely possibility: Failee will have mishandled the incantations, improperly joined the two sides of the craft, and the world will have ceased to exist. In which case we will all be quite dead." His words hung in the air with great finality. To Tristan it seemed there was little more for any of them to say.

But the look in Faegan's eyes told the prince that the rogue wizard had yet more to reveal.

"The only contact I have ever had with the one who calls himself Geldon are the notes I receive tied to the legs of the pigeons," Faegan said thoughtfully. "It is quite possible that there truly is no Geldon, and these notes are simply another way for the Coven to get you—or all of us—to Parthalon, to be killed. I therefore feel it is important that before the two of you depart we attempt to discover the truth. If we are unsuccessful, then I am not sure that I can in good conscience send you there."

"And just how do we accomplish that?" Tristan asked. He appreciated what he was now beginning to recognize as the wizard's honesty, but he couldn't fathom how such a thing might be managed. Looking over at Wigg, the prince could see that the Lead Wizard himself was looking intrigued.

"Assuming that Geldon indeed exists, I plan to search out and find the true intentions of his heart," Faegan said softly.

Wigg's eyebrow came up. "I have never heard of such a thing. Just how do you intend to do it—especially from this far away?"

"There is an incantation of the Vagaries, one that actually allows another to *feel* the intentions of the subject. This is not the same as telepathy. We will not be speaking to his mind, only probing it. He will feel our presence but will be uncertain of what is happening. If all goes as I hope, I will be able to enter the heart and mind of Geldon, and then we shall know. And, as proof to you of my actually doing this, Wigg's mind shall accompany my own in this practice of the craft."

"But if the incantation is of the Vagaries, will Wigg not then die?" Tristan pressed anxiously. "He has both taken the wizard's vows and accepted the death enchantments."

"Wigg will not be harmed because it is not he who will be performing the incantation," Faegan said with another smile. "Only I shall be doing that. Wigg's mind will simply be feeling the same things my mind is, and also sensing my thoughts." The rogue wizard's smile broadened a bit. "Wigg's mind will be, as they say, simply along for the ride."

Tristan remained highly skeptical. "If this so-called testing of Geldon's heart can indeed be accomplished, then why didn't you do so before you started sending him messages?" he asked the wizard in the chair. "Surely that would have made more sense."

"Well done." Faegan smiled at the prince. "But it was not so simple a choice as that. You see, I was hoping that you and Wigg would make your way here. I could have tested Geldon earlier to set my own mind at ease, but then I would not have dared risk doing it again for your benefit. It is conceivable that the Coven may detect the intrusion, especially Failee. If that is the case, then doing it once is all we can afford. To do otherwise might tip our hand. Failee is nothing if not brilliant, you know."

"And how is this accomplished from such a great distance?" Wigg asked. It was apparent that his curiosity was now in full bloom.

"I must be either touching each of you or touching something that is personal to each of you, such as one of your possessions."

"You can certainly reach out and touch Wigg," Tristan responded, "but how can you touch anything of Geldon's? We have nothing like that."

"Oh, but we do," Faegan said. He reached out and picked up the parchment scroll. "We have his handwriting. It doesn't get much more personal than that." The crippled wizard looked across the table at Wigg. "Shall we begin?"

Wigg raised his eyebrow. Then he sighed slightly in resignation. "Very well," he answered.

"Bring your chair next to mine and take my hand," Faegan ordered. Feeling across the scroll's handwritten words, he stopped his fingertips upon Geldon's signature at the bottom. With Wigg's hand in his own and his fingers touching the scroll, the rogue wizard closed his eyes.

"Shut your eyes," he said to Wigg. "There is nothing else for you to do," he added drily, "except to make sure you do not interfere. To do so is to invite the wrath of the Vagaries. Otherwise, I think you will find this to be most interesting."

Almost immediately the familiar azure aura began to engulf them both as it slowly grew in size and intensity, its light eventually blotting out almost everything else in the room. Tristan could barely see the two wizards through it, and sat there spellbound as it increased even farther.

Wigg felt his mind begin to drift slowly, as if it were traveling somewhere, leaving his body behind. Despite the fact that his eyes were closed he could see haze of the brightest azure, and blue and lapis clouds billowing all around his consciousness. *What an extraordinary sensation,* he thought as he took in the added sensation of his consciousness gaining speed, rushing intently toward something, soaring through the billowing, parting azure clouds.

And then, quite suddenly, the Lead Wizard could also sense the presence of Faegan's mind as their separate consciousnesses seemed to search each other out in the luxurious turquoise mist and finally join. Then, as one, they sensed yet a different energy, a separate and distinct intelligence apart from their own.

Will this be the heart of Geldon? Wigg wondered as he rushed blindingly forward into the lapis fog. *Or is Faegan indeed a traitor and I have allowed him to deliver my mind to the twisted, demented soul of Failee?*

Emotions began to pour over him. Powerful, male emotions. *Geldon,* he suddenly heard Faegan's mental voice say. *We have found him.*

As he felt Faegan begin to probe Geldon's mind and heart, the emotions coming to the Lead Wizard became overpowering. But they were not *his* feelings, he realized. Rather, they were those of the other there with them. The one they had been seeking. And it was one sentiment, single and irresistible, that surpassed all others: hatred.

A hatred of women. No, Wigg realized. Not hatred of all women, but only several. Only four. The four sorceresses of the Coven.

But not for Shailiha.

Then, from out of the turquoise mist, another seething emotion erupted into the wizard's consciousness. Pain. But what kind of pain, and why? The agony kept coming and coming, as if it had been there for centuries and its owner never had the slightest hope of ever being released from it. And then Wigg recognized it.

Slavery. The pain, both mental and physical, of being placed into servitude and bondage, with the hideous prospect of it continuing for all eternity.

We have touched Geldon's heart, and his motives are true.

Yes, Faegan's mental voice responded. *Our task here is complete.*

Wigg felt Faegan's mind detach itself from his own, and the magnificent azure cloud banks began to retreat. He opened his eyes to find himself at the rogue wizard's dining table.

Wigg's breathing was short, and his vision was taking its time readjusting to the light of the room; but otherwise he felt fine. He turned his ancient, aquamarine eyes to Faegan's. "Magnificent," he whispered. "I believe you. And I believe in the dwarf who sends you messages. He hates both the Coven and his bondage as much as any one person ever could."

Faegan smiled. "I believe him also," he answered. "An interesting experience, is it not?"

Tristan sat there stunned, still unsure of what had just transpired. "Is it true?" he asked quietly. "Did you really find his heart, from across the Sea of Whispers?"

"Yes," Wigg answered simply. "This much of it I believe."

He turned toward Faegan and looked him hard in the eyes. "But if the prince and I are to put our lives in your hands, there is still one more thing of which I must be sure." He stood from his chair and looked down meaningfully at the crippled wizard. "I'm sure you know what it is," he added. "And if everything you have said is true, you won't mind my request."

Perplexed, Tristan watched Wigg as he stood there waiting for the rogue wizard's response. "I fully understand," Faegan finally said. "Tristan, you might want to brace yourself for what you are about to see. I have had only small success in solving my problem. Even the waters of the Caves did little to heal me of the results of the Coven's cruelty."

Wigg calmly reached down to grasp the hem of Faegan's robe and slowly lifted it up and over the old wizard's knees. It was at that moment that the prince fully understood in his heart what he had known in his mind. And what it was that Wigg wanted to be sure of.

Faegan's legs were a gruesome sight. The skin was gone completely, and much of the muscle mass looked as if it had been literally shredded away by someone or something, as if some awful beast had repeatedly attacked both legs with its teeth and claws. The remaining bright red muscles throbbed visibly, and Tristan could see what he took to be exposed nerves and blood vessels running up and down their lengths. In truth the legs were more than half gone, and the prince initially wondered how the wizard could possibly stand the pain, much less keep from dying of infection. And then he remembered. This was Faegan, the rogue wizard, protected by the life enchantments. "Master," his gnomes called him. Since first meeting Shannon the Small and Michael the Meager, Tristan had realized that the term "Master" was given by them only out of great reverence. Tristan suddenly had a newfound and even deeper respect for the crippled old wizard in the chair, the one who loved riddles so. Wigg replaced the robe and slowly stood back a little.

"I had to know," he said softly to Faegan. "Even now, as it is, I cannot be completely sure you are telling us the truth. But we have no choice." Wigg looked over at the prince. "We go. Now. Agreed?"

"Yes," Tristan said.

"You realize this could be nothing more than a ruse to put us into the hands of the Coven?"

"Yes," Tristan said firmly. "But I believe him." He looked at Faegan. "I have a request before we leave."

"Yes?" Faegan asked.

"I would like to speak to Shannon the Small."

"Very well," Faegan agreed. He turned his chair to face Michael the Meager, who had been standing dutifully in the corner all of this time, hearing everything. "Run and fetch Shannon," Faegan said simply. "Hurry."

"Yes, Master," Michael replied. In a heartbeat, he was gone.

Almost immediately Michael returned with Shannon in tow, and the two of them entered the room. "The Chosen One wishes to speak to you," Faegan said. He turned his chair so that he could look at each of them at once, curious about Tristan's request.

Tristan looked down at the gnome, the same one who had challenged him at the bridge, bitten into his leg, and led him into the Tunnel of Bones. He smiled at the little one. "Wigg and I are going away for a while," he said, taking a step closer to Shannon. "But we will be back soon. I called you here because I want to know you will take good care of Pilgrim for me while I'm gone."

"I already am," Shannon said eagerly, typically puffing out his chest with pride. "Pilgrim is already settled down in our stable. I brushed him real good, and gave him extra oats. I think he likes me." The little man beamed.

"I know he does." Tristan smiled. "Make sure to exercise him, and treat him well. He'll do anything for a carrot, and likes to have his ears rubbed."

"Yes, Prince Tristan," Shannon said.

The prince smile broadly and then narrowed his eyes, deciding. "Oh, and there's one other thing," he said sternly.

"Yes?"

"If I should never come back, Pilgrim is yours. Yours to keep."

Shannon looked as if a storm had just passed through his little face and body. His eyes began to tear. No one had ever given him anything as wonderful as Pilgrim. *The horse of the Chosen One,* he thought, amazed.

"Thank you, Master," Shannon said to the prince. "But I truly hope I never claim that right."

"You called me 'Master,'" Tristan said, smiling to him. "I don't think you meant to say that. There is only one master here."

"Pardon me," the little one said, looking sheepishly at Faegan and then to the prince. "But I'm not sure that's true anymore."

Tristan smiled and walked over to his chair, gently lifting the baldric and dreggan from it and lowering the sword back into place over his right shoulder. He checked his dirks to be sure they were all there, and then slowly walked back to the window to look at the ocean. They had been talking all night, and the sun was just beginning to come up in the east. His nostrils took in the smell of salt that came in on the sea breeze.

Automatically reaching over his right shoulder to grasp the hilt of the dreggan, he felt for the hidden button there. The sword felt good in his hand, despite the fact that it was the same weapon that had killed his father. *Will it also become the sword that kills my sister?* he wondered. He pulled out the medallion that lay beneath his black leather vest and looked at the lion and broadsword engraved upon it. The last gift from his parents. He tucked it back into his vest.

He turned around to see Faegan quietly handing Wigg a pewter locket on a silver chain. It was square, small, and rather flat. Wigg put it around his neck and tucked it into his robes. Too tired to ask, Tristan once again turned his attention toward the sea.

"Where will the portal appear?" he asked without turning around.

"Right in front of you," he heard Faegan say. And no sooner had the words come to the prince's ears than a swirling azure vortex began to appear directly in front of him, only two steps away. It was beautiful.

It revolved constantly before him, an incredible swirling mass of color and light, and he could feel it beckoning, pleading with his endowed blood to enter it.

He then felt as much as saw Wigg standing next to him, also looking into the vortex. He felt the Lead Wizard take his hand, and the two of them stepped forward into the swirling mass and were gone.

PART V

The Recluse

Twenty-one

It is not the absence of evil that perpetuates goodness. That alone is the province of the teachings of the Vigors, and is found to be most true in the hearts of kind men of endowed blood. It is, however, the absence of goodness that allows evil to survive.

—AXIOM OF THE DIRECTORATE OF WIZARDS

Failee stood in silence, slowly looking about the floor and ceiling of the great, round, subterranean room. The First Mistress was dressed in a gown of the palest green, the Pentangle of golden thread clearly visible upon her left breast as always. The Paragon hung around her neck, gently refracting the light of the room and sending out spots of blood red that danced happily about, as if looking for a place to come to rest.

Sister Shailiha stood next to her. Her maternity gown, a deep shade of blue, also displayed the beloved five-pointed star. *For over three hundred years this room has remained unused,* Failee mused. *But in just six more days its purpose will be fulfilled.*

The First Mistress continued to examine the chamber—the room that had been built for one purpose only so long ago. This was the Sanctuary, and it was one of her finest achievements.

The chamber was a perfect circle, some sixty feet in diameter, and the domed marble ceiling rose at least seventy feet into the air. In the center of the dome was a small circular opening about three feet across, from which could be seen the last remaining rays of pillared sunlight as they dashed down into the room. Golden and unrestrained, they brightly illuminated a small spot in the center of the floor. Despite the fact that the Sanctuary was far below the ground level of the Recluse, the opening in the center of the ceiling ran vertically all the way up through each level of the castle and finally to the roof, where it opened to the sky.

The walls, ceiling, and floor were made of the finest white marble, and they glistened as the light from the many wall sconces flickered and began to take over from the slowly vanishing rays that came through the ceiling. Inlaid into the white marble of the floor was a very large, perfectly proportioned Pentangle in the blackest of marble. Each point of the five-pointed star touched the outer edge of the floor where it met the wall, and over each of the points sat a raised throne of solid black marble. In the very center of the Pentangle, directly below the opening in the ceiling, was a raised white altar. As the final rays of sunlight lost their battle with the coming night and slowly vanished away into the softer, more golden lamplight of the room, in the total silence of this place Failee could begin to smell the unmistakable fragrances of long-awaited hopes and dreams. Silent. Waiting. And unstoppable.

She had been coming alone to this room for each of the last three days and would continue to do so for each of the next six until the day of the Communion, and the Reckoning that would follow it. She came here to meditate silently and prepare her mind for what was to come, and to draw upon her knowledge of the craft that she had ripped away from Faegan's consciousness those many years ago. She had begun to realize that she would also need to incorporate much of the Vigors into the incantation for it to prove effective, but was certain that she could do it.

Failee turned to look at Shailiha, who was obviously entranced with the room. Failee had brought her here today to acquaint her with the room and to make her feel at home in this, the most important of her new surroundings. The other three members of the Coven would join them there shortly.

It had been only a few days since Shailiha had successfully endured the last of the Chimeran Agonies, but her ardor to become one of the Coven had already surpassed even Failee's wildest dreams. The young woman was highly intelligent, possessing an unimaginable desire to learn the craft and an equal, if not even higher, desire to see their dreams through to the conclusion—to the victory that they had waited for so long to come. She was one of them now, and it showed in her eyes, her voice, her speech, and her mannerisms. And one day, because of the supreme quality of her blood, she would become their leader. The First

Mistress smiled. They were finally five, and with Shailiha's child, they would be six.

"Beautiful, isn't it?" Failee said to the younger woman at her side.

Shailiha took a few steps forward, speaking as she walked. "The Sanctuary is even more breathtaking than your description, Mistress," she said. Her hazel eyes were alight with curiosity and desire. "Which one is to be mine?" she asked, as she walked to one of the heavy black marble thrones.

"The one to your right will be yours at first," Failee told her. "But when the day comes for you to lead us, your throne will be the one that is now nearest me." She looked back at the black throne in which she would sit during the Communion, the one she would gladly one day give up to Shailiha.

"May I, Mistress?" Shailiha asked.

"Of course, my child," Failee said happily. "It's yours."

The First Mistress watched hungrily as the young woman walked to the first throne Failee had indicated and carefully took the two steps up and into it, gently arranging her maternity gown about her. Where it fell over her satin slippers, the dark-blue gown contrasted strikingly with the highly polished black marble.

Shailiha looked rather commandingly into Failee's face. "I belong here," she said simply. "This is my destiny; I know it. My blood tells me so."

My blood tells me so, Failee thought with an ecstatic heart. *Excellent. Not only have the Chimeran Agonies commanded her, but now her own blood does so, as well. There will be no turning back for this one.* She smiled to herself. *The Chosen One shall come, but shall be preceded by another. The twin. And now she is mine.*

"How appropriate," Succiu's voice suddenly called out from the other side of the room. "You look as if you were born to it, my Sister, which of course you were." Failee and Shailiha turned to see the other three members of the Coven standing in the doorway to the room. There was only one way in and out, and it was connected to a long series of circular steps that led down from the Recluse above. The second mistress was dressed in a black leather vest and breeches, both tight fitting and leaving little to the imagination. Black elbow-length gauntlets and high-heeled knee boots also in shiny black leather completed the picture, and she carried a long riding crop in her left hand. Beads of moisture could be seen on her brow and upper breasts, and Failee knew immediately that Succiu had just come from one of her "training" sessions with some slave from the Stables. But the second mistress' countenance looked frustrated and angry, rather than showing the usual satisfaction that typically followed such an interlude. Vona and Zabarra, each dressed more appropriately in a gown, followed dutifully along behind her as her heels clicked and clacked upon the marble floor, the crisp, staccato sounds resonating commandingly throughout the room.

Succiu walked directly to the throne in which Shailiha was sitting, smiled, and then ran the frayed end of her riding crop up and over the cool, black stone of the great chair, gently brushing first the hem and then the sleeve of the princess' gown. Shailiha recoiled slightly, but showed no fear. The second mistress smiled. "You are indeed lovely," she said, smirking. "Sitting in that throne gives you a certain, how should I say, 'attractiveness.' I look forward to knowing you even better after the delivery of your child."

Succiu turned her head back toward Failee, throwing her long, dark hair over the opposite shoulder. "I have a surprise for you, First Mistress," she said. Her demeanor was beginning to return to something closer to humility. "Tell me, have they been fed yet?" she asked. Failee shook her head.

"Good." Succiu smiled back. "That was the other reason you brought Sister Shailiha here, was it not? To show her the additional use for this chamber?"

Failee looked to Shailiha and saw the expected look of puzzlement upon her face.

"What additional use?" Shailiha asked. "Why was I not told?" *Good,* Failee thought. *She is beginning to assert her authority even in the presence of one as strong as Succiu.*

"There is a second use for this chamber," Failee said. "Beings live here, in this area. Beings that you have not yet been shown. They are additional protection for this most important of rooms."

The First Mistress turned her eyes to Succiu. "And just what is your surprise?" she asked.

"I brought them dinner," Succiu said coyly. She turned back to the empty doorway and the dark hallway that led upward from it. "You may bring him in now, Geldon," she called out. "And be quick about it or you will taste my lash, as he has."

The remaining four mistresses turned to see Geldon emerge from the darkness, holding the jeweled chain that ran from his collar in one hand, and a larger, dirtier chain in the other. The larger chain led into the hallway behind him. Finally a man emerged, beaten and bloody, wearing only a loincloth. The chain was attached to manacles around the man's wrists. Once in the Sanctuary, he collapsed to the floor and curled up into a ball, sobbing. From where she stood, Succiu could see the Pentangle that she had so carefully carved into his back two months earlier with her whip. It was covered in fresh blood.

"He has failed in his duties to me yet again," she said nastily, walking over to the slave, her long legs straddling his body as he writhed about in pain on the cold marble floor. "I am through with him." She looked up at Geldon. "Drag him to the center of the floor."

Geldon strained and groaned against the chain as he drew the slave to the center of the marble floor, leaving a winding path of sticky red blood behind. When he reached the center of the Pentangle, he dropped the slave's chain and then dutifully held up the end of his own jeweled leash to his mistress, wondering if she would chain him down, as usual.

"Not now," she sneered. "I'm having too much fun." She walked over to the slave called Stefan and put the shiny heel of her right boot against his throat, pinning him to the floor. Geldon's mind painfully flew back in time to that night in the Ghetto when she had first found him—when she had also put her heel against his throat, nearly killing him. He looked away in shame. He felt guilty for having brought the slave here, but what else could he have done? He had to make everything seem normal. The Chosen One and the Lead Wizard would be here soon. Master Faegan had promised. Nothing must jeopardize that. Nothing must give any hint of what was to come. *But I swear I will live to see this bitch die,* he thought. *Even if I must somehow kill her myself.*

Succiu turned her exotic, almond-shaped eyes up toward her mistress as she increased the pressure against the slave's neck. "Do you agree?" she asked.

"Indeed," Failee said, pleased. "I think they will be most happy with him."

The First Mistress raised her right hand upward, and the room began to change. A vertical seam in the white marble wall directly opposite the doorway began to split open, and from ceiling to floor the wall slid apart to reveal a dark space beyond. The floor of this new room was so far below the floor of the sanctuary that Shailiha could not see it. Nor could she see any steps leading down.

Failee looked at Geldon. "Bring him to the edge," she said.

"Yes, Mistress," Geldon gurgled.

As Geldon struggled to drag Stefan toward the opening, Shailiha came down off her throne and joined the others at the edge of what she could now see was a pit. At first she could see nothing, but then her eyes began to adjust to the darkness and she was finally able to pick the pit's inhabitants out in the gloom.

They were pairs of eyes, yellow and slanted. They seemed to glow. And there were hundreds of them. Occasionally she could hear low, reptilian hissing sounds, but she could see nothing but the yellow eyes shining menacingly out of the gloom.

"Good evening, my pets," the First Mistress cooed lovingly into the darkness below her. Had she not been one of the Coven, she might just as well have been doting over a friend's newborn child, or some beloved family pet. Shailiha turned to look at her.

"Sister Succiu has graciously brought you a very special dinner for this evening," Failee continued. "If this one is not enough, I shall supply you with more." The hissing became noticeably louder, and the yellow eyes crowded together just below the spot where the sorceresses were standing. Failee turned to Succiu and nodded.

Succiu glared at Geldon, who had by now managed to drag the inert slave to the edge. She narrowed her eyes, smiled, and pointed to Stefan. "Throw him in," she said simply.

Geldon stood there in front of his mistress, speechless. She had ordered him to perform many depraved acts over the course of the last three centuries, but until this moment, she had never ordered him to kill anyone. He looked back at her, through her, as if she didn't exist. He simply couldn't do it.

Succiu's reaction to his doubt was immediate. She backhanded him as hard as she could, sending him sprawling onto the floor, into the bright-red blood that Stefan had left on the otherwise pristine white marble. "Throw him in," she ordered, "or you will follow him."

I have no choice, he thought to himself. *If I die now, our plans will be for nothing, and all will be lost.* Slowly rising to his feet, he forced himself to slap Stefan's face and pull on the chains, finally coaxing the semiconscious man to stand erect on the edge of the pit. Geldon walked up behind him and waited for Succiu's order.

And then the unexpected happened.

"Wait!" he heard one of the women demand. Turning, he could see that it was Shailiha.

All four mistresses simultaneously turned their concerned eyes upon their newest Sister, examining her face for clues. Failee's heart began to race, fearing that some remnant of the princess' past life had somehow come to the fore, repulsed by what was about to happen. She looked calmly into Shailiha's face. "Yes, my dear?" she asked politely.

Shailiha looked down at the many pairs of yellow eyes in the pit and then back at the slave. Her breath was quick and ragged. "Let me do it," she whispered.

Failee cast a knowing, relieved look at Succiu. "Of course," she said to the princess. "You may do the honors. It is perhaps the most fitting thing, since this is your first trip to the Sanctuary."

Shailiha walked carefully to stand behind Stefan, sneered at Geldon, and then rather roughly pushed the dwarf aside, as if to make sure he was not about to rob her of her request. She smiled and closed her eyes, feeling the endowed blood rushing through her veins with more sheer joy than she had ever known.

With a strong, quick push, she sent the slave over the edge.

Immediately the many pairs of eyes descended on the body as it tumbled headlong into the darkness, and the screams from the slave seemed to go on forever as they echoed back and forth in the chamber. Shailiha heard the moist, violent ripping and tearing of flesh, and then more screams radiated upward before all went quiet. Looking up she saw that some of the mistresses had been splattered with blood, she included. Succiu placed an index finger into a blood spot on one of her leather gauntlets and touched it to her tongue, smiling. Shailiha smiled back.

Geldon lowered his head, and a tear began to form in each of his eyes and run down the lengths of his cheeks. *One tear for the slave,* he thought. *And one tear for the princess this new sorceress used to be.*

Twenty-two

I t took Tristan a long time to awaken. Several times he felt himself drifting in and out of consciousness before actually coming to his senses. It had been a maddening experience, knowing that he desperately needed to reenter the world but at the same time also being held back from it. Finally, he woke up completely.

He was lying prone on the dirty, cold, wooden floor of a small dark room. A fetid, animal-like smell hung in the air. He was not in pain from his journey through the vortex, but his senses had been dulled and his mind swam sickeningly, as though he had consumed too much wine. He managed to sit up—and the point of a sword appeared out of nowhere, aimed at his throat, silently daring him to move again. The shiny, silver blade twinkled in the weak moonlight that came through the room's only window.

"Identify yourself," a male voice said calmly.

Before answering Tristan risked a quick look around. Against one wall, he could just make out what seemed to be a great many rows of some kind of small cubicles. The only other furniture was a small writing desk and a chair. Wigg lay on the floor a little distance away, curled up into a ball and still unconscious, the way a child might be seen peacefully sleeping in a crib.

Groaning inwardly, the prince realized that he was defenseless. Having worn the dirks across his right shoulder for so many years now he knew immediately when they were not present. The baldric that normally housed his dreggan was feather light. *It is no doubt my own dreggan that is now at my throat,* he observed cautiously.

A strange noise was coming from the wall that held the cubicles. Turning his full attention to the odd sound, Tristan realized it was the simultaneous cooing of many birds. *Parthalon,* he thought. *The Ghetto of the Shunned. Geldon's aviary. It has to be.*

Moving very carefully, he sat up a little straighter. If he needed to try to overpower this man he would have to move fast. "Is this the Ghetto?" he asked anxiously. "Are you Geldon?"

No answer came. But his eyes were adjusting to the dim light. He could see his robed and hooded captor, and the dreggan that was still pointed at his throat, but he could not make out the man's face.

Finally, the other man spoke. "If you ask one more question before answering mine, you will have a hole where your throat used to be." The dreggan moved even closer to Tristan's neck. "Identify yourself!"

The prince's mind raced. He looked to Wigg, still unconscious on the floor just a little bit away from him. It might as well have been one hundred leagues. Tristan needed the old one now, but there was no way to reach him to wake him up. *If I tell the cloaked one who I am before knowing his identity, I could be signing our death warrants,* he thought. *But the longer I hold out and tell this man nothing, the greater the chance that we will be killed anyway.* And then he had an even more urgent thought. *Wigg is unconscious. While he is like that he cannot hide our blood from the Coven.*

"You must allow me to awaken my friend first," he said brazenly. "Then, if you don't like what I say, you can be as creative as you wish and kill us both any way you want." He wished he could see the man's eyes.

"No," his captor returned angrily. "Insolence does not constitute an answer." Whatever patience his captor once had was clearly gone. Tristan thought he detected a slight movement of the man's right hand; he tried not to flinch as the tip of the dreggan shot out its extra foot, the familiar, deadly ring clanging out into the darkness of the room. The sword's blade now rested coldly against the side of his neck. All the other man would have to do to cut his throat would be to turn the blade slightly inward, and Tristan would soon bleed to death, his jugular severed neatly in half.

"Last chance," the voice said from inside the hood.

Tristan took a deep breath. "I am Prince Tristan of Eutracia."

"Of what House?"

"The House of Galland. Son of Nicholas and Morganna, now dead. Twin brother to Shailiha." At the mention of his sister's name, Tristan thought he saw the other man relax slightly.

"Otherwise known as?" his captor asked.

Tristan's mind went blank. He didn't know how to respond to such a question. Then he realized what the man was searching for.

"Otherwise known as the Chosen One," he said quietly. He suddenly realized that this was the first time he had ever referred to himself as such.

The man in the cloak freed one hand from the sword and reached out to pluck an unlit candle from somewhere out of the darkness. He placed the candle on the floor, about a foot away from the seated prince. Striking a match, the man lit the candle, and the room began to brighten. But it was still not bright enough for the prince to see the other man's face within the folds of the dark hood.

"The Chosen One is said to wear a medallion around his neck," the man said calmly. "If you are he, then show it to me now." He moved the dreggan slightly away from Tristan's flesh.

Tristan bent over slightly and reached into his vest, pulling out the medallion, lowering it over the flame of the candle. The familiar images of the lion and the broadsword twinkled in the dim, golden glow.

"Who gave it to you?"

"My mother, Morganna, queen of Eutracia." Tristan tucked the precious bit of gold back under his vest.

"And who is the old one?" the cloaked man asked, indicating the wizard lying on the floor.

"He is Wigg, Lead Wizard of the Directorate of Wizards. He is also my friend."

The man's hand on the hilt of the sword moved again, and the extra length of the dreggan clanged back into place. The blade was lowered to the floor.

"Thank you," the one in the cloak said, almost kindly. "Please forgive my actions, but we had to be sure."

The man then walked over to the other side of the room, where he gathered several more candles and began lighting them one by one. As the brightness increased Tristan could see that this was not the hunchback Geldon: This man was tall and straight backed. The dark-yellow robe he wore was worn and torn in many places, but seemed to be clean.

"Who are you?" Tristan asked, standing up and testing the muscles in his legs.

"I am Ian, Geldon's friend. I am also the keeper of the birds. It is a great pleasure to meet you finally." Ian turned around, lowering his hood, and looked the prince in the face.

What Tristan saw made him narrow his eyes and take an unconscious step backward.

Ian was about the same age as the prince and had bright blue eyes, but that was where any similarity ended. Those eyes and his straw-colored blond hair were the only normal things about him. His face and neck, where it disappeared into his robe, had been ravaged by some terrible disease such as the prince had never seen. A glance at his hands showed them to be the same—all sores and gray flesh.

"I'm sorry," the prince said immediately. "I wasn't expecting . . ."

"I understand," Ian said gracefully. "It is called leprosy, and it is ultimately fatal. I have had the illness for about two years. Although not everyone becomes infected, there is no cure. But don't be alarmed for yourself or your friend. Your endowed blood will protect you from it—Master Faegan told us so. He also told us that there is no such thing a leprosy in Eutracia," he added a bit wistfully.

"Wrong on two counts," Wigg's familiar voice called out from the other side of the room. Tristan looked over to see the wizard sitting up, obviously in more distress than the prince had been when he first awakened.

Tristan immediately went to him, and could see that the wizard appeared flushed and was breathing more heavily than normal. *This can't simply be the aftereffects of the vortex,* Tristan thought. *Wigg is as strong as I have ever been.* He motioned for Ian to bring him the chair, and he helped Wigg into it.

"What's wrong?" he asked anxiously. "Are you not well?"

"I am well," Wigg said breathlessly. He looked up into Tristan's face. "The vortex was an interesting experience, wasn't it?" He looked quickly around the room, and then directly at Ian. A hint of recognition showed in the wizard's face. He looked back up at the prince. "At least we didn't turn blue, like Nicodemus," he said, one corner of his mouth turning cynically upward.

Tristan smiled. "No, that's true. But why do you seem to be so tired?"

"Can't you guess?"

He is forever testing me, Tristan thought. *Forever my mentor.* But instinctively he knew the answer. "You're hiding our blood, aren't you? That's what is draining your energy."

"Yes," Wigg said simply. "And the effort required is more than I had originally imagined. The quality of your blood is so exceptionally high that it is extremely difficult to disguise. But I should be able to manage, especially after some time has gone by and my gift has accustomed itself to the strain." He gave the prince a harder, more serious look. "It is important that your fabled impetuousness does not get us into anything you yourself cannot get us out of," he ordered. He let out a long breath and rubbed the back of his neck, stretching his muscles. "I will not be able to use my gift to help you. Not and continue to hide us from the

428 † *Robert Newcomb*

Coven. You have a very big heart, Tristan. Just don't put it into the wrong kinds of places while we are here, as you have been known to do." The wizard's infamous eyebrow shot upward.

Wigg's remarks stung, but the prince knew that the old one was right. Wigg was no doubt referring to the day when, against the wizard's better judgment, Tristan had insisted upon helping the woman they thought was Lillith, a decision that almost cost them both their lives. But the hunger to kill the ones who had murdered his family burned as hotly as ever inside him. He knew he would be able to make no promises as to his actions when the time came.

Ian walked over to where Wigg was sitting, obviously in awe of the wizard. "When I was explaining leprosy to the prince, you said I was wrong about two things," he said, obviously concerned. "What were they?"

Wigg looked up into the blue eyes, and then to the lesions and gray skin that covered the young man's face. *I have not seen this horror for almost three hundred years,* he thought. *Everywhere the Coven goes, they bring nothing but suffering.*

"First, there *was* leprosy in the kingdom of Eutracia," Wigg began. "The Coven induced it into the population during the war, and then dispersed rumors throughout the land that it was an intentional by-product of male endowed blood. Their plans proved to be quite successful, and we knew we had to find a cure to reverse both the physical and psychological damage that had been done." He looked at Ian, anticipating the effect of his next words. "We found it," he said compassionately.

Ian fell to his knees in front of the wizard's chair. "You mean to say that there is a cure?" he asked. His eyes were full of tears—both of wonder and of hope—as he looked beseechingly at Wigg. "Why would Master Faegan not inform me of such a thing?"

"I am sure it was because he knew he could never come here himself, and therefore could see no reason to raise your hopes," Wigg said. *But he knew that I would tell you.* He smiled to himself. *Faegan always had other, more compassionate motives hidden beneath the obvious. Even three hundred years ago.*

"There is an incantation that may end your suffering," he explained, affectionately placing one hand on the young man's head. "But please understand, it does not always work. And, of course, I cannot perform it now for fear of the Coven detecting our presence. But if we survive all of this, I may be able to help."

"Your word is enough, Lead Wizard," Ian said. He stood up on shaky legs and smiled slightly, wiping the tears from his cheeks.

Tristan reached down to the floor and recovered his dreggan, which he slipped back into its scabbard. "Where are my dirks?" he asked Ian.

Ian gave him a quick nod of understanding and walked to the small writing desk. Opening the single drawer he removed all twelve of the knives and handed them to the prince. Tristan placed them into the quiver, glad to feel their comforting weight over his right shoulder. He silently cursed himself for not having brought even more of them. These would just have to do.

The prince walked to the wall of cubicles that held the many enchanted pigeons. He had to admit that they were beautiful birds. "How many of them are there?" he asked Ian.

"Over one hundred now," Ian said, his face darkening with concern. "They are becoming quite a responsibility."

Despite Ian's words, Tristan could tell that caring for these birds had become a labor of love. Now he remembered Ian's supposed friend. So far all had gone as planned, but he still had his suspicions. "Where is Geldon?" he asked suddenly.

"He waited for you as long as he dared," Ian said. "He runs a great risk coming here, to the aviary. Even as it is, he cannot be assured that she will send him out of the castle on any given night. Sometimes she requires his presence for her . . . amusements." His face blushed around the many red lesions. "He suffers greatly," he added. "As we all have."

"Is he expected to return tonight?" Wigg asked. He seemed more composed now, no longer flushed, his breathing calmer.

"We are hopeful. I know that is not what you wanted to hear, but it is all I can offer you."

"Beginning with today, there are only six days remaining until the Blood Communion," Tristan said, rubbing his brow. He scowled and shook his head, anxious beyond words to leave this place and accomplish what he had come here to do. "And just what are we supposed to do until then?"

"We wait here, in this room," Ian said. "Going out into the Ghetto for any reason is an unjustified risk. We will wait here all day until nightfall, and then we'll see. When—if—he comes, you will leave with him for the Recluse."

The Recluse. Shailiha.

Tristan looked out the lone, sad little window of the room that was to be his prison for at least two more days as the sun began its slow climb and the rays of his first morning in Parthalon crept silently into the aviary.

Tristan's first day in Parthalon passed with an odd combination of maddening boredom and excruciating tension. Unable to leave the room, the three of them spent most of the day talking. Wigg was especially eager to glean from Ian all that he could about the nation of Parthalon, but it soon became apparent that Ian's helpfulness would be limited, since he had been born inside the Ghetto and had never ventured beyond its walls. Adding to that frustration was the warmth of the day, and the stuffiness of the aviary; the smell of the birds was a suffocating blanket of mustiness, and their cooing eventually became a constant annoyance.

At least Ian and Geldon had had the foresight to keep some food in the aviary. Now, fortified by a meager meal of bread, cheese, and water, Tristan gazed out the solitary window at the dark of night, anxious to be off and away from this confining place. It was close to midnight. The stars in the sky twinkled just as brightly here as they did in Eutracia, the three red moons casting their familiar crimson glow upon the land. *The dwarf must come soon,* he thought, *or we will have lost another entire day.* The wait was becoming interminable.

It was Wigg who first heard the slow, shuffling steps coming up the stairway. He stood from his chair and pointed to the door. As Tristan silently positioned himself behind it and drew his dreggan, Wigg moved off into the shadows, and Ian stood before the door, ready to face whoever it was—in case it wasn't Geldon.

The footsteps abruptly stopped on the other side of the door, and silence reigned for several moments. Then the door began to open slowly, creaking as it turned on its rusted hinges. Halfway through its arc it abruptly stopped, yet no one entered the room. Finally Ian smiled and took a breath. "We were beginning to wonder," he said with obvious relief. He motioned to the wizard and prince that it was safe to show themselves, and as they emerged, a small, hooded figure stepped through the doorway.

The figure standing before Tristan in the relative gloom of the candles was not much taller than Faegan's gnomes. He wore a yellow robe just like the one Ian wore, albeit smaller. Tristan guessed that it had once belonged to someone else—a child, perhaps.

Without speaking, the dwarf named Geldon removed the yellow robe. Tristan could plainly see the hump in his back and the intensity that emanated from his small, piercing eyes. His hair was dark brown, and his ordinary-looking clothes were filthy and soaked through. But it was something else about the dwarf that commanded the prince's attention, and when he saw it he immediately felt empathy for Succiu's slave for over three hundred years.

Geldon's collar.

A wide band of shiny, black metal embedded with jewels encircled the dwarf's neck. Some of the gemstones Tristan had seen before, and some were completely foreign to him. The ornate luxury and obvious value of the jewels contrasted sharply with the intentionally brutal purpose of the collar. From a ring in the front ran a chain of about four feet which the dwarf was apparently forced to carry with him everywhere he went. *Three hundred years of such servitude and humiliation*, Tristan thought. *It is no wonder that he also wants them dead.* Geldon turned to look at the prince and the wizard, and then addressed Ian.

"You are sure of them?" he asked cautiously in a soft, low voice. Tristan watched in curiosity as water dripped from the dwarf's clothes to the floor of the aviary. "You asked them the prescribed questions?"

"Yes," Ian said. "They are who they claim to be."

Geldon walked to Wigg and looked him up and down as though he were examining a horse he was considering for purchase. "I have never seen a male with endowed blood," he said carefully, his eyes narrowed. "The only such experiences I have ever had are with the Coven, so you can therefore understand my apprehension at meeting yet another being with the gift." He paused for a moment, regarding the Lead Wizard as if trying to discern something. Finally he spoke once again.

"For some reason it seems as if I already know you," Geldon said softly as he continued to examine Wigg. "There came upon me a strange feeling today, something that I had never before experienced. Luckily I was not within close proximity to the Coven, for I am sure the look on my face was unusual, to say the least. It was as if a sudden storm passed through my consciousness, a storm that carried with it a ken of its own. It was you, wasn't it? Some use of the craft . . . somehow I can sense it was you now that your endowed presence stands before me."

"Yes," Wigg said, impressed with the acumen of the dwarf. "I was wondering if you would mention it; but if you hadn't, I would have told you. Faegan, your friend from across the sea, wanted to make sure of your motives before sending us here. It was both his consciousness and mine that you felt yesterday. He wanted to test the sincerity of your heart, and my consciousness accompanied his as proof of his task to the prince and myself. An interesting experience, wasn't it?"

Geldon raised an eyebrow knowingly and then, at Wigg's previous mention of the prince, turned his rapt attention to Tristan. "So it is to *you* they have anointed 'the Chosen One'? You and your sister have been the subject of a great deal of conversation at the Recluse over the course of the last three centuries, I can assure you. But I don't see very much that is special about you, except for the fact that you are weighed down with so many weapons I doubt you can move." He looked at the hilt of the prince's sword. "You carry a dreggan," he said rather thoughtfully.

"It was Kluge's," Tristan answered, a hard look in his eyes. "It is the sword that I was forced to use to kill my father." But he was not interested in discussing his weapons. Without further hesitation he demanded, "Tell me of my sister. Now."

Geldon turned and walked toward the pigeon coops with a worried look on his face, as though he could avoid the question by avoiding the man who had just asked it. He knew little of the person they called the Chosen One, but he knew enough from Faegan's messages to understand that this was not a man to be trifled with. He finally turned back to the prince. "Your sister is well," he said. "She has survived the third of the Chimeran Agonies, as I mentioned in my message to Master Faegan. But she is no longer the woman you knew, Tristan. She is one of them now, both heart and soul, and you must prepare yourself for that." The dwarf paused, as if not knowing how to continue. He was fully aware of the fact that the prince might eventually be forced to kill his sister, in addition to having already slain his father.

"She murdered an innocent slave yesterday," he continued, his head lowered slightly. "She enjoyed it, even asked for the privilege. I have seen several examples of her growing depravity, the same scourge of wickedness that inflicts each of the others except for Failee. I am truly sorry."

Tristan felt something deep inside of him slip, and the power of his blood immediately rose to entwine with his anger as his mind rebelled against the impossibility of the words the dwarf had just uttered.

"No!" he shouted at the dwarf, walking menacingly toward him. Instantly a dirk was in his right hand. "She could never have done such a thing! You lie! And if you lie about her, you are probably lying about everything else! I should kill you where you stand!" The razor-sharp knife pointed at the dwarf's throat.

Wigg immediately moved to stand between the two of them and looked the prince hard in the face. *Strong emotions awaken his blood,* he thought. *It will be this way until he is trained to control his gift.* "I think we should hear him out," the old one said compassionately. "It may be of help to us later. And without him we are lost, like it or not."

Tristan's countenance relaxed slightly, and he backed away. "Very well," he snarled through gritted teeth. "But I want to hear it all, every bit. He is to omit nothing. And if the dwarf values his life, it needs to be the truth."

Geldon backed away, realizing that he was truly glad still to be alive. He gave a quick look of appreciation to the wizard. He walked to the chair, sat down, and told them of the Coven's meeting in the Sanctuary, and of Shailiha's execution of the slave named Stefan. He also went into detail about the Recluse and the Stables, where the Coven's slaves were kept, and how those slaves were abused. As the prince demanded, Geldon left nothing out, even the most graphic of his knowledge. When he finally finished, the room was embarrassingly silent.

Wigg was the first to speak. "And just how do you propose to get us into the Recluse?" he asked. "Your message to Faegan said that the Minion guard has been doubled." His right eyebrow arched up. "What do you propose to do, just walk us in through the front gate?"

"Actually, yes," Geldon replied. He smiled, enjoying the looks of astonishment on their faces. "But I have horses hidden in the woods. We'll ride in. It's much more civilized."

"Explain," Tristan ordered. There was little patience in him for a dwarfed hunchback who wished to be cryptic.

"Sometimes I procure their slaves from the towns, and sometimes from the Ghetto," Geldon continued. "Mistress Succiu believes me to be procuring new slaves for the Stables right now." He smiled again. "And that is what I intend do. The two of you are going into the Recluse as slaves of the Coven."

"Are you mad?" Tristan exclaimed. "We will be recognized immediately! They would enjoy nothing better!" He looked at Wigg. The wizard had crossed his arms, placed his weight on one foot, and was scowling blatantly—for once in complete agreement with the prince.

"It is considered quite an ordinary occurrence for me to bring new slaves into the Stables," Geldon said. "And they are most usually taken in through the front gate. In addition, I have a dark cloak for each of you, to cover your bodies and hide your faces. When we have escaped the Ghetto we will discard the leper's robes, put on the darker cloaks, and ride right in through the front gate. I even have chains to wrap about your wrists to add to the effect. Once inside the Recluse we will proceed directly to the Stables, so as not to appear out of context. There you will stay until the two of you decide upon your plans, and I will rejoin Succiu." Sensing their apprehension, he added, "As you have said, the Recluse is doubly guarded by the Minions. Every single entrance and exit is this very moment protected by at least one squad of elite assassins. Either we can try to storm one of the entrances, alert the entire Recluse, and die immediately, or we can simply walk in through the front door, welcomed by the Minions, and let me escort you to your quarters." He sat back in his chair. "The choice is yours."

Tristan narrowed his dark eyes. "And what if any of the Coven wishes to see their new 'slaves'?" he asked.

"There are many slaves there whom the Coven has not yet seen. I will simply take those particular slaves to them. They will not suspect."

"How far is it to the Recluse?" Wigg asked skeptically.

"It is a two-hour gallop on the main road, but we must take another, slower way. The main road is carefully watched by the Minions and is an unjustified risk."

Tristan snorted down his nose at the dwarf. "And walking in through the front gate of the Recluse is not?"

"In my opinion, no," Geldon said simply. "And I remind you both that I have lived there for over three hundred years."

"How long can you be gone?" Tristan asked, slowly becoming more convinced of the plan. "Won't Succiu become suspicious if you do not return by morning?"

"When I come to the Ghetto to procure slaves, it takes me much longer," Geldon said. "The selection is much more limited, due to disease and hunger. Although the only time I am permitted to leave the palace is under her orders, it is not unusual for me to be gone for two or three days when she sends me here."

Wigg sighed and rubbed his chin with one hand. "Why would they want slaves from the Ghetto," he asked, "when they can have healthier, more well-subdued citizens from the towns?"

"Not *they*," Geldon replied. "Only Succiu. It was here, in this place, that Succiu first found me."

Mistress Shailiha. The pain stabbed through Tristan's being as surely as if he had been physically wounded in battle. *This is the first time I have ever heard her referred to as a mistress.* He closed his eyes as he felt his heart tear.

Ian, who had until this moment been silent, tentatively walked closer to Wigg. "There is a problem you must hear about before you leave," he added quietly. The cornflower-blue eyes looked apologetically at the Lead Wizard.

"And that is?" Wigg asked.

"There is only one possible way out of the Ghetto. And to take it, you must use your gift."

Wigg's jaw dropped open, a very rare sight. "I cannot!" he thundered. "Did Faegan not make it clear to you? I am using all my energies right now to hide our blood from the Coven. If I must stop shielding ourselves and use the gift to aid our way, not only may they detect our blood, but they will also sense whatever actions I must perform to aid our escape, as well!" Tristan wasn't sure he had ever seen the old one so angry. "What was Faegan thinking, sending us here knowing this?" the old one said, shaking his head.

"Forgive me, Lead Wizard," Ian said, "but Master Faegan said if anyone could accomplish it, you could. He puts great faith in you, as do we all."

Faegan! The eccentric master of riddles and motives, Wigg thought. "And just what is this supposed route out of here?" he asked angrily.

"There is a stone room not too far away from the aviary, into which rises the moat that surrounds the outer wall of the Ghetto," Geldon said. "I believe it must have been originally used as a refuse portal, perhaps before the Coven installed the moat. There is a grate underneath, at the lower end of the water, through which we must swim. But the grate opening is ancient, and must be widened before the two of you can swim through it to the other side of the Ghetto wall with me."

Wigg looked hard at Geldon. "There is absolutely no other way?" he asked. "You obviously came in through the moat, since you're wet. But if we're posing as slaves, why can't we just go out the front gates with you?"

"The Minions at the front gates always examine whoever I bring out, to make sure they do not have leprosy. They would surely want to examine the two of you. It is simply too dangerous. You might be recognized, and that would mean the end of us. Besides, I did not enter through the gates. To exit that way now would surely invite questions—questions we are not prepared to answer. We will wear the yellow lepers' robes until we come to the moat. I always keep a spare or two here. They are robes that I have taken from the dead. While we are still inside the Ghetto walls, the yellow robes will help to keep unwanted attention from us, and hasten our trip. But after that, we cannot be seen with them outside the Ghetto walls. We would again be questioned instantly."

Tristan watched as Geldon went to a small closet and pulled out two more yellow robes. "I believe him," he said to the wizard. "And if we are going to do this, we must begin it soon, despite the consequences." He looked up at the still-fuming wizard and smirked. "It looks like we're going for a swim."

The old one closed his eyes and shook his head, but finally took one of the yellow robes from the dwarf. Tristan took the other, and both he and the wizard put the robes on over their other garments. Turning to Ian, Wigg said, "It has been a pleasure knowing you. Take good care of the birds. If we are lucky enough to return, I will try to help you."

Geldon and Tristan nodded farewell, and then the three of them were gone.

Two hours later they were standing in the dark, cold stone room that Geldon had described. Their trip through the Ghetto had been largely quiet, despite the beseeching of several of the street whores. They had removed the yellow robes, sinking them to the bottom of the moat with stones. There was very little light, and the stench from the polluted water was overpowering. Wigg looked into the filthy water. "Where is the grate?" he asked.

Geldon pointed. "There," he said, "at the bottom of the far wall. An underwater tunnel leads through the moat, and ends at the grate at the other side."

Wigg looked at Tristan and took a slow breath, his eyes softening. "You understand that if I do this thing it may be the end of us, and of all we know," he said gently.

"Yes, I know," Tristan said. "You have been my teacher for as long as I can remember. But now the student is telling the teacher that he must do his best."

Wigg closed his eyes and raised his hands into the air. Almost immediately Tristan could see the old one's face begin to change, and he knew that Wigg was discontinuing the protection of their endowed blood. The old wizard then opened his eyes and looked down into the water, parting his hands as he did so. He once again raised his arms, closed his eyes, and immediately began recommitting his energies to shielding their blood. At last, he turned to face Tristan and Geldon. He appeared to be more tired than ever. "The grate has been widened," he said. "But I cannot promise that we were not detected."

"Gather all of the air into your lungs that you can muster," Geldon told them. "The swim is long, and the water is both cloudy and thick. Do not try to open your eyes, or they may become permanently damaged. And whatever happens, do not open your mouths. Wigg, I will hold your hand, and you hold on to Tristan's. Together we will approach the tunnel. When you feel the other person's hand let go of your own, that means we have arrived at the entrance, and it is time for each of you to feel your way through. Then swim directly upward until you break the surface of the water. I will be there waiting for you." The dwarf paused to give them a last, hard look. "Whatever you do, do not let go of the other person's hand until we reach the tunnel. If you become separated you will become disoriented, and surely die in this place. Now, take that deep breath!"

Holding hands, the three of them jumped into the filth, and the brackish waters quickly closed in over them. In only moments, the water calmed to its original stillness as though it had never been disturbed, locking its secrets beneath a surface as dark as death.

*W*hen it first came to her it had begun as a warm, distant vibration. Low and almost undetectable, the phantom contact had teased her subconscious for only the briefest of moments, and then was gone.

But it had been long enough.

Failee sat alone on her black marble throne as the last rays of the day cascaded down through the skylight above her. Aside from her silent presence, the room was empty. She had come here to the Sanctuary to practice her daily meditations in preparation for the Blood Communion. But for the last several hours she had been sitting there, quietly contemplating the surprising connection and poring over the ramifications in her mind.

Smiling to herself, she rose from the massive chair, levitated her curvaceous body, and glided over to the white marble altar that sat directly below the cascading light. As she hovered there, the First Mistress took a deep, sweet breath and slowly ran the long, painted nail of her right index finger seductively along the altar's length as though it were the manhood of some long-desired lover.

They are here, she thought to herself. *Male endowed blood is in Parthalon. The Lead Wizard and the Chosen One have come.* She removed her finger from the cool altar to reach up and protectively grasp the bloodred stone that hung around her neck. *They are here for the same things that I took from them: the woman and the stone.*

At first her discovery had caused her concern—and disbelief. The contact with endowed blood that was not of the Coven was the first she had sensed in over three hundred years, and it had come to her in a shielded, protected way, as though the person who possessed it was trying to hide it from her. It had come to her as if it were passing *through* something, and the contact was so brief that she had been unable to discern the medium through which it had struggled to reach her. But in the end it had not mattered, because the presence had possessed a flavor and a texture all its own. She was absolutely certain of its meaning and had already sent a handmaiden to summon Succiu and Kluge to the Sanctuary.

She smiled again, her maniacal, hazel eyes turning up at the corners as she did so. *I am not intimidated, Wigg. It is perhaps fitting that you should be here at this time.*

She was not concerned over how Wigg had survived the stalker, the harpy, and the wiktor. Nor was she immediately perplexed about the method he had obviously employed to cross the Sea of Whispers so quickly. She would discover all of that in due time. All that mattered to her now was that he was here. And when she at last had him in her grasp, she would make him watch as she fulfilled the Coven's rightful destiny, and female endowed blood finally ruled the world.

She pursed her red lips and ran one hand back through the gray-streaked hair that fell to her shoulders. *We have shared much, Old One, and we shall share even more before you die.*

She turned and looked at the white marble altar, shining beneath the last rays of the setting sun. *The Chosen One will watch you die. He carries the very finest of endowed blood within him.* She then narrowed her eyes, as another, even more intriguing concept occurred to her. *Tristan may prove useful, after all. And it will provide the opportunity I have needed to put the second mistress back in her place.* She smiled. *Succiu should be severely punished for defying me,* Failee thought, *but I need her now more than ever, and she is best controlled by giving her the one thing she wants most.*

It was her handmaiden's voice that took the First Mistress from her reveries. The young woman had returned from her errand. "Forgive the intrusion," she said tentatively, "but the second mistress and Commander Kluge wait just outside the door."

Continuing to hover near the altar, Failee did not turn around. "Show them in."

The tall, dark commander of the Minions of Day and Night walked quickly to where his mistress was standing and immediately went down on one knee. "I live to serve," he said. Succiu, dressed in a riding habit of the finest red velvet with matching boots and crop, walked into the room and stood by imperiously, as if angry to have been disturbed.

Failee looked down at the dark, rather unkempt hair that reached Kluge's shoulders; the black, piercing eyes; and the white scar on the left cheek that ran jaggedly into the forest of his black goatee. As always he was fully armed, the tearing points of his gauntlets sharp and ready, the returning wheel at his side, and the ever-present dreggan at his left hip.

"You may rise. Given the nature of the situation, I also grant you permission to speak at will."

"Has something important happened?" he asked quickly, rising to his feet.

"Oh, indeed," she said, smiling again. "The Lead Wizard and the Chosen One have arrived in Parthalon. You may get your chance to kill them after all." She hovered there above him, still as a statue, watching for his reaction.

Kluge was thunderstruck. He couldn't believe his luck, despite the obvious problems this news brought with it. He not only considered his mission to Eutracia unfulfilled as long as the two of them lived, but now had deep, personal reasons as well for wanting to see the prince dead. And he was not a man to leave a job unfinished, no matter what the risks.

Failee could tell that Kluge felt he had a score to settle with the prince. And she knew that it had much more to do with the woman beside him than with her own orders.

She turned her attention to Succiu, and once again the reaction was as she expected. Succiu would be concerned that the wizard and the prince were here, to be sure, but the First Mistress could also easily discern the longing in Succiu's expression—the burning hunger for the Chosen One.

Kluge's hand tightened around the hilt of his dreggan, his knuckles turning white. "Do you know were they are?" he asked breathlessly.

"No, I do not. The contact with their endowed blood was too brief for me to ascertain their whereabouts."

"Shall I organize search parties?" he asked. "There are so many vengeful warriors that I am sure we could find them in a matter of days. They would relish the chance to find the ones who escaped them." He smiled wickedly.

"Again, the answer is no. They are obviously here for the stone and Mistress Shailiha. There is no need to chase them, for they will come to us. They have to. You are to tell no one of these events. I shall inform the other two mistresses myself. I wish no unnecessary confusion in or around the area of the Recluse, especially where Sister Shailiha is concerned. Nonetheless, you shall quietly double her guard. Use only your best assassins. The wizard and prince will be forced to try to enter the Recluse in some way, but they cannot possibly know how or where to enter. Personally inspect each of your squads that guard the entrances."

After the initial shock of the news had settled into his mind, Kluge found himself stunned by the attitude of the First Mistress. The wizard and the Chosen One were in Parthalon, and no one knew where they were or how they had managed to travel here. And yet Failee did not seem upset, but rather looked almost as if she relished the chance to prove herself to Wigg one final time. Kluge's mind flashed back to that day on the Minion training field when he had just killed a fellow warrior and Succiu had suddenly appeared in a white gown and matching parasol, accompanied by her slave, Geldon. She had even then ordered him to double the guard and tell no one, just as Failee was doing now. He could still picture the second mistress standing there in the sun, her white gown splattered with the blood of his latest victim as she calmly gave him her orders. That attitude was typical of Succiu. But what he saw in Failee today was different. What was it Succiu had said that day about the wizard and the prince? *"I fear I may have underestimated them both . . ."*

The commander looked into the First Mistress' eyes, truly not knowing whether her lack of concern was due to an overwhelming confidence of power that he still did not understand, or some form of intricate, endowed insanity. In any event, it did not matter. He would gladly follow her orders at the cost of his life, and he relished the chance to see the wizard and the prince suffer once again. *Especially the one who dares to call himself a king,* he thought hungrily.

"And there is something else that I must discuss with the two of you," Failee said easily. "For some time I have been aware of your—how should I put it?—your 'uses' for each other." She paused for a moment, letting the magnitude of her words sink in. Kluge appeared stunned, as she had expected. Succiu simply appeared angry. The second mistress took a wider, more aggressive stance, her eyes narrowed.

"It is to stop," Failee continued. "Immediately. Kluge, I shall not punish you for these indiscretions, for I believe you were following orders."

Kluge felt as if a storm had just passed through his body. He closed his eyes in hatred. *If she cannot be mine, then I will see to it that the Chosen One, the man Succiu seems so interested in dies slowly, indeed.*

Succiu stepped forward in a rare display of brazenness. She cared nothing for Kluge except that he had been better able to fulfill her needs than the other weaklings of this land. But this was not about caring—it was about power.

"I refuse to be spoken to in this manner!" she hissed angrily.

"Oh, indeed you shall listen," Failee said, almost casually. "For there is more that you must know. Since the Chosen One is here, in Parthalon, I have decided to make use of him, rather than killing him immediately." She smiled, knowing that her plan would not only please the second mistress, but return her to the fold, as well. "You will remain here, while I explain it to you."

She turned to the still-seething Kluge. "That is all. Leave us now. You have your orders." She watched him struggle to hold himself under control, then added, "We are about to have visitors."

Barely able to contain himself, Kluge went to one knee and whispered, "I live to serve."

It was as he was ascending the long flight of circular steps from the Sanctuary that he once again allowed himself the luxury of revisiting his desires. *Very well, Chosen One. Come to me, and we shall finish what we have begun.*

Aside from that awful day on the dais when his family was murdered, Tristan had never in his life felt such horror and revulsion.

He found himself following Wigg, swimming for his life, his lungs on fire, his eyes closed tight. The old wizard clung securely to the wrist of his left hand, limiting its use, making the swim even more difficult. Kicking furiously with his feet and pulling desperately with his free arm, he made his way through the murky filth.

It was not the fact that he was underwater that was so frightening. He had been a strong swimmer all of his life, and as a youth he had always loved diving to the floor of lakes to explore. But this was different. Here, with his eyes shut, he could see nothing; his senses were totally deprived. And his survival was dependent upon Geldon, a man he had known for less than a few hours. The combination of factors was overpowering.

But most loathsome was the water itself. Thick and warm, it was difficult to swim through, and what he could only imagine to be litter, garbage, and human feces struck his face and body as he went along. Occasionally his free hand would brush the floor of the moat, sliding sickeningly through warm, sticky layers of the same awful waste. The foul memory of the stench at the top, before they had plunged in, plagued him. The impulse to vomit was coming upon him, and with it the awful realization that if he did he would likely drown. He had little stamina left, and he knew it.

Suddenly Wigg stopped and let go of his hand.

We're at the other side! his oxygen-deprived mind screamed at him. *Wigg is going through the tunnel.* He could feel himself beginning to collapse under the strain, the deadly urge to open his eyes and mouth becoming irresistible, the pressure in his lungs approaching the bursting point. As he reached out in blindness, his hand came into contact with the dirty, submerged brick wall of the moat. With his left hand finally free of the wizard's grasp, he groped his way along the length of the wall, his fingers slithering in and out of three centuries' worth of filth. Then his hand plunged out into nothingness, and he knew he had found the entrance to the tunnel.

Half swimming, half running along the bottom of the tunnel in his desperate, underwater dash to reach the end, he was overwhelmed by his first real feelings of doom. On he went, a few strokes more, each one double the agony of the last, his lungs about to explode, his vision imprisoned in the fathomless darkness. Until, at last, he reached the tunnel's end.

The passageway had narrowed dramatically despite Wigg's use of the craft, and the end of it was edged with metal shards. There would be just enough room for him to squeeze through. Stretching out his arms, he plunged headfirst into the blackness, toward the tunnel exit.

And then it happened.

He had come to an immediate halt at the exit, and somehow he knew that only his head had come out the other side, his body trapped in the sharp-edged opening. Reaching up in abject blindness, he tried to find the cause of the problem, and panicked when he discovered the answer.

The hilt of his dreggan was wedged against the roof of the tunnel. With his last reserves of strength he reached up, frantically trying to feel for the hilt and pull it free.

The familiar, usually reassuring clang of the dreggan rang loudly through the water as the last foot of its sharpened steel launched itself outward. He had accidentally touched the button at the hilt. Now the point had ripped through the end of the scabbard and impaled itself in the tunnel wall. Again he reached up in the maddening blackness, his lungs bursting, and tried to find the button to retract the blade and free himself. His senses were ebbing. He was becoming disoriented, unable to discern in the pitch-black darkness of his closed eyes whether he was right side up or upside down. With a last, great effort of will he reached one more time to the sword, but his hand fell back in failure and weakness.

He hung limply from the dreggan that stretched across the roof of the tunnel, his arms useless and unmoving at his sides, head turned to one side, his chin against his chest. The pressure in his temples was close to exploding, the beat of his straining heart growing ever louder in his ears. Small bubbles of air began to seep from his mouth and into the black filth of the water.

Before his mind finally surrendered, from somewhere far away the last words of the dwarf came to his expiring consciousness: "*. . . Or you shall surely die in this place . . . or you shall surely die in this place . . . or . . . you . . . shall . . . surely . . . die . . .*" And then finally, from nowhere, he heard his mind whisper, *Shailiha . . . forgive me.*

Twenty-three

He had heard many stories about the Afterlife back when he was alive, but he hadn't realized there was so much fog there. He could barely see anything at all. Then he noticed a father and son splashing about in a stream. *That looks like fun,* he thought. *Is this what we do here in the Afterlife to amuse ourselves? And they have no clothes on, not a stitch. I don't think I have any on, either. Apparently no one wears anything here. How wonderfully odd.* Tristan smiled to himself, wondering if Evelyn of the House of Norcross would be wearing anything, for she would surely also be here, in the Afterlife, along with her parents and his, as well. He began to squirm with embarrassment. *I don't want to have to face her father. But first I must find my own mother and father, and tell them how sorry I am for not better protecting them that day in the Great Hall. The day when the winged monsters came. And how will I explain Shailiha?*

Nervous and fearful, Tristan lapsed back into unconsciousness.

When he finally began to awaken, the two things he heard first were Wigg's voice telling him to wake up, and then his own violent retching as he painfully turned over in the grass in which he was lying to let it just happen. Finally, and with great effort, he sat up to see the wizard and the dwarf both looking anxiously down at him. He was wet, cold, and naked.

As his mind and eyesight began to clear he could discern that Wigg and Geldon were both fully clothed, but that they were also dripping wet. And then he remembered. *The tunnel, the water, my sword against the exit. I was trapped and dying in there.*

Wigg's familiar left eyebrow came up. "I was beginning think that you were never going to rejoin us," he said as he knelt down and looked deeply into the prince's left eye, examining him. "You'll live." The old one snorted. "I could have brought you around sooner had I been able to use the craft, but as it was I had to let nature do the job instead. After I cleared your lungs, of course."

Coughing some more, Tristan looked around to see that he was sitting in the shade of a huge oak tree, alongside the banks of a rushing river. Three saddled horses were tied up to the low branches of the tree, and the high walls of the Ghetto of the Shunned could be seen off in the distance. The sunrise was low in the clear, blue sky, and the birds and insects were just beginning their songs of the day. The stream rushed and bubbled happily, joining into nature's chorus.

"How did I get out?" he asked, coughing. He spat some more water into the grass.

"When Geldon and I surfaced and you did not, it was obvious you had to be in trouble," Wigg said. "But you owe your life more to Geldon than to me. It was he who first saw the bubbles rising to the surface, and dived down to free you." He reached out to pick up the dreggan from the nearby grass. The scabbard end had been smashed through, but the sword itself looked undamaged. The old wizard held it to the sun, admiring the handiwork of the blade and hilt. "Geldon found you dangling helplessly from this. This sword of yours already has quite a history." He laid the weapon back down next to the prince.

"Through some kind of a mist I saw the Afterlife, and a father and son frolicking in a stream," Tristan remembered. He shook his head slowly, as if trying to understand. "They had no clothes on," he added, embarrassed, wondering if Wigg would believe him.

The old wizard pushed his tongue against the inside of his cheek and narrowed his eyes. "What you saw," he said rather mockingly, "was the morning fog beginning to lift. It is rather thick here, in this land. And then you saw Geldon and me washing all of our clothes, not to mention ourselves, in that stream over there." He motioned to the dark pile of clothes that lay next to the prince. "We washed your clothes, too, as well as the rest of you, while we waited for you to rejoin us." The eyebrow came up again. "I suggest you put them on. Do you think you can ride? There were no Minions present when we surfaced from the water, but we shouldn't stay here long."

Coughing again, Tristan turned around to look back at the moat and the filthy water that had almost ended his life. "If it means getting away from here, I can do anything you ask." He looked up into the eyes of the dwarf who had yet to speak to him, and to the collar and the heavy chain that Geldon wore around his neck. *He risked his life to rescue me,* Tristan thought. Whatever misgivings the prince had once felt about the dwarf were now gone. "Thank you," he said to Geldon. "Thank you for coming back for me. I won't forget it."

Geldon smiled down at the wet, naked prince as he collected the chain that ran to his collar. "Don't mention it," he said. "I have a feeling you will be paying both myself and Parthalon back handsomely before we are finished." He turned and began walking toward the horses.

Feeling stronger by the minute, Tristan stood and put his clothes back on. It felt good to have the black trousers, leather vest, and knee boots on again, and he lifted the baldric over his right shoulder and slid the dreggan into it. The point of the sword pushed menacingly out through the ruined end of the scabbard. Wigg handed him his dirks, and he replaced them in the quiver. As an afterthought, he ran his hands back through his wet hair. Then the three of them donned the cloaks that Geldon had brought with him, mounted the horses, and trotted up and away, deeper into the woods that bordered the stream.

The roan mare that Tristan was riding was not the quality of Pilgrim, and he longed for his own horse to be under him. But this one would have to do. He took time to look about the Parthalonian countryside as they went along and found it to be not unlike his native land. The trees seemed to grow taller here and some of the sounds of the forest were unfamiliar to him, but he recognized most of the birds and small animals he saw.

Riding alongside the dwarf, Tristan spent some time in conversation with him, learning more about the nation, the Recluse, and the Minions. At the mention of Kluge and his followers the prince's heart grew dark and hard, and he could feel his blood rise and tingle as if it was responding simply to being in the same nation with the winged monster. The dwarf told him that the route they would be taking ran parallel to what was called the Black River, and that it would take them two days to reach the Recluse at this rate. Tristan objected about the waste of time, but the dwarf was adamant. The area was full of Minion warriors on patrol, he said, and any additional interest caused by galloping up the main road to the Recluse was precisely the kind of attention that they did not need. In the end, the prince was forced to agree.

Whenever their path came close enough to the main road, Tristan tried hard to catch a glimpse of the people who lived in this land, wondering what they would be like. He was not heartened at what he saw. The people of Parthalon seemed to be sullen and sad. They moved with a slowness that gave him the impression that either their lives, time itself, or both were of no importance to them. They were for the most part shabbily dressed, and seemed to be quite poor. Occasionally he would see entire families moving along the road with only a cart and ox to transport what he assumed to be all of their worldly possessions, just like the many Eutracians he had seen on the journey to Shadowood. The muscles in his jaw clenched. *Everywhere they go, the Coven brings nothing but suffering,* he thought. *Now my sister, my very blood, is one of them.* The dreggan suddenly felt heavy across his back, as if reminding him of his responsibilities. *And I must find a way, somehow, to keep myself from taking her life.* They continued on.

It was near the end of the day that Geldon changed their course. He turned his horse to the east, away from the road they had been paralleling, and began to venture deeper into the woods. Tristan gave Wigg a questioning glance, and the old one nodded.

Wigg cleared his throat. "I thought we were to stay alongside the road until we reached the Recluse," he said. The statement was far more a demand for answers than a casual comment. "Where are you taking us?"

"We cannot go any farther in the direction I had planned," the dwarf replied. "We must take a more circuitous route, and avoid a particular area of the woods." He stopped his horse. "It will take us longer, but it has to be."

"Why?" Tristan asked.

Geldon pointed his hand to the sky. "They're the reason why."

The prince raised his eyes above the tree line to see a flock of enormous birds of prey. They looked like a cross between buzzards and hawks, and they were almost twice the size of any such birds he had seen in Eutracia. Black, swift, and menacing, they circled the woods some distance ahead, and it was obvious that they were waiting for something to die.

"What is it that they are waiting to prey upon?" Tristan asked casually.

Geldon turned in his saddle to face them both. "They wait to prey upon people," he said.

"People?" Tristan exclaimed.

"Yes," Geldon said calmly, but the pain was evident in his face. "They wait to prey upon people. It is essential that we avoid this place. I only brought us this way because it is shorter and time is of the essence. But this is as close to the birds as I dare take us. The area beneath which the birds circle is a valley—a place of the Minions."

Immediately Tristan's vows of vengeance came rushing to his mind. His endowed blood was calling out for action, and here at last he was close to the monsters who had slaughtered his family and the Directorate of Wizards. The dreggan that only moments before had seemed so heavy across his back now felt light as a feather, its blade suddenly, surely, calling to him as well. Calling to him in its need to taste blood.

Tristan's eyes narrowed, and his lips curled back into a snarl; his face was as hard as stone. "I will see this place," he said quietly.

Wigg walked his horse over and looked Tristan dead in the eye. "You cannot do it," he said, trying to be sympathetic but still in control. "I forbid it. You must think of the reason we came, and of your sister. Do not risk everything we have gained just for this."

"I understand your wishes," Tristan said slowly. "But this is something I must do, with or without the two of you." He looked up to where the birds were circling in the blue afternoon sky. "I will do it alone, if need be," he told them quietly, through clenched teeth. "In truth I do not need either of you for this, and you both know it. Stay here if you like. You cannot use your powers to stop me or to help, and I do not need the dwarf to find my way. The birds will guide me to the ones I seek."

Geldon looked fearfully at Wigg. "Will he really do it?" he asked. "Is there nothing you can do to stop him?"

Wigg continued to look into the eyes of the Chosen One he had seen born, struggle, and suddenly learn so much about himself. *But there is still so much more to know,* he thought.

"In truth, I cannot control him right now," the old one said. "Because of the nature of his blood, he is partially under the influences of things he will not be able to control until he reads the Tome. And I am unable to use the craft, for fear of being detected." He took a long, resolved breath and turned to the dwarf. "If he is intent upon killing us all, then you should lead us there as safely as you can, since you seem to know the lay of the land. I will not let him go alone."

Geldon relented. There was little else he could do. He needed both the wizard and the Chosen One, and therefore had no choice.

"Very well," the dwarf said reluctantly. "But this is madness. However, if we must do this thing, we do it my way. Take off your robes. It will be easier to defend ourselves without them, if need be. Dismount and follow me. Silently. No talking until I speak to you."

Tristan and Wigg tethered their horses to a tree and tied their robes to the animals' saddles. Then Geldon began to lead them single file through the dense woods.

It was slow going, constantly uphill. Finally the dwarf turned around and put his finger to his lips, reminding them to keep silent. Tristan looked up to see that the birds were circling lower now, becoming more brazen.

Geldon fell to his stomach and indicated that the prince and wizard do the same. Then the three of them crawled up a small knoll and slowly raised their eyes to just above the level of the ridge.

What Tristan saw below him was unimaginable.

There was a clearing in the valley, at least one hundred feet down from where the three of them lay. Geldon, Tristan, and Wigg were poised at the top of a low, rocky hilltop, from which they could see for miles in every direction. At the bottom of the valley, six wooden stakes had been pounded into the ground. Each was at least ten feet tall, with a very large, rough-hewn wooden spoked wheel at its top, mounted horizontally. The very large wheels turned around and around slowly in the silent gusts of wind that invisibly came and went through the valley.

Five of the stakes stood at the points of a Pentangle that had been drawn in blood upon the ground; the sixth was in the center of the star. Yet more blood lay splattered in odd, incongruous patterns around the base of each of the stakes. For a moment the prince wondered why. But then, horribly, he found his answer, and he took a quick breath.

Each of the wheels held a human being.

Straining his eyes, he could see that the bodies had been literally woven in and out between the spokes of the wheels and simply allowed to turn there in the wind, exposed to the elements until they were dead. At first his mind rejected the sheer physical impossibility of such a thing until, looking more carefully, he could see how it had been done. Each of the men's arms, legs, back, and neck had been broken, allowing for the impossible angles that were created as the various body parts had been interlaced between the spokes. In many cases jagged, white splinters of bones could be seen erupting through the victim's skin. The blood pattern on the ground, which at first had seemed so incongruous, now made perfect sense: The prisoners' dripping blood was splattered this way and that by the turning of the wheels in the wind. A ghostly, creaking sound could be heard as they rotated. He had never seen anything like it, and the inhumanity of it was staggering.

It was then that he noticed the person upon the wheel in the center of the Pentangle. It was a woman. She was not, however, an ordinary woman. Heart racing, Tristan stared with wide eyes at what made her different.

She had wings.

They were not the usual wings of the Minions. Her wings were white, and even from this distance he could tell that they were made of feathers like the wings of birds, unlike the dark, muscular, leathery wings of the Minions. Her hair was blond and fell down around her shoulders; her head slumped forward on her chest. A meager loincloth was wrapped around her waist, and her upper body was bare. But the woman was not mounted to her turning wheel of death in the same fashion as the men—she had been simply laced to the top of the wheel, facedown.

Tristan took another look at the five men. Now he saw that they also had white wings and blond hair. He glanced at the dwarf, indicating he wished to speak, and Geldon motioned for the three of them to creep back down out of sight, behind the safety of the ridge.

Still lying on their stomachs, Tristan and Wigg slithered nearer to Geldon.

"What is this place?" Tristan whispered urgently. "I have never seen anything like it! And who are those people down there? What have they done to anger the Minions?"

"It is known as the Vale of Torment, and it is used as a place of execution by the Minions," Geldon whispered back. "The ones you see on the wheels are actually of Minion birth themselves. One of every five thousand children is born blond, with white wings. They are considered to be an inferior race, and are raised in disgrace by the Minions until the age of twenty-five. Sometimes they change to the typical dark wings and hair, and those that do are trained and kept as true Minion. But if they do not, they are considered inferior and are brought to this place to be killed.

"They have done nothing to deserve such treatment except to be born with white wings and blond hair. It is said that they are very loving, another trait that the Minions find to be inferior. They are known as the Gallipolai."

"What is this method of execution?" Wigg asked. "I have never seen it before."

"It is a slow form of death by exposure," Geldon replied. "Their arms, legs, backs, and necks are broken, then they are woven between the spokes of the wheels and are left here to die." Geldon closed his eyes for a moment. "To add to the cruelty, the Minions force the victim to swallow a brew that keeps them from going unconscious for a while, adding to the torment." The pain of his words was clear upon his face. "They seldom survive for more than three days."

"Then the ones we saw are dead?" Tristan whispered.

"Some of them, at least. And not for long, for the birds are just now beginning to come close. Most likely the men are dead; the woman might not be."

Wigg narrowed his eyes. "Why would the woman last longer?"

"You no doubt noticed that she was not woven into the wheel, but simply tied facedown. They probably did not break her bones. If so, she will have lost no blood, and can last longer."

"Why would they spare her?" Tristan asked.

"It is Minion custom that those who brought her here may do anything with her they choose, before killing her outright." Geldon swallowed, as if trying to force down his revulsion.

Tristan was staggered. *An innocent race of the Minions,* he mused.

Suddenly, another thought seized him. "When will the Minion warriors come back to check on them?"

"They do not need to come back," Geldon said tentatively, looking at Wigg. "They never left. They're here."

The prince's endowed blood roared in his ears, and the sword across his back felt as if it had come alive. "Where?" he demanded.

Geldon looked meekly into the prince's eyes and saw the very face of death itself mirrored there. Unsure of what to do, he indicated that the three of them should return to the top of the ridge.

They slithered back uphill, and Tristan cautiously peered out over the valley. Nothing had changed in the Vale of Torment. The only movement came from the grotesque, blood-soaked wheels as they revolved in the wind, creaking with the weight of their victims. No birds sang. The flying predators continued to circle overhead with their soaring, mercenary patience.

Geldon pointed down and to the right where, about eighty feet down the hill, a little overhang covered with rocks and bushes faced the Pentangle. "There," he whispered as quietly as possible. "That small outcropping. It is called Vulture's Row. That is where the two Minion warriors will be waiting for the three days to pass." He turned to look at the prince. "They always send two. No more, no less."

Immediately realizing the importance of what the dwarf had just said, Wigg tried to grab Tristan's arm, but he was too slow. With surprising strength Tristan easily shook off the old one and was gone. Wigg felt something inside of him slip. *He knew what he was doing all along*, the Lead Wizard realized. *What a fool I have been. He knew that once we were at the top of the ridge, I couldn't call out to stop him or move too violently to control him for fear of being seen. And now he is gone.*

Geldon looked at the wizard, terrified. "Is he always like this?" he asked, his lips trembling.

Wigg frowned, shaking his head slightly. "More than you could ever know," he whispered. The two of them crawled back down below the safety of the ridge to wait.

Twenty-four

T ristan moved quickly around the end of the knoll, trying to be silent as he put as much distance between himself and his companions as possible. Stopping for a moment, he looked up to make sure the wizard and the dwarf had had the good sense not to follow him. He was pleased to see that he was alone.

Reaching behind his right shoulder, he checked to make sure his dirks were in place. Then silently, slowly, he drew the dreggan from its scabbard and held it to the sun for a moment, looking at it. Lowering it once again and holding it upright in both his hands, he finally bent his head forward, eyes closed, touching the coolness of the blade to his feverish forehead. *May the Afterlife grant me strength,* he prayed.

He continued to move around the knoll until he was directly above the place Geldon had called Vulture's Row. He could detect no movement from within, but he could hear vulgar conversation and coarse laughter drifting up to him. The last time he had heard such Minion voices, he had been unable to move, he recalled, outraged. He had been chained hands and feet by the monster named Kluge. This time it would be different. He crept to the edge of the outcropping. Taking a deep breath, he leapt off the hill, twirling his body around in midair to face the direction from which he had come—to face his enemies.

He landed firmly on both feet, directly in front of the outcropping. The first Minion to overcome his surprise immediately pulled his dreggan. But Tristan reacted first. He moved in swiftly like a dancer and pointed the blade at the warrior's throat, touching the button on the hilt. The point of the blade immediately shot out the extra foot, the loud, familiar ring careening off the valley walls, and drove itself straight through the warrior's neck, violently exiting just below the back of his head. Tristan immediately turned the blade to the right and pulled his arm over, driving the edge of the sword toward the man's left shoulder, slicing through the side of the neck. The Minion warrior's eyes went wide as his head toppled over to hang only by the skin that had been spared, and he fell to the earth as though his legs had been cut out from under him, blood erupting everywhere.

The second Minion had moved the instant he saw the prince, but his dreggan had been out of reach, propped up against a nearby stool. By the time Tristan had killed the first man, the second was almost upon him, sword raised, screaming. Tristan immediately tossed his dreggan over to his left hand and reached behind his right shoulder for a dirk. His arm a curved blur of speed, he released the blade with all of his strength. The razor-sharp throwing knife completely surprised the warrior as it buried itself to the hilt into his left eye. The force of the impact carried the Minion over and onto his back, dead before he hit the ground.

Tristan stood there panting, glancing about as if it had all been a dream. Looking down he saw that he had been splattered with blood. He didn't care. Using the surrounding grass, he wiped the blade of the dreggan clean. A touch of the button on the hilt pulled the extended blade back in. He resheathed the dreggan.

Walking to the warrior he had killed with the dirk, the prince bent over and removed the knife from the man's eye, watching as the colorless vitreous humor ran lazily from it, down the dead man's cheek and onto the ground, mixing with the blood already there. He wiped the blade on the thigh of his trousers and replaced it in the quiver.

Hearing a sudden sound, he turned quickly, his right hand automatically on the hilt of one of the throwing knives. Slowly uncoiling, he saw that the sounds were the death throes of the Minion he had killed with the dreggan. The body was twitching violently, and the wings were beating against the ground in a pitiful display of what Tristan could only gather to be a desperate, autonomic attempt to rally as the last bit of breath rattled from the lungs. Finally, all was quiet.

Recalling that the point of his scabbard was damaged from his mishap in the tunnel, Tristan found the scabbard belonging to the Minion he had killed with the dirk and traded it for his own. He was just adjusting the baldric when he noticed the returning wheel.

Immediately he recognized the vicious saw-toothed disc that had killed Evelyn of the House of Norcross and several of the wizards of the Directorate. Tristan removed the wheel from the belt of the dead warrior and, using the hook from the man's belt, attached it to his own.

In addition he removed the leaded glove from the corpse's left hand, the glove that safely allowed the wheel to be caught upon its return to its owner. He put the glove on his own left hand, not really knowing why he was taking these things, knowing only that for some reason his endowed blood had directed him to do so. Somehow, it just felt right.

Wigg was probably right, the prince thought as his breathing began to return to normal. *This may have been unnecessary, but I will not apologize for honoring my vows.* He looked at the twisted bodies of the two men he had just killed, wondering whether either of them had been in Eutracia that day. Whether either of them had killed any of the wizards of the Directorate. And whether either of them had contributed to the rape and murder of his mother. *No matter how many of them I kill,* he thought, *I will not rest until Kluge stands before me. Stands before me and dies.*

Turning toward the Vale of Torment, he began walking down toward the six wheels.

*W*hen he finally reached the Pentangle Tristan slowed his gait and approached cautiously. Glaring around in revulsion at the work of the Minions, he wondered if this insane cruelty had been under the orders of the Coven or was simply an amusement of the winged monsters. It also occurred to him that if the Minions were a product of Failee's craft, so then, even if obliquely, were the Gallipolai. *Perhaps that is the reason the Gallipolai are always killed unless their hair and wings turn dark,* he thought. *Their continued existence in this form would illustrate an imperfection in the sorceresses' use of the craft.*

He walked around the perimeter of the Pentangle, examining the five men who had been woven into the wheels. Each of them appeared to be dead, the blood that had once streamed down their many wounds now dried to a dark crimson in the midday sun. Each was young and blond, with wings that were constructed of the most delicate of feathers. The wings were smaller than those of the Minions—and suddenly he realized why. They had been severely clipped back, presumably to make it impossible for them to fly, and therefore to escape. The work was reminiscent of his father's practice of trimming the wings of his hunting falcons when they were young and not yet reliably trained. But this procedure had been much more severe. The dead Gallipolais' feet were much smaller than normal, and looked deformed. *Not only have those bastards clipped their wings,* he snarled silently, *they have also bound their feet. These men could neither run nor fly.* Growing more angry by the second, he walked to the center of the Pentangle to examine the dead woman.

Upon reaching the wheel, he found himself looking up at the most beautiful woman he had ever seen. The long blond hair that hung down between the spokes of the wheel was thick and lustrous, an amazing combination of colors that resembled corn tassels laced with the palest of honey. The similarly colored eyebrows were long and arching; he imagined her eyes were blue. She had a slim, straight nose; pink lips; and a smooth, strong jawline. There was no blood on her face, and Tristan could see the dried rivulets of tears that had run from her eyes, then to her cheeks, and down onto the ground.

Her wings, like those of the men, had been severely clipped back. Her feet, too, were small and deformed, the product of the same cruelty the men had obviously suffered. And yet she was beautiful. *Truly amazing,* he wondered to himself. *Such incredible beauty born of such intense hideousness and cruelty. How could such a creature have been produced by a Minion warrior and his brothel whore?*

When he finally lowered his eyes from the woman, it was only then that he saw the final horror of this place.

His eyes caught a glimmer of white off in the distance, just at the edge of the surrounding woods. Walking over, he was aghast at what he saw.

It was a gigantic display of Gallipolai wings.

Impossibly white and artfully arranged, they had been carefully nailed into the branches of the trees, where they were blown softly back and forth in the breeze, their beauty belying the savagery that had taken place here. There were thousands of them, no doubt the result of centuries of torture. He began to back away, eager for the first time to be gone from the disgusting display of Minion butchery.

"Grotesque, aren't they?" Geldon called out to him from behind. "The Minions do this to the females only, as a sign of their conquests. Many of them are hundreds of years old. Failee was so taken by them that she sends one of the Coven here each time a new pair is added, to enchant them to remain beautiful forever."

Tristan immediately felt his endowed blood rise, the amputated wings a reminder of the dead Eutracian women and girls he had seen literally thrown into piles after the Minions had taken their pleasure from them. *The insanity never ends,* came the whisper in his mind.

Tristan turned to see the wizard and Geldon standing near the wings, the three horses' reins in the hands of the dwarf. Wigg folded his arms upon his chest and slowly looked the prince up and down, taking in the bloodstained clothes and the returning wheel hanging from Tristan's belt. Faegan's words, uttered that night in Shadowood, came back to the Lead Wizard: " 'And the Chosen One shall take up three weapons of his choice and slay many before reading the Prophecies, and coming to the light.' " "Did you accomplish what you wanted?" he asked quietly.

"Yes," Tristan said, the memory of the fight keeping his endowed blood churning. "But sometimes I feel that no matter how many of them I kill, it will never be enough."

Wigg's eyebrow came up. "Geldon tells me there are more than three hundred thousand of them, Tristan." He shook his head slowly. "I doubt you can kill them all."

Tristan said nothing. As he took his horse's reins from Geldon, he noticed more than a little awe registering upon the dwarf's face.

Geldon swallowed hard. "I have never seen a Minion killed by anyone other than a fellow warrior," he said tentatively. "I thought it was impossible to kill one in battle." He stood there nervously fingering the chain from his collar, as if seeing the Chosen One for the first time.

"One should not believe everything he hears," Tristan said angrily. He had had enough of this place, and was anxious to be on his way again.

Then, from behind them, they heard a moan.

Immediately the three of them whirled around, wondering what or who had made the noise. But everything was still the same as before, the bodies motionless upon the wheels, deathly silence reigning once again, the only movement that of the birds of prey as they continued to turn menacingly above them in the morning sky. Suspicious, Tristan walked back to the wheel that held the woman. Drawing his dreggan, he pushed the point of the sword up to press lightly against the top of her right foot.

She moaned again, soft and low, and twisted slightly in her bonds, her eyes still closed.

"Geldon! Wigg!" Tristan shouted, his eyes riveted on the woman's face. "Come quickly! This one's alive!"

The dwarf and the wizard ran to the wheel, and Tristan asked Wigg to go down on one knee. The prince replaced his dreggan in its scabbard and pulled a dirk from his quiver. Stepping up on Wigg's one raised knee, he hoisted himself up to stand on the wizard's shoulders, beneath the spokes. He quickly cut through the rope that bound the woman's feet and then the ones that held her hands. Reaching up, he maneuvered her limp body to where he could hand her down to Wigg, then finally jumped to the ground.

He turned to Geldon. "Go and get some water. And bring back my robe. Hurry!"

Immediately the dwarf began to run back toward the horses. Still holding the woman, Wigg sank to the ground and cradled her in his lap. Transfixed, Tristan bent over the amazingly beautiful creature to examine her. It was then that her sapphire-blue eyes snapped open.

The result was unexpected.

At the sight of the prince's dark hair and the dreggan that protruded behind his left shoulder, she immediately panicked, struggling desperately to free herself from the grip of the wizard. She began trying to scratch Tristan with her nails while beating her wings viciously against the wizard's face.

"Tristan!" Wigg shouted, barely able to hold on to the struggling Gallipolai. "Back away! She thinks you're one of the Minions, and I cannot use the craft to control her!"

Tristan immediately retreated, removing the dreggan from its scabbard and tossing it to the ground some distance away. "Look at me," he said, turning his back to her. Then, facing her again, he opened his palms in a gesture of friendship. "I have no wings. I am not of the Minions. We are not here to harm you; you must believe that. I hate the Minions as much as I'm sure you do."

As quickly as she had begun her struggle, she became strangely quiet. Wigg relaxed his grip on her upper arms, keeping his hands there to control her again if necessary. But the woman had become stone still. It was not out of fear, nor was it a sudden understanding of the prince's words that had broken through her panic. Tristan could see that it was a different, yet equally powerful emotion now at work within her mind.

It was awe.

She dropped her hands to her breasts, covering herself. Her mouth flew open, her sapphire-blue eyes wide and unbelieving. She continued to stare at the prince as if he had just come from another world. After what seemed an eternity, she tore her eyes from Tristan and craned her head around as best she could to look at the wizard who was holding her. The result was the same: complete and utter disbelief. She turned back to face the prince, a strange combination of wonder and surprise still in her eyes.

Tristan gazed down at the beautiful face. "Do you understand what I am saying to you?" he asked.

She nodded tentatively, her arms still covering her breasts. Tristan looked impatiently around to see what had been keeping Geldon. Just then the dwarf approached, carrying the water flask and the dark robe in his arms. At the sight of the hunchback with the collar around his neck and the chain that led from it the woman's eyes went even wider, and she began looking back and forth between the dwarf and Tristan as though she could not decide which of the two of them was the most bizarre.

"Why does she act this way?" the puzzled prince asked Geldon.

"It is simple," the dwarf answered. "All of their lives the Gallipolai are imprisoned within the walls of the Minion fortress, waiting to see whether their wings and hair will turn dark. She has never before seen a man without wings."

Tristan held out the water flask. "Are you thirsty?" he asked gently.

Quick as a flash she snatched the water from his hands and began drinking greedily. Tristan waited patiently until she had drunk her fill, and then decided to try to speak with her.

"Do you have name?"

"I am Narrissa," she said quietly, wiping her mouth on the back of her hand. Her voice was soft and had a sweet huskiness to it that he found attractive. "Narrissa of the Gallipolai."

Tristan looked at Wigg and said, "Let her go."

"Tristan," Wigg began, "I don't think that this is the time to—"

"Let her go," Tristan said more forcefully. Taking a long, exasperated breath, the Lead Wizard released Narrissa. She rose shakily to her feet, still covering her breasts with her hands.

Tristan took the robe from Geldon and held it out to Narrissa. "Put this on," he said. "I'm afraid it's the best I can do."

"I have never seen men without wings," she said cautiously, looking at him with narrowed eyes. "But I have heard about you. The Minion warriors laugh at your weakness. Keep your clothing. I do not wish to be known as one of you."

"You must wear it, my child," Wigg said. He walked out from behind her to stand with the prince and the dwarf. "No one here will hurt you, nor will the simple wearing of it make you one of us."

Narrissa walked closer to Tristan and looked directly into his dark eyes. As she approached, he felt an unexpected wave of compassion go through him. "Do you really hate the Minions as much as you say?" she asked. She watched his face darken in anger.

"Yes," he said, frowning. "They murdered my parents. I killed the two who apparently brought you here." And then, in a kinder voice, he asked, "Did any of them abuse you before placing you upon the wheel?"

She lowered her head slightly, shaking her head no. Finally she reached out to take the robe from him. "You did that for me?" she asked incredulously. "I have never heard of anyone with the skill to kill a Minion other than one of his own brothers." Her face began to soften as she looked at him. "You carry Minion weapons, but your eyes are kind. I will do as you ask. But first, tell me, what is your name?"

The prince thought for a moment. He was well aware of the need for secrecy, but something inside him wanted this woman to know his real name. "My name is Tristan," he answered. "But I must tell you that what I did to those Minions I did as much for myself as for the people on the wheels."

Wigg and Geldon helped her as she struggled to put on the robe. Tristan was pleased that it was several sizes too large for her—otherwise it never would have provided the extra space needed to cover her wings. Of course, giving it to her meant that he would not have one to wear, but he didn't care. He had hated the robe; it had prevented him from quickly reaching his knives.

He stood back a little from the group, still looking at the Gallipolai as he made his decision. "She's coming with us," he said simply. He narrowed his eyes and folded his arms over his chest, waiting for the inevitable explosion from the wizard. It didn't take long.

"Are you mad?" Wigg shouted at him. "We are on the way to a place that may be the end of us all, if we are even lucky enough to gain entrance, the likelihood of which I still seriously doubt!" He spoke cryptically in front of Narrissa, not wanting to reveal too much of their plan. "What are we supposed to do, just ask them if they would like to take her in, too?"

Although deep in his heart he could understand Tristan's reasons, the Lead Wizard was beside himself with anger. *It is all I can do to hide our blood from the Coven,* he thought furiously, *and Tristan knows full well that while I am struggling with that I cannot use my power to overrule him. This is maddening. Just imagine what he will one day be like, when that stubborn streak of his is finally combined with his training in the craft and he has become an adept. This soft spot deep in his heart has gotten him into trouble before, and is about to do so again.*

Tristan knew that he might be making a very bad decision, especially considering his experience with the one he had known as Lillith. He had no reason to trust this Gallipolai. But at the same time he knew that, having cut her down, he could never allow her to be put back upon that hideous device. Nor could he leave her to wander alone, to be found by the Minions again. Deep down, he also realized that part of this decision was due to the fact that this woman reminded him of Shailiha. Somehow, however illogical it might seem, helping her furthered the desperate hope that he might also help his twin sister. No matter the consequences, his mind was made up.

Tristan retrieved his dreggan and slid it slowly back into place in its scabbard. Then he placed his hands defiantly on his hips and scowled at the old wizard. "And what then do *you* propose, eh?" he asked. "If you turn her loose, the Minions will find her and no doubt torture the story out of her—along with my name and a description of each of us. Not to mention subjecting her to the abuse for which she was originally intended. We certainly cannot put her back up on the wheel and leave! And no matter what we do, there is the small matter of the two dead Minion warriors up there. When other warriors come looking, as they're sure to do, they will find their dead comrades." He paused, glaring at Wigg and Geldon. "Then what do you suppose will happen?"

Upon hearing these words, Narrissa moved closer to the prince. She had no desire either to be left here in this place or to have to fend for herself in the world outside of the Minion fortress, a world she had never known. Instinctively she thought that the tall man with the dark hair and no wings would help her.

Geldon cleared his throat and smiled briefly at the Lead Wizard. "I'm afraid he's got you," he said. "There seems to be little choice but to do this his way. I do believe, however, that I can help the situation."

Wigg's eyebrow came up. "And just how is that?"

The dwarf looked at Narrissa. "How long were you on the wheel?"

"I'm not sure, but I think this was the second day," she said. Tired and weak, she reached out to hang onto the prince's arm. He placed his right arm around her waist to support her.

"The Minions sometimes take their pleasure of the women right here, but often they take them elsewhere, out of sight, to abuse them," Geldon explained, rubbing the back of his neck in thought. "If we were to dispose of the guards' bodies, when their brothers come looking they will see both the warriors and the woman gone, nothing more. Nothing will seem out of place to them at first, and no alarm will go out, at least for a while. It will buy us time."

"Very clever," Wigg said. "But what do we do with her when we get close to our destination?"

"I know of some caves on our way," Geldon replied. "They're quite deep, and not well known. We can leave her there with some food and water until we return can return for her." A sudden darkness came over his face. "And if we fail, none of this will matter anyway."

Narrissa clutched the prince more tightly, struggling to remain upright. His arms around her, Tristan lowered himself to the ground, allowing her to rest with her head in his lap. She looked up into his eyes. "Please don't leave me here," she begged. Tears welled out of the sapphire-blue eyes and began to trickle down her cheeks. "Not here, Tristan. Not in this place."

"No one will desert you," he told her gently, pushing some of the honey-blond hair out of her eyes. "I promise you." Upon hearing his words, Narrissa drifted back into unconsciousness.

Wigg looked on disapprovingly as Tristan held the Gallipolai in his arms. *Once again he is thinking with his heart, and has rescued yet another lost puppy,* the old one thought, shaking his head. *No good can come from this.*

"It will never work, you know," he said quietly to the prince.

Tristan looked down at Narrissa's peaceful face and then up at the murderous, inhuman wheels with the five dead bodies still woven through their spokes, listening to the awful stillness of this place. He knew there was no going back for the beautiful young woman in his arms, and that he was the cause of it. He looked up at the wizard. "It has to," he said softly.

Reluctantly leaving Narrissa in Wigg's care, Tristan went with Geldon to dispose of the bodies.

As night approached and darkness started to fall over Parthalon, Tristan was becoming more and more acutely aware of the beautiful woman with the white wings who sat behind him on his mare, her arms about his waist. They had been traveling this way for several hours, Geldon and Wigg in the lead, the prince and Narrissa following behind. Tristan had taken the opportunity to ask her several questions about herself, but she offered little in the way of information, presumably because she had not yet brought herself to trust the strange, wingless men entirely. *She is perhaps the only woman I have ever known who does not know I am a prince,* he mused. He smiled ruefully. *I'm not even sure she knows what the word means.*

As the evening finally fell and the three red moons came into view, Geldon signaled for them to stop, that this would be where they would camp for the night. But at the same moment Tristan felt the Gallipolai behind him stiffen, and heard her take a quick breath as if she had just become aware of something. She leaned closer to him so that she might whisper into his ear.

"Please, Tristan," she said quietly. "Do not let us stop here. It is important that we go on a little farther."

"Why?" he asked skeptically.

"In truth, I cannot give you a full answer, for you would probably think me mad. But please trust me when I tell you that the fact that we must go on a little farther is of great importance to me, just as it would be to any of the Gallipolai. It is only just now, for the first time in my life, that I have felt it."

"Felt what?" he asked.

"The pull of the Myth," she answered.

The prince looked up to see that the wizard and the dwarf had dismounted and were apparently starting to wonder why the prince and the Gallipolai had not already done the same.

"I don't understand," he said. "What myth?"

"I could never expect you to understand something I do not comprehend myself," she replied urgently. "Tell your friends what you must, but please take me farther. I will guide our way. It will be all right, I promise you."

Tristan turned around to search her face. The sapphire-blue eyes were wide and sincere, but tinged with a hint of fear. *She is asking with her heart,* he realized. *But can I trust her?*

"Please," she asked again. "You are the only one I trust to take me there."

Perhaps it was the look in her eyes. Or perhaps the fact that he sympathized with her because she had been through so much, just as he had. But for better or worse Tristan made up his mind. He wheeled his horse around to face the wizard and the dwarf.

"Narrissa has asked me to take her a bit farther into the woods, for some privacy," he said simply. "We will be back soon."

"Why?" Wigg asked skeptically. Geldon was also clearly suspicious.

"Personal reasons," Tristan said smartly. "*Female* reasons. Do I need to say more, or would you prefer that I stay here and that you two brave souls go along with her to supervise?" He smirked at the flustered wizard.

"Uh, er, no, no, of course not," Wigg stammered. "Just be back soon." Geldon's relieved face told the prince that the dwarf was also in complete, if silent, agreement.

"Which way?" Tristan whispered to Narrissa.

She paused for a moment, almost as if she needed to feel her way along for some reason. "There," she said finally pointing her arm. "Over there where the clearing begins in the edge of the woods. I think we should enter there."

Tristan turned his mount toward the small entrance into the woods, and they started to penetrate the forest proper.

"Now that we're alone, my lady, would you care to tell me what this is all about?" he asked quizzically.

"I cannot."

"And just why is that?"

"I cannot explain that which I do not fully understand myself. As I said, it is the Myth, and we can only be sure once we have reached it."

"Reached what?"

"The grave site."

Tristan abruptly stopped his horse in midstride and turned to look at the Gallipoli. "The *grave site?*"

"Yes. The grave site of all of the Gallipolai who have died in the Vale of Torment, on the wheels of the Minions."

Tristan thought for a moment. "If you have never been away from the Minion compound, then how do you know of this place, or where it is?"

"As I said, it is only the Myth. But it has been handed down by our people for hundreds of years. The legend says that the souls of all the murdered Gallipolai have gathered in one place, and that if any of us ever survives the wheel, we will be pulled there by an unseen force." She paused, biting her lip. "I can feel myself being guided there as we speak."

"And just who supposedly buried them all?" Tristan asked, more skeptical than ever. "The Minions leave their victims to rot where they lay, disposing only of their own."

"The dead Gallipolai bury themselves."

"What?"

Narissa placed two fingers over Tristan's mouth, begging him to be still. "Please, no more questions. Just keep on going. I must have my answer. I owe it to so many."

The prince reached back and drew the dreggan. If he had to go, he would go prepared.

"You will not need that," she whispered. "This is supposed to be a place of peace."

"That remains to be seen," he replied. He spurred his mount forward.

Tristan continued to ride according to Narrissa's directions, navigating by moonlight. The night sounds of the woods were all around them, and shiny, translucent dew had started to form on the tree leaves and forest floor. Finally, Narrissa told him to stop. She quickly slid off and beckoned to him to come with her. He tied his horse and cautiously followed.

Narrissa stopped at the edge of a small embankment. Using the tip of his dreggan to part the leaves of a tree, the prince looked down.

In the area below lay a small clearing. There was nothing extraordinary about it. Garlands of holly and juniper completely encircled the clearing, as if to keep it separate and distinct from the encroaching undergrowth that covered the rest of the forest floor.

"This doesn't look like a grave site to me," he commented.

"Nonetheless, I must say the words," Narrissa whispered.

"What words?"

"The ones handed down through the generations. The secret words each Gallipolai learns in childhood, against the day they might be condemned to the wheel and somehow survive. The words the Minions of Day and Night know nothing of. Although our wings and hair may turn, deep inside we are still Gallipolai. And the legend says that none of us, even those whose coloring has turned, has ever divulged the secret. For they remain Gallipolai first, and Minion second." She turned her blue eyes to him and smiled. "It is you who have made this possible, for it is you who have saved me, and I believe I may be the first to persevere."

Without speaking further, she walked to the edge of the clearing, standing near the protective rope of garlands.

"I have come, departed brothers and sisters," she began, raising her hands upward in supplication. "I am the first to have found you. Please rise and show yourselves."

Slowly, the clearing began to be bathed in violet light. In its center the glow grew brighter and seemed to revolve. Tristan watched, transfixed, as Narrissa raised her arms higher.

"I am the first to have survived the wheel," she said. "And I know my duty. Please come to me now and show yourselves, so that you may be freed."

Slowly, tentatively, from between the blades of grass, tiny bright pinpricks of light, of two different colors, began to rise. Some were the most delicate shade of twinkling amber, and the others were a shining silver. As they rose from the grass they grew until each was about the size of Tristan's hand, and then they started to revolve and sparkle as they hovered there in the clearing. There were thousands of them, and they filled the dark night like stars in a moonless sky. It was spellbindingly beautiful.

"They are called the Specters of the Gallipolai," Narrissa said. "Each of them represents one of the departed. The amber ones are the females, and the silver ones are the males. The myth says that these troubled souls shall come to a sacred place after death upon the wheel, to await the one who will free them into eternity." She paused for a moment, remembering. "Each child of the Gallipolai is told of this, and is sworn to come here should he or she survive the Minion wheels." She turned to Tristan.

"So now you understand why it was so important to me to come here, once I felt the pull. I knew it could be nothing else, just as I somehow knew that you, the one who took me from the wheel, was to be the one to accompany me. I also knew that I could not explain it to you in a way you would understand, for I myself have only seen this for the first time. *'And the one who first survives the ravages of the wheel shall also be drawn to the venue of souls, and release them from their bondage,'* " she quoted. "I know now that I am that person."

The prince could see the tears in her eyes as they gently started to overcome the lower lids and run down onto her face. "Thank you, Tristan," she whispered, her voice cracking. "Thank you for sharing this with me."

Amazed, Tristan turned his attention back to the swirling sparks of light.

And then, incredibly, as if with one mind and one voice, they spoke.

"And who is it who comes before us?" they said. Their voices were thousands and yet as only one—the sound of spoken music. Tristan had never heard such a beautiful consonance in his life.

Narrissa removed the dark robe so that her white wings could be seen, her body glistening in the pale moonlight. "I am Narrissa of the Gallipolai," she called out. "And this man without wings is my friend, and the one who released me from my bondage. He is also a slayer of the Minions, having killed the ones who would have first taken and then murdered me." She turned and smiled into Tristan's face, the glow from the Specters highlighting her great beauty. "We have much to thank him for."

"Please approach us, friend without wings," the many voices said together. "Your weapons are not needed here."

Tristan rather self-consciously replaced the dreggan in its scabbard.

"Kneel," the voices said.

Without really knowing why, the prince went down on bended knee before the thousands of the Specters of the Gallipolai, and Narrissa joined him.

"Join your hands," they ordered.

Tristan took Narrissa's hands and looked into her face. He saw fresh tears in her eyes. He, too, was starting to be overwhelmed, but something in her eyes and his heart told him that the specters were not to be feared.

"The fates have brought you together, and in turn have delivered you to us," the chorus of voices said. The twinkling amber and silver lights continued to dance before the kneeling prince and Gallipolai. "It is your act of kindness that has freed us from this place of unrest. It is now time for us to depart this world, and go to another. But know this: Wherever the two of you may go, or whatever you may do, you will always be bound in your hearts by your act of kindness this night. For it is only the good that holds beings together, and only the evil that tears them apart, and in this we thank you for your charity, your courage, and offer to you our blessings."

And then, as quickly as they had come, the Specters of the Gallipolai rose slowly into the sky, faster and faster, until the amber and silver lights began to coalesce, into one stream of light reaching for the heavens.

In a matter of seconds they were gone, leaving the stunned prince and Narrissa on their knees in the moonlight.

She reached over to his face and pulled it close, kissing him lightly.

"Thank you," she whispered. "Thank you for your trust."

Tristan looked back up to the sky, now once again full of the pinpricks of stars, and then back down to the beautiful Gallipolai. Something in his heart told him that what had just happened he would never share with Wigg or Geldon. That what they had shared here this night was to stay theirs, and theirs alone.

Tristan and Narissa rose to leave the forest. As he began to walk, the prince could not escape the feeling that whatever dangers still lay ahead for him—indeed, whether he lived or died in his attempt to find his sister—he had been strangely comforted by having seen the beautiful, twinkling lights ascend into the sky. And equally comforted, he realized, by the graceful, gentle, still-mysterious winged woman who walked quietly by his side.

*T*ristan sat on the ground under a small rocky overhang, reflecting on the amazing last two days. The four of them were now two days' ride from the Vale of Torment, and back to a path parallel to the Black River. They had moved as quickly as possible without attracting attention and had stopped here, at this rocky place on a hill overlooking the river, where they could easily see anyone who might be approaching. After a meager meal of dried meat, water, and cheese that the dwarf had brought with him from the Recluse, Wigg and Geldon had left the prince and the Gallipolai to post guard for the night, a little way down the slope toward the river.

Tristan looked up into the dark night sky, admiring the stars. *They seem closer here than at home,* he thought, looking at the iridescent pinpricks of light. *It seems as if you could reach out and touch one.* He smelled the scent of the pine trees as they swayed gently back and forth in the light wind, and he both heard and saw the undulating darkness of the Black River as it babbled happily northward toward the Recluse. The three red moons cast a subtle, violet hue upon everything as the night creatures added to the gentle song of the river. *The Recluse,* his endowed blood called out to him. *In two days I will reach the Recluse.*

Wrapped in the robe he had given her, Narrissa huddled next to him, trying to stay warm in the cold night air. Wigg had forbidden a fire, and Tristan had agreed. But despite the cold, they all—even Narrissa—were feeling refreshed by the rest, food and water. Narrissa ran a hand through her long blond hair as she looked questioningly at the prince.

"Who are you?" she asked tentatively. "I mean who are you *really*? You do not look like someone from Parthalon. In fact, none of you do. Perhaps it is only because I have never seen a man without wings before, but still there is something unexplained about you, a man with dark hair and no wings, who carries Minion weapons as well as any of the Minions themselves and was willing to take a stranger into those woods last night simply because she asked him to."

Tristan looked into the incredible eyes and thought for a moment. "I am a . . . traveler," he said at last. "I have come to find my sister, and those two other men are my friends. The older one I have known since the day of my birth. I trust each of them with my life."

"How is it that you come to carry Minion weapons?" she asked. She moved a little closer to him, pulling up her knees and wrapping her arms around them. "It is forbidden by penalty of death for anyone in Parthalon even to possess, much less carry, such things. And yet you not only carry them, but kill the Minions with them, as well."

How do I answer? he asked himself. "The sword belonged to Kluge, commander of the Minions of Day and Night. He made me use it to kill my own father." His eyes narrowed with the pain that the memories brought him. "One day, very soon, I will use it to kill him."

At the mention of Kluge's name, Narrissa lowered her head in fear. "I have seen Kluge," she said, her lips trembling lightly. "He is said to be the strongest of them all, followed only by Traax, his second in command. They came one day to inspect the fortress in which I lived. When they were not completely pleased by what they saw they killed the fortress commandant on the spot, in front of his subordinates. It is said that they train by killing their own kind, since there is no one in the kingdom worth fighting." Another look of fear crept into her eyes, and Tristan sensed it was not for herself that she was afraid. "He will not be easily killed."

"I know," he said. "But there is a fire in my blood, both born to me and fanned by the animal named Kluge. I will not rest until it has been extinguished."

She smiled at him. "There is a saying among the Gallipolai: 'It is not difficult to light a flame when the conditions are dry.' "

How true, Tristan thought. In the moonlit darkness he looked over at her face, taking in her beauty, wanting to know more of her life. "Please tell me more about yourself, Narrissa," he said to her. "How is it that one survives being a Gallipolai inside a Minion fortress? Did you have brothers and sisters to help you?"

"Gallipolai are all brother and sister to each other, existing only for the common purpose. That is, to serve the Minions. We are their slaves, our wings clipped and our feet bound. Gallipolai are considered to be worthless because of the color of our wings and hair, even though we may have had the same exact parents as any of the other Minion warriors or whores. No records are kept of who our parents might have been, a rule that is enforced to this day by the Coven. The same is true even for the warriors. In this way, we each consider ourselves to be brother or sister to all. One could almost consider it a noble concept, except for its true reason for being. It is designed to make the Minion warriors unhesitatingly think, act, and die as one in their orders, if need be." She paused for a moment, and then smiled. "The only secret that we had was the Myth of last night, and now those souls have been freed."

"And what if yet more of your kind die on the wheels?" Tristan asked softly. "Will those souls go to the same place in the forest, also waiting to be freed?"

"Yes," she answered sadly. "But now, after these many centuries, there is finally a difference. Now one of us has survived the wheels. And if I can continue to live, then I shall also be able to return there, secretly, and free the souls of the ones who may yet perish."

"Geldon said that it was forbidden for a warrior to be with a Gallipolai woman," he said gently. "Is that true?"

She lowered her eyes and turned her head slightly away. "Yes," she said quietly. "That is true. I have never been with a man. It is not permitted."

He put one finger beneath the point of her chin and lifted her face up to his. Her sapphire eyes seemed to be even more beautiful here in this dark, lonely place. "There is no need to be ashamed," he said. "Where I come from such women are considered highly virtuous, and are often preferred as wives."

Narrissa unexpectedly reached out to take both of his hands, turning them over to reveal the scars that crossed each palm. "I noticed these last night, when we joined hands before the Specters," she said softly, as she began to rub the red lines in his hands. It was almost as if she was trying to heal them faster, or take away the pain that creating them had once produced. "Do they cause you pain?"

"Only in my mind, but no longer in my hands," he answered. He let her soft, gentle hands close around his. "These scars I created myself, when I took an oath to return my sister to our native land. They serve as a reminder to me never to give up." His eyes left hers for a moment and searched the distance as if he had temporarily left this place and traveled far away. "I also wear a medallion that reminds me of my life before." He paused, thinking. "Before the madness began."

"Tristan," she asked, "what is the color of your heart?"

Her question broke his reverie, and he turned back to her. "What do you mean?"

"We have another saying, one that we ask a friend whenever we do not understand what it is that they are feeling. We respond to that question by revealing the color of our heart. Right now, I feel your heart is gray." She placed one hand against his cheek. "For us, gray is the color of sadness. But I do not believe that it has always been this way for you. I sense that one day, before the madness began, as you put it, your heart was golden." She paused, her hand still upon his cheek. "And I believe that once you have accomplished what you came here to do, whatever it is, your heart will be golden again." She smiled, lowering her eyes. "I know that time will come. I care very much for you, and hope that you will allow me to see that day with you."

Golden, he thought. *Yes, that is the perfect description of my life before the Coven came that day. Golden. But I was too selfish to realize it. What a fool I was.* He looked at Narrissa with an even greater appreciation than before. *A simple woman in a faraway land has taught me more in one day than the entire Directorate of Wizards could in an entire lifetime of trying,* he thought. *For the first time in my life a woman truly cares for me because of who I am, not what I am.*

He smiled back at her and held her closer to him. "Do your people have a saying for everything?" he asked.

"There is one of which I am particularly fond," she said.

"What is it?" he asked.

"When you find the one who most pleases your heart, plant your love and let it grow." She raised her eyes back up to his. "Tristan," she asked, "promise me you will return for me. Promise me you will survive whatever it is you must do, and come back for me."

He sat there staring at the beautiful creature before him, wondering in his heart whether there would indeed be any time for them truly to explore their feelings for each other. Whether in fact either of them would survive any of this.

He touched his lips gently to hers. "I promise to come back," he whispered. "On my life."

Plant your love and let it grow, her soft voice echoed in his heart.

Perhaps, Narrissa, he thought. *If we can survive all of this. If we can just survive.*

Twenty-five

The prince lay next to the wizard and the dwarf in the soft grass of the high mountain glade, the night sounds gathering around them as they looked down at the Recluse. *Finally*, his endowed blood seemed to be saying to him. *Finally you are here.*

It seemed like years since he had said good-bye to Narissa, and still more years since he had left the comfort of Faegan's strange house in the trees. They had come upon the dwarf's grotto earlier that morning and had left Narissa safely deep inside with food and water. Tristan had taken back his dark robe and left her with one of Geldon's spare leper robes for warmth and cover. Wigg had forbidden her to light a fire unless absolutely necessary, and instructed her not to leave unless one or more of them came for her. Geldon had supplied the candles and flint he always kept stored in his saddlebag for emergencies, and upon leaving the caves they had disguised the entrance with rocks and brush.

Despite the shininess of the tears forming in her eyes, Narrissa had bravely accepted the situation, giving the prince a kiss on the cheek before he left. It had broken his heart to leave her there alone, but he also knew it had to be. What they had ahead of them she could be no part of. But in his heart he also knew he would somehow see her again. The night before he had promised on his life to come back for her, and he meant it.

Tristan lay as still as death in the wet, cold, evening dew, his eyes glued on the castle, the weight of the dreggan and dirks on his back a silent reminder of their goal. The wizard, prince, and dwarf had been there for some time, Geldon urgently and quietly describing the layout of the amazing structure. Tristan and Wigg knew that should they some-how become separated from the dwarf, they would have to navigate the corridors of the Recluse by themselves, finding the Stables, hiding among the slaves, and finally making their way to the Sanctuary at the time of the Communion.

Tristan's eyes continued to scan the Recluse, his heart beating quickly. *Somewhere inside is Shailiha—somewhere in the depths of that magnificent fortress.* Despite how he hated its purpose, it truly was the most awe-inspiring structure he had ever seen.

The Recluse sat upon a high island, in the middle of a lake. The large body of water that surrounded it was still and tranquil tonight, as there was as yet no breeze to disturb its surface. The castle itself was reached by a long bridge, which seemed to be the only way in or out.

The drawbridge at the end of the arched bridge was lowered, and was flanked on either side by high barbicans. Just beyond, the outer courtyard areas were full of Minion warriors; others manned the portcullis, castle walls, and the drawbridge itself. Beyond the first two gate towers were another two towers, with yet another portcullis between them, banning entrance to the depths of the inner ward. These two inner gate towers seemed to be the only opening in the walls that surrounded the castle itself, protecting the forebuilding and keep, the innermost sanctuary of the Recluse. Unlike the dark and foreboding towers and outer ward areas, the buildings at the heart of the Recluse looked lighter, more ethereal. The walls seemed to be constructed of a very pale blue marble, but it was hard to tell in the moonlight.

Tristan stared in awe. The Recluse had to be at least half again the size of the royal palace at Tammerland. And that didn't even include the huge areas below ground that the dwarf had described. He couldn't imagine how many different rooms and hallways there might be. It was like something out of a dream.

The turrets at the corners of the main structure were very high, and flags carrying the Pentangle could be seen everywhere, waving in the stiffening night breeze. The entire fortress seemed to be ablaze with light, the many torches and lanterns spreading their glow into the night with an almost white-hot, unyielding intensity. The shadows they created flitted along the walls and recesses of the Recluse like haunting ghosts in the night.

Tristan's eyes narrowed to focus on the highest, most well-protected area of the inner structure. It ran upward to an astonishing height, ending in a dome of stained glass. *The keep,* Tristan realized as he looked at the fortress where his sister was imprisoned. *An apt name. That is where their private quarters will be.*

Silence reigned between them for several moments as they took in the splendor of the scene below. It was the dwarf who finally spoke next. "As we cross the drawbridge and go under the portcullis, make sure to keep your hoods over your faces and your heads lowered, and sway in your saddles a bit as if you have been drugged. In addition, make sure no one can tell that the chains around your wrists are not tight. We will be proceeding directly to the Stables. Do exactly as I say, and above all do not speak, whatever happens." He turned to look at them. "Here, in this place, life has no value," he said sadly. "But death sometimes has a price." Silence once again settled in around the three of them like a blanket of fog.

Lying in the grass next to the prince, Wigg could feel against his chest the hardness of the small pewter locket that Faegan had quietly given him just before he and Tristan had left Shadowood. Faegan's last words of advice echoed in the Lead Wizard's mind, and he knew that now was the time to conduct the difficult conversation with Tristan.

He looked at Geldon with determined eyes. "I must speak to the prince by myself," he whispered. "It is no reflection upon you. You have served us extraordinarily well, as I'm sure you will continue to do. But right now the prince and I need to be alone."

Geldon gave a short, reluctant nod of understanding. "Be quick about it," he whispered back urgently. "This area is crawling with Minions, and I have already been gone from the Recluse for a long time. We must enter the castle as soon as possible." He crawled a little way back down the hill and sat up against a tree stump, where he could keep watch on the area below.

One corner of Wigg's mouth turned up admiringly as he watched the dwarf deftly slither down the hill and take up his position. *Despite all that he has been through,* the old one thought, *he makes use of every second.*

Tristan slid closer to the wizard, concern creasing his brow. For hours his blood had been churning with his proximity to the Recluse, and he was in no mood for talk. "You heard Geldon. We don't have time for this! Shailiha is down there! What is it I need to listen to now?" he asked. "Another of your lectures on being prudent?"

Wigg ignored him. There was too much at stake to begin another verbal joust with the prince. "Listen to me," he said sternly. "What I have to say may be the most important thing you ever hear in your life. Three nights from now, when the Blood Communion begins, we must be in the Sanctuary with the Coven. How we are to do this without being detected I have no idea. But you must remember what Faegan said to us that night at dinner. During the Communion is the only time the sorceresses are vulnerable. Until that time I must continue to struggle to hide our endowed blood, a task that becomes much more difficult as I travel closer to the sorceresses."

"That much I already know," Tristan said. He was obviously anxious to be off, but the Lead Wizard continued to be firm.

"What you *don't* know is that should I become killed or incapacitated, you *must* take the pewter locket that hangs around my neck."

Tristan was stymied for an instant, and then he remembered Faegan giving the locket to Wigg. At the time, he'd been too concerned with his thoughts of Shailiha to ask about it. He did, however, remember what it looked like. Small and octagonally shaped, it had a stopper in the top and was hung by a silver chain.

"What does it hold?" he asked.

"That I cannot tell you at this time."

Tristan narrowed his eyes. "Then why tell me of it now?"

"Because if I am dead, you must do as I have told you. Open the locket, look into it, and you will understand. Besides, what you do not know cannot be tortured from you. Need I remind you of my attempts to make you listen to me that night on the dais?"

The wizard's words hurt, but Tristan knew that Wigg was right. Had he listened that awful night, Shailiha might not be one of the Coven. More contrite, he was now ready to hear the rest of what Wigg had to say.

The wizard noticed the change in the prince's eyes. "Do you remember when you first saw the bridge over the cavern to Shadowood?" he asked.

"Yes."

"Whether you realized it or not, that was the first time you ever made use of the craft. And you did so without any previous formal training. That is without precedent." Wigg looked carefully at Tristan. "When Faegan heard of it, he was astounded. That was one of the things we were discussing in private. He told me that he believes if you concentrate hard enough, due to the quality of your blood you *might* be able to use the craft, even if the Coven and I are powerless. Not in any major way, since you are untrained, but hopefully in some small way that might help us. Something simple, such as moving an object or lighting a flame. For most wizards, even these lesser examples of the craft can only be accomplished after years of practice. But you, the Chosen One, may be able to do so by nature." Wigg watched the carefully chosen words sink in, fully aware of the effect they would have.

Tristan felt as if he had just been hit by a thunderbolt of understanding. *This is why my blood calls out to me so,* he thought. *It calls out in its need to be used.* "How do I accomplish this?" he asked breathlessly.

"The same way you managed to see the bridge, but with one difference. In order to see the bridge, you first had to stop *trying* to see it, and let it come to you. Do you remember?"

"Yes."

"And then once you had mastered that, just before you solved Shannon's riddle, you heard the beating of your own heart."

Casting his mind back to that day, Tristan could almost hear it again. He remembered the breeze on his face, and Pilgrim standing quietly next to him as he sat in the grass of the field.

"When you finally hear your heart," Wigg continued, "you must use your mind to will whatever it is you want to take place. Remember, you will not be able to perform great deeds, but you may be able to accomplish something small. It will require a great deal of effort." He hesitated. "It will take everything you have."

The inflection in the wizard's voice as he spoke the last few words ignited a spark of concern in the prince. "What is it you haven't told me?" he asked gently.

I have been his teacher since the day he was born, Wigg thought. *But how am I supposed to counsel him on something that even I myself am unsure of?* He looked down at the ground. "The act of using the craft may have an effect upon you, since you are trying to use it without having been trained first."

"What kind of effect?"

"Even Faegan did not know. But we must be on the lookout for it." Wigg's eyebrow came up in its customary arch. "Your situation, after all, is unique."

Confused, Tristan thought for a moment. "But you said the first time I used the craft was at the bridge to Shadowood. Why did that not change me?" he asked.

"Because that was, in fact, only a very small manifestation of the craft," Wigg replied. "You were only trying to observe something that was already there, not trying to affect it in any way, such as altering its nature, or trying to get it to move. Overcoming your lack of training to accomplish more difficult feats will require an unheard-of strength of will. Even Faegan was not sure whether you would be able to do it. But, if you do, this supreme effort may change you forever. Next to this effort, seeing the bridge will seem mere child's play."

"Anything else?"

"If I have failed in my attempt to stop the Communion, make every attempt possible to kill Failee first. She is the one who holds the most knowledge of the Vagaries. Therefore, if she dies, much of the Coven's knowledge of the Vagaries dies with her." Wigg seemed to turn melancholy. "And, in the end, if none of the aforementioned things can be accomplished, you know what our duty must be."

A cold, inescapable pain shot directly through Tristan's heart. *He's talking about killing Shailiha!* He looked into the eyes that he held so dear and took the old wizard's gnarled hands in his. "I am aware of my responsibilities," he said purposefully. The muscles in his jaw tightened. "But I swear to the Afterlife I will find another way."

"One last thing," Wigg said, his hands still held by the prince. "If I am dead and you have successfully survived all this, once you return to Eutracia, stay close to Faegan. He'll be the single remaining person with enough knowledge to properly train you in the craft."

Without giving Tristan another chance to speak, Wigg glanced down the hill and indicated to Geldon that they were ready to leave. The dwarf rejoined them and, putting a finger to his lips to indicate silence, led them back to their horses. Once the prince and the wizard were in their saddles, Geldon pulled their hoods up over their heads and wrapped the chains around their wrists. He then joined them together with another length of chain and took hold of the end.

Almost as if he were trying silently to say good-bye, Geldon looked into each of their faces in turn and then shifted in his saddle to begin leading the Stable's newest slaves to the Recluse.

Twenty-six

T ristan lowered his head drunkenly in the hood of his robe as he swayed slightly to the left and right in his saddle, his chained hands in front of him. The ride to the Recluse was agonizingly slow. He desperately wanted to raise his face free of the hood to see better what was happening, but he knew he must not. It was conceivable that the Minions guarding the castle could include some of the same troops who had ransacked Tammerland and killed his family. In response to that thought, his blood churned violently. But this time he knew why, and he hoped that very soon now he would have the chance to satisfy its lust.

As they began to traverse the bridge, several of the Minion warriors called out to Geldon, bidding him hello, and laughingly insulting the two apparent captives with filthy warnings of what would happen to them inside the Recluse. Geldon laughed along with them, careful to neither stop to talk nor speed up his advance. The dark, leathery pairs of wings Tristan could see out of the corners of his eyes made him acutely aware of the sword and knives across his back as the three of them continued across the bridge. *So far so good,* he reassured himself.

When they reached the drawbridge and the first portcullis, a squad of five Minion officers, completely armed, began to walk briskly toward them from the gate towers, the heels of their barbed leather boots snapping crisply on the dried wood of the bridge. From their midst emerged another, larger and stronger looking than the rest, carelessly holding a jug of red wine. He was obviously in command.

"Halt!" the lead officer ordered.

Geldon obediently brought his horse to a stop. As the other two horses followed suit, Tristan's knuckles whitened in their grip on the reins to his horse, and his breath momentarily caught in his lungs.

The senior officer smiled. In size, he was almost the equal of Kluge. Looking up at the dwarf with a leering, vengeful sneer, he asked, "So the hunting was good, eh? Mistress Succiu will be pleased. We thought you were never coming back." A loud, wet belch emerged from his mouth, and he wiped his lips with the back of his hand. "I hope these two will be worth the trouble."

He began to walk unsteadily around the rear of the prince's and wizard's horses, his free hand on the hilt of the dreggan at his side as he enjoyed his little game. For a time he surveyed the two cloaked figures as if he were considering a purchase at the market. Then he stopped next to Tristan. The prince stiffened. *He's drunk,* Tristan realized frantically. *This could make things much more difficult.*

As the officer's brow furrowed and his eyes narrowed with curiosity, Tristan heard the clear, unmistakable ring of a dreggan being drawn from its scabbard. Suddenly, the steel blade clanged piercingly into the night as the officer touched the button on the hilt and loosed the tip of the blade forward. Tristan's heart skipped a beat.

The officer raised the sword awkwardly and then gave a sharp, taunting poke to Tristan's ribs. The tip of the blade went through the cloak, piercing his black leather vest and cutting him, drawing blood. Tristan could feel the sticky liquid running down the length of his abdomen in a slow, warm trickle. But still he managed not to flinch, and continued to sway slightly in his saddle as if too drugged to notice. The Minion officer looked skeptically at the dwarf, the point of his dreggan still at the prince's side.

"Men or women?" he asked the dwarf drunkenly. He obviously hoped it was women.

"Men," Geldon said angrily. "And if they enter the Stable harmed it will be you who will answer to the second mistress for it." He glared at the officer as the winged one continued to smile arrogantly back at him.

It was clear the officer was unimpressed with the dwarf's warning as he took another draught of the wine, much of it running sloppily from his mouth and down the front of his chest. Raising the sword a little higher, he pushed harder and then began to twist the blade, smiling in contempt at the dwarf as he did so. It was all Tristan could do to keep from crying out in pain. The steel had gone deeper, through the muscle, and Tristan could feel it twisting and grating against the bone. The pain was excruciating, setting his entire right side on fire. *Hold,* his mind shouted at him. *Ignore the pain, or we all will surely die.* The Minion officer smiled lopsidedly as he watched the trickle of blood that had begun to run down the length of the shiny blade. He looked the dwarf hard in the eye.

"Very well." He snorted, obviously pleased with himself. "You may pass." The bloodstained tip of the dreggan suddenly came out and up in a swift arc to end less than an inch from Geldon's right eye. "But if asked, the slave was injured during his capture. Do you understand?" It wasn't a question, it was a command. "I could make life very hard for you if I chose to. And provided I didn't kill you, you little bastard, I doubt Mistress Succiu would care at all." He laughed and slapped Geldon's horse hard on the rump with the flat of his blade. "Go!" he shouted. He took another swig of the wine. "Go and report to your owner! And take your precious slaves with you."

Geldon waited for no further inducement. He quickly led the prince and the wizard under the portcullis and through the outer ward of the Recluse, heading toward the second portcullis, the one that protected the entrance to the inner ward and the forebuildings that lay beyond it.

The Minion officer turned around to grin at his four smiling troops and lifted the wine jug to his lips. Then, as he watched the dwarf and his two slaves make their way into the main structure of the Recluse, he wiped his dreggan clear of blood. Once the three horses were finally out of sight, he threw the wine jug to his men and replaced the sword in its scabbard, sober once again. Obviously confused, his men watched as he did something unexpected: Climbing the stairs to the top of the gate tower, he lifted a torch into the air and quickly waved it back and forth.

From across the inner yard, at the top of the wall between the second pair of gate towers, the lone Minion officer saw the waving flame, and his eyes narrowed in delight. Smiling, he walked out from his hiding place, stretched his long, muscular wings, and flew effortlessly down into a shadowed area of the inner yard, landing as lightly as a feather.

Kluge turned to look through the inky night and across the broad length of the inner yard as the dwarf, wizard, and prince finally made their way to the side of the forebuilding and through the hidden door that led to the Stables.

Welcome, he thought. *Welcome to the Recluse, Lead Wizard and Chosen One.* He could hardly contain his joy. The officer he had chosen had played his part well, and the Eutracians had been completely unaware. He paused in his thoughts, gazing jubilantly at the three red moons that had finally made complete appearances in the night sky. Lowering his dark head he looked back at the Recluse, its exotic architecture silent and sprawling like a giant spider crouched upon the great courtyard as he stood there alone in the moonlight, his lengthened, muscular shadow stretching ominously across the ground. His hand tightened around the hilt of his dreggan, and his jaw clenched.

Welcome, Chosen One. The small wound in your side is nothing compared to what I shall honor you with.

This is the place where you shall die.

Tristan heard Geldon close the door behind them with a heavy, quiet finality. The dwarf immediately drew his finger across his lips, indicating silence.

"Keep your cloaks on," he whispered seriously as he moved toward the doorway of the little room and peered out into the adjoining hall. "We have entered through a small side door used only to bring in slaves. As you follow me, be sure to continue to appear drugged. The Stables are below ground level, and we must pass through another area first." Stepping back closer to the prince, he saw that the wizard had lifted Tristan's robe and was examining his wound. Blood was dripping down Tristan's side.

"I cannot use my craft to stop the bleeding," Wigg snapped in frustration. It was obvious to Geldon that the struggle to hide their endowed blood was becoming a great strain on the Lead Wizard.

The dwarf produced a small rag from one of his pockets, and Wigg pressed it against the wound. The prince flinched at the painful contact. "Hold this against your side," Wigg said apologetically. "The last thing we need is a trail of endowed blood down the hallways of the Recluse. The more of it there is, the more difficult it becomes for me to hide its presence." He released control of the rag to Tristan. "I'm sorry, but this is the best I can do for now." Then, carefully and slowly, Geldon took up their chains and led them out into the hallway.

Doing his best to look drugged while also holding the rag against his side, Tristan cast furtive glances around him as he shuffled along behind the dwarf. What he saw amazed him. The intersecting hallways of the Recluse were gigantic and seemed to stretch on endlessly, with curved, vaulted ceilings that rose at least thirty feet into the air. The highly polished marble was of the palest blue, shot through with darker indigo streaks that randomly crisscrossed each other like the paths of shooting stars in the night sky. The light in the hallway was very bright, emanating from numerous wall sconces, each of which seemed to be made of solid gold. The warm, rather humid air was scented with what seemed to be fresh lilac. He narrowed his eyes, thinking. The entire effect was one of great beauty and grace, creating a façade of tranquility that intentionally seemed to overlie what he knew to be the true, barbaric nature of the place.

At last Geldon slowed and led them into a much larger, circular room with a stained-glass ceiling, into which spilled a number of other hallways. In the center of the room was a blue marble spiral stairway leading downward. Without hesitation the dwarf headed right for the stairs, and together they descended, single file, into the bowels of the Recluse.

The stairway was as wide as the corridor had been, and as brightly lit. On and on they went, traveling lower with every step, and it seemed to Tristan that the stairs would never end. He could not recall ever having been so far below ground, even in the Redoubt of the Directorate back at the palace in Tammerland. After what seemed like forever, they stopped, their way barred by a stone door. Pushing hard, Geldon swiveled it inward upon its hinges. He peered quickly into the room beyond, and then beckoned them in.

What Tristan saw next made his heart recoil.

The chamber was clearly a place of torture. It was very large and constructed of dark, rough-hewn stone. Flames roared full blaze in a fireplace, and in the center of the room was a blacksmith's hearth, fueled by hot coals. A collection of iron rods and branding pokers had been shoved into the bright, orange embers, their ends aglow with heat. In one corner sat an enormous cauldron.

Tristan stood spellbound as he continued to look around the room, the flames from the fireplace creating menacing, ephemeral shadows that danced lightly across the walls. Scattered around the room were several roughly fashioned wooden chairs, each of which had manacles and turnbuckles attached to its arms and legs for holding a prisoner in place. A long, flat table stood a little way off, with what he could only imagine to be disemboweling tools lying on a wooden tray next to it. The tools were covered in dried, crimson-black blood. Flogging whips and chains of all descriptions hung upon the walls, and a stretching rack angled threateningly up against one of the room's supporting beams. He realized that he had begun to sweat, as much from the heat in the room as from the nature of its purpose. And then, suddenly, he detected the smell.

It was like nothing else he had sensed before, a sweet, sickly aroma combined with a stench like that of raw meat burning. The powerful fragrances slowly curled up and entwined around the three of them as they stood there, in horrified silence, the crackling fire the only sound—at first.

Then Tristan heard the first light drip. It sounded like the familiar soft plop of a raindrop falling upon a broad leaf in the forest. And then there was another, and yet another. He looked down, his first reaction to check the wound in his side, but it had stopped oozing, and was already scabbing over. Following the sounds of the dripping, he finally found their origin. It was blood, and it was dripping upon the three of them from above. And whether he had a full lifetime remaining to him or whether he would die this day in the Recluse, Tristan instinctively knew that what he saw above him would haunt his dreams forever.

At first nothing could be seen; the room was too dark, and the ceiling timbers were so large and recessed into the roof above. But the longer the three of them stood there and looked, the more obvious the nightmare became. Naked people, apparently simple citizens of the countryside, had been hung from the ceiling in between the rafters. But they were not suspended by the neck, as was the usual way of hanging. These poor souls had been disemboweled. Part of their entrails hung crazily out and over the sides of their bodies. Their hands and feet had been nailed to the ceiling, suspending each of them faceup, in grisly human arches of death. In many cases their genitals had been horribly mutilated, and the prince also saw that some had suffered having their eyelids crudely sewn shut with strips of rough leather.

There had to be at least twenty men and women suspended there, twisting and bleeding, their entrails hanging impossibly over the sides of their bodies, the blood dripping casually to the floor. Then, suddenly, he noticed something else.

Each of them had been branded with the sign of the Pentangle. The five-pointed star could be seen scorched into the naked skin of each body at various places. That accounted for the stench, Tristan realized in disgust. Looking again at the room, he made another grisly deduction. *It also accounts for the dried blood on the disemboweling tools, and the iron rods still heating in the hearth,* he realized. *These people have been dead for only a short time.* Looking over silently at the dwarf, he could see that even Geldon was in shock at what he saw.

"What in the name of the Afterlife happened here?" Tristan whispered incredulously.

Geldon hesitated, as if trying to choke down the impulse to vomit. He swallowed hard. "The Afterlife has very little to do with what has happened here," he said quietly. "I have come through this room hundreds of times over the last three centuries, sometimes even when it was in use." He sighed deeply and closed his eyes. "But even I have never seen such savagery as this." Geldon looked to the Lead Wizard for comfort and guidance, as if Wigg always had the answer to everything.

The old one's eyebrow came up as he closely investigated the corpses, silently walking beneath them and examining them much the way a healer would do. "These people have been tortured for a very special reason," he ruminated, half to himself. He returned to stand beside the dwarf and the prince. "Although they could have known nothing, it is possible the poor devils were questioned about *us*."

"There is another reason for their suffering," Geldon said sadly.

Wigg clasped his hands together within the sleeves of his cloak. "And that is?"

"The worst reason of all. The Coven enjoys it."

Tristan's heart recoiled as he wondered whether Shailiha could have had any part in what had happened here. He tried to blot the prospect from his mind.

"We leave here now," Wigg ordered. "How much farther to the Stables?"

"It is a rather long and winding walk from here," Geldon replied. "Behave exactly as you have up to this point. You are still supposedly drugged and bound by the chains. If we are stopped by anyone, be certain not to speak." He took up the chains and led his companions to a stone door at the other side of the room.

It was indeed a long way, through a maze of blue marble corridors identical to the previous ones, and after a time the prince was beginning to wonder impatiently if they would ever reach their destination. His heart beat quickly at the thought of coming closer to Shailiha with his every step. He could almost feel her presence as he followed the dwarf through the great subterranean halls.

They were in a busier part of the Recluse now. From the recesses of his hood, Tristan saw all kinds of people coming and going about their business. Kitchen workers and handmaidens, scullery maids, and even the occasional Minion warrior. The Minions were almost always fully armed and moving with seemingly great intent. No one showed any particular interest in the three of them, however, except for the occasional palace worker or servant who nodded at the dwarf in silent greeting. Geldon always nodded back carefully, never stopping to speak even if the other person appeared to want to.

Finally, the dwarf stopped before a magnificent pair of black double doors. The sign of the Pentangle was inlaid into each of them, glistening brightly in solid gold. A huge, armed Minion warrior stood at attention at either side of the doors. Tristan's heart skipped a beat as the dwarf brazenly walked directly up to the doors as if he owned them and stared defiantly at the winged warriors.

"New slaves for the Stables," he said imperiously. Tristan was suddenly reminded that, despite the dwarf's physical stature, Geldon was nonetheless the emissary of the second mistress and would therefore command at least a modicum of respect, even from the Minion guards.

The guards gave the two figures behind Geldon a perfunctory glance, and then the one on the right stepped before the door on his side and, without a word, opened it to allow them in.

Saying nothing, Geldon led his charges into the next room, and Tristan could hear the enormous marble door close heavily behind them. At a nod from Geldon, the prince and wizard threw back their hoods and looked around. What they saw defied description.

The room they were standing in was huge, rivaling in size the Great Hall of the royal palace in Tammerland. Walls and floor were marble of the faintest rose, shot through with both indigo and white streaks. The ceiling was even higher here, almost double the height of the hallways, and made of the palest blue marble, with the occasional gray streak running through it.

Everywhere he looked the prince saw nothing but opulence and comfort. Chairs, sofas, and loveseats of every shape and size filled the room. Long tables of food and drink were piled so bountifully high that he thought at first some of their contents might fall off onto the highly polished rose-colored marble floors. Handmaidens came and went, refilling the tankards of wine that sat upon the tables and bringing ever-more-appealing food to replace immediately whatever was taken. There were cascading fountains and cool, serene swimming pools. The soft, gentle music of a flute and lyre wafted upon the air. And nearby, with various colored oils warming over low flames standing ready at their sides, stood tables for massage.

Then Tristan noticed the strange scent. A curious combination of sweetness combined with heavy musk, it seemed to wash over the entire room. In fact, the longer he stood looking, the more he could detect the presence of it in the air. It seemed to give the atmosphere in the room a distinctly violet hue.

But of all the amazing aspects of the room, it was the slaves that fascinated him the most. The place was full of hundreds of young people, seemingly equally divided between men and women. Every one was a physically beautiful specimen, dressed only in a scanty loincloth. Lithe and happy, they seemed to care little that they were slaves as they frolicked and swam, danced and laughed, and kissed and stroked each other, occasionally pausing to take some of the food and drink. Each of them had the sign of the Pentangle tattooed upon his or her right arm, presumably as a method of identifying any that should manage to escape. But the prince could not imagine any of them wanting to: They all seemed happy beyond their wildest dreams. Oddly, none of them seemed to notice the three intruders.

In contrast to the revelers, there were a number of slaves lazing on floor cushions in the middle of the room, seemingly doing very little. In the center of them sat a very large device, the likes of which Tristan had never seen. Its base was a large glass bowl, with glass tubes extending upward from it and branching outward into several lines of woven material, each of which ended in a circular piece of brass. To his amazement, one of the slaves took the end of one of the lines, placed the brass piece into his or her mouth, then seemed to inhale deeply. After holding his breath for a time, he blew the violet smoke from his mouth, relaxed and handed the appliance to the woman next to him. Transfixed, Tristan stood watching as time after time the slaves continued this strange practice, each occasionally relinquishing his or her spot to another who had joined them and was waiting his turn. As far as he knew, there was no such custom in Eutracia, and he was fascinated. He looked at the dwarf in confusion.

"It is an addiction," Geldon said softly, his face pinched by the pain the scene brought him. "Whatever you do, do not participate in it. This is the reason they seem so happy. The pipe in the center is filled with the flower of a local plant that is cultivated by the sorceresses, and each new slave is forced to ingest it. The result is initial happiness, followed by addiction, always leading eventually to madness and then death. Its purpose is to keep the slaves under control." He paused, looking sadly out at the spectacle before him. "It is also the reason that the Stables must be constantly replenished with new captives."

Tristan was about to speak when he noticed a strange look upon the wizard's face. His heart froze when he realized it was an expression of stark terror. He took an automatic, protective step toward Wigg, but then, as if in slow motion, the wizard roughly pushed the prince to one side, raised his arms, and stood squarely before his companions as if trying to protect them from something. Suddenly Tristan saw a great azure ball of flame barreling toward them. He had never seen anything so beautiful and terrible at the same time, its giant presence and thundering noise seeming to swallow up everything in his vision. But before he could cry out or move, the great ball was upon them, smashing into them with its noise, heat, and light. A thousand excruciating flashes of pain exploded in his head—and everything went black.

CHAPTER

Twenty-seven

Tristan awakened with a start and a gasp, his eyes snapping open quickly and suddenly. He vaguely remembered hearing women's voices talking and laughing from some distance away, but could neither hear nor see anyone now.

Looking around, he could see nothing but ghostly, ephemeral fog and shadowy darkness. He seemed to be standing upon solid ground, yet at the same time he had the impression that he was turning in mid-air, first this way and then that, at the behest of some unseen power. The air was cold, he realized, as he watched the white ghosts of water vapor leave his mouth with each breath. Yet he remained strangely calm. It was almost as if he were regarding himself in a mirror, uncaring, from some great distance. *Is this what it is truly like to be dead?* he wondered. *Is this the Afterlife?*

"Tristan!" The voice was male, and came to him from somewhere in the gloom. The prince turned to look about, but still could see nothing. "Tristan!" the foreign yet familiar voice called once again. A figure appeared before him, slowly taking shape.

It was his father.

Tristan gasped and immediately tried to run to Nicholas, but found himself held back somehow. The more he tried to reach his father, the stronger the forces that bound him became.

"Do not try to come to me, my son," Nicholas said in the same kind yet commanding voice that Tristan remembered. "It is impossible. For I am dead and you are alive, and it is not permitted for you to cross over in this manner."

Tristan sank to one knee before the apparition and lowered his head. Tears began to form in his eyes. "I am dreaming, aren't I?" he asked.

"Yes," Nicholas said quietly. "Rise and look at me."

Tristan rose on shaky legs. Before him, Nicholas wore the same dark-blue ceremonial robes that he had been wearing when he was killed, and an angry red scar encircled his neck. The dead king's face and hands were the white, lifeless color of snow.

"Where are we, Father?" Tristan heard himself ask. His voice echoed, hollow and never ending.

"It doesn't matter," Nicholas said. "What matters is that I can reach out to touch your mind this one last time. Your mother, Frederick, and the wizards of the Directorate send their love."

The tears were falling freely down the prince's cheeks now, and he clasped his hands together in supplication. "Please forgive me, Father," he begged. "Please forgive me for killing you." He began to sob openly as his mind returned to that hideous nightmare on the dais, the weight of the same dreggan that killed the man before him now impossibly heavy across his back. This time he was sure the pain in his heart was more than he could endure.

"There is nothing to forgive," the dead king said gently. "You had no choice. Both the wizard and I could see that." He looked down at the son he had loved so much. His only son, his heir. "My death is not the reason I have come."

Nicholas then seemed to move closer. Tristan longed to hold his father, even for only a moment, but he somehow knew that the force that was holding him would prevent that.

Apparently the dead king was not so bound. Nicholas reached out and lifted the gold medallion from Tristan's chest. He studied it in the dark, then he let it gently drop back against the prince. "I have come to tell you that you must do everything in your power to save your sister— and, by doing so, also save the world as we know it." He paused, still looking at the medallion as though remembering all that it had once represented. "You and she are the very future of Eutracia," he said. "You must rule, and she must be free of the powers that hold her here, free to go home and raise her child in peace. But also understand this: If you are able to return with her, be informed that there are many problems in our homeland, and your destiny, however difficult, still waits to be fulfilled. You two are the Chosen Ones. But the Prophecies decree that it is you, the male, upon whom the main burden falls."

The dead king's image began to soften and waver, and Tristan instinctively knew that very soon his father's presence would be lost to him forever. He also knew that there was no use trying to fight to keep him here.

But this chance to see his father one last time had granted him not only a modicum of peace and forgiveness, but inspiration, as well. He managed a slight smile though his tears.

As Nicholas' image began to fade away into nothingness, his final words drifted to Tristan's ears. "Sleep now, my son," the dead king said, his voice becoming ever more faint. "Sleep now, that you may once again awake and fulfill your destiny." He vanished.

Tristan gratefully slumped against the unknown forces containing him and surrendered to the need for sleep as he turned and twisted in the cold, dark emptiness.

Twenty-eight

True peace of mind comes only when my heart and actions are aligned with true principles and values. I shall forsake not, to the loss of all material things, my honor and integrity. I shall protect the Paragon above all else, but take no life except in urgent defense of self and others, or without fair warning. I swear to rule always with wisdom and compassion.

The words seemed to come to Tristan's ears from somewhere nearby, and resonated through the air around him in hollow, emaciated tones. The voice sounded much like his own, but he couldn't quite identify the meaning or significance of the words. He knew he had heard them somewhere before, and for some reason he was sure they had great importance to him.

Again he felt his body turning slowly, ever so slowly in the air as his mind began to clear. Then he realized what the words meant. *The voice was mine! I have been reciting the succession oath while I was unconscious.*

His eyes opened slowly, painfully, his mind and vision still cloudy. It seemed every part of him was in pain, and as he took in the scene around him, his first reaction was to scream out in anger.

He was trapped like an animal in some kind of cage. It was fashioned like a bizarre, elongated birdcage and suspended in the air. Black, iron bands curved down from the center of its top to join with the metal floor. He was standing up, his legs and knees trembling in exhaustion. He had no idea how long he had been here, standing like this. Looking around as best he could, he was able to see no door to the cage.

His arms were hanging down, touching the sides of his body, the bars of the cage squeezing in on him from all sides like a cocoon of iron. He realized that both his dreggan and his dirks lay undisturbed across his back, but reaching them was impossible. He felt something slip inside of him, his blood slowly turning to ice as it became abundantly clear that here, in this cage, any movement other than the acts of speaking and breathing seemed to be hopeless concepts. Beads of sweat began to run down from his forehead, maddeningly tickling him as they crept their way down his face and neck and under the leather lacings of his vest.

His eyes slowly clearing, the first thing that he saw outside of his cage was one of the sorceresses.

Failee, he thought. *It has to be.*

She was standing very close to him, before a white marble altar in the center of the room. Slowly looking him up and down, she was examining him as if he were some creature from another world, and he shuddered to realize that he was under her complete control. Tall and shapely, she had dark hair shot through with streaks of gray. The Paragon hung around her neck from the gold chain he knew so well, and she was dressed in a magnificent red gown, the sign of the Pentangle embroidered in gold thread over the left breast. In her own way, she was as beautiful as he remembered Succiu to be. But the most arresting feature about her was her eyes. Sparkling hazel, almost incandescent, they shone with a high degree of intelligence that just barely masked the touch of madness lurking within them. His mind went back to that night in Shadowood when Faegan had warned him of the First Mistress. *"I know you have witnessed some of the evil they are capable of,"* the rogue wizard had said. *"But make no mistake, even though you are the Chosen One. Despite what you have seen from Succiu, she is nothing compared to Failee."*

His vision almost back to normal, he now saw two other sorceresses. They were standing just behind their mistress, in this strange room with the black marble thrones and the huge Pentangle of black marble inlaid into the floor. The light from the many gold oil sconces gave the room a quiet, almost soft sense, and the air was tinged with the scent of lilac, just like the hallways above. Because it was impossible for him to turn around, he had absolutely no idea what was behind him, making him feel even more vulnerable and exposed.

One of the sorceresses had straight, red hair and deep-blue eyes. She, too, was dressed in a red gown, and she wore an emerald-encrusted design of the Pentangle around her neck.

The tall, smiling blond standing next to her was equally impressive. Long ringlets cascaded over the shoulders of her own red gown; her green eyes were level and commanding over a mouth that he instinctively suspected wore a permanently sarcastic smirk. She toyed nonstop with her ringlets as she admired him in his cage, saying nothing.

"So the rooster has finally entered the henhouse!" came a female voice from somewhere out of his line of vision. It was dominant yet familiar, with a nasty ring that meant business despite the flippant nature of the insult. Succiu.

The second mistress entered the room from a small doorway to the left and walked to the center of the floor to join the others. He guessed from the way she was dressed that she had just come from a session of enjoying her bizarre tastes, and blood could be seen on her fingertips and on the toes of her black leather boots. Her matching black leather vest and trousers were stretched tightly around her form, leaving little to the imagination. A long black bullwhip hung from the silver-studded leather belt that was slung low around her hips, and the obscenely high heels of her boots sounded like snaps of the same whip as she walked commandingly across the marble floor to stand directly in front of him in his cage. She looked hungrily up into his face with the same exotic, almond-shaped eyes he had come to remember and hate with every fiber of his being.

Reaching up, she placed one of her long, painted nails through the rent in the side of his vest and then painfully punctured his wound. He could feel it begin to bleed. Smiling, she removed her bloody finger and touched it to her tongue, closing her eyes. "Such blood," she said to him quietly, almost gently, as if she and the prince were the only two people in the world. "I have never known its equal."

Hands upon her hips, she turned back to the other three mistresses. "Beautiful, isn't he?" she asked. "Just as I described him."

Turning back to Tristan, she smiled. "In case you were wondering, the rather unique cage you find yourself in is called a gibbet. We have found them to be useful for a variety of reasons. But where are my manners? I believe some introductions are in order." Extending her arm, she turned back to the Coven. "I give you Failee, Vona, and Zabarra. They have been most anxious to meet you." Tristan remained silent as he stood before them in his tight, unforgiving prison—his gibbet, as she called it. *Let them gloat,* he thought. *It's what they do best.*

"But there are only four of us here," Failee said. "Don't you think it is time to show the prince the one whom he has come so far to see?" Levitating herself, she glided over to where Tristan stood in his cage. "The one who has most recently joined us," she whispered, almost reverently, almost inaudibly. "I believe you know her. The female of the Chosen Ones for whom we have waited so long." She paused, as if the mere mention of his sister's name was cause for a display of reverence. "The fifth sorceress. Your sister, Shailiha."

At the mention of Shailiha's name Tristan's breath caught in his lungs, and a feeling of both anticipation and dread shot through him. His sister had been foremost in his mind since he regained consciousness, despite his concern over the apparent disappearance of Geldon and Wigg. He looked down at the First Mistress with eyes that knew only hate.

"Where is she?" he hissed at her, straining futilely against the bars of the gibbet. He could feel his endowed blood rising in his veins and the dreggan across his back calling out to him to take it in his hands and draw blood. But the only movement he could summon was to bend forward slightly. The gold medallion around his neck slipped away from his sweaty chest and dangled downward, twinkling in the pale light of the room. The combination of his blood commanding him to take action and the gibbet preventing him from doing so made him feel as though his heart were about to burst. He continued to glare hatefully into the hazel eyes of the First Mistress.

"Sister Shailiha," Succiu called out of the room. "Come and meet the Chosen One."

It was then that Tristan saw her.

Shailiha walked out from behind one of the great black thrones to stand directly before him, alongside Succiu. Tristan felt a wave of love and compassion spread across his heart, followed by immediate misgivings. This was clearly not the Shailiha that he knew.

She was dressed in the same red gown as Failee, Vona, and Zabarra, but hers was generously cut to allow for her pregnancy. Around her neck lay a gold chain, each end of which ran down into the bodice of her dress, presumably suspending some piece of jewelry in the valley of cleavage that lay between her breasts. The Pentangle, he assumed. Her abdomen was hugely swollen, and it looked to the prince as though she would give birth at any moment. The same strong, beautiful face that he had always known and loved was there before him, but there was something very different about it. Shailiha now had a look of commanding presence, of the ability to wield great power, and to do so without mercy or guilt. He remembered what Geldon had told him about her having willfully murdered one of the Stable slaves, and sadly he was forced to admit to himself that the person he saw before him looked fully capable of such things. The long blond hair that cascaded down onto her shoulders framed beautiful, narrowed hazel eyes that looked at him with a contemptuousness born of what soon would become true power of a frightening magnitude.

"Shailiha," Tristan begged. He looked desperately into her eyes, hoping that he would find some glimmer there of the woman his sister used to be. "It's me, Tristan. Your twin brother. Don't you remember me?" Tears began to form in his eyes as he saw that she clearly was not responding, and his voice began to shake. "Don't you remember?"

Shailiha walked closer to the gibbet, and for a moment she seemed to focus on the medallion that hung from his neck as though there was something about it that she remembered. But then she smiled and looked at him with a cruelty that froze his heart. "My Sisters said that you would try to convince me of something like this," she said quietly. She began to walk back and forth in front of his cage as if she were examining some exotic animal in a zoo, at the same time rubbing one of her hands over her swollen abdomen in an automatic, strangely mindless gesture of love for her unborn child. She once again looked into his face, and it was clear that she truly did not recognize him. "You are an enemy of the Coven, and your words mean nothing to me," she said with finality. Her eyes began to walk hungrily up and down the length of his body. "Besides," she said nastily, "how could you be my brother when I find you so attractive?" Impossibly, she began to reach out to touch his groin.

"Mistress Shailiha," Succiu said commandingly. The second mistress' voice carried the tone of a mother scolding a greedy child, but Tristan thought he detected a hint of jealousy, as well. "Instead, why don't you show him who it is that you really love?" Succiu stood there, hands on her hips, a look of triumph on her face.

Tristan stood aghast at what he saw next.

Smiling, Shailiha walked to Succiu and took her in her arms. She then kissed the second mistress. Not a kiss upon the cheek or a sisterly kiss of endearment, but a raw, passionate, sexual kiss on the mouth that seemed to the prince to last an eternity. After the embrace, Shailiha lovingly brushed back some of Succiu's hair, and the two stood there before him, arm in arm. Tristan began to feel the need to vomit, as tears welled up in his eyes. His head slumped down to his chest. *The insanity never ends,* his heart sobbed.

"What have you done to her?" he whispered to Succiu as he trembled with hate.

"We have simply unleashed her potential," Succiu purred, "and introduced her to a few of our more sophisticated tastes." She reached over to stroke Shailiha's hair, and the prince's sister did not shy away. "We have finally given her her rightful place in the world."

"*Your* world!" Tristan shouted.

"That's right," Succiu agreed nastily. "The entire world is soon to be *our* world. And soon it shall be the only world that matters—or even exists, for that matter. I'm sure that old fool Faegan told you all about that."

"What have you done with Wigg?" Tristan demanded. He was

careful to make no mention of Geldon, in the highly unlikely event that the Coven had somehow not detected the dwarf's part in bringing them here to the Recluse.

Failee levitated herself closer to the prince's cage. "If you wish to see the old one, that can be easily arranged," she said. She raised her arm, and another pair of gibbets came floating into view from behind the prince. They came to rest, still floating in the air, between Tristan and his captors. Looking at the first one, he saw the Lead Wizard. It was a sight he would never forget.

Wigg had clearly been tortured. He seemed to be in a half-conscious state, and the prince had no idea whether the wizard could even hear them speaking. His face was ashen and sweaty, his breathing labored. The wizard's once all-seeing aquamarine eyes were glazed over with a remote, empty, uncaring stare. Drool snaked slowly from one corner of his mouth, and dried blood crusted each side of his face. Tristan painfully surmised that the blood had poured out of the old one's ears. He stared in horror at the wizard he had loved for so long, his mind racing. *I can't tell if the pewter locket is still around his neck! If only he had told me what it was for . . .* The wizard's gibbet turned slowly, silently, in the air before them, as if Failee wished to keep her sick, twisted prize on exhibition for all eternity.

Tristan quickly turned to look at the second gibbet, and his heart fell again. Geldon. *But how did they know we were already here in the Recluse?*

Geldon had fared no better. Although he was much more animated than the wizard, it seemed he could not speak. Due to his smaller size there was more room for him in the gibbet, and he was waving his arms about wildly, his face red and his eyes bulging in their sockets. It was then that Tristan realized what was happening. *Succiu is tightening the collar around his throat!*

"Stop it, you bitch!" he screamed at Succiu as he watched the life being literally squeezed from the dwarf. "You'll kill him!"

Succiu laughed aloud as she examined one of her long, painted nails. "I have no plans on killing this little traitor," she said casually. "That would all too quickly end my amusement with the little freak. I do this to him a great deal, and I know exactly how much he can take before he comes close to dying. He belongs to me, and now that I am aware of his true loyalties I shall do as I wish with him." Her dark eyes looked up at Tristan from under seductive, heavily hooded eyelids. "I suggest you start worrying about yourself, Chosen One."

Tristan glared with rage at Failee. "What have you done to Wigg?" he snarled. He looked over to the Lead Wizard to see that the old one had regained a modicum of his mental focus and was looking at the prince, although he still did not speak.

"What I have longed to do for over three hundred years," Failee said, almost to herself. "What I longed to do even during the Sorceresses' War. I have taken away his power. The last of the wizards of the Directorate has finally fallen. Your precious Lead Wizard, as you knew him, is no more."

She glided over to Wigg's gibbet and hovered there gently, looking at him. "I took it away from him little by little, over the course of the last day while you were still unconscious. It is said that taking a wizard's power in such a manner, rather than all at once, is much more likely to cause madness or death, just as it did when we transformed some of the other endowed male vermin like him into the blood stalkers of so long ago." She tilted her head a little this way and that as she luxuriated in her memories, some of her madness showing through in her rather languid, almost gentle, gestures. "It took all of us, joining our powers, to accomplish it," she gloated. "The blood that ran from his ears carried his power out of his body and dried in the air, rendering him useless. Near the end, when I was sure he was about to die, he proved to be almost as strong as Faegan, and survived." She smiled. "No matter either way," she said happily.

The lead mistress was clearing enjoying herself. *She has waited over three hundred years for this,* Tristan thought, tears running down his face. He glanced at the dwarf and was relieved to see that Geldon, although unconscious, was breathing normally, his head slumped against the side of his gibbet.

"But enough about Wigg," Failee said suddenly. "He is no longer an issue. I would think you might prefer to learn how it was that we knew you were coming. I have been told by more than one of those present in this room that you have a quick, curious mind."

Tristan said nothing, deciding not to give her the satisfaction of an answer. He stood silently before her, his unforgiving gibbet hovering gently in the incongruous beauty of the room.

"It began when Wigg used his powers to aid your journey here," she began, smiling beneficently at him. "That really was quite foolish of him, although he did a particularly good job of hiding your endowed blood once you were on the move. Sending the Minions out into the countryside to find you could have taken weeks. We knew that you would have to make your way to the Recluse, but it also served our purpose to know when you would arrive, and by what method." The hazel eyes narrowed with pride. "So we arranged a little scheme." She paused, wanting to see his next reaction. "It had to do with the Gallipolai."

Tristan froze. His first thoughts were of Narrissa, his mind careening in several different directions over what part she could have played in this. His heart began to tear with the fear of her possible betrayal of him. *Did she aid the Coven? Wigg warned me that taking her along would lead to no good. Could I have misjudged her so badly?* he asked himself. He felt a strange kind of haunting emptiness begin to build within him.

"I can see by the look in your eyes that you think she betrayed you," Failee said, almost kindly. "No, that was not the case. She had no idea. In fact, I am now told that she genuinely believes herself to be in love with you, poor thing. It's sad, isn't it, that you will never see each other again? But I digress. When I recognized the presence of your blood here in Parthalon I arranged to have six Gallipolai taken to the Vale of Torment, knowing that it would call the birds of prey into the sky overhead, drawing you there. I ordered one of the chosen Gallipolai to be a woman of particular beauty. I felt sure you would spot the birds overhead. Skirting the Vale is the shortest and least traveled way to the Recluse, so naturally the dwarf would take you that way. And, unlike the males, the female was purposefully kept alive. Just as I planned, your curiosity drew you in, and your notorious affinity to help stray urchins didn't fail us." She smiled, her hazel eyes gleaming.

"We had other Minion warriors there, in the hills, watching the whole time, who followed you as you left for the Recluse," she continued. "They sent riders ahead to warn us. But even more illuminating was the unexpected realization that your foolishness in helping the one called Narrissa also alerted us to the fact that the dwarf was a traitor. We simply let the three of you walk into the Recluse, on into the Stables, and then took you at our leisure." She smiled again, her hazel eyes shining with victory. "All that remains is to find whatever person or persons who may have aided you in getting here. And find them we shall."

Tristan was aghast at the sheer simplicity of it, the cold, calculated way in which they had so easily manipulated him. At the same time, he worried about Ian's safety. *The gentle young man who is also the keeper of the birds,* he thought. *He should not have to die simply because he helped us.*

His anger returned, his blood surging in his veins, crying out for action. He glared into the eyes of the First Mistress. "I killed two of your Minion warriors out there. It was easy, and I enjoyed it," he said, the words dripping from his lips like venom. "Do you mean to say that there were other warriors nearby watching, who did nothing to help them? That you let the two of them die simply because you wanted me and the wizard?"

"Of course, you fool!" a deep male voice shouted from somewhere behind him. "Dying is what they were bred for!"

Tristan instantly recognized the voice he so hated. It was so easily identifiable in his mind that it seemed like only yesterday since he had last heard it. He tried frantically to turn in his gibbet, to see the man who had spoken, but he couldn't move. He didn't have to wait long, though, as the monster walked out before him to stand with the sorceresses.

Kluge.

Tristan's heart beat faster with hate as he looked down upon the man he most wanted to kill in the entire world. The same man who had ordered him to kill his own father, and strung the heads of the wizards of the Directorate upon a rope like prizes. The monster who had raped and ordered the multiple rape and ultimate death of his mother. The same man the prince had sworn by his own blood oath to kill. Tristan's endowed blood tore through his veins like never before as he trembled with the sheer, pure hatred of wanting to see another man die by his own hand. Horribly. Slowly.

Kluge had changed little since that day in Tammerland. Tristan took in the long, black-and-gray hair that fell loosely down around the warrior's neck; the dark, leathery wingtips that protruded just above his shoulders; and the blatantly white battle scar that ran from the left eye down into the salt-and-pepper whiskers of the monster's goatee. The piercing, black eyes were as careful as ever. The commander of the Minions of Day and Night wore a glittering new dreggan at his side, obviously a replacement for the one that Tristan now wore in the scabbard behind his back. The prince also quickly noticed the shiny glimmer of the returning wheel hung low on Kluge's hip, ready to be thrown at a moment's notice. The winged monstrosity's black leather vest, breeches, taloned gloves, and boots completed the picture. Silently standing there, saying nothing, he was death incarnate.

I will kill you, you bastard, Tristan swore silently. *Even if I do nothing else in this awful place, I will kill you.*

"I see that in the brief time that has passed since our last meeting, you seem to have developed an affinity for Minion weapons," Kluge said nastily, eyeing both the dreggan across the prince's back and the returning wheel at his hip. "You don't mean to tell us that you actually claim to have a working knowledge of either of them, do you?" The monster laughed aloud at the thought.

Tristan glared down at the winged freak before him. In a low, animal-like tone, he said, "Let me free of this cage, and I will be happy to give you a lesson in each of them." Gathering as much saliva as he could, he spat it all into the monster's face.

Completely unperturbed, Kluge smiled, wiped his face, and then slowly drew his dreggan, pressing the button at the hilt and loosing the tip of the blade, listening to its clear, familiar ring slowly fade away in the great expanses of the Sanctuary. He turned to Failee as if to ask permission, and the First Mistress nodded.

Stepping closer yet to the gibbet, Kluge slowly, ever so slowly, pressed the tip of the dreggan against the wound in the prince's side, and then directly into it, down to the bone of one of the prince's ribs. Tristan's breath started to come out in a rush, but he immediately caught himself, silently swearing he would show no pain before this man. Kluge smiled as he withdrew the bloody tip of the sword and held it high in the soft, golden light of the room, the sticky crimson blood of the Chosen One running down the length of its razor-sharp blade.

"They tell me this is the highest, the most sought-after, the most endowed blood in the world," he said casually, looking at the blade as if it were any other recently bloodied weapon. His lips twisted sarcastically. "Strange, it doesn't look any different to me."

Kluge leaned his head closer to the gibbet to whisper to the prince. "I was there, you know," he said. "There, at Vulture's Row, when you killed the two warriors. I watched you work. You are good, it is true, but not as good as you think you are. And certainly not good enough to kill me." He turned his head slightly, obviously looking forward to the reaction he anticipated from the prince at what were to be his next words. "Tell me, did the Gallipolai ask you about the color of your heart?" He smiled wickedly as he watched the look of extreme anger and hatred wash across the prince's face. "I'm not sure about the color of Narrissa's heart," he said, touching his tongue to one corner of his mouth, "but I have just come from yet another visit with her, and I can safely tell you what color all of the rest of her body is."

Tristan's teeth drew back in an animal-like snarl, and he spoke in such a low tone that Kluge could barely hear. "You disgusting winged freak!" he whispered hatefully, alive with rage as he twisted and turned against the unyielding bars of the gibbet. "What did you do to her?"

Kluge smiled and closed his eyes, as if relishing some recent memory. "What did I do to her? Why, everything I could think of," he whispered. "Slowly. Over and over again." Opening his eyes, he replaced the dreggan in its scabbard. "You do a very poor job of protecting your women, you know," he sneered. He reduced his voice to a whisper. "I was struck by the Gallipolai's beauty as she lay bound upon the wheel, and decided then and there that she would be mine. As the commander of the Minions I alone am granted the right to take a mate for life, and may even choose from the Gallipolai if I am so inclined." He paused, narrowing his eyes. "First your mother, then your sister, and now Narrissa. You failed to protect them all. Instead of the Chosen One, you should be known as the Worthless One! I watched you and the now-useless wizard hide her in the cave, and then went back to take my prize. The sweet, oh, so sweet prize you gave me. Just as you gave me your mother."

Tristan tried to subdue the vicious images in his mind. The twin visions of Kluge first atop his hysterical, screaming mother, and then the gentle, virgin Gallipolai. *I swear by all that I am, I will kill this man.* He glared with hatred at the demon responsible, wishing, willing him to die on the spot as if he could somehow force the fates to comply. *I will show no emotion,* he suddenly thought to himself. *It's what he wants most. To hurt me in any way he can. And until I am free of this cage, all I have to fight him with are my words.*

Tristan forced a false, conspiratorial smile to his lips. "Was the Gallipolai good?" he asked slyly. "You may take her as much as you like. She means nothing to me." The words stung his heart as surely as the dreggan had stung the wound in his side, but he was determined to continue the pretense. He smiled again at Kluge and motioned with his head for the monster to come even closer to his cage.

"You were whelped somewhere near the area of the Recluse, I assume?" Tristan asked, hiding the insult with a look of sincerity.

"Yes," Kluge responded, narrowing his eyes. "What does it matter?"

"You should return there as soon as possible," the prince said, almost politely. "They must need you."

Kluge angled his head with curiosity. "Why?" he finally asked.

Tristan smiled. "Because you're depriving a village somewhere of its idiot."

Kluge snarled viciously at having been so easily drawn into the insult and immediately drew his dreggan. For an instant Tristan thought he was about to die, but Failee's voice cut through the room like the snap of a bullwhip, halting Kluge's sword in midair.

"Enough!" she shouted at Kluge. "You fool! Can't you see what he is doing to you?"

At his mistress' command, Kluge reluctantly lowered his sword. He peered menacingly into the cage, into the deep-blue eyes of the Chosen One, with an almost new, even more intense hatred.

"Soon," he said simply from between gritted teeth.

"I welcome it," Tristan whispered back.

Failee, still hovering in the air, glided over to where Kluge was standing. She peered at the prince with an almost newfound respect.

"Neither the bloodstalker, the screaming harpy, the wiktor, or even a sorceress herself could kill this one," she said over her shoulder to her commander. "Are you so sure you can do the job they could not?"

Tristan looked to the other sorceresses briefly and saw a smirk pass across Succiu's face.

Ignoring Kluge, Failee kept her full attention upon the prince.

"Tell me," she asked rather quietly, "how was it that you were supposedly able to kill Emily? Surely she must be dead, since you continue to live. She was one of us, and would never have given up unless she had been somehow vanquished once and for all."

Thinking it over, Tristan could see no harm in telling her. He smiled, and this time the smile was genuine. "Wigg strangled the bitch to death with a wizard's noose," he said, "and I cut off her head with Kluge's dreggan and threw her body into the river. You won't be seeing her again."

"I see," she said slowly. The First Mistress lowered her beautiful, awful face and seemed to be staring at the marble floor, thinking. When she finally raised her hazel eyes up once again to meet his, they burned with an even greater intensity. "I can see now that we have underestimated you, underestimated your blood. But no matter. You are as yet untrained, and therefore of no danger to us. However, now that you are here, you have something that we want. We could take it from you, of course, but the Vagaries say that if given to us, rather than taken from you, the results will be far more powerful."

Tristan froze. He immediately knew what it was. The same thing that the woman he had known as Natasha, then as Lillith, and finally as Emily had tried to take from him.

His firstborn daughter.

"Ah," Failee said, almost compassionately. "I can see by the look in your eyes that you understand. I have no doubt that it was Faegan who somehow arranged for you to come to Parthalon so quickly. Leaving that old one alive was another mistake that I shall soon remedy. The rapid but as yet unknown method of your travel here intrigues me, but it is a topic better left for another day. I am equally sure that he also explained to you the incantation known as the Chimeran Agonies, did he not?" The look in her eyes had become harder. Tristan saw Succiu smiling at him, seemingly waiting anxiously for something as she stroked Shailiha's hair. Repulsed, he focused once again on Failee.

"Yes," Tristan answered. "He explained the Agonies to me." He stood silent, hoping that he would not hear the First Mistress' next words, for he could guess what they were to be.

"If you will freely submit to the Chimeran Agonies so that we may take your seed from you willingly, whenever it suits us, I can promise you an eternal life of luxury and indulgence, just as Sister Shailiha now has. Resist, and we will take what we want from you anyway, without the mind-numbing benefit of the Agonies, as you spend all of eternity in the dungeons, called for only when we need you. And I tell you now that the process, without the aid of the Agonies, will be quite unpleasant. It is not how we would prefer things, since, as I said, what we wish to take from you will not be as powerful if it is taken rather than freely given, but we will take it if we must. What is your answer?"

"And why would you need my permission to submit willingly to the Agonies when you could always force them upon me?" Tristan asked her blatantly.

Failee closed her eyes, thinking. "Because the Vagaries are not clear on this point. It is possible that, because of the strength of your blood, should you resist any application of the Vagaries the result could be cataclysmic. Despite the fact that you are as yet untrained, you remain a very dangerous man, and we still must be very careful with you. Simply put, the forced use of any aspect of the Vagaries against your blood could result in the destruction of us all. An unstoppable force meeting an immovable object, if you will forgive the rather poor analogy."

She tilted her head to one side in surprise. "Didn't Faegan tell you?" she asked. "Ah, of course not. Faegan, the eternal riddle master. You truly do not know how much power you would command once trained in the craft, do you?"

Tristan ignored the question. *The insanity never stops. Never.* "Why would you want another sorceress of my loins?" he asked. "You have the five you need for the Blood Communion and the Reckoning that follows. There is now nothing standing in the way of your enslaving the entire world, so why bother?"

"Because it isn't your firstborn daughter they now want, Tristan." The familiar male voice had come from the prince's left side, from inside one of the hovering gibbets. "What they want now is your first-born *son*."

Tristan looked over to see that Wigg was alert, despite the obvious trembling of his legs from exhaustion. But something was still wrong. Tristan slowly looked Wigg up and down, trying to get a sense of what it was, when it finally hit him. *It's his eyes,* he realized. *His eyes no longer have the sparkle of the gift. He truly has lost his powers.*

Casting a glance at Wigg's gibbet, the First Mistress glided over to hover before the cruel, suspended cage that housed the old wizard. "So," she said quietly, almost to herself. "You still live, Old One. But not for long, to be sure. Tell me, after over three centuries of power in the craft, how does it feel to be a simple, unendowed mortal?"

Wigg began to cough. His lungs wheezed sickeningly for a few moments, and a final hack expelled a small amount of blood that began to run down his chin and onto the gray robe. Failee smiled.

"The last time we were together it was I who was coughing up blood," she said almost happily. "Do you remember? It was upon the Sea of Whispers, the day you banished us to our lives here in Parthalon. You and your precious Directorate had restricted our nourishment so as to keep us weak and prevent us from using the craft. Your use of the azure bowl from the Caves to push us even farther away was really quite brilliant. I commend you on your ingenuity." She tilted her head maddeningly, enjoying every word. "You should have killed us when you had the chance, Wizard. I told you that day your ridiculous vows would be the end of you all, and with the exception of finally killing you, everything I predicted has come to pass."

"Tell him why you want a male child of his blood," Wigg snarled breathlessly, each of his words an effort. "As for myself, I can already guess."

Failee unexpectedly reached through the bars of Wigg's gibbet and caressed his dazed face, her fingers lingering in the wizard's blood. *The blood that used to be so endowed,* the prince thought. He recoiled at the sight. Failee's touch was clearly not a gesture of affection, or of love. Rather, it was like watching a cat play with a mouse it was about to tear in half with its teeth.

"Ah, Wigg," she said. "So much has passed between us. I will grant you your request for old times' sake. The Chosen One deserves to know, since he is to play such a major part in it all."

She turned to the prince, her hazel eyes gleaming. "It is really quite simple," she said. "From your seed mingled with that from one of us, I mean to acquire your first and only son. Raised by us, he will be much more easily controlled than his father. He will worship us, in fact, and be a male of the Chosen One's blood who, unlike yourself, will do our bidding gladly, without the use of the Agonies. And in turn I shall mate your son with Vona, Zabarra, Succiu, and myself for as long as we choose, allowing only the females to live. The result will be blood and seed that will be of an even higher quality than your own, because it came forth from your son willingly. Then we will be free to kill both you and your boy child at our leisure. Imagine it. An entire race of female Chosen Ones, trained in the Vagaries and under our complete control." She looked almost delirious with the thought of it.

"For over three hundred years I thought that the Communion and the Reckoning would be our finest achievement," she continued. "The most we could ever hope to accomplish. But now, Chosen One, you have delivered yourself to me, and it has given me the opportunity to surpass even those victories." She seemed caught in the grip of a fever as she stood there before him. *Wigg and Faegan were right,* Tristan realized. *She is clearly beyond madness.*

"But there is more, Chosen One," she whispered, keeping her words too soft for anyone else to hear. "Listen carefully. I will also use your firstborn son to mate with Shailiha. Think of it. The purest of male endowed blood, and the purest of female endowed blood, coming together in conception." Her mouth was open and her breathing erratic. Sweat beaded on her forehead as her next words came out in the barely audible whisper. "Their product shall be unlike anything the world has ever witnessed. A super being. Trained in the Vagaries, protected by time enchantments, and loyal only to me. The super being and I, ruling over a population of endowed female beings of consummate perfection, for all eternity. There would be no limit to the reach of our experimentation."

At first Tristan couldn't think, couldn't breathe, couldn't speak. *She actually means to do this,* his mind shrieked at him. *Enslaving the world is no longer enough for her. Now she means to populate it only with beings that she deems worthy of life. And I am the one who shall, willingly or not, provide her with the means.* His chin fell to his chest in pain, his mind too overwhelmed to think, his voice too overcome to speak.

"You have miscalculated, First Mistress." It was Wigg's voice again, seemingly somewhat stronger this time. "Despite the plan you have described, nature will still take her own course. You must realize the result of a union between Shailiha and Tristan's son would be a hideous product of inbreeding! Only the Afterlife knows what the end result of such an abomination would be. Surely even you must see that you will not succeed in creating the super being you cherish, but rather an abhorrent freak of nature, possibly with uncontrollable power. The sick, twisted result of such a union would be horrible beyond description!"

Failee smiled at the wizard and then turned around in midair to face the rest of the Coven and Commander Kluge. "I told you he would not see it," she said proudly. She returned her gaze to Wigg. "Do you think I had not contemplated such a thing? Let me explain something that will enlighten you greatly." She paused. "I will give the former Lead Wizard a lesson in the craft."

Failee gestured to the commander of the Minions. "Where do you suppose the Minions came from?" she asked Wigg simply.

"I always assumed them to be naturally occurring creatures of Parthalon that you enslaved upon your arrival, just as you did the rest of the population," Wigg said skeptically.

"You assume a great deal, Wigg," Failee said. "You and the Directorate always did, and this time your assumption is quite wrong. Until we arrived upon these shores, the Minions did not exist. I systematically bred them. Bred them from humans taken from the countryside and mated over time with the many exotic animals we found here. A disgusting process to watch, I assure you, and requiring use of the craft to overcome nature, but quite effective in the end. After I had the product I desired, I needed to be sure they could only reproduce among themselves, since there was nothing else like them in the world." She watched in triumph as a horrified look of realization began to creep over the Lead Wizard's face.

"Yes, Wigg, that's right," she gloated. "I have formulated an incantation that prevents inbreeding, allowing the Minions to reproduce perfectly among themselves, each one a brother to the other. The Gallipolai are the only aberration, and most of them turn by the age of twenty-five. The ones who do not are dealt with in the Vale of Torment. The same incantations used to prevent inbreeding among the Minions shall also hold true for Shailiha and Tristan's union, as they conceive the being I desire.

"The process was not a simple one," she admitted. "I made many mistakes along the way, and the results were at first often horrifying, even to my seasoned mind and talents. In truth, the Minions have a race of ancestors. My initial mistakes, if you like. I cherish these errors of the craft as if they were my own children, as though they had come from my own womb. There are hundreds of them still living, protected by my time enchantments. And they dwell here, among us, in this room."

Horrified, the three prisoners in the hanging gibbets watched as the First Mistress raised her hand and pointed to the far side of the chamber. Immediately a split began to appear in the wall and the marble floor moved back to reveal a gaping pit, its contents just out of view.

"Please, my children, come out and join us," Failee said lovingly. "Awake from your sleep. I believe there are people here whom you know."

Tristan watched, his mouth agape, as the first of the awful things crawled up and out of the cavern that lay beneath the floor of the Sanctuary.

The wiktor.

At first it appeared, impossibly, to be the very one he had killed that day in front of the royal palace in Tammerland. The same one he had watched die at the point of his dreggan in the dirt beneath him. The same one that had sworn to tear the prince's heart from his body. *It can't be,* Tristan said to himself. *Not only did I kill it, but I also beheaded the awful thing and impaled its lifeless head upon a stick.* But the longer he looked at the Wiktor, the more he realized that it was indeed the same one, despite the fact that there was now many more of them in the room as they deftly continued to clamber up and out of their living area.

Tristan took in the green, scaly creature, seeing the useless-looking dark wings that protruded just above each shoulder. The yellow, slanted eyes looked intently back at him from above a long, pointed snout; its grin showed sharp, yellow teeth arrayed in neat upper and lower rows. It stood upon its two large, powerful lower legs, using its barbed tail for support; and the short, equally powerful arms that ended in black talons moved back and forth nervously, as if anxious to tear into the prince's chest and take what had been denied it at their first meeting. Green drool ran from its mouth to the floor, its pink, forked tongue occasionally licking some of the shiny slime away from its teeth.

But it was the thing's wounds that finally convinced Tristan of its identity. The wiktor had a light-green, recently healed scar that ran vertically down the center of its chest—carved by Tristan's dirk—and another, less ragged one that completely encircled its throat where the prince had beheaded it. *But how did it get to Parthalon?* his emotions asked of his common sense.

Tristan thought about what the First Mistress had said, about how the wiktors were the ancestral forerunners of the Minions. *Her mistakes, her children, she called them.* Except for the wings, he could see little similarity between the wiktor and the Minion commander. But in the two pairs of eyes he saw unmistakable cruelty, and a total, blind willingness to obey the Coven's orders no matter what the risk. But how could it be alive? He had killed it!

"I now realize how it is that the wiktor remains alive, although it gives me no pleasure to have to tell you," Wigg said to the prince, as if reading his mind. "I fear that its survival is the product of yet another of my mistakes." He looked into the puzzled faces of the prince and the now-conscious dwarf, and his face seemed to sadden even further with guilt.

Failee smiled as the Wiktor continued to glare hungrily at Tristan. "Please, Wigg, by all means, enlighten us all," she said nastily. "Perhaps you may even prove yourself to be correct."

"Tristan," the wizard began, "do you remember the day I killed the screaming harpy in the courtyard of the palace? Do you remember the orders I gave to the Royal Guard regarding the disposal of the body?"

Standing in the gibbet, his mind and legs close to exhaustion, the prince thought back to that day as best he could. Wigg had killed the harpy with a wizard's cage, crushing the life out of it, after Tristan had thrown a dirk into one of its eyes. And then he remembered.

Tristan raised his eyes to his friend. "I remember," he said. "You ordered it cut up and buried in separate pieces."

"Yes," Wigg said, "because the harpies had the ability to rejoin their parts and reacquire life if the limbs and organs were left close enough together. The Harpies were a product of the Coven, just as are the wiktors. The wiktor must have been taken to Eutracia in Succiu's flagship as a safeguard against you, I, or any of the royal house or Directorate surviving. The wiktor's job would have been to stay behind and hunt us down. After you supposedly killed it, we must have left the wiktor's head and body near enough to each other, and then, after the rejoining, Succiu took it back to Parthalon with her. But obviously the First Mistress has been unable to bestow that particular talent of coming back from the dead onto the current ranks of Minions, since many of them were killed when they invaded Eutracia."

"Well done, Lead Wizard. Right on all counts!" Failee scoffed. "And, as I am sure you have already deduced, it is because of that failure that I was forced to develop the incantations that prevent the Minions from inbreeding. But Succiu did not leave that day, as you had thought. True, by then all of the Minions had been boarded back on the ships, and only she remained in Parthalon to make a last attempt to find you and the prince—dead, presumably. But when she returned to the palace gates, hoping to find your bodies, instead she found the Wiktor. It is my pet, don't you see? How could you expect me to leave it behind? I simply had to let Succiu retrieve him. And now here he is. Such a shame the two of you and the Second Mistress didn't cross paths that day, isn't it? But that doesn't matter now. Now we're all together once again."

Tristan watched in disgust as she lovingly began stroking the wiktor's head and face, her hands becoming partially covered in the drool that continued to run from the thing's mouth. The green of the wiktor's drool combined with the less-viscous red of the wizard's blood to form a brown-tinted fluid that dripped sickeningly from her fingers onto the shiny, pristine, white marble floor.

"Everything seems to come full circle eventually, doesn't it, my dear Wigg?" she asked the wizard. "Even the Coven's loss of the Sorceresses' War, as you call it, has ironically resulted in your final prostrations here, in Parthalon, before me."

The wiktor continued to eye the prince menacingly, and it was clear that it was anxious to speak. Finally, after a nod from Failee, the words came. "Despite my failure at our initial encounter, it seems that the prospects of your survival are not particularly good," it rasped in a low, guttural tone. "It is also my understanding that they have a use for you first, and that the commander of the Minions of Day and Night has been given the honor of taking your life once your usefulness has come to an end." The pink tongue again lashed out to lick away yet more of the green ooze that continued to run from its mouth. "But no matter," it said with great satisfaction. "I told you that night in Eutracia that we would meet again. By the way, it is I to whom Failee has promised your heart. And have it I shall."

Tristan looked down at the wiktor, wishing with all of his endowed blood that he could be freed of the gibbet. Free to draw his dreggan and tear into this monster he had already killed once and also to strike down the gloating commander of the Minions. But for now all he could use

was his wits. He smiled wryly. "In that case I hope you have been practicing," he said sarcastically, "because you didn't do such a professional
job of it last time."

The wiktor smiled back, comfortable in its position of security next
to the First Mistress. Hissing, it tilted its head slightly. "Look to Mistress
Shailiha, *Chosen One,*" it said, "and tell me what you see."

Tristan raised his eyes to his sister and looked into her face, the same
beautiful face that he had loved for so long, the face for which he had
already braved and suffered so much. "I see a young woman who has
been perverted by the Coven," he said simply, watching her move even
closer to Succiu.

"Is that all?" the wiktor asked. "Then let me ask you a philosophical
question, Chosen One," it proposed carefully. "In your perfect, royal,
privileged world, is it still a perversion if the so-called perverted one
performs such acts of her own free will—indeed, asks to do them, needs
to do them, begs to do them?" It smiled and waited patiently for an
answer.

Tristan was temporarily stymied. "What do you mean?" he asked
cautiously.

"I mean that there was a slave from the stables named Stefan who
failed to please the second mistress," the thing answered. "A truly beautiful specimen, much like yourself. Succiu brought him here, to let us
feed upon him as is her custom with those who have disappointed her
too many times. Satisfying the hunger of the wiktors is another of the
reasons Geldon was constantly forced to seek out so many candidates
from the countryside. Even he did not fully know the reason so many
slaves were required."

Tristan glanced at the dwarf to see him crying, crushed to learn of
the ultimate fate of the people he himself had selected to come to the
Recluse. Tristan looked back at the wiktor.

"But it was not the second mistress nor the ignorant slave named
Geldon who pushed Stefan into the wiktor pit. No, Chosen One," it
continued. The yellow eyes gleamed. "It was Mistress Shailiha. It was
Shailiha who did the job of feeding him to us. She asked, begged to do
it." The wiktor's tail began to snake back and forth with pleasure.

"In fact," it said nastily, "it has been she, rather than Mistress Succiu,
who has performed our feeding rituals ever since, selecting the slaves
from the Stables who are to die, and providing us our sustenance." The
wiktor strode closer to the prince's gibbet, close enough so that Tristan
could smell its awful breath. "There is even a rumor that she has asked,
once you are dead, to be the one to push your lifeless body into the pit,
whereupon I have been given the honor of taking your heart." At the
hearing of this, many of the other wiktors began hissing and snaking

their tails back and forth in anticipation. "So you see," the wiktor said, almost lovingly, "it has all been arranged."

"That is enough for now, my pet," Failee said suddenly. "After all, we wouldn't want to give away all of the surprises that we have planned for our guests, now would we?" She looked at the wiktor once again. "It is time for you to return to your home."

The wiktor hissed an immediate tone of obeyance and then looked once more at the prince. "The next time I see you, you shall be dead," it seethed, its head maddeningly turning this way and that. "I am looking forward to it." Turning, its tail still snaking back and forth, it walked to the edge of the pit and began to lead its followers back down into it, until they were all gone from sight. Failee raised a finger, and the walls and floor returned to normal.

It was the wizard who spoke next, breaking the awful silence that had been created by the revelations of the wiktor. "Tell me," he asked Failee slowly, "how was it that you were able to cross the Sea of Whispers? We put you out to sea with only a modicum of supplies, yet you made it all the way to these shores. Quite remarkable, Failee, even for you. How was it done?" *Wigg is playing for time,* Tristan thought, trying to forget the things the wiktor had said. *Time is the only ally we have.*

The First Mistress shook her head back and forth slowly. "There are things in that sea that even you couldn't imagine. After you and the other wizard bastards had condemned us to our course we discovered what those things were, and overcame them. But I would not tell you the secret any more than you would tell me how it was that the prince and yourself were able to disappear completely that day on the dais, or come to Parthalon so quickly. I would never add to your knowledge—not that you are capable of using it anymore."

Wigg pursed his lips in thought, trying to hide his emotions. "No," he said flatly. "I suppose not."

"But I have spoken of such unimportant things for long enough," she said. Looking into Tristan's cage, she bluntly asked the question he had been dreading. "Do you agree to my demands?"

Tristan broke into a cold sweat, his legs almost beyond exhaustion. *A life of pleasant, mindless servitude forever as their slave, their breeding material, or a life with my wits about me, despite the fact that I am condemned to the dungeons,* he thought. *Time is the only ally we have,* his mind said once again. *And it is quickly running through our fingers.*

"What demands?" he asked politely, obviously mocking her.

"I have no time for this!" the lead mistress said. "Each of us here knows that the Chosen One need not be told anything twice!" The hazel eyes turned cold and hard. "Agree, or I shall take action against the wizard." She smiled. "And I shall enjoy it."

Tristan looked over to Wigg, already knowing what the old one's response would be. Wigg was intently staring back at the prince, his eyes narrowed, a stern look upon his face. He shook his head slightly, indicating no.

Tristan turned back to Failee. "I will not submit to the Chimeran Agonies," he said strongly. "Whatever you take from me will be against my will."

"That remains to be seen," she said cryptically. Gliding back and away from the prince a few feet, she closed her eyes. The light in the room softened slightly, and then something began to take shape upon the floor where she had just been hovering. As it grew more distinct, the prince was not comforted at what he saw before him.

Failee had conjured another throne, like the five others in the room, but this one was white. Its right side faced Tristan. A tall, white marble column extended from the top of the backrest.

Failee opened her eyes, then turned to Succiu. "I don't think white suits the occasion, do you?" she asked. Without waiting for a reply she once again closed her eyes, and the throne and the column behind it slowly turned to black. Opening her eyes, Failee regarded her handiwork.

"Ah, much better," she said. She narrowed her eyes in the direction of the wizard, and immediately Wigg's gibbet disappeared, sending the old one crashing painfully to the floor. *The gibbets aren't real,* Tristan heard his endowed blood shout to him. *They are conjured by the sorceresses.*

Failee nodded to Kluge, and the Minion commander went to the wizard. Picking Wigg up off the floor as if he were no heavier than a feather, Kluge roughly pushed him into the black throne. As Kluge stood near the wizard, Failee again narrowed her eyes, and it became apparent that Wigg could no longer move, imprisoned in the chair by what the prince could only imagine to be a wizard's warp. Obviously pleased with herself, Failee glided over to face the helpless wizard.

"There was a reason why I asked you the method by which Emily was killed," she said to Tristan. "It has to do with turnabout being fair play. We shall see how much you have come to love and respect your teacher." She smiled. "And how much you are willing to sacrifice to see him live another day."

She pointed into the air, and Tristan saw the beginnings of an azure glow. It thinned and stretched into a long line, glowing intensely in the subdued light of the room. With a twist of her fingers, the glowing line began to take shape, coiling itself into the familiar circle of the hangman's knot.

It was a wizard's noose, exactly like the one that had killed Emily, and it hung in the air, glowing ominously, a silent portent of death.

She lifted her hand, and the noose slowly rose higher into the air.

Tristan watched as it slipped itself up and over the column above the black throne, finally slithering down and around the wizard's neck, pulling his head back against the smooth, cold marble. Wigg swallowed hard, raising his neck as best he could to gain a slim margin of room between his skin and the brightly glowing azure circle. His aquamarine eyes went to the prince.

"There are three things that together signify a wizard," Failee said lightly to Tristan. "Do you know what they are?"

Tristan remained silent.

"No? Very well then, I shall tell you. First, of course is his gift. Second is his training in the craft. And third is the ridiculous tail of braided hair that they choose to wear. I have removed from Wigg his gift, and therefore his training in the craft. The only thing left before he dies is the humiliation of removing his wizard's tail."

She extended the palm of her right hand, and suddenly a dagger appeared there, with a silver blade and a shiny, pearl handle. She walked around behind the column and gripped the wizard's braid, pulling the back of his skull viciously against the column. With a quick swipe the tail came away in her hand. Returning to stand before Wigg, she sneeringly dropped it into his lap. Then she turned her insane, hazel eyes to the prince.

"Emily died with a wizard's noose around her neck. Submit to the Agonies, or so shall the Lead Wizard," she whispered.

Tristan closed his eyes, trying to blot out the pain of what he was seeing. "No," he said simply.

"Very well," she said. She closed her eyes, and another azure haze appeared and began to shape itself into a similar solitary length of brilliant blue. Tristan could see that this time the length of light was rigid, instead of pliable as the rope had been. She extended her fingers, and the glowing azure rod flew behind the column and inserted itself into the folds of the rope there. Failee turned once more to look into Tristan's eyes.

Tristan shook his head.

Failee narrowed her eyes, and the azure rod turned itself clockwise one full revolution. The effect was immediate.

The noose tightened visibly around the wizard's neck. Wigg reacted violently, straining for each breath, his face beginning to turn red. Failee smiled, looking again to the prince.

Tristan felt his heart rip, and a tear ran down his right cheek. *I beg the Afterlife, somehow make her stop!* Against his will, he again shook his head no. And again the rod circled an entire revolution.

Blood began to ooze from the wizard's mouth. His body began to shudder, convulsing violently in the chair. He turned his face as best he could to his prince, tears flowing down his face.

"Torture *me*, you bitch!" Tristan screamed at the top of his lungs. He thrashed his body against the sides of the gibbet with everything he had, finding it impossible to believe that a prison so strong had not been built in a smithy's shop, but in the privacy of another's mind. "It's me you really want, isn't it? Then don't make him suffer! Let me take his place if I must. Just stop this!"

"I know you are not stupid; therefore you must not have heard me the first time," she said, the obvious, maddening patience in her voice out of keeping with Wigg's desperate situation. "I cannot put you in the wizard's place because I cannot take the risk of harming your blood. If I must, in the end, take your seed from you, the Agonies are the only way to do it without sacrificing its vast quality." Her eyes narrowed, the hazel irises becoming brighter than ever. "One more turn of the rod will break his neck," she whispered. "Submit to the Agonies."

I killed my father, and now I am just as surely killing Wigg, he cried silently. Then he forced himself to look at the wizard.

Straining with everything he had, Wigg extended his fingers and raised his palms upward. His bulging eyes then went frantically back and forth between his hands and Tristan's eyes, over and over again. *What is he trying to tell me?* the prince wondered desperately. *What is it he wants me to do?*

And then he knew. Looking at his own palms, he saw the red scars that crossed them. The scars of his oath. His promise to return Shailiha to Eutracia, even at the cost of his own life. *Wigg has included himself in my oath. He is telling me to let him die, rather than give them what they want,* he said to himself. *He has more knowledge and wisdom than I may ever possess. I will no longer disobey him. Even if it means the death of each of us.*

He looked at the sorceress with a hatred that burned across the expanse of space between them and into the hazel abyss of her eyes. "No," he whispered.

"So be it," Failee replied softly. The azure rod began its final turn, much more slowly this time. The First Mistress obviously meant to make the wizard suffer as much as possible before the light left his eyes for good.

Tristan stared hopelessly at the wizard as the life force gradually left the old one's body. *Good-bye, my friend, my teacher,* he thought. *I will do everything in my power to avenge your death. Farewell, Old One.*

And then the rope stopped tightening. Tristan's breath caught in his lungs as he watched the wizard violently cough up more blood.

Tristan tore his eyes from Wigg to look at Failee, and saw that his sister was standing behind the First Mistress, whispering something in her ear. Failee's smile widened, and then the two of them looked at the prince.

With a wave of Failee's hand the hangman's noose disappeared, and Wigg's head fell forward to his chest. He was retching and coughing; his eyes looked glazed and his body was trembling.

"You have Mistress Shailiha to thank for the old fool's life. Her logic is quite inescapable," Failee said casually. Tristan's heart leapt in his chest. *Does Shailiha remember? Is that why she asked Failee to spare him?*

"Why don't you tell the prince what it is you have in mind, my dear?" Failee suggested. "Such an excellent idea. I think he will find it most amusing."

Shailiha walked closer to his gibbet and looked Tristan straight in the eyes. "There is a better use for the old one," she said softly, rubbing her abdomen. "The First Mistress tells me that there still may be infestations of male endowed blood in your native home of Eutracia. That set me to thinking." Walking back and forth in front of Tristan, she continued.

"Failee tells me that, a long time ago, there were things in your land known as blood stalkers. That these things were once originally wizards, whom the Coven mercifully rid of their infestations of endowed blood, transforming them into creatures of useful service to our cause." She paused, her hazel eyes shining. "This is what I intend to do with the wizard. After the Communion we shall transform him into a stalker and set him loose once again upon his beloved homeland of Eutracia. He can hunt down for us any remaining endowed blood that exists there. Despite what we feel will be the complete effectiveness of the Communion and the Reckoning that will follow it, it always pays to make sure." Her lush, full lips parted nastily into a smirk. "Such a wise use of the old fool, don't you agree, Chosen One?" She stood there in triumph, daring him with her eyes to contradict her.

I wish they had killed him, Tristan cried silently, *and before it is over, so shall he.* To spend eternity as a stalker, killing the ones he had spent his life trying to teach and protect—it was the worst of all fates that could have been bestowed upon him. And Shailiha was the one they had to thank for it.

He closed his eyes and lowered his head, thinking of Faegan, and of all of the innocent consuls of the Redoubt. He could not look at the face of his once-beloved sister. For the first time in his life, his heart began to harden toward her—toward what she had become. He could literally feel the place in his heart that he had once kept only for her begin to shrivel and die. At last he raised his eyes and forced himself to look at her face. The face that showed so much triumph and cruelty. The face of the woman he realized he no longer knew.

I will kill you if I must, he swore to himself. *Just as Wigg and Faegan told me I may have to do. I know that I can now. I will also forbid the soul of the unborn daughter in your belly to be defiled, as you have been. Given the chance I will kill you both. I will not let you live, my sister, to remain such a creature as you have become, or to give birth to another like you.*

"You . . . will fail, First Mistress." Despite the weakness of Wigg's voice it cut through the prince's thoughts like a knife, bringing him back to the present. "Your knowledge . . . is fragmentary, and you must . . . listen to what I am about to say, or it could mean the end of all of us . . . and all that we know," the old wizard slurred. "The Vagaries . . . you do not possess them all . . . You will fail . . . and take the world with you." His head slumped forward on his chest, bleeding red welts blooming all around his neck.

"Ah, look Sister Shailiha," Failee said. "It lives."

The First Mistress floated to a place behind the throne. Grabbing a fistful of the wizard's hair, she violently pulled his head back against the column. Wigg's skull impacted with the marble so viciously that the blow sounded like a marble cutter's hammer coming down to strike off a piece.

"What are you babbling about?" she asked. "Do you really expect me to listen to anything you could have to say?"

"It's true," he continued. He paused for breath. "You must listen to me. The knowledge of the Vagaries that you took . . . took from Faegan's mind that day so long ago was incomplete. During your torture of him he was able to shield part of his mind from you. The Agonies worked on him, but not to the extent you believe." Again the wizard was forced to pause, more blood and drool running from his mouth to his chest, creating dark blotches on his gray robe. "You only retrieved a small part of the Vagaries . . . He was able to withhold most of the rest. You will fail, and you will take the world with you," he gasped, the breath rattling in his lungs.

"Liar!" she screamed. "My ministrations were complete; I could feel it. No trick of yours now will save you from becoming a stalker, Wizard."

"You do not fully understand what you have become over the last three hundred years," Wigg rasped. "If studied improperly the Vagaries cause not only madness but addiction, leading the practitioner into a false sense of knowledge, infallibility, and an unquenchable lust for sexual depravity." He paused, searching for the words to continue. "The feelings you and the other mistresses are experiencing are therefore both real and false at the same time. And the manner in which you plan to employ your power is totally, irreversibly deadly. If you persist in this ritual of the Communion and the Reckoning, it will be the death of both us and all that we know."

Somehow Wigg found the strength to continue. "It is the Reckoning that is the greatest danger. Because your knowledge is fragmentary, you will be forced to try to combine the Vigors and the Vagaries during your attempt, and it will be cataclysmic. The powers of the gold and black orbs were meant to be combined and employed by only one person: Tristan, the male of the Chosen Ones, as proclaimed in the Prophecies. As the Ones Who Came Before intended it to be." And then Wigg did something unexpected. He smiled.

"Tell me, Failee, have you felt the need to draw upon your knowledge of the Vigors in your daily rituals preceding the Communion? That is exactly what Faegan said would happen. Let me rephrase something you said to me a time long ago upon the decks of the *Resolve*, the night you were banished from Eutracia. Your Sisters all think you have won. Tell me, Sorceress, are you yourself so sure?"

Tristan listened in amazement. Why would Wigg tell her that? It was the only knowledge they had that she did not. And then it hit him. *Wigg knows we are going to die. There is no chance for us now. If he can make her stop the Communion and the Reckoning, then perhaps, someday, Faegan and the consuls of the Redoubt may be able to overcome her and the Coven. But either way, the wizard, the dwarf, and I will not live to see it.*

A storm passed over Failee's face and then seemed to vanish as quickly as it had come. "Liar," she said quietly. "You know my powers are much greater than your own. Who are you to lecture me upon the use of the craft? Both the Communion and the Reckoning shall occur as promised, and both you and the Chosen One will be alive to see the world enslaved to my bidding."

She turned to face Kluge. "Commander!"

Immediately Kluge was at her feet like an obedient dog. "I live to serve," he said.

"A small, yellow leper's robe was found among their things," she said. "Its size indicates that it belonged to the dwarf, the one who led the prince and wizard to the Recluse. There remain lepers only in the Ghetto; therefore the Ghetto has something to do with their arrival here in Parthalon, and it is there that I wish you and the entire Minion force to begin your search. Tear the city down one brick at a time if you must, but find me the ones who helped these three make their way here. There had to be conspirator; I can feel it in my blood."

Geldon must have had another yellow robe in his saddlebags, Tristan realized. *An extra one. And that mistake is about to cost a great many innocent people their lives.*

Kluge asked for permission to speak freely. Failee nodded.

"We have underestimated the prince before," Kluge said cautiously, acutely aware of the Second Mistress's attraction to the prince, not wishing to leave Succiu and Tristan in the same room together without him. "I am uncomfortable with not commanding a force here at the Recluse to guard you."

"The wizard is incapacitated, and the prince has not been trained. Do you forget who I am? We are in no danger. I want their friends in the Ghetto found and dealt with." Her eyes narrowed. "Make their deaths as painful as possible."

"I live to serve," came the reluctant reply. With a final look of hatred toward the prince, Kluge was gone.

Failee raised her hand, and an empty gibbet appeared, hovering in the air next to the prince's. She pointed to the wizard and levitated his body upward and back into the floating prison. Wigg tried to stand but was too weak, instead half collapsing, half kneeling in the cruel cage.

Failee turned to her prisoners as she gathered her mistresses around her. "Sleep well," she said sarcastically. "Especially you, Chosen One. I have decided that there will be a special surprise awaiting you tomorrow."

Tristan looked at each of their faces in turn, ending with Succiu. As she looked him up and down, her almond eyes smiled and the full, red lips parted to allow the tip of her tongue out to touch one corner of her mouth. Smiling, Failee led them out of the room. Once the women were gone, the light from the wall sconces faded, finally dying entirely.

The three captives continued to twist and turn in their strange, hovering prisons, lost in the total, empty darkness of the belly of the Recluse.

CHAPTER

Twenty-nine

I n his strange, cruel prison, Tristan had lost all concept of time. He
knew neither what day it was, nor the hour. Pain wracked his legs,
and a powerful thirst rose with the realization that he could not remember how long it had been since he had consumed food or drink.

The pitch-black darkness of the room was now impenetrable, and
he knew that his vision would not improve in it or become accustomed
to the light, because there was none.

He made a mental note to himself to close his eyes the next time he
heard the Coven enter the room. He remembered stories from near the
end of the war of prisoners who were suddenly released after having
been held in total darkness, only to be rushed out into the sunshine and
immediately be struck permanently blind, their eyes unable to adjust
quickly enough to the sudden brightness. But first of all he had to
know about Wigg.

"Wigg," he whispered tentatively in the dark. For some reason,
whispering seemed the only appropriate tone of voice in this place.
"Wigg," he repeated, "are you all right?"

The reply was immediate. "If you mean having had my gift taken
from me, my wizard's tail removed, and being almost choked to death,
then yes, I'm fine," came the caustic reply. Despite their circumstances,
Tristan managed to smile to himself in the dark, glad to see that the old
one had not completely lost his sense of self.

"We need to talk," the wizard said seriously, "and we must speak
obliquely, if you follow my meaning. There is much to be said, with
perhaps little time in which to say it, for I fear these walls may have

ears." Wigg paused for a moment, and then added, "Geldon, are you conscious?"

Tristan could now hear the soft, low sobbing that came from the direction of the dwarf's gibbet.

Geldon finally spoke, his voice cracking and childlike under the strain. "I am better," he said softly. "Succiu has used her powers to tighten my collar a great many times over the course of the last three centuries, and it is something I will recover from this time, as well." He paused, and both the wizard and the prince could tell he was struggling with his next words.

"I killed them," he said finally. "All of those whom I brought here, to this awful place . . . It is my fault."

"It is no one's fault but the Coven's," Wigg said adamantly. "And I do not have the time to waste to try to convince either of you of that fact. We have other matters to attend to. Remember, Tristan, speak obliquely."

Tristan's mind went back to his education with the wizards—the education he had then thought to be of such little use, and which he now wished he had paid more attention to. *Think obliquely,* he remembered the wizards of the Directorate teaching him. *Try to think as we do. In intricate layers of thought and deed.*

"We have an old friend at home, do you remember?" the wizard began. "He likes to think he lives rather above us all."

An old friend, Tristan thought. *Faegan. Living above us in the tree house.* "Yes," he said.

"He is very generous, do you remember?" the wizard asked.

Tristan was initially stymied. *Generous . . . giving . . . gifts. . . .* And then he had it. *The locket!*

"Yes," he said. "I remember his generosity."

"Good," Wigg said. "I remember it, too. His generosity still touches my heart."

He's telling me that the locket Faegan gave him is still around his neck, lying upon his chest. If only he had told me what it was for. "Open the locket, look into it, and you will understand," *was all he said.*

"I remember. Sometimes one must uncork the stream of knowledge to recognize what is before him," Tristan replied, referencing the unknown contents of the locket.

"Good," Wigg said. "Then you remember what I said of it. But there is something else that our friend said to me, about you, that I passed along to you just before we entered this place."

The prince remembered back to when he had made use of his gift to see the bridge to Shadowood, without having been first trained in the craft, and to the words Wigg had spoken just before they entered the Recluse. "*When Faegan heard of it, he was astounded,*" the wizard had said. "*He told me that he believes if you concentrate hard enough, due to the quality of your blood you might be able to use the craft . . . Not in any major way, since you are untrained, but hopefully in some small way that might help us. Something simple, such as moving an object or lighting a flame . . . When you finally hear your heart, you must use your mind to will whatever it is you want to take place . . . It will take everything you have.*"

"I remember," Tristan said. "Sometimes it takes another to convince one of his abilities."

"Precisely," Wigg said. "And knowing exactly when to do such a thing can always be of the utmost importance. Patience has always been a virtue." He paused. "And sometimes the smallest urging can move mountains."

Wait, Tristan thought. *He's telling me to wait until the right moment to try to use the gift, because there probably won't be a second chance. But what did he mean by the smallest urging moving mountains?*

Pausing for a moment, the old one finally said, "And do you remember the charge that our old friend burdened you with?"

This time he knew immediately what Wigg was referring to. *My charge, my responsibility regarding Shailiha,* he thought. *That the time may come when I must kill her, and not hesitate in doing so.*

"I remember," he said. If either the wizard or the slave had been able to see his expression, they would have known it had become hard and dark with responsibility. "My heart does not reject the duty as it once did," he said simply.

"Good," Wigg said compassionately. "For all things there is a reason." Darkness and silence hung between them like a cloud for several more moments before the wizard spoke again.

"Each time a door opens, another closes," he said simply. "Just like the quest for knowledge, doorways can be elusive."

Doors, Tristan thought. *Faegan's portal. The swirling vortex that brought us here, and the knowledge of it that could take us home. But how many days has it been?*

Panic began to grip his mind. He had no idea how long he had been here, and did not know how many more times the portal would be opened, if at all. *Has the portal opened and closed for the last time?* he wondered.

Tristan decided to play on the wizard's own words. "Each time a door opens, another closes," he repeated to Wigg. "But sometimes, despite the best of intentions, one misses the opportunity." He hoped he was not being too revealing.

"And then again, if one is lucky, one may grasp the opportunity for such freedom of knowledge not just once, but perhaps even twice more," Wigg answered.

Twice more, the prince said to himself. *Wigg is telling me that the portal will open twice more. Two more chances left.*

"We have spoken enough," the wizard said with finality. "I suggest we try to sleep as well as we can. Rest may become our most valuable asset."

As the silence of the room once more surrounded them, Tristan took the opportunity to ask Wigg one last, more blatant question.

"Wigg," he ventured, "what will happen to us?"

"We are alive," the wizard said softly. "And our old friend at home will twice more do his duty. I also continue to believe in his generosity that still touches my heart. Anything can happen."

Sleep finally began to overtake them all as the gibbets turned softly, endlessly, in the depths of the darkness.

*H*e had no idea how long he had been there, half asleep, turning in the dark, but there were now some things softly gnawing at the underbelly of his consciousness; a flurry of noise, and a distinctive, gathering lightness in the atmosphere of the room. Tristan gradually awakened, trying to remember to open his eyes slowly, letting them adjust to the light. As he did so, he could see several people entering the room from the long set of circular stairs that led down to the Sanctuary.

The first to enter the room was Succiu, dressed in the same highly erotic black leather clothing that he had last seen her wearing. A black leather bullwhip hung from one side of the belt slung low on her hips.

Following her came his sister. In stark contrast to the second mistress, Shailiha wore a long, beautiful maternity gown of the palest blue, with touches of white lace at the bodice, hem, and wrists. The gold-threaded Pentangle was sewn over her left breast, and a pair of highly polished, sapphire shoes completed the picture. She smiled at Tristan as she entered the room.

Behind her came six slaves from the Stables. Three men and three women, they were all clad only in loincloths. They seemed singularly detached and uncaring, as if in some kind of stupor.

The wiktors must be fed, Tristan realized.

"I will not watch this disgusting freak show!" he shouted at the second mistress. Wigg and Geldon remained silent, surprised at the prince's sudden outburst.

Succiu whirled to face him, unaccustomed to having males speak to her without first having been given permission.

"Vigorous, isn't he?" she commented to Shailiha, her almond eyes roaming over Tristan's body. "Keep that strength, Chosen One. You will soon need it." She smiled knowingly at him as he twisted in his cage. "But first there are some duties to be performed."

She raised her right hand and Tristan saw the altar in the center of the room begin to glow a soft, radiant azure. Then the glow faded, and an assortment of sumptuous-looking food and drink appeared on the altar. The scent of the food came to his nostrils, quickly reminding him of how hungry and thirsty he was. Again raising her right hand, Succiu watched as the area around the altar began to take on the same, familiar glow, and soon there were three chairs there, as well.

Without warning, the second mistress pointed in the direction of the three gibbets and they dissolved, sending their prisoners crashing down the fifteen feet or so to the cold, marble floor. Despite the weariness in his legs Tristan landed quickly like a cat. He was about to reach for one of his knives when he found suddenly that he could not move. Caught in Succiu's warp, he fell awkwardly over on one side on the floor, paralyzed.

At first the prince didn't know which he hated more, being caught in the gibbet like some prize in a zoo, or being on the floor at Succiu's feet, unable to move his arms and legs. His endowed blood roared in his veins, and he once again made the promise to himself: *I will kill this woman. I will kill them all.* Looking over as best he could to the wizard and the dwarf, he could see that they, too, lay paralyzed on the floor, but appeared to be otherwise unhurt.

"The First Mistress has made several decisions," Succiu told them simply. "First, that you should eat and drink."

"And the second?" Tristan snarled.

"That you should watch Sister Shailiha tend the wiktors," she said matter-of-factly, as though she were discussing the weather rather than condemning six innocents to death.

"Am I to assume there is a third decision?" he asked sarcastically.

Succiu walked over to where he lay, taking the black leather whip from her belt. Holding the woven handle, she bent down and placed it beneath his chin, raising his eyes up to meet hers.

"Oh yes, Chosen One," she said softly, almost lovingly. "There is indeed a third decision. It involves you, myself, and Shailiha. But that we will keep as a surprise."

She backed away from him and narrowed her eyes. Immediately he could sense that his legs had been freed, though his arms were still paralyzed. "Walk to the chairs at the table," she ordered. "Sit down. Do not make any heroic gestures, or I shall kill the dwarf, and then the wizard. Bear in mind I can do so with a single thought." She licked her lips strangely. "Besides, you wouldn't want to deprive them of the up-coming performances, now would you?"

With great difficulty the three of them struggled to their feet, their arms frozen at their sides, and shuffled to the table on trembling, ex-hausted legs. They sat down heavily, hungrily taking in the sight of all the food before them, inhaling the enticing odors. Tristan looked ques-tioningly at the wizard.

"Yes," Wigg said, "we can eat this food. If they wanted us dead, we would have been gone long ago."

"Quite right, Wizard," Succiu said, snapping her fingers. The six slaves walked to the table, the dumb, vacant looks still on their faces. "Serve them," she said simply. Succiu looked briefly up to Shailiha as the slaves began feeding the immobilized prisoners. "You will learn, my Sister," she said, turning her attention to one of her long, painted nails, "that there really is no point in having a slave if you can't tell him what to do."

Another chair had appeared from nowhere, next to the one in which the prince was sitting. Succiu sat down in it, smiled, and crossed her long legs up and over the top of the table, propping her high, shiny, black leather boots close to his face. Tristan felt his skin crawl with her closeness, and could smell the jasmine in her long, dark hair as it fell over the back of the chair and nearly to the floor. Staring at him, she formed a circle with the thumb and index finger of her left hand, and began to gently push the handle of the whip in and out of it, imitating the action of intercourse.

She pursed her lips. "You know," she said coyly, "if you were to submit to the Chimeran Agonies, I could promise you a life of eternal bliss. It is said that coupling with a sorceress is the most intense pleasure a male can receive. Just think of it. You and I, forever."

Tristan stopped eating and turned to look directly into her eyes. *So beautiful,* he thought. *And yet so hideous. How many men have wanted her, only to die for having succumbed and given her what she demanded of them?*

He smiled back at her as he swallowed, and shook his head in quiet ridicule. "I doubt you could live up to your own expectations," he said flatly. "I think you have delusions of adequacy."

The black handle of the whip came around with blinding speed, striking him across his right cheek and sending him crashing to the floor. His arms still locked helplessly against his sides, he looked up to see her standing over him.

"Soon, Chosen One, we shall see who is adequate and who is not," she hissed. She narrowed her eyes and the chairs and altar disappeared, sending Wigg and Geldon to the floor, goblets of wine and plates of food noisily crashing down around them. She waved her right hand and two of the gibbets reappeared, swinging gently in the air. Finally extending two of her fingers, she levitated the wizard and the dwarf back up into cages.

Still lying on the floor, Tristan turned his face toward the sound of the wiktor pit being opened. He could hear the hungry, hissing noises that emanated from its depths.

"Line them up," Succiu said to Shailiha, indicating the slaves. There was venom in her voice. She looked down at Tristan. "Get up!" she snarled. "Walk to the edge to stand with Mistress Shailiha."

Tristan stood with difficulty, dazed and dizzy from the blow she had given him. He stumbled to the edge of the pit and looked down, trying to maintain his balance and not fall in. What he saw there he would never forget.

The wiktor pit was huge. Peering down, he literally could not see the end of it. The floor was covered with writhing, slithering wiktors. Some were standing up on their back feet, some were lying on their stomachs, and most seemed to be in a constant state of agitation. Occasionally one would snap at another as if wishing to start a fight, the other snapping back or snarling and hissing in return. The many pairs of yellow, slanted eyes began to look upward to the edge of the pit in anticipation as their hissing grew louder.

"They are hungry," Shailiha said to the prince as she came to stand next to him at the edge. "And the ones you see here are only a small fraction of the total population. The pit extends far beneath the Recluse. If left alone too long they would begin to eat their own out of sheer survival." She kept her eyes focused straight into the pit, seemingly mesmerized, without turning her face to him. "And we couldn't have that, now could we?" she asked sarcastically.

Looking among them, Tristan was finally able to pick out the wiktor he knew, the one he had thought he'd killed that day in Tammerland. One corner of his mouth turned up. He took great pride in knowing that it had been he who had put the telltale scars on the wiktor's neck and chest, and hoped for another opportunity. The awful thing just stood there without speaking, stone-still in a sea of writhing monsters, and calmly stared up at the prince with its yellow eyes. *This one can actually think,* he reflected.

As if reading Tristan's mind, Shailiha pointed to the wiktor. "That one is the only one that can speak, and is the First Mistress's favorite," she continued. "She uses him to communicate with the others. Those that you see here are his less-intelligent progeny, but they, too, have their uses. Sometimes it pleases us simply to loose them upon the countryside to ravage the population. I'm sure you can see the advantages to such a thing. Besides helping to keep order, it is also an efficient way to feed them." She finally turned her head and smiled at Tristan. "They are also an efficient method of disposing of unwanted Stable slaves," she said sweetly.

Looking farther down into the room, his eyes now more accustomed to the light, Tristan could make out some other objects in the pit. There were tables and chairs scattered around, beakers and vessels of every description lying about, some still containing colored liquids, and charts and scrolls lying discarded on the tables and floors. Huge, long-since-abandoned books were piled floor to ceiling in some places, and everything was covered in a thick layer of ancient dust. It looked as if this place had once been some kind of ancient laboratory. Then it hit him.

This is where she did it, he realized, looking at the awful scene before him. *This is where she created the wiktors and the Minions. Here she could experiment with the very essences of life.*

His mind went to the sickening uses to which this room would have been put, and to the many who had died there so that Failee could practice her version of the Vagaries over the course of the last three centuries. Until she had gotten it right. Until she had created the Minions of Day and Night, finally achieving what she considered to be their consummate perfection.

He could see now many large glass bottles that contained baby wiktors. Here and there a swollen-bellied pregnant female slithered among the bottles, protecting them from the others. Bloodstains covered large portions of the pit walls, and in many places human bones could be seen, picked clean and polished white. A terrible smell loomed up from the pit, much like that of a poorly tended slaughterhouse. Sickened, Tristan turned his face away, looking once again at his sister. The sister he no longer knew.

"How can you do such things?" he asked breathlessly, his heart simultaneously aching for the kind young woman he had once known and hardened toward the monster she had become. "I am your brother. Can't you see that?" he asked her, hoping desperately for a glimmer of light in her eyes to tell him that she understood at least some of what he was saying.

She smiled. Not the same, sweet smile he remembered from their youth, but a cruel, knowing smile of superiority, much like the twisted smiles Succiu always gave him. "I know only that you are the Chosen One," she said. "And that I have never in my life seen you before yesterday, when I first noticed you hanging in your proper place. Your gibbet."

Shailiha reached out her hand to brush the dark hair away from his forehead, her hazel eyes gazing deep into his in a manner to which he was unaccustomed. Her red lips parted slightly. "I do, however, find the Chosen One to be amazingly attractive . . ."

"Enough talk!" Succiu's jealous voice cut through the air like the crack of the whip she carried at her side. "Do what you came here to do," she said to Shailiha, her tone softening slightly. "We have other duties to attend to." Smiling at the prince, she ran the tip of her tongue along her lower lip.

Shailiha dutifully walked over to behind the row of slaves who were standing at the edge of the pit, inspecting them as she went. More of the wiktors hungrily crowded toward the near wall, their tails lashing back and forth in anticipation, drool dripping and pooling into green puddles on the floor beneath them. The hissing rose to a level that would drown out normal conversation.

Tristan looked at the row of slaves as they stood there dumbly, vacantly staring out over the pit. The three men and three women were all young, lithe, and beautiful. *What a horrific waste,* he thought as he stood there, helpless to resist. *How many times over the centuries has this sick, twisted massacre been played out here in this room? And how many more centuries will it continue, with my sister as the head butcher, if I am unable somehow to stop the Coven before the Communion?* He hung his head in shame. *I see no way to fight them. They are too strong,* he thought sadly, his heart squarely facing the truth. *What little manifestations I might be able to perform of the craft could never be enough to do what must be done to stop all of this.*

Without further ceremony Shailiha used her index finger to easily, almost casually, push the slaves one by one into the pit.

The prince could close his eyes against the horror, but not his ears. The wiktors descended upon the slaves immediately, and he could not shut out the sounds of the crunching of bone, the tearing of flesh, and the screams that rose from the pit as the reptile-like things tore into their victims. And then, finally, all was quiet.

Looking up, he saw that blood had sprayed everywhere, splashing high against the upper walls and running slowly back down in sticky, streaming rivulets of bright red. The second mistress touched a splattered blood spot on her right arm and placed the bloody finger to her tongue. Shailiha was looking at Tristan, smiling again.

Tristan ached to seize the weapons that lay across his back, but his arms were still frozen, useless, and at last he understood the cruel logic that allowed him to keep the dirks and dreggan. It was for that same, exact reason: Because they were no good to him. A reminder only. His eyes tore across the space between himself and his sister, his blood alive with rage.

Given the chance I will kill you, he swore to himself. *Any misgivings I may have had because you were once my sister are now gone. I will kill you as surely as night follows day.*

The three of them stepped back as the walls rejoined and the floor covering the pit began to scratch its way back into place, the only remnants of the tragic scene the blood that continued to slither down the white marble walls. Tristan stood there in abject hopelessness, his frozen arms hanging at his sides, wondering what would happen next. Wondering what the second mistress had been referring to when she spoke of "other duties to attend to." He didn't have to wait very long.

Succiu raised her right arm and immediately an azure bolt appeared, striking the prince squarely in the chest and lifting him high into the air. Immediately he was thrown back with stunning force against the marble wall directly across from the altar and impaled there, ten feet in the air. The back of his skull impacted with the wall with a terrible cracking sound, and for several moments he could not see or hear, his eyes blurry and his ears ringing violently. The dreggan and dirks dug maddeningly through the leather vest and into the skin of his back, and the fragile wound in his side had torn open, beginning to bleed again. Testing both his arms and legs, he found he could move neither.

Pinned to the wall and in excruciating pain, his arms and legs drooping helplessly toward the floor, all he could do was to look down upon his tormentor—the impossibly beautiful woman in black leather with the long, silken hair and the exquisitely slanted, mahogany-colored eyes. The second mistress. The one who liked to taste blood. The woman Faegan had said could not rival the evil of Failee. But the woman who, to the prince's mind, was in so many ways so much worse.

Succiu stepped in front of where Tristan was pinned to the wall, the snapping sounds of her black, high-heeled boots following her as she went. She motioned for Shailiha to join her there, and draped an affectionate arm around her as the two of them looked up at him, gloating.

"It is now time to tell you that there has been a slight change of plans," Succiu said, casting her eyes up and down Tristan's helpless body. "This is the ninth day of Failee's deliberations, and she is ready to perform the Blood Communion. Think of it, Chosen One. It is to be this very night." She paused, relishing the words, as if simply speaking them to him could make the ritual happen sooner. "And the other event, the one that the First Mistress so carefully explained to you before, is to take place now."

Tristan froze, his mind reeling.

She was going to rape him, and take from him his firstborn child.

The second mistress raised one of her long, arched eyebrows. "I can see by the look on your face you understand," she said, stepping closer to him. "Good. The First Mistress has determined that one of us should carry your child now, before the Communion commences. Her ruminations of the Vagaries have led her to believe that if one of us has already conceived your child when the Communion occurs, the ritual will strengthen the unborn. I must say that I agree with her." Her eyes narrowed seductively beneath the long, dark lashes.

"It is I who have been chosen to do so," she continued. "A task which I must say I have been anxious to carry out ever since the first time I saw you on the dais, back in Tammerland. Time did not permit such intimacies then, but we shall make up for that now, won't we?" Succiu turned her gaze momentarily to Shailiha, who was standing there dutifully.

"Oh, and there is just one other thing," she added nastily, lowering her voice. Then she smiled. "You should know that Mistress Shailiha has asked to watch," she whispered.

For a moment Tristan couldn't think, couldn't speak, couldn't hear. His mind was simply awash with the horror of what was about to happen, literally floating away upon the impact of her words. There was no one to help him, and no way to stop it. But as soon as the realization that Succiu's words had become clear in his mind, he noticed that something was happening to him. His body was beginning to move away from the wall.

Succiu dropped her arm and the azure bolt disappeared, but the prince remained in the air, a few feet away from the wall. The second mistress then began to manipulate her hands in front of herself as if she were disrobing some imaginary person who might have been standing before her. And his clothes began to come off.

She began with his weapons. Baldric and quiver were removed and lifted up; they fell noisily to the floor, the sword sliding from its sheath and the knives spilling out and skittering across the smooth expanse of marble. His boots were removed, and then his socks. He watched in horror as his arms rose involuntarily above his head and the laces of his vest began to untie themselves. The vest glided up and over him, falling to the floor. Finally, with the mere pointing of Succiu's finger, his breeches unlaced, and they too fell, in a rumpling heap on top of his other clothes. He slumped forward slightly in defeat, the gold medallion twinkling in the soft light of the room as it swung away from his neck, beads of sweat from his chest randomly falling upon it. The blood from the wound in his side dripped slowly onto the floor.

Succiu looked at Shailiha wickedly. "I told you he would not disappoint," she said. "Time to put him in his place."

With a slight movement of her hand, the prince's body gently lowered toward the altar. She turned her palm up, and he turned in the air with it, following her movements exactly until he was lying on his back on the cold, smooth altar. He lay spread-eagled, totally unable to move his arms or his legs. *This is where she means to do it,* he thought in disbelief. *On the altar of the Blood Communion.*

Noticing the medallion resting on his chest, Shailiha walked over to the altar and looked down, first at his naked body, and then at the medallion itself. A strange look of puzzlement came over her face as she stood there, watching the engraved piece of gold rise and fall with Tristan's frantic breathing. He watched as she lifted one hand and touched the bodice of her dress lightly, at about the place where the two ends of the gold chain around her neck would have come together had they been suspending a piece of jewelry. The gesture meant nothing to him.

"You may stand exactly where you are now, Mistress Shailiha," Succiu's voice purred from the other side of the altar. She had suddenly become naked, and a crystal goblet of red wine had appeared in her right hand. "Since you have asked to watch, this will provide an excellent chance for you to learn how it is done." She leaned across the altar, across the body of the Chosen One, and gave Shailiha a soft kiss on the lips. "So that you will be proficient at it when it is your turn. And your turn it shall be. Watch and learn."

Tristan watched as the second mistress, naked, the goblet of wine still in her hand, levitated herself to a position above him and then gently lowered herself back down to the altar so that she was standing upon it, directly over him, one foot at each side of his body. Her magnificent form shone in the soft light of the wall sconces. She raised the wineglass slightly, in the form of an offering.

"Would you like some wine first?" she asked nastily. "I have made it a custom to first offer my partner a refreshment."

"No," he said. His mind was racing, his heart pounding so hard he thought it might come out of his chest.

"You really should be courteous enough to take what is offered to you," she said. "After all, I am a sorceress, and there are always other ways to make you drink."

"No." He spat out the single word as if it were made of poison. "I want nothing from you, including your body. Save it for your Stable slaves."

Succiu pursed her lips. "So you want neither my wine nor my body, eh?" She paused, thinking. "Too bad. Let's see if there is a way to give you a taste of each at the same time, because I think it impolite of you not to drink with me."

She pointed her free hand toward his face, and Tristan felt his mouth opening. He tried to close it, but he could not keep his jaws from parting.

Smiling, the second mistress moved the glass of wine to her lower abdomen, and then down farther still until it pressed against the warmth of her groin. Extending one of her long legs, she pointed her toes and placed them into the prince's mouth, choking him slightly. Pouring the wine from the glass, she silently commanded the liquid to travel between her legs, and then down the length of her right leg and into his mouth.

Tristan began to choke immediately as wine ran down his throat and into his lungs at the same time, bringing him the taste of both her scent and the heavily scented flavor of the grape. Some spilled down the side of his face, ran over the edge of the altar, and splashed on the floor. Tristan arched his back and coughed violently as she poured the wine relentlessly down and into his mouth. Finally she stopped, seeming to enjoy watching his misery as she pulled back her leg to stand over him once again, her arms akimbo. Shaking his head and retching violently, he was finally able to gasp some life-sustaining air into his lungs. When he had finally regained his breath, the second mistress spoke.

"Now that the pleasantries are out of the way, it is time to accomplish what I came here for," she whispered to him, as though they were the only two people in the room, the only two people in the world. A look of undeniable need had begun to come over her face, and her mouth started to twist upward into a vicious snarl. It was almost as if her countenance was changing before his eyes. Turning toward Shailiha, he could see the same strange need beginning to build in his sister, as well.

The prince then turned his face as best he could against the cool hardness of the marble to look at the two gibbets. Wigg and Geldon were still in them, twisting slowly in the air. Wigg was slumped in defeat against the wall of his strange cage, and had tears in his eyes. Tristan watched as the droplets slowly ran down the length of the wizard's face, leaving small, shining trails as they went. *I have never seen the old one cry before,* he suddenly realized. *We are truly finished.*

"The old wizard cannot help you," Succiu sneered. "No one can help you now."

She looked at his groin and narrowed her eyes. Suddenly, without warning, the prince began to feel the longings of desire building within him, and the inevitable physical arousal that always accompanied it. He could feel the heat literally growing in him, greater than he had ever known. He lay there beneath her, powerless, in abject terror of what would come next.

"Ah," the second mistress cooed as she stood above him on the white altar, her eyes hungrily taking in the length of his body. "Now we are finally ready to begin."

Slowly, almost carefully, she lowered herself down upon him just as Natasha had done, until her face was only inches from his own.

Immediately a searing, unrelenting fire shot through him. Not the usual warm, pleasant beginnings of lovemaking, but an unnatural, all-encompassing, and painful burning that started in his groin and reached out to every corner of his body. He tried to arch his back in defiance, but there was nowhere to go and no way to turn from it.

Succiu looked down on him with now unseeing eyes, her mahogany-colored irises lost high beneath her eyelids, her red lips parted seductively as her pleasure intensified. She began to undulate slowly upon him, her cadence increasing as her pleasure began to build.

The pain Tristan felt was becoming unbearable, the burning sensation increasing even farther as his breath came harder. He was bathed in sweat, most of it his own but some of it belonging to Succiu as she continued to ride him, lost in pleasure.

It was the panic of being raped by Natasha all over again, but this time there was no one to save him. No azure wizard's noose would come to his aid, and even had there been dreggan or dirk at his back he would have been unable to grip it. This time the sorceresses would win, and he would give them his firstborn. He knew it in his heart, and there was nothing he could do to prevent it.

And then it happened.

Succiu threw back her head and screamed, and as if she could will it, with that scream came the inevitable waves as they rippled through his groin. But this time, the experience was different.

The pain was beyond anything he had ever experienced in his life.

Every nerve was on fire as he, too, began to scream, his sweat-coated body convulsively dancing and jangling like a marionette at the end of unseen strings, his head thrashing violently back and forth, white foam dribbling from the corners of his mouth. To his dazed and controlled mind it seemed to go on forever, his own screams mingling with hers, joining and careening off the white, spotless walls of the Sanctuary.

And then, finally, it was over. Succiu's eyes returned to normal as she looked down upon him in triumph, her breasts heaving with exertion. She put a hand to one side of his face and stroked it affectionately as his consciousness began to clear.

Finally looking up, he could see that she was still astride him, and her breathing had begun to slow. But there was something different. There was an azure glow all about her. It danced and flickered in the soft light of the room, creating convoluted shadows of violet and blue for a short time before finally receding, and then disappearing altogether. She smiled and lowered her face to within only inches of his own.

"Congratulations," she purred to him. "No man but you, no one but the Chosen One, could have survived what has just transpired between us. This time it was special for me." She tilted her head to one side, to watch her words sink into his consciousness. "For you see, my sweet, I have just conceived."

Tristan tried to stop them, but they just came: tears. He had no clever answers for her. No glib things to say in the wake of what had just happened. He lay there, defenseless, listening to her awful words as she spoke, his tears running wet and salty down the sides of his cheeks. Blood from the wound in his side dripped lazily to the floor.

"Did the old one not tell you?" she asked. "A sorceress can indeed choose whether or not to conceive. For all of my life I have never found a male of sufficient blood quality to justify it. Until now. I'm sure you saw the azure glow that marked the blessed event." She ran her tongue around the outer edge of her lips, wetting them seductively.

"In addition to that there is one thing more that you should now know. A sorceress can greatly accelerate her pregnancy. Already I can feel it growing in my womb. Our child will be born just three days from now."

Tristan felt his heart tearing, wishing that he could will himself to die, die and be gone from this place, this world, forever. *I have given them what they wanted most,* his crying heart called out to him in guilt. *I have done more to further their ends than any other person in the history of my nation. And all because of the blood that I carry in my veins.* He looked over to his sister to see that she seemed to be caught up in some frantic, sexual need to be part of what had just happened.

"Did you not enjoy your time with me?" Succiu asked cattily as she continued to lie upon him. "This is what it shall be like for you throughout all eternity as we protect you with time enchantments and proceed to take your seed. Time after time. Thank you, my prince. Take comfort in the fact that it matters not whether our first child is a boy or a girl. Either way it will be raised as one of us." She paused, looking him up and down with what were now more satisfied eyes. Then those almond-shaped eyes narrowed.

"Either way, my sweet, be sure of one thing," she said as she tossed her head and threw her long, silken hair over one shoulder. "You lose."

And then she was suddenly away from him, standing next to the altar, fully clothed in her black leather. She put an arm around Shailiha, and then once again lifted the prince up into the air. Slowly, one by one, his articles of clothing were replaced upon his body, including the weapons that he was still unable to use.

His gibbet reappeared, and she pushed him back into it, his body somehow passing through the bars until he was once again trapped in his strange, hovering prison of imaginary steel. He slumped against the walls of the cage, his eyes half open, his body and mind still wracked with the pain and terror of what had just happened to him.

Succiu turned to lead Shailiha out of the sanctuary, and as they left, the light in the room slowly dimmed back to nothingness, leaving the three prisoners high in their airborne cages, the prince sobbing quietly into the darkness that surrounded him.

CHAPTER

Thirty

It was Wigg who first spoke. Upon hearing the wizard's voice, Tristan realized that he had no knowledge of how long he had been hanging there in the dark. No idea of whether it had been hours or days, or whether he had been unconscious or awake. Time, life, and his very consciousness seemed to flow darkly into one long, endlessly trailing river of despair, emptiness, and pain. He could remember nothing. The only thing his cloudy mind was sure of was that it was Wigg who was speaking to him.

"Tristan," the wizard whispered in the dark. "Are you awake?"

At first the prince couldn't speak. His mouth wouldn't work, and his mind couldn't formulate the words to transfer them to his tongue.

"Yes," he answered thickly.

"Try to concentrate," Wigg said. "It is vital that we talk, and that you be able to remember what I tell you now." When no answer came he continued, hoping that Tristan had not blacked out again.

"What she did to you could not be helped; you must believe that. There is no one on the face of the earth, including Faegan, who could have fought off the power that Succiu had within her when she raped you. You must believe me. It is not your fault."

A scratchier, more diminutive voice joined the conversation, but in his dazed condition the prince did not recognize it. "It's true, Tristan," Geldon said. "She has been torturing me for centuries. But I still live. Take heart."

Tristan began to sob again, unable to control himself. "I couldn't stop her," he said, the tears coming freely. "I tried, but I couldn't. She now has my child. She was so strong . . ."

"I know," Wigg said softly. "But you must also know that the effect it had upon you is temporary and that you are not permanently damaged. They want you to live and to be healthy, so that they may use you again. Now you must concentrate. The Communion is only hours away."

Tristan laid his head back against the bars of his gibbet. He simply couldn't bring himself to think properly, and he sobbed as his cage turned slowly in the air. *What is the old wizard babbling about?* he thought dully. *Why can't he just let me go back to sleep?*

"Tristan," Wigg said softly. "Feel the palms of your hands."

Why does the old fool want me to do something like that? he wondered. He dumbly rubbed his fingers over his palms, and then it all came flooding back to him on a river of hate.

His oath. His family. His reasons for being here.

Shailiha. I came here for Shailiha. And to stop the Communion.

"I am here, Wigg," he said.

"Good," Wigg replied. "We must once again speak obliquely."

"Very well."

"Sometimes only a small urging is all that is required to move mountains," the old one said. "And sometimes it is easier to let a thing come to you, rather than for you to go to it."

Tristan shook his head in the dark, trying to clear away the last of the cobwebs that clouded his thinking. *I don't know what he is talking about,* he realized. *It doesn't make any sense.*

"Sometimes the student is unable to keep up with the master, and needs further guidance," he said.

"And sometimes the master knows the answer but has said all that he can, and the student must find his own meanings," Wigg responded.

He knows! Tristan shouted to himself. *He knows the answer to stopping the Communion, and he is trying to tell me what it is!*

He continued to struggle with the wizard's words, stymied. *A small urging. . . . Let a thing come to you . . .* "I am sure that you have had students who have failed you," Tristan replied glumly. "It seems that such is once again the case."

"There is little time to reflect upon such things," the wizard said. "And there is little more that I can say. I will now be silent, so that you may be alone with your thoughts."

We are finished, Tristan thought. *Only a few hours until the Communion, and I cannot find the answer to his riddle. Layers of thought and deed. If I do not realize the answer soon, everything we know and love will soon be gone.*

He continued to slump in his cage, near exhaustion, trying to fathom the words of the wizard as sleep started to crowd into the corners of his mind and try to rob him of the precious time he needed to think.

Sometimes only a small urging is all that is required . . . urging is required . . . sometimes. . . .

Sleep finally won over his mind, and the prince once again collapsed into unconsciousness.

CHAPTER

Thirty-one

T ristan regained consciousness just as the light began to come up
again in the Sanctuary. It was somehow brighter than the times
before, the scene before him more alive this time in the large, white
room with the five black thrones and the altar nestled in their center.
The black Pentangle inlaid into the white marble floor loomed up before him ominously.

Again, he had no concept of how long he had been out. Opening
his eyes slowly, he first turned to check on Geldon and Wigg. The
dwarf, like the prince, was still rubbing his eyes, trying to accustom
himself to the light. Wigg was awake and looked as though he had been
for some time. Without his wizard's tail he somehow didn't look quite
like Wigg. When he saw Tristan looking at him, he raised his eyebrow
inquisitively, hoping against hope that the prince would give him some
sign that he had solved his riddle. When none came, he tried to smile
bravely back at Tristan nonetheless, willing him not to give up.

They had no time to speak.

Footsteps could be heard coming down the single, circular stairway that led to this place, and Tristan knew who was about to enter
the room.

Failee led the way, carrying a golden goblet, the Paragon hanging
around her neck. She was followed by Succiu, Vona, Zabarra, and finally Shailiha. *Shailiha,* he thought. *The fifth sorceress. My sister.*

Each of them wore a magnificent black gown with a Pentangle
of woven gold thread just above the left breast. Tristan's eyes were immediately drawn to his sister, and he looked at her with an impossible,

maddening mixture of love and hate. Love for the woman she had once been; hate for the woman—the monster—she had become. His eyes then fell upon Succiu, and the breath caught in his lungs.

She was obviously pregnant, and quite far along in her term.

He crouched there in his cage, staring in wonder at the woman who had raped him presumably only a few hours earlier. The black maternity gown she wore was much like Shailiha's, and her abdomen was clearly swollen. If she had been an ordinary woman he would have guessed her pregnancy to be at seven or eight moons. But it had only been a few hours, a day at the most. Pregnancy somehow made her even more impossibly beautiful, the almond eyes, long black hair, and red lips even more inviting. *Such power. A true sorceress of the craft,* he thought, trying to grasp the incredible fact that she was soon going to deliver his firstborn child. *And then the product of her crime against me will be among us,* he reflected sadly.

Looking into his eyes with a strange combination of what seemed to be triumph and awe, Succiu placed an affectionate hand around Shailiha's waist, pulling her close. His sister smiled.

"Your blood never ceases to amaze us, Chosen One," Succiu said quietly. "The child in my womb grows faster than even we had predicted. Later today, early tomorrow at the latest, you shall have a son. Imagine, the firstborn child of the Chosen One may in fact be born on the day of the Reckoning. Fitting, don't you think? Pity you shall never know him, or any of the other children you shall give us."

My child, my firstborn, carried by such a monster, he thought, the hideousness of it almost bringing him to tears. *And still I have no inkling of the meaning of Wigg's words. "Sometimes only a small urging is all that is required to move mountains. And sometimes it is easier to let a thing come to you, rather than for you to go to it." What does it mean?* His thoughts turned to the pewter locket that the wizard presumably still carried around his neck, hidden beneath his robe. *Does he still have it?* he wondered frantically. *What is it for? Am I somehow supposed to know?*

Failee levitated herself and glided serenely across the room toward Wigg's cage, the hem of her black gown fluttering slightly in the breeze of her passage. Tristan could see the madness in her eyes; the strange, hazel irises seeming to glow more brightly than ever.

Three hundred years, Tristan thought. *Three hundred years she has waited for this day.*

The First Mistress floated higher in the air until she was level with the wizard. "So, Old One," she said softly, "we have now come full circle. There are those of us in this room who believe that you should already be dead, that your continued presence here among us can only be a danger. But I know different. I know how robbed you are now of your power, and I enjoy seeing you this way, the way I wished to see each of the males of endowed blood during the Sorceresses' War, as you now call it." She paused, continuing to look at him through the bars of his cage as she taunted him.

"But I shall let you live, at least for a little while. I wish to have you see with your own eyes that all your attempts to undo what I have accomplished here shall eventually end in ruin for you, and see those failures you shall. And all of this shall happen just before we take the advice of our fifth sorceress and turn you into a blood stalker, to walk the lands of Eutracia for all time."

Wigg reached out and grasped the bars of his cage, pulling his face as close to hers as he could. "I tell you for the last time, woman," he said urgently. "You must stop this. Your knowledge is fragmentary at best, and you will be the ruin of us all. You have known me for eons, and I have never lied to you. I do not lie to you now. This is my last warning! Stop this madness, or we all may die."

"Ah, yes," she said. "A wizard's warning. A tradition of the recently departed Directorate, I believe. How noble. Your oath, again, no doubt. How does it go? 'I shall take no life except in urgent self-defense, or without prior warning.' Yes, we heard the prince recite it several times while unconscious. Do you seriously expect me to believe you?" she asked, almost politely, as she continued to gaze at him.

"No, Wigg, that would be much too easy. I have waited and suffered far too long to be persuaded by a wizard's trick. I told you three hundred twenty-seven years ago, upon the decks of the *Resolve*, that one day your oath would be your undoing, and so here we are."

She turned her eyes toward the prince. "The wizard wasted your time when he spoke to you *obliquely*, because he is quite wrong in whatever it was he was thinking," she said softly. She smiled at him. "There is no way stop me. Soon he will be dead, and you, like your sister, will be one of us."

It's true. They were listening to us all the time, Tristan realized. His mind raced, trying to understand the wizard's riddle, at the same time wondering whether the sorceresses having heard them talk had made any difference. *But there is an answer—there must be—and Wigg knows what it is. Too many times I have not trusted the old one and have paid the price for it. I shall never mistrust him again.* But his thoughts were interrupted by the voice of the First Mistress.

"So as to placate the other members of the Coven, I have devised a little gift for the wizard." She raised her right index finger toward Wigg, and immediately the wizard put his hands to his throat, protectively, and opened his mouth to speak. But no words came. In a flash, his arms were frozen at his sides. Whatever slight amount of room that might have once existed in his gibbet was now obviously gone.

Wigg looked at Tristan with what the prince thought to be an even greater sense of urgency; his mouth moving silently, pitifully, as he hung there in his cage. Geldon, trembling with terror, looked back and forth between the prince and the wizard, as if he could somehow help them communicate. But Tristan could see in the dwarf's eyes that he, too, knew all was lost.

"The Lead Wizard is now unable to speak or to raise his hands or arms to gesture to you in any way," Failee said haughtily. "Qualities I enjoy in all wizards. For your information, the old one is in no pain and is still quite able to watch the ritual that I am about to perform. But any communication that the two of you may have been planning on during the Communion, verbal or otherwise, should now be quite impossible." She turned to look lovingly at the four other members of the Coven standing dutifully before the altar.

"And so it begins," she said quietly, as if to herself.

Without further explanation, she glided back down to the floor, stopping at the altar. Tristan watched as she placed the golden goblet directly in the center of it, beneath the skylight.

Tristan looked again to Wigg, but the helpless wizard could only stare back frantically in return. *Think, you fool!* the prince thought angrily. *What was it that Wigg was trying to tell me?*

Tristan began to try to remember everything that Faegan had told them that night about the Communion. A small amount of blood would be taken from each of the five sorceresses and combined in the goblet. The goblet would then be placed in the center of the altar, directly below the skylight, and Failee would begin the ritual. The stone would be removed from around her neck and suspended over the goblet of blood.

He stopped thinking for a moment to glance at Wigg, as if seeing the wizard would help him to remember. Finally, the tragedy of the Communion came back to him. The mistresses would take their places in their thrones at the five points of the Pentangle, and the combination of the stone and the blood would call the light from the sky. It would strike the stone, refracting it into different colors that would cascade into the goblet, charging the blood, already strengthened by the purity of Shailiha's blood, with the power of the stone.

Then they would each drink, sharing the power, the Communion complete. The Reckoning would invariably follow.

Tristan's head hung down to his chest in defeat, his mind painfully calculating the horrors that the Reckoning would bring. *World enslave-*

ment, he thought. *The death of Geldon and Wigg. The loss forever of Shailiha and her daughter to the Coven. And the enslavement of myself to produce Failee's super being, so that she might rule with it in perpetuity, continuing to "experiment" on the masses. The insanity never ends! And the culmination of it all is almost here.*

Failee beckoned for the other mistresses to gather around her, and they did so silently, forming a small circle around her just before the altar. Then she began to speak in a low, guttural tone, in a language that the prince did not understand.

Each of the four held out their right, upturned wrists in the direction of the First Mistress. Failee narrowed her eyes at the wrist offered first by Vona, and Tristan watched in dread as a small wound opened on the younger woman's forearm. The incision had the appearance of a straight line, no more than one or two inches long. Failee held out the goblet as the blood began to well up, creating a shiny bracelet of red and finally dripping into the golden vessel beneath it. When the First Mistress apparently felt there was enough, she removed the goblet from beneath Vona's wrist and started the process over again, this time with Zabarra.

The bloodletting has begun, Tristan thought in a panic. *In only a few moments she will call the light from the sky. Think! What is the answer to Wigg's riddle?* The old wizard's words raced through his head for the hundredth time. *"Sometimes only a small urging is all that is required to move mountains. And sometimes it is easier to let a thing come to you, rather than for you to go to it." What does it mean? What in the name of the Afterlife is the answer?*

Tristan looked back down to see that Failee had completed the bloodletting of the four other sorceresses and was now performing the same ritual on herself. Her blood dripped slowly, agonizingly, into the goblet as Tristan hung there in his cage, powerless to stop it. His face and body were covered with a light sheen of sweat, and he found himself breathing so heavily he thought his heart might burst.

Failee stopped speaking and gestured for the mistresses to take their thrones. Dutifully, they walked to the massive black marble chairs and sat down, the matching black silk of their gowns flowing down and over their feet, the maternity gowns of Succiu and Shailiha draping elegantly over their abdomens. None of the five looked at the three prisoners in the gibbets. Tristan knew instinctively that at this point in time, nothing existed for them except the completion of the Communion.

Failee gently, reverently, placed the goblet of blood in the center of the altar, directly below the skylight that reached up through the height of the Recluse and to the heavens. Slowly she removed the stone from around her neck and held it in the air above the goblet. She closed her eyes and removed her hands from the Paragon. Because the stone no longer had a host, its deep, bloodred color immediately began to diminish, just as it had that evening on the dais when Tristan's father had removed it and handed it to Wigg. When Failee opened her eyes, the Paragon remained hovering above the goblet. She slowly walked to her throne and sat down, her face a mask.

Silent, unmoving, and totally oblivious to their wounds, the mistresses sat on their thrones as the blood dripped slowly from their arms to pool on the white marble floor. A tear escaped the corner of the prince's eye as he looked down at his sister, resplendent in her black gown. *The fifth sorceress,* he thought. No one moved; no one spoke.

The room had become as silent as death.

Then, almost imperceptibly at first, the Sanctuary began to lighten.

The light crept into the room gradually as it descended through the long tunnel of the skylight. It was the purest, whitest light Tristan had ever seen. Streaming down as if it were alive, it flowed straight into the Paragon. Slowly but dramatically the light grew brighter and brighter until the prince could barely look upon it. It was magnificent.

The blood and the stone are calling forth the light just as Faegan said they would, Tristan thought, not wanting to believe the awful, wondrous thing that was occurring before him. Tearing his eyes from the stone, he looked at the members of Coven. What he saw before him made his breath stop short in his lungs.

Each of the mistresses' eyes had rolled all the way up until only the whites could be seen. The women seemed to be staring lifelessly, unseeing, out into the room as the light pouring into the stone continued to brighten.

They're defenseless, Tristan suddenly realized. *No person of endowed blood is wearing the stone, nor is it in the water of the Caves. "This is the only time you can even think of acting against them,"* he remembered Faegan saying that night in the tree house. And then he realized something else.

The mistresses must be protecting their eyes from the light! And while they do so, they seem to be temporarily blinded. If I am able to do something, they may not be able to detect it.

Think! he told himself as the light continued to rain down upon the stone, its rays increasing to a white-hot pitch. *Think, before the light blinds you for life. The mistresses do not care whether you are able to see, only if you are able to give them your seed. Think!*

The Paragon had become devoid of color, looking almost like a diamond as it hung there in the bright, white glow. Suddenly, without warning, the light completed its journey through the Paragon and shot out the lower end of the stone, refracting into thousands of separate shards of light, each one seeming to have both form and substance, as if one could literally reach out and touch them. Their beauty was dazzling. Each of the shards had its own distinct color, and they all pointed from the stone downward toward the blood in the goblet. As Tristan watched, they began to grow in length like the stalactites of the Caves, creeping lower toward the rim of the goblet. When they reached the mingled blood of the sorceresses the liquid would be empowered, and all that would remain would be for the mistresses to drink it, thus harnessing within each of them both the power of the Paragon and the blood of the female Chosen One for the first time in the history of the world.

In only moments the stretching fingers of light would reach the blood.

What is the answer? he cried to himself. He wanted to look to Wigg and Geldon to see if they were well, but he dared not take his eyes off the scene for fear something would change without his knowing it, despite the incredible pain looking at it was causing him. He could feel it burning through his eyes and into the back of his brain. *What is the answer?* he lamented. *Why is it I do not know?*

Tristan finally closed his eyes against the light, trying to calm his mind and recall all he could about the stone and the Communion. *The stone begins to die if not around the neck of one of endowed blood or immersed in the water of the Caves,* he remembered.

He forced himself to look back at the Paragon as the light shattered his senses. His eyes narrowed in disbelief. The stone's bloodred color had completely returned as it collected the light from above. *The stone needs the host or the water to stay alive, but now it has neither.* His mind rebelled against the truth that lay before him. *Then how is it that the stone can now be red once again?*

And then it hit him. Tristan suddenly felt a door open in his mind, and it all became clear, the knowledge flowing through his consciousness, heart, and endowed blood as if it had been there always, from the day of his birth.

The light is sustaining the stone, he realized.

And he also realized that the knowledge was no longer coming from his mind, but from the endowed blood that now so quickly coursed through his veins.

The light is not just flowing through the stone to empower the blood below, draining the Paragon of its power as Faegan thought, but is actually sustaining the Paragon as it does so. There is a third, before now completely unknown entity, other than the host and the water, that can empower and sustain the Paragon. The light that Failee has called down. That is why the Directorate did not know of it—its description was contained only in the Vagaries. The forbidden, esoteric Vagaries that Failee tore from Faegan's mind with the Chimeran Agonies and was forced to combine with the Vigors to produce this bastardization of the craft. And in her thirst for the Reckoning, the First Mistress herself is not even aware of the danger she has created. In that part of it, Faegan was indeed correct. He felt almost as if an unseen presence was speaking to him from somewhere far away. Once again he heard Wigg's riddle, and now he knew the answer.

"Sometimes only a small urging is all that is required to move mountains. And sometimes it is better to let a thing come to you, rather than for you to go to it." Wigg wants me to use my gift to bring the stone to me, removing it from the stream of light. If I am able to do that, the Communion cannot proceed because the Paragon will lose its sustenance, the light will have no partner, and the Coven will still be defenseless. And then, suddenly, a new fear seized him.

If he took the stone from the light, the Communion would end. But, given enough time away from a host and the water as well, would the Paragon die? He had no water from the Caves in which to submerge it—and that had to be done first, in order to return it to a virgin state so it could be given to a new host of endowed blood, whether that person was Wigg or Tristan. But if he did *not* move the stone, would the improper combination of the Vigors and the Vagaries that Failee was employing destroy everything, as Faegan predicted? Was there really any choice?

The shards of light were reaching past the rim of the goblet now. The mistresses were still unmoving as the blood in the goblet started to roil with the impending power of the light. The Paragon itself was beginning to shake as if it could no longer stand the strain of the improper combination of the Vigors and Vagaries, as if begging for someone to stop the ritual. Tristan knew the time to act was almost upon them all. He could feel his blood beckoning him to remember the wizard's instructions on how to use the rudimentary beginnings of his gift.

"In order to see the bridge, you first had to stop trying to see it, and let it come to you," Wigg had said. *"Let it come to you . . ."* Tristan thought. *The second part of the wizard's riddle. "And then once you had mastered that . . . you heard the beating of your own heart,"* Wigg had continued. *"When you finally hear your heart, you must use your mind to will whatever it is you want to take place. . . . It will take everything you have."*

The intensity of the light reaching lethal proportions, the Paragon itself close to bursting, the prince closed his eyes. He knew he must somehow shut down his mind, shut out the activity in front of him, and join with his blood. He lowered his breathing and tried to hear the beating of his heart.

There was nothing.

Again he calmed himself, trying to imagine only the quiet stillness that he required for the gift to come to him, for the beating of his heart to be heard. But still no sound reached his ears.

He opened his eyes to take a precious moment to look at the Paragon. It was swelling almost to the bursting point, and seemed to be calling to him, begging him to fulfill the demands now being placed on his blood. Tristan closed his eyes. There would be only one more chance.

And finally, almost silently, it began.

The quiet, rhythmic beating of his heart arrived in his mind as his endowed blood surged past his eardrums, telling him to continue. He opened his eyes and found that he could now see the stone clearly, despite the white light that coursed through it.

Continuing to stare at the stone, he willed it closer to him, away from the path of the light. Nothing moved.

Again he tried, straining his mind almost to the breaking point, willing, wishing, demanding that the stone come to him. But still there was nothing. In only seconds now they all would be dead, and he knew it. And then he heard his blood call to him.

No, Chosen One. Do not use your mind. Use me, his blood seemed to whisper to him from somewhere far away.

He relaxed his mind, this time somehow sure of what he was doing, and looked at the Paragon.

It began to move—slowly at first, then more dramatically, and finally completely away from the light. Free of the descending rays, it fell to the marble floor of the Sanctuary.

The result was overwhelming.

The shards of light that had been extending down toward the goblet shattered into thousands of pieces, each one pointed at the end, and began to swirl around the walls of the room in a great circle as an almost-solid mass, a riot of color. It was as if it had suddenly become a conscious mind and was searching for something. The unknowing mistresses remained still, their eyes high and unseeing as the shards gathered speed, turning faster and faster as they circled the walls of the room. Tristan watched in amazement as the colored daggers of light finally found their destination.

The shards tore relentlessly into the bodies of the sorceresses, tossing them from their thrones and onto the floor. The room was filled with a swirling riot of color. Though he was frantic to locate his sister, he could no longer see what was happening. But he could hear the screams of the defenseless women as the shards went round and round, stabbing and slicing through their bodies. Finally, almost silently, the shards of light careened upward, still seemingly of one mind, and exited through the skylight above.

Without warning each of the gibbets dissolved, and the three prisoners fell crashing to the marble floor.

Tristan landed like a cat, despite the weakness in his legs. Dreggan in hand, he crouched, looking around the room with deadly, animal-like intent, ready to kill if necessary. The view was indescribable.

Everywhere he looked there was blood. It covered the floor in pools and dripped long, crimson fingers down the Sanctuary walls. Failee, Vona, Zabarra, and Succiu all lay on the floor, dead. Zabarra had been decapitated. Vona was missing an arm, Failee a leg. Succiu, covered with blood, stared blindly up at the ceiling from where she lay on her back. The prince looked sadly at her abdomen, mourning the child she had carried. *My firstborn,* he thought.

He looked behind him to see Wigg and Geldon gingerly picking themselves up off the hard marble floor, shaken, but apparently unhurt. *The three of us still live,* he thought. *How is it that the sorceresses died, and we still live?* Frantic, he began searching the room for his sister. It was then that the familiar sound of her crying began.

Quickly looking around, he found Shailiha cowering in one corner of the room, sitting on the floor, rocking back and forth, babbling to herself incoherently. Her black silk gown was soaked in blood, and she was rubbing her abdomen frantically, crying hysterically, looking outward but seeing nothing. *Exactly as she was that day upon the dais, when Frederick was killed,* Tristan thought. Sheathing the dreggan, he ran to her as fast as he could and kneeled down to hold her in his arms. She did not fight him, but it was clear that she didn't know him, either. *I have you, Shailiha,* he told her silently. *And I shall never let you go again.*

He opened his mouth to speak to her, but before he could, from the center of the earth came a great clap of noise that sounded something like thunder, and the Recluse literally started to come apart.

Tristan held his sister close as the walls and floor of the Sanctuary began to crack, dust and noise filling his ears and lungs. The cracks in the floor widened, their depths seemingly endless. He pulled Shailiha closer to the wall. The wind howled like thunder, and debris washed viciously in and out of the skylight despite the great distance to the top of the Recluse roof. Covering his sister with his own body, he finally recognized the destruction for what it was.

Just as when we killed Natasha and the sound of thunder and the great gusts of wind came, so, too, it is for these dead sorceresses, he realized.

After what seemed to be an eternity, the shaking and thunder slowly stopped, and the haze in the room began to clear. Dazedly looking around to find the wizard and the dwarf, Tristan saw Wigg first, and what he saw would remain burned into his memory forever.

Wigg was sitting on his heels before the dead body of Failee, seemingly oblivious to the devastation that surrounded him. He was weeping, his hands covering his face as the tears ran blatantly down and onto his gray robe. Stunned, Tristan couldn't find his voice to ask the questions. Once again, as if reading the prince's mind, Wigg lowered his hands and turned his great, wet, aquamarine eyes to the prince.

"I can easily understand your surprise," he said gently, his body still shaking, tears still spilling from his eyes. "You see, Tristan, once, long ago, before the Sorceresses' War, Failee was my wife. I loved her dearly. And, in many ways, I always have."

Tristan simply sat there, shocked, unable to speak, his joy at once again holding his sister at odds with the incomprehensible revelations of the old wizard. *Layers of thought and deed,* he said to himself.

And then he realized how it all fit together. How it had been right there, before him, his entire life. There had always been Wigg's dark reaction each time Failee's name was mentioned, and his reluctance to speak of her. Faegan's offhand references to Failee during their meeting that night, and the Lead Wizard's sad, lonely reaction when he had walked to the window to gaze out at the sea, looking east to Parthalon—just as the prince himself had done that very night when he had thought of his sister. Tristan also recalled the strangely sick, almost loving way Failee had caressed the wizard's face when he was imprisoned in the gibbet. And finally there was the Directorate's decision, centuries ago, to ban the sorceresses instead of killing them—and Wigg having been chosen as the one to take them into the Sea of Whispers, no doubt an appointment made out of reverence and respect for their new Lead Wizard and the woman he had once loved.

"Yes," Wigg said softly. "The signs were always there, despite how hard I tried to hide them. Sometimes it is not a simple thing to put a hand over your heart, even when one is a wizard." He turned once again to look down at the corpse that had once been Failee.

"She first began to go mad during our marriage, and there was nothing I could do to bring her back, no matter how hard I tried. After she left me, she began teaching other women of endowed blood the workings of the craft. But only those women who would blindly follow her insanities." The tears started to come again, and Tristan's heart went out to the old one.

"It was my wife who was responsible for the Sorceresses' War, Tristan," Wigg said, his voice almost inaudible. He looked behind him to see Geldon come up and stand tentatively next to the corpse of Failee.

"I had no idea," the dwarf said.

"Nor did I," Tristan replied.

Wigg turned his attention to Shailiha. "How is she?"

"She is unhurt, but is once again hysterical and doesn't seem to know me," Tristan said sadly. "But she doesn't seem afraid of me, either." He looked down at his sister as she rocked back and forth in the circle of his arms, rubbing her abdomen, still lost in some world of torment all her own.

He thought of the dreggan in its scabbard on his back, wondering if he could ever really use it to take his sister's life, yet also knowing that he still might have to. The sorceresses were dead, but he was unsure whether Wigg would be willing to risk taking her back with them in her present condition. She posed a potential threat, and he knew it. *Come back to me,* he begged her silently. *Come back to me, my sister, or I shall have to take the light from your eyes and leave you here, in a foreign land.*

"At least she is stable for the time being," Wigg said, his countenance beginning once again to show the indomitable spirit the dwarf and prince were accustomed to. "I will attend to her shortly, but first there are things that must be done."

"Your powers have returned?" Tristan asked hopefully, seeing the light returning to the wizard's eyes.

"No," Wigg said, standing up, "but when Failee died, so did most of her incantations. Remember, her knowledge of the Vagaries was fragmentary. Therefore, so were many of its applications. But first we must find the Paragon. Quickly. Too much time may already have gone by."

Tristan left Shailiha in Geldon's care and went to search the carnage. After a few moments he found the stone, still on its chain, lying in a corner. It was completely clear, cold to the touch, and covered with dust and soot. Picking it up, he was surprised at how heavy it was as he handed it to the wizard.

Wigg took the Paragon lovingly in his hands, brushed it off, and held it under the light of one of the wall sconces. The infamous eyebrow came up in concern.

"Pray we are not too late," he said simply as he quickly began to remove his robe.

"What are you doing?" Tristan asked. "You cannot wear the stone until it has been prepared for a new host."

"Who said anything about wearing the stone?" Wigg said, finally allowing a smile to crease his face. He dropped the robe to the floor and reached for the pewter locket that hung around his neck.

The locket, Tristan thought. *I had completely forgotten about the locket!*

Wigg unceremoniously removed the top of the locket, then slid the Paragon from its gold chain. After placing the stone into the locket, he carefully screwed the top back on and hung both the locket and the Paragon's chain around his neck. Last, he put the robe back on. He stood there imperiously staring at the prince, daring him to figure it out.

And then Tristan understood. He found himself smiling at the old wizard. "Water from the Caves," he said simply as the old one stood there before him, smiling back. "From Faegan."

"Yes," Wigg replied. "The rogue wizard in the trees tends to be quite clever, you know." Tristan could tell from the tone in his voice that Wigg had long since decided to forgive Faegan for whatever had transpired between them so long ago.

"But aren't you now wearing the stone?" Tristan asked. "After all, it *is* around the neck of one of endowed blood."

"Oh, didn't I tell you?" Wigg asked impishly. "The pewter insulates the stone from my blood. It is the only substance other than the water of the Caves that can do so. Another nugget of wisdom from the wizard in Shadowood. Shortly, we shall know the fate of the stone, and therefore also the fate of my powers." Then his expression grew more serious.

"By the way, I am most relieved that you were able to decipher my riddle and use your gift to move the stone." He pursed his lips and looked narrowly at the prince. "As you can imagine, there is much to be said of your first use of the craft, but right now time does not permit it."

"But how did you know?" Tristan asked. "How could you have possibly realized that moving the stone was the answer?"

"I couldn't be sure," Wigg told him. "But I did know that the only time the Coven was vulnerable was when the stone was off Failee's neck. And the Communion apparently needed the stone not just to begin the ritual but also to sustain it. Removing the stone *while* the Communion was in progress seemed the only solution. But even I did not know that the Paragon could be sustained by the light itself until I saw its color begin to reappear." His eyebrow came up as he looked at the prince.

"What kept Failee from simply putting the stone back around her neck?" the prince asked.

"Apparently she did not immediately know it had been moved away from the light, or she would surely have tried. Protecting their eyes from the light seemingly kept them unaware. And remember, her knowledge of the Vagaries was fragmentary, and therefore seriously flawed. What ultimately killed the mistresses was Failee's incomplete knowledge of the Vagaries. But what she truly knew or did not know will probably always remain a mystery."

Tristan's mind flew back to the question that had occurred to him upon first seeing the dead sorceresses. "How is it that they died, and we did not?" he asked. "I can see no logic to the pattern."

Wigg pushed the tip of his tongue against the inside of his cheek, thinking. "Without taking valuable time to consider it further, I can only assume that the shards of light, being a product of the Coven, were therefore also a product of the craft itself. When the stone was removed from the light, they too needed sustenance, just as the stone did. In any event, the shards were forced to search for endowed blood to sustain themselves. My powers were gone, so they detected nothing of me, nor of Geldon. And as far as you and your sister are concerned, I can only assume that, ironically, it was the vast quality of your blood that protected you from them. Simply put, your blood may have been too powerful for them to thrive upon, and so they rejected it. In the end, I doubt we will ever really know."

Wigg walked quickly to Shailiha and sat down next to her. The princess had stopped crying but was continuing to stare blindly at nothing. Wigg raised one of her eyelids and peered at her eye. He then placed an affectionate hand on her abdomen and closed his own eyes for a time.

"She is well, at least physically, and so is her child," he announced at last, showing partial relief. "The daughter she is carrying is very near to term. But Shailiha's mind is still haunted by the Agonies. The women she thought were her sisters have all been killed before her eyes, just as were the family and husband she once knew, adding to her trauma. And the Agonies seem to linger, despite the death of Failee. The total damage may be more than even we had assumed." He rubbed the back of his neck in frustration.

"I cannot be sure that she will ever return to us," he continued. "There is much to consider, and despite the urgency to leave, now is the proper time to make such decisions." The wizard frowned and looked at the prince. "*Before* we leave for the portal," he added glumly.

Tristan went cold inside, knowing what the wizard was about to say next.

"If she does not improve, we cannot take her back, Tristan," the old one said compassionately. "To return one of such endowed blood, one who was actually a member of the Coven and still exhibits the effects of Failee's Agonies, would be completely irresponsible, no matter how much we love her. There is very little I can do for her, since I am not trained in the Vagaries. Faegan, perhaps, but not me. And we cannot simply leave her here, like this, to the mercy of the Minions. With the Coven no longer here to protect her, you know what that would mean."

Tristan knew what Wigg was saying, and if ordered to he would obey. He remembered the vow he had made never to doubt the old one again, and he intended to keep it if he must. But not without first trying everything he could think of to save Shailiha.

"How much time do we have?" he asked the wizard.

Wigg turned to the dwarf, understanding what Tristan was asking. "Geldon," he said sharply, "you have lived in the Recluse all of your life, and no doubt have a greater appreciation of the time that may have passed since we entered this room. What day is it?"

The dwarf was taken aback. "What do you mean?" he asked.

"I mean, how many days, in your opinion, have we been here in the Recluse?"

"If you are asking me how many more days will Faegan's portal open in the Ghetto of the Shunned, the answer is this is the sixth day. If we do not reach the Ghetto in time, we will have to wait until tomorrow—and that could be disastrous. The Minions would surely know of our escape by then."

Wigg pursed his lips. "Quickly," he said, "go to the skylight and look up to the sky. Tell me what color it is."

Geldon ran to the skylight, jumped up on the altar, and peered upward. "It is still dark," he said. "But dawn will break soon. Faegan's portal opens for one hour. I estimate we have about seven hours to reach it."

Tristan looked deep into the wizard's eyes. "Wigg, we must take her with us," he said sternly. "If she is not improved by the time we are forced to enter the portal, I will do my duty, make no mistake. But we cannot take her life now. We owe it to her, to my family, and to her unborn child to take her with us and give her every possible chance."

"But surely she cannot ride," Wigg said, putting a finger to his lips in thought. "We would need a wagon. Keeping her calm and comfortable may help prevent her giving birth while we try to get back to the portal."

Tristan thought for a moment, wondering why the wizard would say such a thing. "Would the birth of her daughter before we went back be such a bad thing?" he asked.

"It is not as simple as that," Wigg said simply. It was obvious he had anticipated the question, and just as obvious that he would take no joy in answering it.

Saying the next words came hard for the prince. "But if we killed her, we would also kill her daughter, providing Shailiha had not already given birth." He looked to the dead Succiu, and then, sadly, to her swollen abdomen, thinking sadly of the child that she had carried. He turned his attention back to the wizard.

"But if Shailiha's daughter had already arrived," he continued, "we could take the newborn back with us." *At least one member of my family could be saved from this place.*

"Tristan, you must listen to me," the wizard said sternly, putting a hand on the prince's shoulder. "I will agree to taking Shailiha with us as far as the portal. But it is not so simple a thing as one might think. You see, we must also consider the possibility that the Chimeran Agonies could pass from mother to child. By now you are well aware of the Coven's penchant for creating horrors that lived on and on for centuries. Knowing Failee as I did, I would actually be surprised if such was not the case here, as well."

Tristan looked into the face of the old one. He could see that it hurt the wizard to say these words as much as it did for the prince to hear them.

"Either way we cannot leave living endowed blood here, in Parthalon," Wigg stated with finality. "Removing endowed blood from this place, coupled with retrieving the stone, was the very reason we came. But bringing back with us endowed blood that might be tainted by the Coven is obviously impossible."

The wizard's logic was harsh, but inescapable. "Fair enough," Tristan reluctantly agreed. *Then I must find a way to bring her back to us,* he thought, shaking his head in frustration. *The insanity never ends.*

"Help your sister to her feet," Wigg said. "It is past time for us to take our leave of this place."

Tristan was just bending over to take her in his arms when he noticed the soft shifting sounds, like grains of sand washing smoothly across the shore. Then he saw the white dust and grain of crushed marble falling from between the cracks in the ceiling as the Recluse began to shift once again, the rumblings growing ever stronger. Marble block grated loudly against marble block, the noise blotting out everything as the convulsions knocked all three of them to the floor next to the princess. The room was literally cracking in half, the already-gaping crevice in the floor widening menacingly, its dark, deepening fingers reaching for the far wall of the Sanctuary. The white altar was thrown into the air along with several of the black thrones, and fell back to the earth heavily, cracking in half. Then the far wall began to split open, leaving a gaping, vertical gash in the marble.

A deathlike silence gradually descended over the room, marble dust choking their eyes and lungs as it fell delicately to the floor like the finest of snow. And then all became silent again.

"Aftershocks!" Wigg shouted urgently. "Sometimes it is the same following the death of a blood stalker! We must leave before the entire building comes down around us! We have waited too long already!"

He and Geldon reached for Shailiha as Tristan rose to his feet.

It was then that they heard the hissing begin.

They turned to look at the far end of the Sanctuary, the end that Failee had opened earlier to reveal her "children." The tremors had caused the wiktor pit to become uncovered, and the wiktor that Tristan had fought in Eutracia was coming up the stone steps. It stopped at the edge of the pit, its tail snaking back and forth anxiously as it stared at the bloody bodies of the dead sorceresses now half buried amidst pieces of marble and the dust of the wreckage.

It turned its head toward the four survivors, green drool slipping from around its teeth and dripping down to the floor. Tilting its head toward Tristan, the wiktor smiled.

"And so the Coven is no more," the monstrosity hissed, its tone a mixture of both sadness and a quiet kind of delight. "You have somehow managed to destroy them, but in doing so you have unwittingly released us for all time.

"Feeding upon the populace had always been our greatest pleasure, and after disposing of you we shall all be free to do so throughout eternity, protected by time enchantments as we go," it said, the long, yellow teeth flashing. "I thank you for our freedom. And before we leave the Recluse, I shall take all of your hearts for the murder of our mother and our sisters." The slanted eyes focused upon Shailiha. "Including the heart of the newest mistress."

As it took yet another ominous step forward, Tristan could hear the many hundreds more below it in the pit as they began to clamber up and out. Pushing Geldon and Shailiha behind him, Wigg stepped forward to stand alongside the prince and face the wiktor.

Tristan drew his dreggan, the familiar, reassuring ring of the blade resounding off the Sanctuary walls, as if it meant never to fade away. It quieted eventually, though, leaving only the sound of hissing from the pit. In an unusual move, the prince tossed the sword to his left hand. Wigg narrowed his eyes in puzzlement.

Tristan turned his dark eyes to the wizard, silently telling him not to interfere. He wanted this moment for himself.

There are old scores to settle, even if he dies trying, Wigg thought. *I should force him to obey me, but I won't.* He nodded shortly to Tristan and stepped behind him.

The wiktor took yet another step closer to the prince. Other pairs of slanted, yellow wiktor eyes could now be seen starting to peer menacingly over the edge of the pit. The hissing grew louder still.

This is where we die, Tristan told himself. *There are simply too many of them to kill, even for a wizard. But I will kill this one before they take me, I swear it.*

And then he did something unheard of in battle. He closed his eyes.

The wiktor smiled again. "I can see you have become too much of a coward to look death in the face. Apparently you realize that you were simply lucky the last time," it hissed angrily, running one of its talons along the scar around its neck in a bizarre fondling motion. It licked more of the green drool from its teeth.

"Prepare to die, Chosen One," it said simply.

Wigg now understood what the prince was doing. *He is calling upon his fledgling gift,* the old one thought, *in the only way he knows how.* He nervously looked at the wiktor, wondering how long it would wait before it struck. Wondering if Tristan could ready himself in time.

The answers were quick in coming.

Without warning the wiktor leapt at Tristan, covering half the distance between them in a heartbeat. Tristan's eyes snapped open.

The wizard's jaw fell open at what he saw next. He had seen Tristan use his knives before, but never had he seen him throw his knives with the aid of the craft.

Tristan threw two of his dirks, one immediately after the other, so quickly the wizard couldn't see his arms moving, much less the knives as they whistled through the air with a shrill, shrieking sound.

They hit the wiktor simultaneously—one in each eye.

The impact of the knives was so great that they tore through the back of the thing's head, heaving the screaming wiktor up into the air and back down over the edge of the pit, where it crashed into its brothers as it tumbled down the length of the stone steps, blood and brain matter running freely from its head.

Tristan looked quickly to the wizard. He had accomplished his goal, but the four of them were dead, and he knew it. Dozens of wiktors were clambering uncaringly over the body of their leader, seeking to satisfy their need to revenge his death.

And to feed.

Tristan looked into Wigg's aquamarine eyes for what he was sure would be the last time. "Is this the day we finally die?" he asked.

The wizard's face was hard as stone. "No," he said softly, narrowing his eyes. "This is the day that *they* finally die."

The Lead Wizard walked even closer to the edge of the pit just as some of the winged, green monsters were starting to land upon the floor of the Sanctuary. Taking the locket from his robes, he removed the stone and peered at it in the light. Then he poured a very small amount of water into the palm of his other hand. He stood there for a moment examining the water, collecting himself as the wiktors drew nearer. Leaving the locket open, dangling from its chain, he faced the edge of the pit as hissing wiktors continued to climb up and over.

Then Wigg held his palm up before his face and blew the water of the Caves into the air in the direction of the wiktors.

Tristan couldn't believe his eyes.

The air over and inside the wiktor pit immediately caught fire and began to rage, searing everything around it. Instead of being red and orange the flames were azure blue, just as Tristan had seen with every other important use of the craft the old one had performed. But this time the azure contained streaks of white-hot bolts that shot through the fire as the wizard stood, arms raised, before the burning air.

Amazed, Tristan watched as the fire consumed everything in the pit. He could hear the wiktors screaming, and their bodies bursting as the gases inside them expanded in the sucking heat of the azure maelstrom. More blood splattered along the wall, so much that some of it mixed with the blood of the Coven that was already on the floor of the Sanctuary.

Slowly Wigg lowered his hands. As he did so, the fire subsided, leaving nothing but the smell of cinders and the stench of scorched flesh. Tristan walked to stand next to the wizard and looked down into the pit. He was joined by Geldon, who held Shailiha close at his side. The scene at the bottom of the wiktor pit was horrific.

Masses of organs and bones lay amidst piles of ashes and a sea of blood. Nothing moved, and the sickly sweet death smell that filled the Sanctuary was overpowering.

Tristan was the first to speak.

"So the stone is rejuvenated?" he asked hopefully.

"No, not entirely," Wigg answered. "But when I removed the stone from the locket I hoped there would be enough regenerative power to perform some single act of the craft. Such a thing had never been attempted before. It was a gamble, but it worked." He pursed his lips in thought, and once again the infamous eyebrow came up.

"We were indeed fortunate," he continued. "And I now believe that the stone will completely reinvigorate, given enough time." He returned the stone to the locket once again, replacing the top.

"Can the wiktors rejoin their limbs to come alive once again?" Tristan asked. He had no desire to face another such creature ever in his lifetime.

"No," Wigg assured him. "The fire has consumed them to the point that we shall have no worry of that." No other words regarding the wiktors were necessary. "Time to go," he said simply.

Tristan turned and, with a grateful look at Geldon, took his sister in his arms. With the others by his side, he headed across the destroyed room to the circular staircase. It was incredible that the staircase had survived all the upheaval. With any luck, it would lead them all the way up and out of the Recluse.

And then he stopped short, and the blood ran from his face.

Succiu's body was gone.

A winding trail of dark-crimson blood led across the marble floor and to the staircase. Bloody footprints marked the ascending spiral steps. The other mistresses of the Coven still lay dead where they had fallen.

Tristan stared at the blood trail, speechless. He didn't even know what to think.

Wigg's voice broke the silence. "It's all my fault!" the old one shouted. His hands were balled up into angry fists; his face was dark and threatening. He was literally trembling with rage.

"I should have known; I should have known!" Tears started to come to the old wizard's eyes as he stood there in embarrassment and anger, beside himself with the pain of the shattering revelation flowing through his mind.

"It's your blood," he said, finally lifting his troubled face to the prince. "She carries your child, and therefore her body now also carries your blood. That's why the shards did not immediately finish her, just as they did not harm you and your sister. I was a fool not to recognize the possibility sooner." He turned to look at the bloody staircase she had used to make her escape.

"She was alive the entire time," he said, curling his upper lip in anger. "Probably wounded, but alive. All she needed was an opportunity to run, and when we all faced the wiktor pit we conveniently gave it to her."

The second mistress lives, Tristan thought in shock. *And therefore so does my firstborn.*

Before the wizard could stop him, Tristan handed his sister to the dwarf and ran up the bloody staircase.

Thirty-two

The climb was hard, and the wound in his side had started to bleed again. He ignored it.

Tristan quickly realized that he had no idea how far up he would have to go to reach the first floor of the Recluse, since he had been unconscious during the trip down to the Sanctuary. Parts of the circular hallway looked as though they might give way at any moment. Dust and debris from the aftershocks burned his eyes and lungs as he forced himself on, wondering with every step if he would suddenly look up to see the slanted, almond-shaped eyes of Succiu waiting for him somewhere up ahead.

When the steps finally ended at a landing, he cautiously opened the facing stone door a crack and peered out. He could see no one. Opening the door completely, he walked through, dreggan drawn.

Slowly, he lowered his sword arm as he surveyed the devastation before him. He was standing in a great, circular hall, or rather, he reflected, what was left of one. In the center of the room stood another winding staircase, miraculously unharmed amidst the wreckage. Around it, entire sections of the pale-blue marble walls had been ripped away as if made of paper. Most of the stained-glass windows that had once surrounded the circular chamber now lay in colorful shards on the floor, their twisted lead frames yawning before him, revealing the predawn sky over the still-dark hills of the countryside beyond the Recluse. The soft flames of the wall sconces were flickering from the breeze that carried into the room the clean, fresh scent of an early morning rain. Everywhere there was silence.

Looking down he quickly found the blood trail. The second mistress had likely lost a large quantity of blood by now, and it increased his hopes of catching her. The trail once again led to the spiral stairs, and he began his second long climb upward.

The stairs finally emptied out onto what was a great, flat section of the Recluse roof. It, too, was of the same pale-blue marble. See-throughs lined every side of it, and other structures had been built upon its vast, rain-slickened surface. He stepped out onto the roof slowly, looking around, his dreggan firmly in his right hand. His eyes narrowed. There was no sound other than the rain that fell down upon him, beginning to soak through his clothes. It was then that he saw her, his endowed blood rising in his veins.

She was not as he expected her to be.

The second mistress was standing at one corner of the roof, bent over from her great loss of blood. The tatters of her once-resplendent black gown were completely soaked through from the rain and clung almost seductively to her skin. Her long, wet hair was matted against her face and shoulders, and there was a growing puddle of blood beneath her. Her belly hugely swollen, she looked as if she might give birth at any moment.

But it was her face that he found most arresting. She had a softer, more compassionate look, as if the wounding by the shards or the loss of so much endowed blood had in some way given her a greater sense of vulnerability. The almond-shaped eyes looked at him with apparent sadness in place of the loathing and hatred that he was accustomed to seeing in her face.

It is almost as if the loss of her sorceress' blood has made her more human, he thought. *She almost seems to be a different woman standing before me, rather than the one I know and hate so much.*

Tristan stood his ground, not speaking, lost in a whirlwind of emotions as Succiu continued to crouch in the rain, shivering, watching his every movement like a wounded, cornered animal. *I must kill her now if I can, while she is still weak from blood loss,* he thought. *If I do not, she may somehow regain her powers and be the end of us all. I must not make the same mistake twice. Not with this woman.*

But there was something in her face that he saw as he stood there, something he had never before seen in her, and he wavered, thinking also of his firstborn child. *If she dies now, so does my child,* he thought. *There has never been a more difficult choice in my life.* He lowered the tip of his sword.

She smiled knowingly. "Do not fear, Chosen One. I cannot hurt you," she said softly. "I do not have the strength."

She raised one arm weakly and pointed a finger at his sword. A soft, azure light arced from her hand, but before it could reach its destination, it fell rather pitifully to the roof of the Recluse, dissipating and sizzling into nothingness in the cold puddles of rainwater.

"You see?" she said, almost kindly. "It's true. I am no threat to you unless you let me live. To do so would be a grave mistake on your part." She paused.

"And I can see in your eyes that you already care too much for our child that I carry," she continued. "The ultimate decision, is it not? To kill a defenseless woman and therefore your own child, or let me live and endanger everyone you love, including that same unborn child as well?"

He took a step toward her, still unsure of what to do. She immediately took a weak, matching step backward, closer to the edge of the wall.

Despite all that he had heard and seen, Tristan had made his decision. Although his heart was breaking, there was no other answer. He remembered what Wigg had told him only minutes before, and he had to agree with it, no matter how hard it was to do. *No endowed blood can be left in Parthalon.* Finding the button at the hilt of the dreggan he loosed the blade the extra foot, its clear, slashing sound echoing off the rainy roof of the Recluse. Tears in his eyes, his sword hand trembling, he took another step forward. Soft thunder rumbled across the still-dark sky.

Just then she bent over in agony, screaming. Raising her face to his as best she could, she said the words that would remain in his heart forever.

"Your child, Chosen One," she whispered. "The firstborn child of the Chosen One is coming." And then she stepped up on the edge of the wall.

Her intentions were clear.

He stopped short, the breath coming quickly to his lungs. Dropping to his knees before her, he looked up into her eyes. "Please," he half whispered to her, "please, I beg you, let me give you a quick death after the birth, but do not take our child with you!" He dropped the dreggan to the roof and held his scarred palms up to her, but she only inched herself closer to the edge.

"I'm sorry, Tristan," she said, using his name for the first time since he had known her. "But with the coming of the child, there are no more decisions to be made. Because your firstborn chooses to come now, at this moment, its fate is sealed. Poor Tristan, there is still so much you and the wizard do not know. Just as you cannot let me live, for reasons you do not as yet understand I cannot allow the child to be taken by you and the wizard."

Looking down at her abdomen, she placed an affectionate hand there. "Our child would have been beyond description," she whispered.

Wracked with pain, she looked into his eyes once again, searching his face as if trying somehow to keep the memory of him forever within her.

"Forgive me," she said.

Opening her arms to the arriving dawn, she threw herself off the roof of the Recluse.

Although the sun was beginning to rise in the east, its brightness was obscured by the gray rain clouds. The showers still came, although lighter now, and the air around him was silent and still. The unrelenting drizzle seemed, to him, to almost match drop for drop the tears that came from his eyes as he sat on his heels next to the dead body. The quiet, gray pall of violent death surrounded everything.

He had raced back down the stairways and out of the Recluse as fast as he had been able, stopping for nothing, hoping against hope that there could be some kind of chance. Running out and over the drawbridge, he had finally found her body facedown in the moat that surrounded the castle. It was immediately apparent that she had not yet given birth. Pulling her out as quickly as he could, he placed his fingers against the side of her throat, hoping for a pulse. None came.

He continued to sit there in the grass alongside her body, sobbing, his mind refusing to accept the unbelievable nature of all that had occurred between himself and the second mistress. *Succiu,* he thought. *One of the women I had sworn to kill. And, unbelievably, the mother of my first child.* It was then that he first smelled the smoke.

Looking up he saw a column of unusually dark smoke rising from the roof of the shattered Recluse, and instinctively he knew what it was. *Wigg is burning the bodies of the sorceresses,* he realized, *including that of the one who was once his wife. He wants to be sure this time.* The odor that came to him was the same sickly sweet yet repugnant foulness that he had first encountered about the funeral pyres of the Minions following the attack in Tammerland.

Tristan looked back down at the body of Succiu, and to her abdomen that still contained his firstborn. *Wigg will soon be here,* he thought, *and will want to do the same thing to Succiu. Especially to Succiu. And he is right.* He thought for a moment, trying to make his decision, the tears coming again. Finally, he knew what he had to do.

Removing one of his dirks from its quiver, he steeled his heart for the task that lay before him.

*W*alking guardedly through the rain, Wigg approached the dead sorceress and kneeling prince. There seemed to be no one about, but given what had apparently happened the wizard wanted to make sure that he and Tristan were alone before they spoke to each other.

Everyone associated with the disintegrating Recluse had fled, no doubt terrified at the turn of events, understandably wanting to be as far away from the place as possible. The old one briefly wondered what such people would do with their newfound freedom after having served the sorceresses for so long. The Lead Wizard sighed resignedly. *And the Minions,* he thought suddenly. *With the Coven gone, who is there to control them?* It was then that he saw the grave.

Tristan, his hands bloody and dirty, was sitting on his heels before a small, sad little pile of rocks. Some freshly picked flowers had been placed on top, and a broken piece of wood that served as a make-shift marker had been shoved into the wet earth at one end. As he approached, the wizard could make out the writing that had been carefully carved into it with a knife. It read:

NICHOLAS II OF THE HOUSE OF GALLAND
You will not be forgotten

Wigg looked at the bloody body of the dead sorceress and immediately knew what had transpired here. *Tristan saw the smoke and knew I was burning the bodies,* he realized. *Instead of letting his son be burned with his mother, he decided to give him a proper burial.*

The old wizard continued to examine the corpse that had once been Succiu. Her naked abdomen had been incised, her shredded gown falling around her on either side. Her once-beautiful but now lifeless eyes were staring blankly into the rainy sky.

Tristan did what he felt he must, Wigg reflected. *I cannot blame him for that.* He closed his eyes for a moment, trying to fathom the horror the prince must have felt—and the courage it must have taken to do the deed.

"Is Shailiha safe?" Tristan suddenly asked in a husky voice. He did not turn around to look at the wizard.

"Yes," Wigg answered softly. "She rests in the back of a wagon that Geldon and I stole from the horse barns. We filled the back full of hay for her to lie in, and luckily she fell into a deep sleep." He stopped short, wishing he had not said that just now. In the awkward silence that followed, the old one cleared his throat.

When Tristan didn't respond, Wigg slowly walked around to face him, squatting down to look him in the eyes. Tristan's cheeks were covered with the streaks of dried tears, and he continued simply to look at the little grave, almost as if not seeing it.

"What happened?" Wigg asked softly.

"I followed her to the roof," the prince finally said, still gazing at the little pile of rocks. "She was badly wounded, and had lost a great deal of blood. Her powers were gone, and she couldn't harm me. I was about to take her life when she went into labor. Rather than deliver the child to us she chose to jump, killing both herself and my son." His voice trembled, and he paused, not sure he could say any more right now.

"I'm sorry, Tristan," the old one said.

"It was a boy. A son," the prince whispered softly to himself. "My son." He touched the top of the grave lightly with the palm of one hand. "He will be staying here now."

Tristan gathered himself up and looked into the wizard's eyes. "She said that there was still so much that you and I did not know, that just as we could not let her live, so could she not let us have my firstborn." He wiped one of his cheeks. "Despite how much she wanted the child, she would rather see him dead than with his father. Do you know why?"

Wigg had no idea what the sorceress had been referring to, and he found the prospect unsettling. "I don't know," he said compassionately. "But we have little time, and I must burn the body before we leave. I only pray that the stone has rejuvenated sufficiently for me to accomplish it."

Gesturing for Tristan to rise, Wigg led him back a short distance from the corpse. He produced the locket from under his robe and removed the stone. Pulling his hood over his head, the old one lowered his face and clasped his hands in front of himself. Almost immediately Succiu's body began to go up in flames. The wizard returned the stone to the locket, and hid it once again in his robes.

When the familiar azure fires died down, all that was left of the sorceress was a charred, black, lifeless form. Tristan walked over to it and knelt down. As if trying to retain some memory of the woman who had been his son's mother, he reached out a finger to touch the remains.

Immediately the charred figure collapsed into a long, flat pile of ashes and began to scatter aimlessly on the rising breeze.

"The sorceresses of the Coven are no more," Wigg said simply.

Tristan turned for the last time to look at the grave of his son, and then the two of them began to walk away in the rain.

CHAPTER

Thirty-three

Upon reaching the wagon, Tristan could see that Geldon had hitched a team of two horses to it. "I'm glad to see you are well," the dwarf said. "When you ran from the Sanctuary, Wigg and I were greatly concerned." Tristan smiled back as best he could.

Quickly walking to the back of the wagon, he looked down at the face of his sister. Peacefully asleep, her eyes closed, she seemed to be the same kind, affectionate woman he had known and loved in Eutracia, the long blond hair and strong jawline just as familiar as ever. A blanket had been placed over her and drawn up to her chin.

Tristan was suddenly reminded of the day she and the wizard had come to the Hartwick Woods to find him, the same day he had first found the Caves of the Paragon. She had gladly risked the wrath of both their parents and the Directorate of Wizards because she had been worried about him. He put a palm to one side of her face. *You came to find me once,* he said to her silently. *And now I have come for you.*

Wigg appeared next to him, also looking down at the princess. The infamous eyebrow came up. "There is something I must show you," he said rather sternly. "I am hoping you can shed some light on the little mystery that I have uncovered."

Without further discussion, the wizard pulled down the blanket from around Shailiha's throat. The prince's jaw fell open in amazement.

A gold medallion, identical to the one that lay around his own neck, was around the neck of his sister, lying upon the black silk of her sorceress' maternity gown. The image of the lion and broadsword, the heraldry of the House of Galland, was clearly engraved upon it.

Impossibly, it was an exact duplicate of his own.

"It slipped out of her gown as we put her in the wagon," Wigg said, frowning. "Was this a gift from her mother, as yours was?" he asked. He thought he knew the answer, but he wanted to hear it from the prince.

"It couldn't have been," Tristan answered, thinking to himself.

"Why not?" Wigg asked, testing him.

Tristan reached out to feel the medallion, as if needing to prove to himself that it was real. "The answer is simple," he said. "Shailiha wasn't wearing this at the coronation ceremony when the Coven first took her. I'm sure of it. If we are to assume that she was taken from the Great Hall directly to Succiu's boat, then, impossible as it might seem, this medallion must have somehow originated here in Parthalon."

"Precisely," Wigg answered.

"But how?" Tristan asked. "I know much less than you about the workings of the Coven, but I cannot believe they would purposely allow her to wear something that would remind her of her homeland."

"Of course not." Wigg smiled. "The only answer is that she had been wearing it for only a short time, and the Coven was unaware of it."

"But where did it come from?" Tristan asked, still incredulous. He could remember seeing the chain around her neck for the first time in the depths of the Sanctuary, but he had never been able to see what was at the end of it. He stared at the wizard. "How did it get around her neck?"

"Without time for a greater study of it, I can only guess the medallion to be some oblique manifestation of the Chimeran Agonies, perhaps even left here in the physical world as a result of Failee's fragmentary knowledge. If the Coven did not put it around her neck, as we know they would not, then somehow perhaps the princess did it herself. The only continuing link to her mental condition is the Agonies. And if she does not show any signs of improvement, I fear we shall never know." He paused, hoping that the prince would remember his duty regarding the princess if and when the time came.

"I'm sorry about Failee," Tristan said simply. They were words that he would never have thought he could say, but that needed to be spoken, nonetheless.

"I know, Tristan," Wigg said softly, pain and fatigue showing in his aquamarine eyes. "We have both had our losses in this place. It is perhaps best to leave the memories of them here, as well."

He looked to the sky, where the sun was just beginning to break through the parting rain clouds. "We have only three hours until high noon," he said sternly. "And a hard gallop to the Ghetto will take at least two, perhaps longer because of the princess. We must leave now." Although it showed in his face, the old one made no mention of what all three of them knew to be their greatest challenge.

In her raging, insane hate, Failee had sent all the legions of the Minions of Day and Night to the Ghetto to look for conspirators. The entire force. And the prince, wizard, and dwarf knew in their hearts that despite the power of the Lead Wizard, even he would not be able to overcome all of them. Failee's fateful decision would most probably spell their deaths.

Tristan climbed into the back of the wagon and cradled his sister in his lap, tucking the blanket snugly around her as the dwarf and the wizard climbed up onto the front seat. His thoughts went to Narrissa, wondering where she was and what had actually become of her. His jaw tightened, thinking of the unbelievable treatment she would have received from Kluge. Sadly, he had to admit to himself that with only hours remaining until the opening of the portal, he would probably never see her again.

With a snap of his whip, Geldon charged the horses down the road to the Ghetto of the Shunned.

PART VI

The Ghetto of the Shunned

CHAPTER

Thirty-four

✦

*Of the seeds of the Chosen Ones, one shall live and one shall die, the two having been
conceived of separate, and therefore distinct, philosophies. The mother of the first and
the sire of the second shall both perish before seeing their progeny come to fruition.*

*As such, these lives shall be yet another manifestation of the Vigors and the Va-
garies, those disciplines being two sides of the same coin, namely the craft, wrapped in
the same confines but residing in different worlds. In this way the Vigors and the Vagaries themselves shall resemble the newborns of the Chosen Ones, being of completely
different philosophies, yet each continually aware of the other's presence as they move
through space and time . . .*

—FROM THE WRITINGS OF FAEGAN,
UPON HIS LATER RECOLLECTIONS OF THE TOME

Tristan, Geldon, and Wigg held their breath as they lay on their
stomachs in the grass upon the short rise, surveying the scene below. The sky had finally cleared to reveal a sun-filled morning, and the
wind was calm. For the second time today their noses were assaulted by
the acrid, sickening smell of burning flesh. Human flesh.

Their wagon ride from the Recluse had been harrowing, if for no
other reason than the speed at which Geldon drove the horses and the
constant veering to avoid the great number of people who were on the
road, fleeing the area of the smoldering Recluse.

There had been absolutely no sign of the Minions along the way,
and in this Tristan had been disappointed. Not because he and Wigg

would have tried to stop and kill them—there was no time for that. But because it would have meant the troops had already left the Ghetto, their job there over. The fact that they saw no Minion troops increased even further his concerns for their safety. He instinctively knew that the wizard and the dwarf were thinking the same thing, and the silent dread in their hearts was palpable as they sped along the primitive, twisting road.

Shailiha had stirred more than once in Tristan's arms as a result of the bumpy ride, but blessedly remained asleep. She was still asleep now in the back of the wagon while the three of them crept up to the short rise to look down over the city below.

The Ghetto of the Shunned sat in a rather large bowl, surrounded on all sides by a sloping, grassy hillside. Geldon had explained to them that before the arrival of the Coven the city had been constructed in the center of the bowl for reasons of defense. Men lining the top of the rim could see for miles in every direction and easily warn the city below of danger, allowing the gates to be shut quickly and the drawbridge to be immediately taken up. Until, of course, the arrival of the Coven.

But that same strategic advantage was now making things very difficult for the three of them as they tried to take in the scene. It was impossible to tell what or who might be on the other side of the bowl, and the prospect of the Minions being either inside the city wall or camped around the bowl's perimeter was a distinct possibility. There was no time to scout the area—it was just too large. Faegan's portal would soon open up for the last time, and that was where they needed to be, regardless of the danger.

Inside the Ghetto. In Ian's aviary.

The city had apparently been under siege from the Minions for the last several days, as the flying warriors carried out the last of Failee's orders to Kluge and searched for conspirators who might have helped the Chosen One. The huge iron gates that had once barred entrance just past the drawbridge had been broken apart and dangled drunkenly off their hinges, the drawbridge itself innocently lowered as if beckoning them to enter. Although from this distance and angle little could be seen of the inside, it was apparent that a great many people had already died at the hands of the Minion troops. The traditional funeral pyres had been lit outside the city walls, the charred smoke rising lazily into the sky, carrying with it the remains of the dead. But those pyres could hold few bodies of the Minions, Tristan realized. The starved, weakened citizens of the Ghetto would never have been able to overcome many of the winged soldiers. The fires must have been burning the corpses of their victims, as the Minions made sure that the bodies of both those with and without leprosy alike were reduced to ash.

So many have died, Tristan thought in horror, *simply because Failee was looking for conspirators. And there was in actuality only one. Ian, the keeper of the birds. I pray that he still lives.*

"It is impossible to know whether the Minions are still there without going inside," he whispered to the other two. "No matter how quickly we try to take Shailiha by wagon through the front gates we will be immediately detected, but I see no other way."

"We must know if the interior is deserted," Geldon said with finality. "And there is only one way to do that. You must allow me to swim under the moat and look inside. If I see nothing, I will signal you from atop the wall closest to the aviary. Come directly through the gates as fast as you can and go to the aviary without diversion. Turn immediately to the right and go as far as you can. Then, when you reach the eastern wall and can go no farther, turn left and continue for a few blocks. The aviary will be on the left. Stop for nothing. However, if the reverse is true, then there will be no signal, for I will certainly be dead. The smoke from the Recluse can only mean one thing to Kluge and he will know that his mistresses are gone, giving him license to do as he pleases." The dwarf paused, and silence lay thick between the three of them.

Tristan looked at the wizard, tacitly asking for his opinion. After a moment, Wigg reluctantly nodded. Without giving them a chance to think any longer about it, the dwarf gathered up the chain to his collar and ran quickly down the hillside and around the edge of the wall, toward the area where he would find the underwater gate.

In an instant he was gone, the only trace of his presence the slowly calming ripples of water that closed in around the place where he had gone in.

Such great courage in such a small body, Tristan thought. *We already owe him more than we could ever repay.*

And then they waited. The moments went by slowly, and for a time Tristan feared that he might never see Geldon's face again.

Then, suddenly, there he was, atop one of the walls and soaking wet, waving them forward. As quickly as they could, Wigg and Tristan jumped onto the wagon and charged it toward the city gate, Wigg taking the reins, the prince keeping one eye on Shailiha still asleep in the back.

The way down was harrowing since there was no real road, but they couldn't stop for anything, or dare go any slower. Finally they were across the drawbridge and inside the Ghetto of the Shunned.

Wigg wasted no time as he galloped the charging horses down the main street. Buildings and corners flashed as Tristan looked around for signs of trouble, but the streets were completely empty.

Following Geldon's directions, the wizard reached the eastern wall, careened the wagon to the left, and charged down the street. Finally, after several more blocks had flown by, Wigg skidded the horses to an abrupt stop in front of the building that housed the aviary.

Except the aviary was no longer there. And there was no trace of Geldon. Tristan jumped down from the wagon, his dreggan already in his hand, and stood agape at the silent, awful scene that lay before him.

The buildings in this part of the Recluse had all been razed and burned. The ashes were still warm, the dark, pungent smoke curling up into the sky. Of the building that had once housed the aviary, only the fractured, fragile skeleton of its foundation remained, rising a few awkward feet into the air. And all around the base lay the remains of Faegan's enchanted pigeons, their wings and heads cut off, their bodies scattered.

The Minions had transformed this entire area into a sickening graveyard, a testament to their butchery. Dead bodies lay everywhere, just as they had in the streets of Tammerland, and in the center of the square were two separate piles of naked women, presumably raped and piled as trophies. The Pentangle of the Coven could be seen smeared in blood on each of the few standing walls, the severed arms and legs that had served as the Minion's paintbrushes cast aside after having completed their grisly purpose. The air was hot and humid, with no trace of a breeze, leaving nowhere for the stench of death to escape to as the birds of prey began to wheel effortlessly in their lazy circles above the carnage, waiting for their turn to feed. A palpable, deafening silence reigned as the moments crept silently forward, taking the sun urgently higher in the sky.

Tristan turned to see that the wizard had climbed down from the wagon and was standing silently in the midst of the rubble that had been the aviary. Wigg beckoned to the prince to join him. Walking over, Tristan looked down and saw a mutilated corpse.

Ian lay dead in the ashes, his eyes gouged out, his arms and legs severed, the yellow leper's robe torn and burned.

The gentle keeper of the birds, Tristan thought sadly. *Kluge found him here and probably forced him to talk. The madness never ends.* Looking around, he found a singed blanket and used it to cover the body.

He looked worriedly at the wizard. "I know," Wigg said tensely. "We can only assume that he told them everything. He wasn't strong enough to stand up against very much." He looked around the small square. "But where is Geldon?" he murmured, half to himself. He looked to the sky, thinking. "There is less than an hour remaining."

Tristan walked to the back of the wagon and lowered the gate. Gently lifting Shailiha from the straw, he carried her to a shady spot by the destroyed wall of the aviary. Her eyes opened partially and looked up into his face, but there was still no sign of recognition, and she did not speak. *Come back to me,* he begged her silently as he gently stroked her hair. *Come back to me from the Chimeran Agonies, or I shall have to leave you in this place!*

He looked around, wondering what had happened to the dwarf. The answer arrived with the sound of wings.

Looking up, Tristan saw the sky darkening. The air was soon filled with the sound of many thousands of pairs of swiftly beating wings. At first he could not see, the sun in his eyes, but then winged monsters settled in to cover the walls, rooftops, and streets that surrounded them.

Thousands upon thousands of them came, so many there was no longer any place for them to land. Only a small space was left between the escapees and the growing horde of Minion warriors. Finally they stopped, those that had landed standing silently at attention as if waiting for something. Then, as if by command, those still in the air suddenly flew off, as if trying to find a better vantage point from which to observe what they apparently thought was about to transpire.

Wigg took two steps back to join Tristan in front of Shailiha. The prince looked quickly to the sun. There were only minutes left now.

Despite the thousands of beings crammed into this area of the Recluse, nothing moved. No one spoke.

Tristan looked into the face of his friend and mentor and knew that Wigg, too, realized this was the end. Even the power of the Lead Wizard could not overcome such numbers. This was the place in which they would both die.

And then, finally, the hated voice came, clear and sharp, cutting through the air over the great number of warriors and traveling directly to the prince's heart.

"Chosen One!" Kluge called from atop the wall directly facing them. "Is this what you have been looking for?"

Tristan and Wigg looked up to see the commander of the Minions of Day and Night standing with Geldon, holding the dwarf's chain. He smiled wickedly down at the prince. Traax, his second in command, stood obediently next to him. Geldon, still wet from his swim beneath the moat, stood plaintively on the other side of Kluge, looking frantically into Tristan's eyes, knowing that he had unwittingly condemned them all to a certain death.

Laughing wickedly, still holding the dwarf's chain by his heavily muscled right arm, Kluge kicked Geldon off the wall.

The only thing that kept the dwarf's neck from breaking was the quick-witted way in which he reached up to grab the chain. He dangled helplessly, his arms losing strength as the commander of the Minions continued to hold him there, laughing, waiting for the dwarf to lose his grip and finally choke to death before them all. But then suddenly Kluge let go of the chain, and Geldon fell crashing into the midst of the Minion warriors, who erupted into raucous laughter.

Looking down on his troops, Kluge shouted, "Let the dwarf through to join his friends, so that they may all die together! It is somehow more fitting!"

Immediately Geldon ran through the obediently parting warriors to stand with Wigg and Tristan, tears in his eyes. "There was no one here when I arrived," he said quickly. "And then Kluge himself came flying out of the ruins of the aviary to gather me up and make me climb to the top of the wall. Unknown to us, there were Minion patrols flying very high in the sky, staying between us and the rising sun. It is no surprise we did not see them. Kluge knew we were here, and after my coming into the Ghetto alone it was a simple matter of logic for him to deduce that you were waiting for a signal." He hung his head in shame. "I'm sorry Tristan," he whispered. "I am the death of us all."

"Tristan," Wigg whispered urgently, "I can kill Kluge if you will let me. But I must know now, while he is out in the open. I cannot save us from what will eventually happen—you must see that as well as I do. Even with the help of the craft I cannot defeat such numbers. And because the Paragon is still in the locket, I am without my powers. I must open the locket and remove the stone. I'm sure that by now it has rejuvenated. If we act in unison I can kill Kluge while you give Shailiha a quick death before the rest of them overcome us. It is the only way," the old one whispered, looking into Tristan's eyes with absolute candor. "We will be dead soon, and this is the only way I can see us sparing your sister from that monster on the wall, and still kill him at the same time."

He put a hand on Tristan's shoulder. "Remember," he added sternly, glancing behind him at the inert Shailiha. "No endowed blood can remain in Parthalon."

Tristan considered the wizard's words for a moment, but in his heart he knew he could not agree, no matter how certain Wigg was that he could actually kill Kluge. *Kluge had no magic to use when we first met,* he thought, looking with hatred at the winged butcher that had killed his family. *He made no use of the craft. Therefore I will make no such use of the craft now. Live or die, I will meet this man on my own terms, wizard or no wizard.*

But before the prince could respond to Wigg, Kluge called out to him again from atop the wall. "Chosen One!" he screamed, his voice alive with hate. "See the present I have brought to you this day!"

Looking up, Tristan thought his heart would tear in half. Narrissa was standing next to Kluge, naked. She was crying, the tears running blatantly down her face, and it was more than obvious that she had suffered every kind of abuse. Bite marks and bruises could be seen on her face and body, and dried rivulets of blood trailed down both inner thighs from her groin to her feet. She cowered with fear before the Minions and the prince, shamefully aware of her nakedness. Tristan felt the blood rise in his veins as never before and took a step toward the wall, starting to draw his dreggan.

"Come no closer!" Kluge immediately ordered. "This Gallipolai has been rather disappointing to me. I never did care for women who called out another man's name while they were being taken! In fact, there is much to discuss before you and the wizard die. Allow us to come to you!"

Lifting Narrissa as though she were weightless, Kluge snapped open his leathery wings and flew down to land in the center of the square, his back to his troops, directly facing the prince. Taking a few steps closer, he threw the terrified woman roughly to the dirt at Tristan's feet. She landed hard and curled up into a protective ball, crying. Kluge spat on her as though she were just so much garbage.

Tristan lifted his eyes back up to his enemy without immediately bending over to help Narrissa, despite how much he wanted to. He could not be too careful with this man.

"Don't worry," Kluge said, as if reading his mind. "The time will come shortly for you and me, but first there are things I wish to tell you, so that I may see the look in your eyes before you die. Go ahead, Chosen One. Pick up your white-winged whore." He smiled. "I am done with her."

Tristan lifted Narrissa into his arms and carried her back to the wizard. Wigg sat her up against one of the wagon wheels and began trying to tend to her wounds as best he could. Tristan removed the blanket from Ian's body and wrapped it around the quivering, terrified Narrissa, giving her his best look of hope. She smiled back up at him, saying nothing. There was no need, for Tristan already knew what she felt.

Wigg looked quickly up into Tristan's dark eyes. "You must let me kill him now, before it is too late!" he insisted in a stern whisper.

Tristan gave the wizard a hard look. "No," he said simply. "I do this on my own terms. And you are not to interfere in any way, including the use of the craft."

"Tristan, you cannot kill him!" Wigg whispered back. "Forgive me, but he is just too strong. The only reason we are not dead already is because of his intense hatred for you. He obviously wishes to toy with us. Use that to your advantage and at least make some small use of the craft yourself, to help you live through this!"

"I have given you my answer," he said flatly. He handed Wigg one of the razor-sharp dirks from his quiver. "And now I am going to give you yet another order. It is obvious that either Kluge will kill me, or the others will. When I am dead, use the knife first to take Shailiha's life as quickly as you can. Then Geldon, Narrissa, and finally yourself, if there is time. And above all keep the stone hidden beneath your robes and do not use your powers. The Paragon is of no use to them without knowledge of the craft and the endowed blood to command it, but we must not show Kluge that we have it. Let him think that it perished with the sorceresses in the destruction of the Recluse. There is no other way." He paused, gathering the courage for his next words. "We are lost, and there can be no endowed blood left in Parthalon," he whispered, quoting the wizard. "Including yours or mine."

Tristan looked again into the craggy, intelligent face of the man he had loved and trusted for so long. "Good-bye, my friend," he said. He turned and walked out into the center of the square to face his death. Raising his face, he looked directly into the Minion commander's dark, piercing eyes.

Kluge towered over him, waiting, his arms crossed over his chest, obviously enjoying the situation. "Now it is time to enlighten you, Chosen One, and finally tell you of all the things you have done for me." His smile broadened at Tristan's look of puzzlement. "Oh yes, you heard me correctly, the things you have done *for* me. You don't realize it yet, do you? Then we shall start from the beginning."

Kluge pointed to the sky north of the city, to the smoke that still lingered in the air over the demolished Recluse. "Any fool can plainly tell that the sorceresses are dead," he said menacingly. His face darkened slightly. "I loved the second mistress, it is true, and now she is no more. But there is little I can now do about that. How you managed to kill them is of no concern to me. All that matters now is that she and the rest of them no longer exist to give me orders. And, despite my once-unshakable allegiance to them and the loss of the one I loved, recent developments have persuaded me not to grieve too terribly for them." A wicked smile began to spread across the monster's face. "You see, Chosen One, you have now freed me to take control of the entire nation, with the Minions at my command. Something I could never have dreamed of if any of the sorceresses, including Succiu, still lived."

Unsurprised, Tristan continued to listen cautiously, braced for the huge warrior's imminent attack. He watched hatefully as Kluge began to pace triumphantly back and forth in front of him.

"But there is still so much more to thank you and the wizard for, I hardly know where to begin. My scouts tell me that not only have the two of you dispatched the Coven, but the entire wiktor colony, as well.

Again, I salute you. They would have proven to be a difficult though not impossible challenge to my reign."

Tristan silently stood his ground, the sun rising ever higher in the sky, the time growing shorter. *It no longer matters,* he thought sadly, *for we are already dead.*

Kluge's face suddenly turned serious again, and he walked closer to the prince, his sword still sheathed. "And lastly, you ignorant, royal bastard, I want to thank you for the greatest prize of all." He paused, letting his words sink in for a moment. "Thank you for handing me the kingdom of Eutracia."

Kluge reached into the belt at his waist and withdrew some pieces of paper, which he carelessly let go, watching as they fluttered to the ground. For a moment, Tristan's heart stood still. He immediately recognized what they were: the parchments from the aviary. The collected correspondence of Faegan to Ian, the keeper of the birds.

Tristan froze, his blood running cold in his veins. *Eutracia,* he realized in despair. *Kluge knows about the portal!*

"That's right," Kluge whispered to him evilly. "That weak little leper named Ian talked. It's amazing how persuaded one can become while having one's eyes gouged out. In any event, we also found the parchments, which illuminated far more than our conversation with the diseased bird boy. Apparently the fool was born here, and was so enamored of the outside world that he foolishly took to saving Faegan's correspondence. I now know how you got here, and how you planned to go back. I also know more of the wizard named Faegan who guards the other side in the place called Shadowood. Once you and the Lead Wizard are dead, I plan to send my troops through to subjugate him. Despite his knowledge of the craft, due to our sheer numbers he will eventually find himself in the same position you are now in. Completely overpowered. I shall use his talents to come and go between the two nations as you have done. We will then also be entrenched in Eutracia, and I will stand astride not one nation, but two." He smiled again.

"Since there is no longer any semblance of the Royal Guard in your feeble country," he sneered, "it shouldn't be all that difficult. I doubt Faegan's gnomes will provide much of a challenge." He broke into laughter.

Tristan stood before the winged freak, stunned. Had Kluge chosen that moment to attack him, he would surely have died on the spot. But the commander did not, instead relishing the pain he could see in the prince's eyes.

"And still there is one other thing, Chosen One," he said, stepping even closer. Tristan could almost smell the foulness of his breath, just as he had that day in the Great Hall when Kluge had slaughtered his family and the Directorate of Wizards. The first day he had learned of the horrors that the Coven and the Minions could bring. The day his life had changed forever.

"I must also thank you for what may indeed prove to be the ultimate gift," Kluge continued. "During my reign I shall need a queen, and since I have already tasted women without wings and find them to be highly superior to Minion whores, I believe I shall not only have such a woman again, but also one of royalty, as well. Your sister shall make me a wonderful queen, don't you agree?" He looked hungrily at Shailiha as she leaned up against the foundation, oblivious to the scene, completely unaware of the fate that loomed before her.

"Given her condition, I doubt whether she will be of any mind to object to whatever I choose to do to her," he gloated nastily. "After she gives birth to the weakling growing in her belly I will dispose of the child, because it is not of my seed. I will then make Shailiha mine. Perhaps our children may even have both wings and endowed blood. Such an interesting combination, don't you agree?" The monster leaned in conspiratorially to smile slyly at the prince. "I am most anxious to discover whether she tastes as sweet as her mother." He paused, relishing the obscene luxury of his words. "And thanks to your stupidity I shall have that which I have wanted for so long: to see your endowed blood running into the dirt of the square, and to possess a woman of equally endowed blood, indeed of blood that surpasses even that of my dead Succiu."

Kluge's jaw hardened, making it clear he was close to finishing what he had to say. "Your life, your family, your Directorate, both Parthalon and Eutracia, and your only sister—in one way or another I shall have taken each of them, and all because you were weak enough to hand them to me, you ignorant bastard."

He finally backed away, drawing his dreggan from its scabbard, the blade's familiar ring slowly fading away in the confines of the square. "Gifts," he whispered, "given to a simple warrior born of a Minion whore's bed, from an irresponsible man across a supposedly uncrossable sea. A man who did not want to become king."

The commander of the Minions of Day and Night backed away from the prince cautiously, taking a quick look at the sun. "Faegan's portal arrives soon, Chosen One," he said quietly. The shiny tip of his dreggan pointed menacingly at Tristan's face. "It is at last time for you and me to settle our differences."

Kluge backed farther away from the prince in the hot, sunny confines of the square, his winged troops standing anxiously all around him. Smiling, he touched the tip of the dreggan to the front of his left shoulder where it lay bare next to the leather vest and cut a small incision into it. Blood ran slowly down his arm and onto the dirt.

The challenge had been made.

Tristan took a step forward, and pulled his dreggan from its scabbard, the blade repeating the same deadly song. Slowly he lifted the scabbard and baldric over his head and dropped them to one side in the dirt. He raised the shiny, curved blade to the sky and looked at it for what he knew would be the last time.

Despite being the instrument of my father's death, you have always been true to me, he thought, looking at the blade as it twinkled in the sunlight. *I ask only that you be true to me one more time, and help me slay the thing that stands before us. After that, may the Afterlife do with me as it will.*

He lowered the sword to his side, and he and Kluge began to circle each other in the little square.

Kluge wasted no time, screaming as charged, cutting a wide, angled swath through the air, designed to take Tristan's head from his shoulders. Rather than block the blow with his sword the prince rolled to one side and, coming back up along Kluge's left arm, tried to slash a circle low to the ground to take off the warrior's feet. But Kluge was too fast and jumped into the air, allowing the prince's blade to cut harmlessly beneath him. The two combatants faced each other again, only several feet apart, their breathing coming more heavily now as they continued to take stock of each other.

Again Kluge came, this time his dreggan whistling through the air from straight overhead. The blade came down with such force that despite the fact that the prince blocked it with his sword, the blow literally took him off his feet, slamming him down viciously on his back in the dirt. Seizing the opportunity, Kluge quickly slashed the sword straight down again, but Tristan rolled to the side and out of the way. For a moment, he stumbled as he tried to get up. The mistake cost him a precious second, and Kluge's sword came around again, the tip catching the prince in the upper right shoulder as it whistled violently through the air. The wound was short but deep, and blood began to pour out of it and down the length of the prince's arm, making his grip on the dreggan more elusive.

He is just too strong, Tristan realized, the heat growing in the confining square, the sweat running maddeningly down into his eyes. *I have never felt such power.*

He lunged then at the monster before him, and the two of them crossed swords, their faces only inches apart. Tristan was straining with everything he had; but Kluge simply smiled, took one hand from the hilt of his sword, gripped the prince's face, and threw him backward into the dirt.

This time Tristan was quicker, and thrust his dreggan straight ahead and upward, aiming for Kluge's groin. Although Kluge was fast enough to dodge most of the blow, the dreggan went straight through his inner thigh and out the other side, blood spurting. Screaming more from rage than from pain, Kluge backed away, Tristan's dreggan sliding from the wound, and began hacking maddeningly at the prince as he lay there in the dirt.

Get up! Tristan told himself. *Get up or you will die in the dirt before this creature!*

As the heavy blows rained down on him one after the other there was simply no chance to retaliate, and the best Tristan could do was to try to stand again. Finally, in between the insane, swinging strikes, he somehow once again found the earth beneath his feet and stood there, dazed and dizzy, blood flowing openly from his shoulder.

Kluge then unexpectedly backed away from the prince and reached for the returning wheel at his side. In a flash it was in the air and heading for Tristan's throat. At the last moment Tristan twisted wildly to the side, but the wheel grazed the side of his right cheek, putting him badly off balance.

The point of Kluge's dreggan came directly at the prince, only to suddenly stop a short distance from his throat. Stunned, the prince almost didn't realize the danger as Kluge depressed the button on the hilt of his dreggan. Just as the last foot of sharpened steel launched itself forward, Tristan wheeled to one side, the tip of the dreggan slashing through the space where his face had just been.

I cannot defeat this man, he realized, his arms so heavy that he could hardly raise the sword in his own defense, much less mount an attack against the screaming, half-insane monster that wanted to take his life. For some reason his oxygen-deprived mind flew back to the day upon the dais, when he had used his dirks to kill several of the Minion attackers. *At least I killed the one who murdered Frederick,* he remembered. *Frederick, my friend . . .*

And then some long-forgotten memory of the past began to tug at his mind. Something about that day in the royal courtyard when he and Frederick had been fencing in front of the Royal Guard. The same day they had killed the screaming harpy. The same day his mother had given him the medallion he wore around his neck. *What is it?* he asked himself, trying desperately to dodge Kluge's blows and raise his leaden arms to strike back. *What is it my blood is trying to tell me?*

And then he remembered. *Frederick's technique . . . the one he finally used to defeat me . . . The way he caught me off guard . . .*

The last of his strength was almost gone. *It is the only thing I have left,* he realized. *May the Afterlife grant me the strength for this last act.*

Tristan backed away from Kluge as fast as he could, momentarily lowering his sword. As expected, the commander of the Minions of Day and Night rushed forward, but that tiny instant of time without being continuously attacked was what the prince was looking for. As Kluge dashed in and raised his sword, Tristan purposely left his dreggan pointed to the dirt as if accepting his impending death. Then, suddenly looking up and over Kluge's shoulder, he dropped his jaw with a total look of surprise.

As Tristan had hoped, Kluge quickly turned to look over his shoulder, briefly turning his attention away from the prince to look for what was coming after him from behind.

Exposing his neck.

With a great effort, Tristan swung his sword in a perfect, curving arc, cutting across the monster's throat.

For a moment Kluge simply stood there, looking at him in amazement as if frozen in time. Then the ghastly line of red began to surface across his throat, and the blood stared to pour from it and down the front of his chest.

With a last measure of strength he didn't know he had, Tristan raised his dreggan again and cut across the monster's lower legs, slicing through them at the knees. Kluge collapsed to the ground on his back, one hand still holding his sword, the other reaching to his throat to try to stem the loss of blood.

Breathless, barely able to hold his dreggan, Tristan stumbled over to look down into the face that he hated so much. He had intended to strike fully across Kluge's throat and behead him, but his swing had fallen short and instead cut shallowly across the windpipe and jugular vein, leaving the monster alive. Tristan looked down into the dark eyes of the murderer of his family, watching emotionlessly as the blood ran from the cut throat and into the thirsty dirt of the courtyard.

And then the commander of the Minions of Day and Night spoke.

"Our struggle is not over, Chosen One," he said, his voice gurgling. He coughed up blood. "Even in death it shall go on for me. There are still things you do not know, and even if you should somehow return to your homeland you will be a wanted man, hunted day and night because of me, your forever-damaged sister a mere shadow of her former self. No, Galland, your victory over me here today is far from complete." Somehow, even now, Kluge managed a wicked grin of defiance.

"Our battle goes on, even from my grave."

His arm covered with blood, his mind barely conscious, Tristan pushed the button at the hilt of his sword. He felt the dreggan jump in his hand as the blade launched the extra foot into the air. He looked down into the hated, dark eyes for the final time.

"As you forced me to do to my father," he said quietly. "With the same sword."

He swung the blade in a high arc and brought it down with every-thing he had left, severing Kluge's head from his body. He stood there for a moment, listening as Kluge's lungs expelled their final death rattle.

Then, thrusting the tip of his sword into the dirt before him, he leaned weakly on the hilt of his dreggan and closed his eyes for a mo-ment, the only sound in the little sunlit square the intermittent rush of the wind as it wandered through the charred destruction of the city.

Rest in peace, my father, he called silently. *For we shall be joining you soon.*

Exhausted, Tristan looked up to the wall where Kluge had stood, knowing that at any moment the Minions would descend upon them. Traax, Kluge's second in command, immediately snapped open his long wings and jumped off the wall, flying menacingly down in a straight line toward the prince.

Finally, this is where I die, Tristan thought. *I am too weak even to lift my sword, much less defeat another of these creatures. Dying here is as good a place as any.*

He tried with both hands extended to raise the now impossibly heavy dreggan in his defense but could only manage to bring it as high as his waist, his weak, trembling legs bent at the knees. He stood there abjectly, the blood still running from his shoulder and down to the han-dle of his sword as he finally accepted the fact that he was about to die.

Traax landed lightly in front of the prince and drew his dreggan, its clear, harsh ring seeming to call out the prince's death knell. The curved blade twinkled momentarily in the sunlight.

And then Traax did something that would change the Chosen One's life forever. Placing his dreggan in the dirt at the prince's feet, he went down on one knee before Tristan and lowered his head.

"I live to serve," Traax said obediently.

Stunned, the prince raised his face to see an entire ocean of Minion warriors doing the same thing. As they simultaneously drew their swords from their scabbards the air rang overwhelmingly with their blades' combined songs, and then the troops laid their dreggans on the ground. There was a great rustling sound as they all went down on bended knee and simultaneously uttered the simple, all-encompassing oath of the Minions.

"I live to serve," they said, as if of one mind. The combination of so many strong voices literally shook the weakened foundations of the buildings around them.

Wondering if he was dreaming, Tristan looked down to see that Geldon had run up to stand alongside him.

"It's true!" the dwarf exclaimed excitedly. "You are their new leader, and they will do anything you say!" He was grinning so widely that it looked as if his face might burst. Tristan stared at him, confused.

"Minion tradition says that whoever kills the commander becomes the new commander of the Minions of Day and Night." He smiled sheepishly, his face scarlet. "I had forgotten all about it, since the custom of Minion succession by death had little meaning for me. Had I remembered, I would have told you sooner."

"Is it really true?" Tristan whispered, half to himself, as he looked out at the sea of kneeling troops. He couldn't believe that his eyes were not lying to him somehow.

"Oh, yes, it is!" Geldon exclaimed. "In fact, they know no other way. You are their new lord." He was obviously enjoying seeing the Minions in this position. "I suppose you should tell them what to do before their wings begin to wilt." He snickered.

Tristan looked down at the still-submissive figure of Traax and then out to the vast hordes of kneeling, winged troops before him. *Thousands upon thousands of them.* The thought staggered him. *My sworn enemies, the butchers of both my nation and my family. What am I to do with such numbers?*

He again looked back down at Geldon, and a brief smile crossed his lips as he continued to lean weakly against the hilt of his dreggan. Shaking his head, he snorted a disapproving, unbelieving laugh down his nose at the dwarf. *"You forgot?"* he asked.

"Uh, yes, I mean, no, uh, I'm sorry, Tristan . . . I know it would have made a big difference, but it was just that there was so much happening . . ." He nervously started up his old habit of fingering his jeweled collar. Not wishing to engage the embarrassingly dark gaze of the Chosen One, Geldon's small eyes suddenly began examining his equally small toes.

Tristan looked back at Traax, his eyes narrowing, wondering what it was he should do. "Rise, Traax," he said finally.

Traax quickly came to his feet, leaving his dreggan in the dirt before the prince's feet. "Yes, my lord," came the quick reply. The man was younger than Kluge, almost his dead commander's size, and clean shaven. He looked at the prince with calm but inquisitive green eyes. His face was handsome, his intelligence apparent.

But just as the prince was about to order the Minions, he heard Wigg's urgent voice calling out from behind him.

"Tristan, come here quickly. I need you!" the old one shouted.

Tristan turned to run back to the wizard, wondering what was wrong. When he reached the wagon he found his answer, and his knees began to buckle.

Narrissa rested against one of the wagon wheels, her lower abdomen covered with blood. Kluge's returning wheel lay on the bloody ground next to her. Wigg looked up into Tristan's face with a mixture of sorrow and finality.

"She was struck by Kluge's wheel," he said, standing up and pulling Tristan to one side. "I tried everything, including the use of the Paragon, to help her, but even my strongest healing incantations were not enough. I have stopped her pain, but the wound is too grievous." Wigg's face was pinched and serious, knowing how much Tristan's heart was aching.

"She has little time left now," he said compassionately. "Use it well. There is nothing else I can do for her, so I will attend to your sister." With that, the Lead Wizard reluctantly turned and slowly walked away, leaving the two of them alone.

As if in a dream Tristan sat down on the ground next to her, cradling her in his arms. He took in the bright-red blood that had splattered against the fluffy white wings, and her tiny, bound feet. *No, please!* he wailed silently. *I cannot lose you, too. Not like this!*

Her expression was calm as she managed a light smile up at him. His shiny eyes took in the honey-blond hair and sapphire-blue eyes, richly lit by the warm sun as it approached its impending zenith.

"Tell me, Chosen One," she asked him quietly, "what is the color of your heart?"

Tristan swallowed hard and looked away, the tears coming freely as he struggled to regain his voice. "It's gray," he whispered finally. "My heart is gray."

She placed a fragile hand against the worn leather of his vest and gazed into his eyes. "No," she said simply. "Your heart is golden. It does not feel that way to you now, but I can tell. You have won. You have your sister, and now you can go home."

But I still do not possess what it is I truly want, he thought as he watched her fade. *I cannot take you and Shailiha with me. We will never know what the future could have held for us.*

"Remember me," she whispered, "but also remember that your heart is too special to keep from another." She smiled again.

Reaching up, she wiped a tear from his cheek. "Odd, isn't it, Tristan?" she asked. She paused slightly as if trying to gather her breath to form her last few words, then continued in an even more faint voice. "Had I been able to choose a place to die, it would have been in your arms." Her eyes closed for a moment and then opened again, more slowly this time, the light in them already beginning to fade. "There will be another for you, Chosen One," she whispered finally. "One whom you shall truly have the chance to love. Find her. Then plant your love and let it grow."

Stay, his heart called out to her. *Stay with me.*

Gently, quietly, she closed her eyes, and was gone.

And then he screamed. Screamed aloud at the true, unrelenting insanity of it all.

It was a blind, overpowering, plaintive scream that seemed to go on and on and live in his heart forever as he sat there uncaringly in the dirt, holding her in his arms. An angry scream that rang out not only for Narrissa but also for his family, for the Directorate of Wizards, and for his countrymen. And for the nations of Eutracia and Parthalon, which had virtually perished at the hands of the Coven and the grotesque, winged monsters that now stood before him, impossibly calling him their lord.

She never knew I was a prince, he realized as he looked down into Narrissa's face. *The only woman who loved me for who I was, and not what I was. She was so hard to find, and now so much harder to lose.*

And now I feel truly lost, he thought. *Lost in the arms that once held me.*

Then from all around Narrissa's body light began to gather, finally coalescing into an aura of radiant illumination. It slowly condensed into a small, twinkling amber sparkle of light that revolved in the air before his face as if somehow trying to say good-bye. And then the amber, sparkling light that was Narrissa's soul came yet closer to his face and brushed his lips once, and then twice. Finally, reluctantly, the fragile, amber sparkle ascended into the sky, vanishing forever.

Fly to the sky, his heart cried as he looked to the heavens. *Go and join your brothers and sisters in death, the Specters of the Gallipolai.*

He might never have moved from that spot had he not heard the sound of a baby crying.

He looked back at the old wizard, his heart and mind struggling to deal with all that was happening. Wigg was getting to his feet, holding something in his arms.

"Shailiha's child," the old one said, smiling. "Her daughter is here. The truly firstborn of the Chosen Ones."

Gently laying Narrissa's body down, Tristan stood shakily to look at the baby Wigg held. His eyes opened wide.

From all around Shailiha's newborn daughter came a dazzling, azure light. The baby gazed up at him, exuding a calm, quiet consciousness that the prince had never before seen in one so new, almost as if the child were already aware of her place in life.

Tristan turned to look at Narrissa's body lying there on the bloody ground, and then once more looked into the face of the newborn child. *A life that I cared for has left me,* he thought, *but another that I will love has somehow found me.*

"*. . . and the azure light that accompanies the births of the Chosen Ones* *shall be the proof of the quality of their blood . . ."* Wigg quoted as he rocked the child gently. He looked into the prince's eyes. "It is from the Prophecies. The Prophecies that you will soon read." Holding the newborn in the crook of one arm, Wigg looked to the sky, taking note of the position of the sun. It was directly at its zenith in the bright, Parthalonian sky. He then reached beneath his robes with his free hand and removed the Paragon from the locket, placing it on its chain about his neck. As soon as he did so, Tristan could see the sparkle of the gift returning to the old wizard's eyes.

And then, almost immediately, the wizard's face darkened, and Tristan knew why. He could feel it in his blood, and it seemed almost as if his entire body was in some kind of harsh, stark awareness of it.

He turned with the old wizard to see Faegan's portal starting to form at the base of the destroyed aviary.

On and on it came, swirling in a magnificent circle of azure, turning faster and growing in strength. Tristan could feel the warning of its arrival rising in his blood. Finally the portal stopped growing, and its turning slowed. The sky-blue light beckoned to them.

Realizing what the appearance of the portal meant, Tristan went directly to where his sister was sitting on the ground, her eyes still lifeless, unseeing. Her hair was soaked with perspiration, and her black, bloodstained gown was torn. Her medallion, the duplicate of his own, still lay upon her chest, suspended from the chain around her neck. Tristan's heart went cold, knowing that the time had finally come to take the responsibility for her into his hands.

Wigg handed the baby to Geldon and quietly walked up behind the prince. "She has shown no improvement," the old one said. "She cannot go back with us, Tristan. You must see that now. To infect Eutracia with one who was once a sorceress and still so overcome with these remnants of one of Failee's incantations would be unforgivable." He paused for a moment, letting his words sink in.

"And I'm afraid the child must now be dealt with, as well," he continued, his heart heavy. "Although the baby appears normal, there is no way to tell for certain, and there may never be until she has matured. Only if the princess were to show some awareness of her former life could I then in good conscience take with us both her and her daughter." Wigg hung his head as a tear came to the corner of one eye; he brushed it away, trying to keep command of his feelings.

"It is time," the old one said.

As much as he wished to contradict the old wizard and simply take his sister back through the portal, the prince knew he could not. Wigg was right. But the reality of it all made Tristan's endowed blood feel like ice in his veins, as if he were no longer human.

Because the task he had to perform was so inhuman.

"How do you wish to proceed?" Wigg asked softly.

Tristan looked away. "I will tend to Shailiha," he said, his voice shaking. "She is my twin, and my charge. You do what you must with the baby." Biting his lip, he paused.

"I will bury the bodies of my sister, her child, and Narrissa in the cemetery of my family, and in this I will hear no disagreement." He gave the wizard a cold, resolved look. "I wish to speak no more of it until it is done."

He walked back to Shailiha and knelt down before her, looking her in the eyes. Stroking her wet hair, he pulled some strands of it off her face and looped them behind an ear. Then he spoke to her for what he knew would be the last time.

"Know that I did all that I could," he said, the tears once again starting to come. "We were fortunate to have come this far, but now your journey with us is over. I promise you that in my remaining days I will see Eutracia whole again, and restored to her past glory. You are and will always be my sister, and I shall love you with all of my heart until the day I die." He kissed her softly on the lips.

He stood, taking the dreggan from his scabbard, knowing that a clean strike with his sword would be the most painless way. The sword sang its usual, oftentimes reassuring, song as it came out of its sheath. But this time the sound was one of sadness, rather than one of protection.

Raising the dreggan high into the air, he held it there and momentarily closed his eyes against the pain. The sword's blade caught the midday sun just before beginning its deadly path downward. His gold medallion, the gift from his mother, dangled off his chest as he bent forward, its glossy surface reflecting the light across his sister's blank, emotionless eyes.

"Forgive me," he whispered.

And then Shailiha blinked.

Gasping, Tristan was just able to stop the downward cut of the blade as he stood there in shock, looking at his sister.

She blinked again, and then she looked down at the medallion upon her chest, and back up at the one the prince was wearing.

Tristan dropped his sword and fell to one knee before her. Grasping her jaw with one hand, he held up his medallion, forcing her to look at it.

"You know this!" he half asked, half exclaimed, as he continued to hold it in front of her eyes. "Tell me you know this symbol!"

She looked directly into his face.

"It is somehow familiar to me . . ." she said, blinking in the sunlight.

She looked into his dark eyes, searching his face.

"Tristan . . ." she said weakly. "Your name is Tristan . . . I do not know who you are, yet your face is so familiar . . ."

The joy he felt at hearing her speak his name was cut short by the grisly image of the task that the Lead Wizard would be performing right now.

"Wigg! Stop!" he shouted. He stood up and whirled around, in a panic to find the wizard and stop him from destroying the child.

"Over here," Wigg said calmly. "There is really no reason to shout."

Tristan ran back to where Wigg was standing, still holding the baby in the blanket. With a great gasp of relief, he smiled into the wizard's eyes.

"You didn't kill her," he breathed. "Thank the Afterlife."

The old one's infamous eyebrow shot up into its familiar arch of annoyance. "Of course not." He winked. "The truth is, I was watching you. Watching and waiting to see if, at the last moment, there might be a miracle." He smiled, continuing to rock the baby.

"And we got it. Sometimes one does not need the craft to produce the greatest of victories." He smiled again and handed the baby to the prince. "Take the child to her mother. Given all that she has been through, I think it is exactly what she needs most right now."

Tristan took the baby, walked over to where Shailiha was sitting, and knelt in front of her once again. His sister's eyes went to the new baby, in that ages-old way that only a new mother's can.

"Whose child is this?" she asked, still dazed.

"She's yours," Tristan said, handing her the baby girl.

Shailiha took her daughter in her arms and instinctively started to rock her, cooing slightly as she did so. Then she looked at Tristan again. "What is her name?" she asked him rather blankly.

Tristan thought for a moment of the sad little grave that he had been forced to abandon at the edge of the Recluse and then said, "Morganna. Her name is Morganna the Second, of the House of Galland. Named after her grandmother."

"Hello, Morganna." Shailiha smiled.

Suddenly remembering the waiting Minions, Tristan reluctantly took his eyes from his sister and looked back to the square, to the hordes of winged warriors who were still obediently kneeling before him in the heat of the midday sun. He had to address them, he thought. Give them orders. He could not leave them to run amok in Parthalon. He had to think of something to tell them—even though the mere idea of addressing the murderers of his family and nation revolted him.

Beckoning Wigg to join him, he walked back to where Traax and Geldon were standing, the Minion second in command still at attention before the dwarf.

"You may all rise," the new lord of the Minions ordered.

The entire Minion force stood, their dreggans still at their feet. Tristan knew that all of the troops could not be here in the square; the others must have been standing outside the city walls, thousands and thousands of them, waiting for the orders to be passed.

"They are a very potent and well-trained force," Wigg whispered into the prince's ear. "Despite their bloody history, it is still a fact that they were obediently following orders, and did so exceedingly well. You would also do well to remember that the Eutracian Royal Guard is no more, and we cannot be sure of the conditions we will find upon returning home. Circumstances have changed dramatically, and we have no choice but to change with them. As difficult as it may seem to be at this moment, do not let your hatred of the Minions color the judgment of what you do here today." His eyes narrowed. "I suggest you put them to good use," he added slyly.

Tristan thought for a moment. *The old one is right,* he realized, trying to adjust to the magnitude of all that had had happened that day. *He always is.*

"I am Tristan of the House of Galland, ruler of Eutracia," he began awkwardly, finding it difficult to use such grand words in his own description. He pointed to the headless corpse of Kluge where it lay in the blood-soaked dirt of the square. "I am also your new lord. The orders I am about to give you are to be followed to the letter." He took another step forward and stood next to Traax, motioning to the second in command to turn around and face the legions with him. To the astonishment of the warriors, the prince bent down, picked up Traax's dreggan, and gently handed it to the man. The same dreggan Tristan had been so sure was to have been the instrument of his death.

"In my absence, Traax is to be your undisputed leader. First, I wish all of the Minion brothels to be opened, and the women there to be freed. They are to live among you as equals. The warriors of the Minions are now allowed to take wives, providing the women are in agreement. They are in no fashion to be coerced. In addition, no permission is needed to have children. However, birth and death records are now to be kept."

He could see the looks of astonishment gathering in their faces, as they first stared at him and then at one another. He gave them a moment to let his words sink in before continuing.

"Second, the areas holding the Gallipolai are to be opened. They, too, are to be freed to live among you as equals. Unions between Gallipolai and Minion are now to be allowed, following the same rules that I have just described. No longer are their wings to be clipped or their feet to be bound. In this there is to be no room for disagreement. Anyone of you who violates these orders shall be subject to punishment."

Upon hearing this, even Traax turned and looked at him in disbelief. Tristan continued to regard the legions sternly, as they stood absolutely speechless in the confines of the square.

"No more violence is to be visited upon the population of this country," he added, shouting more strongly so that there would be no possibility for misunderstanding in his words. "The people here have suffered enough. Although you are to remain a fighting force, you are forbidden to take up your swords against anyone without explicit orders from myself, and the custom of succession by death is hereby outlawed. To that end, you are to commit part of your legions to rebuilding the Ghetto as a proper Parthalonian city, freeing the people inside and tending as best you can to the leper colony that exists here. All of the people who died here this day you are to burn, rather than bury.

"The Recluse is to be rebuilt, and all signs of the Pentangle and the existence of the Coven are to be eradicated," he continued. "We shall one day perhaps use the structure for the common good, and I will expect it to be finished before the turn of the year."

"And lastly, know that I will soon return here, to Parthalon, to see that what I have ordered this day has come to pass."

He turned to Traax. "Face me," he ordered his second in command.

Traax obediently turned to look his new lord in the eye. Despite the fact that this warrior had been one of the butchers of his family and his nation, Tristan was beginning to realize that he would also be completely loyal to whomever he recognized as his lord.

"Do you understand the orders that I have given you this day?" Tristan asked him sternly.

"Yes, my lord," Traax responded.

"Good. You are dismissed. I wish you and the legions to return to your various fortresses and make plans for what I have ordered to come about. Go now."

"I live to serve," the short reply came. Immediately Traax sheathed his dreggan and took off into the air, followed first by his officers, and finally by the rest of the legions. As the sky began to darken with their numbers, Tristan stood there, almost speechless, trying to become accustomed to the fact that he was their new lord.

Once they were gone, the wizard took a step closer to him. "Well done," he said dryly. "It should be interesting one day to see the results of their labors."

"Yes," Tristan said blankly, the sadness of Narrissa's death suddenly revisiting him. So much had happened so quickly that not only his head, but also his heart had been overwhelmed—lost, swimming through the concurrent mazes of new life and sudden death.

Wigg laid an understanding hand upon his shoulder. "We have the stone, Shailiha, and her firstborn. In addition, the Coven is destroyed. It is all we could have asked for."

Tristan turned to look at the body covered with the blanket, thinking not only of the woman with the white wings who had cared for him so much, but of the little grave that lay next to the Recluse.

"Perhaps not all," he said softly. With a blank look on his face, he went to Narrissa's body and sat on the ground beside it, his back up against the wagon wheel, looking out at the awful carnage in the square. Taking her in his arms, he pulled the blanket away from her face and began to rock back and forth gently, as if he and Narrissa were the only two people in the world.

Wigg looked cautiously at the glowing vortex as it continued to revolve. He could easily envision Faegan as the rogue wizard sat in his chair on wheels on the other side, waiting anxiously to see whether anyone could be coming through as he held the vortex open for the last time.

The Lead Wizard then turned to Geldon, the hunchbacked dwarf who had been so brave and true. He paused for a moment, smiled knowingly to himself, and then pointed a long, bony index finger at the dwarf. A narrow azure bolt of pure energy immediately scorched through the air and onto Geldon's collar. With a snapping, cracking sound, the iron collar split instantly in two and fell to the dirt.

His eyes wide as saucers, Geldon unbelievingly rubbed his neck where the collar had been, finally free of it after more than three hundred years. "Thank you, Wigg," he said, crying unashamedly. His voice was breaking, and he was barely able to get the words out. "Now I can live as a free man, and no longer a slave."

Wigg placed his hands into his sleeves. "It is we—the nations of both Eutracia and Parthalon—who should be thanking you," he said simply. "For your services to this cause."

Then the Lead Wizard looked down at Tristan, still sitting in the dirt. "It's time to leave," he said quietly.

"You, Shailiha, and the baby go now," Tristan said gently, without looking up at the wizard. "And take Geldon with you. He deserves a better life, a life away from this awful place. I have almost an hour before the vortex closes. I wish to stay here for a time, and be alone."

Wigg was about to speak again and order the prince to come, but then he stopped himself. *I can no longer give this one orders,* he realized.

"Very well," the old one said reluctantly. And, at that moment, his eyes widened in disbelief. Tristan's blood, still trickling from the wounds in his shoulder and side, was glowing.

No longer red, the prince's blood was a radiant azure that twinkled and sparkled as it dripped from his body. And the wizard instinctively knew that it was due to the fact that the Chosen One had made his first real use of the craft.

Wigg's mind was immediately sent back in time to that night in Faegan's tree house, just before the rogue wizard had sent the two of them to Parthalon, and to the words Faegan had whispered after giving the Lead Wizard the locket of water from the Caves.

"It may be possible for the prince to perform some small use of the craft, despite the fact that he is untrained. If you are dead or incapacitated, it may be his only salvation. Although they do not say how, the second volume of the Tome affirm that after he has accomplished it, he will be forever, inalterably, changed. You must stay on the lookout for this change, whatever it is to be . . ."

Wigg continued to look down at the prince, thinking of the Tome of the Paragon, the book that he had so long ago found with the stone, and to one of the many lines written therein: *"The azure light that accompanies the births of the Chosen Ones shall be the proof of the quality of their blood . . ."*

He placed his hand on the prince's shoulder once again, and Tristan turned his face up to him, smiling slightly through the pain in his heart. "I know," the prince said quietly. "This feeling has been with me for several hours, although I could not discern its meaning until just now. It began when you first opened the locket and removed the Paragon, exposing it to my blood. And I could feel the change strengthening even further just now, as the Paragon came closer."

With fresh, tearful eyes Wigg took a newfound look at the man who sat before him and then, without speaking, went back to gather up the princess, the baby, and the dwarf. Without looking back, Wigg, Shailiha, her baby, and the dwarf named Geldon walked into the vortex . . . and vanished.

It was only then, as Tristan sat finally alone in the dirt, holding Narrissa in his arms, that the full realization came to him. Not gently, as if upon silent cat's feet, or whispering softly upon the flutter of the afternoon breeze, but suddenly and fully, from his blood.

And then he understood.

Understood what his mind had come to accept, but until now his heart had not. Understood, finally, that those things his family and the Lead Wizard had been asking of him, he had ultimately achieved. *You have survived, and ascended to manhood,* he heard his endowed blood call out to him. *Your careless ways are no more. And you have become, truly, the Chosen One.*

He looked down to the brilliant azure blood that dripped from his shoulder. It was his transformed, endowed blood and his transformed, matured heart that spoke to him, he now knew. Speaking, somehow, from the Prophecies of the Tome, the great book that he still knew so little about, but was nonetheless destined to read. *The Chosen One shall come, but shall be preceded by another,* he could hear it saying to him. *And the Chosen One shall take up three weapons of his choice and slay many before reading the Prophecies, and coming to the light . . .*

Looking down at the gentle woman who lay dead in his arms, his mind was taken back to what the monster Kluge had said, just before he died. *"There are still things you do not know, and even if you should somehow return to your homeland you will be a wanted man, hunted day and night because of me, your forever-damaged sister a mere shadow of her former self. No, Galland, your victory over me here today is far from complete . . ."*

Tristan sat there silently, hugging Narrissa, and looked out at the charred and broken landscape, and upon the bodies that lay there. And then, just as he had sworn to avenge the deaths of his parents that rainy night in the graveyard, he made a new covenant with himself.

I will not rest until I have discovered who has poured such endowed blood into my veins, and why. I shall know why I have become the vessel that contains the blood of the fates. And the answers lie with the Tome.

Looking down into the soft, gentle face of the Gallipolai, he felt the tears once again begin to roll down his cheeks.

Picking her up, he turned and walked up the little knoll, into the swirling light.

Epilogue:
The Recluse

The following day the weather surrounding the Recluse turned harsh and cold, the wind whipping steadily through the cloudy air, wheeling the cold rain into heavy, swirling patterns before it hit the already soaked and muddy ground. Thunder and lightning barreled across the sky from time to time as the Vagaries continued to mark the passing of the Coven, unleashing yet more wind before finally relenting. They were soon followed by a dense fog that had slowly snaked into and around the once-magnificent structure, carrying with it a silent, foreboding kind of impenetrability. With the slow, final cessation of the wind, nothing moved and there was no sound. The deserted, ruined Recluse rested awkwardly, split open and broken, on the island in the center of the surrounding lake.

And from the fog now came, slowly, an azure mist, glowing ever more brightly as it deepened in both size and density. The azure haze swirled and gathered, then slowly, silently, began creeping across the surface of the moat and started to approach the little grave with flowers upon it.

The grave that was marked Galland.

The sapphire radiance swirled and began to coalesce, forming itself into an ethereal, yet partially human aspect. Two human, glowing azure hands hovered bodiless above the grave and then slowly began to beckon to the stones.

The small, carefully piled rocks began spilling down over the edges of the grave and onto the ground, finally exposing the little body that lay there, wrapped in the simple cloth. With a smooth turn of one of the ghostly hands, the dead, exposed infant in the grave rose into the air and floated over to settle in an azure palm.

With a wave of the other hand, the rocks piled themselves back into a cairn, the marker remaining untouched, the grave completely taking on its previous appearance.

Then a combination of voices from the sky spoke aloud. Their words seemed to encompass the entire land, although there was no one near to hear it.

Our servants, the Coven, defeated by what was once an irresponsible prince, the voices said as the child rested peacefully in the cupped palm. *A mere prince no longer. Now the fully realized male of the Chosen Ones. But all was not in vain. The blood, the male heir of the Chosen One, shall be ours.*

The hand without the child gathered upon its glowing fingers yet more of the swirling, lapis mist and guided it to fall gently upon the dead infant's face.

Slowly, the baby's chest began to rise and fall, his breathing beginning to quicken, the color returning to his cheeks.

Finally, his eyes snapped open.

His hair was dark and thick, his expressive eyes blue, slanting slightly upward at the corners in a rather exotic fashion, his face the perfect embodiment of the man who was his father and the sorceress who had been his mother. He continued to gaze calmly, almost wisely, into the dark night sky. He was quite unafraid.

The firstborn son of the Chosen One lives, and now he is ours.

The thunder and lightning of the Vagaries came once again, even more violently this time. The wind howled, and the lightning cascaded across the sky in unimaginable streaks, now more a portent of what was to come than an homage to the death of the Coven.

Turning toward the heavens, the pair of azure hands holding the baby began to ascend skyward, toward the stars, and disappeared.

FANTASTIC STORY.
FANTASTIC COMPETITION.